GLOBAL MEDIEVAL CONTEXTS 500–1500: CONNECTIONS AND COMPARISONS

Global Medieval Contexts 500–1500: Connections and Comparisons provides a unique wide-lens introduction to world history during this period. Designed for students new to the subject, this textbook explores vital networks and relationships among geographies and cultures that shaped medieval societies. The expert author team aims to advance a global view of the period and introduce the reader to histories and narratives beyond an exclusively European context.

Key Features:

- Divided into chronological sections, chapters are organized by four key themes: Religion, Economies, Politics, and Society. This framework enables students to connect wider ideas and debates across 500 to 1500.
- Individual chapters address current theoretical discussions, including issues around gender, migration, and sustainable environments.
- The authors' combined teaching experience and subject specialties ensure an engaging and accessible overview for students of history, literature, and those undertaking general studies courses.
- Theory boxes and end-of-chapter questions provide a basis for group discussion and research. Full-color maps and images illustrate chapter content and support understanding.

As a result, this text is essential reading for all those interested in learning more about the histories and cultures of the period, as well as their relevance to our own contemporary experiences and perspectives.

This textbook is supported by a companion website providing core resources for students and lecturers.

Kimberly Klimek is Professor of History at Metropolitan State University of Denver, concentrating on medieval women and intellectual history.

Pamela L. Troyer is Professor of English Literature at Metropolitan State University of Denver, specializing in ancient and medieval mythology and manuscript culture.

Sarah Davis-Secord is Associate Professor of History at the University of New Mexico, specializing in the medieval Mediterranean and cross-cultural exchange.

Bryan C. Keene is Assistant Professor of Art History at Riverside City College, Los Angeles, and former curator of manuscripts at the Getty Museum.

Global Medieval Contexts
500–1500: Connections and Comparisons

For additional resources please visit the companion website for *Global Medieval Contexts 500 – 1500: Connections and Comparisons*:
www.routledge.com/cw/klimektroyer

Perfect for use in the classroom or as an aid to independent study, the companion website includes:

- Videos with the authors **Kimberly Klimek, Pamela L. Troyer, Sarah Davis-Secord and Bryan C. Keene** as introduction to the book.
- Three timelines which highlight key events, people and locations in global medieval history.
- Introductions, research questions, and further reading for each chapter.
- An image gallery containing pictures of art, manuscripts, objects, people, and places.
- A gallery of maps to explore the geography of the medieval world.
- Weblinks to exciting online resources.

GLOBAL MEDIEVAL CONTEXTS 500–1500

Connections and Comparisons

KIMBERLY KLIMEK

PAMELA L. TROYER

WITH

SARAH DAVIS-SECORD

BRYAN C. KEENE

Routledge
Taylor & Francis Group

NEW YORK AND LONDON

First published 2021
by Routledge
605 Third Avenue, New York, NY 10158

and by Routledge
2 Park Square, Milton Park, Abingdon, Oxon OX14 4RN

Routledge is an imprint of the Taylor & Francis Group, an informa business

Library of Congress Cataloging-in-Publication Data
Names: Klimek, Kimberly, editor, author. | Troyer, Pamela, editor, author. |
Davis-Secord, Sarah C., editor, author. | Keene, Bryan C., editor, author.
Title: Global medieval contexts 500–1500: connections and comparisons /
Kimberly Klimek, Pamela Troyer, with Sarah Davis-Secord, Bryan C. Keene.
Description: First edition. | New York : Routledge, 2021. |
Includes bibliographical references and index. |
Contents: Growth of Monotheisms – Caravan and Dhow –
The sword and the pen – Sustainability and climate change – Pathways
to Paradise – For sale – Soldiers and civil servants – Class rites –
Devotion – Golden opportunities – World connected –
Everyone believes it is the end of the world.
Identifiers: LCCN 2020055462 | ISBN 9781138103382 (hardback) |
ISBN 9781138103399 (paperback) | ISBN 9781315102771 (ebook)
Subjects: LCSH: Middle Ages–Textbooks. | Civilization, Medieval–Textbooks. |
Middle Ages–Study and teaching (Higher) |
Medieval, Civilization–Study and teaching (Higher)
Classification: LCC D118 .G54 2021 | DDC 909.07–dc23
LC record available at https://lccn.loc.gov/2020055462

ISBN: 9781138103382 (hbk)
ISBN: 9781138103399 (pbk)
ISBN: 9781315102771 (ebk)

Typeset in ITC Stone Serif
by Newgen Publishing UK

Access the companion website www.routledge.com/cw/klimektroyer

For our students, who inspire us to be better every semester.

Contents

Maps

Maps created by Christy Bouchard

Who We Are

Kimberly Klimek, Ph.D.

Pamela L. Troyer, Ph.D.

Sarah Davis-Secord, Ph.D.

Bryan C. Keene, Ph.D.

The four primary authors wrote this text to provide students with a basic foundation from which to consider the rich global connections in the period 500–1500. These connections still resonate in our present-day experiences across the world; each author teaches diverse and multicultural communities of students.

Both Dr. Kimberly Klimek and Dr. Pamela Troyer teach at Metropolitan State University of Denver, on a large urban commuter campus. The student population is diverse in ethnicity and age range. The average student is non-traditional, and the university is the largest Hispanic-serving institute in the state of Colorado. Many MSU Denver students work full time or study online while managing a busy schedule with families, work, and children. There is also a significant number of first-generation college graduates, LGBTQIA2+, and veterans in the student body.

As a historian, Dr. Klimek regularly teaches general-studies courses in early world history and women in world history. She writes and presents on the intersections between gender and intellectual history, with a particular focus on women and their impact on historical writing. She is also interested in medieval concepts such as mysticism and crusading, particularly as they relate to philosophical, intellectual, and gendered identities. Her teaching interests include women and gender, crusades and the ideas of masculinity, and the craft of history writing. She is interested in exploring the cultural and intellectual history of the medieval and early modern periods, particularly as these cultural ideas relate to the larger political and intellectual forces of the period.

Dr. Troyer is a professor in the English department, teaching courses such as Myth and Literature, Medieval Mythologies, and Legends of Troy, which explore ancient and medieval storytelling and how these narratives are adapted and applied to contemporary cultural aesthetics, events, and concerns. Trained in Middle English literature and history, she researches manuscript culture, writing systems, and material artifacts of writing and learning. In recent projects, she has considered how many twenty-first-century students identify with experiences of people from a thousand years ago because of linguistic isolation, forced migration, loss of community, and powerlessness. Modern students are enthusiastic about discovering how present-day creative environments are informed by literature and art from these long-ago communities.

Dr. Davis-Secord draws on her experience as a historian at the University of New Mexico, a public research university with one of the US's largest populations of Latinx and Native American students and faculty. She is a historian of the early and central Middle Ages, particularly interested in economic and cultural exchanges within the Mediterranean Sea region. She has published books on intercultural relationships between Greek Christians, Muslims, Jews, and Latin Christians in early medieval Sicily (*Where Three Worlds Met: Sicily in the Early Medieval Mediterranean*, Cornell University Press, 2017), and on migration across the medieval Mediterranean (*Migration and Movement in the Mediterranean*, Arc Humanities Press, 2021).

As an art historian, Dr. Bryan C. Keene teaches at Riverside City College, a Hispanic-serving community college in Los Angeles with a diverse student body. His wide-ranging research interests include Italian art and music, medieval fantasy (from the Brothers Grimm to *Game of Thrones* and from Disney to video games), and the ways in which queer contemporary artists (LGBTQIA2+ individuals) have drawn inspiration from medieval art. As a former curator of manuscripts at the Getty Museum, he organized and presented exhibitions for an international public of learners. His exhibitions have helped define the concept of a global medieval period. Among his many publications is a seminal work in the field, *Toward A Global Middle Ages: Encountering the World Through Illuminated Manuscripts* (Getty Publications, 2019).

Acknowledgments

In any long and sustained work, the list of acknowledgments grows like vines flourishing around the larger tree. Some people have propped us up when we swayed too far in the wind, some have wrapped themselves around us when we felt like the task was too large; all of them aided us with their support and advice.

Many helped us with editing and reading the text, offering their advice and critiques at various stages of the work. Lou J. Berger's careful editing kept our prose concise and clear, while his insightful and gentle criticism helped us see where our themes got lost in the words. Diversity readers Abby Ang, Sally Hany, Miguel Valerio, and Adam Vazquez Cruz all gave us invaluable advice on sections of the text. Many thanks go to Sally Hany and Nicole Lopez Jantzen, who were instrumental in the development stage of this work. Nayhan Fancy and Monica H. Green read and commented on portions of the final chapter of this work, as did several other plague historians. Joanna Quargnali-Linsley gave helpful explanations of traditional medicines and Ayurveda. Graham Abney, Donald Burke, Cynthia Colburn, Suzanne Conklin Akbari, Morgan Conger, Paula R. Curtis, Frederick Paxton, Amanda Respess, Michael A. Ryan, and Maya Soifer Irish read and commented on portions of other chapters. We thank Patrick McGovern for his help and advice on the archeology of alcohol. We included as many of their critiques as possible.

We are grateful for the careful work of alums of Metropolitan State University of Denver who helped us craft portions of the book. Christy Bouchard, our cartographer, designed our wonderful maps. Morgan Huston and his company, The Arcana Research Initiative, researched and aided in the creation of our bibliographies. Our librarians and researchers are essential in any academic work, and Morgan's thoughtful additions kept our bibliographies up-to-date and inclusive. Aaron Jackson took time from his own dissertation to comment on our sections on warfare. Siet Wright, Carter Hilty, and Tiarra Refosco contributed writing, ideas, and feedback. Current students at all our institutions read, commented on, and answered the student questions. We could not have done this without them.

Our editors at Taylor & Francis, Laura Pilsworth and Kirsten Shankland, steadfastly supported us throughout the project. We cannot thank them enough for their guidance. Emma Brown patiently marched through miles of image-permissions tasks. We also owe a great debt to our anonymous batch reviewers, whose thoughtful critiques and comments propelled us to greater concision and truthfulness. We are buoyed knowing how many students also benefit from professors such as these.

The families of academics are long-suffering, ours no less than any others. Computers traveled on every vacation as we woke early and worked late. Spouses good-naturedly listened to and commented on portions of the text. Our children were patient with their parents having too much screen time. We thank our amazing spouses for being easygoing parents and our children for being such great kids. Grandparents and friends also came to the rescue, picking up the slack while we, yet again, worked.

Kim thanks Kevin and Anya for living through this project with such grace and for advising on everything from word choice to images; Carole and Jon Boyers and Marion Klimek, for being wonderful and reliable grandparents; her sisters (Stacie and Delania) for their encouragement; and the dozens of aunties and friends who made sure Anya still had plenty of attention.

Pam could not have done this without Bob's provision of strategies, sentences, and soup – much love to him. She is grateful for creative inspiration and encouragement from Cody and Clara Troyer, Ken and Joyce Luff, Sally and Tom Troyer, and many friends and colleagues who sent clippings, recommended reading, suggested exhibitions, and advised on process, including Kara Kirk, Steven Luff, Dr. Mary Kohn, Frances Wehner, and Dr. Gloria Eastman.

Sarah thanks Jon and Sage for their love, support, and enthusiasm; her parents Terry and Catherine Davis, especially for childcare at critical moments; and her students who have listened to her go on and on about shipwrecks, coins, and commodities.

Bryan is grateful to Mark, Alexander, and Éowyn for their intrepid willingness to venture to remote petroglyph sites across North America; for his students who have read and commented on chapters in this volume; and for his educator relatives, especially Epaminondas James (Pete) Demas, Laurence Keene, and his parents, Rosemarie and Kenneth Keene.

Sarah and Bryan also thank Kim and Pam for welcoming them into this project, which has been one of the most fruitful and enjoyable collaborations of their career. In turn, Kim and Pam thank Sarah and Bryan for so enthusiastically embracing this project. Zoom calls, mountain retreats, Getty galas – we could not imagine a more encouraging, engaging, and lively group of colleagues and friends. Thank you all for joining us in this project.

We also honor Paul L. Sidelko, who believed in this book from the beginning and worked tirelessly for our students at Metropolitan State University of Denver, encouraging them to see the world as a bright place where they all belonged. One of his final academic projects was this work, and his words live on in Chapter 7. His untimely death is a great sadness in many ways, not the least of which is that he did not see our finished project. *Requiescat in pace, amicus.*

Instructor Preface

Why This Book?

We designed this book to support lower-division or general studies courses for the history and culture of the period 500–1500. This book is not a world civilizations textbook; instead, it is a history from a global perspective, showing connections and comparisons among peoples across political boundaries and geography, across religions and languages, and at the intersections of various economic systems. Through this book we introduce the rich and exciting events, artifacts, documents, literature, and art of the period, and offer students from diverse places a chance to encounter their heritage and consider it alongside other cultures. This is not medieval history as it is traditionally presented – we hope it will show students how they, no matter their backgrounds, have something at stake in the study of the past.

The authors teach many sections of this type of course each year in History, English, and Art History departments. For many of our students, a course such as this will be the first, and often only, view they have of premodern interconnections and transcultural networks that inform the present day. For many of our immigrant and refugee students, it is often the first, and maybe only, time they will see the artifacts and history of their native cultures in a formal classroom setting. Some of these students will be the next generation of scholars, others will move on to degrees outside the humanities, and our hope is that they all will be challenged to think creatively and expansively about the role history continues to play in their lives and professions.

Theoretical frameworks grow and shift; individual instructors will always have the delight and responsibility of providing fresh ideas. To support those efforts, we provide frequent theory boxes that address contemporary debates. This book also has a companion website with additional resources, new discoveries, and up-to-date information. History is all about formulating questions, and our students will ask different questions from the ones we ask them. Our job is to spark their curiosity and provide critical thinking tools to carry them forward.

Global Medieval Contexts 500–1500: Connections and Comparisons has three sections: 500–900, 900–1300, and 1300–1500. Occasionally, evidence provided in a chapter will be earlier or later than the period designated for that specific section – this flexibility is necessary to provide context. In each of the three sections, the chapters are organized by a general topic: religion, economies, politics, and society. The chapters can be used in chronological order or by general topic; for instance, an instructor may want to follow economic change over the period by having students read the three chapters that focus on economies: chapters 2, 6, and 10. But in all cases, we intend the chapters to interlink and reference each other. In keeping with our interdisciplinary teaching, each chapter has two sections: the first provides a historical overview and the second offers cultural expressions of those themes and events.

The introduction, "Orientation," is meant to "re-orient" students' understanding of time, geography, and the cosmos as perceived by different cultures of the period. (We also use the word orientation as a demonstration of how a word in one context is positive, but in another has negative connotations of racial prejudice.) Overall, the book covers eight major geographical regions, although not every region will appear in each chapter. In the chapter introduction, we indicate which regions, cultures, and trends will be used as examples of the chapter theme. The primary regions are Mesoamerica, North and sub-Saharan Africa, the Mediterranean basin, western and eastern Europe, the Middle East, Central Asia, the Indian subcontinent (and Indian Ocean), East Asia, and Oceania. In order to make the material lively and relevant, we find it most effective to begin with themes such as trade, worship, warfare, survival, exploration, and migration, and work from there to map geographies and comparative chronologies.

This text is best used alongside a sampling of primary sources in translation. At the beginning of each chapter section, we include a category called "Evidence," which contains a select list of primary sources. In almost every case, there are inexpensive versions of these texts or images of these objects accessible online. At the end of each chapter, we offer sample research and discussion questions along with additional reading. We know that instructors will follow their own expertise in choosing materials to round out the course. If you do not see a topic you need, we suggest forming a research question. Instructors will also develop their own assignments, but one suggestion is to have each student choose a culture or region to follow throughout the course, creating a record of its religious, economic, political, and social history according to the themes offered in the book. Students could present their work at the end of the semester, providing their peers with knowledge about that specific culture or geographic area. Students could be guided to cultures or regions with lesser representation in the book.

What Words Should We Use?

A primary challenge we faced in writing this book is that terminology is undergoing much-needed and rapid change. As scholars around the world work to put the histories of conquered, suppressed, and even lost cultures on a par with those of the European colonizers, we know long-used terms, methods, and assumptions will be challenged and displaced. Take, for example, two words in the title: medieval and global. As we know, "medieval" is particularly tied to European history and not necessarily applicable to the major events of non-European cultures nor to the way those cultures defined historical time. However, "medieval" is pervasive in Western scholarship and has been applied by many cultures to their own history. It is also a term prevalent in internet searches for the period, and for most students reading this textbook in English, it conjures up the centuries under discussion. Until there is consensus on an alternative, we use the term because it is familiar to students for the period 500–1500. The use of "global" is also under construction; we use it here because it communicates to students that the text provides information about people from many parts of the globe.

We are hyper-conscious of terminology used comfortably and unselfconsciously for centuries. For example, the use of Western in the previous paragraph and its "opposite" Eastern are shorthand for differentiating distinct cultures, but what are these cultures? The terms are reductive, inaccurate, and formed by racist Euro-superiority. East and West change with the vantage point. For instance, the famous Chinese text *Journey to the West* records the trials of a monk going west to learn more of the ancient teachings of the Buddha. The "west" he seeks is India; from a European perspective, India is not the West.

Flawed as they are, until there is widespread agreement on new terms that help us negotiate and discuss the topic of global history and culture from 500 to 1500, we use, with humility, "medieval", "global", and sometimes "West" and "East", because otherwise we would risk the unintended consequence of stifling or silencing discussion entirely. We expect that terms and words will be under constant discussion and scrutiny in the classroom. We hope that you will have frank discussions with your students about which terms are most useful and appropriate; you may decide as a class not to use a term that we have used here. To that end, we have also framed theoretical questions in each chapter. These "theory boxes" are indicated by a question title ("Is it wrong to recover and move the human remains and sacred objects of Indigenous peoples? or "How is new technology changing maritime archeology?) and can be used to begin discussions on the important issues facing scholars today.

Can We Include All Languages in One Language?

In writing *Global Medieval Contexts*, we faced another language challenge: every instructor of world material cannot know all the languages from which the information is derived. We can feel uncomfortable and even illegitimate about interpreting translations, but if we are caught up in that quandary, we cannot offer students a wide-lens perspective that takes into account the constant and vibrant transcultural and translingual environments in which people lived from 500 to 1500. The primary goal of this book is to provide an introduction to the period and, as such, we stand on the shoulders of scholars who spend and have spent their lives decoding texts. By offering an introduction informed by this wealth of scholarship, maybe we will inspire the next generation to study ancient languages, thus preserving and amplifying these voices in the historical record.

So too, we know that interpretations of text-bearing objects and images will evolve. Some of these objects and images accompany texts, others are informed by textual sources, and still others are more imaginative or evocative of many possibilities. When introducing and examining works of art, we offer information for students to understand the media, contexts – religious, economic, political, social – and the figures or events depicted. We will not be able to decode the purposes or potential meaning of every aspect of a work or its longer visual tradition, but students can explore further through class discussions, recommended readings, and our companion website.

Yet another linguistic challenge is determining how to spell words from languages other than English. We have tried to use those spellings scholars use most commonly in the present day, but even then, there is variation. We trust that readers will be flexible about spelling conventions. In addition, since students reading in English will not understand diacritics for all the languages represented nor understand their use in the period 500–1500, we do not use diacritical marks. We want names and terms to be searchable so that students and instructors can most easily find information on topics that interest them. As for pronunciation, a guide seemed too involved for this text, especially when students and instructors can look to the internet for spoken representations.

We are aware that many of our examples are still weighted toward European history and culture, that we use terms that are actively being debated, and that we cannot translate all languages and visual imagery for ourselves. We believe this to be true of many instructors teaching this type of introductory course. But by beginning with recognizable constructs, we capture students' interest and have the opportunity to extend their knowledge to other ideas, cultures, and geographies. Like you, we are always listening to our diverse student populations and incorporating their historic "pasts" into what we teach. We cannot do it all, but can do something to advance a global view of the period and pass on our enthusiasm to the next generation of students, wherever they are from and whatever languages they know.

We expect that instructors will expand and add topics according to their own research and their student audiences. What we provide is foundational content on which current debates can be layered. We suggest connections and comparisons to welcome new students and potential scholars into those conversations.

Student Preface

How Did a Buddha Get to a Swedish Island?

The tiny Indian Buddha featured on the cover of this book was found in 1954 in a hoard of treasures, mostly gold coins and jewelry, buried during the medieval period on Helgö Island in Sweden. For the authors, it represents the goal of this book: to show the amazing connections across geography and time during a distant past when those connections might seem impossible. This small bronze figurine was made in the sixth century, possibly in Kashmir, a region in the far north of present-day India. It was carried by hand, or many hands, from the heights of the western end of the Himalaya mountains, across many rivers and landscapes to the edge of the North Sea. It was valuable enough to be interred along with precious gold and other treasures such as a large spoon or cup probably made for Christians from far off Egypt. How and why were such objects valued enough to be carried over long distances and buried as part of a treasure hoard? Questions like this one form the basis for the book you have just opened.

Medieval Global Contexts 500–1500: Connections and Comparisons emphasizes the organization of individuals into larger social groups that experienced global developments, changes, and practices common to all cultures, such as trade, worship, warfare, survival, exploration, and migration. We work with two kinds of systems. The first is connections: evidence of networks of actual exchange and communication across cultures. The second is comparisons: to show that because all human beings are biologically the same, communities that have no direct interaction develop and sustain similar practices and customs. For instance, all people need food and water, shelter from heat and cold; they organize themselves into social hierarchies, have families, worship divinities or the supernatural, and tell stories to explain phenomena. In this book, we are interested in describing connections and comparisons, providing opportunities for students to consider the view from different locations, perhaps even close to home.

This book has four sections. Section I contains Orientation, which provides a broad overview of the book's subject matter. Section II covers the period 500–900. Sometimes, to emphasize a point about travel or trade from 500 to 900, we need to explain earlier events or provide examples from a later period. This is true for Section III (900–1300) and Section IV (1300–1500) – occasionally it is important to stretch the envelope of time in one way or the other. Sections II, III, and IV each have four chapters: one focused on religion, one on economies, one on politics, and one on society. These chapters necessarily overlap and inform each other; no one perspective can be considered without the other three.

The chapters on religion consider answers to such questions as: What were the spiritual beliefs that inspired and motivated people in their individual and social lives? What were their worship practices, and how did they pay respect to the divine? How did they celebrate blessings or cope with tragedy? How did different religious systems face similar questions about how to live the best life? And how did religions, sacred texts, and objects such as the Helgö Buddha move from place to place around the premodern world?

Through economic systems of trade and travel, we think about what people harvested, created, and sold in order to survive and even prosper. What were they interested in having or buying that they could not produce themselves? How far did goods travel, carried from one culture to another, finally arriving at a place so far from the start that the object became a great wonder and a symbol of the owner's status and honor? And what else traveled alongside commercial merchandise? Technologies, people, texts, ideas, and even disease traveled these same routes.

Politics is the study of how people organize in groups to compete or cooperate for resources. It is also the way a society creates a sense of identity that separates it from other ones. Which groups had power, and how did they acquire it? How were they governed – by tribal blood feud or centralized justice systems? How did spiritual beliefs and economic needs inform government systems and the ambition of rulers? What drove a society to war, and what are the lasting effects of those conflicts?

Each section concludes with a chapter on society, introducing ideas of how individuals, families, and communities survived and behaved. What were the social roles they were meant to fulfill? How were class systems structured? Who had a voice, and which voices were silenced? How did they deal with adversity and diversity? What was their treatment of those perceived as outsiders? How did they accept and absorb ideas and innovations from other cultures or transmit knowledge of their own innovations?

These questions and more are explored in this text, often leading to more questions that we hope will encourage further discovery. Although it is not possible to examine and compare each culture over this era, we hope that students will continue to develop their own knowledge by exploring ideas or geographies that are not fully covered in this book.

Section I
Orientation

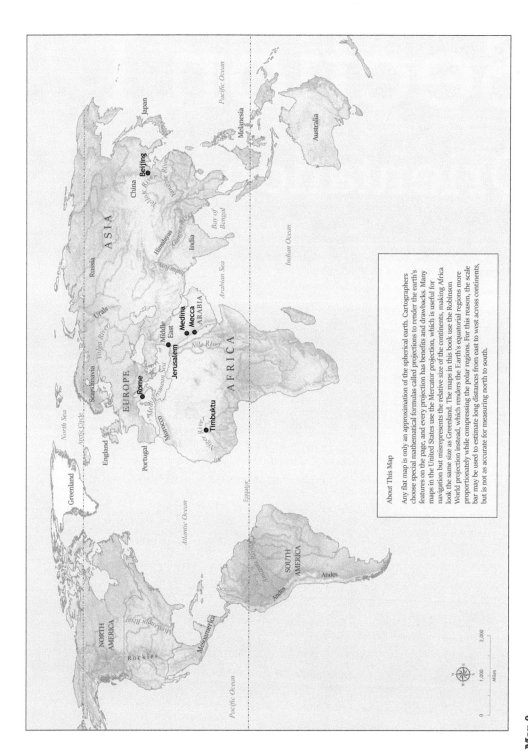

About This Map

Any flat map is only an approximation of the spherical earth. Cartographers choose special mathematical formulas called projections to render the earth's features on the page, and every projection has benefits and drawbacks. Many maps in the United States use the Mercator projection, which is useful for navigation but misrepresents the relative size of the continents, making Africa look the same size as Greenland. The maps in this book use the Robinson World projection instead, which renders the Earth's equatorial regions more proportionately while compressing the polar regions. For this reason, the scale bar may be used to estimate long distances from east to west across continents, but is not as accurate for measuring north to south.

Map 0
Orientation

Orientation

Introduction

In this first chapter, we investigate how different cultures across the globe understood time and place during the period 500 to 1500. People viewed, and still view, time and geography from culturally specific points of reference. Take, for instance, the term "medieval." This word is particularly tied to European history and not necessarily applicable to the major events of non-European cultures nor to the way those cultures define historical time. Medieval is Latin for middle age, typically used for the period between the fall of the Western Roman Empire (around 500) and the rise of the early modern period of Europe (around 1500). An Islamicate historian might refer to this period as the Rise of Islam (ca. 632) and the Golden Age (ca. 786 to 1258). For a Chinese historian, 500–1500 is a portion of the Imperial Age, which includes eight different dynasties, one of which is called the Five Dynasties and Ten Kingdoms (907–979). The Postclassical period of Mesoamerica is 900–1521 and the historical periods of the Andes (present-day Peru) are Middle Horizon (600–1000), Late Intermediary (1000–1470), and Late Horizon (1470–1532). Japanese historians consider Medieval Japan to extend from around 1100 to 1603. In this book, we use the term "medieval" because it is familiar to the audience reading this book in English, but at some point in the future, there will be a new term, or no term at all, that encompasses a global period between 500 and 1500. There are many ways to think about time.

In Section A, we discuss how different societies imagined and organized time. In direct collaboration, astronomers from China, the Islamicate world, and India found ways to use the motions of the moon, the sun, and the stars to plan and coordinate systems for planting fields, observing religious rituals, collecting taxes, and recording history. European systems emerged from the solar Julian calendar, standardized in the time of Julius Caesar (d. 44 BCE) which, though fairly accurate, gained an extra three days every 400 years. During the period 500–1500, innovations and debates about telling time culminated in the development of the Gregorian calendar, named for Pope Gregory XIII, who introduced it in 1582. Today, it is widely used throughout the world, independently or in correspondence with particular religious calendars. Across the Atlantic Ocean and unknown to these other cultures, Mesoamericans similarly synchronized planting and rituals to the movements of celestial bodies.

In the above examples there is a sense of defining and labeling time, and that time is connected to location. In Section B, we examine maps and mapping systems. In addition to the various ways of marking time, groups defined social identity and claimed resources by naming the features of the immediate geography according to their own legends and events. Maps that survive from communities across the world tell us a lot about the individual cultures that created them. They were tools of political actors and religious leaders for controlling territory, and at the same time they were guides used by merchants and average people to find their way around that territory. What is at the top of a map? That depends on one's perspective.

WHAT WORDS SHOULD WE USE?

Throughout the book, we will explain current theoretical debates about relevant topics and describe new research methods or historical discoveries. In this first theory box, we address how important it is to use care in our word choice, working against both intended and unintended bias and prejudice. Take, for instance, the word orientation. We chose it as the title of this section as an example of how words change meaning in different contexts.

In one sense, orientation in this meaning is our sense of location and direction. When we arrive in a new place, we get oriented to that setting and its community. We use maps to orient ourselves in a new city or on a hiking trail. We attend university or workplace orientation to understand the expectations and opportunities of that new culture. Orient comes from the Latin word *oriri*, to rise, which is related to *oriens*, Latin for where the sun rises, a reliable way to know if one is facing east. Orienting ourselves is knowing where we are, and that is a good thing.

Medieval Europeans called the cultures east of Europe the Orient; they were closer to where the sun rises. But, over time, the words orient and oriental became loaded with prejudiced stereotypes informed by European suspicion and contempt of people living to the east, for instance, in India or China. In one sense, orient is a wonderful word indicating certainty in location and direction. In another sense, Orient is an unacceptable term that communicates derogatory information about non-European peoples. Similarly, we pay attention to the use of words like "west/western" and "east/eastern" as they suggest a binary that did not exist. It is useful to use compass directions, and to relate cultures to one another geographically, but often these geographic words have become more than place, they have cultural significance attached to them (think of the differences brought to mind when we say "East Berlin" and "West Berlin" for example).

Words mean different things in different contexts at different periods of time. Many words commonly used for people in the period 500–1500 are now identified as derogatory and inappropriate. In the past, English words for Muslims were Moors, Saracens, or infidels, all of which carried disparaging judgments about those who practice Islam. Likewise, because they have been used to stigmatize and diminish pre-Christian or non-Christian peoples, pagan and heathen are unacceptable words for non-Christian societies. Originally, pagan and heathen referred to rural people and had connotations of rustic and uneducated. As city dwellers converted to Christianity earlier than their rural neighbors, they used these terms to belittle believers in older, nature-based spiritual systems. They considered pagans to be ignorant and heathens to be sinful instead of simply non-Christian or pre-Christian.

Another example of cultural bias is in the word *ferenji*, which in Arabic referenced the Frankish tribes but came to be used for Western Europeans in general. It still brings connotations of crusade imagery to the minds of many Arabic speakers and is used pejoratively in some African countries.

Even as we reject some words from the mainstream historic conversation, they may appear in medieval texts and in scholarship from not too long ago. Throughout the book we provide examinations of language and invite you to challenge language as well. As we work toward inclusive language accepted by the people it represents, phrasings and definitions will change.

A: TELLING TIME

Introduction

Between 1022 and 1026, Mahmud of Ghazni, the ruler of the Ghaznavid dynasty in the region of present-day Iran and Afghanistan, campaigned in India, seeking to expand his empire. Alongside his military traveled members of his court, including Abu Rayhan al-Biruni – a mathematician, linguist, geographer, and historian. Al-Biruni availed himself of the opportunity to study in northern India, and in his short time there he learned Sanskrit and wrote several books on Indian geography, history, and mathematics. Al-Biruni described for his readers the rivers of India, their sources and courses, the languages, the people, and the relationships among neighboring communities. As an adventurous and curious historian and scientist, he detailed the customs and innovations of a culture new to him. He is an inspiration for the global connections we will make in this text.

Al-Biruni was also interested in the way the people he encountered kept track of months and years. In our modern environments, timekeeping and calendrical devices are ubiquitous – we read a chapter because it is due next Tuesday for a class that starts at 11:00 am. We know how old we are and celebrate our birthdays and anniversaries on particular dates. The calendar most of us use today, the Gregorian calendar, marks the beginning of the year in January; yet, even in this system, there are many ways of marking a year. A fiscal year in the United States can run from July to June. Students and professors often think in terms of academic years, with US students attending school from September to May, Australian students from February to November, and Japanese students from April to March. Precise time-telling is such an integral part of our daily lives that it is almost impossible for us to imagine life without it. For many of us, our calendars are as close as our phones or our wrists.

People of the Middle Ages rarely knew how old they were, counting things like births and deaths in conjunction with a king's rule, the passing of the seasons, a remarkable weather event, or a social calamity. They created periodization and naming techniques that corresponded to and supported survival of the core group. As we mentioned above, no people under discussion in this text ever felt as if they were living in the "medieval" period – that periodization is a modern construct. They thought they were living in the present age, believing themselves to be at an important moment in time, facing an uncertain future.

Evidence: Bede, *On Time* and *On the Reckoning of Time*

Abu Rayhan al-Biruni, *India*

Bernardino de Sahagun, *Florentine Codex*

Shao Yong, *The Book of Supreme World Ordering Principles*

Al-Khwarizmi, *On the Calculation of Hindu Numerals*

Moon, Sun, Stars

Time itself is culturally relative: that is, each culture had and, to some extent still has, its own way of grouping days into units (such as months) and grouping those units into larger units (such as years). Despite this relativity, all cultures use the largest celestial objects (for example, sun and moon) as their first ways of configuring a calendar. Therefore, every calendar is a sign of scientific exploration – knowledge of astronomy and the Earth's relationship to other heavenly bodies requires mathematic and scientific thinking. There are three major empirical ways for understanding celestial time on Earth: lunar, solar, and sidereal (having to do with the stars and planets). The first calendars were lunar, that is, based on the behavior of the moon, the brightest and largest celestial object moving regularly across the night sky. The lunar calendar tracks the moon's phases and bases a year on a certain number of lunar cycles, generally 12, adding up to approximately 354.3670 days. Solar (or tropical) calendars track the seasons from equinox to equinox. An equinox is a point when day and night are of equal length, which happens twice a year, in March and in September. The solar year is approximately 365.2422 days. Sidereal calendars track smaller celestial objects, like the star Sirius, as they appear and reappear in the same place. This cycle equates to the time it takes for the Earth to rotate once around the sun. The sidereal year is around 20 minutes longer than a solar year. Today, most societies use the solar day as the basis of their calendars. However, some cultures in Africa and Eastern Europe have additional variable months related to the lunar month that range in time from one to 29 days.

Medieval astronomers and calendar creators spent much time and effort in intercalation, attempting to reconcile lunar and solar calendars – a difference of 11 days a year – or mesh solar and sidereal calendars, showing the movement of stars across the night sky and the sun across the horizon. Noting the movement of sun, moon, and stars, studying their physical natures, and attempting to understand the universe in which we live became the scientific fields of astronomy and cosmology. For many scientists today, astronomy is considered the "first science," as humans began observing and measuring the stars as early as 30,000 years ago. Cosmology is the subset of astronomy interested in the origins and evolution of the universe, which we see in the earliest forms of astronomical science. Astronomy was usually called astrology in the ancient and medieval worlds and was what we could consider both a science and a pseudoscience. While astrologers carefully recorded the movements of celestial objects to understand the physics and motion of the Earth, they often did so at the behest of leaders who sought to understand the will of the gods through the alignments and arrangements of the stars. Scholars often debated whether astrology, and by extension astronomy, were legitimate sciences. By the seventeenth century, European scientists deemed astronomy a science and astrology a pseudoscience.

Obviously, the most significant way people kept track of time was by the light and dark of day and night and by the cycle of seasons, which determined the sources and abundance of food, but calendars informed by scientific observation of the cosmos were further developed for religious and political purposes. In order to honor and worship on significant days, religious administrations created calendars that were in turn used by powerful rulers – emperors of Chinese dynasties, European Christian kings, Mediterranean and Arab caliphs, and Mesoamerican leaders of the Maya and Aztec – who sought to standardize important dates for their subjects. Distribution of standardized calendar systems (along with standardized weights, measures, coinages, and other aspects of daily life) was considered an important part of creating strong and centralized political leadership. Kings and emperors wanted and used calendars, which academics and scientists designed. Political groups later used calendars to organize their societies, to collect taxes, to create rituals, and to unify people within their realms. We move through time here, beginning our discussion with the cyclical time systems of the Chinese, before moving to the linear systems of the European Christian and Islamicate worlds, and conclude with the cyclical structure of the Mesoamericans.

Chinese Calendars

From the Han dynasty (206 BCE–220 CE) forward, China's strong centralized government published calendars to be used around the country, and the strongly literate bureaucratic class assured that most Chinese people were well acquainted with these calendars. The Tai Shu calendar (ca. 100 BCE) was the

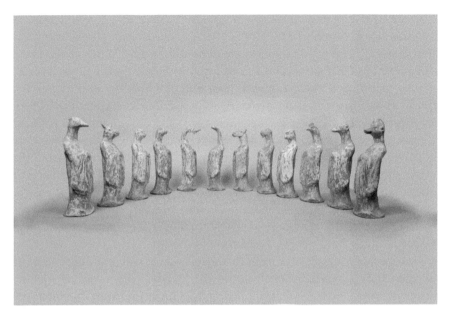

Fig 0.1
These earthenware statuettes from the eighth century are the animals of the Chinese zodiac figures dressed in robes. While some are damaged – for example the rabbit (fourth from the left) has lost its ears – the dragon and snake in the center are recognizable. The semi-human creatures are arranged from left to right in order of the 12-year cycle of the Chinese calendar: rat, ox, tiger, rabbit, dragon, snake, horse, sheep, monkey, rooster, dog, and boar.
Metropolitan Museum of Art, Gift of Charlotte C. Weber, 2000, 2000.662.7a–l

first complete calendar published by the Chinese government that officially connected astronomical events with astrological symbolism. The cultural and religious connections to astrology, that is the belief that the movement or appearance of celestial objects affects human events and behaviors, were important for both the aristocratic and the average Chinese person. The 12 astrological signs date from at least 200 BCE and, by 600 CE, most Chinese people calculated dates almost exclusively from the zodiac. Zodiac has the same Ancient Greek root as zoo and means an array of animals. People born within a particular year, say that of the dog or the monkey, were said to share character traits of those animals.

In the Chinese calendar system, birthdays, marriages, deaths, and important economic and political transactions were all checked against the astrological signs and the date. Years were numbered 1–10 and named along the zodiac, like 1-Rat or 2-Ox. The year was also numbered according to the emperor's reign, so a year might have a four-part name: Year Five of Empress Wu, 3-Tiger. Daily and yearly time was marked with astronomical events, although the exact reckoning changed by both region and era. Days generally began at midnight and months began at the new moon, so the Chinese followed solar, lunar, and sidereal reckoning points. Their year began on the second or third new moon after the winter solstice and was therefore a moving date, announced by the central government and followed by most of the Chinese provinces.

The 12-year cycle may have been related to the planet Jupiter, important within Chinese astrology, which rotates around the Earth every 12 years. This sidereal rotation does not, however, account for the solar/lunar drift, and various methods of intercalation developed in China. The most popular was a complicated 24-point system devised during the Tang dynasty that counted the movement of the Earth around the sun. To accurately figure these movements and account for the difference between solar, lunar, and sidereal years, the Office of Astrology kept detailed records of the night sky. These cosmologists also added important historical data to their logs, creating for historians a significant record of both earthly and astronomical events.

THE BOOK OF SUPREME WORLD ORDERING PRINCIPLES

Shao Yong (d. 1077), one of the most learned men in Chinese philosophical history, wrote on Neo-Confucianism, poetry, and cosmology. His work, *The Book of Supreme World Ordering Principles*, used astrology, astronomy, and the calculation of time to explain the philosophical principles that underlay the Chinese ideas of heaven and Earth. Numbers lay at the heart of Shao Yong's perception of the universe, as he felt they were the principle by which all the world was ordered. The idea that the universe could be understood mathematically also had a deeply spiritual aspect. His numerology (the belief that numbers hold important spiritual or divine value) was complex, and he developed numerical systems to explain many philosophical ideals, such as predestination. His most famous mathematical principles were additions to the ancient text of the *I Ching*, where he added a hexagram arrangement with a binary representation of the numbers 0 to 63. This was the first use of binary within history, 600 years prior to Liebniz and about 900 years before the digital computing revolution.

All these ways of reckoning time were important to the empire, both in secular and spiritual matters. The emperor himself was the link between the Heavens and the Middle Kingdom (as the Chinese empire was known), and his divine mandate to rule (The Mandate of Heaven, explained in chapters 3 and 7) ensured that he must keep the equilibrium between heaven and Earth, between the gods and humanity, between himself and his subjects. A correct calculation of time confirmed that the emperor and his court held the Mandate of Heaven, which legitimized his rule. One of four major duties of the emperor was to sustain the effective operation of the government administration, and this was aided by accurate timekeeping. The calendar was a sacred document, created by the imperial court and held up as proof of the emperor's divine right to rule.

From the eleventh to the early fourteenth century, mathematics became one of the most important topics for scholars in China. Mathematicians held

```
                          1
                       1     2
                    1     4     4
                 1     6    12     8
              1     8    24    32    16
           1    10    40    80    80    32
        1    12    60   160   240   192    64
     1    14    84   280   560   672   448   128
```

Fig 0.2
Pascal's triangle for computing square and cube roots.

honored places in the Chinese court and these scholars excelled at mathematical place value and algorithms. Jia Xian (d. 1070), a court mathematician of the Song dynasty (960–1279), published a *Mathematics Manual* in 1050 (now lost) that described the algorithm for root extraction, a history of Chinese and Islamic mathematic methods, and other principles. He also invented the Jia Xian triangle, which allowed him to calculate square and cube roots. In European science, this triangle was independently invented in 1654 by the French philosopher Blaise Pascal (Pascal's triangle), six centuries later.

The later Song mathematician Yang Hui (d. ca. 1298) described multiplication, division, root extraction, quadratic equations, and computation of figures like triangles. He acknowledged his debt to Jia Xian's earlier works (including his triangle), and he stressed understanding the theoretical principles behind the mathematics. These mathematicians influenced court astronomers, who used the new mathematic equations to figure better answers to combining solar and lunar years. New mathematic and calendrical information from Islamic merchants also informed Chinese systems. An unnamed Syrian astronomer who was invited to the Yuan court brought the systems of the Greeks, Christians, and Muslims to the Eastern Empire. He spent time at various observatories along the trade routes from the Middle East to China and was hired by the emperor to help correct the Chinese calendar. The Shou Shi calendar of 1281 was the result of the efforts of these Chinese and Islamic scientists. They calculated the solar year as 365.2425 days, which is only .003 off modern calculations. It was also completed 300 years prior to the Gregorian calendar reform of Europe, which would also find the year to be 365.2425 days long.

European Calendars

The Gregorian calendar of 1582 is the calendar most recognized by students today, as the majority of the world uses this calendar for economic and political purposes. (This is also the calendrical system we use in this textbook.) Brought into use by Pope Gregory XIII of the Roman Christian Church, the calendar was the culmination of Muslim and Christian refinements of the Roman Julian

Calendar, introduced by Julius Caesar in 45 BCE. The Julian calendar fixed the "wandering" dates of the earlier Roman calendar by setting the solar year at 365.25 days and adding an extra day every four years to account for the odd quarter (.25) of a day. Unfortunately, this calculation was not quite correct; the Julian calendar gained an extra three days every 400 years. Over 1,500 years, those odd days added up and distorted timekeeping. The Gregorian calendar "fixed" this Julian drift by dropping ten days from the calendar (so with a pen stroke in 1582, October 15 followed October 4) and changing the number of leap years. While these changes reduced the Julian shortfall, the Gregorian calendar is still slightly off in a way that will result in an extra day every 3,300 years. For most of the European Middle Ages, however, regular people had no access to, or little interest in, either the Julian or Gregorian calendars, dating instead by religious events, natural phenomena, seasons, or the reigns of secular or religious leaders. For these calendars, scientific and mathematic reckoning worked in service to the religious needs and planting cycles of the culture.

Setting the Date of Easter

Instead of seeing time as the Chinese had (a series of repeated cycles), Christians and Muslims saw time as linear, leading from events mentioned in the Old Testament (Jewish Tanakh) to events in the New Testament and/or Qur'an, and from current events to the end of the world. The need to create universal histories (histories from the beginning of humanity to current times) led religiously inspired scholars to work on dating systems. They used mathematical calculation to reconcile astronomical phenomena with biblical events (for example, proving the time of Christ's birth and death and anticipating the apocalypse that would effectively "end time"). One of these projects was standardizing the dating of Easter. The observance of the persecution and death of Jesus and his resurrection as the divine Christ was the most solemn religious event within the Christian liturgical year. It also lay near the Jewish festival of Passover (the Jewish festival to celebrate the escape from slavery from ancient Egypt). Since the Council of Nicaea in 325, Christian bishops actively worked to disassociate Easter from Passover, urging their congregations to disregard customary Jewish dating systems. This created a need for a fully "Christian" calendar.

By the sixth century, there were two competing dating schemes for Easter. The Christian Churches of Europe and the Greek East followed this formula: Easter was to be observed on the first Sunday after the full moon after the vernal equinox (in the Northern Hemisphere), so long as that date was not the first day of Passover. The second scheme, followed by the Celtic Church in Northern Europe and the Christian Church in Ethiopia, fixed the date of the equinox as March 21, rather than following the actual and changeable event of the equinox as indicated by the position of the sun. Easter shifted significantly depending on where one worshipped, and since the Julian calendar that all the churches followed also had drift, it became necessary for the Christian bishops to ensure some sort of consistency of celebration.

PASCHAL FEAST

The Latin for Passover was "Paschalis." The New Testament books of Matthew, Mark, and Luke all describe the last supper Jesus shares with his disciples as a Passover feast. John describes Jesus's supper as happening prior to Passover, and *paschalis* remains the root word for Easter in most European languages outside of German and English. The German and English word "Easter" comes from "Oster," or east, and has the meaning of aurora or dawn. It was associated with the spring season and renewal. Both Passover and Easter have their beginnings in spring fertility rituals emphasizing the hope for a fruitful and bountiful growing season.

During the sixth century, a monk named Dionysius Exiguus (d. 544) created a new calendar that calculated the date of Easter for the next 95 years. Wanting to keep the focus on Jesus Christ and Christian ideals and not pre-Christian fertility rituals, Dionysius was the first to introduce the idea of *anno domini*, or "in the year of the Lord" as a beginning point of Christian history. The year Jesus was born would from then on be called the year 1; thus, he imposed a Christian framework on the counting of years, decades, and centuries. BC (before Christ) and AD (*anno domini*) were taken for granted in large parts of the world as the system of historical dating until very recently, when non-Christian peoples protested against this Christianizing of time. However, since 2,000 years of events are organized within this system, it is thought impossible to discard it. The compromise is the change to BCE (before the common era) and CE (common era).

Another of Dionysius's major improvements to the calendar was his Latin term for "nothing" or "none" – *nihil* or *nulla* – used as a word, not a mathematical number – which he used to date the vernal equinox more precisely. The more precise the vernal equinox, the more accurate the date of Easter. Christians in the Greek East accepted the new Easter tables but not the calibration of them from the zero of *anno domini*. Byzantine Christianity continued to use older ways of figuring years, labeling them by the years of reign of particular emperors. They also continued to use the *anno mundi*, or year of the beginning of the world, system that tracks the history of the world to events described in the Jewish Bible (Christian Old Testament).

Dionysius's dating system and his more precise Easter tables gained credibility and were picked up and spread by a scholar-monk in northern England known as the Venerable Bede (d. 735). In reading Dionysius, Bede finally found a system for computing the date of Easter that he could use as a framework for his own historical studies and writings, such as *On Time, On the Reckoning of Time*, and *Ecclesiastical History of the English People*. His works were highly popular, with hundreds of copies of his manuscripts still to be found in monasteries across Europe. As more scholars read Bede's work, they used his Easter tables, and his dating schema became more popular throughout the Western Christian world. The success and widespread appeal of his treatises did more for changing calendars in Europe than Dionysius had done with specific papal approval.

These eighth-century calendars aided religious authorities in Europe and the Greek East in their consolidation of Easter celebrations, and a unified Christian calendar helped in the foundation of the new European governments; however, the new calendars did not fix the Julian shift, and the Gregorian calendar, introduced in 1582, attempted to correct the deficiency of the Julian calendar by changing the solar year's duration in days from 365.25 to 365.2425 – a reduction of almost 11 minutes per year (and finally in agreement with the Chinese calendar). Better astronomical observations and improved mathematical knowledge, led by the medieval Islamic introduction of zero and invention of algebra, allowed for these changes to the modern calendar.

Islamic Calendars

The extraordinary expansion of Islam from a small central core of believers in seventh-century Arabia to a tenth-century empire stretching from Spain, through northern Africa, and to India, gave Muslims the unique opportunity to mesh different calendrical systems. Rapid conquest meant Muslim leaders ruled disparate people of many faiths and cultural traditions, and there was a strong need for one calendar system to unify the activities of the converted peoples.

Islam's "common era" or CE begins with Muhammad's flight from Mecca to Medina in 622 CE (called the "hijra," of which more below). This is the Islamic year 1, known as Anno Hegirae 1. The Islamic calendar is lunisolar, based on a combination of movements of the moon and the sun. A Muslim's use of the solar calendar is daily prayer – a Muslim should pray five times daily (*salat*). The first prayer is at sunrise, the second when the sun is at its zenith (noon), the third at mid-afternoon, the fourth at sunset, and the fifth at night. To keep Muslims in concord with each other, a *muezzin* recited the *adhan*, which called Muslims within hearing to the prayers. Islam used, and still uses, a lunar calendar for holidays and rituals, the most important being Ramadan, the lunar month of fasting, where Muslims should abstain from food, drink, and sexual intercourse during the daylight hours. It happens during the ninth month of the lunar year, begins with the sighting of the crescent moon, and lasts either 29 or 30 days. Since the lunar calendar is about 11 days shorter than the solar calendar, this ritual moves each year. As Muslims traveled and settled around the globe, this ritual was celebrated at different times, depending on the first sighting of the moon, which is different in various places around the Earth. Modern Muslims often joke about their far-flung families starting their fasts on different days; some areas still rely on sighting the moon, while others rely on astronomical calculations. This ritual is an interesting amalgam of solar and lunar uses of the calendar, as the fasting is set to be from dawn to dusk, using the twilight to determine the daily timing (just before the sun appears or just after it disappears), and is one lunar month in duration.

In addition to using astronomical events as markers of ritual events, Islamic imperial governments quickly saw the benefits of having a solid, central calendar that brought into alignment the spiritual calendars of conquered North African Christians, sub-Saharan polytheists, and Persian Zoroastrians. Leaders also understood that calendars based on secular needs allowed an empire to operate more efficiently, and as Muslim traders moved and sold goods throughout the large swaths of land in Eurasia and Africa, they benefited from a common calendar. The solar calendar used by almost all groups in Africa and Eurasia was often used for primarily secular, and not spiritual, reasons. It therefore seemed the best foundation for a common calendar as it did not elevate one religion over another, and left the lunisolar religious calendar of the Muslim faith intact. Although there is no evidence showing us who chose to use the solar calendar first for economic purposes, we do find evidence that the solar reckoning of time became the norm in trade during the period 500–1500.

Mathematics and the Zero

So far we have discussed how peoples used celestial events such as sunrises, lunar sets, and star crossings as a basis for the creation of their calendars, and as these groups came into contact with each other their knowledge of the world expanded and changed. Muslim merchants brought their systems into China, and, as we saw above, later Chinese emperors requested Muslim scientists to come to China for more in-depth study. Muslims used lunar systems like their Jewish neighbors but added the solar calendar to meet the needs of their constituents. Christians worked to link solar and lunar calendars together for events like Easter, so that they might be consistently celebrated across far-flung areas. But the most important scientific addition to calendars came out of India.

Understanding time is really about understanding mathematics. By attempting to order years, days, and hours, we are practicing the scientific language of numbers and their relationships to each other and the physical world. The most important mathematical development of this period was the invention of the notational idea of zero. Both the Mesopotamians and the Maya invented a notational place keeper, meaning a symbol that represented nothingness; however, in the period 500 to 1500, Indians really understood how the zero could be used in a mathematical sense. Adding zero to mathematical equations allowed scientists to figure out the length of a solar year with much more precision, and this knowledge spread throughout the expanding Muslim world and also changed how other Asian societies and Europeans computed annual time.

An important player in this transmission of Indian numerals to Muslim lands outside India was al-Khwarizmi (d. ca. 850), a Persian intellectual who was a member of what is called the House of Wisdom – a general center of scholarship in the Muslim capital of Baghdad that bustled with philosophers, linguists, and scientists translating into Arabic a vast collection of texts in Greek, Latin, Indian, Persian, and other languages. His major work, *On the Calculation of Hindu Numerals*, was the first introduction of the Hindu numbering system outside India. We only have one extant (surviving) copy of this important work, but its many later translations show us how important these mathematical concepts became. Al-Khwarizmi also worked on astronomical tables, figured the circumference of the Earth, created a map that included eastern Asia and Africa, and invented algebra. In fact, the word *algebra* comes from al-Khwarizmi's book on the topic, which translates into English as *The Book of Calculation by Completion and Balancing*, but is also known by one word in the Arabic title, *al-jabr*. (A tenth-century Persian mathematician, al-Karaji, would invent algebraic proofs, much to the delight of middle-schoolers everywhere.) Taken together, this prolific scholar aided in the transmission and use of Hindu numerals.

Al-Biruni (d. 1048), an Islamic scholar and mathematician born near the Aral Sea, began his mathematical career early, around age 17, when he calculated the latitude of his home city by observing the altitude of the sun. Traveling around the far eastern reaches of the Islamicate, he kept detailed accounts of astronomical events. When he was about 50, he went into India with his patron, who was attempting to conquer sections of northern India. There, al-Biruni learned Sanskrit and began translating Indian texts into Arabic. His work, now known as *Tarikh al-Hind* (*The History of India*), covers social, cultural, political, and, of course, mathematical information garnered from his time spent there. Based on his own interests, he wrote extensively on Hindu mathematics, astronomy, and

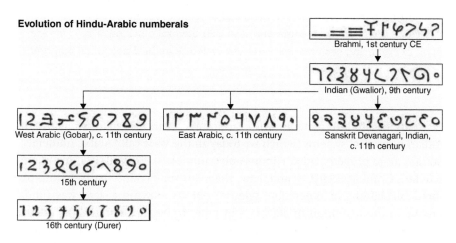

Evolution of Hindu-Arabic numerals

Brahmi, 1st century CE

Indian (Gwalior), 9th century

West Arabic (Gobar), c. 11th century

East Arabic, c. 11th century

Sanskrit Devanagari, Indian, c. 11th century

15th century

16th century (Durer)

Fig 0.3
The evolution of Hindu numerals into the Arabic forms that became a standard mathematical symbol set across the world.

calendric calculations. His most important mathematical work is contained in *The Exhaustive Treatise of Shadows*, which details the mathematical principles behind shadows and shade, and how to use shadows in calculating astronomical events. In this text, al-Biruni combines theoretical concepts with examples of their practical uses, and his careful observations on mathematics, astronomy, and physics show us the sophisticated state of scientific thought in India and the eastern Islamicate.

Al-Biruni's translations of Indian calendars are evidence that the Indian astronomers synchronized the lunar and solar calendars into complicated and comprehensive systems that were almost impossible to follow. We know, for example, that the Indians calculated over 26 different calendars aiming to keep the calculations correct. It was also important for religious observation to measure time from the smallest concept of the day to the largest hypotheses of cosmological time; these cyclical creations, lasting thousands of years, struck al-Biruni as interesting, and his treatise, *Tarikh al-Hind* dedicated over 12 chapters to the Indian conceptions of time.

BASE 10

In a base-10 numbering system, there are ten integer possibilities (0 to 9). "Ten" becomes the "basis" of the system, hence base-10. It is, today, the most widely used and understood system. We have ten fingers on two hands, and modern science shows us that the human brain can only conceive of five objects at once before we start to group them into smaller clusters. Nonetheless, different systems have been, and continue to be, used. Other base systems have different numbers as their basis. So, a base-18 uses 18 integer possibilities; base-20 uses 20 integer possibilities. In the West, we also use a base-7 system – for counting the days of the week. And computers use a base-2 (or binary) system for digital computing. Philosophers of Ancient Babylon used a base-60 system, which is still evident in the geometry of a circle and the 60-second clock. Degrees of an angle are base-360. Several other base systems are in use in encryption or ciphering systems. All these are called "standard positional numeral systems."

Translations and interpretations by Islamicate scholars helped to popularize the Indian numerical systems (which we today in the West call "Arabic numerals," but are more properly titled Hindu-Arabic numerals). This allowed for Islamic scholars, Chinese scientists, and, later, their Christian counterparts, to improve their calculations of observable celestial objects. Having a zero was fundamental to the invention of algebra – in order to begin finding for a variable, zero and negative numbers become necessary. Once mathematics included algebra (around 800), algebra was included in astronomy. Using algebraic equations allowed astronomers to measure speeds and movements of celestial objects with more specificity; this aided in fine-tuning the measurements of the solar and lunar years, which was of importance to the Abrahamic faiths, who used equinoxes and moon phases to dictate when their religious rituals would happen.

Mesoamerica – Maya and Aztec

The Mesoamerican civilizations of the Maya (ca. 250 to 1500) and Aztec (ca. 1400 to 1500), had calendrical systems that accommodated both spiritual and secular usages. The spiritual calendar tied the leaders, government, and the people together, and rulers who had the power of creating and controlling the calendars used them to support economic practices and secure political power.

The historical Maya of Central America kept amazingly accurate calendars that showed their concern with the past, the present, and the future. They primarily followed a lunisolar model (similar to the Muslim calendar described above), with the solar calendar used for agrarian purposes, the lunar calendar used for ritual purposes, and both calendars used in service to the government and ruler. The authority and power of the king was tied to his ability to regulate and enforce time – that is, he had to maintain and promote ceremonies on the specific dates and times required by their religion. In a similar fashion to the Chinese emperor's Mandate of Heaven being tied, in part, to his maintenance of the calendar, proper observation and protection of the Mesoamerican calendar was a king's main administrative duty. Failing to do so could endanger the community, as the gods may see fit to cease the progression of time for a people who did not worship properly and punctually.

The Maya used base-18 and base-20 systems (as opposed to our base-10 system) for their numbering and calendars. The solar calendar had 18 months of 20 days, with an extra 5 days added to the end to account for the sun's cycle, adding up to a 365-day solar year. The lunar year held 20 months of 13 days each, for a 260-day lunar year. There were 38 named months: each lunar and solar month was named after a god, such as Imix and Sip. Every day was also numbered, but lunar and solar months were numbered separately: 1–13 in lunar months and 1–20 in solar months. Therefore, every date was expressed using the lunar day and month and solar day and month, for example: 1 Imix (lunar day and month) 3 Sip (solar day and month). The years were counted in 52-year cycles of 260-day lunar years. We do not know if these time periods were meant to mirror life spans (52 years was the average life span of most Mesoamericans) and pregnancies (the length of visible human gestation is about 268 days) but the coincidence is there. The Maya idea of zero was the creation of mankind, according to Maya mythology. This date corresponds roughly to 3114 BCE, and events were dated from that time forward in what is called the Long Count calendar.

An important facet of Mesoamerican time, then, is its relationship to the continuation of the universe and the connection between the gods and humanity. The Maya and other Mesoamerican astronomers tied their dates to the names of the gods and the paths of celestial objects. These astronomical and calendrical observations imposed some order on the ineffable nature of the gods – if the gods were tied to the stars, and astronomers could predict the motion of the stars, then they might also be able to predict the will of the gods. This allowed the astronomers to create detailed genealogies of the gods: since the gods were stars (and other environmental phenomena like fire and water) and humans could observe the environment for patterns, then perhaps they could discern the history of the gods themselves. Like many cultures, the Maya rulers claimed to be descended from gods, so the genealogy placed the current kings in direct line with the heavens: they ruled by divine right. Nevertheless, Maya astronomers were concerned not just about history and its relationship to rulers, but also about cosmology: the history of all things, of all time, and how it related to and proved the importance and legitimacy of rulers and civilizations. They sought the origin of time to establish and preserve the authority of their aristocracy.

In the postclassical period of 1300–1521, another Mesoamerican people, the Aztec, created the grand city of Tenochtitlan and founded an empire stretching from the Gulf of Mexico to the Pacific Ocean. Through the European men who wrote about the Nahua, we read their horror at Mexica practices of human sacrifice (which, as we detail below, had solemn significance for perpetuating the people and the environment for another 52-year cycle), about Mexica militaristic conquests, and about the "barbarity" of their religion and people. European commentators wrote about Mesoamerican practices in a way that demonized the conquered, in particular using the idea of Aztec human sacrifice to further their own conquest. Because Europeans destroyed much of Mesoamerican artistic and written records, especially because they considered these records as representations of a malevolent religion, we know very little about how the Nahua felt about their world, their rulers, or their calendars. But subsequent archeological and linguistic work has been done to recover a history of these people, and deeper study into the Nahua people shows a vibrant and diverse culture just beginning to form a strong bureaucratic government when the Spanish arrived.

AZTEC, THE PEOPLE OF AZTLAN

Today, we use "Aztec" to refer to the people and culture that controlled Central Mexico from the fourteenth to the sixteenth century. The people of central Mexico spoke the Nahuatl language, and, although the Aztec were only one of many groups within this region, modern people often use the term Aztec to refer to all the Nahua peoples who occupied Central Mexico. The Aztec are more properly the Mexica (pronounced *meh-she-cah* in Nahuatl) – the particular subgroup that ruled this area. "Aztec" was coined by the Prussian historian Alexander von Humboldt in the nineteenth century. He combined the names Aztlan and the suffix *tec(atl)* to create a name that means "the People of Aztlan." European historians of the nineteenth century, in particular, renamed colonized peoples without their knowledge or consent; these names would not have been recognized by those people so named. We use "Aztec" here because it is recognizable to students, but "Mexica" is the more proper term for the Nahua rulers of Central Mexico, and Nahua refers to all the people of the region, both the rulers and the ruled. We will use Aztec in generalities, but Mexica when we refer to the rulers of the area, and Nahua to refer to the peoples of Central Mexico.

Despite the wanton destruction of Aztec documents, their carved stone calendars show us a packed schedule of rituals and festivals. Inscribed in the calendar is both the lunar 260-day year and the solar 365-day year – each associated with differing celestial and earthly events. The entire calendar was set in the 52-Year Cycle, the end of which was a fateful and dangerous period. To forestall the imminent destruction of the world at the end of each 52-year cycle, the Aztec performed the New Fire Ceremony. People put out their fires, destroyed pottery and household tools, and sacrificed a human to the gods. This was an important point in Nahua cosmology – they believed their gods had sacrificed themselves in order to bring life and food to the people; therefore, it was a fair

Fig 0.4
Carved in the Piedra del Sol or the Stone of the Sun are figures of the days, weeks, and months of the Aztec calendar. Etched in the central disk is the name of the Aztec ruler Moctezuma II, who reigned between 1502 and 1520. It weighs 54,210 pounds, about 25 tons.
Deposit Photos

exchange for them to sacrifice a human for their gods. Bernardino de Sahagun (ca. 1499–1590), a Spanish Catholic priest, wrote of this in the *Florentine Codex*. He explained how the Nahua believed the blood of the gods created humanity, animals, and foodstuffs. Then the gods reaffirmed their sacrifices for humanity by destroying the old era and bringing in the new era. Through the sacrifices, both human and divine, the end of the world was postponed for another 52 years.

Mexica priests wrote and kept their calendars as a way to mark the religious needs of their community. The calendars served as reminders that, venerated correctly, the gods would provide for their people. Throughout the year, Nahua celebrated and worshipped at various temples of a selection of gods associated with particular months and seasons. For example, people left offerings of cornhusks, tamales, and woven mats to the corn god Cinteotl during the beginning of Hueytozoztli (our month of April) as a way of asking for a good corn harvest that year.

WHAT ARE HISTORIOGRAPHY AND PRESENTISM?

As we are talking about time, here we introduce the concept of historiography and a qualification about "presentism." As constructed by human beings such as scholars and philosophers, the history of any group or phenomenon is not necessarily truth, but instead, an effort to create a truth by taking deep and extensive research and determining and interpreting what it tells us about that topic. One historian may look particularly at the spiritual documents, objects, and practices of a certain group to make judgments about that culture based on its religious history. Another may study the trading practices, monetary systems, and economic power of the same culture to determine a different truth about it.

While all historians use sources, their ideas about what constitutes a valid source may, and does, change over time. The questions they ask of their sources also differ, as do the methods they use for interpreting source materials. The differences in interpretation of that evidence lead us to the expanding world of historical and literary analysis – each one of us can approach the past, read and analyze the evidence, and advance an interpretation for others to use and critique. Techniques for interpreting history change as well, as do ideas about what constitutes a valid topic of study. The study of how people have produced history is called *historiography*.

Since this text looks back in time anywhere from 1,500 to 500 years, our historiography seeks to avoid *presentism*, which is imposing present-day, anachronistic values on the evidence the people of the past have left behind. Our goal as researchers of the past is to avoid presentism and embrace *cultural relativism*, that is, considering that people are products of the prevailing social norms and cultures in which they live. That said, we can also consider that, as human beings, people of the past certainly had similar needs to our own. For instance, they sought psychological and spiritual comfort, useful tools and interesting art, fair and reasonable justice, and fellowship. Some ideas are universal across cultures and time.

Conclusion

Having one or two major calendars could create a sense of identity among a population and unity in their habits and customs, even if that population was dispersed. Once the calendars were centralized, Muslims fasted together throughout their wide-ranging empires every year. In Europe, Christians were assured that they all celebrated Easter together. When Jews sat down to Passover Seder, they did so knowing that Jews all over Europe and western Asia did so roughly at the same time. When the Fire Ceremony began at the end of the 52-Year Cycle, the Nahua gathered together to renew their world. Designed from spiritual pretexts and for religious use, calendars became tools for kings and bureaucracies. Holidays, festivals, and taxation were regulated and controlled by a central bureaucratic calendar. These practices of naming and controlling time fit well with the next concept, that of naming and controlling space through maps. Intercultural exchanges of mathematic and astronomical information led to refinement of scientific methods that would be used increasingly by cartographers and travelers to expand the spread of religions, the networks of merchants and markets, the claims of rulers, and the spread of ideas. By the end of the sixteenth century, innovations in calendaring and mapping led to the ability of sailors to navigate the world, thus bringing Eurasian and Mesoamerican concepts of time and space into comparison and collision.

WHOSE HISTORY?

Throughout this book, we aim to demonstrate that there is no single right way to describe the world – globally or locally – and the events from the period 500–1500. There have been and continue to be unbalanced narratives that privilege one group over another, as well as countless attempts to silence some voices from telling their stories, or to censor accounts or images that might be considered offensive to some but which are liberating for others. Scholars, curators, activists, and citizens of the world or the World Wide Web have worked to champion equitable presentations of the past, as painful as it may be in some instances, with the hope of a brighter future. This theory box considers a few of the scholarly approaches to studying the past with an equity mindset.

Social history and class studies – This is the study of all people, especially those not in the highest echelons of society. The ways that individuals and groups organize themselves can reveal information about class systems, working conditions, and the relationship between urban and rural areas in a local context. We might also compare aspects of social history on a global level, for example, by considering the role that children played in one region or how those with pre-existing medical conditions were treated by a community. This purview falls under social history and class studies.

Feminism – Global feminism includes a range of movements and efforts to combat gender stereotypes and, more importantly, to dismantle gender inequalities. For historians, one feminist approach is to foreground women's voices and perspectives. We generally look at four "waves" or milestones in feminism: the first centered on women's suffrage, or voting rights in the early 1900s; the second is often synonymous with the Women's Liberation Movement of the 1960s that sought equity for women under the law; the third arose in the 1990s and looked to the diversity of women's experiences (especially in relation to Kimberlé Crenshaw's ideas about intersectionality; see below); and the fourth began online around 2012 with #MeToo and other calls on social media to combat sexual harassment.

Gender and queer studies – Perspectives about gender and sexuality continue to expand and to be at the forefront of global discourse. Academic studies of each rely upon class studies, feminism, postcolonial discourse, critical race theory, and others, including religion, politics, economics, and the law. What we have just described is an intersectional approach to a global Middle Ages, one that considers how systems of power oppress or disenfranchise people based on their multiple intersecting identities. Queer studies is a blanket term that examines the often-overlooked lives of individuals who identify as lesbian, gay, bisexual, transgender, queer, intersex, asexual, two-spirit, and other gender nonconforming or nonbinary identities (often abbreviated by the acronym LGBTQIA2+). Just as the term "medieval" is a modern construct, so too are the words "homosexual" or any of the terms used in the previous sentence. We cannot always know how an individual in the past might have identified – and we have to be careful not to "out" someone – but we can widen our field of focus by looking at expanded ideas about gender or sexuality that push beyond the male/female binary or that see heterosexual as default.

Postcolonial discourse – Studying the legacy of colonialism and imperialism – especially of European powers and of the United States – is the remit of postcolonial discourse. Scholars apply numerous approaches, drawn from the fields mentioned in this theory box, as well as from anthropology and postmodernism, the last of which rejects grand ideas about progress or knowledge-based inquiry. One approach that critiques the colonial enterprise is referred to as Indigenous Ways of Knowing, which may involve oral history, Native traditions and cultural practices, and an understanding that individuals and land are symbiotically connected. Another approach is called "Southern Theory," which considers perspectives from societies in the global South (including sub-Saharan Africa, Latin America, India, and Austronesia). The term "decolonize" is often used in relation to institutions and even to the teaching profession – the inherent meaning behind the term is to assess imbalances of power, to address histories of exploitation, and to work toward justice for all.

Critical race theory – Identities are often linked to a place and time. As the title of Section B states, "Where I am is who I am." During the period covered by this book, people around the world often defined themselves in relation to those around them, especially those who looked, acted, or believed differently. Epidermal race or somatic difference – that is, societal constructions of identity based on the color of one's skin – was a category for defining and describing oneself and others. This colorism often involved ideas about climate and geography – through which writers and thinkers understood links between temperature and skin tones, for example – but could also include confessional categories of one's religion or creed. Thus the words Saracen and Moor could at times be used interchangeably and derogatorily to refer to a Black African and to a Muslim (or to a Black African Muslim). Critical race theory examines the history of race and the ways in which racial categories are discussed throughout time.

Disability studies – Many of the above methodologies deal with the human body and how it is understood or described according to beliefs, laws, science, or medicine. As we have seen, these ideas are not without biases. Disability studies takes a close look at how societies and medical fields have historically understood cognitive, developmental, intellectual, mental, physical, and sensory conditions of ability or disability. Scholars using this perspective might look at deafness, mental health, the autism spectrum, or illness and disease. It is important to take care not to attempt to diagnose conditions of people in the past but to approach a text or image with empathy, to analyze the role that shame and stigma play in relation to an individual's abilities, and to be alert to ableist narratives or stereotypes.

As you read each chapter, take note of which approaches have been taken in order to tell inclusive and equitable stories about the past. Sometimes a combination of methods is needed, depending on the type of evidence being considered. Sometimes the perspective may need further development. Begin to think about how you construct ideas about history and about the world and the people around you.

23

B: WHERE I AM IS WHO I AM

Introduction

As we have seen, calendars and the organization of time are fundamental to communal stability and identity. Maps from the period under study demonstrate the cultural beliefs and concerns of the people who created them. Groups look for lands with resources from which to make and maintain shelters. They need access to fertile soil for sowing, sustainable vegetation for flocks and herds, and access to water and land where there is plentiful fish and game. They need terrain that provides defensible positions against hostile invaders. Each community draws its maps according to its spiritual and economic needs, its perceived claims to territories, and its remembered connection to those spaces.

These boundaries between groups are political and relative; they have nothing to do with the impersonal geography and geological forces of planet Earth. Seen from space, Earth does not have boundary lines separating nations, provinces, counties, and neutral zones, nor does it have a north/south or east/west orientation. A spaceship is not under or over the planet. It is always *next to* some point of reference and *inside* or *outside* the Earth's gravitational pull. Astronauts in space do not navigate by north or south or up or down except as defined for them, in a spaceship, with a floor-to-ceiling design, created on Earth. Our sense of our location is relative to the culture with which we identify. For example, in Egypt, the Nile River flows from the south (in the mountains) to the north (in the delta), so for Egyptians, up-river is going south, and down-river is going north. This section considers some important maps and what they tell us about the cultures that produced them. There are other examples throughout the book.

Evidence: Yu Ji Tu (Map of the Tracks of Yu)

Hereford *Mappa Mundi*

Pliny the Elder, *The Natural History*, Book 2, "The Wonderful Forms of Other Nations"

al-Idrisi map

Map of the Tracks of Yu

By the mid-eleventh century, Chinese mariners could exploit the magnetic properties of lodestone (a naturally occurring magnetite) to create the earliest known magnetic compass. It may have been developed during an earlier period, but is first mentioned in texts from the 1040s. In 1088, scientist Shen Kuo

(1031–1095) described how an iron needle could be rubbed with a lodestone and then either floated on water or suspended on a thread of silk. The needle pointed to a pole, north or south, allowing sailors to find their way even when poor weather obscured the sun, stars, or coasts – the preferred reckoning points at the time for navigating all waters within the Eastern Hemisphere. The creation of a lodestone spoon, which would be placed on a bronze plate, allowed navigators to travel with this important piece of technology.

The lines of transmission are unclear, but many historians believe that the introduction of the magnetic compass into the Muslim world (earliest references from the mid-thirteenth century) and Latin Europe (from the twelfth century) may have come from the Chinese through contact in the Indian Ocean region. By the early fourteenth century, Mediterranean sailors developed the "dry compass," featuring a fixed needle that rotated over a wind rose inside a glass box. In the fifteenth century, Europeans used deck-mounted compasses, mariner's astrolabes, improved ship technologies, and enhanced charts to dominate not only Mediterranean Sea trade but also to navigate into and across the open waters of the Atlantic Ocean.

Early Chinese compass makers privileged south over north, and the compass ladles they wrought were weighted according to that correlation. As a result, until the fourteenth century, medieval Chinese maps often depicted south at the top of the page. But in the fourteenth century, Beijing had grown in importance as a cultural capital, and Chinese cartographers regularized map orientation as depicting the world with north at the top, which placed Beijing "above" most parts of China. Despite this modern change, the Mandarin Chinese phrase for compass is *jur nan jun* or "south-pointing needle," and the modern Chinese word for a guidebook or a tourist map is a "point south."

The *Yu Ji Tu*, or the Map of the Tracks of Yu, is the oldest comprehensive map of the Chinese domain known to exist. This detailed map of China, including clear depictions of the Yellow and Yangtze rivers and the remains of the Great Wall of China, was etched on a stone tablet in 1137 CE just as the Song dynasty (960–1279) court and its people were driven south of the Yangtze River by an aggressive northern rival. While the map is useful as a way-finding tool, it is also a symbolic "empire map," a representation of the Song dynasty's political claim to the northern territories lost to the nomadic invaders, the Jurchen Jin. The empire map was a feature of imperial administration (as was the Chinese calendar) and was a claim of ownership, power, and rights to all the land depicted. It was also a powerful connection to one of the Five Classics, writings from before the fourth century BCE that constitute the canon of Confucian writings. One of these, the *Book of Documents*, includes a description of the journey of the Great Yu, the mythological first emperor of China. Although no maps from this period of China's history exist, Yu's legendary sojourn became the primary prototype of mapmaking in China and is honored in the title of the map featured here. In other words, his travels defined the nine provinces (or domains) of China. By connecting the geography with this legendary character

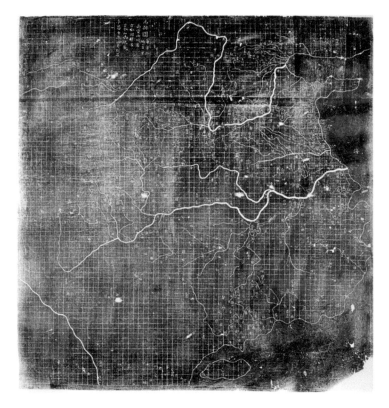

Fig 0.5
A photograph of the twelfth-century stone etching known as the *Map of the Tracks of Yu*.
© Wikimedia Commons, public domain

and with the sacred teachings of Confucius, the map links past with present and legitimizes the Song dynasty's claim to the nine domains.

Maps, like calendars, can be used by a government or an elite group as propaganda to convince both supporters and enemies of a political or divine right to territory. They can also evoke highly personal emotions of birthright over the land and nostalgic emblems of missing "home." This thirteenth-century poem by Chen Yinglong, an official of the defeated Song court, is an elegy, a poetic expression of loss:

> In youth, I handled the brush,
> For a while I was a scholar of texts.
> In the middle of the night my sword's bright rays shine forth,
> Its bright rays shoot through the imperial avenues of the sky.
> I want to dispel the emperor's sorrow;
> I light a lantern and read the map.
> Even though the landscape in the south is exquisite.
> I still miss my old home.

Conflating the power of written expression with that of a warrior, the poet laments the loss of a homeland he cannot take back by pen or by sword. The feelings are projected into the image, concentrating and justifying fantasies of ownership; the loss of identity is transposed onto the geography.

Another important map of the period is the Kangnido (or Gangnido) Map produced in Korea in 1402. It was the most accurate map of its time, showing Africa, western Asia (Persia, Arabia, and Egypt), China, Korea, and Japan, as well as some European place names. This extensive knowledge of the Eastern Hemisphere was the result of the influence of Muslim merchants in Mongol Yuan China. Muslims brought to China more than trade goods and coins: they also participated in intellectual exchange, offering the Mongols knowledge of cartography, geography, medicine, and navigational technologies. Figure 0.6 is a Mongol-era map that shows the Mongols' intellectual interest in the wider world.

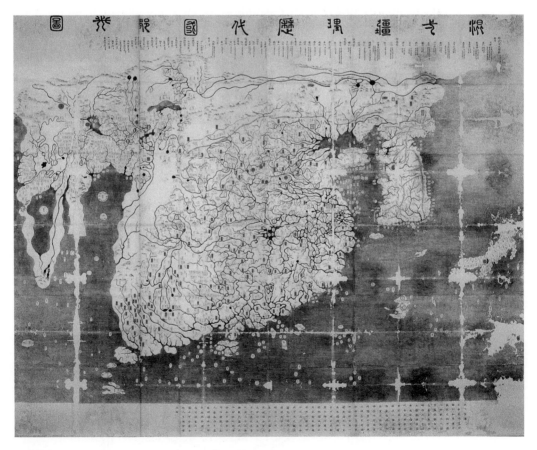

Fig 0.6
Based on two Chinese maps from the 14th century, this Korean Kangnido (or Gangnido) Map of China was copied in 1402 on paper.

Source: Honkoji Tokiwa Museum of Historical Materials, Shimabara, Nagasaki

European T/O Maps and Mappae Mundi

Although, in modern times, we are accustomed to thinking of the North Pole as the top of a globe or map, and the South Pole as the bottom, in fact the north does not have to be at the top. At the beginning of the chapter we noted that the word "orient" comes from the Latin word *oriri*, to rise, which is related to *oriens*, Latin for the "east where the sun rises." For European Christians, the sun was set in motion by God. Because east was closer to the divine (and for most Europeans, the direction toward Jerusalem), it was often given pride of place at the top of what are called T/O maps, the dominant category of extant maps of early medieval Europe.

They are called T/O maps because from a distance they look like the letter T inserted inside the letter O. These letters also form the initials of the Latin phrase "orbis terrarum," or "globe of the Earth," which is how early medieval cartographers conceived of their product. The surface of the Earth is depicted as a large circle (the O of T/O), within which are two dominant bodies of water (they make the T of T/O). The vertical line of the T, from top to bottom, is the Mediterranean Sea, dividing the European continent from the African. The horizontal cross stroke is formed on the left side by major European rivers such as the Don, connecting with, on the right side, the Nile River. The intersection of these land masses was sometimes shown as the city of Jerusalem, considered within Christian cosmography to be the "navel" of the world. Most T/O maps are not highly decorated, typically featuring only written labels for the continents and sometimes written descriptions of the people who were believed to have lived in Asia or Africa.

Fig 0.7
T/O map diagram. Drawn in the seventh century by the Spanish intellectual, Isidore of Seville.

T/O maps are configured according to Christian geography. In the later Middle Ages, the T/O map developed into a fuller picture of the Earth and cosmos called a mappa mundi (Latin for map of the world). On most, Christ is depicted at the top as the source of light for the world, with Eden, the earthly paradise, just below. From Eden emanate the four rivers of paradise, which, as they flow down the page, become the Nile, Tigris, Euphrates, and Ganges. The great ocean is south of the four seas: the Caspian Sea, the Red Sea, the Persian Gulf, and the Mediterranean. Jerusalem remains prominently in the center and often other cities and regions are labeled, but there are also spaces filled with fantastical beasts and monsters. The Hereford *Mappa Mundi*, ca. 1300, is one of the largest extant mappae mundi, but there were also many others

Fig 0.8
The Hereford *Mappa Mundi* was drawn around 1300. on a remarkably large single calfskin or deer hide of about four by five feet. It is the largest medieval map known to exist. Alongside geographical features and historic cities are biblical figures and mythical beasts.
Chapter of Hereford Cathedral

Fig 0.9
The Hereford *Mappa Mundi* is oriented with East at the top of the map, where Christ sits in majesty.
Chapter of Hereford Cathedral

found in manuscripts from the later Middle Ages. Another is the contemporary Ebstorf map.

Later medieval mappae mundi often featured unknown places between Christ in heaven and the earthly world, where mythical beasts and legendary monsters resided. To this end, the Hereford cartographer drew a unicorn, the Minotaur (from the ancient Greek myth), and a mermaid. He also included creatures featured in the writings of Pliny the Elder, a Roman philosopher of the first century CE. In his *Natural History*, Pliny described such creatures as the Cynocephali, people with dog heads, the Blemmyae, creatures with no head but a human face on their chests, and the sciapods, a race with one leg and a giant foot. The sciapods were said to live in nearly uninhabitable desert regions, where they survived the scorching sun by using their large foot for shade. Mappae mundi depicted the world as created by the Christian God and dominated by His son Christ, yet they acknowledged that many non-Christian peoples and creatures lived there, too.

Portolan Maps

In the fifteenth century, Portuguese and Spanish sailors ventured further into the Atlantic Ocean and further away from the safety of the known coasts, and practical cartographers enthusiastically diagrammed the newly discovered

Fig 0.10
Cynocephali, the dog-headed people, as featured on the Hereford *Mappa Mundi*.
Chapter of Hereford Cathedral

Fig 0.11
Sciapods were semi-human creatures with one leg and a giant foot. To shade itself
from the hostile desert sun, a sciapod lay on its back and used the foot for shade.
Chapter of Hereford Cathedral

territories and their people so explorers could find these lands again, and so
monarchies could demonstrate their claim over the new lands and their commodities. Many Europeans felt the "new" lands to be free to the first armed
group who invaded, and mapping and naming these territories established
their claim to ownership over them. Astronomy, as we saw earlier, blossomed as
a science with the addition of the Muslim mathematical invention of algebra.
Used for both calendric calculations and mapping, these innovations also
aided European sailors on their voyages. Navigating as they were by the reliable
North Star, these late medieval European sailors typically followed maps that
positioned north at the top and south at the bottom and detailed coastlines
and ports. Often, these maps have notations identifying the authorities in control of each port to enable sailors to plan their expeditions with a reasonable

expectation of finding hospitable landing, supplies, and a potential for taking over new territories.

At the end of the fifteenth century, a Spanish cartographer named Juan de la Cosa (ca. 1460–1510) traveled with Christopher Columbus on his first two expeditions and went on to make five more voyages to the Caribbean. He was intent on making maps for King Ferdinand of Aragon and Queen Isabella of Castile (regions in modern-day Spain), identifying new lands they could claim as their own. This was the beginning of the great land grab that developed into the European colonization of the Western Hemisphere. For his project, de la Cosa drew on (as all explorers, cartographers, and scientists of this period did) the scientific knowledge brought to Spain through the Islamic occupation. We should note that in 1510, Indigenous people of Colombia killed de la Cosa with poisoned arrows, a violent and fatal global connection.

Maps from the Islamic Golden Age

Islamic cartographers of the Golden Age oriented their maps with south at the top, placing the Arabian Peninsula in the center, with emphasis on two cities important to the life of the Muslim prophet Muhammad – Mecca and Medina. In 622 CE, Muhammad was spreading the word of God in his hometown of Mecca. Always under some threat by those who did not accept him as a prophet, and subject to the dangers of clan rivalries, he learned of a plot to assassinate him, and he and his followers fled north from Mecca to the town of Medina, where he found protection with people who accepted him as the prophet of God. Later in his life, he returned to his birthplace and converted its citizens, too, thus elevating the status of his birthplace slightly over the town that had been his temporary refuge. The escape to Medina and subsequent return is called the *hijra* and set the precedent for the *hajj*, the pilgrimage to Mecca every Muslim is meant to do once in a lifetime. On a contemporary map, Medina is north of Mecca. By inverting the presentation so south was at the top of the page, early Islamic cartographers placed Mecca above Medina, privileging the slightly higher spiritual significance of one city over the other.

In the twelfth century, a talented geographer and mathematician named Muhammad al-Idrisi was commissioned by King Roger of Sicily to produce an atlas of the world. Born in Morocco and educated in Cordoba, the capital of Muslim Spain, al-Idrisi spent most of his career working in the royal court at Palermo in Sicily, a bustling center of learning under the direction of the Norman (North French) King Roger. The *Al-Kitab al-Rujari*, or the *Book of Roger*, included a world map with south at the top. The *Book of Roger* was later lost, but the maps survive in a copy made by al-Idrisi for Roger's son, William II. These are called the *Little Idrisi*. It is important to note here that, in the tradition of a thousand years of cartographers, al-Idrisi knew the Earth was round. So too did Christian thinkers throughout the Middle Ages – the myth of the "flat Earth" is the product of the modern, not the medieval, period.

Fig 0.12

The Little Idrisi, a copy of the 1154 Charta Rogeriana, or map of King Roger. In order to privilege the holy city of Mecca above Medina, the map is oriented with south at the top. Notice the Arabian Peninsula is "upside down" in the top center.

Everett Collection Historical / Alamy Stock Photo

Mapping the Heavens

As we discussed in the first section, medieval cultures looked to the position of the celestial bodies to gauge important events, such as the beginning of planting season or the coming of the monsoons, to mark important religious festivals, to predict the future and to navigate their way over land and through seas. People looked for clues in the heavens to anticipate natural phenomena or human behavior and events. A profound example of the human need to impose our beliefs on the physical universe is the way we "map" the night sky. In order to make the vast, unknowable cosmos less frightening to us small human beings, we organize the visible stars by familiar stories. These stories become part of the astrological and cosmological understandings of a particular culture's worldview and are often incorporated into the calendric elements seen above.

Because ancient Greek knowledge was revered in the Roman Empire, medieval Europe, Byzantium, Arabia, Persia, and beyond, those cultures and others commonly mapped the stars in terms of Greek mythology, diagramming the night sky as the extensive neighborhood of such mythological heroes as Hercules and Perseus. For instance, a recognizable constellation in the Northern Hemisphere, and to some extent the Southern, is Ursa Major (Latin for Great Bear), which Europeans and others interpreted in terms of the myth of Zeus and Callisto. As a maiden, Callisto took a vow of chastity in order to join the inner circle of the hunting goddess Artemis, but, one day, Zeus spied the beautiful girl as she roamed through the forest of Arcadia. Knowing she would run from a man, Zeus approached her in the likeness of Artemis. Thinking she was in the presence of the goddess, Callisto allowed him to embrace her, and he assaulted her.

Polaris (North Star)

Fig 0.13
Ursa Major (the Great Bear) includes the star formation known in the United States as the Big Dipper. Ursa Minor (the Lesser Bear) includes the Little Dipper. At the tip of the handle is Polaris, also known as the North Star.
McDonald & Woodward Publishing Company

When her son from Zeus was born, Artemis shamed and exiled Callisto. In addition to this traumatic punishment, she was harassed by Hera, Zeus's jealous and vengeful wife, who turned the poor girl into a bear. One day, as she roamed the woods in lonely misery, Callisto was discovered and chased by a hunter and his dogs. The hunter was her very own son, Arcas, and at the moment he was to kill her, Zeus felt some pity and swung both mother and son into the heavens. As they ascended, Arcas was also transformed into a bear, and the tragic Callisto and her son are immortalized as Ursa Major and Ursa Minor, a testament to the casual attitude of this ancient patriarchal society toward the rape and humiliation of women.

Embedded in the two bear figures are what US Americans call the Big and Little Dippers. For those navigating in the Northern Hemisphere, Ursa Minor was particularly important because the tip of the handle of the Little Dipper is Polaris, the all-important North Star. Nevertheless, while this is the ancient Greek interpretation of this particular cluster of stars, not all cultures see the same image in the sky. The seven stars Americans know as the Big Dipper have long been called the Plough in the United Kingdom, and other Northern Europeans see them as the Great Wagon or the Three Horses. The ancient Babylonians also interpreted this constellation as a wagon, while North Africans diagram it as a camel. Many cultures – Arabs, Hindus, Native Americans, and more – perceive this constellation as a stretcher for carrying an injured warrior or a sick elder.

In China, the so-called Big Dipper is interpreted as a meeting of a heavenly bureaucracy, presided over by the Emperor Wen-chang, the god of literature. Others in attendance are Kuei, minister of literary affairs of the world; Mr. Red Coat, a minister who helps struggling students pass their exams; Mr. Gold

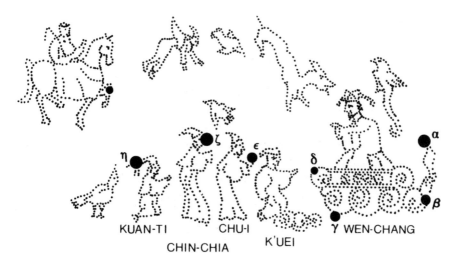

Fig 0.14
The Chinese interpretation of the seven stars of the Big Dipper, the Emperor Wen-Chang and his advisors.
McDonald & Woodward Publishing Company

Armor, who searches for talented young people to serve in the state bureaucracy; and Kuan, a protector of the kingdom. The Chinese cultures considered the North Star the Purple or Imperial Star and connected it with the Imperial City and, by extension, all of Beijing, the Celestial City. For the Chinese cartographers, the heavens are mapped as a celestial imperial court with three "enclosures" or sections. The first section is the Purple Forbidden Enclosure and contains Ursa Major. It is the seat of divine justice, considered the center of the heavens. The second enclosure is the Supreme Palace, containing stars most visible over China in the spring and early summer. The third is the Heavenly Market Enclosure, stars visible in fall and early winter. In fact, each of the nine domains identified in the ancient Chinese story of Yu is associated with a particular constellation.

Although the constellations discussed above are visible in the Southern Hemisphere, there are others with more significance. A good example is the Crux or Southern Cross. In Greek astrology, these four stars are merely a part of the hind leg of the mythical half man/half horse figure called the Centaur. But for those living nearer to the South Pole, they stand out as a constellation of their own, an iconic and significant feature of the southern night sky. Said to have been revealed to Europeans by Amerigo Vespucci, the Crux is not as reliable for reckoning travel as the North Star but is helpful in finding a southern orientation. In the present day, the image of this constellation is used on the national flags of Australia, New Zealand, Papua New Guinea, Samoa, and Brazil.

Looking Forward

The significant theme of this chapter is cultural relativity, recognition that each culture has its own beliefs, practices, and perspectives, all of which we must evaluate within the context of that culture. Nevertheless, these cultural ideas were often based on common empirical phenomena not particular to one group: the sun, the moon, and the stars, the oceans, and land masses. No set of beliefs and practices is inherently better or worse than another. Cultures form their identities based on their circumstances, including the way they keep time, organize spiritual practices, and survive in geographical landscapes they claim as "home." Even the constellations are imaginatively discussed in terms of the stories and legends of the Earth-bound communities that view them.

Whether a culture mapped the stars to determine the proper time to perform a religious ceremony or the proper direction to travel, its routines and traditions were based on careful observation, which today we call science. To that end, this chapter demonstrates the connection of science and mathematics to history. We may think of history as a written narrative of the past, but the fields of mathematics, science, archeology, anthropology, and others form important foundations for our appreciation of how people in the past viewed their worlds. In the three sections to follow, there are four chapters, each organized primarily to focus upon a specific point of view – religion, economies, politics, and society – but all perspectives will be involved in every discussion; they are inevitably intertwined.

Research Questions

1. How does algebra aid in the understanding of astronomy?
2. Choose one of the cultures discussed in the chapter and look further into its calendar systems. What gods and events were celebrated? How is history charted and remembered? Who influenced these calendars, and what were their political purposes?
3. Choose a constellation and research the stories attached to it by different cultures. What are different interpretations of this star configuration?
4. In 1569, a Flemish man named Gerardus Mercator created a new method of drawing maps on flat surfaces that more accurately portrayed the size of landmasses closer to the poles. Watch a video or read a description of the Mercator system. Use this system to determine any distortion in the earlier maps discussed here or another map in this book.
5. Research the trade routes used in medieval Eurasia. How many calendar systems would a merchant encounter on a journey from China to Italy? Why might a solar calendar work best for this merchant?
6. Choose one of the maps discussed in the chapter and learn more about it. What is the knowledge the cartographer wished to highlight? Why? Was there a political purpose to it? Scientific? What does the map celebrate? Does it reveal any fears about unknown or unfamiliar places or peoples?

Further Reading

Aveni, Anthony. *Empires of Time: Calendars, Clocks, and Cultures*. Boulder: University of Colorado Press, 2002.

Barber, Peter, ed. *The Map Book*. New York: Walker and Company, 2006.

Brown, Victoria. *Feminism, Time, and Nonlinear History*. New York: Palgrave, 2014.

Cohen, Jeffrey Jerome, and Linda T. Elkins-Tanton. *Earth (Object Lessons)*. London: Bloomsbury Academic, 2017.

Divakaran, P. P. *The Mathematics of India: Concepts, Methods, Connections*. New Delhi: Springer and Hindustan Book Agency, 2018.

Duncan, David Ewing. *Calendar: Humanity's Epic Struggle to Determine a True and Accurate Year*. New York: Avon Books, 1998.

Harvey, P. D. A. *Mappa Mundi: The Hereford World Map*. Hereford: Hereford Cathedral, 1996.

Hassig, Ross. *Time, History, and Belief in Aztec and Colonial Mexico*. Austin: University of Austin Press, 2001.

Hayashi, Takao. "The Units of Time in Ancient and Medieval India." *History of Science in South Asia* 5, no. 1 (July 2017): 1–116.

al-Khalili, Jim. *The House of Wisdom: How Arabic Science Saved Ancient Knowledge and Gave Us the Renaissance*. London: Penguin, 2010.

Reingold, Edward, and Nachum Dershowitz. *Calendrical Calculations: The Millennium Edition*. Cambridge: Cambridge University Press, 2001.

Rice, Prudence. *Maya Political Science: Time, Astronomy, and the Cosmos*. Austin: University of Texas Press, 2004.

Rosen, Ralph M., ed. *Time and Temporality in the Ancient World*. Philadelphia: University of Pennsylvania Museum of Archeology and Anthropology, 2004.

Sorabji, Richard. *Time, Creation, and the Continuum*. Chicago: University of Chicago Press, 2006.

Staal, Julius D. W. *Patterns in the Sky: Myths and Legends of the Stars*. Granville, OH: McDonald & Woodward, 1988.

Steele, John M., ed. *Calendars and Years II: Astronomy and Time in the Ancient and Medieval World.* Oxford: Oxbow Books, 2011.

Waugh, Alexander. *Time: Its Origin, Its Enigma, Its History*. New York: Carroll & Graf, 2000.

Section II

500–900

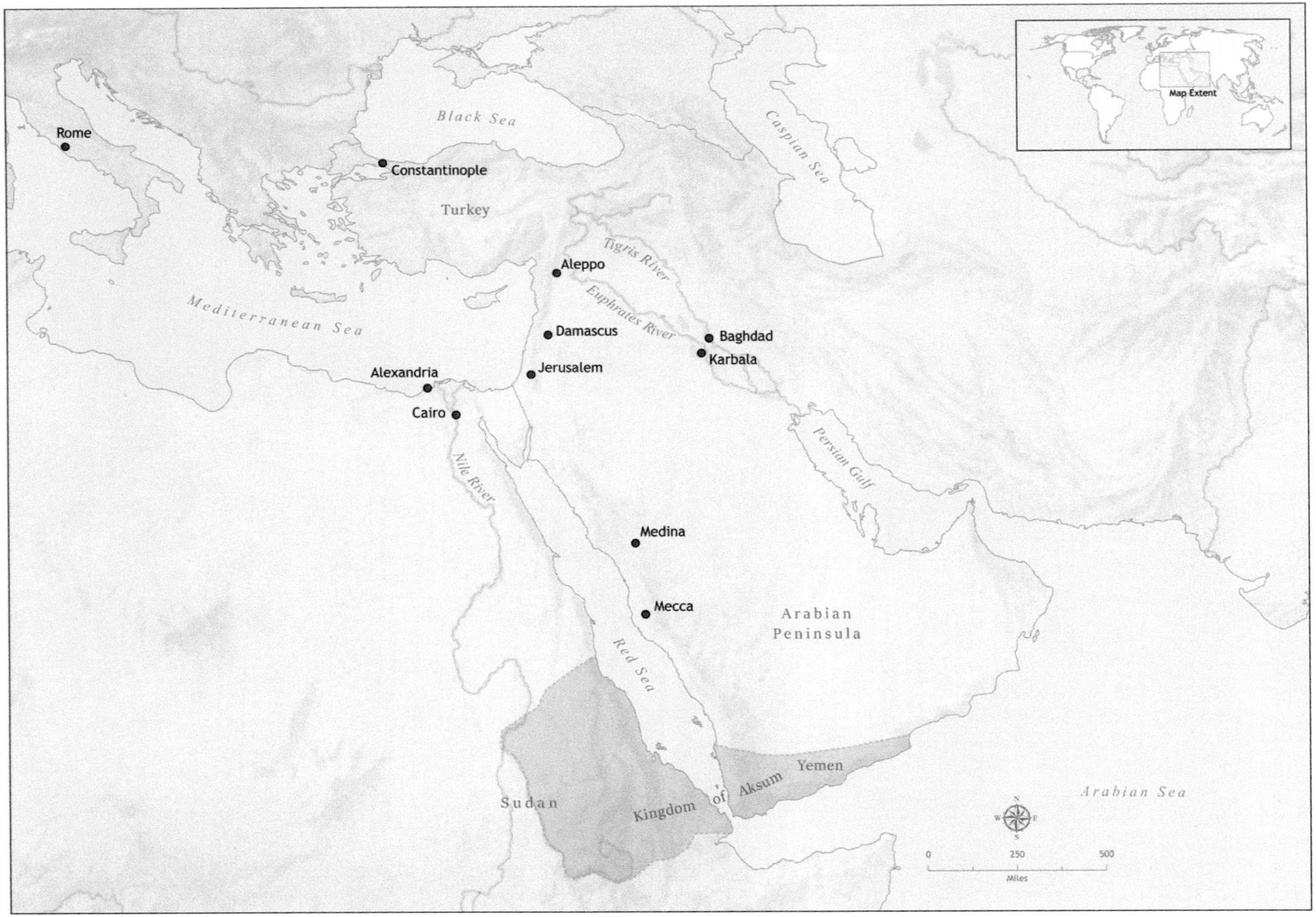

Map 1
Growth of Monotheisms

1 Growth of Monotheisms

Religion, 500–900

Introduction

Spiritual and theological concerns governed, justified, and animated the behavior of people throughout the world and, as such, we begin our journey with faith and religion. In the period 500–900, the spread of monotheistic religions created a profound cultural influence across the Eurasian landscape. Monotheistic religions are those defined by the doctrine that there is only one god, omnipotent (all-powerful), omniscient (all-knowing), and omnipresent (present in all time and space). In the global medieval period, Europe, the Near and Middle East, and North Africa were dominated by three primary monotheisms: Judaism, Christianity, and Islam. These faiths and their various, and often conflicting, sects inspired people to their greatest works of artistic and philanthropic achievement, but also motivated them to their most debased acts of conquest and cruelty.

These religions were formed by interaction with other religions and groups. None lived in isolation from other faiths. For example, although many see medieval Europe as a Christian space, cosmopolitan European Christians knew the Jews in their cities, and Christians along the Mediterranean and in the Middle East lived and worked alongside Muslims and Jews. Muslims in the Middle East knew Jews and Christians, as well as Zoroastrians and, to the east, Hindus. In later chapters, we extend this discussion to Hinduism, Buddhism, Jainism, Confucianism, Daoism, and Shintoism, but in this chapter we focus on the eventual domination of two of these monotheistic religions: Christianity and Islam.

There was not one "true" practice of any of these faiths and we will introduce some of the early controversies and schisms. Since all faiths under discussion in this text are still living religions with adherents and practitioners worldwide, it is important to note that modern practices may be strongly related to their ancestral faiths, but there will be differences. Section A introduces the four major monotheistic faiths, including debates that led to separation of worshippers into sects, and discusses how political leaders adopted, adapted, and developed religious administrations for their own political and economic goals. Section B discusses the sacred textual traditions of Judaism, Christianity, and Islam, all of which include the patriarch Abraham and thus are called the Abrahamic religions. Because the written word of God, Christ, or Allah is a centerpiece of these faiths, by extension each culture was dedicated to recording divine and human knowledge in scrolls and manuscripts and preserving them in libraries. They are the People of the Book.

A: POLITICS AND FAITH

Evidence: Einhard, *The Life of Charlemagne*

John of Damascus, *In Defense of Icons*

Genesis

Avesta, Zoroastrian text

Russian Primary Chronicle

The Monotheistic Faiths

The four major monotheistic religions of the Middle East – Judaism, Zoroastrianism, Christianity, and Islam – began in the deserts east of the Mediterranean Sea, and each one believed that the world was created by a single God, whose will was revealed to humanity through prophets. Shared aspects of all four include the importance of sacred, written texts, a focus on the ethical behavior of its adherents, and an eschatological view of time – a belief that there will be an end of the world or of humanity, such as an apocalypse. After our brief introduction to all these faiths, we will focus on the religions of Christianity and Islam in the period 500–1500, looking at how each spread throughout the Mediterranean and beyond. A cursory look at several theological disputes shows us that neither of these faiths existed in a vacuum but were shaped by people from a wide variety of cultures, including civic leaders and ambitious rulers who used religious ideology to advance their political aspirations.

Judaism and Diaspora

The oldest of the four faiths is Judaism, formed as early as 1500 BCE. The early stories describe Abraham, a migrant from the Mesopotamian city of Ur, leading his followers to the land that would become Israel. The earliest written Jewish texts are from the sixth century BCE (when we officially begin using the term

Judaism), and these form the basis of the Hebrew Bible (or Tanakh). Followers of a strict set of ethical and ritual laws, Jews often separated themselves or were separated from the larger communities in which they lived. As was typical in the ancient world, Jews passed on their history, beliefs, and traditions through oral storytelling, but by 500 there were written accounts of sacred literature and laws in a number of languages.

WHY ARE THESE CALLED *ABRAHAMIC* RELIGIONS?

Judaism, Christianity, and Islam are often called Abrahamic religions. Christianity and Islam claim descent from early Jews and both use Jewish texts (the "Old Testament" in Christianity, and the Torah and Psalms in Islam) within the understanding of their own faiths. These texts form the backbone of the Abrahamic faiths, those religions that purport Abraham to be a direct ancestor of their people. All three worship the God of Abraham and trace their origins to Abraham's sons. Isaac, the youngest son of Abraham, is said to be the ancestor of Jews and Christians; while Ishmael, the eldest son, is the ancestor of Muslims. These religions differ greatly; their stories, cultures, and ideals are distinct from each other at every stage and continue to change over time. Nevertheless, they all believed and believe in an omnipotent and omniscient God who created the universe and favored Abraham and his descendants above all peoples.

As it developed in tandem with the political power of Israelite kings like David and Solomon (ca. 1000–900 BCE), religious worship by Jews came to be focused on the temple in the city of Jerusalem. The building of the First Temple by King Solomon, its role as the home of the tablets of the law (in the Ark of the Covenant), and the focus of Jewish ritual life and festivals in that temple, all became central aspects of Jewish faith and identity. Alongside the focus on the temple was the development of a priestly class, which came to play a central role in Hebrew society and politics. The First Temple was destroyed in 586 BCE by the Babylonians, at which time many Jews were deported from Israel to the central lands of Babylon. Exiled from their ancestral land and temples, Jews developed a strong sense of their collective identity as focused on the worship of YHWH (Yahweh – a statement of identity, or name, for the God of the Israelites, meaning "I am") and their unique common culture as Hebrews. Even after returning to Palestine in the sixth century BCE, Jews maintained their communities in the larger sense that they were a unique people of God who could maintain their religious life even without claim to territory or sacred buildings.

After the destruction of the Second Temple by Roman imperial invaders in 70 CE, the Jews of Israel were scattered around the Roman world in what is known as the Diaspora. Jews during the medieval period did not control a political, religious, or cultural state of their own, but lived as minorities in a wide variety of places around the Eastern Hemisphere. As they lived, worked, worshipped, and studied in territories that were predominantly Muslim or Christian, medieval Jews were often victimized and uprooted, making it difficult to preserve religious objects and sacred documents. For that reason, there is not as much material witness to medieval Jewish culture as there is for Christians and Muslims, and there exists, for example, very little architecture.

Zoroastrianism

The earliest record of Zoroastrians comes from the Ancient Greek historian Herodotus, who described the practices of the followers of Zoroaster – people living in what is present-day Iran – in his *Histories* (ca. 440 BCE). Zoroastrians followed a dualistic cosmology that described the universe as split between good and evil. All goodness and purity came from the supreme God Ahura Mazda; evil and chaos emanated from an alternative spiritual force called Angra Mainyu (Ahriman). The Zoroastrian holy book is the Avesta and it details how the principles of light and dark were in continuous conflict, and would eventually do battle at the end of days, and that humanity had a key part to play in this conflict. This apocalyptic view played out daily, as the sun and moon fought for control over the lands but, as the sun always returned to defeat the night, Zoroastrians believed that goodness would always prevail over evil. Ahura Mazda gifted humanity with free will, and, with every action, humans had the ability to choose to follow either a righteous or a wicked path, and with every righteous choice they prevented the end of days.

Fire was essential to all aspects of Zoroastrian belief, and still today sacred fires burn constantly in Zoroastrian temples and homes to connect the faithful with Ahura Mazda, the God of Purity and Light. Zoroastrians do not worship the fire itself but consider it a symbol of the radiant purity and goodness of the creator god. Zoroastrians continued to practice in Persia and throughout the Roman Empire until their almost complete displacement by Islam in the seventh century. A minority of Zoroastrians in Persia maintained their faith and were granted protected status under Islamic rulers, so that they were not forced to convert to Islam and could maintain their traditions. Zoroastrians still worship in Iran, Iraq, India, and other places around the globe.

Christianity

Christianity formed in the Levant region (modern Syria-Israel-Palestine) of the Middle East during the first century CE. Although begun as a Jewish sect, early Christian theorists struggled with whether their new faith would use Jewish ideas, texts, and laws. Because this new religion was formed in a province of the Roman Empire, it was also based heavily on Roman life and thought. In fact, the first 300 years of Christianity are really a study of early Christian scholars attempting to decide exactly how "Roman" and how "Jewish" this new religion would be. By the medieval period, basics texts and principles of Christianity were established, but there was much to be determined and many different ways of living a Christian life.

Many people today think of medieval Christianity as a united, European, white institution. That is not true. Medieval Christianity emanated out of the Middle East, traveled along the Roman roads, and in its earliest stages reached such distant regions as Ireland and Ethiopia. In fact, the early theology was more influenced by philosophers from northeastern Africa and Asia Minor (modern Turkey) than Europeans. A history of medieval Christianity is one of cross-cultural theological debates, battles waged on individual words and their meanings, civic and cultural adoption and change, and of syncretism, which is the way spiritual traditions are absorbed by and blended with other ones.

Over the course of the fourth century, Christianity became the primary religion of the Roman Empire, with an administrative structure based on urban Roman bureaucracy. Priests and deacons ministered in local churches; bishops administered all the churches within a city; archbishops governed the many churches in a region; and patriarchs ruled over major territories. Separate from this bustling, urban hierarchy, there also arose a movement that stressed a quiet, contemplative religious practice withdrawn from worldly affairs. Monasticism, as it was called, became a prominent mode of religious devotion in both eastern and western Christianity. Both men and women could live in isolated settings with a small group of like-minded worshippers.

The daily routine in a medieval Christian monastery revolved around a regularized course of prayers throughout the day and night. The various rules that governed monastic life demanded strict adherence to a life of obedience (to the rule and to the abbot), labor, humility, chastity, and poverty. Monasteries and abbeys were also repositories of books, and centers of education for the boys and girls of elite families who could afford to place their children within ascetic walls.

Islam

The final monotheistic religion to form was Islam, which developed in the Arabian Peninsula in the early seventh century CE. Muhammad, the Prophet of God (ca. 570–632 CE), was born into a region highly influenced and sometimes governed by Jews or Christians, particularly Christians from Ethiopia across the Red Sea. The Christian kings of Aksum controlled the southern reaches of Arabia, in Yemen, and raided and traded north into Mecca. Jewish merchants moved from the Yemeni area into Mecca for safety, bringing trade as well as their monotheistic religion. Various Arab tribes fought for control of Mecca and other port cities along the coast, as the trade networks expanded during the sixth and seventh centuries.

Although Muhammad was born into a branch of the ruling tribe, he derived little benefit from his family connections. Orphaned young, he spent much of his youth bouncing between family members and living with Bedouin traders in the desert. Muhammad grew up seeing the damage wrought by increasing warfare and strife in his city. He became a mediator, using diplomacy to settle personal and economic conflicts. Many sought his advice on their family, business, and political dealings. He married a wealthy young widow, Khadijah, and ran her family's trade networks, and as his wealth grew, Muhammad began a series of social programs for widows, orphans, and the poor, but his social activism was often in conflict with ruling authorities. To recuperate from his busy life as father, husband, merchant, and arbitrator, he often sought out solitary spaces for reflection.

In the year 610 CE, Muhammad went to the caves outside Mecca where he began receiving divine messages from God (Allah in Arabic), through the angel Gabriel (Jabril in Arabic), a phenomenon that continued for 23 years until his death in 632 CE. Gabriel outlined God's will for the Arab tribes and tasked Muhammad to bring the message of a single God to his people. Muhammad understood himself to be the Prophet of God and began preaching this monotheistic vision to his family and close associates. Consistently emphasized in these revelations was the importance of absolute submission to God's word and will (Islam is an Arabic word meaning submission). The imperative of God's message was to reach as many people as possible with prophecies and commandments. At the heart of many of these teachings was dedication to bringing justice to the poor and marginalized within Arab society.

Some of the major differences between Islam and its predecessors came as a direct result of early Muslim thinkers wrestling with what they perceived as problems in the two older faiths of Judaism and Christianity. For example, the Oneness of God is an integral and important part of Islamic theology and came in conflict with the concept of the Christian definition of the godhead as the Trinity (God, Son, and Holy Spirit). Islamic beliefs were intensely popular and in one century spread throughout the Middle East, North Africa, and into Europe.

Politics of Christianities

In the medieval period, several dominant Christian sects emerged as culturally and doctrinally separate from each other: Roman (or Latin) Christianity, Byzantine Orthodox Christianity, and Oriental Orthodox Christianity. We use the term Roman Christianity to refer to the sect that has become the Roman Catholic Church and is led by a pope living in Vatican City in the center of Rome. The Byzantine Orthodox church began in the eastern Roman Empire and developed separately as part of the Byzantine Empire. Russian and Greek Orthodoxy come out of this tradition. Sometimes referred to as "pre-Chalcedonian" because these groups split away from other Christian churches at the Council of Chalcedon in 451 CE, the Oriental Orthodox faith was practiced in Ethiopian, Coptic, Eritrean, Syrian, Armenian, and Indian Christian communities. While today we do not refer to Asian peoples as "Oriental," members of this specific faith still refer to it as the Oriental Orthodox Church.

Because Christianity was prohibited by Roman law for about 300 years, the faithful worshipped in secret, often unaware of the practices of Christians in communities far from theirs. Once Constantine declared that this religion was favored by the Empire (ca. 325), Christianity developed a structure of administration that to some degree paralleled the secular administration. It also developed theologically through conversations and debates among the founding members of the early hierarchies. Debates raged about the largest and smallest of ideas within Christianity, and out of these arguments and deliberations came orthodox beliefs, or those beliefs that were accepted as sacred, standard practice. The most hotly debated beliefs were difficult for lay people to understand, such as the earthly versus the divine nature of Christ and his body (the Christological debates) or the concept of whether the Trinity was three separate entities or three parts of a whole (the Trinitarian debates). In the first seven ecumenical councils (held between 324 and 787) many of these primary doctrinal questions were decided, but not without significant factionalism.

Several major theological disputes began with the bishops in the African churches of North Africa and Ethiopia. Although many of these debates were centered on minute and intricate details of theology, at their core they were often about individual churches asserting independence against a growing centralization around the emperor and the patriarch of Constantinople. The most serious early conflict brought the African patriarch of Alexandria into direct dispute with Constantinople. Their dispute lay at the heart of the Council of Chalcedon (451).

Like earlier Church councils, the Council of Chalcedon was charged with debating theological issues and declaring an orthodox position on them. The African bishop of Alexandria brought a Christological debate to the Council ("Christology" is the study of whether Jesus is both human and divine). Many African and Assyrian Christians understood Jesus to be both completely human and completely divine, with neither essence mixing with the other. Christians in other spaces believed him to be only divine, while yet others believed him only human. The patriarch of Alexandria represented his churches and their positions at Chalcedon and directly challenged the authority of the patriarch of Constantinople, and through him, the emperor himself. Neither the patriarch of Constantinople nor the Byzantine emperor condoned the African bishop's position, and they removed him, replacing him with their own agent. The African priests refused to accept the newly appointed leader and reinstated their archbishop. Thus began the Chalcedonian Schism of 451, with several churches rebelling against the political and religious power of Constantinople. For many churches, the arrogant and high-handed attitude of the Byzantine emperor in their affairs, both temporal and spiritual, angered them enough to walk out of the council. The original patriarch of Alexandria and his priests returned to Africa, declaring that they would remain in exile until the other patriarchs accepted their hierarchical line of succession. This did not happen, and those churches who chose to follow the patriarch of Alexandria formed a sect of Christianity known as Oriental Orthodoxy. These included the churches of Africa, particularly those of Egypt, Ethiopia, Sudan, and the Middle Eastern churches of Syria and Armenia.

The arguments at Chalcedon had important and far-reaching consequences. Inherent in much of the schism was the problem of hierarchy: which patriarch should hold the ultimate power over all patriarchies and therefore over all Christians? The patriarchs (also known as archbishops or metropolitans) included Jerusalem, Antioch, Constantinople, Alexandria, and Rome. The five patriarchies were centered in powerful cities with strong ties to the earliest Christian communities. All five had an authoritative archbishop who ruled over church decisions and clergy in that region. The patriarch of Constantinople felt he held the most authority, as archbishop over the largest city and the seat of the Byzantine Roman Emperor. The Roman patriarch disagreed, arguing that his city was more important than Constantinople, historically, and that his position as bishop of Rome put him in a direct line of succession from Peter, one of Christ's main disciples, and as such, he should wield more authority. The patriarchs of Alexandria and Antioch split from the other three after 451, although new men, loyal to Constantinople, were formally placed in those positions.

The African Christians continued to follow their archbishop, sending missionaries south and also across the Red Sea to Yemen, taking Christianity to southern Arabia where it had a presence until overwhelmed by Islam in the 630s; however, as Islam forbade forced conversions, Christians remained (and remain) in Yemen throughout this political change. By 641 CE, the Oriental Orthodox churches in Africa were under the authority of the Muslim Umayyad Caliphate, as were the Patriarchs of Jerusalem and Antioch (by 637). Among the eastern patriarchates, only Constantinople and Rome resisted Muslim conquest, and as Islam moved across North Africa in the seventh century, Ethiopian Christians fled south, creating the Kingdom of Ethiopia, which centered itself on its Oriental Orthodox Christianity and lasted well into the twentieth century.

AKSUM

The Aksumite (or Axum, Axumite) Kingdom, which encompassed the regions of present-day Ethiopia, Eritrea, and portions of the Tigray region, was centered on its largest city, Aksum. Ethiopian tradition says that, in the fourth century, a group of nine saints led by the prophet Abba Garima brought sacred texts from the Mediterranean basin to the African region and translated them into a language and writing system known as Ge'ez. The Ethiopian monastery complex at Debre Damo and Abba Garima Monastery were part of these legendary foundations. The earliest illuminated gospels, the Garima Gospels (prominent in the next section) were created here. Aksumite kings facilitated trade between the Roman and Indian empires, enriching their rulers and populace. Powerful from around 80 to the early 900s, the kings authorized minting of coins in bronze, silver, and gold. They also encouraged scholarship and writing in Ge'ez. Jews, Christians, and later Muslims, all lived within this large empire.

Fig 1.1
Our Lady Mary of Zion in Aksum is a place of worship for Ethiopian Christians. It is believed that the first structure was built in the fourth century. It has been rebuilt many times since.
© A. Savin, WikiCommons

Another formative early conflict in Christianity was instigated by an Alexandrian priest named Arius, who stressed God's unity and uniqueness, arguing that Jesus was created by God and therefore was not co-eternal with God and hence the nature of the Trinity was as three distinct figures (Father, Son, and Holy Spirit). His thesis defied the fundamental nature of monotheism. Arius was condemned and excommunicated by the established leaders of the church in Africa. He fled from Africa to Palestine, continuing to write and argue for his theological stance.

The Roman emperor Constantine called a council to decide the question, as the emperor was as important in the Church as the leading patriarchs. At the First Council of Nicaea (325), Arius's views were declared heretical (or false), and a statement of orthodox belief was issued. This statement became known as the Nicene Creed, which stated that Jesus was "begotten and not made, of one essence with the Father." Nevertheless, Arianism flourished in many Germanic and Balkan areas, particularly as emperors in the Eastern and Western halves of the empire sought to shore up political support, either discrediting or bolstering Arian or non-Arian bishops and patriarchs, depending on their needs. Arian Christianity remained an important sect in Europe until the seventh century, especially among the Germanic kings of Europe.

A third divisive conflict in early Christianity was the Iconoclastic Controversy of the eighth and ninth centuries when icons (sacred images) had become a large part of Christian religious practices by the seventh century. Christian icons were representations in paintings, murals, or mosaics that had the likeness of Jesus Christ, his human mother Mary, saints, or narrative scenes of Christ's life. Many Christians believed that artistic representations of religious figures could easily lead to the worship of the image (the icon) in place of the divinities themselves, which would break the holy commandment that one shall not worship idols in place of God. This theological debate led to a very significant political change, as icons were outlawed in the eighth century by some Christian rulers. This "iconoclastic" movement caused a deep rift, particularly in Byzantine society, and helped the Roman church establish its independence from the emperor. In 726, the Byzantine emperor Leo III (r. 717–741) forbade the creation of any new icons and issued further edicts removing prominent public ones, even outlawing the private use of icons in homes or monasteries. This was hugely disruptive to the religious life of many Greek Christians at the time, and the emperor's efforts to enforce his edicts in Rome were met with stiff resistance. Battles broke out between Byzantine and Italian forces in Italy, which caused several Italian churches to turn their allegiance from Constantinople's patriarch to Rome's.

The Iconoclastic Controversy ended in 843, when the Byzantine Empress Irene (r. 780–802) called the Second Council of Nicaea (787) where it was determined that Christians were allowed to venerate but not worship icons. The patriarchs of Rome had consistently favored icons, mostly to rebel against imperious Byzantine leadership and heavy imperial taxation in southern Italy. Without the same heavy pressure from Islam, the European patriarchs could afford to defy the Byzantine emperor. And, by the end of the controversy in 843, most European bishops sided directly with the patriarch of Rome and against the Byzantine emperor. This debate continued to cause serious theological and political conflict between the patriarchates and the Byzantine emperors, and it may have contributed to the rancor felt between the European patriarch and his Middle Eastern cousins. While it did not yet cause a formalized separation between the two regional Christianities, the Roman patriarch (or pope) began to look to the north for military and political support, eventually finding a protector in the Frankish kings.

Charlemagne

The most powerful Frankish king was Charlemagne (d. 814 CE), who successfully used Christianity to consolidate an empire that included almost all of western Europe, except Spain, which was part of the Islamicate empire. At his death, he controlled territory from the Elbe to the Ebro rivers and from the English Channel to Rome. It was the largest kingdom in Europe since the dissolution of the Western Roman Empire 300 years earlier. Charlemagne even styled himself "Roman Emperor," going so far as to be crowned emperor by the Roman patriarch, Pope Leo III, on Christmas Day, 800 CE. Like Constantine in the early fourth century, Charlemagne used Christianity to bind his territory into a unified whole. This was not only conceptual: Charlemagne used church officials – like bishops, who governed all the churches within a city region, or archbishops, who governed all the churches in a multi-city region – to administer his far-flung territories and govern the people of their flocks.

The size of his new empire dictated that he could no longer rule by persona alone – he needed literate people who could record his decrees and relay them to wide areas. This idea brought on educational reform in Europe. The "Carolingian Renaissance," a rebirth of art and culture under Charlemagne's rule, was a result of his program to raise and support literacy, specifically writing and reading in Latin with a simplified script and standardized grammar. By the fifth century, Latin had become the preferred language of the Christian church in the Western Empire and the dominant language for writing (spoken Germanic and Celtic languages were rarely written down in the early medieval period). The handwritten letter shapes of Carolingian script are the basis for the text you are now reading.

Charlemagne recognized what the Romans had discovered early on: literacy makes it easier to rule a large area. Germanic kings prior to Charlemagne ruled

Fig 1.2
Pope Leo III crowning Charlemagne Roman Emperor, 800 CE. The image is from a mid-fourteenth-century *Les Grand Chronique de France*, a history of French kings from legendary beginnings to the thirteenth century. A digitized version of the manuscript, Royal MS 16 G VI, can be viewed on the British Library site.
Album / Alamy Stock Photo

through the force of their presence and their armies. They were peripatetic, moving about their kingdoms to announce laws, hold courts, dispense justice, and be seen by their subjects. Charlemagne's kingdom was too large for him to cover in one year, especially as he regularly campaigned into far-flung corners to expand his territory. The written word could stand in for Charlemagne when he could not personally be in any one place. To make this happen, Charlemagne needed notaries. He found them in the churches, but he needed more than educated clergy. He needed men who could act as his bureaucrats and not be tied to their bishop over their king. He needed schools.

Charlemagne found his educational director in Alcuin of York, a Northumbrian trained in northern England who understood the difficulties inherent in teaching Latin to a Germanic audience. Alcuin himself was a bureaucrat, trained in dealing with the early English kings and their courts. He understood the nature of rule and men who ruled. When called by Charlemagne, Alcuin moved south to France to begin Charlemagne's new educational campaign. Schools for bright boys were organized in larger cities that had numerous churches and established clergy. These "cathedral schools" were the centerpiece of educational reform in Europe during the ninth century. (Girls occasionally could be educated in monastic settings, and several nunneries, like Wilton Abbey in southern England, became well known as schools for girls and young women.) Charlemagne used Christianity's emphasis on the written word to create secular bureaucrats who would aid his rule.

Alcuin wrote on the nature of kingship for Charlemagne, expounding on the ways he felt a good king must rule: "A king should be strong against his enemies, humble to Christians, feared by pagans, loved by the poor, and judicious in counsel and in maintaining justice." Within this one sentence, we can see how this medieval Latin-educated monk created a type of kingship that merged the Frankish ideals of a strong and just leader with the Christian ideals of humility and compassion. Charlemagne took his position as a Christian ruler seriously, and sponsored churches in Jerusalem, aided pilgrims, and sent his own emissaries to the holy city and to Constantinople. In other arenas, Charlemagne continued the roles of Germanic kingship, through warfare and economic support, among other traits.

Germanic and Slavic Conversions

The official and final separation of western European Christianity, as controlled from Rome, and Byzantine Orthodoxy, as controlled from Constantinople, is called the The Great Schism of 1054. It was not a dramatic rupture; instead, it was the formalization of divisions and disagreements that grew steadily from the mid-fifth century on. For centuries, the two institutions had been actively competing for new communities of believers in north and eastern Europe, and by 1000 CE, the pre-Christian Germanic and Slavic peoples had converted to one or the other. The Scandinavians largely converted to Roman Christianity, as did some Slavic peoples such as the ancestors of present-day Poles, Czechs, and Slovenes. Bulgarians and Serbs converted to Byzantine Christianity, as did the Rus – a mixed culture of Slavic peoples and the Vikings who ruled over them.

Tightly connected through conquest and marriages, Slavic and Norse nobles ruled the large cities in Kievan Rus: Novgorod and Kiev. The first Slav to rule Kiev, Sviastoslav I, ruled an increasingly Christian people, including his mother Olga, who converted late in life. At his death in 972 CE, he divided his realm among his three sons: Iaropolk and Oleg, both of whom had Christian sympathies, and Vladimir, who did not. (Iarapolk's wife had been a nun and she would later dig up and baptize her husband's body.) Iaropolk killed Oleg in 977 CE and the ongoing animosity among brothers ended in 978 CE, when Vladimir killed Iaropolk. Vladimir was unapologetically anti-Christian, allying himself with the pre-Christian deities worshipped in different areas of western Russia and actively persecuted Christians until this practice backfired and threatened his royal control. Needing a way to unify his rule, Vladimir began considering monotheism.

In 987 CE, he sent envoys to representatives of the major faiths and also sought input from his nobles on the best choice for himself and the Rus. Russian chronicles detail Vladimir's reasoning for rejecting or accepting a faith. The Jews, he felt, had lost God's favor in both the loss of their territory in Jerusalem and because the Muslims were so successful in attracting converts, an indication that God favored the Muslims over the Jews. However, he thought Islam was too conservative, particularly in its rules against pork and drinking alcohol. As wild boar was a staple protein source for his people, the proscription of both Judaism and Islam against pork was a problem. Moreover, alcohol, he declared, was the great joy of the Russian people. This left two branches of Christianity. Vladimir's envoys found Latin Mass confusing and joyless, and believed the Roman patriarch had too much political power, but his agents in the Byzantine churches wrote to him that the Mass held such beauty that they were not sure if they were in heaven or on Earth. It helped that the powerful nobles of Kiev had numerous contacts with the Byzantine Empire and several of their wives had already converted to this faith.

The final reason for conversion to Byzantine Orthodoxy, however, was much more political and practical. The Byzantine emperor Basil II was fighting a two-front war against the Bulgarians and needed additional military support. He promised his sister Anna in marriage to Vladimir for his aid. Vladimir agreed, but Anna refused the marriage unless Vladimir converted. He was baptized in 988 CE and 6,000 troops immediately moved south to Byzantium. When Basil reneged and refused to send Anna to Kiev, Vladimir invaded Constantinople and forcibly took her back to his capital. Once home, he employed Christianity and his status over the Byzantines to consolidate his rule, converting his people, building churches, and beginning a program for literacy. His acceptance of Christianity provided a divine sanction for his rule, something he had earlier sought in his alliances with polytheists, and Christianity became the centralizing force of this new empire. The Byzantine patriarch established the office of the Metropolitan of Kiev. Metropolitans became the most important religious figures in this domain. When the Ottoman Empire conquered the last remnant of the Byzantine Empire in 1453, this patriarch pronounced Moscow (the new head of the Russian Empire) as the "Third Rome" and the center of all Christianity.

In broad terms, the Slavs who were Christianized by the Roman Church and took Latin and the Roman alphabet as the language of liturgy are present-day Poles, Czechs, Slovenes, and Croats. Medieval Slavs who chose Byzantine Christianity as their spiritual system received scripture in vernacular languages written with the Cyrillic alphabet (named after one of the two monks, Cyril and Methodius, who were missionaries in the region and first wrote down the languages of the people). These are the Russians, Ukrainians, Bulgarians, and Serbs. The different national alphabets are still a source of some cultural division.

Early Islam

Arabs were often a marginalized group in the early period, militarily weaker and economically disadvantaged against the larger empires of Byzantium (to the north) and Persia (to the east). In the few centuries before Muhammad brought God's instruction to the Quraysh (the ruling tribe), control over Mecca and the region along the coast of the Red Sea was fought over by the peoples of the Mediterranean Basin: Jews, Persians, Byzantines, and the African Christians of Ethiopia. As Muhammad explained, God had sent his word to the Arabs and his message of monotheism and inclusion – every person, regardless of birth, status, or gender, could convert – appealed to various people in and around Mecca. Impressed by Muhammad's perseverance and conviction, many members of the tribe converted and accepted him as a prophet of God, but others felt threatened and retaliated against those who converted. In 615 CE, some of Muhammad's early followers were forced to flee across the Red Sea to Aksum. Several years later, in 622 CE, a larger group fled with Muhammad north from Mecca to Medina. This emigration from Mecca to Medina is called the *hijra*, Arabic for "flight." (As discussed in the previous chapter, 622 CE became year one in the Islamic calendar, to praise the dedication of Muhammad and his small band of followers). For the next several years, Muhammad set up a new center of worship in Medina – one dedicated to God and focused on improving the lives of common people, economically as well as spiritually. At the heart of Islam is the belief that one's spiritual life cannot, and should not, be separated from one's political, economic, and social dealings. One is Muslim in all aspects of life, not just the religious parts, and Islam is a way of life that permeates political and economic dealings.

In 630 CE, Muhammad and his followers returned to Mecca and took control of the Kaaba, the spiritual and political center of Quraysh rule. Muhammad "cleansed" the Kaaba by removing idols and dedicated it to his new faith, as the place where Abraham (Ibrahim) and his son built a place of worship (masjid) to

God. Muhammad quickly set up a new political order, one centered on his new faith, for which he was the spiritual, military, judicial, and cultural leader of the community. He died in 632 before he could fully implement his ideas or select a successor, and the 30 years following the prophet's death were internally tumultuous. Despite the civil conflict, the subsequent four leaders (or *caliphs*, from the Arabic *khalifa* for successor) continued their process of conversion and expansion.

MUHAMMAD SUCCESSION

After Muhammad's death, four caliphs led Mecca:

632–634 CE Abu Bakr (Muhammad's father-in-law)
634–644 CE Umar ibn al-Khattab (Muhammad's brother-in-law)
644–656 CE Uthman ibn Affan (Muhammad's cousin, not of the Quraysh clan, but Umayyad)
656–661 CE Ali ibn Abi Talib (Muhammad's son-in-law, elected after Uthman's death)

Muhammad's death caused both political and religious divisions. Since he had died without a male heir, several men argued that they were best served to rule. Abu Bakr, Muhammad's father-in-law, convinced most of those close to Muhammad he was best suited, and he ruled from 632 until his death in 634. This short reign did not solve the succession problem and the next several years were fraught with political instability. Many people believed that succession should go to Muhammad's closest male relative (in this case his son-in-law and cousin, Ali), while others believed that the community should be ruled by a person selected for his capabilities as a ruler. In the 20 years after Muhammad's death, four different men ruled Mecca and the surrounding territory.

Despite the internal debates, they also continued to expand their reach far past traditional Arab territory. The first three rulers extended Islamic hegemony north and west, and, by 637 CE, disparate militias had formed into a state organization, with a standing army, a structured hierarchy and system of pay for its soldiers. Known as the Rashidun Army, this military force allowed Muslims to conquer more territory throughout the Byzantine and Persian empires. Taking a page from Alexander the Great, Muslim leaders allowed conquered soldiers to enter their army if they converted to Islam. Twelve thousand Persians converted and entered the army by 636, which certainly aided in the capture of the Persian capital and the fall of the Persian state to the Muslims in 651 CE. By 650 CE, northern Africa had also been conquered. Discontented with Byzantine rule and taxation, many people in Asia Minor and Africa welcomed the Muslims as liberators, which explains the lower death toll from these conquests than we see from later wars. Jews and Eastern Orthodox Christians welcomed Islamic rule, especially as the Muslim rulers accepted these older Abrahamic peoples and often used local men as officials within the state government.

As religion and politics were explicitly tied together, doctrinal issues also plagued the early caliphate. These differences began directly after Muhammad's death and reached a tipping point in 656 CE, when Ali was chosen as successor to Uthman. Many felt Muhammad had designated Ali as his heir and that this selection made Ali divinely sanctioned. Despite this designation, when Muhammad died, his companions elected Abu Bakr over Ali as the next caliph. This caused dissension both inside Muhammad's family and among others who felt that succession should go through lineage or felt slighted by this choice. Abu Bakr ruled for two years prior to succumbing to illness and dying. He chose as successor Umar, a strong leader who focused on social programs and expansion. Umar was killed by a Persian assassin, an event brought about because of his expansion. Umar had appointed a group of six men to choose a successor in the event of his death; they chose Uthman, a popular leader who sought to bridge the divide between the caliphs and Muhammad's family. His assassination in 656 CE (by an Egyptian group angered at expansion into Egypt) brought Ali back into the inner circle, as he was elected soon after Uthman's death.

Ali's election was contested, and he fought civil insurrections during his seven-year rule. He was assassinated in 661 CE, while at prayer. His sons attempted to rule but were met with fierce opposition and, at the Battle of Karbala in 680, Ali's younger son Husain and around 70 family members were killed. This became the major dividing point between the Islamic sects of the Sunni and Shia. Shia Muslims, also called Shi'ites (the *Shia Ali* or the "party of Ali"), felt that only people within Muhammad's family could be legitimate caliphs. Sunni Muslims (those who follow tradition, *sunna*) felt that rulers should be chosen based on their ability to rule. Both groups had similar religious and doctrinal beliefs, although these differed more over time, as Shia and Sunni ruled and lived separately. Shia Muslims were, and remain, a minority of Muslims, but differences between the two sects would mark important variances within the Muslim world during the premodern period. One example is that Shia Muslims would venerate Imams and others as saints, making pilgrimages to tombs and other holy places.

The practice of Islam, as in other monotheistic faiths, emphasizes both personal ethical behavior and a set of required practices by individuals who owe loyalty and belief to a personal God. The basic requirements among Sunni Muslims are often called the "five pillars of Islam," some of which take place once in a lifetime and some of which are daily or annual. Various sects of Shia Islam nuance these five pillars, adding other requirements for ethical behavior and allegiance to the Imams. The five pillars are foundational beliefs and acts of faith in God and the prophet Muhammad, five daily prayers, a requirement of charitable giving, annual fasting during the holy month of Ramadan, and pilgrimage to Mecca. That final pillar, called the *hajj*, is to be undertaken at least once in a Muslim's lifetime (although the disabled and destitute are exempted); it commemorates the return of Muhammad and his followers into Mecca after their period of exile in Medina. The *hajj* requirement meant that many medieval Muslims from around the Eastern Hemisphere traveled long distances and thus needed technology, mapping, and transportation networks available to make it possible.

Islamic Expansion

At the prophet's death, many regions defied the political and spiritual leadership in Mecca, and Islam, just like Christianity, quickly separated into various sects that shared a fundamental commitment to the same God, but with significant differences in practice and theology. Yemen and Oman, two states with long histories of independence and outside connections (Yemen to the Kingdom of Aksum and Oman to the Persian Empire), openly rebelled against Abu Bakr, the next leader. Abu Bakr spent his reign fighting the Ridda Wars (632–633), a series of conflicts in Arabia intending to pacify the Arab tribes and bring them under the aegis of Meccan political power, while also continuing excursions north to the Byzantine Empire. Although few Arabs renounced their faith, Abu Bakr understood that he needed to consolidate the new groups, politically, for both civil and religious purposes.

During Muhammad's lifetime, his armies sought control of the regions both north and south of Medina. When he reentered the city of Mecca in 630 CE, he had gained influence over most of west Arabia. An ill-fated foray north into Byzantine territory resulted in the death of several top generals and family members. At his death, Muhammad instructed Abu Bakr to continue fighting the Byzantines, which his successor did directly after the Ridda Wars. The biggest gains came with the military-minded caliph Umar, who pressed into the southern reaches of the Byzantine Empire while also moving east into Persia. By 636 CE, his armies controlled Syria and commandeered Damascus as their new political capital (Mecca would remain the religious capital). In 637 CE, his armies captured the Persian capital of Ctesiphon and the disintegration of the Persian Empire began. The Muslim armies had a distinct advantage over the Persian and Byzantine empires, weakened as they were by almost constant conflict with each other over resources and territory.

Most Persians followed the religion of Zoroastrianism, although Oriental Orthodox and Eastern Orthodox Christians also lived within their environs. Centuries of conflict with the Roman and, later, Byzantine empires left the Persian Sassanian Empire unable to repel the new incursions by the Muslims. Many Persians readily converted to Islam, and Islam absorbed much of Persian culture. Some, however, kept their native religion, and Zoroastrians continued to live under Muslim rule in Iran and, later, the Gujarat province in India. Nevertheless, Zoroastrians were often persecuted and, over time, many converted to Islam. But many in the Middle East and North Africa saw the Muslims as liberators, particularly North African Christians, who felt disregarded and oppressed by their Byzantine neighbors. Umar's armies moved into Egypt by 639 CE and Uthman continued this expansion when he became caliph, conquering most of North Africa by 646 CE. Burdened by heavy taxation and absentee leadership, local populations in the Middle East, Africa, and Spain welcomed the new Muslim political leaders who had, by this time, settled on taxation rates that favored Muslims, but did not overburden

Christian and Jewish adherents. Uthman's caliphate began the Umayyad dynasty (named for his family clan), which ruled the Islamic territories from 661 to 750 CE. Centered in Damascus, the Umayyad brought peace and stability to areas under their control. They developed administrative forms learned from the Byzantine's administration in Damascus and translated huge numbers of Greek texts into Arabic.

DOME OF THE ROCK

The Umayyad period also saw the development of a particularly Islamic style of art and architecture, including the building of the Dome of the Rock mosque in Jerusalem. This site held, and holds, significant meaning for Muslims and Jews. It is an Islamic shrine but is built on the

Fig 1.3
Dome of the Rock.
Photo: Andrew Shiva

Temple Mount, the site of the Second Jewish Temple, which was destroyed by the Romans in 70 CE. Muslims consider it to be the place where Abraham went to fulfill God's commandment to sacrifice his son. In the Qur'anic verse known as "Muhammad's Night Journey," Muhammad flies to the site on a winged horse. Constructed in 691, the first building collapsed in the eleventh century and was replaced by the current building in 1022.

The English word *mosque*, which denotes a Muslim house of worship, comes to English from the French and Italian words for *masjid*, the Arabic for "place of prostration (in prayer)." The Arabic word for a mosque used for communal Friday prayers is *jamia*, or *masjid jamia* from the word meaning "gathering." Various English words for mosque (*moseak*, *meseache*, *muskaye*) were used as early as the fourteenth century. Premodern Christians used words like "churches" to describe mosques.

Umayyad forces continued expanding and, by the early eighth century, they had moved further east and west. Afghanistan and the Indus River valley fell to Islamicate armies as the Indian military retreated further east. Chinese expeditions by the Tang empress Wu Zetian fought against the newly established Umayyad dynasty in Afghanistan in 751 CE, but they were over-extended, and the Muslims handily defeated them at Talas. In Europe, Tariq ibn Ziyad fought the Visigothic king Rodrigo, defeating him in 711 CE. During the next three years, Tariq's army moved across Spain with little opposition and, by 714 CE, Umayyad rule was well established. Al-Andalus, as Muslim Spain was known, became a strong central player in the medieval European sphere, with a vibrant intellectual and artistic community.

From Muhammad forward, Islamic political leaders combined the ideals of their religion with their government – one strove to be a Muslim in all areas of life, not just in the masjid. They established taxation principles that differentiated tolls based on religion: although not forced to convert, monotheists who were mentioned in the Qur'an (first Jews and Christians, later Zoroastrians) paid an annual head tax, with Muslims taxed at the lowest rate. This may have led to conversions for economic reasons. Although begun in Arabia and for Arabs, by 650 CE Islamic leaders believed that a person of any ethnicity or previous faith could convert to Islam. They set up rules and regulations within their districts to ease the transitions for new converts, with codes on how business and political dealings with peoples of different creeds and backgrounds should be undertaken.

Conclusion

Here we introduced the major monotheistic faiths of the western Asian sphere: Judaism, Zoroastrianism, Christianity, and Islam. Between 500 and 900, Christianity coalesced into several major sects: Roman, Byzantine

Orthodox, and Oriental Christianity. Disputes on the nature of Christ and the theological basis of icons, along with political infighting and cultural differences, caused most of the controversies until, in 1054, the separation of the Roman and Byzantine churches was clearly defined. Along with Oriental Orthodoxy, there were three distinct Christian Churches. Increasingly, the Roman Church looked to western European kings for military and economic support, while the Byzantine missionaries converted Slavic peoples as far north as Kiev.

As Christians dealt with large internal arguments and competition that partitioned the early Church of the Romans, they also had to contend with the growth of Islam. In the early seventh century in the Arabian city of Mecca, Muhammad the Prophet spread the word of God, quickly attracting large communities of followers to a religion called Islam, "the submission." By 661, Muhammad and the four caliphs who succeeded him had spread Islam outward from the Arabian Peninsula, conquering territory throughout the Middle East and northern Africa. By 750, the Islamicate world included territory from the Indus River to Spain, but it was not without its own destructive and complicated power dynamics. The split between Sunni and Shia sects of Islam was originally political in nature, but involved increased theological and ritualistic differences as well.

One reason these religious institutions came to dominate western Eurasia is because of the connection between political leaders and the power of faith. Political leaders needed divine authority to attract public support, which was required to fight for land and resources. Religious leaders needed the safety that stable political units brought to their institutions and worshippers. Medieval leaders such as Charlemagne, Vladimir, Muhammad, and the four caliphs combined spiritual imperative with political and economic ambition.

B: PEOPLE OF THE BOOK

Evidence: *Aleppo Codex*

Codex Aureus

Cairo Geniza

Garima Gospels

Amajur Qur'an

In this section, we focus on Jewish and Christian Bibles and Islamic Qur'ans, the sacred texts of their respective religions and symbols of knowledge and literacy. A centerpiece of each of these faiths is a sacred respect for writings, through which the adherents contemplate the most absorbing questions of life: why do I exist? What does God want from me? How can I live the most principled life?

How should I treat my neighbor? And how should I treat my enemies? For all three faiths, the written presentation of the spoken word of God was honored with all the artistic sophistication and material resources a community could provide. These books were the center of life, providing instruction to individuals and societies on how to live according to God's plan. They had other uses as well: witnesses of divine oaths, talismans to ward off evil, luxury items to display the status of a powerful ruler, or objects to awe illiterate non-believers and inspire their conversion.

A Shared Tradition

The most influential monotheistic faiths from 500 to 1500 CE were Judaism, Christianity, and Islam. A significant foundation of both the Christian Bible and Islamic Qur'an is the Jewish holy text, the Tanakh. The Tanakh is what Christians call the Old Testament; thus, Christians share with Jews reverence of all the characters of the Tanakh, including Abraham, Moses, and Joseph – but they see Jesus as the final messiah (God's anointed one) of this tradition. Islam considers all these holy figures, including Jesus, to be prophets in a line that preceded Muhammad, who is the Prophet, God's last messenger on Earth. Qur'anic writings record this relationship by frequently referencing People of the Book, or the Jews and Christians who share many of the same prophets, texts, and their stories. Because of the importance of Abraham in all three, they are cumulatively referred to as the Abrahamic religions.

Tanakh is an acronym of the words for the three sections of the Hebrew Bible: TNK. T is for Torah, the first five sections: Genesis, Exodus, Leviticus, Numbers, and Deuteronomy. N is for Nevi'im, or the Prophets, such as Isaiah, Ezekiel, and Jeremiah. K for Ketuvim, the Writings, including Psalms and Proverbs. Originally a sect of the Jewish faith, Christians accepted the Tanakh as prophecies of the coming of Jesus and his mission on Earth. Later Christian theologians accepted the Tanakh as the holy word of God, calling it the Old Testament. They added to it a New Testament, which includes accounts of Jesus's life, along with the letters of St. Paul and other messengers of Christ's miracles and teachings.

The Qur'an also references material from the Hebrew and Christian Bibles. God's messenger to Muhammad, the angel Gabriel, is an important spiritual being in both the Hebrew and Christian sacred texts. He revealed to Muhammad information about major figures of the other traditions – Abraham, Noah, Lot, Mary, and Jesus – and how the Jewish and Christian people misinterpreted and denigrated the experiences of these figures and of the original message of God. By the end of the eighth century, these revelations were recorded and consecrated as the Holy Qur'an, or "recitation" (from the orality of Muhammad's revelations). Caliph Uthman ordered scribes to copy the oral history as it had passed down from Muhammad. This "Uthmanic" text was produced in a very short time, which is quite different from the emergence over a thousand years of the Hebrew books and over 400 years for the Christian holy book. One reason for the quick agreement on the contents was, as we saw above, that the newly united and inspired people of Islam wanted to spread out, find additional resources, absorb new ideas, and create a vigorous, energetic culture in the name of God. Formerly adversarial communities were united by the common language and lessons of the Qur'an.

The concept of God's covenant with Abraham as expressed in the Tanakh is often interpreted in Christian belief as foreshadowing the covenant God makes with Christians by sacrificing his Son for their sins. The Qur'an is very serious about this same covenant but claims that Jews and Christians have willfully disdained and broken the compact between God and Abraham. As the messenger of God, the angel made it clear that the people of Muhammad's tribe and others who worship and submit to God's will would be honored.

Invention of the Book

The form of the book as we know it – a stack of pages (also called leaves or folios) joined together at the edge or spine – is called a codex. During the Roman Empire, the codex (pl. codices) became the common form of recording information in writing. Because the pages of a codex are easy to flip through and mark for later reference, it was the preferred form for documenting Roman legal and administrative "codes." The Romans also used scrolls made of papyrus, a reed harvested from the Nile River and rivers of Mesopotamia. The reeds were sliced and pulped, beaten into thin mats that were overlapped and glued together, and rolled into scrolls. These rolled books were called *uolomen* in Latin, which becomes volume in English. At the time of the Roman Empire, the Chinese used a similar process to make paper (see later chapters); nevertheless, the English word paper is derived from papyrus.

Unlike scrolls, codices were portable, easy to store, and more durable – they could be bound in leather, wood, or precious materials and stacked without the pages being crushed or soiled. Additionally, codices were often made of parchment instead of the less resilient papyrus. Parchment is made from animal skins, typically sheepskins or calfskins that are soaked, stretched, and scraped into thin, smooth sheets. Scribes sometimes used skins from goat, deer, or even rabbit. Especially fine pages made from the supple skin of lambs and young calves is called vellum. Parchment was usually too thick and unwieldy to glue together, end to end, into long scrolls. Instead, a prepared skin was folded, trimmed, and bound into a codex. Parchment and vellum manuscripts are sturdy and resilient. These documents are called manuscripts, which tells us that they were written (Latin, *scriptus*) by hand (*manus*).

Before the codex was invented and popularized, Jewish texts were recorded on scrolls. By the seventh century the codex was the form for some of the Jewish holy books, but scrolls remained a preferred form especially of the Torah or Pentateuch, the first five books of the Hebrew Bible. These are called Sefer

Torahs – scrolls that are carefully prepared with text solemnly copied by hand. They are stored in a Torah ark, a special space or cabinet in a synagogue, and are still the foundation of Jewish weekly worship. No scroll contained the entire Hebrew Bible; most contained just a few biblical books. The oldest Sefer scroll known to exist is at the University of Bologna and was produced around 1200. The oldest surviving complete Hebrew Bibles are codices: the *Leningrad Codex*, copied on parchment in 1009 CE, and the *Aleppo Codex*, copied about a century earlier.

Before a manuscript, scroll, or codex had any writing or designated purpose, it was already a luxury item. Animal hides could be used for a variety of purposes, such as durable, waterproof leather for shoes, bags, and shelter. They could be used as warm, windproof garments and blankets. However, honoring God was the most important project of all, and so communities desired to show their devotion through the creation of beautifully written and decorated texts. In a premodern manuscript, illustrations are called illuminations, a term that comes from the fact that so many of the decorations and paintings were accentuated with gold leaf. When the book was opened, and the gold leaf caught the light, it looked to viewers as if the images were either reflecting the light of God or generating the light of God's knowledge from within. Rich blue was made from ground lapis lazuli, a mineral found in the hills of Afghanistan and transported along the trade routes at great expense. Lapis was as precious as gold, but the most luxurious color of all was the reddish purple harvested from a Mediterranean shellfish called a *murex purpurea*, which created the color purple (see Chapter 8).

RANSOM

In addition to valuable hides, rare pigments, and gold leaf, it took great amounts of time, skill, and labor to produce a book. If the content of the book was religious, then the manuscript was elevated from a precious commodity to a sacred object worth dying for. Stories of the life of two manuscripts demonstrate the importance of them to their communities. In 1099 CE, at the height of the First Crusade, European Christians succeeded in taking Jerusalem from its Muslim rulers. The crusaders slaughtered the Muslims and many of the Jews living in the city, but some were spared because they could be held for a ransom. Crusaders also captured Jewish religious texts, including the *Aleppo Codex*, a full Hebrew Bible. A year later, a Jewish community paid a high price to recover it and other religious objects. The codex was then taken to Aleppo, Syria, where it remained protected in the Central Synagogue of Aleppo until 1947 CE when the building was destroyed and the manuscript damaged. The remaining portion has been in Jerusalem since 1957.

The Aleppo Codex   Deut. 4:38 — 6:3
From J. Segall, *Travels through Northern Syria* (London 1910) 99

Fig 1.4
A 1910 photograph of a page now missing from the *Aleppo Codex*, once a full Hebrew Bible or
Tanakh that was copied ca. 1008 CE. It was looted during the First Crusade and held for ransom.
It survived intact until 1947, when it was damaged in a raid of the synagogue in Aleppo, Syria,
where it had been kept.
© Wikimedia Commons, public domain

Another dramatic story of kidnap and ransom involves the *Codex Aureus*, named for the
Latin word *aurea* (gold) because of its extensive gold-leaf decoration. A century after it was
captured by Viking raiders, it was bought at great expense by a nobleman who presented it
to Christ Church Cathedral in Canterbury, England. Anxious to record the details of his good
deed, Alderman Alfred wrote on the page for the gospel of Matthew in Early English:

> In the Name of our Lord Jesus Christ. I, Earl Alfred, and my wife Werburg procured this
> book from the heathen invading army with our own money; the purchase was made
> with pure gold. And we did that for the love of God and for the benefit of our souls, and
> because neither of us wanted these holy works to remain any longer in heathen hands.

The inscription is signed for Alfred, Werburg, and their daughter Alhthryth. Over time, the
manuscript traded hands and is now at the National Library of Sweden.

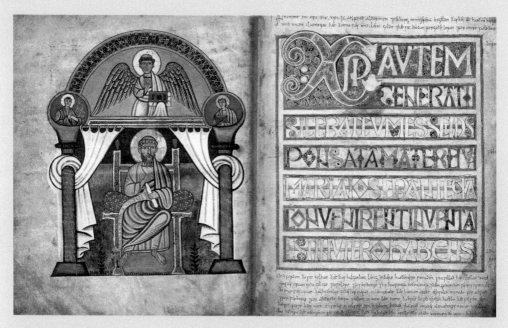

Fig 1.5
The opening page of the gospel of St. Matthew in the *Codex Aureus* (mid-eighth century), which has an inscription in Early English written by the nobleman who gave his own hard-earned money to get the manuscript back from the Vikings who stole it.
The Picture Art Collection / Alamy Stock Photo

Cairo Geniza

During the Middle Ages, the Jewish people did not have a homeland and lived in communities all over Europe, the Middle East, and Africa, always vulnerable to persecution, expulsion, and massacre. This precarious, unsettled existence made it difficult to preserve books over generations, and thus there is less material evidence of Jewish religious texts than for the other monotheisms. But there is one cache of written documents that provides incredible evidence of Jewish life and worship, a *geniza* (pl. *genizot*), which is a special kind of storage bin: a consecrated space where medieval rabbis temporarily stored any old and tattered religious parchments in the Hebrew script, both religious and non-religious, just in case the name of God was written in them. They were considered worth saving even if the language underlying the Hebrew script was not Hebrew. Some *genizot* were rooms in a synagogue. Others were holes in the earth much like graves.

Diasporic Jews often used the Hebrew alphabet to record their spoken languages, which were those of the society in which they lived. For example, medieval Jews who lived in the Arabic-speaking lands of the Islamic world spoke Arabic just like their neighbors, but often wrote theological and business documents in what is known as Judeo-Arabic – the script of Hebrew recording the language of Arabic. Even when these documents were considered illegible, if words were written in Hebrew characters and if they were or could possibly have been about God, the manuscripts were considered holy, and it was blasphemous to destroy them.

At the end of the nineteenth century, a Jewish scholar from England's Cambridge University was invited by the rabbis at the Ben Ezra synagogue of Fustat (Old Cairo) to look through its *geniza,* which contained parchment fragments going back as far as the eleventh century. Although these bits of parchment shared space with vermin, odd bits of organic refuse, and deteriorated building materials, they had been preserved by the incredibly dry climate. At the Ben Ezra synagogue, the practice had been to treat any writing in Hebrew letters as consecrated (sacred), so in addition to religious texts, the collection contained fragments of contracts, receipts, and correspondance – much of it in Judeo-Arabic. Solomon Schechter was not the first scholar to examine manuscripts from this sacred stash, but he was held in high esteem by the Ben Ezra rabbis, and they allowed him to bag up some of the contents – mouse droppings, fleas, fallen ceiling plaster, and all – and take them to Cambridge, where it has become the world's largest single collection of medieval Jewish manuscripts. In addition to its high value in the field of Judaic studies, the collection is a record of daily life in medieval Cairo and its Mediterranean trade that has no parallel in any other culture from the Middle Ages.

Some of the parchments are palimpsests, manuscripts that have been erased or scraped by a scribe wanting to use the surface to write a new text. A famous palimpsest found in the Cairo Geniza is on its face a Sabbath hymn in Hebrew, but underneath the writing is a barely visible substrata of Greek lettering. Upon close examination, scholars have determined the Greek to be a late fifth- or early sixth-century copy of passages from a book in the Tanakh.

Spreading the Good News

Like Hebrew scripture, copies of the Christian gospels were produced in a wide geographic area. The gospels are the first four books of the Christian New Testament, which are the experiences of Jesus according to the apostles Matthew, Mark, Luke, and John. Because these men and their missionaries spread the story of Jesus, they are known as the Evangelists, from an ancient Greek word meaning "to announce good news." When the tribes in Britain were Christianized in the eighth century, they translated the term into Early English, calling these biblical narratives "gōd spel," the good story, which soon became "gospel." Because of their focus on the life of Jesus, books containing just these four stories were very popular across all Christian denominations. They were also portable and took fewer resources to produce.

We have examples of these scriptures ranging from a monastery on the coast of the North Sea to the city of Aksum in Ethiopia, and from the Iberian

Fig 1.6
Produced in the sixth century for the Byzantine Church's celebration of the conquest of Italy, the Rossano Gospels is a luxury manuscript with red/purple parchment pages and writing in silver ink. Along with the Abba Garima Gospels, the Rossano Gospels has early examples of images of the four Evangelists. Rossano Gospels, Rossano Cathedral, Italy.
© Wikimedia Commons, public domain

Peninsula to western Syria. These books are evidence of the different traditions among the Christian faiths. In the medieval Roman Christian tradition, gospels are in Latin, and the Evangelists have iconic representation. Matthew's symbol is a winged man, Mark's is a winged lion, Luke's is a winged ox, and John's an eagle. This imagery was derived from passages in the book of Revelation, the last chapter of the Christian Bible, in which four winged creatures surround the throne of God. The Byzantine Orthodox and Oriental Orthodox Christian gospels are usually in the vernacular, the language of the local people for whom the book was produced. Byzantine Orthodox gospels are often in Greek, but are found in other languages as well, including Old Church Slavonic. Surviving Oriental Orthodox gospels are written in Armenian, Georgian, Coptic, and Ge'ez, the liturgical language of the Ethiopian Christians. There are even gospel books in Arabic, reflecting the large number of Arabic-speaking Christians who remained unconverted under Islamic dominion.

Garima Gospels

A remarkable example of the gospel tradition is the Garima Gospels, named for the Ethiopian monastery, Abba Garima, where the treasured manuscripts have been kept and are still used for ceremonies. The Garima Gospels are three full texts of the gospels. Until 2005, two books were combined in one binding (Abba Garima II and III) and another bound separately (Abba Garima I). In 2013, it was announced that parchment samples from the three books had been radiocarbon tested, with the astonishing results that these manuscripts are much older than scholars thought; in fact, they are possibly the oldest gospels in existence. Abba Garima III is dated between 330 and 650 CE, and the Abba Garima I parchment is dated to 530–660 CE. The text and decoration of the third gospel book, Abba Garima II, indicates that it is not as old as these first two, but considerably older than any other surviving Ethiopian gospel book. Abba Garima III contains illuminations of Matthew, Mark, Luke, and John. This means that it is the earliest reliably dated gospel book, in any tradition, to survive with intact portraits of all four Evangelists.

Before this discovery, the Garima Gospels were relatively unknown outside Ethiopian Studies. Given this inspiring new evidence, scholars were able to free themselves of preconceived notions about the manuscripts and come to different conclusions; specifically, they have begun to consider that there were centers of Christian manuscript production other than those in Europe and the near Middle East. It is certainly possible that these gospels were produced in Aksum, the cultural heart of the Aksumite kingdom of Ethiopia. Aksum was a vigorous cultural center, with enough mercantile contact with the late antique and early medieval Mediterranean world to develop an Ethiopian version of Christian culture. Illuminations and decorations of

Fig 1.7
Mark the Evangelist. Abba Garima III.
History and Art Collection / Alamy Stock Photo

late antique Mediterranean manuscripts are the closest comparison to the art of the Garima Gospels.

The monastery at Garima was founded by the Christian missionary Abba Garima. Abba Garima and nine other men entered Ethiopia from the north (probably from Egypt or the Middle East) sometime in the fifth century, after the Council of Chalcedon and the schism that created Oriental Orthodoxy. The monasteries and churches they founded have been continuously occupied since the ninth century. The Ethiopian language, Ge'ez, is a synthesis of Arabic, Ethiopian, and Greek. The knowledge and use of the Greek language tied the Ethiopians to the northern Byzantine Empire, while the Arabic language tied them directly to the Arabian Peninsula. As the Ethiopian Christians traded with and raided both the Byzantine Orthodox and Islamicate territories, competence in the languages common in those areas was necessary and helpful.

Qur'an

As with the Judaic and Christian scriptural traditions of honoring God with the highest artistic presentation of His holy word, Muslim patrons and artisans devoted their resources and talents to producing beautiful Qur'ans. A significant feature of Qur'anic design is the lack of divine or human figures. There is no specific rule against representing these characters in the Qur'an, but the tradition is much like that of the Byzantine Christian iconoclasts who interpreted God's commandment – that humans will not worship false idols or graven images – as disallowing artistic representation of divine figures. Therefore, scholars believed it to be hubris to imagine and depict what God, Muhammad, or the prophets might have looked like. Instead, the art of a Qur'an is the script, which is called calligraphy. Since the written record of these revelations and instructions was compiled in Arabic after Muhammad's death, Arabic is considered the only human language that is worthy of the word of God. Qur'anic Arabic is now called Classical Arabic.

Calligraphy itself, surrounded by abstract designs in gold leaf and expensive pigments such as lapis lazuli and Tyrian purple, is symbolic of respect and devotion. Because Muslims memorize the Qur'an (or at least large parts it) and listen to it being recited poetically and almost musically, the books were not always used for verbatim reading but as an inspirational reminder of the surah, or verse. One sentence could occupy an entire bifolium (two facing sheets of parchment). Early in the history of Islam, scribes and illuminators developed a special style of writing called *kufic*. With exaggerated lines and spaces, it was used to distinguish Qur'ans from any other books. Later scribes expanded and elongated the horizontal lines, a design element called *mashq*. Extra marks used to distinguish one Arabic letter from similar-looking ones gave an illuminator another opportunity to embellish the writing.

Although parchment was the traditional writing material for early Qur'ans, paper was also used from the ninth century forward. Since about the first

Fig 1.8
An inscription at the top of this folio of the Amajur Qur'an indicates that it was
donated to a religious community in Tyre (Lebanon) in 876 CE by Amajur al-Turki,
a powerful governor of Damascus, Syria, during the Abbasid Caliphate. The large
kufic script and generous empty spaces on this page display wealth and power;
parchment was expensive to prepare, and this artist did not worry about covering it
with writing or images. Although not all of it survives, it is estimated that a full text
of a Qur'an in this style would be many volumes with an overall number of 6,500
leaves, or pages. In that case, the book required at least 1,600 sheep or calf hides, an
extraordinary luxury, especially in a time when the Abbasid Empire was expanding,
and the military needed those hides for saddles, bags, shoes, and other uses.
Heritage Image Partnership Ltd / Alamy Stock Photo

century CE, Chinese communities made paper by mashing tree bark and other
plant fibers in water and pressing the mixture onto screens where it would dry
in flat, thin sheets. Around the eighth century, Islamic culture imported papermaking technology from China. Papermaking did not reach Europe until later
in the medieval period, with only minor usage in the twelfth century.

Looking Forward

In this chapter we discussed the power of the primary monotheisms, organized,
documented systems of religious belief that galvanized and mobilized great
societies to both creative innovations and destructive pursuits. In the period
500 to 900 CE, the consolidation of monotheisms in a large portion of western
Asia happened quickly, in no small part because of the connections between
religion and politics.

   During the first 500 years of Christianity, there were many different factions
arguing for their points of view, attempting to codify a set of beliefs into one
"Christianity." This chapter included several distinctions among those Christian
churches. As we continue, we will have more discussion of monasteries, which
became wealthy and powerful institutions as lay elites donated lands and
wealth (or paid to have their children become monks and nuns) to gain the
spiritual benefits of being associated with these holy men and women and their
constant prayers. We will also discuss the religious life of women. At the end
of the book, we encounter another massive shift in Christian ideology: the
Protestant Reformation.

After a swift ascendence to regional domination, Islamic leaders solidified and extended their territories. In the next chapters, we will see dynasties change and be replaced, but Islam will continue to a be a powerful religious, economic, and political force across Eurasia, North Africa, and Europe. At the same time, dynamic Jewish communities will exist, innovate, and operate within many dominions, but always be subject to intense stigmatization, persecution, and sudden expulsions.

The bureaucratization of the Abrahamic hierarchies into formalized offices required literacy, and book arts became a primary object of devotion and of status. In Western Europe, Latin became the major clerical language, and in areas where literacy dropped to near zero, Latin was the only language left to the literate. Mass in Western Europe was almost exclusively sung in Latin, while in areas outside Europe, Mass was nearly always in the language understood best by the congregation. North Africa maintained its literate culture, with Latin, Greek, and Coptic (contemporary Egyptian) languages used almost interchangeably. Literacy held fast in the Middle East; Islamic schools trained boys in Classical Arabic, Hebrew, Greek, and other local languages, and Muslims produced major texts, both religious and secular. Collections like the documents of the Cairo Geniza demonstrate the highly literate and learned traditions of Jewish culture.

The emphasis on literacy within these faiths accelerated consolidation and standardization of practices, which supported the economic and political activity we discuss in the next few chapters. In the next chapter on religion (Chapter 5), we expand our subject to the spiritual practices, texts, and objects of India and East and Southeast Asia. Among the topics of our third chapter focused on religion (Chapter 9) is the religious experience of women and the texts they patronized, produced, and used for prayer.

Research Questions

1. What factors allowed for the expansion of Islam in the early centuries?
2. How did early medieval Christian or Islamic political leaders use religion to achieve their goals?
3. Compare and contrast Charlemagne's and Vladimir's uses of Christianity. What might account for the similarities and differences?
4. Investigate Jewish manuscripts from 500 to 900. Compare this to the creation of the Christian Bible and the Islamic Qur'an in the same era. What is similar in construction? What differences are there?
5. Look into the history of Zoroastrianism and Judaism during this period. What limited the growth of these two faiths?
6. Discuss the relationship between literacy and the spread of monotheistic religions. How did the manuscript production in the second half of the chapter help the religious and political expansions detailed in the first half?

Further Reading

Ahmed, Akbar. *Discovering Islam: Making Sense of Muslim History and Society*. London: Routledge, 2002.

Blair, Heather. "Religion and Politics in Heian-Period Japan." *Religion Compass* 7, no. 8 (August 2013): 284–293.

Brown, Michelle, ed. *In the Beginning: Bibles Before the Year 1000*. Washington, DC: Smithsonian Institution, 2006.

Cox, George. *African Empires and Civilizations: Ancient and Medieval*. New York: Pan-African Publishing Company, 1992.

DeHamel, Christopher. *A History of Illuminated Manuscripts*. London: Phaidon, 1986, 2001.

Hoffman, Adina, and Peter Cole. *Sacred Trash: The Lost and Found World of the Cairo Geniza*. New York: Schocken Books, 2016.

Isichei, Elizabeth. *A History of Christianity in Africa: From Antiquity to the Present*. Trenton, NJ: Africa World Press, 1995.

Kennedy, Philip. *Christianity: An Introduction*. London and New York: Palgrave MacMillan, 2011.

McKenzie, Judith S., and Francis Watson. *The Garima Gospels: Early Illuminated Gospel Books from Ethopia*. Oxford: Manar Al-Athar Monographs, 2016.

Robinson, Chase. *Islamic Civilization in Thirty Lives: The First 1,000 Years*. Berkeley: University of California Press, 2016.

Schimmel, Annemarie. *Islam: An Introduction*. Albany, NY: SUNY Press, 1992.

Settagest, Mary. *When Zarathustra Spoke: The Reformation of Neolithic Culture and Religion*. Costa Mesa, CA: Mazda, 2005.

Small, Keith. *Qur'ans: Books of Divine Encounter*. Oxford: Bodleian Library, 2015.

Soskice, Janet. *The Sisters of Sinai: How Two Lady Adventurers Discovered the Hidden Gospels*. New York: Vintage Books, 2010.

Stausberg, Michael, and Yuhan Sohrab-Dinshaw Vevaina, eds. *The Wiley Blackwell Companion to Zoroastrianism*. Hoboken, NJ: John Wiley & Sons, 2015.

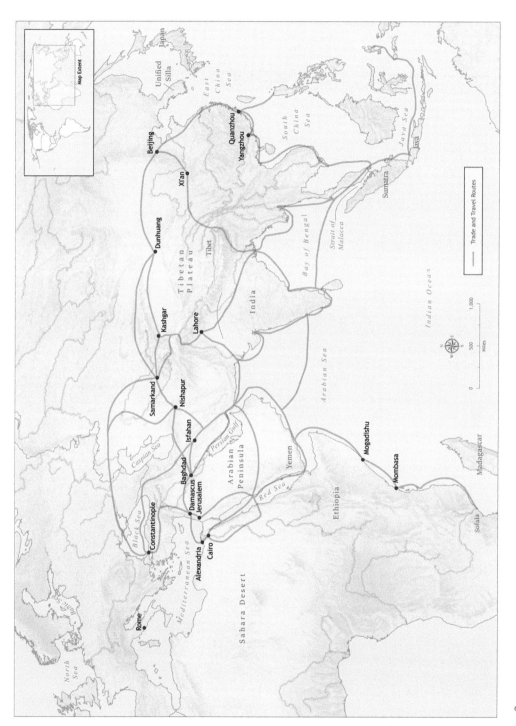

Map 2

Caravan and Dhow

2 Caravan and Dhow
Economies, 500–900

Introduction

People have been traveling long distances throughout human history – seeking new places to live and valuable goods from far away. Some of the oldest discovered human settlements provide evidence that, as early as the Neolithic period (ca. 10,000 BCE) in the eastern Mediterranean, humans were exchanging obsidian (a naturally occurring black volcanic glass, useful for hand tools) from Asia Minor for shells from the Levant and the Red Sea. And cowrie shells made their way from the Indian Ocean to gravesites in Central Asia and northern China, similarly, far back into prehistory. Such valued items are found thousands of miles from their places of origin, indicating the very early development of long-distance trade within human history, and as human settlements became more complex, so too did the networks of exchange that connected them.

One of the most important reasons that historians are interested in long-distance trade is because exchanges between communities living far apart give us a sense of what people in the past valued, and how they interacted with each other. How did people in the premodern world relate to others across differences of religion, language, and culture? What did they desire enough to spend huge amounts of time and expense to acquire? What foreign items did they want to imitate, to bury alongside their beloved dead, or to adapt to their own cultural needs? The history of economies and trade is really a history of cultural connections and meaning in human societies.

This chapter introduces the trade patterns of the early medieval period, highlighting the most active trade routes and the most highly desired commodities. In some ways, the early medieval period can be seen as laying the foundations for the massive economic growth and expansion of trade that characterized the later Middle Ages. However, in other ways, the early Middle Ages should be considered economically vibrant in its own right, with ships and caravans covering distances both long and short to bring coins and commodities (both luxury and subsistence goods) to people around the globe. And, indeed, by 900, various routes for long-distance trade in the Eastern Hemisphere were connected to each other at one or many points, making for globalized connections at least across this hemisphere and, at one point, even into the Americas.

The first section introduces some of the connections between ports, cities, and entrepôts (trading centers) in these various territories where deals were made, both luxury goods and utilitarian items were bought and sold, and representatives from various cultures and languages interacted, learned from each other, and exchanged ideas, technologies, and traditions. Travel over long distances, whether by land or by sea, was difficult, expensive, and often dangerous during the medieval period, but people continued to consider it worth the time, effort, expense, and danger. Travel by sea, despite its dangers, was much faster than overland travel and allowed for much larger cargoes, and was therefore often preferred by medieval traders. Consequently, we see that the early medieval economy was vibrant, despite periods of political decentralization, especially in the Indo-Pacific region, and increasingly in the Mediterranean and North seas. The second section takes a closer look at some of the trade goods themselves and the ideas, artistic styles, and cultural concepts that traveled with those goods.

A: NETWORKING

Introduction

Economic connections do not always follow political connections – or the absence of them – but politics and economics do influence each other. By the middle of the sixth century, several longstanding, powerful empires had diminished or collapsed entirely. Nonetheless, in many parts of the globe, the centuries from 500 to 900 were ones of economic vitality and thriving local and long-distance trade. In 220 CE, the Han dynasty in China ended, and with it went unification of China and Central Asia, but caravans still traveled sections of the silk roads, and Chinese state control returned to the region by the late sixth century. A much-reduced eastern portion of the Roman Empire still controlled Constantinople and the extensive trade routes connected with that city, even while, by the end of the fifth century, the western half was entirely under the authority of Germanic kings (see later chapters). Theirs was a primarily agricultural subsistence economy, but long-distance commerce continued at the hands of Viking traders in the north and Italian merchants in the Mediterranean Sea. Around 590, the Gupta Empire of northern India broke up, but the southern states of India and nearby islands were enriched by substantial maritime commerce conducted at their ports. These Indian Ocean entrepôts were active sites of local exchange, and facilitated trade between the Chinese and other peoples of Southeast Asia, with first the Sassanian Persian Empire (until 651) and, later, the peoples of the Islamicate world.

ENTREPÔTS

Many interactions between distant groups of merchants occurred at entrepôts, commercial trading centers situated along a long-distance trade route, where foreign merchants could meet to buy and sell goods. Merchants could thus acquire products from far away for resale at home, without the time and expense necessary for traveling the entire length of the route. Many medieval entrepôts became quite wealthy and powerful due to their commercial importance and the cultural interactions they fostered.

A similar concept is that of the emporium (pl. emporia), which was a town specializing in trade that could be either a seasonal marketplace or permanent town. This word is used in the early medieval period particularly for coastal towns in the North Sea and Baltic Sea that facilitated trade carried out across the northern coasts and along the land routes of Russia that connected to the Black Sea. Some of these early medieval emporia were later abandoned, while others developed according to the political environment or market changes.

Evidence:	Coinage from China, Persia, Byzantium
	Huaisheng Mosque
	Changsha pottery
	Byzantine jeweled bracelets

Silk Roads

One of the most famous routes for long-distance trade is the series of over-land passages through Central Asia known as the "Silk Road." This route was made up of many roads, an intertwined and complex series of unmarked paths that were rarely traveled from end to end by a single merchant or caravan. For this reason, we refer to it here as the "silk roads." The complete network covered thousands of miles, with important nodes at Samarkand (in modern Uzbekistan) and Xi'an in central China, but stretching far beyond, along a variety of branching pathways. From these and other trading cities, products moved further afield – across northern Iran, south into India, and across China and Southeast Asia.

Despite being known as a conduit for massive amounts of luxury cargoes, for much of silk roads' history the caravans were small – between five and seven pack animals – and carried daily-life commodities like grain, foodstuffs, livestock, slaves, and paper between towns located along mountain passages and desert roads. While some luxury items like silks, metalware, glass, and coins moved between China and distant power centers – for example in India, Tibet,

Persia, and the Roman (Byzantine) Empire – much of that happened through indirect exchange between various entrepôts. Rather than being one straight path for an exchange of goods, then, most silk roads' travel and commerce took place across shorter-segmented, but overlapping, routes. There are records of diplomatic embassies between China and political entities such as Byzantium, and those groups also would have carried valuable diplomatic gifts.

WHY IS THIS ROUTE CALLED THE "SILK ROAD"?

The term "Silk Road," describing the long caravan paths that crisscrossed premodern Central Asia, is an invention of the nineteenth century. The name was based on the idea that the route was developed as a thoroughfare for huge caravans of expensive silk fabrics that were exported across Central Asia from China to Rome. It was first coined by a German geographer in 1877, whose knowledge of Central Asia was of use to the German government, which wanted to build a railroad between China and Europe. While it was politically useful for them to imagine they were reviving an ancient superhighway for high-value commerce, the ancient and medieval reality was much less direct and much less romantic. Nonetheless, the term (often nuanced as "silk roads") is widely used today in the titles of books, films, and museum exhibitions because it evokes a transnational, transcultural space of exchange for goods, peoples, and ideas. It has also been adapted for use in other contexts, such as the Indian Ocean trade routes, which are often called "the maritime silk road" or the "maritime ceramic road."

China's Tang dynasty (618–907), building on the expansion of the Sui dynasty (581–618), unified control over the Western Regions (Tibet and westward into Central Asia), thus allowing them to maximize the economic potential of the route and the valuable commodities available there. The Tang capital of Xi'an was an important eastern node of the route, and it grew to be a rich and multicultural city. For several centuries before the reunification of China by the Sui dynasty, the lands along the silk roads had been broken into smaller territories ruled by various nomadic groups. For those centuries, most trade along the route was limited to regional and small-scale trade in food, wine, and other subsistence goods, but also some high-value items. The Tang established army garrisons throughout the Western Regions, which also fostered exchanges of horses and their feed for bronze coins, silks, and grain – all of which served as currency for payments, salaries, and taxes.

When Chinese state control of Central Asia was strongest, we see a greater volume of state-sponsored journeys of high-value luxury goods along the silk roads. At times when the Chinese army presence was withdrawn due to political weakness, invasion, or disunity, however, goods were more likely to follow shorter routes and be exchanged at entrepôts. For example, the Tang government's control of the Western Regions was challenged both by the An Lushan rebellion (755–763) and by the Tibetan kingdom's expansionism. But when the Chinese held strong control over Central Asia, the silk roads were a thoroughfare for Chinese military troops, taxes, costly goods, technologies (such as production of ceramics, paper, and silk), and religions (like Buddhism, Manichaeism, and Islam), along with pilgrims, missionaries, and sacred texts. At other times, it is more proper to speak of short-distance regional trade in subsistence goods along desert paths than of one continuous conduit for east–west commerce. Nonetheless, it is important to note that valued items had been moving between China and the Middle East and Africa for millennia, much of it along these various pathways, independent of Chinese governmental control.

Tang domination of Central Asia also meant that commerce along these routes employed more coins than previously. The Chinese government exclusively minted bronze coins, but regional commerce also used measures of grain, and bolts of undyed silk, as currency. Silver coins from Persia – found in high numbers in archeological sites along the silk roads – could also be used for trade, but primarily on the western part of the route and only by the wealthiest traders. Silk was lighter and more stable in price than bronze coinage, and thus shows up more often in documents detailing trade, property disputes, taxation records, and payments, especially for smaller transactions.

Travel along the silk roads required official passes that specified the exact number of humans and animals in a caravan and the precise route they intended to follow. Although paper was available – the technologies for making paper and silk originated in China and entered the Islamicate world via the silk roads, and then into Christian Europe after their eleventh-century conquests of Muslim Sicily and Spain – these passes were typically written on

Fig 2.1
The Chinese minted copper and bronze coins as early as the fourth century BCE. By the Han period (202 BCE–220 CE) coins looked like this, round with square holes. They were often carried on strings of up to 1,000 coins. They were regularly used throughout China for commerce and payment of taxes. This particular coinage – called Kai Yuan Tong Bao – was minted from 621 in the Tang period and often imitated by Central Asian peoples such as the Sogdians.
© Wikimedia Commons, public domain

slips of wood, which was less expensive. Permissions were checked at regular guard stations, and merchants were fined for deviating from what was specified. Preserved passes show that the size of most caravans was modest, with goods transported on a variety of animals (camels, donkeys, cattle, and horses) and bound for nearby market towns. Unfortunately, most passes did not specify the commodities being transported, but we know that common goods traded along these roads were paper, silks, leather, metalwork, pottery, spices, perfumes, precious gems from India and Southeast Asia, grains, wine, and other foodstuffs. Archeological finds and reconstructed documents also show that Central Asian horses were highly desired by the Chinese and that enslaved women were exported eastward for the sex trade.

While the silk roads are famous for connecting the Roman Empire and China, those links were mostly indirect ones. In fact, the silk roads were much more significant for trade between China and Persia. Ruled by the Sassanian Empire (224–651) and later by Muslim caliphates, Persia offered goods and artistic innovations that were desired in the East. Sogdian merchants based in Samarkand, and other groups speaking Iranian dialects, transported metalwork, silver coins, and art throughout Central Asia and China. At one time the wealthiest region of Central Asia, Sogdiana also exported its own textiles, metalwork, foods, wine, and music and dance styles, which became popular in Tang China. The western silk roads were also one route for the dissemination of Islam eastward into Central Asia, and the spread of Buddhism and other eastern religions westward. In this way, the silk roads facilitated multidirectional human migrations and the transfer of cultural elements, like religious texts, decorative motifs, and languages, making medieval Central Asia and China richly multicultural places.

SOGDIANS

Much of the long-distance commerce along the silk roads was conducted by people called Sogdians. One of many ethno-linguistic groups in Central Asia, the Sogdians spoke a language from eastern Iran and are known for traveling long distances as merchants and diplomats. The center of Sogdian population was Samarkand, an opulent city in the western part of the silk roads. Famed in Tang China for being successful traveling merchants (especially in the lucrative jewel trade), the Sogdians' language became a common dialect along the silk roads. Sogdians were also known in Tang China for their distinctive hats and clothing fashions and their particular styles of music and dancing, which were notable for their energetic leaps and whirls. Troupes of entertainers traveled along the silk roads and were sometimes paid to perform at the Tang royal court.

Far from only being merchants or entertainers, however, Sogdians also settled in China (many in Xi'an) and in towns along the silk roads, engaging in farming, military, craft production, and other occupations. After the Muslim conquest of Samarkand in 712, Sogdian migration eastward intensified. At the same time, most people in the Sogdian heartlands began the process of conversion to Islam (many from Zoroastrianism, but others from Buddhism, Manichaeism, and eastern Christianity). A rebellion against Tang rule led by the Sogdian-Turkish general An Lushan (755–763) prompted attacks on Sogdian communities in Xi'an. Discrimination, violence, and more massacres led to further migration and attempts at assimilation, such as Sogdians changing their names to hide their Sogdian origins. Conversion, migration, and integration meant that, by 1000, the Sogdians were losing their distinctive language and culture. A minority group in modern Tajikistan, called the Yaghnobi people, speak a descendant version of the medieval Sogdian language.

Fig 2.2
Five musicians wearing hats in the Sogdian style ride on a Bactrian camel, which is indigenous to Central Asia. Sogdian entertainers – musicians and dancers – were popular along the silk roads and at the Tang imperial court. This ceramic figurine was found in the grave of a high-ranking military officer named Xianyu Tinghui (660–723). It is decorated in the three-color style typical of Tang-era ceramics, although this one features an additional color, blue, which came from the highly prized mineral cobalt, mined in western Central Asia or Iran – thus indicating that this piece was expensive and meant to reflect the very high status of the person in the tomb.
National Museum of China

As for direct trade between China and the Roman Empire, there is little firm evidence before the sixth century. The Romans were familiar with silk from at least the first century CE, and Roman glass has been discovered in Chinese tombs from as early as the first century BCE. It is not clear how these items were transported in the earliest periods; they may have arrived by seaborne rather than overland trade, either as diplomatic gifts or through indirect trade at entrepôts. The earliest Roman gold coins discovered in China date from the reign of Theodosius II (r. 408–450), who ruled from Constantinople, suggesting to some historians that it was only from the fifth–sixth centuries that direct China-to-Rome trade developed. Other Chinese finds of Byzantine gold coins were mostly counterfeits, perhaps made not for trade but for use as ornaments or grave goods. Imitating valued foreign goods was one way to demonstrate reverence for those items and the status that ownership of them could convey.

In the late sixth century, Sogdian merchants arrived in Constantinople, where they sought and received permission from Emperor Justin II (565–574) to trade silk directly, thus circumventing the Sassanian Persians, who were enemies of the Byzantines. It was around the mid-seventh century that the Eastern Romans (Byzantines) may have first sent official envoys to the Chinese court, establishing diplomatic relations that enriched both parties and lasted through the eleventh century. Chinese silk and silkworms were highly desired in Byzantium, even after the Greeks developed their own silk industry in the sixth century. Constantinople was connected with trade networks into the Mediterranean and Black seas, and pieces of Sogdian silk have been found in early medieval European sites. But it was primarily Byzantine silks that were distributed as diplomatic gifts and sold for high prices in the early medieval Mediterranean Sea region. After the Islamic conquests of the southern and eastern shores of the Mediterranean, these were joined by Muslim silks, produced at important silk-manufacturing industries in places like Egypt and the Levant.

Overland travel in the silk roads region also intersected with that network, leading to the bustling Indian Ocean markets and moving finished products and raw materials both north and south. Movement between western Central Asia and India fostered trade in spices, cowrie shells, incenses and aromatic woods, ivory, gemstones, and corals from southern India and the islands of Southeast Asia, incense and horses from Arabia, silver from Persia, glass from the eastern Mediterranean, and gold and ivory from eastern Africa, all of which and more traveled between the Central Asian paths of the silk roads and the maritime routes of the Indian Ocean.

Indian Ocean

During the medieval period, the Indian Ocean became the most active – and lucrative – route for long-distance trade in the Eastern Hemisphere. By the central Middle Ages, these routes came to be dominated by traders from Muslim communities. But they did not originate seaborne trade there – rather, they took advantage of millennia of local seafaring traditions. For example, Indian sailors were plying the waters of the Indian Ocean during the ancient Harrapan civilization (ca. 3300–1700 BCE). By the third–fourth centuries BCE, mariners from Southeast Asia had developed trade and travel networks stretching across the South China Sea, reaching into both the Pacific Ocean and the Indian Ocean, and trading directly with both China and India. Some of this long-distance trade was conducted by means of direct voyages, and some within regional trade networks that met and overlapped at active trade emporia.

In the medieval period, several maritime empires controlled the trade and connection between China and the Indian Ocean: Funan (at the southern tip of modern Vietnam) from the third to seventh centuries, followed by Srivijaya (based on Sumatra, in the Indonesian archipelago). By controlling the Straits of Malacca, which connected the Indian Ocean and South China Sea, they grew rich and powerful. In the western Indian Ocean, prior to the rise of Islam in the mid-seventh century, the Sassanian Persian Empire (224–651) was deeply involved in maritime trade, as demonstrated by hoards of silver Sassanian coins found in India along with products imported from the eastern Mediterranean. By the sixth century, the Persians appear to have dominated trade in the western Indian Ocean; over the seventh and eighth centuries, Arabs joined these networks. Many of these routes and trade connections later became part of the wider Islamicate world, with Arabs, Persians, and Arabic-speaking Jews and Christians integrated into the broader economy of the Indian Ocean and China Seas.

The Tang period was an especially important one for Chinese maritime technology, knowledge of wind and current patterns, and the growth and safety of Chinese shipping activity. Even so, Chinese ships and merchants were not the only ones – or even the majority – sailing from Chinese ports to those in the Indonesian archipelago, Ceylon (Sri Lanka), and the Maldives, where they met Persians, Indians, Malay, Javanese, and other merchants. Southeast Asian peoples captained many of the ships and controlled many market centers, especially at the critical juncture of the Straits of Malacca. Multiethnic and multicultural communities developed in these trade emporia along the sea routes – the religious cultures of Buddhism, Hinduism, and Islam mixed and mingled, as did the languages, people, and material cultures of the many peoples who sailed these waters.

It was also this period that saw the growth of what is sometimes known as the "maritime ceramic route" (or the "maritime silk road"), across which highly desired Chinese products such as ceramics were distributed from ports like Guangzhou and others to markets far and wide. One Tang-era Chinese ceramic style is known as Changsha ware, after the area where it was produced. Archeologists have found Changsha pottery in India, Sri Lanka, the Red Sea and Persian Gulf ports, Cairo, the Levant, and the islands and ports of southeastern Africa. Other goods traded along these routes include Chinese silks; African ivory, iron, and gold; spices, aromatic woods, gemstones, pearls, corals, and perfumes from Southeast Asia; pearls and coins from the Persian Gulf; and, to a lesser degree, Byzantine coins, glassware, beads, textiles, and gold and silver metalwork.

GUANGZHOU

Ships sailing eastward from the Indian Ocean through the Straits of Malacca aimed to arrive at a Chinese port, such as Guangzhou (Canton), Yangzhou, or Quanzhou. Located at the Pearl (Zhujiang) River Delta on the South China Sea, Guangzhou connected river passageways through China with the Indian Ocean shipping lanes, and thus was a wealthy and important trade emporium. Market officials at the port checked travel passes – required of travelers entering China by land or sea – and collected import taxes on arriving cargoes. Nonetheless, foreign seafarers were able to make enormous profits from the Chinese goods – silks, precious metals, pearls, gems, and ceramics – they acquired there in exchange for incense, ivory, and other foreign goods.

The religion of Islam arrived at Guangzhou and other Chinese port cities in the seventh century, spread by merchants from the Islamicate world. Guangzhou is believed to have been

Fig 2.3
The entrance to the Huaisheng Mosque (ca. 1873), also known as the Great Mosque of Guangzhou. Tradition claims that this mosque was built in the 620s or 630s by one of Muhammad's closest associates, although this may only be legend. It is certainly true that by the late seventh century Guangzhou had one of the largest communities of Muslims in China, and mosques were probably built there and in other port cities during the Tang dynasty or early Song dynasty. This mosque was rebuilt several times during later periods.
Wellcome Library no. 29893i, Wellcome Collection

the site of one of China's earliest mosques, called the Huaisheng Mosque, and one of China's earliest Muslim settlements. These Muslims and other foreign merchants were the target of a massacre in 878, carried out by Huang Chao, a rebel fighting against Tang authority. An earlier massacre of foreign merchants at Yangzhou in 760 was also a part of a revolt against the Tang, by An Lushan. After the last Tang emperor was killed in 907, and their capital at Xi'an destroyed, long-distance trade with the West by both land and sea routes began to decline; it would revive under the later Song dynasty.

The Indian Ocean, however, was as much a center of trading activity in its own right as a conduit for high-value goods between Asia, Africa, and the Mediterranean. Shipping activity has long been a defining feature of the Indian Ocean's cultures, and regional sailors and shipbuilders were quite experienced in their crafts. Sewn-plank rafts and dugout canoes were built to connect seaports with inland markets via river transport, and many different types of seafaring ships sailed in various Indo-Pacific regions. One prominent style of seafaring vessel in the western Indian Ocean and Arabian Sea is called a *dhow*, which refers to variously sized boats with long, thin bodies, made of wooden planks sewn together (usually by coconut-fiber ropes). These were treated to become watertight and had tall, triangular "lateen" sails. Although the origin of the dhow in place or time is unknown, by the medieval period the Kerala region on the Malabar Coast of India was one place known for its shipbuilding industry, in part due to the availability of timber and rope material. These boats were crafted to take advantage of the regular winds and currents to sail in circuits along the coastlines of the Arabian Sea and beyond.

Indeed, wind and weather patterns dictated sailing seasons and routes. It was the discovery by Southeast Asian sailors of the seasonal monsoon wind patterns that allowed them to make long journeys at sea, connecting the regional circuits of the Indo-Pacific waters. These predictable winds and currents determined both the direction and the schedule of voyages. They allowed for southwestward sailing in the summer (February–September) and northeastward in the winter (October–January). A voyage from the Arabian Peninsula to China took about six months, as did the return journey. Round trips could take up to three years, accounting for the need to stay at port waiting for the sailing season to change. But, not all ships had to make the entire journey in both directions: trading entrepôts in India and Southeast Asia facilitated shorter, segmented trips and enriched local merchants. Voyages in the western Indian Ocean, from the Persian Gulf and Red Sea ports along the eastern shores of Africa, were also timed to coincide with the monsoon winds. Ships from the central Islamic lands sailed to the eastern coast of Africa at the beginning or end of the monsoons, in April/May and August; in June and July, storms made sailing in the western Indian Ocean too dangerous to be attempted.

LATEEN SAIL

One example of a premodern technology that has traveled around the world is that of the triangular ship sail called the lateen sail, after its prevalent use by Latin sailors in the later medieval Mediterranean Sea. The origins and development of the lateen sail is contested among historians of naval technology, but it is clear that the Latin sailors of the Mediterranean did not invent this type of sail. They probably adopted it from ships piloted by Muslim sailors, who learned it from Southeast Asian sailors in the Indian Ocean. This sail shape is now typical on sailboats all over the world. The dhow's lateen sail allowed sailors to take advantage of monsoon wind patterns by tacking against the wind (heading into the wind instead of with the wind) and utilizing the currents to create predictable sailing routes along the coasts. Although a square sail gives a ship more stability and power, the triangular sail allows for more precision and maneuverability.

In the China Seas, the Tang government maintained tributary relationships with many of its neighbors, in which China demanded payments – tribute – from otherwise independent powers or kingdoms. In exchange, China sent official envoys and Chinese goods, as well as translators, artisans, Buddhist missionaries, merchants, and other people and objects. Chinese commercial activity was closely tied to these tributary relationships: they sent and received massive cargoes to and from these neighbors. One such tributary state is called the Kingdom of Unified Silla (668–935), which became a wealthy maritime trading power in the China Seas. The peoples of the Korean peninsula had maintained relationships with the Chinese since at least the third century BCE, adopting Chinese language and script, along with Buddhism and Confucianism. And yet, they remained independent from Chinese authority, having organized into three separate kingdoms by the fourth century CE. In 668, one of those states, the southeastern Kingdom of Silla, conquered the other two. This ushered in a period known as the Kingdom of Unified Silla, which lasted until 935 when a competing dynasty took control after a period of disunity. They were a tributary state of the Tang Empire, meaning that they were required to send tribute to the Tang court, but the Silla also engaged in private trade and were active merchants in seaborne exchange among Korea, China, and Japan. Seafarers from Unified Silla were also deeply involved in the maritime networks coursing across the East China Sea and into the Indian Ocean; the kingdom became wealthy from such trade.

In Southeast Asia, China had a tributary relationship with Funan (68–550), in the southern area of Vietnam and Cambodia) from the third century. Funan also maintained an independent maritime trading empire of its own. They subjugated nearby ports and controlled the waterways between China and the Indian Ocean until the late seventh century, when that role was taken over by Srivijaya. The Srivijaya Empire dominated sea trade along the maritime silk road until the twelfth century, when it was rivaled by other regional powers. It was a trading empire rather than a strictly political one, with its seat at Palembang on Sumatra. By controlling the ports stretching from today's Thailand to the western coast of the Malay Peninsula, Srivijaya controlled the sea route between the Indian Ocean and the China Seas. Although the Srivijaya Empire encompassed a mix of ethnicities, the dominant culture adopted Buddhism and was an important player in its spread across Southeast Asia. Weakened in the eleventh and twelfth centuries by challenges from the Chola Empire in India over control of the Straits of Malacca to the west and by new powers on Java to the east, their empire collapsed by the end of the fourteenth century.

By means of both direct voyages and exchanges at entrepôts throughout the Indian Ocean, trade was conducted between China, Japan, Vietnam, Korea, the Indonesian archipelago, and various other states of the Indian Ocean region, with ports to the west – in the Arabian Sea and along the eastern coast of Africa. From the Persian Gulf and Red Sea ports, merchants carried goods to be traded in the Mediterranean basin (especially in Egypt, North Africa, and the Levant, but also north to Constantinople), creating linked networks stretching thousands of miles. Ports located along these routes meant that no one merchant ship had to take the entire voyage from the Persian Gulf to China, although some did. Even if no individual merchant traveled the whole route, such overlapping circuits allowed objects to move between China and the Mediterranean or the North Sea areas (discussed further below).

During this period in the western Indian Ocean, Persians, Christian Ethiopians, and Arabs and Jews from the southern Arabian Peninsula (Yemen) participated in exchanges via the Red Sea. From there, overland traders carried valuable goods to the peninsula's trading cities, such as Mecca, and then north into the eastern Mediterranean or further north to Constantinople. From 476 to 800, the only imperial capital in the Roman Empire, Constantinople, was a thriving hub for urban economic, cultural, and intellectual activity. With a population of around one million people by the sixth century, Constantinople was (until 1204 when it was ransacked during the Fourth Crusade) filled with markets, aqueducts, baths, gardens, places of entertainment like the Hippodrome, imperial palaces, churches, and monasteries filled with rich ecclesiastical ornaments and icons (until the Iconoclasm movement, 726–787 and 815–843, during which countless sacred images were destroyed by imperial decree; see Chapter 1).

Even though the traditional narrative of the Roman Empire claims that the early medieval period was one of economic decline, the commercial world of Constantinople (capital of the Byzantine Roman Empire until 1453) tells a very different story. The Golden Horn, Constantinople's busy port on the Bosporus, sent and received ships from the Aegean, the Mediterranean, and the Black Sea, and the city's warehouses were filled with goods produced both locally and afar. The major boulevard through Constantinople was called Mese Street, where markets offered silks, gold items, clothing, furniture, jewelry,

Fig 2.4
These impressive bejeweled bracelets were made in Byzantine Constantinople from materials imported from around the Eastern Hemisphere: the gold may have come from Africa via Islamicate-world traders, the pearls were from the Persian Gulf, and the gemstones from Southeast Asia.
Metropolitan Museum of Art, Gift of J. Pierpont Morgan, 1917, 17.190.1670 and 17.190.1671

and more. Running from the Hagia Sophia westward, past imperial forums, baths, and cisterns, the most luxurious products were sold closest to the imperial palace and the more commonplace items were found farther along the road. Some of these products were manufactured there in Constantinople, and some were imported from China and Southeast Asia, via traders bringing goods from the Indian Ocean to the ports of the Red Sea, and northward to Constantinople.

Trade in the late Roman Byzantine Empire continued even though, by 500, its political and economic influence reached no further east than the shores of the Mediterranean. Over the following two centuries, Byzantine economic and political power would be threatened again and again, first by the Sassanian Persians (for example, Sassanians conquered across the Levantine region during the early seventh century; they attacked Constantinople in 626, and the failure of this foray allowed Byzantine emperors to recover their territories in Damascus and the Palestinian area), and then by Muslims from the Arabian Peninsula, who would take advantage of the destruction wrought by the Byzantine-Sassanian wars to triumph over both empires, rapidly, in the mid-seventh century. Thus, the Islamic world began its rise to political, economic, and cultural ascendancy across a huge swath of both land and sea.

The Islamicate World

With the establishment of Islam as a religion and a political power in the seventh century, economies and cultures across the Eastern Hemisphere were transformed. Many historians use the term "Islamicate" to refer to the expansive territories in which the religion and culture of Islam were dominant, but not exclusive. The Islamicate world of the medieval period was filled with diversity of language, culture, political rule, and religious expression: many sects of Christians, Jews, and Zoroastrians lived and worked alongside Muslims, both Shia and Sunni, and their lives and cultures contributed to the broader culture of the Islamicate world. The term is often used interchangeably with "Islamic world," as we do in this book. Both terms are intended to convey the cultural and political diversity of the regions in which Muslim rulers held power and the religion of Islam was practiced by the majority of the population. The Islamicate world stretched, at its greatest extent, from western China and northern India to the far western edges of North Africa and Spain, but the influence of its arts, culture, and people reached far into the Indian Ocean, China, and the Mediterranean Sea, with colonies of Muslims established in China, Indonesia, India, Italy, Iberia, and much of eastern Africa. Over the next several centuries, the Arabian Peninsula would become the major midway point, controlling trade routes from the Indian Ocean to the Mediterranean Sea, as well as the overland routes that connected east and west.

Within the lifetime of Muhammad (d. 632), the peninsula's mostly nomadic Arabs swore allegiance to Islam, including those who lived in ports along the Red Sea and in Yemen, such as Aden. Thus, from quite early in its history, the Islamicate world developed seafaring interest. Under the second caliph, Umar (r. 634–644), Muslim-sailed ships began crossing the Persian Gulf, both raiding the Indian coast and establishing a Muslim presence in the active Indian Ocean trade. Direct trade with China was a development of the eighth and ninth centuries. By 713, Muslim merchants and ambassadors had reached China, where they appear to have been active in regional commerce until 878, when foreign settlers at Guangzhou were massacred by Chinese groups rebelling against Tang authority. After this time, direct trade with China was halted in favor of segmented journeys and transactions at entrepôts in India and Southeast Asia; it resumed about a century later.

From the eighth century, Islamicate merchants also sailed along the eastern coast of Africa as far south as Sofala (modern Mozambique) and Madagascar. East African port cities – among them Mogadishu, Mombasa, and Kilwa – exported gold, ivory, timber, and enslaved persons. Known in Arabic as *zanj* ("black"), African slaves were profitable enough to give their Arabic name to the southeast region of Africa (Bilad al-Zanj, or Country of the Blacks) and to a massive slave revolt in Iraq from 869 to 883. This lucrative trade in humans promoted the economic and political power of the African rulers of the Swahili coast – themselves mostly Muslim by the ninth century – and boosted the economy of the central Islamic lands, where enslaved Black Africans were highly valued as military, agricultural, and domestic laborers.

ZANJ SLAVE REVOLTS

Beginning in late 869 and continuing until 883 in the Tigris-Euphrates valley, a series of uprisings of enslaved Africans (Arabic *zanj*, "black") threatened the political and economic structures of the Abbasid Caliphate. For a century, Bantu-speaking peoples had been shipped from eastern Africa to the agricultural fields of Iraq, where they were forced to drain swampy salt flats in the southern region of the Fertile Crescent. Their lives were extremely harsh and short, so when a religious leader from an egalitarian sect of Islam promised freedom to any who would support his war against the caliph in Baghdad, many thousands of the enslaved revolted against their Muslim overseers. The Abbasid government was, at the time, facing political disputes and military coups, making it difficult for them to quell the rebellion. After 15 years of battle and disruption to agriculture and commerce, the caliph's armies were triumphant and conquered the rebel capital; their leader was captured and killed, his head sent to Baghdad. This lengthy rebellion – the largest slave revolt in Islamic history – caused insecurity for Abbasid military, economic, and political control in the area, and may have contributed to a decline in Abbasid central authority and in the Indian Ocean slave trade. Nonetheless, slave markets in Islamic lands continued to be filled with enslaved Blacks and other imported people who filled demands for domestic and agricultural labor.

Among the eastern goods most valued in the Islamicate region were ceramics, spices (especially pepper, cinnamon, nutmeg, dyestuffs, and medicinals), pearls, jewelry, gemstones, silks, and silkworms. Muslim traders also gained knowledge of many agricultural products – including rice, sugar cane, citrus fruits, eggplants, and cotton, some of which they helped to introduce to new regions ("sugar" comes to English through the Spanish azucar, from the Arabic al-sukkar). Trade in foodstuffs, coins, timber, and textiles was also significant. Islamicate merchants also learned about and transferred several important technologies from China to the central Islamic lands, including technologies of silkworm care and textile arts, porcelain pottery, and paper production. Over the coming centuries, many of these commodities, products, and technologies would enter European cultures via the conquests and communications between Muslims, Christians, and Jews in the multicultural Mediterranean Sea region.

Islam itself, as a religion and a culture, was transmitted into Southeast Asia, Africa, and China by merchants who established colonies and spread the religion along their trade routes. By the ninth century, Muslim colonies existed all along the Indian Ocean sea lanes – from the Persian Gulf to the Malabar coast, the island of Ceylon (Sri Lanka), the Maldives, the Straits of Malacca and the Malay coast, and from there into Indonesia and China, and, likewise, along western Indian Ocean routes to southeastern Africa. Muslims and their culture thus had the opportunity to interact with and influence the various Buddhist and Hindu cultures of China and India, while traders and commodities also moved back and forth between cultures. Often intermarrying with locals, settling in new lands, and sharing ideas with foreigners, merchants could thus be agents of cultural transmission as much as of economic exchange.

The Umayyad Caliphate (661–750, capital at Damascus) conducted most of its seaborne trade via the Red Sea and the Mediterranean. After the Abbasid revolution overthrew the Umayyads in 750 and the new dynasty established their capital at Baghdad in 762, the bulk of trade shifted to the Persian Gulf route. From ports near Basra, Muslim-sailed ships could travel up the Tigris to Baghdad, or out to the Indian Ocean via the Persian Gulf. Under early Abbasid rule, trade from the Persian Gulf into the Indian Ocean became even more lucrative, and a northern route was developed via the Tigris and Euphrates Rivers to the Black and Caspian seas, and thence to the Baltic Sea. The creation of a canal between the Tigris and the Euphrates aided the transportation of goods and the development of this northern trade route and helped to enrich the caliphal city of Baghdad, featured in many tales of the *One Thousand and One Nights* as an opulent and prosperous city filled with markets, libraries, schools, and gardens.

The Abbasid caliphs (750–1258) oversaw the development of a strong, stable, and extraordinarily active economy across their expansive territories. From their impressive capital at Baghdad, to smaller cities and towns around the Islamicate world, urban settlements became the centers of craft production, trade, culture, education, and communication, and a common language

Fig 2.5
This gold dinar minted under the Umayyad caliph Abd al-Malik (r. 685–705) was one of the first set of Islamic coins to have only words and no images. Earlier coins had been based on Byzantine and Sassanian models, which included images of the emperor. The earliest Islamic coins also displayed human images, but caliph Abd al-Malik's coinage reform did away with the use of pictures on money. This coin contains the Muslim profession of faith: "There is no god but God, and Muhammad is the messenger of God."
Metropolitan Museum of Art, Bequest of Joseph H. Durkee, 1898, 99.35.2386

and religious culture facilitated travel across long stretches of land and sea – even in places outside Abbasid political control or governed by rival Muslim rulers. And, because they took over places with well-developed industries – like glassmaking and silk production in the eastern Mediterranean, silverwork in Persia, and papermaking in Central Asia – medieval Muslim lands came to be known for the manufacture of goods that were highly valued in both East and West. Similarly, the demand for exciting new products – especially those from the East – that was fostered by the monetized economies of Abbasid-era cities fueled production, trade, and travel.

It is often said that medieval Muslims developed technologies for long-distance travel because of the religious requirement that all Muslims who are financially and physically able must take at least one pilgrimage (*hajj*) to Mecca in their lifetime. And, while it is certainly true that the religious obligation for pilgrimage meant that many medieval Muslim men and women traveled over long distances, it is also the case that medieval Muslim culture promoted travel for intellectual purposes (for example, the study of God's creation – the Earth, the cosmos, and human cultures – was highly valued) and for economic purposes. Arabic-speaking merchants, mostly Muslims, but also Christians and Jews who lived and worked within the Islamic world, traveled extensively by land and sea, both promoting the spread of Islamic cultural influence and enriching the traders and the cities in which they operated. Because they traded and traveled so widely, Islamic-world merchants also connected various commercial orbits that otherwise operated independently. For example, by controlling the Red Sea and Persian Gulf ports and the land routes into Egypt, they helped to transfer Indian Ocean products into the Mediterranean economy.

Europe and the Mediterranean Sea

Europe in these centuries provides a strong contrast to the booming economies of the Islamicate world, the Indian Ocean, China, and Central and Southeast Asia, with their long-distance trade networks crisscrossing the land and sea routes. The local economy and trade connections within western Christian Europe during the early Middle Ages were limited, local, and, at most, low level. After the Roman Empire effectively split into two halves following the death of Emperor Theodosius I in 395, the eastern half, with its capital at Constantinople, continued to conduct international trade by both land and sea, while the western part fell into economic decline. While the Islamicate world, Byzantium, and China had large bustling cities filled with merchants and many buildings, the Roman west (Latin Europe) was primarily rural, and based on subsistence agriculture in the early medieval period.

In many ways, the theory of western European economic backwardness in the early medieval period has been overstated, but it is nonetheless true that the city of Rome lost its primacy as a site of far-reaching trade connections, which it had been during the heyday of imperial Rome. Western Christian rulers in Late Antiquity and the early Middle Ages minted very few coins – virtually none in gold and only limited issues of debased silver deniers (Latin, s. *denarius*, pl. *denarii*) – and conducted only limited trade. The only truly long-distance trade networks intersecting with western Europe at this time were those developed by the Norse (Vikings) over the northern arc and a few Italian mercantile city-states in the Mediterranean basin.

Many factors caused the downturn in western Europe's economy. The basis of the Roman imperial economy was agriculture, carried out on huge estates, which were worked by enslaved persons. As imperial expansion halted, the influx of slaves was reduced, and the brutality of their lives meant that few among the enslaved population reproduced. As the large estates broke up into smaller plots of land – called manors, where a lord lived in a manor house and oversaw the agricultural labor of peasants – subsistence agriculture took the place of large-scale commercial agriculture.

In addition, the Mediterranean lands that had been the source of much of ancient Rome's grain supply (which entered the city through either private commerce or the imperial grain tax) – especially Egypt, Sicily, North Africa – were no longer politically or economically tied to western Europe, as the power of Rome declined. Their grain was shipped first to Constantinople and, later, to markets in the Islamicate world. Without the distribution hub of Rome, the European economy became far less tied to cross-Mediterranean shipping, and many ports silted up or welcomed fewer ships. Likewise, many of the ancient Roman roads around Europe fell into disuse because of the drop in regional or long-distance trade. Vikings used their longships to develop an intensive river transport in the north, both for raiding and trading activities, transforming both the pathways and the methods of travel within Europe and at its borders.

Europe also lost access to gold metal, with which high-value coins could be minted and luxury trade carried out. The Roman gold mines in Spain were depleted by the third century, and anyway, by the early eighth century Spain was part of the Islamic world. No other European gold mines were discovered until the thirteenth century. With few manufactured goods of high value to export, Europeans were limited in their ability to trade for African gold. Trade continued on a smaller scale between individual city-states in Italy and the Byzantine and Islamicate networks, but this was limited in scope and volume. While both the Byzantine and Muslim economies had access to African gold and were based on tri-metallic coinage systems – gold for expensive luxuries and large cargoes; silver for most of the mercantile activity; and bronze for low-cost daily expenses – the economy of Latin Christendom was barely monetized at all. In late antique Europe, coins were minted sporadically by local, rather than centralized, authorities. Germanic rulers in Gaul and England instituted reforms of their kingdoms' silver coinages in the eighth century, but it is unclear how many people had regular access to such coins. Most Europeans, even among the elite, ate food that had been grown locally, and perhaps engaged in local barter with their extra produce. Charlemagne (742–814), crowned emperor in 800, sought to restore aspects of the Roman imperial system; he issued a silver *denarius* imprinted with his image in the style of ancient Roman imperial coins. Few of these coins have been found, however, perhaps suggesting that they were not widely used.

Accompanying this decline in the complexity of the European economy was a change in settlement patterns. Across the eighth to tenth centuries, Europe experienced regular invasions from several directions. Vikings from the north, Magyars (Hungarian horse nomads) from the east, and Muslims from the south attacked in waves and, without the Roman army to hold them back, the western European population was exposed to repeated assaults on their lives and properties. It is likely due to these factors that the European peasant population began to exchange their freedom for security. They clustered on manors as serfs – land-bound agricultural workers who owed service to their lords – and were unable to move freely or control their own labor (see later chapters).

This ruralization of the populace was accompanied by a marked decline in cities, where only bishops and the very poor remained, if the city survived at all. Many cities that had flourished in Roman times were abandoned; many others were reduced in size and population. The impoverished urban populations could no longer support the taxation system that had allowed the imperial Romans to fund urban governmental institutions, such as a state-funded military, and the Germanic kings of Europe stopped trying to collect urban taxes around 600. With most of the European population working at subsistence agriculture, and virtually no urban artisans creating craft goods for trade, there was little to attract Muslim merchants from the Mediterranean, who were interested in gold, silks, spices, porcelain, and other high-value goods from the East. It has been suggested that enslaved Christians were the major export item to the Islamicate.

At the same time, developments in early medieval western Europe were laying the foundation for future economic growth. Advancements in iron technology – most notably the heavy plow – and the three-field crop rotation system, combined with extensive clearing of forests, led to increased food security and, by around 1000, a booming population. The increased population would lead to urban growth in the central Middle Ages, which would also lead to growth of commerce and industry, and thence to increased long-distance trade by the later Middle Ages.

Even in the early medieval period, however, long-distance commerce thrived at Europe's edges. Far from exclusively being raiders as they are often depicted, Vikings (or the Norse) carried out substantial trade in the North Sea and along the inland river systems of northern Europe. In Scandinavia, Ireland, and the continental coastlines of France and the Netherlands, trade emporia were established and thrived along this northern arc. Coming from as far away as Byzantium, the Islamicate, and Asia, products like colored glass beads, Islamic silver coins, wine, pottery, and silks were exchanged for raw materials such as timber, animal furs and skins, amber, enslaved humans, and walrus ivory. This long-distance exchange was conducted both by means of the Viking longships and by overland traders who arrived in the Baltic and North Sea regions via the route through Kiev.

THREE-FIELD CROP ROTATION SYSTEM

One of the most important developments in European economic history was a simple revision in the way agricultural land was managed. Romans farmed huge estates with slave laborers working the land, typically producing single crops for sale rather than for subsistence. Ancient Romans knew that grain crops depleted soil of its nutrients, so these estates were typically divided into halves: half to be planted while the other half lay fallow, allowing it to recover. At some point in the early Middle Ages it was discovered that partitioning into three plantings – one for a fall crop of wheat or rye, one for a spring crop of nitrogen-depositing legumes or oats, and the third to lie fallow – utilized land more effectively and resulted in greater crop yields. They also discovered that peas, beans, lentils, and other legumes replenished nutrients, especially nitrogen, that were pulled from the soil by crops like wheat. By rotating fields through these three assignments, each plot had healthier soil and produced more food. And, by farming two-thirds of their land rather than half, more land was productive at any given time. As farmland thus became more productive, excess yield could be sold or traded at local markets, which contributed to the rise of commercial exchange within Europe. More food also meant more people surviving to adulthood. This population boom would fuel the growth of cities, monetized economies, and long-distance trade networks that characterized the later medieval European economic expansion.

The Norse were also known to have sailed around the Atlantic coast and into the Mediterranean Sea, raiding in the Iberian Peninsula and even reaching Constantinople, where some served as mercenaries in the elite Varangian Guard. Viking longships also reached North America by the late tenth century, sailing from their Greenland settlement and trading with natives whom they derogatorily called Skraelings (but were probably the Dorset or Thule Inuit).

Vikings were not Europe's only long-distance traders, however. Cross-Mediterranean trade continued between southern Italy's mercantile city-states and Muslim merchants at Mediterranean ports in the Islamicate world. While cities declined elsewhere in Europe, urban structures persisted in southern Italy and Sicily because these territories continued to be closely connected to the monetized economies of Byzantium and the Islamicate world – at least until Ravenna fell to the Lombards in 751. Naples freed itself from Constantinople's control in the eighth century, and Sicily was conquered by North African Muslims in the ninth century. By this time, merchants from Venice, Naples,

Amalfi, Salerno, Genoa, Taranto, Syracuse, and other Italian cities had established mercantile connections with Muslim-held ports along the southern shores of the Mediterranean Sea.

Gold coins – albeit small and debased ones (heavily alloyed with lower-value metals) – continued to be issued by the Byzantine provincial mint at Syracuse until the city was conquered by Muslims in 878. At that time, the mint was taken over by the new rulers of the island and small Byzantine gold coins were transformed into a new denomination called the quarter-dinar that would come to be minted widely in the Muslim world and Mediterranean. It was such a successful coin that even some Christian cities of southern Italy, such as Salerno, decided to mint their own copies complete with "fake" Arabic inscriptions.

It is not clear from the historical record what the Italian merchants had to offer Muslim traders in exchange for their gold, silks, spices, and other eastern commodities. Europe exported timber, helpful for shipbuilding in the ports of North Africa, and tin, furs, and eventually wool cloth. It has also been suggested that the primary European exports, virtually invisible in the Latin written record, were enslaved Christians who were captured and shipped to the Muslim world. Venetian traders had to be warned more than once by early medieval popes to halt their trade in Christian persons at the markets of Rome. Otherwise, however, early medieval Christian texts appear reticent to admit that Christian merchants profited from the sale of fellow human beings.

Muslim Sicily continued to produce grain for export, as it had during the Roman Empire, but after the ninth century its economy was tied to the bustling commercial trade of the Islamicate world and its grain was directed there. Traders and ships from Islamic lands came to dominate early medieval Mediterranean commerce. Muslims and Jews who spoke Arabic sailed on ships originating from ports in Egypt, modern Tunisia, and the eastern Mediterranean. Overland traders from Muslim Spain and Morocco caravanned westward across northern Africa to Egypt and beyond. Camel caravans crossed the Sahara Desert along north–south routes, doing business at trading towns such as Timbuktu. There, copper, textiles, and salt from the Mediterranean Sea were exchanged for gold, ivory, and enslaved Africans. This trans-Saharan trade enriched the rulers of the Ghana Empire (in the western African region of Mali) and introduced them to the religion of Islam. It also provided the gold needed for the Islamicate world to maintain a high-value currency, which they used to trade silks, spices, and other costly goods within the Mediterranean Sea and between there and the commercial realms of the Indian Ocean, Byzantine Constantinople, and the Central Asian silk roads.

Conclusion

As this section has shown us, the connections between people and places allowed for the exchange of technologies, traditions, and ideas. Despite the collapse of several Eurasian empires, thriving trade continued. Merchants traveled along local and regional roads and across the oceans, trading with their counterparts and fueling economic growth in several important cities along their paths. Movement through Central Asia and across the oceans created opportunities for economic growth for both governments and individuals. Although travel was expensive, difficult, and time-consuming, the people who moved along these routes found the trade in commodities and ideas worth the perils and struggles. We now turn to a closer look at the goods and ideas themselves, focusing on what the commodities tell us about the people who used and traded them.

B: RARE FINDS

Introduction

Archeologists, historians, art historians, and museum curators can point to thousands of objects created and traded, both near and far, during the centuries of the early medieval period. Far from being a period of economic backwardness or decline, as often claimed, 500–900 was a time of intense interaction across the Eastern Hemisphere. It was also a time of great creativity in many parts of the globe, with new technologies being developed and old ones transmitted to new places. Items produced in one part of the Eastern Hemisphere were not only carried to other parts, but they were often copied there to give the impression that the object's owner had access to goods from remote locations, even if they did not. By taking a closer look at some of the items and ideas that moved back and forth along these routes, we can see how long-distance networks linked cultures and allowed them to share and transmit technologies, styles, commodities, and beliefs.

Evidence:	Han Gan, *Night-Shining White*
	Diamond Sutra
	Chinese and Islamic ceramics
	Sassanian dishes
	The Jewel of Muscat dhow
	Chinese, Byzantine, and Sassanian silks
	Batlló Majesty

Paper

Although known since the nineteenth century for their most famous commodity (silk) as exported from China, the silk roads product that has had the greatest impact on history is actually paper. Paper – which most people today take for granted as cheap and disposable – was produced in China, but it was expensive. It was also durable, light, and highly desired. Papermaking technology was developed in China during the second century (during the Han dynasty) and it would eventually spread across the globe – but not until many centuries had passed. First paper and, later, papermaking technology, spread from China to Japan, Korea, and Central Asia along regional trade routes. It entered the Islamicate world in the eighth century, after the Umayyad conquest of Samarkand, which had an active paper production industry. By the ninth century, paper was being used and made across the Islamicate, and after Muslim Spain and Sicily were captured by European Christians in the eleventh century, paper mills were established in Europe.

Paper was so valuable in China that some documents recording early medieval silk roads commerce and legal disputes were reused for other purposes, such as for ceremonial burial clothing and shoes. This practice preserved them so that scholars today can read them by stitching together various pieces and thus recover information about property disputes, small-scale commercial transactions, and complaints made by regular people along the silk roads.

Other paper objects from Tang China were highly prized pieces of artwork that were carefully saved for centuries. Figure 2.7 is a painting by the renowned Chinese artist, Han Gan (active ca. 742–56), mounted on a paper scroll more than 37 feet long. It depicts a horse of Emperor Xuanzong (r. 712–56), who was deposed by the An Lushan rebellion. Horses were a valuable trade item along the silk roads. The Tang aristocracy particularly prized horses raised by Central Asian nomads, considering them stronger and faster than native Chinese horses, with an otherworldly energy like dragons. This painting was so valued that it was not only preserved for centuries by Chinese emperors, but also augmented by their personal seals (the red stamps) and explanatory inscriptions.

Numerous among the paper documents traveling both overland roads and maritime routes were religious texts. Buddhism and Islam spread to China along trade routes via land and sea, along with their adherents, missionaries,

Fig 2.6

A scrap of paper with early Chinese writing was recycled as the sole of a shoe for dressing a corpse for burial.

Courtesy of the East Asian Library and the Gest Collection, Princeton University Library

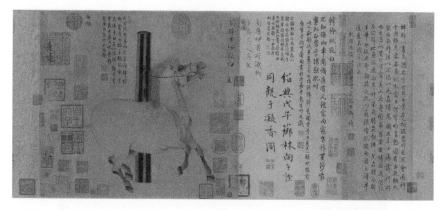

Fig 2.7
Horses raised by the Central Asian nomads were highly prized in Tang China.
This horse, Night-Shining White, was the personal property of Emperor Xuanzong
(r. 712–756).
Metropolitan Museum of Art, Purchase, The Dillon Fund Gift, 1977, 1977.78

and sacred writings. Buddhist pilgrims from China and Southeast Asia traveled
to India to visit places from the life of the Buddha and Buddhist temples, monasteries, and centers of learning, often to obtain or translate sacred Sanskrit
texts. As we think about long-distance trade, we must carefully consider all the
other elements that traveled alongside people and their commodities.

One silk-roads site, the caves at Dunhuang, held hundreds of sacred texts
in a wide variety of languages: Sanskrit and Chinese, but also Tibetan, Uighur
(a Turkic language), Sogdian, other Central Asian languages, and even Hebrew.
Mostly these were Buddhist texts, since Dunhuang was the site of a Buddhist
monastery-school. But the paper scrolls also included Zoroastrian, Manichaean,
Christian, and Jewish texts. This find demonstrates the intensely multicultural
and multiethnic nature of the silk roads, and the fact that it was not only commercial goods that were exchanged along these paths, but also spiritual beliefs.

Perhaps the most famous item found in the Dunhuang caves is identified as
the earliest complete printed book in history – the woodblock-printed *Diamond
Sutra* (see Chapter 5). Dated to May 11, 868 by an inscription, it consists of a 16-
foot-long scroll created by pasting together seven sheets of paper. The text is a
Chinese translation of the original Sanskrit, one of hundreds of sacred Buddhist
sutras translated and disseminated during the heyday of Tang-era travel and the
possibilities it provided for pilgrims and missionaries – as well as merchants and
envoys – to move between distant lands.

Ceramics

One of the Chinese products most desired in the Islamicate world was pottery,
especially the fine white ceramic types grouped together as whiteware. In

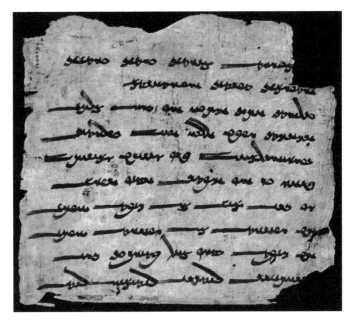

Fig 2.8
Prior to the arrival of Islam, most Sogdians practiced Zoroastrianism, but others were
Buddhists, Christians, or Manichaeans. Their mercantile activity across the silk roads
meant they knew many religions and languages, and Sogdians were known for their
translations of sacred texts. Here is a Zoroastrian prayer, the Ashem Vohu, in Sogdian
language and script, copied in the ninth century and found at Dunhuang. Later, many
Sogdians converted to Islam.
© British Library

the later Song period, Chinese artisans produced significant amounts of the
finest white – nearly translucent – ceramic called porcelain. In later medieval
centuries, porcelain technology would be popularized and produced widely
in the Islamic lands. Before they could make porcelain themselves, however,
artisans in the Islamicate world imitated the appearance of Chinese whiteware
through glazes and decorations. Islamic-world ceramics, through both trade
and post-conquest plunder, arrived in western Europe in the late Middle Ages,
where they were used both as vessels and as decorations and were imitated by
European artisans.

Archeological finds from around the Indian Ocean region and beyond show
that there was also a massive trade in ceramics that were less finely made (in
earthenware or stoneware rather than the more delicate whiteware or porcelain). We know that Chinese ceramics moved along land routes as well as the
sea lanes that some historians call the "maritime ceramic routes," both because
Chinese products have been found in archeological sites and because they were
imitated in faraway places. But it is also clear that the movement of technologies and styles did not only go in one direction at a time. Ceramics produced
in Tang China were often modeled on metalwork exported from Sassanian

Fig 2.9
Fashioned to look like Chinese whiteware, this ninth-century bowl is one of the
earliest attempts in the Islamic world to copy the look of Chinese ceramics. It
features vibrant blue Arabic calligraphy, a style that would become characteristic of
Islamic art in later centuries. The Arabic word "happiness" is repeated twice in the
center of the dish.
Metropolitan Museum of Art, 63.159.4, Harris Brisbane Dick Fund, 1963

Persia, demonstrating that influences and transmissions were moving in multiple directions at once. Persian metalwork was highly desired in China, especially platters, bowls, and long-handled jugs called ewers. The designs on these
silver items also show links between Persia and the ancient Greek world of the
Hellenistic kingdoms as well as with Central Asia and China.

Other popular types of ceramics produced in southeastern China have
been found in archeological sites ranging from the islands of Southeast Asia
to the Persian Gulf – as far west as Cairo, and as far south as Mogadishu and
Zanzibar in eastern Africa. Historians surmise that much of this ceramicware
was produced only for export, and not for local use. Shards of Tang-era Chinese
ceramics have been excavated from sites on the eastern coastline of Africa, in
modern Kenya. Later ceramics, from Song-era Chinese kilns, have been found
as far west as Cordoba, Spain.

One of the most important archeological discoveries showing the mag-
nitude of the ceramics export trade is a shipwreck discovered in 1998 called
the Belitung wreck. This boat sank off the coast of Indonesia around 830 with
more than 60,000 pieces of ceramicware on board, nearly all of it produced
at the Changsha kilns, one of southeastern China's most productive pottery-
producing regions. Also among the cargo were gold and silver items and valuable spices such as star anise. The boat itself was a dhow, a common vessel along
the Persian Gulf and western Indian Ocean sea lanes. This fact has suggested
to scholars that the boat had been sailed by Muslims from the Persian Gulf to

Fig 2.10
Persian Sassanian ewers (pitchers) like this one from the sixth/seventh century often had imagery from ancient Greek myths and stories. The figures here – dancing women holding grape leaves and branches – are linked to the female worshippers of the ancient Greek god of wine, Dionysus. Called maenads, they danced in frenzies that caused their clothing to slip off, a provocative image often found on ancient Greek and Hellenistic wine jugs. The maenads may have been translated to signify worship of the Iranian goddess Anahita in the local context and are evidence of centuries of deep interconnections between the Persian and Greek societies.
Metropolitan Museum of Art, Purchase, Mr. and Mrs. C. Douglas Dillon Gift and Rogers Fund, 1967, 67.10a, b

a Chinese port such as Guangzhou or Yangzhou, where its original cargo was sold, and local goods were purchased and packed carefully on board for the return trip westward. It is unclear why the boat sank where it did – quite a bit south of the expected route from China to the Persian Gulf.

Silk

Even though historians and archeologists emphasize that many products and goods besides silk circulated around the premodern Eastern Hemisphere, we cannot ignore the importance of silk – medieval traders and artisans certainly did not. Highly desired both in China and abroad, silk textiles, technology, and silkworms were transmitted, borrowed, copied, and sometimes stolen by those who wanted them. Silk, in the form of measured undyed bolts, was even used as currency in Central Asian trade, paid out by the government as salaries, and sent abroad as diplomatic gifts.

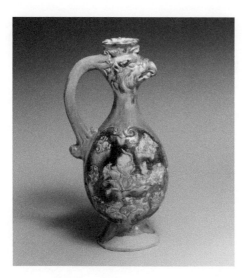

Fig 2.11

This late seventh–early eighth-century Chinese-made pitcher is modeled on the shape and style of Sassanian or Sogdian metalware but crafted in ceramic and decorated in the Chinese three-color glaze style. Green, brown (or amber), and off-white glazes were combined to create the "three-color" style, with a topcoat of lead-based clear glaze that created a shiny, waterproof surface. This decorative style is found on pitchers, bowls, trays, and figurines showing humans and animals. This pitcher has a phoenix's head, and the body has an image of a horse-mounted warrior shooting an arrow backwards over his shoulder. This so-called "Parthian shot" was a skill associated with Persian and other horse warriors of western Central Asia. Metropolitan Museum of Art, Gift of Stanley Herzman, in memory of Adele Herzman, 1991, 1991.253.4

The Chinese had developed the technology for domesticating silkworms and weaving silk thread into cloth as early as the third millennium BCE. Even after silk-production knowledge spread – first to Japan, Central Asia, and Persia by the third–fourth centuries CE and, later, to Byzantine Constantinople – the silks produced by the Chinese were considered the finest and most valuable fabrics. A legend says that the Byzantine emperor Justinian I (r. 527–565) asked Christian monks to steal silkworms from China so that silk could be produced locally. This is likely a fiction, but the story reflects both the high value placed on silk and the belief – also probably fictional – that the Chinese were fiercely protective of their technology. Silk production and trade spread across Central Asia and the Islamicate and, by the central Middle Ages, silk production and exchange was one of the most important commercial trades in the Mediterranean region.

Early medieval silk textiles demonstrate a multidirectional transfer of technologies, motifs, and fashions similar to the ceramic evidence above. While the process of harvesting and weaving silk started in China and later moved westward, one popular image woven into textiles – a mirrored image within a circle, of animals, birds, dragons, or hunters on horseback aiming arrows at

Fig 2.12
The Jewel of Muscat is a dhow built in Qantab, Muscat Governorate, Oman, between 2008 and 2010 as a joint project of the governments of Oman and Singapore. It was modeled after the Belitung shipwreck. It is now housed in the Asian Civilisations Museum in Singapore.

Fig 2.13
A seventh/eighth-century painting from a Buddhist sanctuary in Khotan depicts the story of a wily princess who smuggled mulberry seeds and silkworm eggs across the Chinese border into the ancient Kingdom of Khotan. The Khotan king wanted to know the closely guarded technology of Chinese silk production, so he requested a Chinese princess as wife. She arrived at his court with the precious items concealed in her hair and headdress.

prey – originated in Sassanian Persia or Sogdiana and spread eastward. Many silk textiles from the early medieval period show a uniquely Chinese image like the dragon, mixed with the Persian-derived style of the mirrored figures inside a circle. Such multidirectional transmission of images and technologies

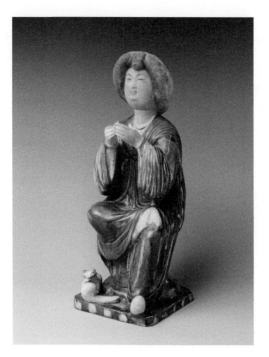

Fig 2.14
This eighth-century ceramic figurine is one of many similar statues produced in
Tang China. Glazed in the typical three-color style, it shows a young woman of
the Tang imperial court sitting with a small pet dog at her feet. She wears vibrant
clothing and sits on a stool imported from Southeast Asia. The Tang era was one of
great innovation in Chinese clothing fashions, with artisans, weavers, and wealthy
patrons working together to create an elite culture focused on fashion and style.
Metropolitan Museum of Art, Purchase, The Vincent Astor Foundation Gift,
2010,2010.120

is characteristic of early medieval cultures in contact with each other. The
Chinese-produced cloth thus incorporated images that they had adopted from
their trading partners, and which would appeal to foreign markets, like we have
seen with the ceramic evidence.

The image of mirrored figures inside a circle also spread westward to
Byzantium, where eastern silks were sold directly by Sogdian merchants from
the late sixth century and, later, produced locally. Once in Byzantium, this
decorative style picked up other connotations associated with Greco-Roman
culture or with Christianity. One example was the ancient Greek myth of the
Amazons – fierce female warriors portrayed as fighting on horseback with bared
breast – who, on some textiles, took the place of the double hunters inside
the roundel. In later Byzantium, the image was also often Christianized, as in
images depicting holy warriors rather than hunters. They use a cross and spear
to attack a serpent, a common early Christian image of the devil.

Egypt and Syria were important centers of silk production in the Byzantine
period and, after they were conquered by Muslim forces, became sites of silk

weaving within the Islamicate world. There, the scene was often Islamized, where the hunter is shown on horseback as in earlier examples, but with the addition of the Arabic phrase *bismillah* ("in the name of God") above the hunter's head. Similar decorations – rounded borders containing mirrored hunters or animals – are found on silk textiles produced and exchanged throughout the early medieval Mediterranean world, both Muslim and Christian.

Silks entered western Europe first from Byzantium and, in later periods, through trade with the Islamicate world. Byzantine textiles may have come to Europe through trade links, which continued on a small scale to bring goods and people from Constantinople to ports in Italy, even after the decline in Roman-era trade across the Mediterranean. More likely, these sumptuous silks found in Europe are evidence of diplomacy between Rome and Constantinople, which may have sent highly prized textiles and other valuable goods to popes and kings to court their favor. Many such silks were so valued in Europe that they were used to wrap relics – the remains of the saintly dead – or to line the coffins of queens and kings. One such example, housed in the Vatican Museum, employs the repeated circular design to showcase a scene of the biblical story of the annunciation, with the angel Gabriel and the Virgin Mary mirroring each other in the fashion of the hunters. This ninth-century Byzantine silk fragment was used to line a reliquary casket in Rome containing what were believed to be Jesus's sandals.

Fig 2.15
A richly decorated wooden statue of Christ, created in mid-twelfth-century Christian Catalonia (northern Spain), shows Jesus wearing a bright robe painted to resemble Mediterranean silks. With red circles around blue floral patterns and golden starbursts, the tunic recalls the long tradition of decorative silk textiles, patterns, and styles that moved between East and West during the early Middle Ages. *Batlló Majesty*, twelfth century, Catalonia, Museu Nacional d'Art de Catalunya, Barcelona. Photo by Sarah Davis-Secord

Looking Forward

By the twelfth century, Mediterranean silks – whether of Byzantine or Islamicate origin – were the height of luxury in Europe. They were used to wrap relics and adorn kings and were imitated in both textiles and in paint. But it was not only silk textiles or other high-value luxury goods from the East that were transmitted across the Eastern Hemisphere. Technologies (like those used to make paper, silk, and ceramics) and the ideas that went along with them were also transferred, borrowed, or imitated by faraway groups. And, importantly, these transfers of knowledge, creativity, spiritual beliefs, and goods were multi-directional and complex, often overlapping in time and space. As the Middle Ages went on, the volume and pace of this long-distance trade accelerated and brought disparate cultures into ever closer contact.

Research Questions

1. What is the relationship between gold and trade? How did the minting of coins aid in long-distance trade?
2. Why did trade slow down in Europe? What aided in increasing that trade?
3. Look at the slave trade throughout Eurasia during this period. How important were slaves to the economies under discussion? Why and where did slavery thrive? Where didn't it? Why?
4. Describe the process for moving goods along the silk roads during this period. What was traded? Who did the trading?
5. Discuss how ideas and technologies moved along the land and sea routes. What seemed to be the most influential ideas to move along the merchant byways?
6. Pottery from archeological sites tells us quite a lot about how people of this period lived. Stoneware and earthenware vessels provide information about how food, oils, and medicinal extracts were processed and stored. Glazed porcelain expresses the artistry and aesthetics of the communities that produced them. Archeologists and cultural historians work all over the world, and their projects are limitless. Research an active archeological site of one of the cultures discussed in this chapter and report on new discoveries.

Further Reading

Chaudhuri, K. N. *Asia Before Europe: Economy and Civilization of the Indian Ocean from the Rise of Islam to 1750.* Cambridge: Cambridge University Press, 1990.

Chen, BuYun. *Empire of Style: Silk and Fashion in Tang China.* Seattle: University of Washington Press, 2019.

Flecker, Michael, et al. *The Tang Shipwreck: Art and Exchange in the 9th Century.* Singapore: Asian Civilisations Museum, 2017.

Hansen, Valerie. *The Silk Road: A New History*. Oxford: Oxford University Press, 2012.

Hourani, George F. *Arab Seafaring in the Indian Ocean in Ancient and Early Medieval Times*. Princeton, NJ: Princeton University Press, 1951/1995 expanded edition.

Kennedy, Hugh. *Great Arab Conquests: How the Spread of Islam Changed the World We Live In*. New York: Da Capo Press, 2008.

McGrail, Sean. *Boats of the World: From the Stone Age to Medieval Times*. Oxford: Oxford University Press, 2004.

Power, Timothy. *The Red Sea from Byzantium to the Caliphate: AD 500–1000*. Cairo: American University in Cairo Press, 2012.

Price, Neil S. *Children of Ash and Elm: A History of the Vikings*. New York: Basic Books, 2020.

Stein, Stephen K., ed. *The Sea in World History: Exploration, Travel, and Trade*. Santa Barbara, CA: ABC-CLIO, 2017.

Wang, Helen. *Money on the Silk Road: The Evidence from Eastern Central Asia to c. AD 800*. London: British Museum Press, 2004.

Wells, Colin. *Sailing from Byzantium: How a Lost Empire Shaped the World*. New York: Delacorte, 2006.

Whitfield, Susan. *Silk, Slaves, and Stupas: Material Culture of the Silk Road*. Oakland: University of California Press, 2018.

Ziaii-Bigdeli, Layah. "Medieval Globalism: Fragments of Chinese Ceramics in Nishapur, Iran." Blog post, August 31, 2017. www.metmuseum.org/blogs/ruminations/2017/medieval-globalism-chinese-ceramics-iran.

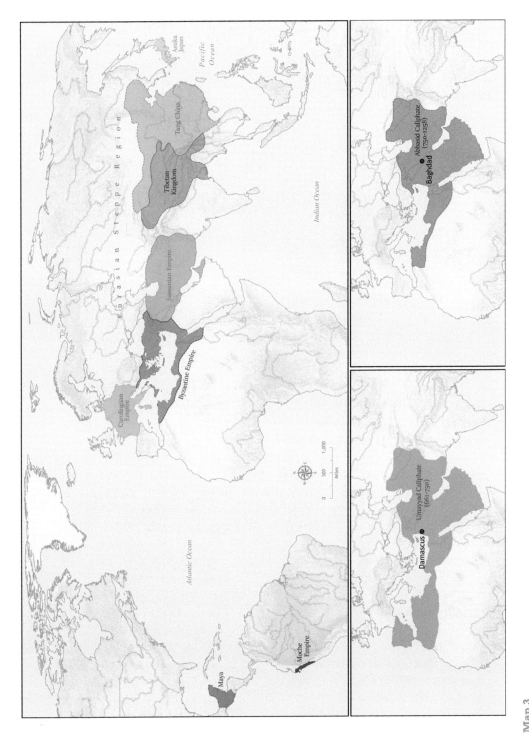

Map 3

The Sword and the Pen

3 The Sword and the Pen

Politics, 500–900

Introduction

In our three chapters about politics in the medieval world, we are concerned with how leaders gained and sustained authority through creating common identity and communications among the people they ruled by creating bureaucracies for taxation and trade and by securing and maintaining stable borders. We also look at how disruptions (wars, famines, plagues) affected political consolidation. Each politics chapter will not cover all of these points, but these ideas are the cornerstones to the growth of strong, centralized states that emerged after 1500. In this chapter, we briefly outline these concepts and focus particularly on royal authority and communication, while also showing how disruptions of the early period by Central Asian steppe nomads helped to create new medieval centralizations.

Political leaders in most of the world were also military figures – using might to secure their right to rule. In the first section of this chapter, we consider how political boundaries were fluid and often chaotic, as differing factions fought to control productive and defensible territories. Warfare had political and economic purposes: rulers sought to create and then defend their territories while using conquest as an economic stimulus. To do this effectively, medieval rulers solidified their military forces, using new technologies and social norms to create stronger armies. Even areas generally seen as politically stable, like China, had continuous movement within their geopolitical boundaries and were pressured by the nomadic peoples of the Central Asian steppes who moved south and west, eventually making their way from the Scandinavian fjords to the southern Indian peninsula.

As we discuss in the second section, the written word was an important tool for any ruler's control and legacy. Some cultures inherited writing systems and significant literate traditions from before 500 (for example, those that came out of the Roman Empire and those informed by China's long writing tradition), while other cultures operated almost entirely through oral language. However, by the end of this period, languages such as Japanese, Arabic, and Russian had written forms, and the knowledge and stories of those cultures were written for and about great leaders and dynasties that used literacy to solidify their rule.

Educational translation projects produced texts from older Persian, Greek, and Roman sources, but languages and histories that were not written down were lost. Through writing, rulers and their religious counterparts sought to hold onto their distant pasts, memorialize their present, and subsume or erase the histories of those whom they conquered.

A: CREATING A SUCCESSFUL DYNASTY

Evidence: Shotoku's *Seventeen Article Constitution*

Shoku Nihongo

Einhard's *Life of Charlemagne*

Anglo-Saxon Chronicle

Introduction

Despite its reputation as the Dark Ages, the early medieval period was one of great growth and change. The Frankish kings (in the Merovingian dynasty) created a strong and stable state in the area of France that lasted for several generations. As their power waned, a new family gained ascendancy. Charles Martel, Pepin the Short, and Charlemagne created a new, more powerful state known as the Carolingian Empire. Charlemagne, a great Germanic warlord, also helped change Christianity within Europe and fostered knowledge with his insistence on education. Further north, Britain saw waves of invasions by Germanic tribes and Scandinavians. Eventually, several stronger kings were able to control most of the island. In the south, Muhammad and his message spread quickly throughout the Arabian Peninsula and, although his life was short, his ideas had resounding effects in the Near East, Central Asia, Africa, and Europe. The caliphs who followed Muhammad created multiethnic empires across large swaths of territory. In eastern Asia, the Chinese and Japanese political entities also consolidated their territories and peoples under single rulership. Although the Chinese Tang dynasty is considered a period of political stability, it was also a time of conquest, as there was a consistent influx of nomadic peoples and unrest, as in the An Lushan rebellion that helped bring the dynasty to an end. Japan, meanwhile, created an imperial political rule by emulating Chinese ideology while still holding true to its nature.

   Although we cannot call the entities of the early medieval period nation-states, we can see the beginnings of the modern nation within these early political entities. The rulers under discussion took advantage of five strategies for strengthening and extending their authority: 1) creating a common identity among their people, 2) using effective communication for administration,

3) ensuring steady revenue streams, 4) establishing and maintaining borders, and 5) controlling rivals and planning for succession of power. This chapter focuses on how early medieval rulers implemented these strategies.

Creating Common Identity

In earlier chapters, we saw how political leaders used religion and faith to create a sense of identity in their growing territories. In many places, the creation of a common identity between disparate people happens through religion. For example, the adherents of Islam were able to use their new faith to create a common identity that stretched from the Indus River valley to the Pyrenees, and from Syria to Africa. Western European leaders used Christianity to bind together the various tribes of Europe into more coherent groups, while also using the textuality of the religion as a way to create more effective communications across their large territories. East Asian political leaders used the new religion of Buddhism as a way to create a common identity, in addition to using the religious ideologies of Daoism and Shintoism, along with the philosophical precepts of Confucianism – all chosen for their strong ideals of obedience and duty.

Using Effective Communication for Administration

The ability to communicate across large distances is incredibly important for the creation of a strong political state. Particularly in areas like Charlemagne's Europe, the Islamicate world, and in Tang China, where the geographical distances were too great to cross on horseback in several days, having solid ways in which a leader could communicate to aristocrats and bureaucrats was vital to the continued success of any government. One of the key elements to this kind of political communication is the maintenance of roads and post systems by which messages could be sent and received rapidly. One of the earliest medieval postal systems was the *barid* in the Islamic world, which was a relay system built and managed by the Umayyad and Abbasid caliphates. Official communications were sent along these networks; likewise, information about far-flung provinces traveled these networks and allowed the caliph to keep a watch on them from his capital. Other early medieval road networks, like those of the Maya (called *sacbe*, pl. *sacbeob*) in Central America or the Pueblo people of North America, may have had more ceremonial and economic functions. In still other places, like the regional lordships of early medieval Europe, the maintenance of roads, bridges, and mountain passes depended completely on the power and will of the local ruler.

Instituting a common language is another of the key factors in long-distance communication and political control. Latin became the lingua franca, or common language, in many areas of Eurasia, despite the fact that many people who lived in Europe spoke a Germanic language rather than Latin as their native tongue. Those who did speak a Latin-derived language used types of proto-Romance languages quite different from the written Latin of Church and administration. Arabic became the common language across the huge expanse of the Islamicate world, even while some native groups maintained their spoken languages (for example, Persian) at least in ritual contexts. Other groups adopted Arabic, even as sometimes they maintained their original language's script (as in Judeo-Arabic; see earlier chapters). And, even though there were dialectic differences between Arabic-speakers in various regions, traders and administrators could understand each other using a standard written Arabic. Likewise, China, Japan, and Silla (Korea) used the Chinese language and scripts. All these areas maintained their native tongues, but found that having stable and understandable written systems was important to ruling large territories.

The creation of writing systems aided in the construction of effective bureaucracies, which were not yet fully formed in most areas in the world. The most effective bureaucratic state was China. Its civil service examination was the most rigorous of this period and the expansion of the examination system was an important tool in Tang rule. The Carolingian Renaissance and Islamic ideals of education all pointed to the knowledge that written languages helped leaders in political, economic, and social ways (as seen in the second half of this chapter), but neither the European nor the Islamicate world had professional bureaucratic systems during this period. In places like Europe, Japan, and the Islamicate, the use of a single language and writing system aided in royal communication, which in turn fueled the need for an efficient and working bureaucracy within the governments.

Ensuring Revenue Streams

None of the above would be possible without the ability for a leader to make money. The creation of a strong and stable state cannot occur without a steady economic system. Although taxation and tribute payments took many forms – as war booty, material goods, enslaved people, and agricultural produce as often as coinage – political leaders found many ways in which to increase their treasuries and support their growing states. Both European and Middle Eastern territories used expansion as their primary means of gathering revenue – controlling more lands meant they could gather the wealth of those lands and use it as they saw fit. Even if the ruler's war leaders, administrators, and governors were not paid in coinage, they did need to be compensated, and they were, usually in land and the revenues derived from that land. Rulers also built impressive palaces for themselves, patronized scholars, poets, and artists, and commissioned luxury manuscripts, robes, and jewelry – all aimed at demonstrating their power, glory, and wealth. The early medieval period was also one of vibrant long-distance trade and economic growth in many regions of the world, allowing rulers to take advantage of the networks of travel and communication as well as the wealth that such trade fostered.

Few areas in the early medieval world, however, had steady streams of income. As all these cultures centered themselves on agricultural economies, collecting revenues was difficult, particularly in areas without strong coinage systems. Many rulers supplemented their meager coffers with conquest. Charlemagne's empire faltered once his expansion stopped; without new areas to conquer, his empire was left without new influxes of people and income. Islam dictated a tax on each follower to be paid to the poor, and Islamicate caliphates collected head taxes on non-Muslim subjects, and, in both these cases, the poor themselves were excluded from paying taxes. This did not garner enough income for any caliphate, and soon the need for new taxation systems arose. These early taxes created the need for efficient and effective bureaucracies, which formed throughout the medieval period. Even the large and bureaucratic state of China struggled with consistent income. The Tang taxed each household a "land tax" and instituted increases on salt taxation throughout their rule. Rebellions, like that of An Lushan detailed below, halted the collection of the land tax. In all these cases, having a professional bureaucracy aided in gathering revenue. The first section of Chapter 2 details how early medieval states traded, sold, and taxed their way into consistent economic stability, and how this occasionally failed.

Establishing and Maintaining Borders

Another important aspect of the creation of a premodern state is that of its borders. The definition of a modern state is an organized territory with geographical boundaries recognized by other states. Recognized and established boundaries are not common in the premodern period, and many borders were porous and contested, even as some are still today. It was particularly difficult in the time from 500 to 900, because there were so few consolidated states with the power to militarize their borders. It took strong military leaders to create respected borders, and, oftentimes, this was at the expense of neighboring tribes and other, weaker political entities. Many boundaries were natural – rivers, mountains, great plains – which divided groups into different territories. Other boundaries were less fixed and, often, more contentious. Einhard tells us, in his *Life of Charlemagne*, that borders of Charlemagne's empire were often unstable and given to lawlessness, which created the need for warfare. The subsequent sorties into contested territory led to conquest, to gains and losses, and the widening understanding of a "border" as something that needed to be defined and defended.

Controlling Rivals and Planning for Succession

In order to create and control their borders, a major political entity must have a large, organized, and disciplined military force. Conquest, in turn, fueled economic stability, as treasuries were often filled with looted goods, and new colonies became places of trade and taxation. Aristocracies were also created by these military societies; noblemen who accumulated wealth and prestige on the battlefield often held important political posts around their king or emperor. Nevertheless, one king pitted against many nobles is dangerous; therefore, it served kings to have good relationships with their men, but also to reduce the power of the aristocracy as a whole. This struggle between royal and aristocratic authority plays out throughout the premodern era, in most areas across the world. Political leaders sought to strengthen their own authority while weakening the authority of the wealthy aristocrats under their control.

Another aspect of strong political leadership is that of a smooth succession. How does the next leader become the ruler of the land? Today, we think of empires and kingdoms in which primogeniture, inheritance by the first-born son, is the rule of succession. But, during the early medieval period, most of the regions discussed here did not practice primogeniture – that was a product of the late medieval period. Most Eurasian men, particularly of the upper classes, were polygamous, that is, they had multiple wives and multiple sons who could be their heirs. Although one son would still be first, the plethora of children often led to partible inheritance, in which all sons received a part of their father's patrimony.

Disruptions

Throughout the early medieval period, leaders sought to formalize their borders and the territory over which they ruled. Few groups had strong borders, and there were a few factors that kept people from having consolidated states, not the least of which were the consistent disruptions caused by internal and external foes. Disruptions include external invasion (by rival powers), attacks by nomads and other raiders (Vikings, Huns, Magyars, Muslims, and others), and internal dissension (coups, attempted coups, and the inability of a central ruler to impose his will on regional lords far away). In this section, we talk about the invasions by the Central Asian steppe nomads into both the western European and eastern Chinese empires. The superior military technology of these nomadic tribes overwhelmed the nascent states in Europe and briefly halted the progress of the Chinese empire. The organized and highly trained nomadic cavalry moved easily across the Eurasian plains to disrupt states on both sides of the continent.

War and battles help to both destabilize and to centralize – strong leaders can rally their armies to fight against a common enemy, unless that enemy has superior weaponry, tactics, or strategies. Military technology is regionally specific, but also very similar across Eurasian cultures: swords and shields, pikes and lances, bows and horses. Warfare is both a catalyst for change and an indication of the differences between people. War is disruptive, it causes great change, and often brings new ideas and approaches. In this early period, we see invasions by raiders across Europe and Asia. The Vikings changed naval travel and warfare in northern Europe (discussed in later chapters), and the steppe nomads of Eurasia changed martial warfare by advancing the cavalry.

The Cavalry

Cavalry are soldiers on horseback, trained to fight with and from their mount. From early evidence, we know the peoples from the Central Asian steppe not only lived with, but also trained from, their horses. Looking at the advancements of the stirrup and the saddle shows us how these nomadic groups created a strong cavalry and how their raids and conquests brought this military idea across Eurasia. Early artistic representations of horses and riders show bareback riders, sometimes with a simple blanket placed between them and the horse. The earliest indicators of stirrups, from India, show the "toe loop"; this simple stirrup allowed the rider to place their big toe in a leather loop that connected across the horse's back. This style of stirrup was not long used, as it was highly uncomfortable for both the rider and the horse. Advances in stirrups moved alongside changes in saddle making, and better stirrups and saddles allowed for more advanced cavalries to form.

As the engineering of the stirrup improved throughout the early medieval period, it allowed a greater number of people to be involved in cavalry warfare. The platform stirrup, invented around 100 CE, enhanced the toe loop by creating a larger place for the foot to rest. The platform was shaped like a large

Fig 3.1
A stirrup from the Mongolian or Tibetan regions was made in the late medieval period. Fierce dragon heads decorate the arch, and the bottom is a sturdy and practical platform. Objects like this are a rare find. They were well used and then melted down and recycled.
Metropolitan Museum of Art, Purchase, Arthur Ochs Sulzberger Bequest and Arthur Ochs Sulzberger Gift, by exchange, 2014, 2014.73

L, which allowed the rider to place their foot in the bottom portion of the stirrup. The open styling was not, however, stable enough for a rider to stand up securely in the stirrup.

The invention of the ring-style stirrup changed mounted warfare in Eurasia. By 300 CE, the L platform was enclosed to create a full ring-style stirrup, providing a platform for the front of the foot to rest on – much like a bicycle pedal does. With the foot bracketed on both sides, the rider would not risk slipping off the stirrup when standing or moving on the horse. The first material evidence for this stirrup is from a grave dated to the Eastern Jin dynasty, from 322 CE, a period when the Chinese military fought against northern Asian steppe nomads.

The Huns introduced the ring-style stirrup to Europe when they began invading in the fifth century. The fully enclosed stirrup moved westward across Eurasia with the seminomadic peoples, and, as their mounted cavalry met with the foot soldiers in the Middle East and Europe, the importance of the stirrup became immediately apparent. In addition to their stirrups, the Eurasian steppe nomads brought with them their recurve bows. These bows were much shorter than the bows used in Eurasia, as the long bows could not be easily handled on horseback. The size of the bow allowed a warrior to shoot from the left or right side of the horse, freeing the rider to fight at more angles. The curve of the bow propelled arrows a great distance (later Mongolians were said to hit targets over 500 yards away from horseback). This bow, used for hunting and warfare,

Fig 3.2
A Mongol archer on horseback as depicted in a Chinese painting on paper from the fifteenth or sixteenth century.
© Victoria and Albert Museum, London

118

demanded a more stable saddle and stirrup, as the archer needed a secure base to shoot from. We have no direct evidence that Attila and his Huns used a ring-style stirrup during their invasions, but the recurve bow and the stability of the archers lead us to believe they did. And fear of these mounted conquerors was extreme.

The earliest written record of the stirrup in Roman territory dates from 580 CE when Tiberius II, Byzantine emperor, wrote of his need for stirrups for his near-constant wars against Italy and the Avars, another seminomadic group from the Eurasian heartland. It would not be until around the year 800, however, during Charlemagne's reign, that the ring-style stirrup became prominent in Western Europe. We know, for example, that Charlemagne himself rode bareback for the majority of his life, as his skeleton shows bone spurs on the inside of his knees. Despite his own riding habits, we can assume that Charlemagne and his mounted warriors were, at least by 778, using the "new" stirrup. Einhard, his official biographer, wrote of a decisive battle Charlemagne's men (the Franks) lost at Roncesvalles in Spain. "The Franks," he wrote, "fought at a disadvantage in every respect, because of the weight of their armor." Men could only have fought in heavy armor on horseback if they had a stirrup and saddle from which to stand and fight.

Saddles also changed significantly throughout this period. During the Roman Empire, most saddles were "four horn" style, with a sloping cantle (rear) in the back and a low pommel (front) to keep the rider on the horse: one "horn" in front and one in back for extra stability. Although Roman riders rode horses into battle, we have little evidence that the men consistently fought from horseback. With the addition of a more efficient stirrup, the need grew for a more robust saddle system. By the sixth century, European saddles had higher cantles and pommels to create a steadier base from which to fight. This addition of the stable saddle and the ring-style stirrup, brought into Europe and China by nomadic cavalry, created the movement to cavalry-based armies that grew in these areas from this period to the industrial age.

Eurasian Nomadic Movements Westward

Western Europeans feared the arrival of the Huns, as they named the nomadic people who arrived in Europe in the fifth century. There is a long tradition of western peoples fearing – and being fascinated by – the nomads of Central Asia. The ancient Romans and Greeks were terrified by a horse-warrior people from the steppe whom they called the Scythians. Like the Scythians, the Huns were fierce fighters on horseback, moving quickly and fighting with bow and arrow. This gave them the ability to outflank and outmaneuver the slower and more cumbersome infantry forces of the settled societies. Although we cannot say for sure what caused the Central Asian steppe peoples to move westward in the sixth century, an important possibility is that of climate change (see Chapter 4).

WHO WAS ATTILA THE HUN?

Little is known for sure about the origins and identity of the Central Asian nomads called the Huns. The Hunnic language seems to have been related to Turkish or Mongolian, and the Huns share many characteristics with the Mongols. The majority of the Central Asian steppe people were pastoralist in nature. They kept herds of cattle, horses, goats, and sheep, which they followed into different pastures in the summer and winter. Expert archers, the Huns fought and hunted with bows from horseback. They were multiethnic and polyglot peoples, albeit preliterate, and the majority of information we have about them is from either Chinese or Roman sources until the Mongol invasions, when they appear in the histories of other cultures.

The famed and feared leader of the Hunnish confederation (from 434), Attila, threatened the Persian Sassanian Empire and both western and eastern halves of the Roman Empire at a time when it was already losing its centralized state power. Attila and his warrior band (which included both Huns and a variety of other Germanic tribesmen) raided and plundered near both Constantinople and Rome, but was unable to conquer either city. Because they were fearsome warriors who moved quickly on horseback, they were able to lay waste to large swaths of territory quite rapidly.

The Roman historian Jordanes wrote that Attila was "born into the world to shake the nations, the scourge of all lands." At the Battle of Chalons (451 CE), the Italian king Theodoric was thrown from his horse amidst the carnage (possibly for a lack of a good stirrup?) and trampled by his own men. Thousands died in the battle, as Hunnic bowmen shot from their horses into the mass of foot soldiers. Attila and his men found themselves surrounded by day's end, and Attila was worried enough that he created his own funeral pyre, covered "in horse trappings … that none might have the joy of wounding him." He escaped the next day to invade and harass Rome and Italy for the next two years before dying on his wedding night in 453 of a stroke. The Hunnish confederation broke up after his death, but the fact that external invaders could so threaten both the city of Rome and the power of the centralized Roman government marked the end of the Western Empire.

By the end of late antiquity, horseback warfare was the norm, and would remain so until the modern era. The technological advancements of the stirrup and saddle made cavalry warfare not just plausible, but preferable. Saddles and stirrups gave added stability to riders, allowing them to arm themselves with shield, sword, lance, and bow and creating, essentially, the medieval version of the modern tank. It also created a new class of warriors – elite equestrians. Horses – their purchasing, equipping, stabling, and training – are expensive. Only the wealthiest could afford to keep horses, and these horses aided in the creation of a new aristocracy throughout Europe, one tied to mounted warfare. From this point forward, cavalry would be a major feature of armies throughout Eurasia. But, even so, not every cavalry force is equal: the European knights, who fought with long swords on large, heavy horses, were surprised when they encountered the Turks during the crusades, who fought with bow and arrows on much faster, lighter horses and were able to surround formations of knights, barrage them with showers of arrows, and then quickly gallop away.

NOMADISM

The cultural differences and military clashes between settled societies and nomadic ones have been a nearly constant factor in human history. Even as far back as the ancient Mesopotamian *Epic of Gilgamesh*, we can see the fear with which urbanized, settled populations regarded the migratory and nomadic peoples that they thought were attacking their borders. Nomadic groups of the medieval period – such as the Huns, the Avars, the Magyars, and the Mongols – were viewed with terror by the polities whose borders they threatened and whose centralized power they disrupted. Because most of these nomadic groups had no written language, however, the historical perspective we have on them is skewed by their portrayals in hostile sources. The idea that such nomads were uncultured barbarians must be revised, but this process depends upon the archeological recovery of material remains of their cultures. Such archeological study often shows these cultures to be rich in material goods and highly developed cultural practices.

Many non-settled communities practiced what is known as nomadic pastoralism. These groups base their economy on the movement of domesticated livestock – such as cattle, goats, yaks, camelids, sheep, and reindeer – which needed to move around to find grazing land. Rather than depending upon large-scale agriculture, as in permanently settled communities, pastoralists rely upon the milk, meat, and blood of animals, with supplementary fruits, nuts, and grains from foraging or small-scale farming. Pastoralism is found in all parts of the world, even today, particularly in areas where climate and soil make farming difficult. Transhumance is a form of pastoral nomadism in which a community migrates seasonally between fixed pasturelands – often in the mountains or highlands in summertime and at lower valleys during the winter.

Eurasian Nomadic Movements Eastward

The Chinese also experienced invasions by the nomadic Asian tribes. Particularly in the period of 200 to 400 CE, there were almost continual invasions into northern Chinese territory. Some of these assaults had major impacts on the political and cultural history of China. For example, early invasions of the Xiongnu led emperors to create the Great Wall of China. At other times, invasions of nomads contributed to the disintegration of centralized Chinese dynastic rule. The later Xiongnu (200–400 CE), the Khitan (907), the Tangut (1032), the Jurchen (1115), and the Mongols (1206) were all Turkic/Mongolian tribal peoples who traded with, invaded, or ruled in China.

The Xiongnu, a nomadic pastoralist tribe, moved in and out of the Southern Chinese Empire for years – arriving when weather and trade dictated. The historian Pangu wrote that they prized youth and strength and, although they had a very militaristic culture, they only really fought when they knew they could win. With the collapse of the Han dynasty in 220 CE, civil strife created a space for new invasions into Chinese territory. The "barbarian" tribal peoples – ethnic minorities within the larger Han Chinese world – lived and traded along the borders of the Chinese Empire, paying taxes and trading livestock for finished products of silk and food. Their cavalrymen fought in Chinese armies, and they paid taxes and tribute into the Chinese government. In the fifth and sixth centuries, with the cooling temperatures across Eurasia, and the Huns pushing both east and west, the Xiongnu and others established their own dynasties within China. This period, known as the Uprising of the Five Barbarians (as it included several different tribal groups), created the Sixteen Kingdoms, a series of kings with short reigns who attempted to control Northern China. Han Chinese moved south, leaving the Northern Chinese Empire open to near-constant invasion by tribal peoples.

Much effort has been put into determining whether the Chinese of this period used the ring-style stirrup and pommel/cantle saddle. No evidence suggests whether the Asian steppe tribes or the Han Chinese invented these important technological advancements, but we do know that the Eurasian steppe peoples did use their superior cavalry skills on the Chinese imperial army to great effect. Nevertheless, the Xiongnu and the other "barbarian" tribes effectively defeated larger and better-trained armies during this tumultuous period. The Chinese favored the cup-style stirrup, which held the entire front of the foot, until well into the 800s, which does suggest a tribal invention of a ring-style stirrup.

Creating Kingdoms

Tang China (618–907/970)

Around 581, the warrior Wen-di gained the support of nomadic men and used this support to create a new, solidified Chinese Empire. The Sui dynasty (581–618) conquered the nomads in the north and the Han Chinese in the south. Tribal peoples entered into many areas of the bureaucratic government, much to the consternation of the xenophobic Han Chinese. Despite these tensions, Wen-di used his northern men to establish a solid kingdom, free from civil and external warfare. Yang-di, Wen-di's son, sought to remove the "barbarians" from governmental service, but, during his invasion of Korea, he actively recruited tribal cavalry and tribal strategies for his armies. He also included them in the building of the Grand Canal, which connected the Yangtze and Yellow rivers and allowed for easier travel and commerce (see Chapter 6).

The Tang dynasty emperors considered themselves strictly ethnically Chinese and sought to rid China of all nomadic "barbarian" influences. They expelled nomadic bureaucrats and seized all the property in China for imperial purposes, redistributing it to Han Chinese loyalists. Despite these moves, when the Tang Empire expanded westward, it hired Asian tribal cavalry and bred tribal horses for uses within their armies, as the Chinese favored the nomads' horses. Their military zenith occurred in the mid-eighth century, as Chinese armies moved across the Eurasian steppe toward the Middle East and Chinese navies sailed through the Southern Sea.

One of the most significant battles of the early medieval period took place in the Western Regions (Central Asia) between Tang troops and Muslim forces, along with their allies in the Tibetan Kingdom. At the Battle of Talas (751), the Tang advance was stopped in the Syr Darya region of Russia by an Abbasid Muslim army. It was a crushing defeat – only 2,000 Chinese soldiers escaped, and many Tibetan and Mongolian mercenaries defected to the Muslim side. This victory by Muslim-led armies was followed by a significant expansion of Islam into Central Asia; many of the Turkic peoples in the region converted to Islam. Following the loss at Talas, the Tang faced another challenge – this one from within, via internal revolt. The An Lushan rebellion of 756 stopped further westward expansion by the Tang. General An Lushan, of Sogdian nomadic and peasant descent, conquered northern China, and all armies were recalled to China to defeat the revolution. The Tang dynasty lost control over northern and western China, economic stability declined, and public intellectuals bemoaned the lack of a stable government. The An Lushan rebellion was one of several rebellions during the Tang dynasty, all of which caused disruption and instability. The Huang Chao rebellion of 874–884 continued the cycle of revolt, when bands of disaffected Chinese fought against the Tang government after years of famine and climate disasters. These two rebellions both had roots in the severe social stratification and heavy taxation of the Tang empire (rebels wrote that the Tang rulers "had no sympathy for our lives"); add in a shifting climate (see later chapters), and the disruption was bound to occur.

While the Tang may have wanted to remove "barbarian" culture from the purity of the Han Chinese world, it remained an impossible task. Expelling nomads proved to be too difficult, as many were now settled and had become part of Chinese culture. The tribal influences in the military (cavalry, technology, and strategy) became central tenets of the Chinese army. Language, fashions, foods – all made their way into Chinese culture. Moreover, the expansion westward, into tribal territories, opened up China and Central Asia to new merchants and finished goods, such as those imported from Persia and other Western Regions by the Sogdians (see Chapter 2). The interior canal system grew, as did internal commercial development, as merchants sought ways to improve civil and foreign trade. Peace across Central Asia brought new merchants and new goods both east and west, expanding the economies of both the Chinese and the Muslim empires.

So, while Tang China is known as a period of political stability, that stability was not guaranteed. Tang Tai-tsung founded the dynasty and renovated the Chinese government underneath a strict hierarchy. He created three administrative units to remove the influence of barbarians and aristocrats: the Council of State, the Council of Military Affairs, and the Censorate. The redistribution of land also broke up the power of the wealthy nobility – land became a means of praising loyalty and punishing disloyalty. Tang Tai-tsung merely handed land back to the wealthiest and most loyal of his military men. By rewarding his loyal military men, the emperor was able to strengthen his own authority, surrounding himself with a loyal cadre that could easily raise an army. At the same time, as he moved aristocratic families around China, the emperor's power was further increased.

An excellent example of how Chinese leaders personified the qualities needed for the premodern state can be found in Empress Wu (684–705). Wu rose from the position of concubine to sole ruler of China. An able and astute ruler, she expanded the military and ordered men to counter the threat of the nomads at her borders. Like her predecessors, she included nomadic warriors within her military in order to fight effectively against those strong men from the north. Her robust military presence allowed Tang China to effectively defend their northern borders during her reign. She also expanded the civil service examinations in order to increase her bureaucracy and turn it away from the

Fig 3.3
Empress Wu Zetian (625–705) was a concubine and then a lady-in-waiting, but eventually became the Empress of China in the Tang dynasty. This fresco was made in the seventh/eighth century.
Heritage Image Partnership Ltd / Alamy Stock Photo

hereditary nobility. Prior to her reforms, only men with high social status could sit for examinations. Wu opened the process up to any Chinese male who had the ability to take the exam, which strengthened her authority over the hereditary aristocratic families. She created an ideal of meritocracy, where ability and service mattered more than wealth and birth; however, in reality, few poor Chinese sat for the examinations, as education was an expensive luxury.

Wu also used Buddhism to reinforce her power, solidifying her connection to divinity by using the Buddhist title "Divine Empress Who Rules the World." Thus, she aligned herself with this important religion and gained divine providence. Empress Wu was a strong patron of Buddhism, using it to bring Tibetan and other southern peoples more fully into Chinese society. She patronized monasteries and the arts, and colossal statues of Buddha began appearing under her reign, like the Buddha in the Fengxian Si Cave (Longmen Grottoes). She sought to make Buddhism a state religion. Wu also recognized the rising influence of Daoism in Chinese culture, so she also promoted this philosophy within her realm. Despite these positive actions, the Chinese aristocracy feared a female ruler, and she was deposed in 705.

While Buddhism did create a sense of identity, Buddhists and other non-native Chinese were seen as threats to the state after the An Lushan rebellion in 755, as many rebels were either Sogdians or identified as Buddhists. Confucianism reemerged after the rebellions as the central ideology of China. Confucianism stressed the duties of the subject to the leader, which aided new

Fig 3.4
The Empress Wu Zetian sponsored the construction of Buddhas at the Longmen Grottoes.
platongkoh / iStock

Chinese imperial stability, for to go against an emperor was tantamount to denying the universe itself. These ideals set the tone for all relationships in China, where the person on the lower rungs of society owed obedience toward those on the upper rungs. Lady Zheng (ca. 730) personified this in her *Book of Filial Piety for Women*, where she outlines the duties of the wife to the husband: she must be an example of rectitude and virtue who should never cross her husband, but she is expected, if only through her tone and deeds, to admonish her husband if he strays.

By the end of the Tang period, the Chinese aristocracy had regained their authority, but the imperial house was forced to share control with the powerful families of China. The backlashes against Buddhism, against nomadic military personnel, and against the power of women within the imperial courts, all created a space where invaders from the north could use the political disruptions to cause internal splits, bringing about the next stage in Chinese politics – northern nomadic and southern traditional cultures.

Asuka (538–710) and Nara Japan (710–794)

Chinese and Buddhist ideals took hold outside China, through the trade and artistic connections China had with other countries, like Korea and Japan. One of the more important aspects of the Asuka dynasty in Japan was the close ties the Japanese emperors made with the Chinese Sui dynasty (581–618). Empress Suiko (r. 593–628) and Crown Prince Shotoku (574–622) were instrumental in solidifying the use of Chinese culture in Japan. Shotoku was a devout Buddhist who studied in China in his youth. He brought Chinese literature, language, and ideas into the Japanese upper classes. Buddhism was fairly new to Japan (introduced around 538) and the Crown Prince's promotion of the new faith aided Buddhism's spread through the royal courts. Prince Shotoku's most important writing is the *Seventeen Article Constitution*, where he modeled Japanese imperial politics on those of the Chinese Mandate of Heaven. The sinicization of Japan expanded greatly under his mother Suiko's reign; the Chinese calendar, Chinese road system, and Chinese language became important aspects of Japanese society.

After Suiko and Shotoku's deaths, the government fell to rival aristocrats, until the Taika Reforms of 645–649. These reforms, again influenced by Chinese systems, strengthened imperial authority in Japan. The reforms set out to redistribute agricultural land and remove the strongholds of large aristocratic families by making all land and all people subject to the royal court. Personal and corvée (conscripted labor) taxes created a stable economic base for the imperial household, which further centralized the royal authority in Japan. The leader of Japan also became known formally as *Tenno* or Heavenly Emperor; this was a translation of the Chinese *tien-huang*, and it was another aspect of sinicization of the Japanese imperial court during the Nara period. The imperial line legendarily began in 660 BCE with the emperor Jimmu, who was a direct descendent of the Shinto sun goddess Amaterasu, and, like other political leaders, the

Fig 3.5
Emperor Shotoku of Nara Japan (574–622) and his two sons as depicted on an
eighth-century hanging scroll in the Museum of Imperial Collections in Tokyo, Japan.
© Wikimedia Commons, public domain

Japanese emperor held the position of high priest, elevating his status to the
semidivine.

Until the Nara period (710–794), Japanese capital cities changed with each
new ruler. The site of death was linked strongly with negative energy that could
disrupt the natural order and destroy the new ruler, so each new leader chose
a new capital city. This was expensive, time-consuming, and difficult. Empress
Genmei established a new capital city at Nara in 710, announcing that Nara
would be the permanent capital city, which held until 794, when the emperor
Kanmu moved to Heian-kyo (modern Kyoto), ending the Nara Period.

Having visited China as a young woman, Genmei directed her new city to
be a carefully planned grid along the lines of the Chinese capital of Chang-an.
She also brought Confucian ideals to her government, and championed the
Seventeen Article Constitution written by Prince Shotoku in 604, which outlined
the virtues necessary for bureaucrats and government officials. Shotoku based
his constitution on Confucian and Buddhist ideals, and, when Genmei adopted
this document as the basis for her government, she aligned herself more
strongly with China and Chinese-style ruling.

The *Seventeen Article Constitution* is often labeled the first written constitution in history. Although very dissimilar to modern constitutions, it does

outline a set of principles by which Shotoku felt Japanese political society should be organized. In this sense, the *Seventeen Article Constitution*, written specifically for Japanese government, is a proper constitution. Shotoku's third precept states "do not fail to obey your sovereign, for he is like Heaven, which is above the Earth, and the vassal is like the Earth, which bears up Heaven." He also clearly states that there should only be one lord – the emperor – whom the aristocrats as well as the lower class must serve. By affiliating her new rule so closely with China, Genmei broke the Japanese aristocracy from their traditional roots – both physically and religiously. Forced into the new city and into new rules, the aristocrats lived far from their homes. Although neither she nor any other ruler stripped Shintoism from Japanese society, the imported religion and philosophy did force the native religion into a secondary space.

After the disruptions of the prior dynasty, the Nara rulers used Chinese ideology to create a common identity. The two major ways in which the Nara rulers used Chinese ideology was in the acceptance of Confucian and Buddhist ideals within the governmental structures, as outlined by their promulgation of the *Seventeen Article Constitution*. The second major way in which the Nara emperors used Chinese culture as a way to create authority for themselves was in the use and spread of Chinese *hanzi* as a writing system. Chinese and Japanese are from different language families (Japanese is actually a language isolate, meaning there are no known languages related to it); however, during the Nara period, Chinese became the lingua franca of the Japanese government. We see this most strongly in the government's patronage of the first major history of Japan, the *Shoku Nihongo*, written in *kanbun*, a mixture of Japanese and classical Chinese. The Nara government's dedication to the use of Chinese as a written and spoken language created a way for them to communicate effectively with people outside the city center. It also tied them directly to the Tang Empire, which gave them a ready economic partner in addition to creating a burgeoning and successful intellectual expansion. Following Chinese economic principles, the Nara emperors collected taxes and used them for infrastructure, agriculture, and support of the imperial family.

The adoption of Chinese culture worked in many senses, but the depreciation of native Japanese ideology and custom frustrated Japanese aristocrats and commoners. This disruption can best be seen with Empress Koken (r. 749–758), who focused on Buddhism by building shrines and publishing sutras. She was one of eight ruling women in Japanese history, and her ostracization of the aristocracy and flouting of succession rules were the reasons given for why women were no longer allowed to rule – it would take 900 years for another woman to rule Japan as empress. Although she abdicated in 758, Koken insisted on staying involved in court politics, which caused an uprising by the aristocracy. Her armies defeated theirs, and she began ruling as Empress Shotoku (r. 764–770). She continued to flout tradition by allowing her personal Buddhist priest,

Dokyo, unlimited access to the courts. She created a palace in his hometown and lived openly with him (Japanese empresses were not to marry if they inherited the throne as a single woman). She then declared him her successor and moved back to Nara. She died in 770, and Dokyo was immediately exiled. The nobles appointed Konin (r. 770–781) as emperor. He followed the traditional Japanese succession route by abdicating in favor of his son in 781.

The Nara emperors sought to extend their authority by focusing on Chinese systems and ideals. This connection to China also increased their economy, as it created a ready trading partner. Nevertheless, without clear rules of succession and acknowledgment of the importance of the Japanese aristocracy, the later Nara period was fraught with internal conflicts. The next periods of Japanese history saw the emperors ruled by aristocratic factions, with a rise in the Samurai classes and *bakufu* (military) governments.

Umayyad Dynasty (661–750)

Much of the early history of politics in the Islamic world arises from Muhammad's sudden death in 632, which did not leave him enough time to create a succession plan for his new government. This lack of clear succession created 30 years of disunity in the early Muslim world. Despite this, the early caliphs did begin expanding outside the Arabian Peninsula into the Middle East. The first three caliphs extended Islamic hegemony beyond the Arabian borders, and, while this was not a calculated expansion, it was definitely unprecedented.

Even prior to Muhammad's death, Arab-Islamic armies begin attacking the southern portions of the Byzantine Empire; soon after his death they conquered broad expanses of both Byzantine and Sassanian Persian territory. By 636, the caliphal armies had conquered Byzantine Syria (including Jerusalem, a city sacred to Jews, Muslims, and Christians alike), and were also taking on the Persian Empire to the east. By 637, they destroyed the Persian capital and, by 650, most of the Persian Empire fell under Muslim control. The Byzantine and Persian empires had been at war for several generations, and internal and external conflicts made it easier for Arab armies to conquer their territories.

Islam then became the most important cultural touchpoint throughout the Middle East and North Africa. It created a common identity that stretched from Afghanistan to Spain, and from Syria to Yemen. Arabic became the lingua franca of the entire region. As a written language, Qur'anic Arabic of the mid-seventh century spread widely across the new Muslim territories. The simplicity of the spoken and written language of the Qur'an aided in its diffusion and its acceptance by different peoples. Islam was carried by merchants and by troops into new territories. In these ways, Islam became the common identity, and Arabic an effective means of communication for the new ruling parties.

WHAT DO TERMS LIKE "CALIPHATE" AND "DYNASTY" MEAN?

Political systems are categorized in different ways by those who study them. Some terms are based on historical context, while others are conventions created by nineteenth- and twentieth-century historians who established norms for studying these past cultures. For example, we use, throughout this book, the term "dynasty" for various periods of political centralization in China. Periods of Chinese history discussed as a "dynasty" indicate that there was a high degree of centralization and imperial control over extensive lands beyond those in the core Chinese heartlands. When centralized control over the Western Regions (Central Asia) and other regions had declined, or when northern and southern China were ruled separately, it is referred to as an intermediate period. For example, the Chinese dynasties most commonly referred to in this textbook are the Tang dynasty (618–907), the Song dynasty (960–1276), the Yuan (Mongol) dynasty (1279–1368), and the Ming dynasty (1368–1644). The Tang and Song periods are separated by several decades of noncentralized rule, not simply by a change in the ruling dynasty of the state.

Another common term used in this book is "caliphate" for one of the three different religio-political states that ruled large swaths of the Islamic world. The term *caliph* means "successor" in Arabic and refers to the leaders who followed the Prophet Muhammad as the political, religious, judicial, and military leader of the Islamic community. Because of debates over how succession should be decided (see Chapter 1), Islam broke into two sects (Sunni and Shi'ite), each believing they had the right to follow in Muhammad's leadership roles. This led eventually to the establishment of a Shi'ite caliphate (called the Fatimid Caliphate, 909–1171, based in Cairo from 969) to rival the Sunni caliphate (led first by the Umayyad dynasty, 661–750, based in Damascus; after a revolution in 750, by the Abbasid dynasty, 750–1258, based in Baghdad). To make things even more complex, at the time of the Abbasid revolution in 750, a man who claimed to be part of the ousted Umayyad family fled westward and established political rule in al-Andalus, the Muslim-ruled territory of Spain and Portugal. His successors eventually declared themselves a rival caliphate (the Umayyad Caliphate, or the Caliphate of Cordoba, based in Cordoba, Spain, 929–1031). These three rival caliphates overlapped in time, each claiming to be the rightful successor to Muhammad.

Other terms are used for rulers within Islamic lands who did not claim caliphal power. Rulers like a governor, or prince (*emir* or *amir*), or a sultan ruled smaller areas of territory and nominally owed allegiance to one of the caliphs. Because it was always difficult for caliphs to maintain strong control over distant lands, the emirs and sultans often had a free hand at ruling their territories. These terms correspond to ones used in the Latin Christian world for regional rulers: titles like lord, prince, duke, or count. The medieval period also saw plenty of political rulers who claimed the power and title of king or emperor.

The first dynasty of caliphs, called the Umayyad dynasty, ruled between 661 and 750 from their capital at Damascus, a former Byzantine provincial capital. The Umayyad government often used non-Arabs in positions of local power and adopted many of the local Greek (and later Persian) administrative techniques. This was of twofold importance: it gave the local elites power in the new governmental structure, and it also threatened the control of wealthy Arabs from the south. The Umayyad Caliphate quickly controlled North Africa and Spain, creating an empire that stretched across the southern Mediterranean. When they took formerly Byzantine port cities like Alexandria, they also took over their naval fleets and the sailors who piloted those ships. This allowed them to gain military dominance on both land and sea.

Ruling such a large and diverse group of peoples is difficult, but the Umayyad caliphs were able to do so by using the common identities of religion, language, and communication (as in the *barid* network described above). They established local governors (emirs) who ruled semi-independently but owed allegiance to the caliphs (as demonstrated by putting the caliph's name on their coins and listing his name during Friday prayers at the communal mosque). Although they did not force conversions on conquered monotheists, they did offer tax breaks and preferential treatment for Muslims and for those who converted, so many people converted to Islam out of both religious and economic need. With a large trade network and a steady stream of taxation, the Umayyad caliphs created a settled and flourishing dynasty.

Battle of the Masts, 654/655

As Muslim forces moved rapidly into Syria and northern Africa over the seventh century, Muslim authorities gained access to seaports at Beirut, Alexandria, and Carthage. When they took those ports, they also acquired the Byzantine ships docked there, complete with the Christian sailors who knew how to maneuver them. Thus, horseback warriors from the Arabian Peninsula were able to gain control over a fleet of galleys for use in both warfare and commerce. The newly-Muslim fleet – possibly numbering 500–600 ships – was able to defeat a Byzantine naval force at the 654/655 Battle of the Masts, a momentous event that foreshadowed the shifting balance of power in the Mediterranean and on its shores. The Muslim navy had already taken the island of Cyprus in 649 and, over the course of the next century, raided and conquered other islands and shores of the Mediterranean Sea. In the ninth century, they took over Sicily, Malta, and Crete. By that time, Muslim dominance of the Mediterranean sea lanes was complete.

Sea battles in the Mediterranean were fought by ramming an enemy ship and trying to board it for hand-to-hand combat, or, from the late seventh century, by throwing onto the target boat a flammable substance known as "Greek fire." Composed primarily of naptha, Greek fire was launched at ships and burst into flame, where it continued to burn even after contact with the water. It was the Byzantine use of Greek fire that protected the city of Constantinople from attack by Muslim sea forces in 674–678, and again in 717–718. Both these sieges ended with the destruction of the Muslim fleets, and, thereafter, Muslim

Fig 3.6
An illustration of Greek fire from a twelfth-century manuscript in Greek now held at
the Biblioteca Nacional de Madrid.
© Wikimedia Commons, public domain

naval attacks on the Greek capital ceased. However, this did not mean the end
of Muslim naval power: their fleets recovered and thrived, and they continued
to dominate the Mediterranean Sea for several centuries.

Carolingian Empire (814–948)

In Europe, the fall of Roman hegemonic power led to a power vacuum from
which different Germanic tribal leaders attempted to amass as much power as
possible. The Merovingians, a group of Franks, were able to conquer and control
most western portions of Europe (in the area known today as France) beginning
around the year 500. Their first king, Clovis I (r. 481–509), who is considered
the founder of the Merovingian dynasty, also converted to Roman Christianity.
Other Germanic kings were practitioners of Arian Christianity, a sect that had
been declared heretical in 325 (see Chapter 1). Clovis's conversion led to widespread conversion by his subjects and by other Germanic rulers of Europe.
Christianity provided a sense of common identity (that only faith could provide) to a diverse population of Romans and various Germanic peoples, each of
which kept their unique languages and sets of laws. However, acceptance of the
religion was rather shallow for the first several hundred years of Christian contact in Europe, with many in Europe not practicing or accepting the new faith,
or doing so in combination with their pre-Christian practices.

When the Merovingians fell to the Carolingian kings, the new rulers
attempted to rectify some of the problems of the Merovingians by solidifying
control over their territories. The most famous of these kings was Charlemagne
(r. 768–814). Like earlier kings, Charlemagne was a warlord who extended

his reach across most of western, and parts of eastern, Europe. Charlemagne sought to create a stronger common identity among his wide-reaching territories, and he chose Roman Christianity as one of his most important unifying elements. Newly conquered peoples were forced to convert, like the Saxons and the Avars; in both instances, when people did not convert they were ruthlessly eliminated. Charlemagne claimed that the point of his conquests was to convert those pagans in his region, and conversion, while not the only aim, was used as a justification for warfare and conquests. His biographer, Einhard, wrote of his king's borders, calling the pagan frontier regions "lawless" and prone to warfare. Charlemagne wanted to consider himself a Christian king, ruling a Christian people, and therefore he needed all the peoples he ruled to be Christians. He felt a responsibility to the Church, and he wanted all the priests and monks within his territories to be literate, educated, and faithful.

His concern for the welfare of the Church led him to the creation of an educational reform program we call the Carolingian Renaissance. He relied on the educator Alcuin of York to create this new program. Although we today call this a renaissance, the major importance was not artistic, it was its insistence on the creation of a literate class. Literacy had all but died out in Europe after the Roman withdrawal, and Latin became the lingua franca within Charlemagne's territories as he sought to create a literate class of priests, monks, and courtiers who could act as bureaucrats within his large empire. Although he was eager for education for others, Charlemagne could not write, but he did insist that all his younger children be educated, girls and boys alike. He used his newly literate subjects to aid in the governance of his territory. The agents of the king, traveling in twos (one layperson and one cleric), visited districts around the empire, handed down decrees and formal writs from the king, and reported to the king on the behavior of the aristocrats. This allowed Charlemagne to control continental Europe through the written word as well as by the sword.

He was never able to create a very deep or loyal bureaucracy, however, and most of his government was filled with landholders and warlord-aristocrats. His economy was based on plundering neighboring tribes, and he had only a small amount of trade between Muslim and Byzantine worlds in the south. The nobles who served as regional lords were given land and the spoils of war as reward for loyal service – they were not paid in coinage, as the notion of a paid administrative staff was not part of the tradition of Germanic kingship. Charlemagne depended on the competence and the loyalty of his nobles, which meant that the royal authority of the Carolingian kings could be weakened if a noble became especially powerful (each had military followers of his own) and decided to assert his independence. Carolingian royal authority was also weakened by the end of expansionism: because supporters were "paid" in land and plunder, when those sources of wealth dried up as the kings stopped conquering new places, no new assets were available to compensate the nobles who provided administrative and military service to the kings.

To be a strong and stable state requires having a clear line of succession and a peaceful transition of power. This idea of succession and transition changed in many areas during the early medieval period. Most cultures of the early medieval world followed a patrilineal succession; that is, property and goods transferred from fathers to sons. Women, in many areas, were given dowries (property she brought into the marriage from her natal family) and sometimes this property was hers to dispose of (like in Islamic law), but, in most places, that property became her husband's (like in English common law). Many cultures also practiced partible inheritance, where all the children of a father received some form of inheritance at his death. Boys received more inheritance than girls, who were often only given their dowries at marriage. Women's inheritances moved to another family, whereas men's inheritances stayed within the same paternal name – this led to a preference for male children in many societies. Polygamy in elite families was the rule, rather than the exception, in much of history. China, Japan, Rome, France, Germany, Persia, Arabia, India, and Maya and Aztec America – all these areas and others practiced some form of polygamy by their ruling elite men. (Commoners were almost always in monogamous marriages, as polygamy is expensive to maintain.) Some cultures had one primary wife and several secondary ones; some had a primary wife and called the other women "concubines" or "consorts" (the *Rites of Zhou* in China dictated that the perfect number was 1 empress and 120 concubines), but, in all these areas, regulations and traditions insisted that sons by multiple women had some expectation of inheritance from their fathers.

The purpose of polygamous relationships was not sexual excess – it was meant to show potency and power. A man chose women who brought him wealth, who secured political or military ties, who brought peace with an enemy, and who could bear him children. Wives were political, military, and economic means to an end. Many women ensured that there would be at least one adult male heir, in a time when roughly half of children lived to adulthood. Nevertheless, it also caused political instability. In a period when most men of status had children by more than one woman, partible inheritance led to the dissolution of property in short order. This practice often led to internecine warfare, in which brothers fought each other to increase their own chances of gaining more land, power, and wealth. It also pitted elite women against each other, as they fought for their sons to gain and maintain more land and wealth.

Creating a clear line of succession and ensuring a peaceful transition of power were paramount to the success of a state. The problem of succession plagued most early political entities, and few groups ensured smooth transfer of leadership for more than a generation or two. As one historian of China notes, "Harmonious polygamy and smooth succession were weighty ideals too heavy for practical use." Charlemagne forbade polygamy within his realm, but this did not stop the ideas of partible inheritance. Charlemagne had one living son, Louis the Pious, but Louis had four sons, all of whom expected a portion of their grandfather's empire.

MURDEROUS MOTHERS

Elite women in the early medieval world lived more luxuriously than their lower-class counterparts, but they also had difficulties less present in farming or merchant lives. Often married as a teen to a man double her age, a young wealthy woman was trained from early childhood for the roles of wife and mother. In an age where polygamy was common, she might also have to maneuver and manipulate to make sure that her son gained his rightful inheritance. Confucian and Christian precepts dictated that sons should care for their parents, and, after a father's death, the son was responsible for his mother, culturally and, in many cases, legally as well. As an elite woman was often married young, she may also have been closer in age to her son than his father, and it behooved her long widowhood to work hard for her sons. This meant that royal and elite women had considerable power politically, which often brought them into conflict with men who felt threatened.

In Merovingian France and Tang China, where polygamy and partible inheritance were the norm, many royal women were forced into conflict to ensure their sons' inheritances. One famous feud happened in the late sixth century between Brunhilda and Fredegund, two queen consorts of the early European kingdom of Austrasia. It lasted for 30 years, during which Fredegund had Brunhilda's sister murdered, and Brunhilda imprisoned Fredegund. One chronicler accused Brunhilda of murdering ten kings, and another accused Fredegund of murdering rivals' children in their beds. To prevent further bloodshed, Fredegund's son had his mother drawn and quartered. Several Tang Chinese consorts and empresses were also charged with killing off rivals and their children. And, yet, another problem likely to cause conflict among wives was favoritism, where the ruler was seen as "entranced" or "trapped" by a woman. Emperor Xuanzong (685–762) was so enamored with one concubine, Imperial Consort Yang Guifei (719–756), that he ignored palace politics and elevated Yang's family to positions of power in Xuanzong's court. Yang herself is said to have controlled several political posts. When Xuanzong's rule ended with the An Lushan rebellion of 756, court officials blamed Yang for distracting the emperor and bringing down the empire. She was strangled, and Xuanzong fled the city.

Charlemagne revived the idea of empire – specifically the idea of the Roman Empire – in western Europe and laid the foundations for many later political developments in Latin Europe. He encouraged a strong sense of communal identity through Christianity within his realm, he created a base of men and women literate in Latin, through whom the nascent ideas of bureaucracy in Europe were formed, and he merged traditions of Germanic kingship with those inherited from the Roman system of rule. The empire itself, however, was too dependent on Charlemagne's strong leadership and the ability to expand to new places. His successors were less able to control the knights (elite warriors on horseback) who served under regional lords, and they had less new land and war booty to distribute to followers. His grandsons fought among themselves for control of larger portions of his kingdom. These factors, combined with the effects of Viking invasions from the north, meant that few of his successors had the same level of power as Charlemagne himself. Within 50 years of his death in 814, the empire had broken into regional states, ruled by separate kings. It would not be until the tenth century that one of those successor kingships (the Ottonian dynasty, in the region of modern Germany) could again claim to be "emperor of the Romans" in the West.

Conclusion

While we cannot rightly say that these areas were nation-states in the modern sense, all these rulers placed their territories on the path to statehood during the late medieval and early modern periods. Because of the early invasions by the Central Asian steppe peoples, European leaders gained the ideas and technology for the creation of cavalry. This allowed them to create larger and more specific armies, which, in turn, fueled their territorial and economic growth. It often led them into conflict with their nobles, as these wealthy men, with military followers of their own, could rebel against the king. Without a paid state army, rulers like Charlemagne were dependent upon the loyal service of armed warriors on horseback known as knights. The Tang and Nara dynasties struggled with similar issues, including succession and aristocratic troubles. Nevertheless, the Chinese did create long-lasting and fairly stable traditions of government. All these areas sought to create common identities for their people, often using religion and philosophy to give the population core rituals, customs, and goals. Religions aided in identity and communication, as many who were literate were also members of religious communities. Religion, writing, military power, and political authority were all necessary elements in the creation and maintenance of centralized power.

B: WRITING RULES

Evidence: Bede's *Ecclesiastical History of the English People*

Code of Justinian (*Corpus Juris Civilis/Body of Civil Laws*)

Einhard's *Life of Charlemagne*

Rule of St. Benedict

Abolqasem Ferdowsi's *Shahnemeh: The Persian Book of Kings*

Translations of Hunayn ibn Ishaq

Introduction

The first part of this chapter discussed the factors that contributed to, or worked against, political consolidation, as groups sought to establish power and authority over other groups, their territory, and their resources. The evidence we used was physical or material: horsemanship, stirrups, weaponry (or artistic depictions of them). This is what we refer to as archeological evidence. We also used the few extant written records available to us. In this part of the chapter, we consider evidence provided by written texts, the process of making that written record, and also the people who made it and preserved it. We must keep in mind that documentary evidence is mostly provided by those cultures that had a long tradition of recordkeeping, which means that there is more known about those cultures than about nonliterate groups, and thus history is written from their point of view. Conversely, those people without a written tradition – because they were nomadic, because they did not have a way to store and transport records, or because their written tradition was destroyed by a conquering power – were not in control of how their history was perceived or interpreted, and often their history is mostly lost. Writing is an important tool for achieving and preserving political power. Historians, intellectuals, and poets write the decrees, statutes, permissions, and heroic poems that justify the ruling class and legitimize its power. The states and empires that had power during the period 500–900 either had or developed strong written traditions.

Power of the Pen

Sustained written communication across geography or time relies on three factors. First, even if the literate community is small and elite, which was usually the case in the medieval period, the culture must have a writing system understood by that community of readers. No matter how careful or practiced an oral storyteller is, information passed on in this way changes unpredictably over time. A writing system stabilizes transmission of information (which is not always good; sometimes writing is erroneous or purposefully false). Examples of writing systems are phonetic alphabets (Latin or Cyrillic), abjad/consonantal alphabets (Arabic and Hebrew), and logographic systems (Chinese and Japanese).

Second, the culture must have leaders and traditions that value literacy and writing and encourage it as an honorable and often sacred social practice, as we saw with the Buddhist monks at Dunhuang (see chapters 2 and 5) and will see below with the court of Charlemagne. The writing community did not have to be large or prestigious, but it had to be a tacit part of dutiful religious life and a legitimate government. Stable and dominant societies have a literate class of librarians, scribes, and bookmakers, in addition to notaries and archivists who keep track of business and administrative affairs. Finally, there must also be a cultural imperative – moral, nationalistic, nativist, spiritual, or philosophical – that written documents from the past are valuable and should be protected and preserved. Although sometimes sheer luck and a perfect climate have preserved documents in caves, ice, and desert sand, most documents were preserved in monastic libraries, royal treasuries, and schools, precursors to modern museums.

Cultural Hegemony

While alphabets and writing systems are crucial to the development of ideas, the expansion of intellectual scope, and the transfer of knowledge, it is unfortunate that alphabets and writing systems can also be, intentionally or not, an aggressive weapon of cultural suppression and extinction. There is, in some sense, a "tyranny" of writing. Our knowledge of any historical period is limited to what was written down, what was saved, what was preserved. For instance, the Huns, discussed above, did not have a written language, so all we know about them came from the literate societies who were the targets of their attacks. We do not even know what the Huns called themselves, or how they understood their own culture and perceived the world.

Similarly, one way of dominating and enslaving a conquered people is to degrade, subsume, and sometimes destroy their customs, stories, languages, and artistic practices. Cultures without a means to record history or without the stability and security to preserve records are eclipsed by those that do or did. The power of one group to diminish, assimilate, or eradicate the traditions and practices of another is called cultural hegemony. We saw this in Orientation and Chapter 11 when the Spanish destroyed Aztec texts and written materials during the conquest of Mexico. As we will see below, in many early medieval cultures the arrival of literacy came with Christian missionaries, who sought both to create alphabets for oral languages so that the Bible could be written in them, and to eradicate the native so-called pagan traditions and replace them with Christian practices and beliefs. Additionally, producing written texts was often an expensive endeavor, and most written works had patrons, so formal histories were often paid for by the ruling class, which caused authors to write a version of history that flattered and extolled their patrons.

OLD ENGLISH

This book is written in English, which is now a worldwide language of scholarship. It began as the language of the Germanic tribes, primarily Angles and Saxons, that invaded the British Isles in the fifth century. We now call that version of the language Old English or Early English. In 597, the Benedictine monk Augustine was sent by the pope to Christianize the

Angles in Britain. He chose Canterbury for his cathedral and became the first Archbishop of Canterbury. He brought with him Latin and its alphabet, and, over the next few centuries, his successors adapted the Latin alphabet to Old English, including a few runes – Germanic symbols used for rudimentary inscriptions on wood, stone, or metal. The scribe who copied down the Early English oral epic *Beowulf* around the year 1000 CE interspersed Germanic symbols with Latin letters. For the "w" in the name Beowulf, the scribe used *wynn* (ƿ). It stood for the sound of "w" but also meant joy. Also featured are thorn (Þ), eth (ð), and ash (sort of like this æ).

Even though Latin remained the venerated religious language of the British Isles, the learned king Alfred the Great (r. 871–899) was also committed to preserving and promoting the language of his people. He believed in promoting literacy and education in English and commissioned scribes to translate Latin texts into Old English. He participated in the literacy movement, presiding over translating, among other works, Boethius's *Consolation of Philosophy* and St. Augustine's *Soliloquies.* No other early Germanic language in Europe was widely used for writing sacred or literary texts (a very few examples in Gothic survive), so Old English is unique in the early medieval period.

Writing Secular and Divine Law

Byzantium

Much of the success of the Roman imperial system was due to its emphasis on keeping administrative records: head counts of taxable citizens and military-aged men; inventories of resources and slaves from conquered territories; and contracts and legal documents. The importance of recording proceedings, decisions, and histories continued in the practices of the Roman Christian and Byzantine Orthodox Churches. Monasteries had sacred spaces and skilled scribes dedicated to composing, copying, and preserving scripture and evidence of the world around them. Later in the period, universities were established to train young men in biblical languages and exegesis (critical interpretation of a religious text), the prestige knowledge of these Christian theocracies.

In 476 King Odoacer deposed the Emperor Romulus Augustulus, and historians use this date to mark the separation of the western and eastern Roman Empire. At this point, Constantinople was the administrative center of the greater empire and continued to be the hub of the thriving, cosmopolitan trade economy of the Mediterranean basin. In 527, Justinian became emperor and commissioned a project that came to define the Byzantine Empire and secure its authority over a vast region: a law code. The *Corpus Juris Civilis (Body of Civil Laws)* is a collection of all the laws of the empire in three parts: 1) a code that includes all documented laws since the rule of Hadrian (d. 138), a ruler concerned with standardizing and reforming legal practices across the empire; 2) a manual on legal procedure and principles; and 3) a summary of legal opinions. Guided and authorized by this monumental work, Justinian and his successors secured a centralized justice system and fortified their power over a growing empire. The Code became the model of most European legal systems.

Justinian thought of himself as emperor over the entire Roman Empire, east and west, and he sought to regain lands in Europe and the Mediterranean that had been lost to "barbarian" Germanic invaders. A native Latin speaker at the helm of an imperial capital that mostly used Greek, Justinian had his Code written in both Latin and Greek. Greek had long been considered the more learned and important language of the Mediterranean, even by the ancient Romans. During Justinian's reign, Greek became the language of the ruling classes and the Byzantine Church, and thus the two Christianities, Orthodox and Roman, were further distinguished from each other by language, Greek and Latin.

As Orthodox missionaries traveled to convert and assimilate pagan groups that challenged the northern borders, they were in direct competition with Roman emissaries trying to fortify their territories in the same way. One significant factor of this contest was language. Roman Church doctrine held that Latin was the holy language of the Christian God. Despite this, portions of the Bible were translated into Old English, Gothic, Irish, and a host of other native tongues. Language, however, became a means of control: the Roman Church hierarchy came to regulate the teaching and practice of Christianity in the West, and they used this control over language in sacred texts as a way to exploit that teaching. Those older translation efforts faded, but never truly died out, despite the fact that Latin became the lingua franca of Roman Christianity. Byzantine and Oriental Christianity went a different way, determining that holy scripture was sacred in any language. They authorized translation into vernacular languages.

Nevertheless, there was a significant impediment to the translation process. Pre-Christian groups did not have writing systems elaborate enough for biblical texts. In the ninth century, the missionary brothers Cyril and Methodius invented a modified Greek alphabet with which to write Slavic languages (they both would be sainted for their work and known as "Apostles to the Slavs"). Their original writing system is called Glagolitic and the language for religious practice is Old Church Slavonic. With a few changes over time, Glagolitic evolved into the Cyrillic alphabet. Later missionaries, sent from Constantinople to convert the Slavic peoples, were successful, in part, because they allowed the Slavs to conduct services and worship in their own languages and helped them to transcribe vernacular stories. For instance, in the late tenth century CE, Vladimir the Great used the Cyrillic alphabet to create the first writing in the language of his people, and his commitment led to the "golden age" of Kievan Rus, where much knowledge was translated into Russian.

European Contexts

As we have seen, many early medieval kingdoms coalesced around a unifying religion and its texts. As writing and literacy fortified and justified the growing Byzantine Empire, it also reinforced the definition of western Christendom and its people. After the disintegration of the centralized Roman state, the western empire fragmented into tribal networks operating locally along the remaining substructure of roads and towns. The unifying written language was Latin, with many people descended from Roman citizens speaking proto-Romance dialects (descendants of Latin), which eventually evolved into Italian, French, Spanish, Portuguese, and Romanian (the modern Romance languages or, languages of Rome). Other peoples who arrived with the Germanic invaders spoke one of a variety of Germanic languages – for example, Frankish, Burgundian, Vandalic, and Gothic. The only one of these languages for which a written corpus, albeit a small one, exists is Gothic. The Gothic language was first written down when a fourth-century Arian Christian bishop named Wulfila (or Ulfilas) commissioned a Gothic translation of the Bible. The most famous surviving manuscript in Gothic is a sixth-century copy of that Gothic Bible, called the *Codex Argenteus*, a luxurious manuscript written in silver ink on purple pages.

Regardless of church affiliation, most of the people of Europe were Christian. Almost all Germanic tribes that gained power in these regions – for instance, the Saxons, Franks, Lombards, and Frisians – had converted to Christianity by the seventh century. As we have seen above, the powerful Christian monarch Charlemagne (Charles the Great, 768–814) was proclaimed "emperor of the Romans" in 800, but his subjects included a wide variety of linguistic and ethnic groups, from Romans to Franks, Goths, Avars, and Saxons. Christianity was one important tool by which he could unify these disparate peoples, and Christian Church officials (such as bishops and archbishops) were useful in governing localities across Charlemagne's expansive territory. Church officials were also literate, which meant that they were necessary to Charlemagne's administrative schema for issuing, promoting, and circulating his laws and edicts.

Charlemagne valued literacy and learning, perhaps recognizing written education as essential to an enduring, civilized rule. He assembled a court of learned advisors and set about creating a class of scholarly administrators. As discussed above, one of the recruits was the Englishman named Alcuin, who was trained in a monastery in England by a disciple of the Venerable Bede, author of the *Ecclesiastical History of the English People*, itself important evidence of early medieval life and politics. Work by Alcuin and others circulated through Church and monastic networks in what is called the Carolingian Renaissance – a reform of culture and the arts sponsored by Charlemagne, with improved literacy and a simplified script at its heart. The narratives of his intellectual and learned pursuits magnified his deeds and fortified his power. In his own time he became a legend, and his biographer, Einhard, secured that legend for the centuries that followed. Einhard knew Charles personally and wrote the biography of his king and emperor in the manner of a saint's tale, highlighting the ways Charlemagne fought for a Christian ideal. Einhard presented Charles as a pious and blessed agent whose mighty deeds were possible because of Christ's blessing.

It is typical for a culture to raise successful rulers to divine status. In the Christian tradition, narratives of king's great deeds appeared predominantly in three genres: saints' tales (also called hagiographies), *gesta* (acts or deeds), and chronicles (also called annals). Stories of great kings that imitated saints' tales were modeled on Old Testament heroes such as Solomon (a great leader), or Joshua (a soldier of God), or on New Testament saints such as Christ himself, and also the apostles and evangelists such as St. Paul. Other biographies of great leaders were written as *gesta*, stories of great deeds, for example, The *Gesta Koralina magni* (*The Great Deeds of Charles the Great*), written in the ninth century by a Swiss monk named Notker of St. Gall. *Gesta* could include religious leaders – for example abbots and bishops – but were especially used to extol heroes and aggrandize the achievements of kings. In addition, court scribes recorded acts and notable events of kings in annals and chronicles. These became more and more detailed until it was a standard way to record the past, particularly in monasteries.

Rise of Monasteries

The extensive and organized bureaucratic system of the Roman world depended upon a literate class of recordkeepers and historians. These same practices and the hierarchy of leadership carried on as the administrative structure of the Roman Church and in monasteries. Although the monastic orders worked closely with and overlapped with Church bureaucracy, they were independently organized and defined by charters and internal codes. The first of these was the *Rule of St. Benedict*, a treatise written to establish and define the monastic professions and communities. It became the basis of an expansive network of monastic houses, and it authorized a cloistered religious lifestyle – one isolated from the social life of the everyday community – as a divinely approved mission. Monastics devoted their energies to praying for the souls of the rest of a community, living frugally, and rejecting material possessions as had Christ.

St. Benedict knew that people living in a community needed regulation – and his rule sought to give examples and rules for everyday living in a monastic house. He believed first that all monks should *ora et labora*, that is, pray and work, every single day. To counter what he saw as the immorality of early medieval behaviors, Benedict believed that every monastic should work within the monastery for the good of the community. St. Cassiodorus, an Italian monk who lived just after the *Rule*'s inception, declared that transcription and translation was worthy work. By 600, the monastic initiative of copying and creating books, both religious and secular, was a major occupation of large monastic communities. Monks and nuns illuminated manuscripts with beautiful designs, human and divine figures, and strange, fanciful creatures. Occasionally they copied down literature and folk tales performed by oral storytellers. The Early

English epic poem *Beowulf* is one of these vernacular texts, as is the earliest surviving copy of the French epic about a hero of Charlemagne's army, *Song of Roland*, copied in Anglo-Norman in the mid-twelfth century.

> A medieval European book curse: "Whoever steals this book let him die the death; let be him be frizzled in a pan; may the falling sickness rage within him; may he be broken on the wheel and be hanged"

Precious manuscripts had to be protected and cared for. Finding that visitors often left with these cherished works of art tucked away in their travel cases, the monks at Hereford Cathedral, on the remote border of England and Wales, secured its valuable treasures by outfitting the bindings with loops for chains. At the end of a shelf of books, padlocks secured the chains.

Reverence of written history in North Africa is apparent in Timbuktu, Mali, where an estimated 700,000 manuscripts were and are preserved and protected in private homes. Many of these are medieval manuscripts produced in West Africa and the Sahara. Families are right to keep their books to themselves and keep them hidden. In 2013, rebels set fire to a historic library in the center of Timbuktu, destroying the manuscripts housed there, but those still in the hands of private citizens were smuggled out. Throughout this book, you will notice that much of the documentary evidence of the medieval period available for study has survived by accident. Another good example of this is the Cairo Geniza discussed in Chapter 1.

Fig 3.7
Chained library at Hereford Cathedral.
RDImages / Epics / Getty Images

Writing in Service of the State

China

At the end of the third century BCE, China's first emperor, Qin Sinhuangdi, established a system of bureaucratic governance fortified by a uniform legal code. For 2,000 years, this system was largely preserved, and the educated classes served as civil administrators and military advisors. In order to break into the bureaucratic system, young men studied a set of traditional texts heavily informed by the teachings of Confucius and took state-sponsored placement exams. As a form of government, bureaucracies are intricate networks of officers and committees obeying a strict hierarchy of communication and decision making, all of which is recorded in writing; thus, those who had a comfortable and influential role in China and its various tributary regions were literate and well versed in a specific canon of sacred and secular texts. In contrast to Europe, where documents were written on treated animal hides (parchment and vellum) into the 1500s, in China papermaking was invented around 100 CE and the process traveled to the Middle East in the eighth century, but it was not widespread until at least the 1300s. Paper became inexpensive and plentiful, but it does not have the longevity of parchment and vellum.

The Chinese writing system borrowed by Japan and areas of Southeast Asia is called *hanzi* (or *kanji* in Japanese), and it was fashioned of symbols that represent sounds, syllables, whole words, or whole concepts. These shared characters created a mutual literacy among the literate people of Asia even when they could not understand each other's oral language. Instead of being bilingual, they were biliterate; for instance, while the Chinese and Japanese used the same symbol for "field," the spoken Chinese word and the Japanese word for field are not the same. As a result, Chinese and Japanese diplomats negotiated through "brush talk," writing their different languages in mutually intelligible symbols. China's Buddhist monasteries were significant centers of writing and knowledge because Buddhist monasteries prized literacy (see Chapter 5).

Arabic Translation Movement

Like the Roman and Cyrillic alphabets, Arabic is a distant descendant of an early Phoenician writing system. In the century after Muhammad's death, the Arabic alphabet was put to significant use in the intellectual and administrative expansions across the Umayyad and Abbasid dynasties of caliphs, from the mid-seventh to the mid-tenth centuries CE. This explosive period of learning was inspired by a large-scale translation project championed most significantly by the caliph al-Mamun (d. 833). Scholars translated ancient Greek texts, such as those of Plato and Aristotle, alongside texts from Persian scientists and Indian

mathematicians. Some of them translated ancient treatises on medicine, mathematics, and astronomy from intermediate languages such as Pahlavi, a Persian
language subsumed by Islam in the seventh century. The effect of so much
spontaneous revelation of centuries of knowledge was rich and effective in producing a learned and contemplative culture, the basis of the quickly expanding
Islamic empire.

Al-Mamun's sponsored translation movement was part of a great think-tank
in the Abbasid capital of Baghdad, called the House of Wisdom. This period is
considered the Golden Age of Islam and the spirit of it pervaded all social classes.
The inventions and innovations made possible by this expansion of texts and
ideas endowed an enlightened and prosperous culture. From the House of
Wisdom came information about how to grow and sustain better crops, build
better and sturdier bridges and buildings, understand the geology and physics
of the Earth, and how to develop medicine important to the growing cosmopolitan success of Baghdad and the neighboring settlements. During this period,
there was an accepted writing system, a dynasty of great patrons, and a cultural
belief that those who participated in writing and learning would prosper spiritually and materially from the effort.

Wealthy patrons sent explorers out to search for documents and sponsored
scholars to learn the languages of the manuscripts and translate them into
Arabic. From China, Arabs imported knowledge of papermaking and book-
binding, and the book arts became a sophisticated art form. Calligraphers
earned high status, as did those who perfected the chemistry of dyes, glues,
and leather treatments. Much of the knowledge of the ancient world that was
first translated into Arabic was then translated into European languages. In
this exchange of knowledge, many Arabic words were absorbed into Western
languages, including sugar, coffee, mocha, algebra, and algorithm. It was
also through the Arabic translation movement that much of the legacy of
ancient Greek, Persian, and Indian scientific knowledge was transmitted to
the modern world.

The most famous translator of the age was Hunayn ibn Ishaq. Raised in the
ancient Christian city of Hira near Baghdad, Hunayn never converted to Islam;
however, he and his group of translators were given space and protection to
produce a vast library over his long life. His subsequent biographers presented
him as a great adventurer, searching the known world for manuscripts to copy.
And while these accounts appear to be legendary rather than historic, his contribution in preserving and advancing knowledge throughout the Muslim world,
Europe, and Byzantium is irrefutable. For instance, Hunayn kept a list of his
translations of the Greek physician Galen, 129 of them, and referred to them
to provide the first fully detailed anatomical drawings of the human eye in
Ten Treatises on the Eye. Later Arab-Muslim scholars elaborated on this Galenic
medical knowledge, developing their expertise through both academic study
of texts and practical knowledge. Ophthalmology, for example, became one of
the most important medical sciences of the Arab-Islamic world. Texts about the
eye and its diseases built upon that of Hunayn ibn Ishaq; tools and methods for

treatment of eye diseases were also developed and practiced, including removal of cataracts.

A Conquered Empire Lives in Story

Defeated and oppressed cultures do not always have the opportunity to record and preserve their mythologies, heroic epics, remembered history, and daily customs and rituals. These narratives are either assimilated into the culture of the dominant power or altogether lost. Often, the language disappears as well, leaving behind odd words and phrases whose origins become obscure. This could have been the fate of ancient Persians, except that the Arab Muslims were infatuated with the highly refined and cosmopolitan culture of the Persians whom they conquered, and they incorporated the culture into their own. While the armies of the Umayyad dynasty (661–750) conquered the Sassanian rulers and mostly replaced Zoroastrianism with Islam and Persian with Arabic, the cultural Persian heritage lived on in objects and stories.

Persian history begins in the sixth century BCE and the founding of the Achaemenid Empire by Cyrus the Great. For a thousand years, it was a significant rival of the ancient Greeks, and then the Romans, and a powerful force in the Middle East until its territories were subsumed into the Islamic Empire from the mid-seventh century forward. In this millennium of triumph and relatively stable state authority, generation upon generation built a storied and sophisticated intellectual and artistic tradition, which the new and aggressively expanding Arab nation admired. As a result, the second wave of Arab rulers, the Abbasids, claimed Baghdad as its capital, and tied itself culturally to the older Persian empire. The region was, however, too large for all areas to be uniformly controlled from Baghdad. In some regions, ethnic Persians continued Zoroastrian worship and folk customs for which we have some written witnesses (Zoroastrians still practice today; the largest populations are in India, Iran, and the United States).

An invaluable and unparalleled document of Persian cultural history is *Shahnemeh*, also called the *Persian Book of Kings*, which was finished in 1010 by the Muslim Persian Abolqasem Ferdowsi (b. 940). Writing in the service of nostalgic memory of a lost golden age, Ferdowsi produced 50,000 poetic lines of Persian history – mythical, legendary, and factual – beginning with the creation of the world according to Zoroastrian scripture, moving through the legendary and historical kings of Persia, and concluding with the final, deposed ruler of the Sassanian dynasty, Yazdegard III (624–651).

Ferdowsi's epic is an invaluable and unique repository of Persian lore. Although he references a few sources, nothing survives that equals the size and scope of his project. And while he includes customary praise of Muhammad at the beginning of the book, he resists superimposing Qur'anic or Arabic information on the Persian material. In its entirety, the *Shahnemeh* includes 50 rulers, and evaluations of their success or failure as leaders of their people. The heroes are not immortal or pure; they suffer and learn from their mistakes and faults. Bad rulers define core Persian values by the negative – a good leader does not behave that way. Several stand out. One is Rostam, a hero from the mythical past, who was destined from birth to be a great warrior and protect his people from aggressive foes and fantastical demons. Much like Hercules from Greek mythology or the knights of King Arthur's Round Table, Rostam faces challenges that define him as a semidivine defender of a righteous and superior people. In the Seven Trials of Rostam, he overcomes a fierce lion, incapacitating thirst, a dragon, a sorceress, the White Demon, and along the way makes a friend of an enemy, Olad. From there he rises to power and leads the Persians to many victories.

Another exceptional character is Sekandar, known in the west as Alexander the Great of Greece (Macedonia). In 330 BCE, Alexander conquered Darius III, the last king of the Achaemenid Empire and subsumed its territory into his great empire. From the Balkans to the Indus River, Alexander's armies conquered an impressive number of regions, including modern-day Armenia, Iran, Turkey, Iraq, Kuwait, Syria, Jordan, Israel, Palestine, Lebanon, Afghanistan, major parts

Fig 3.8
As the most popular hero of *Shahnemeh*, Rostam is often depicted in Islamicate literature. This mid-fifteenth-century illumination depicts Rostam taming Rakhsh, the foal that will grow to be Rostam's mighty steed and constant companion.
Metropolitan Museum of Art, The Grinnell Collection, Bequest of William Milne Grinnell, 1920, 20.120.240

Fig 3.9
Because the first of his great feats is killing a massive lion, Rostam is often shown in
a lion's skin (or here, more of a tiger pelt). This early fourteenth-century illustration
shows his enemy Olad (who will become his friend) tied to a tree. Olad knows the
secret to defeating the White Div (the Persian/Iranian word for demon) and his evil
cohort and helps Rostam to overcome the monster. In Ferdowsi's epic, Rostam cuts
out the demon's heart and liver and gives the liver to Olad as a sign of truce and
friendship.
Metropolitan Museum of Art, Rogers Fund, 1969, 69.74.7

of Egypt and Libya, the Black Sea coastal regions, and much of Central Asia. In
Persian lore, Alexander became a legendary leader and hero. He is also a great
figure of Islamic prehistory, appearing in the Qur'an as Dhul-Qarnayn and in
Arabic legend as al-Iskandar.

The final chapters of *Shahnemeh* are dedicated to the Sassanian dynasty, starting with its founder, Ardishir (180–242), whom Ferdowsi presents as an enlightened ruler, and extending to the inglorious death of the last Sassanian king, Yazdegard III (624–651). According to *Shahnemeh*, Yazdegard's forces were overwhelmed by the numerous and fierce Turks. Unhorsed and alone, he stumbled into a miller's barn. Coerced by Yazdegard's nemesis, Mahuy, the miller snuck up behind the king, stabbed him between the ribs, and threw his naked corpse into the mill pond. Monks happened upon the undignified scene and pulled the body from the pond. They tended to the body and created a proper burial place. And that marks the end of history.

In the last decades of the tenth century when Ferdowsi began the project, the ruling Samanids governed a population of mostly Sunni Muslims, with a small Shia minority, and even smaller and isolated Zoroastrian holdovers. The capital had moved to Samarkand, and there was some freedom to recover and appreciate pre-Arab Persian culture. However, by the time he finished his profound project, invaders known as the Ghaznavid Turks, a rival dynasty, easily deposed the ruling family, which was weakened by a succession crisis. The new leader, Mahmud of Ghazneh, had no interest in the poem or project, possibly because it often recounts Persian defeat of Turks, and Ferdowsi died impoverished and unappreciated. Nevertheless, his vast epic poem, written in the Persian of his time, is a significant witness to Persian history, mythology, language and its writing system and is one of the most frequently illustrated literary texts in the Islamicate world.

Looking Forward

The efforts to gain, extend, and maintain political authority and control over people, land, and resources was long and arduous. Rulers sought to bring regions under submission through warfare, through the control and dissemination of information, knowledge, and justice. Using religious and philosophical precepts aided emperors and kings in the creation of common identity among their disparate peoples. Although few dynasties resolved their succession issues, the structures these groups put in place allowed later groups to define and solidify their territories into more modern states.

Latin is written in the Roman alphabet, and in medieval Western Europe it was the language of scholarship, religion, and diplomacy. As Roman Christianity spread throughout the region, the Roman alphabet was adapted for writing languages that had very little written tradition. A different writing system was favored by the Byzantine Orthodox Church. Across Eastern Europe, the Cyrillic alphabet was fitted to Slavic languages and dialects of this region. Chinese culture continued to use and adapt an ancient system of symbol writing, which Japan and Southeast Asian cultures borrowed and adapted. And, as the Islamicate world grew, the Arabic writing system as used in printed

Qur'ans became the prestige script, replacing and eclipsing pre-existing writing practices, some of which are now undecipherable.

Research Questions

1. Women feature prominently in Chinese and Japanese empires. Research why those areas allowed for female rulers. Why is female rule the exception and not the norm?
2. Explore writing systems. How have they changed over time? What has stayed constant?
3. Look at examples of cultures that have been oppressed or ignored but are now taken seriously by historians (for example, the Sogdians or Tocharians) and compare them to current oppressed or ignored groups, like the Uighurs or Zoroastrian Iranians.
4. Research minority religions within one of the empires/kingdoms mentioned in the text. How did Zoroastrians fare in Iran? Jews in Spain? Christians in China?
5. Focus on one character in the *Shahnemeh*. What are the strengths and weaknesses of that character? If the person is heroic, what are the features of his or her success? Are his or her deeds physical (strength in battle), moral (devotion to the divine), or intellectual (promotion of learning). If the person is bad, what is the definition of his or her failures? From this evidence, determine how Ferdowsi and his people defined a good ruler or person.
6. A thesis of this book is that even though cultures across the globe between 500 and 1500 may have had very little direct contact with each other, there are connections to be made across cultures that are worth considering. What are challenges to our historical method and thesis?

Further Reading

Bloom, Jonathan. *Paper Before Print: The History and Impact of Paper in the Islamic World*. New Haven, CT: Yale University Press, 2001.

Camille, Michael. *Image on the Edge: The Margins of Medieval Art*. London: Reaktion Books, 2004.

Dabashi, Hamid. *Authority in Islam: From the Rise of Muhammad to the Establishment of the Umayyads*. New Brunswick, NJ: Transaction Publishers, 1989.

Ferdowsi, Abolqasem. *Shahnemeh: The Persian Book of Kings*. Translated by Dick Davis. New York: Penguin Books, 2016.

Friday, Karl F. *Samurai, Warfare and the State in Early Medieval Japan*. New York: Routledge, 2004.

Hammer, Joshua. *The Badass Librarians of Timbuktu: And Their Race to Save the World's Most Precious Manuscripts*. New York: Simon & Schuster, 2017.

Karam, Jonathan. *Sui-Tang China and Its Turko-Mongol Neighbors: Culture, Power, and Connections, 580–800*. Oxford: Oxford Scholarship Online, 2012.

McKitterick, Rosamund. *Charlemagne: The Formation of a European Identity*. Cambridge: Cambridge University Press, 2008.

Robinson, Andrew. *The Story of Writing: Alphabets, Hieroglyphs & Pictograms*. London: Thames & Hudson, 2007.

Sonn, Tamara. *Islam: History, Religion, Politics*. Chichester: Wiley, 2015.

Timbuktu Manuscripts. Manuscript Project organized through the University of Cape Town. Tombouctoumanuscripts.org.

Yamamura, Kozo, ed. *The Cambridge History of Japan*. Vol. 3. Cambridge: Cambridge University Press, 1990.

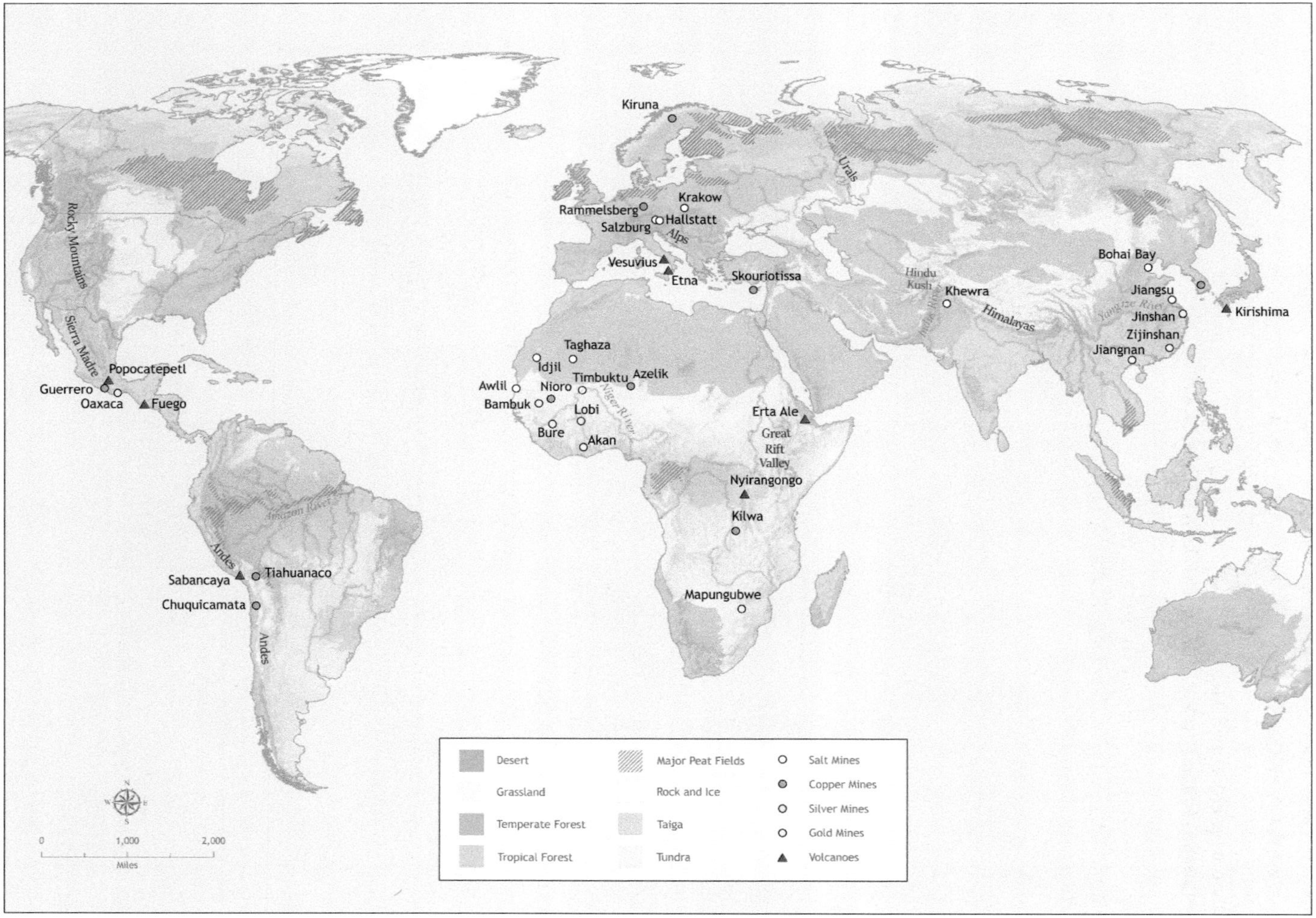

Map 4

Sustainability and Climate Change

Sustainability and Climate Change

Society, 500–900

Introduction

Textbooks on human history typically introduce students to the grand events, colossal structures, and life-changing processes that have the most impact on the ages that follow. However, humans have survived largely because of the regular and methodical repetition of basic life-sustaining practices by everyday people and their innovations in horticulture, livestock breeding, and construction of dwellings, irrigation systems, and fortifications. Even though they are unnamed and unmentioned in the chronicles of the great kingdoms, working people made life possible for those who made history. Peasants enabled the lives of the ruling and educated classes and received almost no attention unless famine and plague reduced circumstances for everyone, or peasants rebelled against heavy tax and labor burdens or military conscription. In this chapter on society, we explore peasant cultures in Europe and East Asia.

The medieval laboring classes were often indistinguishable from slaves. Sometimes they *were* slaves, captured by traders and put to work in fields, rice paddies, and hunting grounds far from their birthplaces. These peasants (subsistence farmers, agricultural laborers, and slaves) were acutely attuned to the cycle of the seasons. In the first half of this chapter, we describe farming methods that supported population growth in Europe and in eastern Asia from 500 to 900. Population growth resulted from innovations in sustainable environmental practices and favorable climate change. In the second half, we look to the imaginative ways average people managed their anxiety about weather disasters, agricultural failures, and raids by invaders. They had customs, rituals, and ceremonies to thank the gods and spirits for an ample harvest, or to appease the threatening and angry forces of nature. They had ways to celebrate unexpected bounty and to cope with equally unexpected losses. Often, when natural disasters happened, survivors were forced to migrate to new lands, taking their spiritual beliefs, histories, and talents with them. Their folk stories and customs overlapped and blended with those of the communities where they settled.

A: PEASANT NATURE

Introduction

It is difficult to capture information about the life of a premodern common person. Most texts were written for and about the secular or spiritual elite. Much of the archeological evidence we have for this period is from the buried grave goods of high-status nobles and rulers or the ruins of castles and temples. Average people survived because of sustainable practices that did not leave behind much to see. They used and reused organic materials that eventually decayed or rusted away. They melted down old tools and repurposed the metals. They restored and repaired wooden furniture, carts, and ship masts until they degraded or were used for parts. They patched together woven fabrics or animal hides until they disintegrated. Nothing was wasted, not even feces, human or animal. Across Eurasia, villagers had a constant need for fertilizer, and both human and livestock waste was "cured" (left for a time to release harmful gases and pathogens) in pits or pots and placed on the fields at regular intervals. Since human waste was a vital resource, all foods collected from fields fertilized with it needed to be boiled to kill off any parasites lingering in the grains.

Despite the intense recycling and repurposing, archeologists and historians have recovered material evidence about the lives of these peoples whose agriculture provided the basis for all economies, and for most social, cultural, religious, and political practices. By clearing forests, moving water, terracing land, and enclosing pastures, peasants manipulated their landscapes to provide food for themselves, local markets, their immediate lords and spiritual leaders, and, ultimately, their kings or emperors.

Evidence:	Bernuthsfeld Man
	Mummy (Momia) Juanita or the Lady of Ampato
	Calendar pages of Ms. Ludwig IX 18, The J. Paul Getty Museum, Los Angeles
	Soy sauce

Mummies

Despite the scarcity of historical records and archeological evidence pertaining to the lives of medieval peasants, some naturally occurring processes provide a small window into the lives of commoners. We know about the ancient Egyptians and their practice of mummifying the pharaohs, but there are also natural ways that human bodies can become mummified: if the body is frozen; if the body is buried in a very dry place with preservative minerals, such as a salt mine; or if the body is submerged in a peat bog. Bodies of premodern people have been found in all three situations, and they provide a glimpse into the life of that regular person. Here, we discuss the evidence left to us by a "bog body" from south Germany known as Bernuthsfeld Man, and the body of a young girl entombed in ice in the high Andes.

A peat bog is a low-lying, waterlogged area of land that, over time, becomes filled with decaying plant matter (peat). Typically, peat bogs are covered in a layer of moss that soaks up all of the area's oxygen, meaning that the layers of plant matter beneath the top layer receive little to no aeration. This process slowly but steadily increases the acidity of the bog, making the area inhospitable for living organisms, even bacteria. Because of this acidification, the bacteria responsible for decomposition cannot easily survive in the bog, which causes a near full-stop in the decay of any organic matter within the bog itself. While the organic matter within the bog typically consists solely of plant matter, occasionally peat farmers will make more shocking discoveries as they dig through the layers, including mummified human remains, called "bog bodies," some having died tens of thousands of years ago.

One example of a "bog body," called Bernuthsfeld Man, provides some insight into the lives of medieval peasants. In 1907 in Lower Saxony, Germany, teenage brothers, aged 16 and 18, were digging for blocks of peat that their family used as fuel for cooking and heating fires. They unearthed a strange, clothed skeleton, which spooked them. Because the boys thought they might be accused of a crime, they reburied it elsewhere. Local authorities found out, recovered it, and determined that it was of archeological importance. Although the body itself was not extraordinarily well preserved, the clothing the man wore was almost completely intact. His outfit consisted of a well-worn tunic, a wool cloak, leg wrappings, and a sheath for some sort of knife.

When he was submerged in the peat bog, Bernuthsfeld Man wore a tunic patched together from over 40 pieces of hand-spun, hand-woven wool from 20 fabrics of different patterns and colors. In analyzing the details of his outerwear, we learn about medieval clothing for an average person with access to sheep's wool. It is an amazing sampler of the ways premodern peoples spun yarn from fleece and wove different patterns for textiles for everyday use. The fact that his tunic was almost entirely patched highlights the importance of sustainable practice for medieval peasants: it took weeks for a person or people to craft a new piece of clothing, gathering and spinning the wool, weaving the threads back and forth through the warp, and sewing the completed pieces. Because clothing materials were expensive, and the crafting itself was time-consuming, it was important for peasants to maintain their clothes as best they could and to recycle old clothing, getting the most out of every bit of material gathered or purchased. In his moss-lined peat grave, Bernuthsfeld Man was also wrapped in a thick, wool coat. Why the tunic and coat were not saved for someone else is curious: the clothing is a rare find.

Most bog bodies are from the Iron Age (ca. 500 BCE–100 CE), usually sacrifices, carefully killed, arranged, and buried in moss within the peat. But

Bernuthsfeld Man is different – he did not live in the Iron Age. Analysis of his head hairs places his death in the seventh or eighth century – much later than other bog bodies. The science of forensic pathology becomes more sophisticated all the time, providing added and different information about finds such as this, but the current thinking is that this man was in his forties when he died from cancer. He lived a life with considerable pain, as both hips had osteo-arthritis, and he had at least one healed rib fracture. Also, his spine showed blockage, possibly from an inflammatory disease. Why his corpse ended up in the bog is a mystery.

Another mummy who has provided insight into the lives of people outside written history is Juanita, the Inca Ice Maiden. Juanita was discovered atop Mount Ampato, a mountain near the Hualca Hualca volcano in the Peruvian Andes. She and several others were sacrificed in the 1470s, after a series of volcanic eruptions from the nearby volcanoes Misti and Sabancaya, which had been erupting since 1440. These eruptions likely added to the climatic changes that scholars call the Little Ice Age, where global temperatures dropped precipitously, particularly in the Northern Hemisphere. Like the Moche and the Maya in the earlier Medieval Climate Anomaly, Inca sought to placate their gods by sacrificial acts. After the volcanic eruptions, a series of devastating droughts affected the Inca highlands, and famine and insurrection threatened the Inca leaders. Sacrificing children, the purest gift, was an act they hoped would appease the gods, calm the volcanoes, and create rain.

Fig 4.1
Juanita/Lady of Ampato.
JAIME RAZURI / AFP via Getty Images

Juanita was dressed royally, another proof of her importance as a sacrifice, and her clothing was also exceptionally well preserved. She was found wearing a *lliclla* – a rectangular shoulder-wrap still worn by people in the Andes – as well as an *aksu* (a sort of tunic) and a belt. These textiles are beautifully patterned in gold, red, white, and purple, which together constitute the royal colors of the Inca. All her garments are sized too large for Juanita, as the Inca believed death to be more of an entryway than an exit; scholars believe this indicates that the Inca who clothed Juanita before the sacrifice assumed she would grow in her next state of being and wanted to ensure her clothes would still fit. Although Juanita went to her death wrapped in royal garments, underneath she wore plain clothes in simpler colors, chiefly gray. The outer robes, of royal quality, were a gift to honor the gods, as was the peasant girl herself.

Much like Bernuthsfeld Man's clothing, scholars believe Juanita's simpler garments had been repaired several times. This indicates that, rather than being born into royalty, Juanita was a peasant selected by the royals and priests to be sacrificed, whereupon she was dressed in more expensive and intricate clothing. Juanita also had a knapsack with some small items, such as shells and hair clippings. Scholars believe that these clippings are from Juanita's first haircut. In many rural areas of coastal Peru today, parents plan elaborate feasts for their children's first haircuts, and the hair is gathered to be used in magical ceremonies; could Juanita's hair have been from a similar custom, hundreds of years ago? Judging from the clothing she was wearing, Juanita immediately rose in sacrifice from a peasant to a princess.

IS IT WRONG TO RECOVER AND MOVE THE HUMAN REMAINS AND SACRED OBJECTS OF INDIGENOUS PEOPLES?

Juanita is one of the most well-preserved mummies known, and people were, and still are, very interested in seeing her. Her discovery has inspired ethical debates across the fields of archeology and anthropology about who owns and can exhibit a 500-year-old body. For several years after she was found, her body was exhibited in Japan and Washington, DC, until Peruvians demanded that she be repatriated. She is now on display in the Andean Sanctuary Museum in Arequipa. The people of Cabanaconde, Peru, the village where Juanita was discovered, have enjoyed heightened visitor populations and the interest of the entire world since the mummy was unearthed, but many of the villagers view Juanita as a sacred member of their own history and culture. Some believe that Juanita's removal from the village has angered the mountain deities and will lead to misfortune.

On the other hand, Juanita's discovery was only made possible by the eruption of a nearby volcano: the eruption triggered a melt on Mount Ampato, which exposed Juanita's body. Had the researchers who discovered the mummy *not* removed her, the body would have decomposed and been lost to the world forever. Which is the more important consideration: the intent of the mid-fifteenth-century Andean community or the historical information to be learned from the rare find? This paradox is a microcosm for a much larger debate across numerous research fields about the ethics of removing artifacts from their original setting for study. Is it more or less ethical to do so when, if not removed, the artifacts would be destroyed? There are no clear answers, and scholars have only begun seriously wrestling with these questions. Until recently, the custom has been for the politically stronger culture to take what it wanted.

Another example of this debate relates to the removal and study of objects from Native American cultures of North America. Chaco Canyon, for example (see later chapters), is the subject of ongoing debate between the archeologists and museums who want to study the objects, human remains, and DNA of the Ancestral Puebloans. Modern Pueblo people insist that all such studies must be done in collaboration with the modern descendants of the Chacoans and with respect for their traditions.

These debates relate more broadly to the issue of removing objects from their contexts. Many items that end up in museums are decontextualized, and their display may contradict the wishes of the modern nations where they were discovered, or those of the descendants of ancient Indigenous peoples – some of whom wish to have their ancestral material objects returned to the earth rather than be archeologically recovered. Other objects in museums have been looted or improperly removed from their country of origin.

Agricultural Neighborhoods

Most peasants lived in villages, social and geographical units whose members worked together. A village generally included outer fields (where the large farming occurred), houses and close fields (for family horticulture), and community buildings. Pre-industrial farming required substantial communal cooperation. All cereal grain farming (like rice, oats, barley, and millet) was labor-intensive. Land was cleared and plowed by hand, seeds were planted, tended, and reaped by hand. Wooden and metal tools aided the process, but these tools also required specialized labor (blacksmithing) to create and repair. Draft animals took on some of the labor, but their purchase and upkeep were also expensive (animals eat grain that could, instead, be used to feed people). In many villages, farm equipment and animals were held as common property, which distributed their cost and their effectiveness over the whole village. Pre-industrial farming was burdensome and expensive, and the group needs outweighed those of any individual. Fields tended to be close to the villages, within easy walking distance, and, while men managed the heavy labor, women and children were no less vital to seeding and harvesting. Most villages held between 30 and 60 families, with some villages gaining prominence as crossroads and spaces for markets. Nuclear families were the norm in most agricultural groups in Eurasia, with a man marrying only when he had enough money to build a house.

In Europe, parents lived with their children in a one- or two-room house, with an open fire pit in the center. Packed-dirt floors, grass thatch roofs, and wooden walls mostly kept out the elements and vermin, but peasants still dealt with cold, heat, mice, and lice, indoors as well as out, in addition to suffering from injury, illness, fatigue, poor sanitation, and starvation. A wattle and daub home was constructed by interweaving a series of vertical wooden pillars (or wattles) with sticks and "daubing" the structure with mud as a sealant. This method of home building was used not only in medieval Europe but all over the world. It is a relatively simple and inexpensive process, lending well to the seminomadic conditions of European society, but without windows and with only one door, the interior of the hut was dark, dank, and smoky. The fire pit served as the house center, a source of warmth, pest control, and a food preparation area. Chimneys were not invented until the twelfth century and were not common in Eurasia until the sixteenth.

Peasant homes were intentionally constructed with the inevitability of relocation in mind, but this inevitability was, nonetheless, undesirable. Staying in one place longer offered protective advantages, as well as increases in productivity. Prepared soil enriched by human and animal waste, as well as sustainable farming techniques, progressively increased the productivity of small plots that surrounded a family's hut, as well as larger plots of land used for wide-scale agriculture. Leaving a village behind meant that the villagers would have to start new gardens and new farms, without the enriched soil, somewhere else. They had to adapt to new ecosystems and establish new support systems, as they were heavily reliant on communal living – if a village community was accustomed to the resources available in a nearby forest, but reestablished in an area surrounded by meadows and pastures, each person in that village must adapt to new agricultural methods; for example, where there may have been honey to gather and game to hunt in the forest outside the village they left, there may not be such food sources in a new environment with rivers or near the sea. Relocating often meant encroaching on another community's resources, leading to hostilities and violence.

As we saw in earlier chapters, the increased raids and conquests of the early medieval period disrupted peasant communities and seminomadic peoples alike. These groups could not defend themselves against invaders and needed to be defended by stronger warlords around them. They traded their freedom for safety, and the trade-off turned into economic, political, and social systems. European peasants lived under the protection of a local elite nobleman on what is known as a manor. Depending on the particular region, the noblemen and their families either owned the land outright, or were given it by their kings as a reward for service. Agricultural workers were bound, through their labor, to a local lord in what we call the manorial system. Every adult peasant had obligations – legal, political, and physical – to the nobleman of the region.

Tools, animals, streams, and lakes were all used in common by the community of villagers. Despite the obligations owed to the lord, peasant villages in Europe were often in flux; depending on the health of the land or the whims of the nobles, the village itself might change size or move locations. Most of the structures in a village were insubstantial, and houses generally only survived for a single generation. Archeologists continue to work on uncovering the lives of peasants and their communities, learning that local resources, climate, and economics affected the types and durability of the structures.

Peasant Foods: Salt and Beer

Peasants adapted to change constantly; weather, famines, wars, raids, and other events disrupted planting cycles. Nevertheless, these peasants innovated their agricultural practices and technologies over time, absorbing new ideas from other communities and cultures while expanding their own knowledge. They came up with sustainable practices and survival tactics that, in the present day, we take entirely for granted. Take, for instance, the tremendous usefulness and importance of salt, a mineral not only essential to cell function in the human body, but also useful in hundreds of everyday ways that make life possible and even comfortable. These applications are the result of centuries of cultural exchanges of field workers, kitchen servants, and merchants, who observed the useful properties of salt and applied them in clever ways.

Salt flavors food, but more important is its function in preserving food through dry, cold winters, hot monsoon seasons, long sea voyages, desert camel caravans, and military campaigns in enemy territory. Until the invention of refrigeration in the mid-twentieth century, pickled vegetables, fruits, and cured meats were essential food sources across the globe. Pickling and curing require salt, which was a valuable commodity – so valuable that Roman troops were partially paid in salt (Latin *sal*), thus giving us the words *salary* and *soldier*. Salt was a major trade good, fueling much of the trans-Saharan exchange in Africa, and, in many areas, such as China, salt was used for taxation purposes.

Soaking fruit and vegetables in heavily salted water (a brine bath) is part of a process called lacto-fermentation. As food begins to decay, salt kills harmful bacteria and encourages beneficial bacteria to convert sugars in the fruit or vegetables into lactic acid. Lactic acid preserves not only the flavor and texture of food but also its nutrients. Salt is also the main ingredient in curing meats; it prevents decay by drawing water from cells. A medieval person would take a clay jar or barrel and layer in cuts of meat with generous amounts of salt, store the containers in a temperate place, and let the chemistry happen. In addition, the meat could be smoked, which enhanced the preservation process and required less salt. As long as a community was stable (for instance, not disrupted by disease, natural disaster, or looting), both of these processes were efficient and easy. By using salt, medieval people were able to preserve foods without refrigeration, keeping food safe and healthful for human consumption.

Asian cultures used, and still use, lactic-acid fermentation to preserve fish, making a condiment generically called fish sauce or Asian garum (after the fermented fish sauce that was wildly popular in the ancient Roman world). Each culture has a name for its own variety. In Thai food, for instance, it is called *nam pla*. To make fish sauce, fish innards and other unused portions of fish are soaked for some time in brine. Eventually the solid parts are strained out, leaving a flavored liquid that lasts a long time and travels well. The Chinese often mixed soybeans in with the fish parts, eventually removing the fish entirely, inventing a soy-based flavoring. Around the sixth century, the Japanese adopted it as soy sauce.

As testimony to the preservative properties of salt, the dried-out but rec- ognizable bodies of workers who died in salt mines have been found by later generations. In 1993, workers in the Chehrabad Salt Mine in Iran found the mummified body of a man dating to about 300 CE. Perhaps because of its power to prevent decay, salt had a major role in the spiritual practices of premodern folk cultures. As a giver of life, it was used as an essential ingre- dient in fertility potions. It was thought to turn away the evil eye, and there- fore was placed in charms and set on mantles as a good luck talisman or used as a protective circle around homes. (Does anyone you know throw a pinch over their shoulder if they spill some salt?) Some cultures equate salt with truth and wisdom – to be the "salt of the earth" is to have practical, humble, good sense.

Because of salt's many practical and spiritual uses, those areas where salt was readily available had a trading advantage over other cultures. China was the first state to organize a monopoly on salt production and trade, and, for the Tang dynasty (618–907), salt was responsible for half the state revenue. Its importance increased in the tenth century, when the Chinese mixed a salt called potassium nitrate with sulfur and carbon, inventing gunpowder. Where it occurred as a mineral deposit, salt mining was a vigorous and important business. Named for its productive salt mines, Salzburg, Germany, was one of the areas that benefited from the salt trade, as did regions in present-day Poland.

There were other ways to harvest salt. It could be gleaned from the edges of salt-water lakes and tidal pools or soaked out of the desert sand. For example, Africans living south of the Sahara Desert needed to import salt from the communities who mined it from salt flats in the desert or from farther north, along the Mediterranean shore. In fact, the exchange of Mediterranean salt for African gold fueled one of the most vibrant commercial networks in the medieval period, trans-Saharan trade (discussed in later chapters). The peasants who tended to these salt works developed many creative ways of recovering salt. They dug systems of solar evaporation ponds, where incoming sea water was funneled and left to evaporate, leaving behind salt crystals. In their effort to reach underground brine springs, Chinese workers became experts at deep well drilling, sometimes discovering natural gas along the way. In all salt works, labor was organized by the physical difficulty in harvesting the deposits; for

Fig 4.2
The Wieliczka Salt Mine near Krakow, Poland, is an example of the power of salt
to stabilize economies and fund grand projects. For most of the medieval period,
surface salt springs enriched the regional economy near Krakow, but in the eleventh
century salt springs began drying up. At that point, the Wieliczka miners dug
underground, eventually creating an intricate 100 miles of tunnels, the deepest of
which is 1,000 feet. Backed by revenue from salt, Casimir the Great (1310–1370)
founded the first university of Poland.
ewg3D / iStock

instance, in the salt marshes of western France, women skimmed off the light
salt crystals that drying winds formed on the top of salt pools. This delicate sea
salt is called fleur de sel. No matter the economic power and elite politics, the
working classes perpetually innovated to increase and streamline the production of salt and put it to use in new ways.

Beer, ale, and other alcoholic beverages also contributed heavily to diets in
the Middle Ages. It is a myth that medieval people did not drink water and that
most water was "bad" and therefore medieval men and women quaffed alcohol
for its safety. There is no doubt that the fermentation process does aid in making
questionable water safer, but there is no evidence that medieval people avoided
water. Medical texts from China to Europe praised the benefits of water for
their patients, and urban centers worked to ensure clean water supplies for their
inhabitants. The early English historian Bede (d. 735) wrote that the king of
Northumbria ordered wells in public thoroughfares to have bronze cups to help
travelers quench their thirst. Nevertheless, water never engendered the poetry
and the praise saved for wine, ale, and other alcoholic beverages.

The earliest brewed beer is Chinese, from ca. 7000 BCE, although beer could
be at least as old as bread. From the earliest written records in Mesopotamia to

the modern world, brewed and fermented beverages occupy space within the legislative and personal accounts of empires and individuals alike. Almost all cereal grains in the Middle Ages could be fermented to create alcoholic beverages of different strengths and consistencies. Rice ferments in 48 hours and can be drunk in as little as 72 hours. Barley was a favorite grain to ferment in northern Europe, and grapes in southern Europe became a luxury trade item across the region. Ales are the oldest brewed beverages, made with a top-fermenting yeast that produces "small beer" in around seven days. This thick ale was about one percent alcohol and could be mixed with grain to create a porridge.

Almost all these beverages were brewed at home by women. Peasant women across the world created beverages for their families and, occasionally, for profit. Brewing was a weekly process and, if a woman could produce excess, or her ales/wines were known to be delicious, she might sell the surplus for additional income. Most weekly beverages were probably low alcohol, while higher-alcohol-content drinks were brewed for special occasions. A particular strain of ale known as "groaning beer" was created in Europe for birthing women, which included sweeteners and was served to midwives and mothers during the birthing process. Some areas, like Syria and Germany became known for their beer production.

Like salt, beer and alcohol were consumed for more than just flavor. Functionally, these beverages were also nourishing, adding calories and carbohydrates to the diet. Scientists speculate that the average non-industrialized farmer today expends between 3,000 to 4,000 calories daily, meaning that they need to eat at least that much to maintain themselves. Rice and breads average about 80 calories a serving. Beans and fish average about 100–150 calories a serving. Adding beer, ales, and rice wines (between 80–100 calories per serving) to these meals increased the caloric intake, while also providing carbohydrates and some fiber. Beer and rice wine were not just recreational drinks but essential nutritional supplements for a largely peasant community.

Agricultural Revolution in Europe

In Europe, as in China during the period 500–900, land clearing and cultivation increased. Wet weather, plagues, and wars of the sixth and seventh centuries had curtailed population growth, and, in northern Europe in particular, peasants lived in small population pockets surrounded by wilderness. Since, at any moment, war and disease could disrupt or destroy the planting and harvesting cycle, peasants continued to innovate new labor-saving devices. In Europe, the large farming estates of the ancient Roman world were divided into smaller plots of land, meaning that peasants who farmed that land needed to do more with less. They could not depend upon urban food markets for variety, so they had to plant all the different foods they needed for their villages. Early medieval Europeans increased the area of land under cultivation (clearing forests and bog lands), planted new types of foods (particularly important were wheat, rye, barley, hops, legumes, and oats), and innovated crop-rotation systems (see below), which resulted in more agricultural yield and, therefore, a rise in population.

We often think of inventing something brand new as a dramatic revelation by an individual genius, but great inventions are usually a product of many, many moments of imagination by ordinary people that add up to a dynamic, unforeseen result. It is easy to overlook the important, life-sustaining creativity of countless generations of people going about daily chores. For example, the heavy plow was one of the most important innovations in European agriculture. Prior to the eighth century, most Europeans used a "scratch plow" or a light plow that merely scratched the surface of the soil. A man pushing this plow created a very shallow furrow in which to drop seeds. We cannot think of "Europe" as being a singular space any more than we can think of "China" or "Africa" as being singular spaces. Even within short distances, differences in terrain, weather, and culture created distinct agricultural regions. The plow worked well in the sandy soils of southern Europe, but very poorly in the clay soils of the north. The larger, heavier iron plow allowed for a completely turned furrow that cut through the thick turf and provided drainage for the wetter, heavier soil of northern Europe.

A single man, however, struggled to push this heavier plow, and draft animals became more important. Slight increases in fodder allowed some peasant families to afford livestock, which improved their ability to work larger fields, get bigger yields, and grow more food. Livestock also allowed a farmer to work more quickly and to farm more land in a single day; oxen and horses were the most important plow animals. Technological innovations related to farm animals in the early medieval period helped make those animal-human partnerships more effective. One important example is the horse-collar harness, which rests on both the horse's shoulders and breast rather than the back, neck, or throat. This allowed the horse to use its power without putting any pressure on its neck, and thus pull the heavier plow for longer. Another example is the iron horseshoe, which protected horses' feet from injury and allowed them to pull carts and plows over a variety of terrains.

Additionally, a new system of farming that began during the ninth and tenth centuries greatly increased both the food production of medieval Europe and the nutrient production for medieval peasants. Most medieval farms grew cereals like rye, millet, buckwheat, and oats; wheat was a more difficult and more expensive grain to grow. These grains worked well in northern European climates and created almost enough nutrients to sustain a peasant family, but they depleted nitrogen from the soil. Continually using the same fields year after year would eventually exhaust the soil and grain would not grow. Nitrogen can be introduced back into the soil by using fertilizers (human and animal) and by letting the soil "rest" for a year. This resting, or letting strips lie fallow, created a "two-field" crop rotational system. Half of the land was cultivated, the other rested in order to replenish some of the nutrients in the soil. With a general lack of draft animals, fertilizer was expensive and highly prized.

A major innovation by medieval peasantry changed this system from a two-field to a three-field rotation. The land was separated out into three sections: one to lie fallow, the second to grow grains, and the third planted with legumes. Legumes – such as peas, lentils, or beans – made their way into the fields and diets of the peasants and had a massive positive impact on the agricultural and nutritional profile of early medieval Europe. The beauty of legumes is twofold: they are nitrogen-fixing and protein-enriching. More legumes meant improved nitrogen to nourish grains; and more food and more protein meant healthier peasants who live longer lives.

Medieval Europeans lived mostly off grains, in the forms of porridge, bread, and beer: wheat (as produced by the lower classes) for the upper classes, and millet, oats, and rye for the lower classes. Vegetables like cabbages, onions, turnips, and carrots enhanced their diets (these vegetables added fiber, vitamins, and folate). Most nobles, however, avoided "peasant fare" such as beans and lentils. The upper classes could afford meat on a regular basis, so much so that gout (a form of arthritis that flares up when one consumes too much meat and alcohol) was a special problem of the wealthy. Peasants ate meat only rarely. The poorer folk ate fava beans and peas, protein- and nitrogen-rich legumes. Milk and cheeses also added protein to their diets.

This increase in food production led to an increase in population. Although this seems like a simple mathematical equation – more food equals more people – both the amount and the types of calories are helpful here. Additional protein strengthens the body and creates a better diet overall, which particularly helped European peasant women. More calories allowed women to be stronger entering into pregnancy, supported their stamina during the labor process, and increased their children's birth weight. This meant that more women and children survived the birthing process. Healthier mothers produced breast milk for longer, and, subsequently, more of these well-fed children survived to adulthood. Although we do not have hard data, we estimate that the population in Europe increased substantially between the end of the Roman Empire to the beginning of the early modern period, with the majority of that growth happening between 1000 and 1300: the population of Europe was about 50 million in 600 and 90 million by 1500; for comparison, Germany in 2020 had about 83 million people. This population increase led to other incredible advances in European societies, economies, and intellectual and political systems, which we will discuss in later chapters.

Urbanization

By around the year 1000, the increase in population that resulted from these agricultural innovations had created a serious burden on peasantries. These communities could not handle the excess population, and young people began to move out of the family village. In some areas, this led to the clearing of new and marginal lands for settlement. Particularly in places like Holland

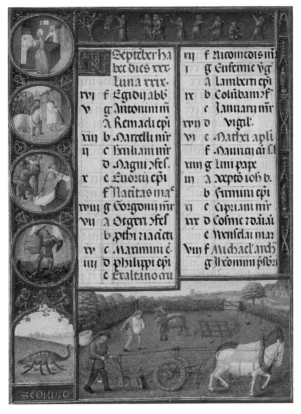

Fig 4.3
A late medieval calendar page shows peasants preparing the soil for fall planting. In the foreground is the heavy plow, which was better able to turn over the heavy, wet soil of northern Europe than the ancient Roman "scratch plow." In the back, a harrow (consisting of a frame with tines) is dragged across the soil to break up clods and weeds. Both are horse-drawn, although medieval farmers also used oxen. The horses wear a padded horse collar, which protected their necks from injury and fatigue and allowed them to sustain significant pulling power over longer periods.
The J. Paul Getty Museum, Los Angeles, Ms. Ludwig IX 18, fol. 5v

and Germany, swamps were drained and forests cleared to accommodate new peasant communities. But there was also an increase in the populations of urban centers. Although peasants who lived under the bonds of serfdom were required to stay within their village confines unless they had the lord's permission to leave, the increased population meant that it was difficult to sustain those new lives, and many moved to find work, causing urban growth that had not been seen since the Roman Empire. The Roman world was a network of cities, but, by 600, most of the people living in the cities were religious clergy and the urban poor, and European kings could no longer collect urban taxes, which resulted in the decline of monetization within Frankish kingdoms. Around 1000 CE, as more peasants moved to cities and others desired the safety of town walls, cities began reviving. Some cities grew out of old Roman towns, like Cologne in Germany, and others grew in places that fit the needs of the local population – at a new shrine, a market center, or near a bridge.

Cities offered the possibility of more personal freedom, which encouraged many to flee their farming roots. The population explosion within the cities created new markets, which peasant villages could supply with food. Many early medieval cities grew up around Christian pilgrimage sites, meaning that the population size fluctuated as pilgrims came and went. Around those sites arose a number of institutions that served such populations: markets, taverns, entertainments, and trinket-sellers. As city populations continued to grow, an artisanal class arose, along with the workshops and markets where they produced their goods. Markets opened to sell surplus food, finished goods, and luxury items gained from the trade routes that crisscrossed Europe, the Mediterranean, and deep into Asia. Early medieval European traders had furs, amber, timber, tin, silver, and finished textiles (particularly woolen ones) to offer, and they imported goods like silk, sugar, linen, dyestuffs, and spices.

This increase in trade led to a new need for coinage, and greater access to the metals needed to mint them. As shown above, the monetized economy of the Romans faded under the European kingdoms, as kings could not collect taxes in coins and many could not yet mint their own coins. The monied economy developed in tandem with the growth of both regional and long-distance trade. This increase in trade fed the growth of the economy, which would, in the central period, lead to increasingly bureaucratic state systems staffed by paid administrators. Typically, these clerks were educated at cathedral schools, but, by the twelfth century, there were an increasing number of universities in urban centers.

Chinese Agriculture: Rice

> "Rice is vitality, rice is vigor too, and rice is indeed the means of fulfillment of all ends of life" (Indian Krishi Parashara, ca. 500 BCE).

Despite China having the most and largest urbanized spaces in the medieval world, most people lived in rural communities. Several cities had populations near 500,000, but all their food was imported from surrounding farms. Although not every village had its own market, there was generally one within an hour's walk. Within these smaller markets, peasants could buy and sell produce and finished products; they could also visit teahouses and meeting areas, and find scribes willing to write out contracts, wills, or other important documents. These smaller markets connected villages to large urban centers, creating a symbiotic relationship between the large rural and smaller urban areas of China.

Chinese peasants built "rammed earth" homes made by compacting soil into forms with tiled floors and thatched roofs. Commonly one large room with only a door and maybe one window, these houses were less susceptible to vermin entering through the walls, but all thatched huts allowed animals in through the ceilings. Most houses faced south, which in Asia is the spiritually favorable direction, and, as families grew, houses could too, with wealthier Chinese living in winged homes surrounding a courtyard. In all regions, peasants also provided food for local elites, warriors, and faraway government officials, and family units were imperiled when lords and kings called the men to arms.

Chinese villagers farmed mostly rice, which grows bounteously in wet conditions, and is hardy enough to grow in arid, semi-arid, and wet conditions. (Rice has been cultivated for over 8,000 years in Asia and Southeast Asia.) The Chinese also farmed wheat and millet, but rice provided more calories per acre than those grains (37 calories an ounce versus 24 for wheat and 34 for millet), and it adapted better to new environments. Growing rice in paddies was labor-intensive and required considerable communal cooperation to soak the paddies, plant, and fertilize them, and then harvest the grain. Chinese families often worked long hours in the fields together, planting, transplanting, and weeding. Women and children aided in spreading seed and gleaning fields for remaining food. In the premodern period, and even today, it both required and supported a large population.

Rice produces a higher grain yield than most other cereal grains and can support more people per hectare of land than can wheat. With proper fertilization, some areas of Asia could grow two and three crops of rice every year. Prior to mechanization in the twentieth century, farmers sowed rice by hand and then transferred seedlings to a flooded paddy. After about three months, farmers cut the rice stalks with hand scythes and threshed the grain with a hand-flail (a flail that breaks the seed heads apart and removes the seeds from the stems; this process was used worldwide until the Industrial Revolution). Most rice was also milled – that is, because the oil in the bran causes uncooked brown rice to spoil much more quickly than uncooked white rice, the brown hull was removed either by hand or by rubbing the rice between stones. Rice loses fiber, protein, carbohydrates, and calories when the hull is removed, making white rice a longer-lasting but less nutritional grain. Despite the loss of nutrients, white rice was preferred by all classes early in Chinese history for its refined taste and texture.

The idea of "fried rice" developed early in Chinese history, possibly during the Sui dynasty (581–618 CE) as frying rice could stave off the effects of early molding. After two hours at room temperature, boiled rice (brown or white) begins to spoil, growing a bacterial toxin that causes vomiting and diarrhea. Frying rice kills off some of the bacteria and ensures that rice made for breakfast can also be eaten for lunch. Rice left in water will ferment in 24 hours, and this fermented rice can be cooked safely the next day or sprinkled with yeast and left to make rice wine, which takes another 48 hours or so. During the Tang dynasty (618–907), home brewing of rice wine was ubiquitous and wine drinking itself a common enough activity that poets like Li Bai often wrote about its effects.

DRINKING ALONE BY MOONLIGHT

Li Po or Li Bai (701–762) was a poet of the eighth century (Tang dynasty) in China. Although he had jobs working for the Emperor Xuanzong, he was fired and participated in revolts after the An Lushan rebellion of 755. Arrested for treason, he was pardoned and wandered throughout the Yangtze river valley, composing poems about the common yet complicated emotions of everyday life. He wrote over 2,000 poems, 1,800 of which are still extant. A frequent motif of his poetry is loneliness. In this one, his only companion is rice wine.

Drinking Alone by Moonlight

A cup of wine, under the flowering trees;
I drink alone, for no friend is near.
Raising my cup I beckon the bright moon,
For he, with my shadow, will make three men.
The moon, alas, is no drinker of wine;
Listless, my shadow creeps about at my side.
Yet with the moon as friend and the shadow as slave
I must make merry before the Spring is spent.
To the songs I sing the moon flickers her beams;
In the dance I weave my shadow tangles and breaks.
While we were sober, three shared the fun;
Now we are drunk, each goes his way.
May we long share our odd, inanimate feast,
And meet at last on the Cloudy River of the sky.

Translated by Arthur Waley

Unfortunately, rice grown in wet paddy fields is the perfect breeding ground for mosquitoes and, therefore, for malaria. Classical Chinese medical journals repeat and emphasize malarial symptoms – fevers, chills, and enlarged spleens – and note that these are consistently present for peasant women, whose continual tending of the fields had them knee-deep in water daily. European doctors were also familiar with malarial symptoms and some believed rice paddy fields to be responsible for the "miasma" (noxious vapor) that caused malaria (the word itself derives from *mala aria*, or "bad air" in Latin).

Chinese peasants realized early that adding fish to their paddies increased their yields, as fish fertilized the water while keeping down the bug population. Peasants also kept ducks and other waterfowl near their fields for similar reasons – in addition to bugs, fowl also ate small vermin attracted to rice fields. The peasants then ate the protein-rich fish and fowl, which aided in the steady rise of the Chinese population throughout the medieval period. Unable to hunt larger game (a privilege available only to the wealthy), Chinese peasants found ingenious ways to increase their rice production while simultaneously increasing

169

Fig 4.4
This peaceful moment of ducks under a rice panicle (spikelets that contain the seeds) would be a common image in a medieval rice paddy. The Song dynasty artist celebrates its simple beauty in India ink on silk. National Palace Museum Taipei.
INTERFOTO / Alamy Stock Photo

their protein intake. Like Europe, the agricultural increases in China during this period also caused a rise in population. At the end of the Tang dynasty (ca. 900), China had a population of about 60 million people. This increased to about 100 million by the Song dynasty (ca. 1100). China's population would hover between 50 and 100 million during the entire medieval period.

As in Europe, owning productive land was the way to wealth and power. Nobles controlled the peasant communities on their properties, using agricultural products created by the peasants for themselves, selling them at a profit, and often amassing great wealth. Peasant men could be pressed into military service, forming a militia for any war-minded lord. Even after the creation of a formalized military class, peasants bore the burden of self-defense and militia service.

Emperors rightly feared the nobility's power bases, and they often sought to break up the monopolies powerful lords held over their properties and laborers. While dividing lands could help prevent civil conflict, it could also bring about warfare – in either case, the destruction of lands, peasant properties, and agricultural fields caused far-reaching devastation and often famines. Chinese emperors and government officials understood the need for strong and stable peasant communities, and often created systems to keep agriculture successful. During the Tang dynasty (618–907), Emperor Tai-tsung (d. 649) confiscated all property in the empire for himself, taking away the power base of several wealthy and competitive nobles. He redistributed the land to those men he called "the most able" cultivators, but in truth they were rewarded because they were loyal; they had no interest in farming and rarely visited their estates. This appanage had its intended effect; the emperor increased his power by proving that he held the ultimate control over land, the primary source of wealth. Peasant production continued almost unabated throughout this redistribution, mostly because of the nature of the absentee landowners, who stayed in the urban centers, near the emperor and away from their estates.

Rice in Western Asia

Rice moved westward on the silk roads, carried by merchants and traded from India and China into the Persian and Islamicate world by the eighth century CE. The cookbooks of Ibn Sayyar al-Warraq from around 950 have over 600 recipes, listing the nutritional, medicinal, and healthful benefits of different foods. Alcohol-free beers made from rice and several other rice recipes show us that rice was eaten and used by this period. Rice is given as healthy and safe for those with gastric problems (much the way the BRAT diet is used today – bananas, rice, applesauce, and toast), sweet rice for desserts, and a couple of recipes for meats and grains including rice. By the Abbasid Caliphate (750–1258), the elite ate rice as a luxury food.

Galenic texts (ca. 200 CE) in Europe also mention rice as a medicinal plant and, as late as the sixth century, rice was prescribed to pregnant women in the Mediterranean as a simple grain to help with pregnancy-induced illness. Rice production probably moved into Europe by way of Spain, with some cultivation of rice in Italy, by the twelfth century. Rice was limited to the Islamicate areas of Europe and adjacent communities until later in the medieval period, and so remained a luxury food for the elite classes within Europe throughout this era.

Climate Change

Physical environment plays a crucial role in our lives; how we as humans alter that environment to fit our needs is the basis for this section. Various climates around the world allow for a wide diversity of agriculture and, throughout the medieval period, humans depended on stable, seasonal weather patterns. We must first begin by discussing a flawed historical idea. Beginning around 1965, textbooks and monographs on medieval Europe discussed the "Medieval Warming Period," describing it as a shift in temperatures that drastically changed agricultural, economic, and physical landscapes. This "warming period" of the tenth to the thirteenth centuries preceded the "Little Ice Age" of the fourteenth to nineteenth centuries (the Little Ice Age was a culmination of several volcanic eruptions that also affected Arctic sea ice). The common line of thinking was that the Industrial Revolution helped to end the Ice Age, bringing about a warming period that continues today. While historical writings formed the basis for this interpretation of these climatological events, modern scientific analysis shows us a different, broader picture.

Since instrumental scientific data for climate change is only about 100 years old, scientists have looked to other measures – tree rings, ice core samples, and lake sediment – to understand the climatological changes of the past. Scientists have also looked to the historical record of those who lived through the periods in question for ideas on what and where to search for clues. Presently, there is serious scientific contention when discussing a Medieval Warming Period, as several prominent climate science deniers use this as evidence that modern Global Climate Change is not a human-created occurrence; instead, they argue, it has a precursor in the Warming Period of the pre-Industrial period. They are wrong. Current scientific analysis shows that temperature swings are fairly normal across the globe and across time, and that the modern change is much more than a shift; instead, it is a wholesale Anthropocene rise in temperatures. Scientists describe the graph as a "hockey stick," which shows temperatures fairly consistent for a thousand years, then undergoing a great leap upward in the latter half of the twentieth century. In this chapter, we look at how the smaller shifts affected medieval people – how the changes in their weather patterns pushed people to make significant changes to their living environments.

Paleoclimatologists (scientists who study past climates) say that the warming effect and the later cooling effect of the Little Ice Age were *regional* disruptions – affecting the Northern Hemisphere much more directly than the Southern Hemisphere, although we have more recorded historical works and scientific data on Europe, China, and India regarding the climate shift during the medieval period than we do for the Americas and the Southern Hemisphere. Some scientists have suggested calling it the "Medieval Climatic Anomaly," to remove the idea of temperature or weather as the centerpiece, and instead focus on the changes in climate around the world. As climatologists point out, weather is constantly changing, but climate does not change easily. We can say, with a degree of scientific certainty, that from about 900 to 1250, world climates shifted, with temperatures in the Northern Hemisphere warming and those in the Southern Hemisphere cooling.

The highest temperature rise in the Northern Hemisphere occurred in the eleventh century, from 1010 to 1090. Solar radiation, volcanic activity, and wind patterns may all have contributed to the changing weather seen in Europe, Russia, and Mongolia. This period of warmer and drier weather greatly affected the agricultural and pastoral communities across the northern span of Eurasia, as well as those in North Africa, with a series of devastating droughts and subsequent famines. The drier weather gave European peasants the benefit of longer growing seasons and Chinese peasants the ability to clear new land for rice.

Paleoclimatology has a longer history in the Eastern and Northern hemispheres, probably because of the longer written record and larger

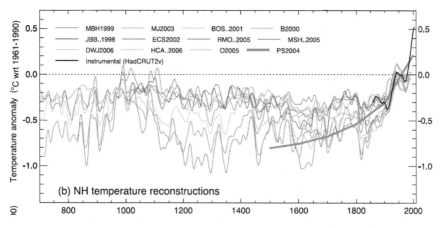

Fig 4.5
Chart with data on medieval warming period produced by the OSS (Open Source Systems, Science, Solutions) Foundation.
OSS Foundation

populations in these areas. Science is also not a neutral tool in that it follows the same biases as other research fields, and only recently have scientists turned with more intention to studying paleoclimates in the Western and Southern hemispheres. This new scientific data shows us severe droughts in the Western Hemisphere, and persistent rains and droughts in the Southern Hemisphere, which point to shifts in the temperatures outside Eurasia as well. Without robust written sources from the Southern Hemisphere to guide them, scientists must examine the material evidence the Earth has left for us. As more research emerges from the Southern Hemisphere, we may, yet again, change our perspectives on the regional changes in the Northern Hemisphere during the medieval period. Historians, looking at the written, artistic, and scientific evidence, see that droughts and heavy rains in the Southern Hemisphere created disruptions in the Maya empires, perhaps contributing to the decline of the Maya kings and the rise of fragmented kingdoms in Central America. The Moche Empire in South America also experienced severe rains around 550, and again around 850, which may have led to a reduction in their empire and the growth of the Chimú Empire in modern Peru.

CLIMATE MIGRANTS

Around the early fifth century and lasting into the sixth century, the world began to cool slightly. The cooling temperatures in the Northern Hemisphere may have led to droughts in the steppes, causing a migration of pastoralist peoples (such as the Huns; see earlier chapters) as they sought out fodder for their animals and more hospitable landscapes. These climate changes also weakened the areas the Huns sought to invade, as Eastern and Southern Europe and Western China all had serious, destabilizing famines.

Climate migrants, or environmental migrants, are groups or individuals who migrated either in response to the natural destruction of their homeland (through flooding or drought, for example) or in search of more favorable climatic conditions (seeking better pastureland for their livestock or richer soil to farm). Climate migration may be invisible in the written historical record, but archeologists, paleobotanists, and paleoclimatologists have worked to reconstruct the ways in which ancient and medieval environmental changes impacted human societies.

Several large-scale population movements took place during the medieval period that may be attributable to climate changes and environmental needs. Without written records, it is impossible to be sure, but some historians believe that the Migration Period (ca. 300–800) may have begun because of the extreme weather events of the early sixth century. This period was a centuries-long process of Germanic tribal groups moving southward from Scandinavia, first into southern Germany and then across the borders of the Roman Empire, along many fronts. The resulting political realignment saw the rise of Germanic kingdoms inside the boundaries of the former Roman Empire (for example the Vandal Kingdom in North Africa, the Visigothic Kingdom in Iberia, and the Frankish Kingdom in Gaul). Later, waves of Germanic invasions pushed into the Mediterranean, as when the Lombards took Italy, and westward into the British Isles. The westward movements of the Magyars, Bulgars, Slavs, and other peoples across the Eurasian steppe may also have been related to these patterns.

Later medieval climatic changes also impacted where and how people could live and farm. One example is migration of the Ancestral Pueblo people of the southwestern United States, whose highly complex settlements were abandoned during the twelfth and thirteenth centuries. In the mid-twelfth century, Chaco Canyon (see later chapters), the center of the Puebloan world at the time, lost its centrality and much of its population. By 1300, likewise, the Puebloan site of Mesa Verde, home of impressive cliff dwellings, was abandoned after more than two decades of drought. The Pueblo people probably decided to move for more suitable locations for farming.

Conclusion

There have been a number of changes wrought by members of society considered beneath the notice of most of the ruling elites and literate classes. Peasants and villagers were the majority of the population in Eurasia, and we know so very little about them; however, historians and archeologists continue to gather information about the lower classes from preserved bodies, occasional archeological finds such as plows, and in the legacy of their innovations. From 700 to 1200, changing climate aided the European peasant in creating new agricultural technology, which further led to an increase in food production. This same climate shift forced nomadic tribal peoples off dwindling pasturelands and into the heart of the Chinese Empire. This changed dynastic succession for 400 years and brought nomadic ideas and ideals into Chinese society. We also see glimpses of the lives of peasants as told in popular stories and as depicted in the margins of great works of art.

B: CULTIVATING GOOD FORTUNE

Evidence: *Mabonogion*, "Manawydan, son of Llŷr"

Mae Phosop

Wat Phra That Doe Suthap

Ganesha

Laxdaela Saga

Introduction

Premodern communities were dependent upon the food cultivated and hunted in their immediate environments. They developed elaborate schedules and customs in sync with the natural world, including rituals focused on appeasing the spirits of weather, plants, and animals. Even when there was an abundant harvest and plentiful wild game, there was no assurance that the next season would be as fruitful. There could be a sudden calamity, such as crop blight or the dreaded "murrain of cattle" seen so often in monastic annals (*murrain* means death, generally caused by infection). There could also be a slowly unfolding disaster like a long period of drought. Premodern cultures acted out rituals of gratitude and respect for the natural world, many of which are still practiced. Here, we provide some examples of folk customs and cultural practices that comforted people, giving them ways to measure and manage their worries about survival. These practices traveled with believers and blended into new environments to create rich cross-cultural traditions.

Managing Unmanageable Nature

With much depending on successful harvests and robust herds and flocks, there was profound fear of the unexpected. A way of managing fear was to anthropomorphize the natural world. Anthropomorphizing means projecting human physical features and emotions on inanimate objects or non-human animals. We do it all the time; for instance, if we take a pair of googly eyes and attach them to a rock or a sock, we think that the object is looking at us. We imagine that it has a personality. We name it and begin to wonder if it needs friends, or a snack, or a blanket. We talk to it and feel uncomfortable leaving it in the dark. Likewise, we imagine animals to have far more human emotion and motivation than they are likely to have. Medieval folklore includes stories and rituals that involve anthropomorphizing weather – projecting human appearance, motivation, and emotion on storms, droughts, tsunamis, and earthquakes, so these powerful "beings" could be approached in understandable terms. Much of peasant life was spent in appeasement gestures for these beings, trying to calm them down or befriend them by leaving offerings: a plate of food, a seat at the table, the first fruits of the season, and the best bowl of rice. These are apotropaic gestures, customs intended to turn away evil. Depending on your perspective, an apotropaic gesture is one that brings good luck; by averting misfortune and evil, we maintain good fortune.

The most important folk practices revolved around the cycle of life and fertility of the general ecosystem. Springtime was the high point – new seeds in warm earth, the birth of baby animals that will grow to provide food and fur, fish energized by the runoff of melting mountain snow. (Remember that spring and fall, or planting season and harvesting season, differ across the globe; for example, spring and fall in Australia are opposite from spring and fall in Europe.) But the rituals of spring were the culmination of a long period of worship that began with the last harvest. If that harvest had been good, a village could store enough to get through to the next planting cycle, and thus autumn rituals included grateful celebrations to the gods. If the harvest had been poor or blighted, the prayers were desperate apologies to the fertility deities, and people made offerings of gifts and objects. Fertility rituals are the most powerful and common of folk customs, and, over the centuries, there has been intermingling of these rituals. This blending of spiritual beliefs is called syncretism.

As we discussed in Chapter 1, in the period 500–900 most peoples living in areas that had been part of the Roman Empire had converted to Christianity; however, many Indigenous pre-Christian fertility customs were absorbed into Christian ritual. For instance, Christianity was introduced in Ireland before the sixth century and has been a defining cultural presence from then until now, but we have an indication of pre-Christian fertility practices in the story of beloved St. Brigid. Along with St. Patrick, Brigid is a patron saint of Ireland, and has come to be especially important as a saint of livestock, midwives, and newborns. She began as a saint of grain and the harvest, reflecting that in the early centuries of Irish Christianity the grain harvest was the most important food source for each village community. Her role evolved along with the Irish economy. As time passed, she became associated with sheep and shepherds, and a later version has her tending cattle.

The fact that St. Brigid's feast day is in February may point to her earlier role as a pre-Christian fertility goddess. Her feast day is February 1, which corresponds to the pre-Christian Celtic celebration called Imbolc, a time of spiritual cleansing in preparation for the spring celebration called Beltane. A symbol of St. Brigid's worship is a woven cross made with wheat stalks from the end of

Fig 4.6
Small traditional type of St. Brigid's Cross.
imarly / iStock

a harvest. The form of this cross is four arms of equal length, which is not a Christian looking cross, but is close enough to be easily translated from early Celtic imagery to Christian iconography. This talisman honors St. Brigid's blessing over the recent harvest and protects the household until spring, when the next fertility cycle begins. Even today, many Irish Catholics hang a St. Brigid's cross in their homes for good luck.

Folk rituals in the Northern Hemisphere often included some kind of spiritual house cleaning in the period between the winter solstice (around December 21, when the days are short and cold and it feels as if spring may never come) and the vernal equinox (around March 21, when day and night are equal). People have struggled through the heart of winter. Their stores are running low, and their livestock needs new fodder, but winter is not yet over. They desperately worry the gods will not bring the Earth back to life and thus perform purification ceremonies to the spirits. Between 500 and 900, the Germanic peoples were only beginning to transition from native belief systems to Christianity. As they converted, some of their folk fertility rituals syncretized with Christian practices; for instance, the Germanic goddess of spring was called Eostre. Worship of her included fertility symbols such as eggs, an obvious icon of new life, and rabbits, because they produce large litters in a short amount of time. In Germanic cultures, Christian leaders accepted Easter as the name of the celebration of the resurrection of Jesus; however, in other parts of Europe, this holiday is referred to with some form of the word *paschal*, derived from the Hebrew term for Passover. Another example of syncretism of Germanic yuletide customs with Christian practices is the Christmas tree, a tree that is evergreen, an indication of life in the heart of winter. Holly berries also show life in winter with their green leaves and brightly colored berries. Lighting candles around the evergreen boughs brought to mind the reviving warmth of the returning sun.

Starvation and Migration

As discussed above, in the period 500–900, climate change was a perilous reality. Peasants were constantly in fear of starvation and projected these fears into their storytelling. One of the four myths in the Welsh collection, entitled the *Mabinogi*, describes the desperation and terror of famine and drought. In "Manawydan, son of Llŷr," two couples enjoy a great feast and set out for an after-dinner stroll. All at once, there is a great noise, followed by an obscuring mist. When the mist clears, they look in the places where there had been flocks and cattle, houses, official buildings, men, and women. All that is left is a deserted, desolate space. All animals have vanished. All plants have been stripped of their foliage. Quite suddenly, their environment has become a wasteland, expressing a cultural fear of catastrophic weather events that threaten human existence. Although the extant copy of these folk tales was written down in the fourteenth century, we know it represents a much earlier storytelling tradition.

The men do the only thing they can, travel to another place to find work, which, in this case, is to England. They arrive at thriving towns with citizens who need practical goods, and Manwydan and Pryderi try their hand at making saddles, then forging shields, and finally crafting shoes. In each case, their skills are superior to those of the locals, which infuriates the townspeople, who conspire to murder them. The two men represent urbanization of the farming class. They are outsiders, subject to suspicion and distrust. After escaping the third town and the third death threat, the two men return home, and the narrative snaps back into the mythical format we expect from *Mabinogi*: an enchanted fountain, revenge, and the near hanging of a magical mouse on a tiny gibbet made just for her. But, preserved within the Welsh myth is a real concern about environmental sustainability. The mystical land of Dyfed experiences an environmental catastrophe – a blight on the crops, the devastation of livestock, and mass depopulation. Underneath the fanciful language of dark enchantment, the core story examines and lingers on the reality of forced migration. Once nobles in their own land, Manwyden and Pryderi become refugees searching for a new home. They are displaced peddlers whose foreign ways and rare skills destabilize and aggravate the locals.

Human Trafficking

Embedded in the Welsh tale from *Mabinogi* is a hint of idealism, as the characters have a choice about migrating and about their destination. More often, the disempowered classes of the medieval period were involuntarily dislocated by slave traders, who used them as currency along the major medieval trade routes. As we have pointed out, planting, harvesting, and building required intense physical exertion; slave labor was the most useful and desirable commodity. No farm, town, or city was above the practice, and all societies took advantage of war captives and vulnerable populations for that purpose. Enslaved persons captured from the Turkic tribes of Central Asia were moved through Samarkand to Afghanistan, and then on to China. African traders captured villagers from the interior of the continent and brought them to the eastern ports of the Swahili Corridor, where they were sold to Islamic middlemen who transported them to wealthy regions in Persia.

In medieval Europe, the Vikings were vigorous enslavers. Operating from Kievan Rus, Viking settlers continuously pillaged and abducted the Slavic inhabitants of the major river systems – the Danube, Volga, Don, Dniester, and Dnieper – selling them throughout Byzantium and the Islamic empire. The Arabic and English words for slave are both adapted from the Greek *sklavenos*, for Slav. The men of the lands around the North Sea constantly raided each other, carrying away goods and people, particularly women. In the Icelandic *Saga of the People of Laxardal*, a respected chieftain named Hoskuld travels to an annual assembly of his kinsman on an island close to Sweden. He participates in arbitrations and legal proceedings, catches up with relatives from Denmark and Norway, and indulges in feasts and games. When it is time for him to depart, he visits a slave trader named Gilli the Russian. In his highly decorated tent, Gilli offers 12 women for sale. Hoskuld chooses the healthiest and best looking, but she has a flaw: she cannot speak. This does not deter Hoskuld from paying more for her than he would for the others. Far from a deal breaker, he considers her silence an asset. He buys other commodities, receives blessings and gifts of gold from the King of Norway, and sails for home. Buying a woman is business as usual. Although his wife does not welcome the concubine and makes life difficult for her, the purchase is socially acceptable.

The enslaved woman gives birth to Hoskuld's son, and at last Hoskuld discovers that she can speak. As it turns out, she is Melkorka, the kidnapped daughter of Myrkjartan, the king of Ireland, and her son becomes the hero of Iceland. Because of her noble birth, exceptional son, and her dignity and talents, Hoskuld respects her. Eventually, the community does, too. Of course, it helps that Melkorka is high-born, but her social position improves mostly because she contributes to the good of the whole; the community needs her participation. In this isolated, far-northern island with a very short growing season, Icelandic communities needed the labor and abilities of every person.

The Saga of the People of Laxardal was recorded in the fourteenth century but is representative of events as early as the ninth century. At the beginning of the tale, a matriarch named Unn the Deep-minded leads her clan from a settlement in Scotland to the west side of Iceland. She claims a large territory and eventually apportions out her lands to members of the community, including enslaved people, who are given their freedom. Their service is rewarded in a way that incorporates them as allies of the community. Thus, the story acknowledges two possibilities for women under duress: Unn takes control as the wise leader of her clan, and Melkorka earns status and freedom after being abducted and sold into slavery. While these outcomes would be rare and may be wishful thinking of the early storytellers, in other places in this book we discuss slave revolts and the political and social effects of slave trafficking.

Mae Phosop

Medieval Southeast Asian cultures provide many rich examples of syncretism – the blending of religious and spiritual traditions. The myths and rituals of Thailand, for instance, are a combination of Hindu and Buddhist mythologies mixed with pre-existing ancient folk practices. The area is sometimes called Indochina, which recognizes both the Indian cultural influences that came from the east across the Andaman Sea and the Chinese influences from the north and east. This mixture of cultures is apparent in folk practices. Throughout the medieval period, Southeast Asian people were dependent on rice. Like all sustainable, foundational crops, rice is grown and harvested according to expected weather patterns, a cycle of a dry season followed by a monsoon. If all goes as planned, rice paddies are seeded during the drier seasons, brought to maturity during the monsoon flooding, and then harvested, threshed, and dried during the next sunny cycle. That is, *if all goes as planned.*

A rice crop can be ruined by too little or, more often, too much rain, or completely swept away by floods. Lack of sunshine to dry the rice kernels means the rice might mold and decay. Vermin are always a threat – rodents and insects must be perpetually fended off. In addition, the growing season can be interrupted by raiders from a neighboring village or a larger-scale war.

In Thailand, a spirit called Mae Phosop (Ma Posop; Me Posop), the rice mother, was worshipped in order to protect against these threats. She was thought to enliven the paddies with bountiful grain and to protect the crop from insects and mice. She was a fertility goddess, the embodiment of the rice harvest, whose favor or disfavor determined the food supply for the village. To demonstrate their appreciation and respect, villagers would (and still do) offer her meals during significant stages in the rice growth cycle. They might also create an effigy of her and place it in a special altar in the rice barn. These figures were often made of leftover rice stalks from the harvest and protected and honored in the barn until the next season. Since the effigy of crop spirits was usually made from the plant material itself, there are no examples from the Middle Ages, but we know that these traditions existed because they have remained part of Thai culture during the modern period. Prayers are said to Mae Phosop, and young village women may dress as her during local rice harvest festivals and celebrations. Rice dolls are kept in careful but humble sanctuaries in the barn.

Dragons and Snakes

Southeast Asia is surrounded by the Indian Ocean and South China Seas, and, except for the Northern Highlands, is below or at sea level. Runoff from the

Fig 4.7
Flooded rice paddies, Ubud, Bali, Indonesia.
Deposit Photos

Himalayas, to the north, creates an extensive freshwater system of tributaries that flow into the great Mekong River. Although the culture is prepared for the annual flooding from the monsoon rains – rice cultivation depends on it – the tipping point between life-sustaining irrigation and destructive flooding is delicate.

Peasants had no control over the weather, but they could channel their anxiety into rituals about creatures thought to control the rainfall or the river systems. The *Phaya Naga* are a dramatic example of these river spirits. Naga is the Sanskrit word for snake, and, in Buddhist and Hindu cultures, nagas are also mythical serpents and dragons, which can be both protectors and destroyers. They are semidivine gods, occupying the unseen depths of rivers and lakes, and the uncanny space between the human and spirit world. Serpents could be blamed for unusual currents, sudden flooding, and even atmospheric changes beyond human understanding.

Yet, just as these unpredictable mythical serpents had the power of death, they also had the power of life. When satisfied and contented, they were the guardians of the fish-giving pools and crucial waterways. They were also guardians of the Buddha. From as early as the fifth century, we find Southeast Asian representations of the seated Buddha, deep in meditation under the protection of a serpent, often one with many heads. Like so many of the legends of this region, this one originates from India and has been incorporated into Southeast Asian culture for at least 1,500 years. The name of this protective great cobra is Mucalinda. Just a few weeks after the Buddha began his practice of meditating under the great Bodhi tree, he achieved a spiritual state of

Fig 4.8
Buddha in meditation with a seven-headed naga, Mucalinda. Seventh/eighth century,
Central Thailand, National Museum of Bangkok.
Placebo365 / iStock

detachment that lasted a week. During that time, a storm moved into the area
with heavy rain, wind, and cold. Struck by the majestic calm of the Buddha,
Mucalinda coiled himself as a cushion for the Buddha and spread his hood (or
hoods) to shelter him from the rain.

The importance of nagas in the history of Southeast Asia is expressed in
Wat Phra That Doi Suthep (Temple of Relics) in the medieval Northern Thai
kingdom of Lan Na. Mount Suthep rises above the present-day city of Chiang
Mai, which, in the thirteenth century, became the thriving center of Lan Na.
A century later, a Buddhist monk from the neighboring kingdom of Sukhothai
brought a small bone of the Buddha to the Lan Na ruler, King Kuena, who
resolved to build a temple to house the auspicious relic. To determine a location, he placed the relic in fine silk on top of a glorious white elephant and
followed the elephant's path. The elephant stopped many times to eat and contemplate, eventually arriving at the top of the mountain, where it trumpeted
mightily, collapsed, and died. Wherever the elephant paused, King Kuena
erected a temple or monument in honor of the Buddha. Where the elephant
died, he built a shrine for the relic – the first structure of the Wat Phra That
complex.

The shrine dates to 1368 and has been a primary pilgrimage site for Buddhists
of all classes ever since. Visitors begin their ascent to the temple at the foot of

Fig 4.9
Dragon-protected stairway leading to Wat Phra That Doe Suthap temple outside
Chiang Mai, Thailand.
Pakpoom Phummee / Alamy Stock Photo

a 309-step staircase, which is framed on either side by elaborate handrails in
the form of serpentine nagas. Nagas are often connected with the rainbow –
probably because snakes appear after or during rainstorms, and water is the
element of the serpent. The rainbow is a path from Earth to heaven; thus, serpent handrails guide the worshipper up and up toward the temple, closer to
the sky.

Ganesha

Sometimes spirits or gods do not require elaborate shows of gratitude and gifts
in order to bless the community. Some, like the elephant-headed god Ganesha,
consistently represent happiness and security. Originally a Hindu god, Ganesha
has been widely worshipped across Asia since the 400s. Called the Playful
Protector or the Remover of Obstacles, he dissolves strife and grants wealth
and success. There are many versions of the creation of this loveable character.
A prominent one is that Parvati, the Hindu goddess of love and fertility, created
a chubby boy to be her companion. Some stories claim she created this guardian
from mud, others claim that she created him from her laughter, still others say
Parvati pulled lint from behind her ear and rolled it into a being; regardless, at
some point, Ganesha came between Parvati and her consort, Shiva, and Shiva
beheaded him. To appease Parvati, Shiva brought him back to life, replacing
Ganesha's head with that of an elephant.

Fig 4.10
This 29-inch-tall statue from Cambodia is one of the oldest surviving Ganesha icons in mainland Southeast Asia. He is a symbol of jolly prosperity, reaching into an ever-present bowl of candy. His round, chubby body contains the universe, and it is good luck to rub his belly. As a god of arts and learning, Ganesha is often shown with one tusk missing. As the story goes, when the sage Vyasa began reciting the Hindu epic *Mahabharata*, the elephant god cut off his own tusk and fashioned it into a writing tool. Seventh/eighth century, Musee National de Phnom Penh, Cambodia.
Ruth Hofshi / Alamy Stock Photo

Most representations of Ganesha feature him with four or more arms. Sometimes he is represented standing with one foot touching the Earth and the other raised in dance. The planted foot shows his connection with the material world, and the free foot is connected to divinity. Often, he sits on top of a mouse or rat, a nod to his ability to perform the impossible, and another common feature is a serpent or rope wrapped around his generous belly, symbolizing the forces of energy that surround the universe. The inclusion of a rodent and a snake in Ganesha's iconography is a nod to the kind of threat he neutralizes: rodents steal crops, and dangerous snakes lurk in watery rice fields; both animals work in the service of the great problem-solver and are hopefully more interested in pleasing him than in destroying the rice paddies.

Looking Forward

A changing climate aided European peasants in creating new agricultural technology, which further led to an increase in food production from 700 to 1200. In Asia, this same climate shift forced nomadic tribal peoples off dwindling pasturelands and into China, thus changing dynastic succession and bringing nomadic ideas and ideals into Chinese society. Even though we do not have much direct testimony about the lives of peasants, they are present in the margins of texts, the edges of ruins, and the folk practices and stories they used as protection against the unknown. Despite suffering from the exhausting labors of agriculture, the terrors of siege and battle, and the constant peril of abduction and abuse, their innovations sustained the lives of their immediate communities and wealthy leaders. The agricultural changes and advances created by early medieval peasant communities led to other developments in the societies of Eurasia and China. Those are the centerpiece of Section III, as we look at religious systems in Asia, the extension of economies, intellectual and political systems, and class divisions within societies from 900 to 1300.

As everyday people depended on growing cycles of fields, flocks, and herds, they used stories and art as a way to process the mystery and unpredictability of their natural environment, both its beauty and its life-threatening danger. Religious festivals, folk tales, and apotropaic images demonstrate a show of humility before the power of nature. Folk customs are still observed all over the world, either as religious ritual or often converted to secular "good luck" practices. They are syncretized, that is, they are combinations of elements from many cultures and faiths.

Research Questions

1. How does the physical environment define peasant life and traditions in that area?
2. Trace a meal you recently had from farm to table. How were farmers involved? How is technology involved? Where was it grown? Who grew it? Who harvested and shipped it? How many steps away are you from the making of your own food?
3. Look at the recent evidence concerning the Medieval Warming Period. How do modern concerns about global climate change affect how we view the past? How does a change in temperature equate to an increased or decreased population?
4. Just as in Southeast Asia, snake imagery is common and crucial to mythologies all over the world, many times magnified into either protective or destructive dragons. Whether the snakes, serpents, or dragons are welcomed or feared, they are venerated. Further explore the mythology of the naga or snake stories from another culture. What are the different ways in which snakes/serpents/dragons are treated? What does that tell you about the culture and its geographic environment?
5. In premodern cultures, salt was used for everything from healing wounds to dyeing textiles. Research common uses of salt and consider the chemical reactions it permits.

6. Attracting good fortune often happens through the warding off of evil. As we discussed in this chapter, humans express this duality through apotropaic gestures. While we may think these are only the practice of ancient people, consider the present-day "good luck" rituals and gestures of sports fans and athletes (for example, not shaving until the playoffs are over, wearing lucky socks, spitting sunflower seeds in a certain pattern). What are some apotropaic gestures you have seen or do?

Further Reading

Albala, Ken. *The Food History Reader: Primary Sources*. London: Bloomsbury Academic, 2014.

Benn, Charles D. *Daily Life in Traditional China: The Tang Dynasty*. London: Greenwood Press, 2002.

Brooke, John. *Climate Change and the Course of Global History*. Cambridge: Cambridge University Press, 2014.

Dehai, Huang, Xiang Jing, and Zhang Dinghao. *Illustrated Myths and Legends of China: The Ages of Chaos and Heroes*. Translated by Tony Blishen. Shanghai: Shanghai Press, 2018.

Ford, Patrick. *The Mabinogi and Other Medieval Welsh Tales*. Berkeley: University of California Press, 2008.

Frankopan, Peter. *The Silk Roads: A New History of the World*. New York: Vintage Books, 2017.

Deal, William E. *Handbook to Life in Medieval and Early Modern Japan*. New York: Oxford University Press, 2007.

Kerlansky, Mark. *Salt: A World History*. New York: Penguin Books, 2002.

Mazoyer, Marcel, and Laurence Roudart. *A History of World Agriculture*. New York: Monthly Review Press, 2006.

McGovern, Patrick. *Uncorking the Past: The Quest for Wine, Beer, and Other Alcoholic Beverages*. Berkeley: University of California Press, 2009.

Pilcher, Jeffrey. *Oxford Handbook of Food History*. Oxford: Oxford University Press, 2012.

Phillipson, David. *Foundations of an African Civilisation: Aksum and the Northern Horn, 1000 BC–1300 AD*. Rochester, NY: James Currey, 2012.

The Saga of the People of Laxardal. Translated by Leifur Eiriksson. New York: Penguin Books, 1997.

Sharma, S. D. *Rice: Origin, Antiquity, and History*. Boca Raton, FL: CRC Press, 2010.

Tauger, Mark. *Agriculture in World History*. New York: Routledge, 2010.

Unger, Richard. *Beer in the Middle Ages and Renaissance*. Philadelphia: University of Pennsylvania Press, 2007.

Section III
900–1300

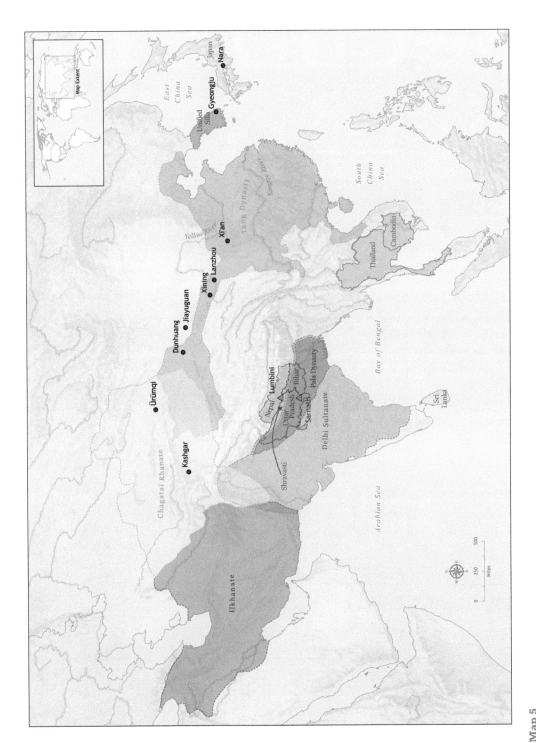

Map 5
Pathways to Paradise

5 Pathways to Paradise

Religion, 900–1300

Introduction

The word paradise often describes an earthly or heavenly place of unmatched beauty, but the concept can also refer to a mindset of harmony and bliss. Many world religions imagine such perfect places or enlightened states of mind, but the pathways for locating these sites – whether physical environments or spiritual modes of transcendence – vary greatly. In the Middle Ages, people journeyed across continents and oceans to uncover and retrieve precious materials believed to be auspicious, holy, and miraculous. Many of these objects were associated with sacred sites, specifically centers of pilgrimage. We know of these quests through the stories people recorded about them in hand-made books or manuscripts, as well as xylographic books or scrolls (xylography is printing made from carved wooden blocks). In this chapter, we encounter sacred texts from major world religions – sutras in Buddhism, the Bible in Judaism and Christianity, the Qur'an in Islam, and others – in order to counter the outdated idea of the "Dark Ages." As we will see, this period can be more accurately referred to as the Illuminated Ages, given the significant quantity of book arts on paper, palm leaves, and parchment that were produced across Afro-Eurasia on topics ranging from religion to medicine to history.

Studying religion in a global medieval framework often involves understanding how faith communities comingled, which may involve considerations of politics and economics. In our first religion chapter, we outlined developments in the monotheisms of Judaism, Zoroastrianism, Christianity, and Islam across Afro-Eurasia, with a focus on sacred structures and scriptures. We saw how the Islamicate world began to expand and how the Christian world experienced dogmatic divisions. In this chapter, we look at visions of paradise and pilgrims' journeys as recorded on paper, palm leaves, and parchment books made for Buddhist, Hindu, and Jain communities across India and East/Southeast Asia, as well as for the People of the Book of the Abrahamic traditions. The theme of paradise allows us to consider ideal states, but we will also look at the realities of religious fragmentation and pluralism.

Section A addresses the ways stories of the Buddha found new audiences across Eurasia, from monastery caves in China, to a powerful Muslim empire in greater Persia, to mercantile communities in the Mediterranean. The intermediality of manuscripts – that is, the relationship between text, images, devotional practices, and other media, such as painting or sculpture – varied by region and yet often invoked symbols of gems, gestures, or color to convey ideas about paradise. Section B examines the role that pilgrimage routes played in connecting distant religious communities as they sought relics or commodities, such as gems and spices, which were thought to bring an individual closer to serenity. In both sections, we will journey across Eurasia – with a few stops in Africa, coastal and interior – during the centuries 900 to 1300, with some examples into the 1500s that demonstrate the pursuit of paradise.

A: IN THE FOOTSTEPS OF THE BUDDHA

Evidence: Buddhist sutras

Hindu puranas

Jain *Kalpasutra* (*Book of Sacred Precepts*)

Jami al-Tawarikh (*Compendium of Chronicles*) by Rashid-al-Din Hamadani

Majma al-Tawarikh (*Compendium of Histories*) by Hafiz-i Abru

Barlaam and Josaphat by Rudolf von Ems

Buddhism Basics – Bodhisattvas and Blessings

Prince Siddhartha Gautama, also called Shakyamuni or simply the Buddha, was born in Lumbini in present-day Nepal and lived sometime between the sixth and fifth centuries BCE. His father, a king, raised him in an opulent palace and endeavored to shelter him from the hardships and suffering of the world, but in his late twenties, he witnessed poverty, sickness, old age, and death for the first time. As a result of these encounters, he vowed to renounce earthly goods and ambitions in favor of mindfulness and detachment from worldly care. Sitting and meditating beneath a bodhi tree at the site of Bodh Gaya in Bihar, India, the Buddha reached enlightenment, and this place is still a major pilgrimage site. The Buddha then traveled and taught a message that can be encapsulated in the Four Noble Truths: everything is suffering; the cause of suffering is desire; removing desire ends suffering; and the Eightfold Path is the way to this end. This spiritual pathway includes having the right view, right resolve, right speech, right conduct, right livelihood, right effort, right mindfulness, and right meditation. The enlightened Buddha first preached this message at Sarnath (also called the Deer Park), where several disciples began following him. It is also a key pilgrimage site for the faithful. A final place for pilgrims to visit was Kushinagar (India), where the Buddha reached paranirvana, a state of enlightenment (nirvana) after death.

Contemplation on the definition of "right" practices is a central part of Buddhist faith, and it varies across communities and individuals, but several specific schools or traditions developed within Buddhism. Mahayana Buddhism (mainly in parts of Southeast and East Asia) was and still is concerned with various figures of veneration, including bodhisattvas – compassionate beings who forego nirvana, which is when the soul (in a process called *moksha*) is released from the cycle of birth-death-rebirth known as *samsara*. Instead of pursuing nirvana, they help suffering beings through their process to nirvana. Theravada Buddhism (mainly in South and Southeast Asia) viewed and still views salvation as becoming an *arhat*, meaning a worthy one with an incorruptible nature. Vajrayana Buddhism (mainly Central Asia and specifically Tibet) developed out of Mahayana traditions and focused on texts called *tantras*, which can be described as esoteric (imparted from teacher to student), magical, or at times sexual, views and practices. Finally, Zen Buddhism is a Mahayana school that emerged in China in the Tang dynasty (618–907 CE); it is still centered on detachment from worldly cares through rigorous meditation.

The Buddhist world was, and is, vast and diverse. Mahayana Buddhism spread from India through the Himalayas and into China by the later Han dynasty (25–220 CE). From China, this tradition moved into Korea from the fourth century CE, but primarily during the Unified Silla Kingdom (668–935 CE); into Japan during the Asuka period (sixth century CE); and into Indonesia by the fifth century CE. In Southeast Asia, Theravada Buddhism emerged in Sri Lanka by the third century BCE and in Thailand and Cambodia by the first century CE. Throughout South, Southeast, and East Asia one finds a long history of texts and images about bodhisattvas. For example, Avalokitesvara, the bodhisattva of compassion, is called Guanyin in China or Kanzeon in Japan and Quán Thế Âm in Vietnam. Another prominent bodhisattva is Maitreya, the Buddha-who-is-yet-to-come, often depicted laughing (Mile Pusa in Chinese; Miroku Bosatsu in Japanese; and Di-lac in Vietnamese). This section primarily focuses on Mahayana Buddhism in its Asian contexts in the period 900–1300, and then considers ways in which other regions and religions incorporated the Buddha into their histories or teachings.

Despite the Buddha's renunciation of material worldliness, his legacy traversed vast distances across medieval Afro-Eurasia through a range of rather lavish art forms. Decorated books – bound as a codex, rolled as a scroll, or folded in a screen-fold format – are primary evidence of how far the Buddha's narrative spread. Two vastly distant sites on the medieval map form geographic bookends for the outset of our journey to paradise: the network of 735 Buddhist cave temples at Dunhuang in China, where we will begin below, to a mercantile artist workshop in Alsatian Hagenau in present-day France, where our voyage in Section A ends. The transmission or translation of tales of the life of the Buddha covers a chronological arc from roughly the eighth century (or perhaps slightly earlier) to the fifteenth century. These literary traditions and the images that accompany them reveal ideals about states of paradise, physical and meta-physical, that many individuals still pursue.

Buddhist Pathways

As mentioned above, Buddhism spread into South and East Asia during the first centuries of the Common Era. Very few handwritten manuscripts survive from this early period. Woodblock printed texts were produced during the Tang dynasty in China (618–907) before the eighth century CE, but painted or illustrated Buddhist manuscripts would not appear until about the year 1000 in India. Sutras are core texts of many Indian religions, including Buddhism. Sutra is the Sanskrit word for thread or sew (related to the English words "sew" and "suture"), indicating teaching, aphorisms, or sermons that are sewn together metaphorically or sewn together into a text. For a Buddhist devotee, commissioning a sutra manuscript is considered a worthy act, one that allowed patrons to accumulate blessings for themselves and for their ancestors. We will look at three sutras – from China, Japan, and India – to get a sense of the various ways in which Buddhist teachings spread.

Printed Blessings: A Fortuitous Find in a Chinese Buddhist Cave

The Diamond Sutra (*Vajraccedika Prajnaparamita Sutra*) is one of the earliest sermons to circulate in print. A verse in chapter 6 of the text states, "Any person who awakens faith upon hearing the words or phrases of this Sutra will accumulate countless blessings and merit." The acts of reading, handling, hearing, and perceiving the words or phrases of the text were considered auspicious. This quality of personal, spiritual interaction with the written word, and at times the accompanying images, is shared among the faith traditions that we encounter throughout this chapter. Furthermore, in chapter 12 we read,

> If any person in any place were to teach even four lines of this Sutra, the place where they taught it would become sacred ground and would be revered by all kinds of beings … Wherever this Sutra is honored and revered there is a sacred site enshrining the presence of the Buddha or one of the Buddha's most venerable disciples.

From an inscription in one copy of the Diamond Sutra, we know that in May 868, a person named Wang Jie commissioned the remarkable book for his parents and deceased ancestors. Known as the earliest dated printed book in the world, this copy of the Diamond Sutra was among a trove of textual treasures found in the early twentieth century in the so-called Library Cave (referred to

Fig 5.1
This printed image from the Dunhuang copy of the Diamond Sutra (868) shows
the Buddha in the Jetavana Monastery (in Shravasti, Uttar Pradesh, northern India)
preaching to his elder disciple, Subhuti, who engages with the Buddha in dialogue
throughout the scripture. Deities and monks attend the dialogue, and two lions lie in
front of the Buddha's lotus-throne. The mulberry paper was mounted as a handscroll,
which developed throughout East Asia as a primary format for preserving
Buddhist sutras (printed or painted alike), whereas painted palm leaves and paper
manuscripts emerged in India and Southeast Asia.
FLHC 8 / Alamy Stock Photo

as cave number 17) of the Mogao Grottoes in Dunhuang, China. Within this
remarkably small space – about nine feet high by ten feet square – were hidden
and preserved at least 400,000 rolled scrolls.

The languages and writing systems of all the Dunhuang manuscripts provide
a window into the cross-cultural diversity of this holy site along the silk roads.
The languages of these texts include Sanskrit, Tibetan, Uighur (spoken by a
Turkic ethnic group still living in Western China), Tangut (both a language and
a script used by a people of the same name in northwestern China), Tocharian
(the language used by a people who lived close to Dunhuang), Khotanese (an
Eastern Iranian language), Sogdian (a language of a Persian people living in
Sogdiana, present-day southern Uzbekistan), Hebrew, and two writing systems
of ancient India called Brahmi and Kharosthi. In 1907, a Buddhist monk
introduced the Library Cave to British archeologist Sir Marc Aurel Stein (1862–
1943), who bought a portion of them for his government. Today many of these
invaluable documents are housed in the British Library in London, some of
which can be viewed online. The preservation of this material is a testament to
the spiritual beliefs of those who stopped at Dunhuang before the journey west
around the Taklamakan Desert, or on their way east just after making the desert

crossing, but their presence in London is a reminder of the legacy of British colonialism and imperialism.

Paper Offerings in Japan and Korea

Around the seventh or eighth century CE, Mahayana Buddhism spread to Japan, becoming an official religion there alongside Shintoism, and the printing of Buddhist texts supported the spread of this faith to the highest levels of society. An example of printing that predates the Dunhuang Diamond Sutra may be a Buddhist talismanic scroll of about 764–770 from the Japanese capital at Nara: the Sutra of the Great Incantations of Pure Immaculate Light (*Mukujoko daidarani kyo*), simply known by the Japanese term *Hyakumanto Darani* (the Dharani in a Million Pagodas). *Dharani* is a Sanskrit word meaning a long-form mantra, that is words, sounds, or phrases that are repeated during meditation or concentration. The *dharani* were transliterated from Sanskrit to Chinese and then into Korean and Japanese. The Empress Shotoku (718–770), a devout Buddhist who is often remembered today for her relationship with a Buddhist monk, commissioned the construction of a million small-scale, wooden votive pagodas (temples containing a prayer), each with a block-print text of the mantra – one of four prayers that each began "the purity of prayer" – rolled and deposited into a hollow cavity at the top of each pagoda. These mini pagodas fulfilled the role that life-sized temples played in the spiritual lives of Buddhists: they served as a proxy for the Buddha and inspired the owner to enact a mental pilgrimage. The million offerings were distributed to Japan's ten

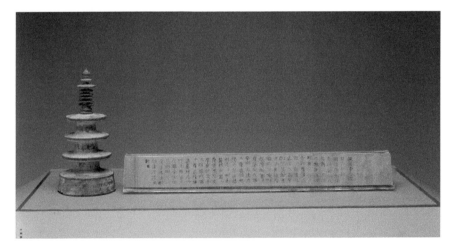

Fig 5.2
The charm text of a mantra found in a wooden pagoda commissioned by the Japanese Empress Shotoku ca. 767–770.
Middlebury College Museum of Art

major temples. Scriptoria at the Empress Shotuku's court also provided temples with copies of Buddhist texts.

About 1,771 of the pagodas associated with Empress Shotoku survive in museums, libraries, and archives around the world. These objects bear witness to an early phase of textual innovation and religious transmission and testify to the importance of new technology – printing – for the spreading of ideas. Indeed, most of the earliest printed texts from China, Korea, and Japan are Buddhist. Printing in Japan would flourish again in the late eleventh century during the Heian period (794–1185), a time when illuminated texts were also produced there.

Similar votive pagodas with inscriptions from the Sutra of the Great Incantations of Pure Immaculate Light have been found at sites from the Silla Kingdom of Korea (eighth and ninth century), such as the Hwangnyongsa Temple complex (Gyeongju, South Korea). We also learn about Korean Buddhism from manuscripts at Dunhuang. For example, a certain Hyecho (born 704 in Silla) left Korea for China at age 16 and later took a pilgrimage throughout India in order to visit sacred sites of Buddhism. He wrote about his journeys in a famous travelogue, which French archeologist Paul Pelliot removed from Dunhuang in 1908. The Korean author wrote about everything from devotional practices across regions to the climate, both of weather and politics.

Illumination in India: Beyond Buddhism

Spreading the message of spiritual revelation of the Four Noble Truths was central to the Buddha's mission – as it was for other religious and political leaders throughout the ancient and medieval world – and the movement of people, ideas, and indeed materials, contributed to the transmission of his teachings. Dunhuang and China's Gansu Province are over 1,000 miles from the Buddha's birthplace in Lumbini; Korea is more than 2,600 miles away, and Japan more than 3,000 miles. Closer to the Buddha's birthplace was a great center of Buddhist practice and manuscript production in Bihar, India, the seat of the ruling Pala dynasty (800–1200; the dynasty also ruled from Bengal). While Buddhist temples were decorated with sculptures and paintings for centuries from the ancient to medieval periods, illuminated manuscripts only survive from about 1000 CE onward.

One of the most important texts to receive decoration is The Perfection of Wisdom (*Prajnaparamita*), which describes the path toward enlightenment in 8,000 verses. In India, scribes and artists used palm leaves to create long, horizontal manuscripts joined in two or more places with strings that passed through holes in the pages before being knotted around wooden boards. This format was used for Buddhist texts, as well as for sacred writings of Jainism and Hinduism, both ancient Indian religions still practiced today. Painted pages and covers from The Perfection of Wisdom often visualized scenes from the

Fig 5.3
A pair of wooden book covers with scenes from the life of the Buddha – including his meditation beneath the Bodhi Tree in Bodh Gaya (Bihar) – was produced in Bihar around 1025. The two holes in each board once accommodated knots and binding strings that held the pages, likely made of palm leaves, of the manuscript together. Los Angeles County Museum of Art, from the Nasli and Alice Heeramaneck Collection, Museum Associates Purchase (M.72.1.20c-d)

Fig 5.4
This page shows Maitreya, a bodhisattva of the future, who will come to Earth to complete Buddha's teachings of enlightenment. It comes from a manuscript of the *Prajnaparamita*, made in Bihar, Kurkihar, India, around 1100–1125.
Los Angeles County Museum of Art, from the Nasli and Alice Heeramaneck Collection, Museum Associates Purchase (M.72.1.19a-b)

life of the Buddha and could include images of bodhisattvas. These subjects find visual counterparts in all Buddhist art forms throughout Central, South, Southeast, and East Asia. Such images in manuscripts were meant to enliven the texts and connect to the other artistic expressions of faith that one would encounter in life and on travels. These manuscripts survive because they are so portable, allowing devotees to transport them, especially during times of political and social change or unrest.

Buddhism influenced, and was influenced by, other religions of India and the Himalayan region, particularly Hinduism and Jainism. We can glimpse these influences through diagrams known as mandalas, which are shared by all three faiths, and through the design and format of manuscripts. A mandala represents the cosmos and usually takes the form of repeated geometric patterns, whether circular or square. In manuscript form, mandalas could be printed or painted and could be consulted to help guide meditation practices by focusing on a holy figure or site, such as Mount Meru – the center of the physical, metaphysical, and spiritual universes in Indian religions.

Fig 5.5
These wooden covers from an eleventh-century manuscript associated with Shiva contain depictions of Hindu deities.
The Walters Art Museum, Baltimore

Hinduism is a diverse, polytheistic tradition with many sects, which mainly agree that an eternal being created three primary deities: Brahma (the creator), Vishnu (the preserver), and Shiva (the destroyer). These individuals can take many forms, or avatars (for example, the Buddha is considered an avatar of Vishnu). Other key deities include the goddess Parvati, wife of Shiva; Ganesha, the elephant-headed god and son of Parvati and Shiva; and Krishna, the blue-skinned avatar of Vishnu. Texts associated with this celestial lineup are similar to the format of palm leaf manuscripts, exceptional examples of which came from Nepal. We can explore the theme of paradise through Hindu texts known as *puranas*, meaning ancient stories. The blue-skinned Hindu deity Krishna and his wife Satyabhama are said to have transplanted a sacred tree from the celestial heaven to Earth. In Section B, we will see just how prevalent sacred tree imagery is in relation to the theme of paradise. Illuminations from the sixteenth century in Northwest India provide a vivid glimpse into Hindu painting practices.

Jainism centers on the teachings of 24 spiritual guides known as *jinas* or *tirthankaras*. The two main sects are the Svetambara (meaning "white clad," referring to the robes worn by monks) and the Digambara (meaning "sky clad," as they do not wear clothes). Jains take five vows: non-violence (*ahimsa*), truth (*satya*), non-theft (*achaurya*), celibacy (*brahmacharya*), and non-attachment (*aparigraha*). A central text for Svetambara Jains is the Kalpasutra (Book of Sacred Precepts), which records the lives of each *jina*. These paper manuscripts often included a painted circle to emulate the string hole found in the palm leaf manuscript tradition. Gujarat province on the northwestern shore of India was a significant center for Jain manuscript production.

One pathway to paradise for Svetambara Jain culture follows the story of Mahavira. The *Kalpasutra* recounts how a queen named Trisala has a series of 14 auspicious dreams related to her desire to have a child. Consulting with astrologers, her husband, King Siddharta, predicts that she will give birth to Mahavira, who will become the twenty-fourth *jina*. The text describes Siddharta as being adorned "like a wish-granting tree." Eventually their child Vardhaman becomes Mahavira, a hero who subdues the serpent-god Sangamaka in a sacred grove. This act is one of many that testified to Vardhaman-Mahavira's bravery. In his enlightened state, Mahavira was often shown surrounded by a mandala of cosmic spheres, jeweled gates, and a flowering tree, all of which combine to form a symbol of paradise.

India's religious diversity in the medieval period included several other faiths. In the first centuries CE, Christianity arrived in India, and, from the

Fig 5.6
Vardhaman (Mahavira) and the Snake-God Sangamaka. Page from a Kalpasutra
manuscript, Gujarat, India, about 1475.
From the Collection of Carrie and Tadzio Wellisz

eighth century CE onward, Islam was also practiced there. From 1206 to 1526,
portions of the Indian subcontinent and environs were ruled by five Persian-
speaking Muslim sultanates (so called after the ruling sultan), known inclu-
sively as the Delhi sultanate since they were primarily based in Delhi. These
included the Mamluk dynasty of greater Egypt and Central Asia (1206–1290),
the Turko-Afghan Khalji dynasty (1290–1320), the Turko-Indian Tughlaq dynasty (1320–1414), the Sayyid dynasty of Multan (Punjab, Pakistan; 1414–1451),
and the Lodi dynasty also of Punjab origin (1451–1526). During this period
of Muslim rule, many east Indian manuscripts (Buddhist, Hindu, and Jain)
were taken to Tibetan monasteries for preservation and safekeeping, especially
during the early formation of the sultanate.

The Buddha and the Khans

There are Arabic and Persian texts from 900 to 1300 that locate the Buddha
within local and regional histories of Islam and of the world. During this
period, the Islamicate world continued to expand, with manuscript culture
flourishing at the Abbasid capital of Baghdad (until 1250), with textile and
luxury arts being traded in Fatimid Egypt (from 969 onward), and with political states stretching from India to the Iberian Peninsula to West Africa by the
1300s. Muslim presence is also attested to in Southeast and East Asia through
reports, chronicles, and the establishment of mosques. The historical context
in which we find stories about the Buddha is the empire of the Mongols, an
East-Central Asian ethnic group that emerged in the thirteenth century under
the rule of leaders who took the title of *khan*, the first of which was Chinggis
Khan (born Temujin; ca. 1162–1227). While the easternmost branch of the
empire – the Yuan dynasty in China (1271–1368) – adopted Buddhism and

local traditions, the westernmost territory in Central Asia was partitioned into three principalities that each adopted Islam: the Chagatai khanate (1226–1241/ 42; present-day Kazakhstan, Uzbekistan, and Turkmenistan, among other areas), the Golden Horde (1240s–1502; from Eastern Europe along the Danube River to Siberia), and the Ilkhanate (1256–1335/1353; including territories in present-day Iran, Iraq, Armenia, Turkey, and beyond). The text and images within the Arabic *Jami' al-Tawarikh* (*Compendium of Chronicles*), compiled by the Jewish-to-Muslim convert Rashid al-Din Hamadini (1247–1318) during the reigns of the Ilkhanid rulers Ghazan (r. 1295–1304) and Oljeitu (r. 1303–1316), provide glimpses into the Buddha's journey toward nirvana as recounted in a place vastly distant from his homeland. The author locates the Buddha within a universal history that begins with the biblical Adam in the Garden of Eden (a site to which we will return in Section B of this chapter) and continues to document the lives of prophets from the shared Jewish, Christian, and Muslim traditions, as well as historical figures that include Shakyamuni Buddha, Muhammad, and the Mongol khans. The surviving portions of the manuscript are now divided between the Khalili Collection in London and the Edinburgh University Library.

In the manuscript, a sequence of three images across several pages depicts Shakyamuni compassionately providing food to a devil, followed by a depiction of the grove of enlightenment (of the Buddha or of Maitreya), and a third image featuring the sites where the Buddha reached nirvana (Kushinagar, Uttar Pradesh, northern India). Rashid al-Din Hamadini likely relied on Tibetan, Nepalese, and Sanskrit sutras – like those discussed and seen in the above sections – for these narratives. The pictorial style across the manuscript, however, relies on Chinese painting, a testament to the trade relationships between the Ilkhanid and Yuan courts. Incidentally, there are 15 pages with images of Chinese emperors (from the Liang dynasty [502–557], for example) spread between the two portions of the surviving manuscript.

One of the most famous Turco-Mongol rulers of Central Asia was Timur (r. 1370–1405), known as Tamerlane in European sources. The Timurid dynasty, which lost most of its power by 1500, is named for him. He was born in Transoxiana (in present-day Uzbekistan) and eventually ruled over the Chagatai khanate, among other areas. During the reign of his son, Shahrukh Mirza (r. 1405–1447), the historian Hafiz-i Abru (d. 1430) chronicled the history of the world up to the present reign of the Timurids. One section of his *Majma al-Tawarikh* (*Compendium of Histories*) includes stories about Shakyamuni Buddha, who, the author recounts, rose from the dead and appeared to his followers. This narrative detail is not found in Indian sources but can be located in certain Chinese texts. The writer may have even conflated Christ's death and resurrection with the Buddha's posthumous manifestations. Manuscript images showing the Buddha in the act of reclining in nirvana could have drawn inspiration from larger-than-life sculpted Buddhas, which existed at the time at various sites within Timurid territory, including present-day Tajikistan, Uzbekistan, and Afghanistan. It was precisely the movement of people, goods, and ideas that contributed to the spread and reinterpretation of stories about the Buddha from his homeland to worlds beyond.

A Christianized Version of the Buddha Story in the Mediterranean

Throughout numerous kingdoms of Afro-Eurasia, manuscript stories abound about an Indian prince who became an enlightened teacher. Some of these accounts present the protagonist as a Christian convert from "paganism" or "idolatry," rhetoric that fell in line with imagined ideas about India from Christianized Europe, western Asia, and North Africa at the time. The etymology, or linguistic origins, of his name can be traced to the Sanskrit word bodhisattva: in Arabic we meet *Budhasaf*, in Georgian we read about *Iodasaph*, in Greek he becomes *Ioasaph*, which in Ge'ez is *Yewasef*, and in Latin is *Josaphat*. We also learn about his spiritual mentor, Barlaam, a name which may derive from the Sanskrit word *Bahgavan*, meaning "lord," a title of the Buddha. Barlaam and Josaphat would become Christian saints and were granted feast days in the Christian calendar (August 26 for the Eastern Orthodox traditions and November 27 in the Western Roman Church).

One of the enduring tales of these saints is by Rudolf von Ems (ca. 1200–1254 CE), a prolific writer who situated Josaphat in his Christian worldview. In his version, Josaphat's father kept the young prince in isolation in the royal palace for many years; however, one day, Josaphat witnessed illness, poverty, old age, and death for the first time. Distraught by these encounters, he meditated beneath a tree, met a Christian monk called Barlaam, and ultimately renounced earthly pleasures and converted to Christianity. Rudolf von Ems was one in a long line of historical writers to recount this tale, which might be traced as far back as the Christian theologian John of Damascus (seventh century, Syria), whom Rudolf refers to in his prologue. In the intervening centuries, we can trace the linguistic transmission of the story through an Arabic version by Buddhist scholars from India during the reign of Yahya ibn Khalid (ninth century, Bactria), a Greek translation by the monk Euthymius of Athos (eleventh century, from Georgia), a French tale by the popular writer Gui de Cambrai (twelfth century, France), and later still to the Jewish-to-Muslim convert we encountered earlier, Rashid-al-Din Hamadani (thirteenth century, Persia). Even the famous world traveler Marco Polo (fourteenth century, Italy) described the figure of the historical Buddha, whom Polo referred to as Sagamoni Borcan according to local customs in Ceylon (Sri Lanka), commenting that if the Buddha been a Christian he would have been a saint. The Christian writers fit the narrative into the expected format of a saint's life: Josaphat renounces worldly goods and spreads his teachings (like the Buddha) while debating perceived heretics and non-Christians. After his death, Josaphat's bones were considered sacred relics by the Christian faithful, as we are told in the manuscript sources.

Numerous illustrated copies of texts by some of the above writers have survived, including Rudolf von Ems's text (ca. 1469 version) from Hagenau, France. A thirteenth-century illuminated copy in Greek, from the library at the Holy Monastery of Iviron on Mount Athos in Greece, contains French translations in the margins, added later but likely indicative of the kinds of encounters a pilgrim or traveler might have with a manuscript. An opening inscription in the manuscript reveals the fluidity of geographical thinking at the time: "A story profitable for the soul from the innermost country of the Ethiopians, called of the Indians." Another account, from 1553, preserves the tale in Ge'ez, the official language of historical kingdoms and courts in Ethiopia and today the liturgical language of the Ethiopian Church. The author's preface mirrors the account of Gregory Jeretz (the Presbyter), a twelfth-century Armenian chronicler, suggesting additional pathways by which the Christianized account of the Buddha's life co-mingled throughout Byzantium.

The connection between shared events from the life of St. Josaphat and the historic Buddha (Shakyamuni) was only realized in the sixteenth century by the Portuguese humanist Diogo do Couto (ca. 1542–1616), and yet serious study of the Josaphat-Buddha connections emerged only in the nineteenth century. The long history of this textual tradition of the life of St. Josaphat now encompasses accounts in Armenian, Dutch, English, French, Ge'ez, German, Greek, Hebrew, Icelandic, Italian, Latin, Polish, Spanish, Syriac, Tagalog, and Yiddish, among others. The story of the Buddha and the spiritual practices associated with his teachings are possibly the best example of global connections and comparisons across the period 500 to 1500 and beyond, even in regions and communities dominated by the monotheisms of Judaism, Christianity, and Islam.

Conclusion

As we have seen, tales of Buddha disavowing and renouncing worldliness in pursuit of enlightenment traversed the globe and connected vast geographies through local interpretation and expression. Vastly different manuscript cultures helped ensure this preservation, even as equally varied confessional communities borrowed from the practices and modes of production of their neighbors. One point to keep in mind is that although many cultures wrote things down and guarded knowledge in safe spaces – from monasteries to libraries and now also museums and archives – many more texts have likely been lost to time due to the very nature of the organic supports on which they were written and the climate conditions of an environment. It is especially difficult to preserve such artifacts in tropical realms. Moreover, other cultures did not use writing as a mode of transmission but instead practiced oral story-telling. We will look at ways to address these differences a bit more in the next section. The role played by language – spoken from person to person or written down – in the shaping of history is a theme that can be explored today by considering how we communicate in multiple ways all of the time: face to face, online through e-mail and social media, through congregational prayer, and through scholarship.

B: SENSING THE SOUL'S JOURNEY

Evidence:	The Crusader Bible/The Shah Abbas Bible
	The Sephirotic Tree
	Qur'anic passages about paradise
	Hajj certificates and pilgrim badges
	Herrad of Landsberg, *Hortus deliciarum*
	The Rothschild Pentateuch

Ideas that Bridge Heaven and Earth

Manuscripts give us information of complex beliefs about the human relationship to otherworldly domains or beings, inviting readers to connect with spiritual realms or to envision the afterlife – states of paradise beyond the Earth. In the centuries between 900 and 1300, writers across Afro-Eurasia endeavored to compile the fullness of human knowledge – at least from within their realm or grasp – into extensive volumes that may appear to readers today as a blend of secular and sacred. But these categories were not entirely separable in the medieval period. Study of manuscripts at madrasas in the Islamicate world, preparatory academies for imperial examinations in China, or universities in the greater Mediterranean context, advanced the education of wide cross-sections of society, and this instruction often involved oversight from religious leaders and certainly included sacred concepts.

The texts discussed in this section concern theological beliefs about a range of physical spaces and metaphysical phenomena, such as gardens and auspicious gems, each of which will expand our understanding of paradise by addressing the journey of the soul. We begin with our feet firmly planted on the Earth in gardens and green spaces, then we will examine the properties of jewels as metaphysical objects; next we will follow in the footsteps of pilgrims to a few holy sites, and finally we will look to the stars and reflect on abstract ideas about what lies beyond the contours of the Earth.

Gardens and Tree Imagery

The veneration of sacred trees and the cultivation of gardens as symbolic spaces are themes shared by many cultures and faiths, but this common ideology does not necessarily indicate borrowing or a reciprocal relationship. The connection between green spaces and divinity or transcendence is a human universal. On a basic level, gardens are enclosed or protected plots of earth in which a variety of plants are cultivated. Even if gardens are blessed with miraculous beauty, this idyllic condition needs human maintenance. Tending a garden is a meditative practice that brings one closer to creation and to nature, a metaphor for spiritual communion. There are many ways to envision a garden, and equally numerous varieties of sacred plants, including trees that produce flowers and fruits, and some that blossom with mystical gems. A look at a few traditions provides a comparative approach to the study of religion in a global Middle Ages.

Earlier in this chapter we explored the central role that trees played in Indian religions: as the site of the Buddha's enlightenment, as a gift to humankind from Krishna and Satyabhama, and as a place of testing for Mahavira. At Buddhist, Hindu, and Jain temples, the devotional practices known as *puja* can include offerings of flowers, food, incense, or precious material items such as coins. The tale of a garden with a sacred tree resonates with the Abrahamic religions of Judaism, Christianity, and Islam. For members of each faith, the Garden of Eden epitomizes earthly paradise. The biblical book of Genesis describes Eden as a site of lush vegetation, containing every seed-bearing plant. Vegetal and arboreal imagery in art of all three religions could remind viewers of Eden, just as cultivating a garden was a practice associated with proximity to the divine. Four sacred rivers were said to flow from Eden or Paradise, refreshing the world: the Pison (possibly in Syria), the Gihon (said to be in Ethiopia), and the Tigris and Euphrates (primarily in present-day Iraq). Fountains in the courtyards of synagogues, monasteries, cloisters, and mosques evoked the calming qualities of Eden.

Christian writers and theologians believed Eden to be a physical place. Mapmakers often attempted to locate it, sometimes in Africa, India, or elsewhere, often at the extreme end of the Earth (depending on the vantage point of the writer or artist). For example, Vincent of Beauvais (ca. 1190–1264), a Dominican theologian of the monastic order established by St. Dominic, wrote a comprehensive history of the world up to the year 1264 called the *Miroir historial* (*Mirror of History*). In the text, he located the Garden of Eden beyond the land of India and the Island of Taprobane (Sri Lanka), far from the world of the people he referred to prejudicially as "idolaters."

The opening page of a luxurious mid-thirteenth-century Crusader Bible visualizes the story of Creation according to the Abrahamic traditions. The uppermost scenes remind us that people in the Middle Ages knew that the Earth was round, an idea that can be traced back to ancient sources across the globe. The figure of God stands beyond the contour of the world, surrounded by angels, but transcends heaven and Earth by spinning the orb with his hand or touching the arm of the first man, Adam, or below by creating Eve and instructing both individuals not to eat from the sacred Tree of Knowledge of Good and Evil at the garden's center (note the four rivers at God's feet). The final quadrant shows the episode commonly known as the fall of humankind, in which the couple is tempted by the devil in the form of a serpent (here shown

Fig 5.7
These four scenes from the Morgan Crusader Bible/Shah Abbas Bible (ca. 1244–1254) show God creating the world, creating Adam and then Eve, and warning them not to eat from the Tree of Knowledge.
The Morgan Library and Museum

with wings and a woman's face, as the word for serpent is gendered feminine in Latin-based languages). It is worth noting that this manuscript has been assigned many names, each of which reveals aspects of the book's provenance or ownership history. Sometimes it is called the Saint Louis or Crusader Bible, both of which reference King Louis IX of France (1214–1270), who may have

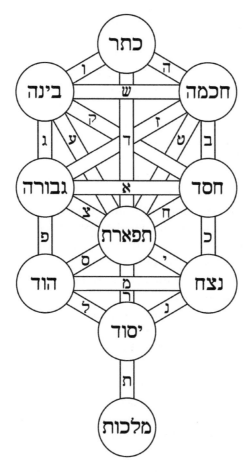

Fig 5.8
This diagram presents the *Sephirotic Tree* with 10 orbs and 22 channels starting with
the Divine at the top and Earth or humankind at the bottom.
© Wikimedia Commons, public domain.

commissioned the manuscript and was considered a pious crusader king. The
codex is also referred to as the Shah Abbas Bible, as it was gifted by European
Carmelite missionaries to the Safavid ruler in the early seventeenth century,
at which point Arabic and Judeo-Persian inscriptions were added. A book
depicting God's creation has traveled all over it.

During the Middle Ages, many Jewish rabbis expounded theology about
paradise as an Edenic garden of spiritual enlightenment, especially in mystical
contexts. Tree and orchard metaphors can be found in the Talmud, rabbinic
writings central to the study of Judaism, and in the esoteric discipline of the
Kabbalah, which seeks to gain insights into the nature of the divine. The general shape of a tree was envisioned as a diagram for exploring how humankind might know God. This arboreal structure consists of 22 branches, each
signified by a letter of the Hebrew alphabet. These pathways connect ten orbs

called *sephirot* (meaning emanations) that represent beyond-consciousness (a state similar to enlightenment), the intellect, and emotions through which the Infinite (the one God) becomes manifest to creation. This school of thought developed in the 1100s and 1200s in Spain and southern France with the writings of Moses ben Maimon, known as Maimonides (1135–1204), and Isaac the Blind (1160–1235). The ideas were later developed in the 1500s by intellectuals of the Jewish diaspora who were expelled from the Iberian Peninsula in 1492 and who migrated across North Africa to Jerusalem or to northern Europe – it is to those later manuscripts that we look for visualizations of the tree as reaching toward God in heaven – a tower for the soul to climb.

Arboreal images like this one and those discussed above reveal commonalities of cultures that were intricately connected but which developed unique expressions as linkages to the divine. The abstract sephirotic tree-diagram is similar to visualizations of *chakras*, that is, centers of spiritual power in the human body in Indian religions, or to the so-called Zodiacal human forms in medieval Christian and Islamic thought, in which the 12 signs of the zodiac are mapped onto the human body.

The word "paradise" is used frequently in the Qur'an to refer to a heavenly place whose sensorial pleasures evoke the image of a garden. A page from a Qur'an produced around 1300 in North Africa – written in the so-called Maghribi script common across present-day Morocco, Tunisia, Algeria, and surrounding areas – contains a passage from surah (chapter) 5:65: "And if the People of the Book had believed and guarded [against evil], we would certainly have covered their evil deeds and we would certainly have made them enter gardens of bliss." Throughout the Islamic world, verses of the Qur'an were incorporated into manuscripts, woven into textiles, minted on coins, painted onto ceramics, and embedded into architecture (as mosaics, wooden carvings, and so forth). Carefully written text, known as calligraphy, was considered a sacred act; the soul traveled to paradise through the formation of blessed words.

One early fourteenth-century mihrab, or prayer niche, in the collection of New York's Metropolitan Museum of Art, contains Qur'anic inscriptions that refer to paradise, thereby suggesting the cosmological importance of sacred landscapes within the Muslim tradition. The inscription reads, "Indeed, the righteous will be within gardens and springs. [Having been told], 'Enter it in peace, safe [and secure].' And We will remove whatever is in their breasts of resentment, [so they will be] brothers, on thrones facing each other." Here the text is written in cobalt, a pigment often sourced from Egypt or Persia, further establishing the Islamic world as central to the networks of material exchange across trade routes from east to west.

Sacred Jewels and Treasure Bindings

As demonstrated in the chapters on economies, cross-cultural trade was ubiquitous in the medieval world. In Chapter 2 we observed how silk and silk textiles

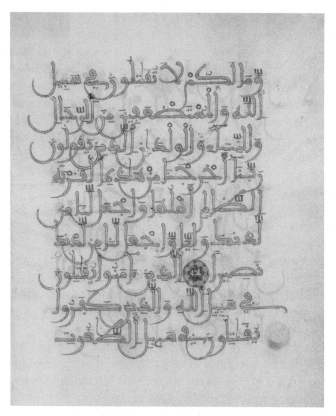

Fig 5.9
The text of this copy of the Qur'an reminds devout Muslims to guard against evil
so that they might enter "a garden of bliss," a phrase for paradise. The words were
written in brown ink, and diacritical marks in blue and green indicate vowel sounds
and other guides to pronunciation. The golden trilobed motif marks the verses.
Metropolitan Museum of Art, Rogers Fund, 1937, 37.21

were used as money, tribute gifts, diplomatic exchange, and signs of status and
luxury across the silk roads. Silks were also commonly used as robes and decorative cloths in religious ceremonies that brought the humble worshipper closer
to the divine. Sacred patterns and motifs were transmitted through weaving
designs. Examples of these propitious symbols are that of the powerful lucky
gem called a *çintamani* (from the Indian subcontinent to China and the British
Isles), as well as the lotus blossom (seen from China to Byzantium, by way
of India), and the *swastika* (also called the *gammadion* or *wàn*). Found in many
Indian traditions and beyond, the *swastika* was traditionally a symbol of harmony and good fortune, unfortunately adopted by Adolph Hitler and the Nazi
party as a symbol of superiority. For medieval people, the soft touch of silk, its
rich colors and polished luster, and the quiet sounds it made as it moved were
a sensory connection with paradise, especially when the fabric was embellished
with cherished symbols – a visual reminder of spiritual delight.

Silks were also used to wrap and enshrine holy manuscripts and their precious illuminations, a practice found from Ireland to India. Other valuable commodities were used as coverings for books as well. Ivory plaques, likely from the tusks of African elephants or Arctic walruses, were carved to adorn the covers of gospel books in Europe and Byzantium. Precious stones – such as rubies and emeralds – were often added to these so-called treasure bindings. The raw materials were generally sourced from India and South and Southeast Asia; for Christians these gems referred to descriptions of Heavenly Jerusalem in the biblical Book of Revelation. While some precious goods – such as jewelry, amulets, and reliquaries – were highly portable and therefore had the potential to traverse great distances, other objects – including crowns, oil lamps, and votive statues – could serve local audiences at court, in temples, or in shrines. The raw materials of sapphires, turquoise, gold, and silver, among others, were highly prized trade goods. Many cultures and religions ascribe magical or healing properties to gems or metals, and these associations often involved ideas about the divine and the afterlife. Buddhist priests in Nepal, for example, wore crowns shaped to recall the division of the universe into Earth, atmosphere, and heaven – a cosmological theme complemented by gem settings that symbolized paradise.

Auspicious gems feature prominently in the teachings and art of Indian religions, specifically Buddhism. The Buddha is said to have imparted his wisdom at the request of Vajradhara, the primordial Buddha whose name means "diamond holder." According to Mahayana Buddhist practice, achieving a state of Vajradhara is synonymous with attaining nirvana or release from suffering. Additionally, three precious jewels known as *triratna* symbolize the Buddha, the dharma (teachings of the Buddha), and the sangha (monastic order), but they also represent the body, speech, and mind of all Buddhas past, present, and future. Perhaps most well-known is the *çintamani*, a wish-fulfilling jewel that often takes the form of three circles closely grouped in a pyramidal composition and which are offered to the faithful by bodhisattvas. The word *çintamani* could indicate numerous bodhisattvas, such as Çintamani-Lokesvara (an avatar of Avalokitesvara, the bodhisattva of compassion), but the term could also describe a pattern of three dots in a triangle. This decorative motif can be found in every form of Buddhist art. On a page from a thirteenth-century charm text from Nepal, the Buddha Shakyamuni sits on a throne above a textile with the *çintamani* design, which also appears against the red background.

The concept of a wish-granting or protective jewel originated in Buddhist and Hindu sacred texts, and eventually the motif became a favorite pattern on luxury textiles throughout South and East Asia, the Persian Empire and the greater Islamicate world, and western Europe. Pictorial depictions of the design appear in Buddhist paintings from Dunhuang to Tibet, Bihar, and elsewhere, as well as architectural reliefs at the Great Stupa at Sanchi. Representations in sculpture can be found on the Sassanian tombs at Taq-e Bostan (meaning Arch of the Garden) in Northwest Iran. The textile pattern was also represented on garments of holy figures as early as the ninth century in the *Book of Kells*,

Fig 5.10
Part of a seventh-century mural found in the Magao Caves in Dunhuang, this
kneeling figure holds the *çintamani* gem and wears a green garment with the
çintamani design and floral motifs.
© President and Fellows of Harvard College

written and illuminated at a monastery dedicated to St. Columba (sixth century) in either Britain or Ireland.

Pilgrimage

Many spiritual leaders and revered individuals traveled to distant places, and
the followers of several religions often held special observances to remember
journeys of faith. We have discussed several sites of significance to the Buddha's
journey toward enlightenment, from Bodh Gaya to Kushingar. Similarly, each
year in the celebration of Passover, Jewish communities commemorate the
exodus out of ancient Egypt by the Israelites and the hope for a Promised Land
to come. In Christian scripture, Christ instructed his followers to make new
disciples of all nations, inspiring missionary journeys by prominent people,
such as St. Paul. And the Prophet Muhammad famously traveled from Medina
to Mecca, an act that Muslims emulate through *hajj* (pilgrimage) to the holy
city. For members of each of those faiths, visiting sites where God, prophets,

and saints walked or taught was and is still considered a transcendent experience and opportunity to connect with the sacred. Looking upon, touching, or even kissing relics – sanctified bodily remains of an individual or items that they touched or used – is another pious act. The theme of pilgrimage allows us to consider the ways that medieval people sought purity and renewal beyond the everyday experiences of life.

When pilgrims returned from sacred locales, they often brought with them reminders of their time abroad – we might call these items souvenirs today (from the French word "to remember"). Pious individuals could also make donations to shrines, just as Empress Shotoku of Japan sent a million votive pagodas to the ten major Buddhist temples on the island (see Section A above). At Bodh Gaya, small-scale versions of the Mahadoghi Temple there were produced in schist and other stones. In Christian tradition, St. James the Greater was thought to have walked from Jerusalem to northwestern Spain, reaching the Atlantic Ocean and picking up a shell to take back with him. The Church of Santiago de Compostela is named after him and the pilgrimage route leading there is called the *Camino de Santiago* (the path of St. James) – you will recognize wayfarers committed to the trip because they often wear a shell. Saint Thomas was believed to have preached in India, where churches and mile markers still bear his name, while St. Catherine of Alexandria in Egypt, a learned royal woman whose skills in rhetoric and debate bested many male competitors, ended her travels when angels transported her body to Mount Sinai in Egypt. Today the Monastery of St. Catherine is home to a library with hundreds of volumes in a vast range of languages used by the Christians, Jews, and Muslims who crossed paths there. Through the images and texts about saints and other holy figures in manuscripts, as well as the occasional pewter emblem acquired by a pilgrim that could be sewn into a book, readers could metaphorically map themselves to sites far beyond their homeland and remember their own journey to a distant land or the travels of an ancestor.

WHAT DID THE MIDDLE AGES SMELL LIKE?

Think about the words that we might use when speaking about the sense of smell: aroma, fragrance, odor, scent, whiff, perfume, and more. Many of the manuscripts throughout this book contain descriptions about the world that evoke those sensations. The Hebrew and Christian bibles and the Qur'an reference myrrh, aloe, and the "scent of paradise," with its sweet-tasting waters and every kind of flower or fruit. The most devout Buddhists are believed to have clarity of mind that allows them to enjoy the myriad fragrances all around them and to mediate between Earth and heaven. Consider also the scents of the materials used to make the manuscripts described in this chapter: eggs (white and sometimes yolk) for tempera paint that would be combined with pigments (organic, mineral, and chemically produced);

palm leaves harvested from groves; animal skins for parchment (soaked, scraped, and hung out to dry); and paper (produced from plant fibers in a mill). The act of making and later opening a new book is a fragrant process. Have you ever smelled a book?

Smell played a role in devotional practices, specifically pilgrimage. Incense – dried plants or hardened resins – could be burned at temples, chapels, or shrines. Some common types of incense include frankincense, myrrh, camphor, and sandalwood. These are also popular essential oils today. Perfumes were also quite popular in the medieval world, especially musk, which could be created from the glandular secretion of a musk deer or from some plants with subtle but seductive aromas such as the monkeyflower. We might alternatively refer to the silk roads as the incense routes, since many of these raw materials were traded along the roadways and waterways of Afro-Eurasia.

Religious and scientific texts throughout the Middle Ages conveyed an interest in and deep understanding of the way our bodies process smell, and some of these ideas still resonate today. The medieval diet, although varied around the world, often relied upon theories about food and the medical benefits associated not only with their taste or consumption, but also with their aroma. The Greco-Roman-Arabic concept of temperament understood the body as having four humors or fluids that needed to be balanced for healthy living: black bile was thought to produce melancholy in excess (we might say depression or anxiety today), yellow bile would result in cholera (think "hot tempered"), (red) blood yielded a sanguine personality (imagine the jovial life of the party), and white phlegm led to a phlegmatic bent (consider this type as being calm, almost sedate). This approach to healing asserted that all consumable natural materials had properties of wet/dry and hot/cold, and the right combination of foodstuffs, beverages, and perfumes could help bring one's body into alignment. For example, roses, as a cool plant, could be used to treat fevers, either as rosewater or simply a bouquet in one's bedroom. Or the warming quality of cloves could aid in digestion and fortify the body even from a simple whiff. In what ways do you regulate your diet or the scents in your environment to improve your health or mindset? And in keeping with the theme of this section, in what ways do scents connect you with a transcendent state of being, even one as simple as happiness?

Other forms of proof of pilgrimage could also be acquired. Certificates were issued to those who made the *hajj* to Mecca, and for those who could not travel, proxy scrolls could allow the person to virtually undertake the journey or for another to complete the trek on their behalf. On these documents, the major geographic markers along the way to Mecca are mapped, such as Jerusalem, Medina, or Mount Arafat overlooking the Ka'aba (the most sacred site in Islam). Often blessings and passages from the Qur'an are included. For Christians journeying to Jerusalem or Rome or other places associated with Christ or the saints, small pewter or lead-alloy badges were sold at shrines. These emblems sometimes featured an image of the holy figure, such as former archbishop of Canterbury, Thomas Becket (martyred in 1170). Others are

Fig 5.11
This document demonstrates the importance of *hajj* for Muslims: in it we read that
Maymunah, daughter of Muhammad ibn Abd Allah al-Zardali, made the pilgrimage
in AH 836/AD 1432/33.
© British Library

symbols of the cross, the monogram for Jesus of Nazareth the Savior (INRS)
or Jesus of Nazareth the King of the Jews (INRI). In the 1400s, pilgrim badges
were sometimes sewn into illuminated manuscripts known as Books of Hours,
which contained prayers to be read throughout the day, and some artists
painted versions of them as well. Finally, ceramic vessels in the shape of flasks
or water-storage devices were popular among pilgrims, so much so that luxury
lines of these objects were produced in painted earthenware and glass for
purely decorative purposes.

Fig 5.12
This fifteenth-century Book of Hours made for use in Bruges contains 23 pilgrim badges sewn into the final page of the manuscript.
National Library of the Netherlands, acquired with financial support from various foundations from antiquarian bookseller F. Knuf, Buren (Gld.) 77 L 60

Cosmos

In the year 1054 and for a few years to follow, people around the globe witnessed a bright light on the horizon – the lustrous remnant of the Crab Nebula supernova (referred to scientifically as SN 1054). The cosmic event may have been described in the writings of Ibn Butlan (1038–1075) in Iraq or later in the diary of Fujiwara no Teika (1162–1241) in Japan, and perhaps further afield recorded in petroglyphs of the Ancestral Puebloan people of the American Southwest (at Chaco Canyon or elsewhere). This single occurrence demonstrates how people from different places could look and respond to the same thing, and how knowledge of such a sighting could be passed down through time (indeed there are later historical records about the strange astral phenomenon). As this textbook demonstrates, the writing of history is always a process of the present, as scholars and students try to make sense of the past with the knowledge and perspectives that they have in mind today. This final section therefore encourages us to think about universal knowledge and about memory, as both processes encouraged medieval people to consider ideal states of mind and body.

Before addressing the concept of universal knowledge, it is helpful to be reminded of how medieval people envisioned their place in the cosmos.

In Indian religions, mandala diagrams were guides to meditation but also metaphorical maps of the sacred universe, one made up of spiritual guides (bodhisattvas or *jinas*, for example). In medieval Christian cosmology, the cosmic spheres or planetary orbits were often depicted as concentric circles held by the Trinity (God the Father, Christ the Son, and the Holy Spirit). The heavenly spheres closest to God include angels, prophets, apostles, saints, and clerics in descending order before finally reaching the Earth. The Qur'an describes the wondrous cosmos as a realm inhabited by angels and jinn (spirits). According to hadith literature (accounts about the Prophet Muhammad), angels were said to be created from light – a characteristic that denotes their function as messengers of God. Because in Islam gold was associated with the light of Allah or word of God, the use of chrysography, or gold lettering, was solely reserved for the pages of the Qur'an. In all these traditions, the complexities of creation involved as many things that could be experienced or sensed with one's body as could be pondered or felt with one's mind and spirit.

The boom in manuscript production across Afro-Eurasia during the Illuminated Ages of 900 to 1300 witnessed the expansion of the encyclopedia as a compendium of universal, or total, knowledge. In this genre, we might consider the text *The Ultimate Ambition in the Arts of Erudition* by Al-Nuwayri (1279–1333), who intended to record all thinking that had come down to people living in Mamluk-ruled Egypt, with references as far afield as the Indo-Malaysian archipelago. Several global encyclopedia traditions rely upon garden and plant imagery in organizing ideas, such as *The Forest of Gems in the Garden of the Dharma*, written by the Chinese Buddhist monk Dao Shi in 668 or *The Paradise of Wisdom* by Persian scientist Ali ibn Sahl Rabban al-Tabari from about 860. Women also contributed to this genre, and our focus here will be on the abbess Herrad of Landsberg.

In the Alsace region between present-day France and Germany, the Monastery of Sainte-Odile (referred to also as Hohenbourg) sits atop a rocky precipice and is surrounded by a lush forest setting. Other religious houses dot the surrounding hilltops, while the more populated cities lie in the valleys below. In the second half of the 1100s, the abbess Herrad of Landsberg began writing a universal history centered on Christian salvation called *The Garden of Delights* (or *Hortus deliciarum* in Latin). She began with the creation of the world, with Adam and Eve in Eden, and continued with charts and diagrams about geography and cosmology, animals and astronomy, and more. Herrad knew classical Greek and Arabic sources and describes her research process as follows: "Like a tiny bee inspired by God, I collected from the many flowers of holy scripture and philosophical writings together in this book." In a diagram for the liberal arts, the illuminator of the volume depicted personifications of arithmetic, geometry, astronomy, grammar, rhetoric, dialectic, and music surrounding a figure of philosophy, beneath whose throne sit Socrates and Plato and beyond which sit unnamed poets and sages.

At points throughout this book, we have called attention to later events in history. We do so in order to provide reminders that medieval ideas and

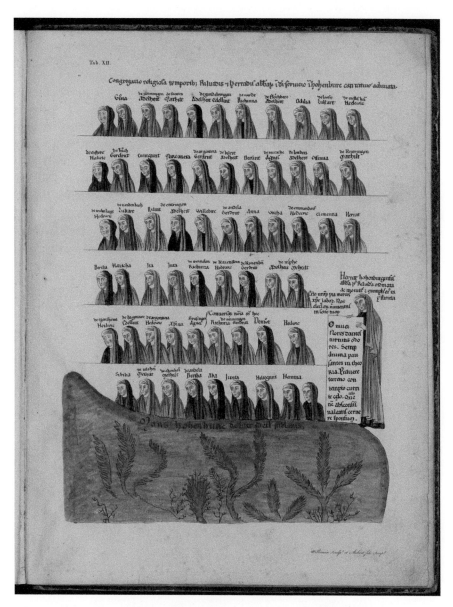

Fig 5.13
On this page from *The Garden of Delights*, abbess Herrad of Landsberg presents the sisters of her order to God. The original manuscript was made between 1167 and 1185 but was destroyed in 1870 during the Franco-Prussian War. In 1979, a modern version was created from tracings of some of the images and descriptions of the contents.
© Wikimedia Commons, public domain

objects survive into the present through the care and preservation of individuals and institutions, but to also alert you, the reader, to just how rare some of the documents and works of art are and how much has been lost. In the context of this chapter, we have seen that paradise was often conceived as a fleeting and fragile ideal. For diasporic communities, memory often provides a link to another place and time. We will take just one final example: a Hebrew study Bible.

The Rothschild Pentateuch is a survivor, a manuscript that has had an eventful life from its place of creation in central Europe in 1296 for the patron Joseph ben Joseph Martell to its escape from the hands of the Nazis during World War II, at which point the volume was housed in Frankfurt, Germany. The main portions of the text at the center of the page are the writings of the Torah (Genesis, Exodus, Leviticus, Numbers, and Deuteronomy), which are surrounded in the inner margin with Aramaic translations, and in the upper, lower, and outer margins with commentary by Rabi Schlomo Itzhaki (Rashi) (1040–1105). For members of Joseph Martell's family and community, the volume would have been considered a luxury – the lavish texts may have been undertaken by itinerant Jewish scribes and the illuminations by local

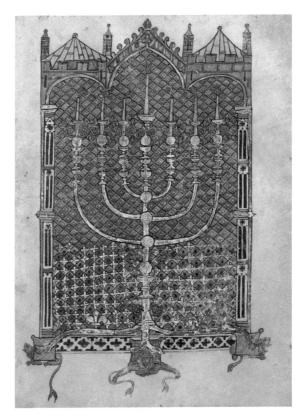

Fig 5.14
The vibrant red and blue colors used across this page are reminiscent of French and German Christian manuscripts. Here they are the background for a Jewish menorah. The stunning use of gold leaf adds to the veneration of the sacred image and reveals the wealth and piety of the patron of the Rothschild Pentateuch (1296).
The J. Paul Getty Museum, Los Angeles, acquired with the generous support of Jo Carole and Ronald S. Lauder, Ms. 116, fol. 226v

(sometimes Christian) artists. The glittering seven-branch menorah in the volume reminds viewers of the Temple, the dwelling place of God on Earth, that once stood in the holy city of Jerusalem, both of the biblical history of Solomon and his ancestors there, but also of a hoped-for future when the central structure of Jewish worship would be rebuilt. The building was destroyed by Roman emperor Titus in 70 CE, and, from that time on, studying the Torah has represented one way to commune with God. At an intervening moment in the middle of the 1400s, the manuscript was in Italy, where Joel ben Simeon, the most famous Jewish artist-scribe, replaced a page showing Moses leading the Israelites out of captivity in Egypt and into the Promised Land. Even amidst migrations and movements, there can be a glimmer of hope. Even when paradise seems worlds away, one can still remember and imagine.

Looking Forward: Paradise Now

The manuscripts explored in this chapter are today located in museums or libraries whose missions support open access to their treasures, onsite and online. Each of the pages discussed can be downloaded free of charge or viewed in close detail on a computer, tablet, or smartphone. Numerous other institutions are moving in the digital direction with open content, including the Vatican Library, the British Library in London, the Bibliothèque nationale de France in Paris, and more. This commitment to access has the potential to not only reunite dispersed pages of the past but also to connect people and ideas at the crossroads of the World Wide Web.

Paradise is a place that can be reached, sometimes as a distant point on a map (real or imagined) and still again as an internal state of bliss and mindfulness. As we have seen in this chapter, there were many pathways to paradise across Afro-Eurasia: some routes led to places of great spiritual importance, while others transported the faithful to metaphysical realms. Manuscripts and luxury goods, as well as other portable objects, aided individuals in reaching these sites, at least in their thoughts and prayers. Today, we may turn to our smartphones or laptops to explore distant and seemingly untouched places around the globe, or to make travel arrangements to a marketed "paradise." As the literary and artistic works from the Middle Ages teach us, paradise is a unique pursuit reached by a multitude of possible pathways.

Research Questions

1. Explore some of the pilgrimage sites of Buddhism and their relationship to the Buddha's life: Lumbini (Nepal), Bodh Gaya, Sarnath, and Kushinagara (India).
2. Consider the spiritual uses of plant products such as dyes (for example, saffron and indigo) or aromatics (for example, frankincense and myrrh).

How was the dye or aromatic extracted and processed? How was it used in different regions?

3. Coins, textiles, pottery or ceramics, and manuscripts often traversed the globe during the Middle Ages. Select two of these types of portable objects and consider how their manufacture or messages (textual or visual) compare and how they contrast.

4. We have looked at three primary materials used for making books in this chapter: paper, palm leaves, and parchment. How did these materials affect the development of the book and what are the lasting challenges for the conservation or preservation of these examples of cultural heritage?

5. In the medieval period, gardens were considered heaven on Earth. They were settings where people could feel closest to the blessing of a divine power, and each feature of the gardens was symbolic: the design, the trees, flowers, and water features. Choose a culture and investigate its idea of a sacred garden.

6. Research tree diagrams in the writing of St. Bonaventure (the so-called Tree of Life) or Moses ben Cordovero (the Orchard of Pomegranates). What features do they share? How are they different? How might we connect them to Indian diagrams of bodily chakras?

Further Reading

Blair, Sheila, and Jonathan Bloom. *Images of Paradise in Islamic Art*. Austin: University of Texas Press, 1991.

Bodin, Helena, and Ragnar Hedlund, eds. *Byzantine Gardens and Beyond*. Uppsala, Sweden: Studia Byzantina Upsaliensia, Uppsala Universitet, 2013.

Keene, Bryan. *Gardens of the Renaissance*. Los Angeles, CA: J. Paul Getty Museum, 2013.

Keene, Bryan, ed. *Toward a Global Middle Ages: Encountering the World through Illuminated Manuscripts*. Los Angeles: J. Paul Getty Museum, 2019.

King, Anya. *Scent from the Garden of Paradise: Musk and the Medieval Islamic World*. Leiden: Brill, 2017.

McHugh, James. "The Incense Trees of the Land of Emeralds: The Exotic Material Culture of *Kamasatra*." *Journal of Indian Philosophy*, no. 39 (2011): 63–100.

McHugh, James. "Gemstones." In *Brill's Encyclopedia of Hinduism*, edited by Knut A. Jacobsen, Helene Basu, Angelika Malinar, and Vasudha Narayana. Leiden: Brill, 2012.

Pal, Pratapaditya. *Indian Paintings: A Catalogue of the Los Angeles County Museum of Art Collection*. New York: Harry N. Abrams, 1993.

Pal, Pratapaditya. *Puja and Piety: Hindu, Jain, and Buddhist Art from the Indian Subcontinent*. Oakland: University of California Press, 2016.

Ruggles, D. Fairchild. *Islamic Gardens and Landscapes*. Philadelphia: University of Pennsylvania Press, 2008.

Scafi, Alessandro, ed. *The Cosmography of Paradise: The Other World from Ancient Mesopotamia to Medieval Europe*. London: Warburg Institute, 2016.

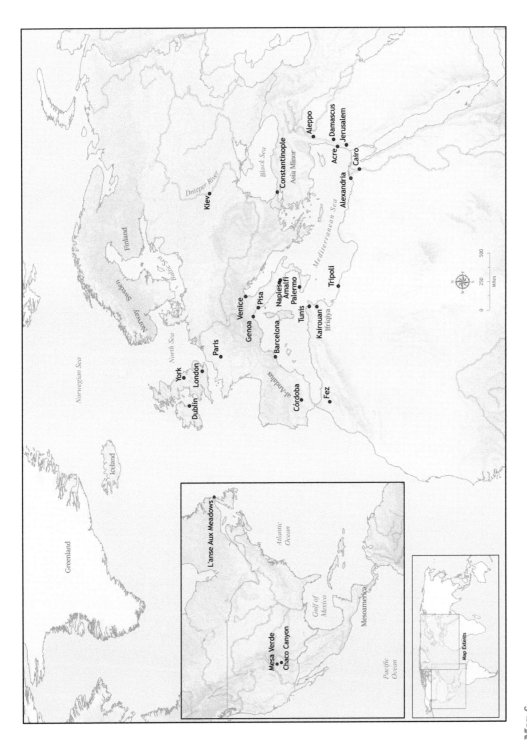

Map 6
For Sale

6 For Sale

Economies, 900–1300

Introduction

As we saw in the first economics chapter, the early medieval period was one of intense trade and travel over long distances, with connections created between peoples interested in products, foods, arts, and technologies available in other parts of the world. From 900 to 1300, the volume and pace of exchange accelerated, especially in high-demand goods and along established trade routes. New routes also arose or flourished in innovative ways, and even more cultures became involved in long-distance commerce. By the central Middle Ages, new and growing routes developed into busy pathways for people, raw materials, finished goods, and technologies.

Beyond the intensification of existing routes and the growth of new ones, a major characteristic of this period was the dynamic commercial traffic along water routes. Naval technology continued to advance and more ship traffic meant both longer journeys and greater cargoes. Nonetheless, land routes like the silk roads continued to be vital spaces of exchange. Section A of this chapter introduces some medieval regional networks, over both land and water, and how these linked with others in transcontinental and intercontinental systems – from China's Grand Canal to North Africa, Viking Iceland to Greenland, and up and down the Americas.

These centuries also show an upsurge in the number and type of commodities, demonstrating that people were willing to sail over long stretches of water to buy and sell, even when seafaring was dangerous and the outcome uncertain. Sea travel was faster than overland travel, and allowed for larger cargoes, but it was also riskier; much of our evidence for long-distance trade goods comes from recovered shipwrecks. Section B considers the maritime archeological record and some of the most abundant products that traveled along these many commercial routes. The products sought out and exchanged in this period were not simply mundane items for daily life, but included vibrantly dyed cloths and dyestuffs, an incredible variety of spices and perfumes, ivory carvings, games, and many other high-value items.

A: SAILS FORCE

Introduction

Although travel along overland routes continued, between 900 and 1300 long-distance travel and trade was increasingly conducted by sea. Maritime lanes across the Indo-Pacific and around the Mediterranean were not new in this period, but we can see greater traffic in commodities, raw materials, and people along the sea routes. Chinese-controlled fleets were particularly active in the China Seas and Indian Ocean, as were ships under the control of the Southeast Asian maritime empire of Srivijaya. Meanwhile, merchants from Muslim-ruled territories sailed throughout the Mediterranean Sea and Indian Ocean, and Scandinavian voyagers, commonly known as Vikings, dominated the North Sea routes. These merchants were intermediaries of long-distance trade and communications, both within and between regions. Along their paths, they met and interacted with many different peoples and their cultures. We find evidence of these extensive networks of land and sea travel from not only historical documents but also extant literary texts, archeological remains, transcriptions of oral traditions, and modern DNA science (using what is known as "aDNA" for "ancient DNA" evidence). These artifacts can help us reconstruct the voyages and pathways by which the transmission of goods, technologies, and people moved across the medieval world.

Evidence: Quanzhou shipwreck

Cairo Geniza

Chaco Culture National Historical Park, New Mexico, US

The Saga of Eirik the Red

L'Anse aux Meadows, Newfoundland, Canada

Saga of the Greenlanders

Silk Roads and East Asia

During the collapse of the Tang dynasty (the last Tang emperor was deposed in 907), China entered a period of political disunity that negatively affected long-distance commerce along the overland silk roads. Chinese state control over much of Central Asia during the Tang era, combined with active trade routes coming from Abbasid lands, had facilitated trade across the full expanse of the silk roads. In contrast, political disintegration curtailed movement and commerce conducted across the whole route. At the same time, regional and local exchanges of food and subsistence goods, which had long been the principal form of silk roads commerce, continued.

In 960, new Chinese rulers gained imperial power as the Song dynasty (960–1276) and ushered in a time of expanded trade and an economic boom. The Song oversaw the development of a fully monetized economy, with active markets in cities and towns as well as expansive networks of foreign import and export. The expansion of China's market economy meant that residents of rural villages began using money to buy and sell goods, rather than living on subsistence agriculture. Likewise, official missions by diplomat-traders continued bringing tribute to the Chinese court from foreign lands.

Across this period, however, land-based long-distance commerce was outpaced by seaborne trade along rivers and coastal waters, and Chinese mariners became major players in maritime trade in the South China Sea and Indian Ocean – joining the Malay, Indian, Javanese, Sumatran, Thai, Vietnamese, and many other communities who had been active in Southeast Asian trade in the earlier period. Chinese trade with Korea and Japan likewise flourished. Chinese kilns increased production during the central Middle Ages, and shipwrecks from this period attest to a massive trade in Chinese ceramics as well as items like iron and silk. These were exchanged for spices (especially pepper, but also other culinary and medicinal products), ivory and other animal products, timber, glassware, incense, pearls, and many other items from near and far. Song-era ceramics have been found in eastern Africa and as far away as Spain.

In the mid-twelfth century, a series of invasions by seminomadic Eurasian groups (such as the Jurchen, who conquered northern China by 1127) disrupted China's politics, economy, and direct trade with Central Asia. Nonetheless, tribute missions and trade with western and northern regions continued, although these were mediated by these new foreign rulers. In the thirteenth century, China was taken over by the Mongols, a confederation of various nomadic groups from the northern steppe that formed around 1200 and would conquer China and Central Asia by the end of that century. Mongols also pushed westward, conquering Kievan Rus, threatening eastern Europe, demolishing the Abbasid capital of Baghdad, and advancing toward Egypt before they were stopped by Egyptian forces in 1260 (see Chapter 7). The Mongols were as interested in commercial trade as conquest, and they built upon the strengths of the Song trade economy over both land and sea.

Song China experienced massive economic growth, at least in the first half of the era, but also periods of political disorder, foreign invasions, and environmental disasters, such as flooding and crop failure. China's population soared during the eleventh and twelfth centuries, rising from around 85 to 110 million people between 1080 and 1110. The Song capital of Kaifeng (until 1127) grew to contain a population of one million people. Along with demographic growth, this period saw expanded agriculture (in rice, wheat, and millet), a huge increase in the production of money, growing commerce in regional markets within China and at merchants' stalls in cities and towns, and extensive trade between China and her neighbors. By the time the Song were overthrown by the Mongols, they had overseen the development of the world's wealthiest economy at the time.

Along with population growth and increased technological sophistication in China, the cultivation of silkworms, weaving of silk textiles, and production of ceramics and foodstuffs also grew. Mining and metalwork improved, which gave rise to an enormous increase in the number of coins minted. This economic vigor meant that a greater share of the population was involved in some level of production and sale of artisanal goods than had been true earlier. Even smaller towns in rural districts developed markets for the sale of goods. Market towns proliferated, and so did services for traveling merchants like inns, restaurants, and warehouses. Trade was no longer restricted to government-sponsored urban commercial centers, as it had been during the Tang period. Merchants offered their wares in open city streets and in markets in rural villages.

Because many of these industries were based in family homes, women were central to both production and distribution. Women raised silkworms, wove the fabrics, prepared and sold foods and beverages, and decorated ceramics. Urban women might run an inn or manage the family restaurant, make and sell wares at market stalls, or work as a courtesan or professional entertainer. All these trades were taxed by the Song government, giving working Chinese women an economic and civic position within Chinese society. While upper-class women were increasingly expected to remain at home, managing the household and producing poetry or calligraphy, middle- and lower-class women were often expected to work – sometimes as servants in elite households or on the family farm or production facility.

Along with expanded trade in manufactured products, this period was one of increased sale of women for use as prostitutes and concubines, and higher dowries for the daughters of wealthy families. Women from foreign tributary states (for example, Vietnam and Korea) and from Central Asia were shipped to Chinese cities as sex slaves, where prostitution districts and the practice of concubinage (in which a woman was kept by a man for sex and who had a status lower than wife) proliferated. Poor families were known to sell their daughters for cash or hope they would reap the benefits of their daughters marrying into a higher-status household.

The Song period is also when the Chinese government first began issuing paper money. The *jiaozi*, the first known paper currency in history, had its roots in the Tang period. The Tang government conducted official commerce for supplying military garrisons along the silk roads, using as currency either minted bronze coins, bolts of silk, or measures of grain. Because some commercial transactions between private merchants were also quite large, merchants in Sichuan province developed a system to use paper instead of the much heavier strings of coins. Acting like a letter of credit, the paper would inform the receiver how many coins it could be exchanged for. In 1023, these privately printed notes were replaced by government-issued bills that were woodblock-printed and stamped with official seals. Bills did not replace the use of bronze coinage and silver metal (valued by weight) but complemented them during this period of rapidly growing commercial economy. The Song outlawed private paper money, attempting to consolidate their governmental power to issue and manage currency. They also attempted to restrict the outflow of metal money in the export trade to keep valued metals within China.

By the mid-twelfth century, however, China's population growth and economic expansion had slowed. A series of harvest failures and the conquest of northern China in 1127 caused widespread disruption to both lives and the economy; the Song capital of Kaifeng fell to the nomads in that year. Crop failures, floods, and epidemics led to famines, the destruction wrought by the Jurchen invasion decimated mulberry trees (the food source for silkworms) and emptied towns of their populations. Jurchen control of the north meant that the Song lost access to important copper mines. This period also featured the mass migration of millions of Chinese from the north to the south, and the relocation of the Song capital to the southern city of Hangzhou, on the southern terminus of the Grand Canal.

GRAND CANAL

China's network of rivers, including both the Yellow and Yangtze rivers and their tributaries, were actively traveled by river boats for centuries, moving goods and people between inland towns and the China Seas. Complementing these waterways is an artificial river called the Grand Canal that connects the northern Yellow River and the southern Yangtze River. Running 1,115 miles from Beijing to Hangzhou, the Grand Canal linked both river and land passages within a dense network of trade routes. Sections of the canal had been built as early as the fifth century BCE, but were connected only in 610 during the Sui dynasty. Private merchants and government boats shipped tons of commodities along the rivers and the canal: heavy boat traffic an important part of China's economy by the eleventh century.

The Song exploited the canal's possibilities most intensively, shipping huge amounts of grain (as taxes) from southern agricultural fields to their capital of Kaifeng (until 1127), and transporting salt, copper, and other commodities from the north. They expended considerable resources to maintain the canal and keep it safe for boat travel. In the mid-twelfth century, after the Jurchen invasion displaced the Song from their domain, the Song lost control over the northern part of the canal. They focused their attention on the southern section, where many boats sailed to and from Hangzhou (the capital of the Southern Song), thus integrating the intense river trade along the Yangtze with the bustling seaborne commerce along the coasts of the South China Sea and into the Indian Ocean.

Perhaps the greatest impact the Song economy had on global connections was its active river and sea trade. The Song period was a high point for Chinese navigation, cartography, and shipbuilding. Chinese ships became technologically advanced, growing in size and speed. The connection between the Yangtze River traffic and the ocean allowed China's trade connections to extend from inland Central Asia far out into the seas, where Chinese merchants sailed directly to Korea, Japan, the Philippines, around Southeast Asia, and as far west as the Malabar Coast of India. Foreign merchants also continued to sail into Chinese ports, from regions both near and far, exchanging a wide variety of items – silks, ceramics, glass, iron, beads, foodstuffs, animals, animal products, silver, and much more.

Indian Ocean

The period from 900 to 1300 was one of unprecedented Chinese mercantile activity at sea, and a high point for the status of merchants in Chinese society. During the Tang era, China had monopolized trade in the China Seas, mainly through its tributary relationships with local powers – in which many of China's neighbors sent tribute missions with huge cargoes and received gifts of Chinese products in exchange. But, Chinese merchants were outnumbered in the Indian Ocean by Koreans, Persians, Arabs, Malays, and many other peoples. During the Song period, however, Chinese merchants sailing on Chinese ships came to dominate the waters between the China Seas and the southern coast of India, even while other peoples continued to sail and trade in the region. In the Indian Ocean – from Indonesia to the Red Sea and Persian Gulf ports – merchants from the Islamicate world were in the majority.

Song China minted enormous numbers of bronze coins, both for the booming market economy inside China and for the export trade. These were used as currency in places like Japan, Java, and Cambodia, and have also been found in eastern Africa, southern India, and the Persian Gulf. Song traders exported silks, aromatic woods and spices, printed books, and fine porcelain ceramics. They also imported a wide variety of products: gold, silver, steel swords, lumber, ivory, pearls, wine, salt, dyestuffs, furs, linen and cotton cloth, and enslaved women for the sex trade. These were imports from Japan, Korea, India, Persia, and many places in Southeast Asia. Incenses and spices from Arabia and eastern Africa were among the luxury imports most desired in China's highly commercialized markets, but so, too, were foreign glassware (Islamicate glass was highly desired in China), metals (especially silver), and animals and animal products.

Chinese ships developed in size and technological sophistication during the Song period. Referred to generally as "junks" (from the Portuguese interpretation of a Malay or Javanese word), Song vessels ranged in size from smaller river boats to ocean-faring ships capable of carrying huge cargoes. Employing multiple sails that raised and lowered on pulleys, and using both sight and the magnetic compass for navigation, junks were built both for cargo and for war. Chinese naval strength was quite strong in this era, numbering at least 100 warships, which could fire projectiles at enemy boats along rivers and seacoasts, thus strengthening Chinese military and mercantile control over the seas.

Fig 6.1
Recovered in 1973–1974, the shipwreck known as the Quanzhou ship (after its discovery near the southeastern Chinese port of Quanzhou) is dated to the end of the Song period (roughly 1272) based on coinage evidence found on board. The ship itself was a merchant ship with about 120 tons of cargo capacity and three masts – larger than ships in the Mediterranean Sea or North Sea would be until later centuries. The cargo aboard primarily came from Southeast Asia, although some may have come from further west in the Arabian Peninsula: cowrie shells, incense, spices, dyestuffs, and ambergris. Archeologists suspect that the ship was sunk intentionally by the sailors who intended to return later in order to recover the goods.
Zhang Peng / LightRocket via Getty Images

While Chinese ships dominated the eastern half of the Indian Ocean route (from the Straits of Malacca to China), the western part was primarily sailed by ships from the Islamicate world. Southeast Asia was the site of many active trade emporia, and, by the early Song period, Muslim merchants were again sailing directly to China, a practice that had been brought to a halt after the 878 massacre of foreign traders in the Chinese port city of Guangzhou. In the meantime, Islamicate merchants had patronized a series of intermediary ports in the Indian Ocean, so there had been no slowdown in the exchange of Chinese ceramics, silk, and other items for incenses and other products from the Middle East. In the later Middle Ages, direct exchange between China and traders from the central Islamic lands flourished, with Islamic law the prevailing legal framework in the western Indian Ocean. Arabic became the common language of traders in the western Indian Ocean, and Persian that of the eastern Indian Ocean.

In the later Middle Ages, the Indian Ocean was quite significant to the economic and political power of the Islamicate world. Both the Abbasid Caliphate and the Fatimid Caliphate were enriched by the import of eastern luxury goods (especially spices and porcelain, but also silk, timber, metalwork, and more) and the taxes collected at the ports. Both were concerned with protecting their shipping interests in the Indian Ocean: the Abbasids and their governors promoted the Persian Gulf ports, while the Fatimids redirected much of the sea traffic to the Red Sea ports. The Red Sea ports were particularly important for transporting pilgrims to the holy cities of Mecca and Medina. Fatimid involvement in Indian Ocean trade also helped promote the spread of Shi'ite Islam along the coast of eastern Africa, where it predominated until the fourteenth century.

The Indian Ocean also saw the rise of a new naval power, the Chola Empire of India. In the ninth century, the Tamil Chola kingdom of southeastern India expanded to control most of southern India, and then invaded Ceylon (Sri Lanka) in 993. The Cholas developed a fleet of ships used for both trade and naval warfare, and they conquered other islands in the area. With attacks starting in 1025, they also weakened the sea power of Srivijaya – a coastal state based in Sumatra that had controlled transit through the Straits of Malacca since the seventh century. Despite successful naval raids, the Cholas were unable to replace Srivijaya as the dominant Indonesian sea power. While the two states continued to vie for a monopoly on trade with China, Srivijaya dominated the eastern part while Chola controlled seaborne trade between southern India and the entrepôts of Indonesia. Both states became wealthy and powerful as mediators of trade between the Chinese and Islamicate mercantile zones. The Cholas maintained diplomatic and commercial ties with both the Song court in China and the Abbasid Caliphate in Baghdad, and a tense, but working, relationship with Srivijaya. Over the twelfth and thirteenth centuries, land-based conflicts in India reduced Chola territory, and in 1279 the final Chola ruler was unseated by the Pandya dynasty of Tamil rulers based in southern India.

Islamicate World and the Mediterranean Sea

From the mid-seventh century, Muslim rulers took over formerly Byzantine North Africa, along with those ports, ships, and sailors. This allowed Muslim seafarers to begin to dominate the Mediterranean Sea and its commercial world (see Chapter 3, Battle of the Masts). For the next several centuries, ships and merchants based in the Islamicate world – Muslims, but also Arabic-speaking Jews and Christians – controlled the waters of the Mediterranean and profited from commerce at its seaports. Latin Christians traveled across the sea, especially as pilgrims to Jerusalem, taking passage on Muslim ships. For example, in 867 Bernard the Wise, a monk, traveled overland from Francia (modern France) to Rome to obtain permission for a pilgrimage to Jerusalem. From Rome, he and his companions traveled through southern Italy to the Muslim-held seaports of Bari and Taranto. His group was able to purchase seats on one of six Muslim ships heading for Alexandria, which, he claimed, had on board a total of 9,000

Fig 6.2 and 6.3
Byzantine ships were built in the galley style, relatively shallow boats propelled
by both oars and square sails. Top: This sixth-century mosaic from the Basilica
of Sant'Apollinare near Ravenna, Italy, shows Byzantine ships and lighthouses.
Bottom: This image is from the Cathedral of Monreale, Palermo, Sicily (late twelfth–
mid-thirteenth century). It depicts Jesus calming the waters for St. Peter and his
companions and gives a sense of the shape (although not the size) of these vessels,
which became the common form of Mediterranean boat for both commerce and
naval battles. In the fourteenth and fifteenth centuries, maritime states like Genoa
and Venice built large fleets of galleys that could carry cargoes of 100–300 tons. By
the end of the Middle Ages, galleys were joined in the Mediterranean and Atlantic
waters by a variety of larger sail-based ships.
www.BibleLandPictures.com / Alamy Stock Photo; imageBROKER / Alamy
Stock Photo

Christians who had been captured in southern Italy and were being exported as slaves to Muslim Africa. Even if these numbers are an exaggeration, as is likely, many historians believe that enslaved Europeans were a common export to North Africa at this time. Bernard and other early medieval pilgrims like him still sailed the Mediterranean, but the ships, sailors, and seaports they used were under Muslim control.

Because Muslim powers also dominated the overland passages between the Mediterranean Sea and the ports of the Red Sea and Persian Gulf, it was their merchants who mediated access to highly desired eastern luxury goods in the Mediterranean. Spices, silks, pearls, gems, and porcelains from China and Southeast Asia commanded high prices at Mediterranean ports. But, an intense trade in locally produced commodities also developed within the Mediterranean basin in locally produced commodities. Wheat grown in Sicily – under Muslim control from 827 to 1061 – became a primary food source for Egypt and North Africa (modern Tunisia, Libya, and Algeria). The merchant letters from the Cairo Geniza, discussed in Chapter 1 also mention other foodstuffs (for instance, dried fruits, fruit juices, cheeses, and almonds), spices, medicines, dyestuffs, silk and other textiles (such as linen and cotton, both Egyptian products), and gold and silver coins minted within the Islamic world, which circulated both as currency and as commodities. The trade routes that developed between Mediterranean commercial centers facilitated the transfer of huge amounts of goods and enriched the merchants who carried out the trade.

While the "trade triangle" between Sicily, Egypt, and Tunisia was one major regional trade network, it was by no means the only such network. Traders from Muslim Spain (al-Andalus) traded extensively with their neighbors in the Maghrib (modern Morocco). From there, they had access to goods from across the Sahara in the areas of Mali and Ghana – gold, ivory, and enslaved Africans, which were traded for salt, indigo, copper, and other Mediterranean products. These caravan routes also extended eastward toward the markets of Tunisia, Egypt, and the eastern Mediterranean, where products from Asia were available. Such routes made it possible for objects and technologies from the farthest eastern places in the hemisphere to circulate in the farthest western part of it, like ceramics in a style from Song China that have been excavated in Cordoba, Spain.

Likewise, the eastern Mediterranean was a region of vibrant commercial activity. Byzantium's capital of Constantinople continued to be a wealthy and opulent city, where goods and enslaved peoples from many foreign places were available for purchase. The city lay at the nexus of many different trade routes: the eastern Mediterranean traffic that sailed along the coast of Muslim Syria and into the Aegean; Venetian trade coming into the Aegean from the Adriatic; overland routes from Central Asia; and the land and river routes northward to Kiev, and thence to Scandinavia. Until it was conquered in 1204 during the Fourth Crusade, Constantinople was by far the largest, most luxurious, and wealthiest Christian city in the world, with a population of around one million, and rivaling only the Chinese cities of Xi'an (capital of the Tang dynasty) and Kaifeng (capital of the Northern Song dynasty) in number of inhabitants.

Christians from Latin Europe also participated in Mediterranean trade and, by around 1100, were starting to take it over. Italian city-states such as Venice, Genoa, Pisa, and Amalfi maintained some level of commercial connection with the highly monetized economies of Byzantium and the Islamic world, even when the rest of Europe was primarily engaged in subsistence agriculture. Pisans, Florentines, Genoese, and other Italian merchants established trade connections with Islamicate traders in Egypt and North Africa, while Venetians concentrated on the eastern Mediterranean and exchange with Byzantine Constantinople. By the twelfth century, many Italian city-states had established mercantile inns and warehouses in port cities across the southern Mediterranean basin, meaning that at nearly all times there were colonies of Latin Christian foreigners living and trading in majority-Muslim cities along the Mediterranean coasts.

A major reason for European ascendancy over Muslim merchants in the later medieval Mediterranean was the advance of Christian military presence and political power into the southern and eastern shores of the Mediterranean basin. In 973, the Fatimid Caliphate moved its capital to Cairo, from where they ruled over much of northern Africa and eventually the holy cities of Mecca, Medina, and Jerusalem. From this vantage point, the Fatimids focused their attention eastward, placing an increased significance on Red Sea commercial traffic with the Indian Ocean – and, to some degree, ignoring the Mediterranean political and commercial realm. This decreased attention to the Mediterranean basin allowed Christian merchants and fleets to begin to take over.

After the eleventh century, the balance of military power in and around the Mediterranean Sea tipped solidly in favor of Christian states. Already in the 960s, the Muslim islands of Crete and Cyprus had been taken by the Byzantines. The crusades in the eastern Mediterranean (from the conquest of Jerusalem in 1099), the Spanish *reconquista* in the western Mediterranean (starting with the conquest of Toledo in 1085), the Norman conquest of Sicily (1061–1091), and the establishment of Italian trade outposts across the Muslim-held shores of the Mediterranean, all contributed to the political, economic, and military advance of Europeans in the Mediterranean region. The Spanish Muslim territories of al-Andalus were steadily conquered by Spanish Christian kings, so that, by 1250, the only Muslim state left in Iberia was Granada (conquered by Christians in 1492). These territorial losses, in turn, contributed to the decline of Muslim sea power in the Mediterranean.

Several Italian city-states also profited significantly from the crusades. Since they were the primary Christian naval powers of the period, the Pisans, Genoese, and Venetians managed troop transport and resupply missions

Fig 6.4
Interior courtyard of the "New Funduq" in Granada, Spain. The fourteenth-century
structure is the only surviving Spanish example of this type of facility, which was
common throughout the multicultural Mediterranean world of the later Middle Ages.
They were used as inns and warehouses for foreign merchants visiting a city, usually
in the Muslim world. Each such facility in a city was reserved for merchants from a
particular point of origin; they slept in rooms organized around an interior courtyard,
which had space for the storage of goods and pack animals.
Photo by Sarah Davis-Secord

to the eastern Mediterranean by sea (as opposed to the more dangerous and
lengthy land route). In exchange, they were offered trade concessions, such
as tax exemptions and market monopolies, in crusader-held port cities along
the eastern Mediterranean coast. Thus, they gained control over ports in historically Muslim territories and obtained direct access to even more eastern
commodities. Likewise, European demand for eastern luxury goods enriched
the Italian merchants who controlled supplies. By 1200, for example, Venice
dominated not only most of the trade routes in the eastern Mediterranean, but
also many of the ports and islands along the Adriatic coast. After the Fourth
Crusade, they ruled territory in the Byzantine Aegean, as well.

In the later Middle Ages, Arabic-speaking Muslim and Jewish pilgrims,
scholars, and merchants still sailed across the Mediterranean, but they did so
almost exclusively on ships owned and captained by European Christians, a
reversal of the situation in the early medieval Mediterranean. By the end of this
period, this shift in the balance of power was complete.

Europe

The extraordinary advances in agriculture during Europe's early medieval period had resulted, by around 1000, in surplus food supplies and an expanding population – both factors in the rise of cities and a commercial economy in the following centuries. Extra food could be traded at temporary markets, many of which became permanent settlements over time. In other cases, towns sprang up around saints' shrines and churches, where relics were held. Pilgrims visiting these holy sites would often reside in the vicinity for days or weeks at a time, seeking healing and needing urban services such as inns and markets. Some shrines attracted pilgrims from surrounding areas, but others gained far-reaching fame. Travelers took regional and long-distance trips to pray at sites such as Compostela in Spain, Tours in France, or Canterbury in England. Merchants, food and drink purveyors, trinket-sellers, and other vendors gathered where pilgrim visitors did, and hostels and other services grew up along popular travel routes.

The increasing number of cities was accompanied by the growth of urban infrastructure and specialized labor and crafts. The population boom meant that some rural manors had more people than available land for them to farm, which led many people to migrate to cities and learn new trades and skills. Although, under the manorial system, peasants were considered serfs who had no freedom of movement, we know some serfs left their manors and that such migration must have fueled urbanization in this period. And, because they no longer needed to grow their own food, city-dwellers developed trades like cheese-making, baking, brewing beer and cider, textile production and dyeworks, shoe cobbling, metalwork, masonry, and others. Many food- and drink-related industries, such as brewing, were originally dominated by women but were taken over by men by the end of the Middle Ages.

By the twelfth century, most craftspeople and specialized artisans in Europe were organized into guilds. These labor and social organizations were based in individual towns and regulated all aspects of an individual craft – for example, guilds determined who could practice a skill, how it was to be done, how artisans were trained and advanced in skill level, what materials were used, what quality of product was produced, and how much workers earned. Guilds not only set wages, but also prices for their products, ensured the quality of the merchandise, and prevented non-guild members from trying to sell "knock-off" products in town. Guilds also assumed important social functions in the urban setting, fostering a sense of community for members of the profession and their families, holding social and religious gatherings, practicing charity both within the guild and in the city as a whole, and providing for the families of deceased guild members. Many guilds were restricted to men, but some allowed select women to join (like wives or daughters of guild members). Others were specific to women – for example, several women-only guilds for silk production were active in Paris by the late thirteenth century.

Related to the rise of professional artisans in these new urban settings is the development of the *bourgeoisie*, or what is often referred to as a "middle class." In the medieval sense, *bourgeoisie* (burgesses in English) simply meant urban dwellers: people who lived in bourgs/burgs (towns), rather than those who lived in rural areas, where both nobility and peasants resided. But because the majority of the inhabitants of these new medieval cities were merchants and craftspeople – those who earned income in coin by producing or selling commodities – they were effectively a new economic group somewhere between the nobility with inherited land-based wealth, and the rural peasantry who farmed to feed themselves and owed rents in produce rather than money.

Not all the burgesses were wealthy – urban poverty was an ever-present reality – but many who rose to the top of their crafts or were successful as merchants could accumulate significant wealth and, with it, social capital and political power (especially in independent cities ruled by elected councils). And, all of them, whether wealthy or less so, participated in what had become a highly monetized economy: goods and services were sold for coins rather than bartered or produced for sustenance of one's own family. By around 1300, European counts and kings began to levy direct taxes on their subjects in coin. For example, French King Philip the Fair (r. 1285–1314) began assessing taxes on the property (rather than on the commercial activities) of Paris's bourgeoisie. Extant taxation records from 1292 to 1313 provide significant information about the growing wealth of many sectors of the Parisian population.

The growth of craft production guilds and a monetized economy was connected both to an increase in regional commerce and trade networks across Europe and to the rise of professional merchants. In addition to urban markets serving a town's population, this period saw the development of regional fairs that facilitated long-distance trade by serving as meeting spots for merchants from distant lands. The most famous example of these were the Champagne fairs, a series of temporary markets held in six towns in northeastern France, beginning sometime before the twelfth century. Each fair lasted for six weeks before moving to the next town. These fairs developed under the protection of the Counts of Champagne, who were independent of the kings of France. They provided security for both the lives and properties of merchants in attendance at the fairs. Under such conditions, the Champagne fairs became a major node of connection for the mercantile zones of northern Europe and the Mediterranean. Merchants from England and the Low Countries brought furs, tin, and the wool cloth that quickly became their dominant export industry. Those from the Mediterranean basin brought dyed and finished textiles (a specialty of several towns in Italy) as well as products like spices and silks purchased from merchants from the Islamicate world.

Entrepôts like the Champagne fairs brought together merchants from distant regions, using a wide variety of coinages, meaning that money changers were also in demand. As in the earlier period, Europe had no single centralized authority that monopolized the minting of coins. Rather, local rulers either assumed or were granted the authority to mint coins, and this meant coins from even nearby cities or principalities could vary widely in their value. To facilitate trade with such disparate currencies, money changers tested the fineness (purity) of the metal and then weighed the coins to compute their value in pure metal. In such a way, exchange rates were calculated and trade between strangers managed. By the end of the Middle Ages, many money changers were either Italians or Jews, who capitalized on their skills and connections as long-distance merchants. This system of money changing also laid the foundations for the development of moneylending and, eventually, the development of modern banking practices.

Higher levels of urban commerce and regional trade also meant that Europeans in this period minted and used far more coinage than in earlier centuries. Most of Europe continued to mint exclusively silver coins, while both the Islamicate and Byzantine worlds maintained a gold standard. The legacy of Muslim rule in Sicily and parts of southern Italy meant that gold coins circulated there even after Christians conquered the area. Latin Christian warriors from Normandy began invading Muslim Sicily in 1061, and, by the end of that century, controlled both the island and mainland southern Italy – all incorporated into the new Kingdom of Sicily, proclaimed in 1130. The Normans adapted the Sicilian Muslim gold coins valued at a quarter of a dinar (the standard gold

Fig 6.5
A gold coin minted by Roger II, the first Christian king of Norman Sicily, crowned in 1130. His coinage system adopted the gold and silver denominations minted by the previous Muslim rulers of the island. The obverse (right) of the Norman coin retains the circular Arabic inscription (stating that Roger is king by God's grace) while the reverse (left) has an image of a Christian cross surrounded by the Greek phrase "Jesus Christ conquers."

coinage across the Islamic world), keeping the tradition of Arabic inscriptions for royal titles, but also adding Christian imagery. Gold coinages were not introduced into the rest of Latin Europe until the middle of the thirteenth century, as we will see in Chapter 10.

The North Sea

Europe's most active long-distance merchants continued to be Scandinavian voyagers, commonly called the Norse or Vikings, who raided, traded, and settled across Europe's northern coastlines. They were active along the river routes between the Baltic Sea and the Black Sea, into Greenland and North America, along the Atlantic coast, and into the Mediterranean Sea. In fact, for much of the 900–1300 period, they were the primary intermediaries of exchange across long stretches of the northern part of the Eastern Hemisphere. Across land and river routes, Norse traders were active on the lanes between Scandinavia, Kievan Rus, and Constantinople. This was one of the most productive and lucrative land-based networks in the Eastern Hemisphere, and it complemented the Vikings' seaborne activity in the greater North Sea region.

Viking ships were highly advanced, crafted to sail quickly across open waters and along rivers even with large cargoes (including livestock and horses). Although known for their destructive raids – across the eighth century they ransacked monastic settlements along the eastern coastline of England, raided the Irish coasts, and plundered towns and monasteries along France's inland river system – the Vikings also established trading colonies and settlements, some of which became permanent. For example, the Duchy of Normandy was given to them by the King of France in 911 in a bid to stop their raids on Paris. Other Viking groups founded cities such as Dublin (in 841), which became a flourishing site of regional commerce and a primary market for the trade in enslaved Celtic peoples. From there they began moving northward, settling the Faroe Islands and nearby islands in the early ninth century. Norse bands also moved southward along the Atlantic coastline and into the Mediterranean Sea during the same years. All these movements allowed them to access faraway products, which they traded regionally and over long distances.

In the ninth century, Iceland, which may have been previously uninhabited, was thoroughly colonized by the Norse and their Irish and Scottish slaves. DNA analysis shows that most of the female population of Iceland's settlers came from Celtic populations, suggesting that Scandinavian men migrated with enslaved women taken from the British Isles. However, the sagas – the literature of the early Icelanders – also depict Norse women leading expeditions and participating in voyages. For example, *The Saga of Eirik the Red* recounts the tale of a woman named Aud, the widow of King Oleif, who herself assembled a crew of both free-born and enslaved men to sail from Norway to Iceland. She laid claim to numerous territories there and distributed farms to the men of her crew, freeing some of the enslaved and arranging marriages for them.

Greenland was colonized about 980 and then, around 1000, some of the Norse Greenlanders made their way even further, to North America (see Chpter 11). The foundation of Viking colonies in Greenland and North America is described in literary texts that were written down in the early thirteenth century, but clearly represent previous centuries of oral tradition. These stories are known now as the Vinland Sagas. The name "Vinland" derives from the purported discovery of grapevines in these areas new to the Vikings. The sagas describe communities of Norse who farmed and sailed on trade voyages, seeking adventure, exploration, and wealth. Archeological evidence supports some of the basic elements of the saga's accounts of exploration.

The first story of an intentional voyage from Greenland to North America, related in the *Saga of the Greenlanders*, was that undertaken by Leif Eiriksson (ca. 970–1020), following an earlier accidental sighting of the unfamiliar coastline by another sailor. That man, Bjarni Herjolfsson, was chided by his friends for not being curious enough to explore further; he sold his boat to Leif, who hired a crew of 35 men and set sail. Upon arrival, Leif's crew built structures and began exploring. They loaded their ships with vines and timber and returned to Greenland. This expedition sparked intense interest in the new land and led to several seasons of voyages by different sailors. The sagas describe later explorers seeking permission to borrow the buildings that Leif had built, suggesting that the Vikings repeatedly reused the same settlements.

While historians caution that these texts post-date the events they describe by hundreds of years, archeology has confirmed some of the essential details about Norse settlement in North America. At the farthest northern end of the Canadian island of Newfoundland, archeologists have uncovered a Viking settlement dating to around the year 1000. L'Anse aux Meadows appears to have been a temporary settlement – perhaps a winter camp, a transshipment post, or a base for further exploration in North America, much like that described in the sagas. Several buildings have been excavated, including homes, warehouses, and workshops for blacksmithing, carpentry, and boat repair. These buildings, coupled with the absence of evidence of agriculture or barns for domesticated animals, suggest that the site was not inhabited by the Scandinavians for very long; it was likely used as an overwintering camp so that goods could be stored before export and boats could be repaired for longer journeys around North America and back to Greenland. The sagas describe precisely this kind of activity – summer voyages to Vinland and reuse of established settlements as winter camps (when the seas were unsafe for sailing) and as bases for exploration. However, several Norse daily-life items were discovered at the site, including a sewing needle, a spindle whorl (for spinning yarn), and parts of a loom, which suggest that women also lived in these settlements.

Unlike Iceland, the Canadian Arctic was not previously uninhabited. That may be one reason that the Norse did not attempt more long-term settlement in North America. The sagas describe combative encounters with Natives they called "Skraelings" (probably either the Dorset or Thule Inuit peoples). Still, there is some evidence of trade between the Vikings and the Indigenous peoples of North America, particularly in furs and walrus ivory. Recent DNA analysis has proven that most of the imports of walrus ivory into Europe – popular for carved artworks and game tokens such as chess pieces – from the 1120s through the fourteenth century came from walrus populations in western Greenland and Canada, a trade the Vikings monopolized. The sagas also portray Vinland trade in milk products and red cloth, which the Natives desired highly, and weapons, which the Vikings did not want to provide to their enemies. According to the sagas, battle erupted between them after a group of Skraelings stole some Viking weapons. After several deadly conflicts with the Natives, the Greenlanders gave up on North America. Greenland itself was abandoned by the Norse by the fifteenth century, perhaps due to the declining trade in walrus ivory, which had been a major source of wealth for the Greenlanders.

The Americas

Although direct connection between Eastern and Western hemispheres was limited in the medieval period to one small part of the northern Americas, it is important to remember that goods, both natural products and crafted items, were traded, and advanced technologies were transmitted, often over long distances across the Americas. Much of this exchange took place in urban settings, where people gathered for administrative, economic, and ritual purposes. And people with access to highly valued goods were able to use them to display their status and increase their power within those settlements.

In the northwestern corner of the US state of New Mexico lies the historical site of Chaco Canyon, what we might think of as a large city, even though its infrastructure and organization differ from cities found in the Eastern Hemisphere. Archeological evidence shows settlement on the site of Chaco Canyon flourished between 850 and 1150, although most of the largest buildings (known as Great Houses) were constructed between roughly 1050 and 1115. Chaco was the center of a complex system of settlements inhabited by the Ancestral Pueblo people, serving as the ceremonial, cultural, economic, and perhaps administrative heart of communities spread miles throughout the surrounding region of the San Juan basin (modern southern Colorado and Utah and northern New Mexico).

The Chacoans and their satellite communities had a primarily agricultural economy, but there is also clear evidence that they maintained long-distance exchange networks with Mesoamerica through the city-states of northwestern Mexico – and perhaps even as far as South America. Without written records, historians rely on archeological remains and the oral storytelling traditions of the modern Pueblo peoples, such as the Hopi, to understand Chacoan culture and connections. The neighboring Diné (Navajo) people also retain memories of Chaco and the migrations of people to and from the site. The convention of passing down history through oral recitation is part of what we call Indigenous ways of knowing.

From tree-ring dating, archeologists date the first structures at Chaco to the mid- to late ninth century. These include both homes and public buildings like the multistory Great Houses (multifamily complexes with possible ritual and administrative uses) as well as huge public plazas and kivas (round buildings, often below ground-level, used for ceremonial and public gatherings). The high number of kivas at Chaco and the range of sizes, from quite small to very large, indicate the significance of the Chaco site within Puebloan culture.

Different phases of construction and reconstruction continued until the mid-twelfth century, by which time almost everyone had left the canyon. Archeologists are not certain why Chaco was deserted. Most likely, a mass migration from Chaco moved the canyon's population to nearby Pueblo settlements like Mesa Verde (in today's southwestern Colorado), which was a growing community of around 30,000 people in the mid-thirteenth century. Mesa Verde may have usurped Chaco's primacy between 1150 and 1300, but a changing climate – the end of what is often called the "Medieval Climatic Anomaly," which had drastic effects on agriculture and disease in Europe, as discussed

Fig 6.6
Pueblo Bonito, ca. 850–1115, is the largest complex at Chaco Canyon (Chaco Culture National Historical Park, New Mexico, US) and is considered to have been the central structure in the settlement. Thousands of artifacts have been recovered from the site, including jars containing drinking chocolate and piles of scrap turquoise from a workshop.
Matt Champlin / Getty Images

elsewhere – brought extensive drought to this region, causing further migration and the abandonment of Mesa Verde by 1300.

Chaco's role as a hub for distribution of products throughout the Americas is revealed by archeological finds at the site. One of the largest finds is that of turquoise, in both finished products and fragments. Over 200,000 pieces of turquoise have been unearthed throughout the canyon and nearby sites. Some of these were finished items – many were grave goods – but others were found in piles of turquoise scrap. This has led archeologists to suggest that Chaco functioned not only as a market or distribution site for products made elsewhere, but also as a place of production. Turquoise stone was imported to Chaco, where it was manufactured into jewelry and other items that were then sold, distributed, or traded to other places – perhaps in exchange for products imported from far away. According to scientific analysis of the stone, the turquoise itself came from a variety of mines. Some was imported from the Cerrillos Hills, about 125 miles south of Chaco. Other turquoise came from even farther away, such as mines in Nevada and southern California. Raw turquoise thus came into Chaco via multiple pathways from different directions, and it is similarly likely that finished products left the canyon along multiple routes.

Timber from mountains up to 50 miles away, shells from the Pacific Ocean, raw copper and copper bells from western Mexico, as well as obsidian, maize, precious stones, and other non-local goods also testify to the extensive network of connections that brought objects to Chaco from both near and far. But the items with the most distant origin were chocolate and macaw feathers from Mesoamerica. Residue of cacao has been found at Chaco Canyon in a cache of tall cylindrical jars dated to between 1000 and 1125, suggesting that the Chacoans were drinking the beverage in a ritual manner like contemporary Mesoamericans of the same period. For example, the Maya drank a cacao beverage that had been spiced, frothed, and poured in highly decorated cylindrical jars. The beverage was an important part of public ceremonies, such as royal coronations, important marriages, and political negotiations. It was also an offering to the gods and drunk during religious rites.

The discovery of cacao at Chaco represents the furthest north chocolate has been found in the pre-Hispanic American Southwest – 1,500 miles or more away from the most northern point of the tropical regions in Mesoamerica where cacao trees can grow. Given that consumption of cacao was a ritually significant act in Mesoamerica, with prescribed tools, actions, and order of events, archeologists have suggested that it was not only chocolate as a product but knowledge of chocolate drinking as a practice that spread so far northward. Probably only elites had access to the chocolate custom, and participation in such a high-status ritual may also have helped to shape who was and was not part of that Chacoan elite.

Also found at Chaco were the remains of scarlet macaws, a tropical bird native to Central America and northern South America. The bright red, yellow,

Fig 6.7
In the last decade of the nineteenth century, the brothers Benjamin Talbot Babbitt Hyde and Frederic Erastus Hyde, Jr. financed a series of excavations in the American Southwest known as the Hyde Exploring Expeditions (HEE). In 1896 the HEE undertook the excavation of Chaco Canyon, whose artifacts were sent to the American Museum of Natural History but have since been dispersed and disconnected from their archeological context. Their discoveries both furthered knowledge about pre-Hispanic American cultures and stirred controversy about the treatment of items considered sacred by Pueblo peoples. In cylindrical jars like this one, archeologists have found the residue of cacao.
George H.H. Huey / Alamy Stock Photo

and blue feathers of the scarlet macaw were ritually and socially important in the Chacoan hierarchy and ceremonial culture; they remain so in many modern Pueblo cultures. Some of the birds' skeletons found there can be dated to the very beginning of Chaco's rise to prominence in the mid-ninth century. One study of the macaw DNA suggests that all the birds were from one breeding colony outside their native ecosystem; the location of that breeding colony is unknown. It has also been surmised that, because cacao and macaws come from similar locations, they may have at times been traded together along with other valued Mesoamerican items.

Some archeologists theorize that perhaps one reason for the central importance of Chaco within Ancestral Pueblo culture was precisely because of its people's ability to access prized items like cacao and macaw feathers from such faraway places. It is not clear what the Chacoans offered in return, however, or whether this was considered commercial trade, tribute, or some other form of exchange. While in some Mesoamerican cultures the cacao pods were used as currency, we do not know whether the Chacoans used them or any other items as currency in exchanges.

Another question about Chaco's networks is how this long-distance exchange was conducted. Chaco is unique among pre-Hispanic North American sites for having a series of human-crafted roads moving out in all directions from the settlement. This network of roads covers more than 400 miles throughout the San Juan basin. The roads are quite broad, with the main branches as wide as 30 feet and spurs about half that width. They are also perfectly straight, with sharp turns rather than gentle curves. These were clearly created with intention and skill, but archeologists have not settled on an answer as to why.

One problem is that we do not know where they all led. Many of the roads' terminuses are unknown, due to degradation of the remains and modern road construction, leaving us guessing about the full extent of the network. For a culture without wheeled vehicles, the meaning and purpose of such wide, engineered roads is uncertain. A possibility is that smoothed roads made foot travel and pack-animal passage over long distances much easier, especially for messengers and others carrying goods. The width of the roads also may have signaled the presence of Great Houses and thus called attention to the multidir-ectional connections that defined the Chacoan polity. A Mesoamerican parallel was the Maya *sacbeob* (sing. *sacbe*), white-paved roads that held ceremonial significance by connecting temples and pilgrimage sites but were also used for trade and communication over long distances. Despite all the unknowns, it is clear that perhaps as early as the mid-ninth century and through the mid-twelfth century, items were being exchanged in the Americas across incred-ibly long distances – hundreds or even thousands of miles between North and Central America. During these centuries, cultural transmission, exchange, and transfer of goods, peoples, and ideas were taking place, just as they did across the Eastern Hemisphere.

Conclusion

The central Middle Ages were a time of bustling trade over land and sea, but also one in which political power over merchant fleets and commerce shifted in many regions: the Song dynasty replaced the Tang, but were themselves disrupted by invasions from the Jurchen and Mongols; the Srivijaya and Chola empires rose and fell; and Europeans steadily overwhelmed Byzantine and Muslim-ruled territories in the Mediterranean Sea. As we have seen, this period was also one of increased regional and long-distance networks despite those political upheavals. Central marketplaces in urban centers and regional exchange hubs, such as Chaco Canyon or the Champagne fairs, facilitated the movement of goods across long distances. Regional economies such as China's Grand Canal network, Indonesian trade empires, and the Sicily–Egypt–Tunisia trade triangle show how such local and regional networks were woven together into lucrative intercontinental, interocean webs such as the maritime trade of the Indo-Pacific. Increased production of coinage (and, in Song China, of paper money) was part of the strength and stability of markets, as was improved mari-time technology. But what mattered most was curiosity about and desire for new things and the profits their sale could bring.

B: RISK AND REWARD

Introduction

Sea travel was dangerous in the era before modern naval technology. Despite the incredible knowledge sailors had about wind patterns and coastlines, nature still had the capacity to take them by surprise. Fierce storms and winds could drive ships hopelessly off course and capsize them; lack of wind could be just as fatal, leaving a crew weakened and dying from hunger and thirst. Ships that drifted too far from shore could become lost at sea, since navigation depended primarily upon sightlines. One way of acquiring merchandise was to steal it from someone else, and pirate ships operated along busy commercial routes. Even when a ship arrived safely at its destination, burdensome import taxes could be levied by officials; smuggled goods could be discovered and seized; or a port under siege could disrupt the landing of merchant vessels. This section includes evidence from several sunken wrecks that met with disaster, whether natural or human-caused. Maritime archeology is a field with ever more sophisticated ways of recovering sunken vessels and their cargo and learning what happened to them and their crews.

Despite these and other challenges to long-distance commerce, the rewards could be astounding. Merchants and investors earned great fortunes for themselves and their rulers. Not everyone who traveled over long distances did so for profit: some sought knowledge of the world, the excitement of seeing foreign places, the spiritual benefits of pilgrimage, or healing at distant shrines. But those who traveled for commercial reasons could bring back fabulous wealth in foreign goods, like the fictional Sindbad the Sailor in *One Thousand and One Nights*. Sometimes those goods made it safely to market, but sometimes the ships or caravans met with disaster. At other times, the threat of danger inspired merchants to bury caches of goods for later recovery; sometimes, those hoards were not recovered until modern archeologists located them. Both sunken treasure and buried hoards demonstrate the immense wealth – in coins and in valuable goods made of expensive materials – that some of these traders amassed.

Evidence: *The Travels of Ibn Jubayr*

                One Thousand and One Nights

                Gokstad Ship

                Serçe Limanı wreck

                Vale of York hoard

                Isle of Lewis Chess Pieces

                Libro de los juegos (*Book of Games*) or *Libro de ajedrez, dados e tablas* (*Book of Chess, Dice, and Tables*)

Dangerous Seas

Because there was extensive sea traffic in the 900–1300 period, we have much evidence of just how very dangerous sea travel was. Although the Vikings are known for their seaworthy ships and their ability to sail across open water, their sagas also include references to boats being (temporarily) lost at sea. For example, *The Saga of the Greenlanders* relates the difficulty Thorstein Eiriksson had in sailing from Greenland to Vinland in order to recover the body of his brother Thorvald. He and his crew "set sail and were out of sight of land. They were tossed about at sea all summer and did not know where they were." Only after winter set in, and the sailing season was over, did they finally find land – but not the land they were looking for. Instead, they had only made it to a different Norse settlement, on the western side of Greenland.

Mediterranean and Indian Ocean sailors were even less comfortable with open waters than were their Viking contemporaries. The preferred method for Mediterranean and Indian Ocean navigation was by sight, so boats stayed close to the shores. More advanced technology – like the magnetic compass and mariners' astrolabe – were common in the Indo-Pacific, allowing for some open-sea voyages, but these were limited to short trips. It was not until the later fifteenth century that European sailors regularly used the mariners' astrolabe, a technology adopted from the Islamicate world that allowed them to determine latitude at sea. During the Middle Ages, all Mediterranean sailors tried to keep within sight of coastlines and used captain's books that described the physical features they could expect to see at particular locations.

The dangers of Mediterranean seafaring are well illustrated by a number of firsthand accounts from this period. Several letters preserved in the Cairo Geniza recount perilous journeys, shipwrecks, and encounters with pirates and enemy warships. For example, one letter is from a merchant who had sailed from Egypt to Palermo, Sicily, around 1025, when the Muslim island was under attack by Byzantine Christian forces. Joseph bin Samuel arrived in Sicily only after a harrowing journey that first took him to Tripoli, Libya, after a shipwreck along the North African coast that left him "without a [gold] dinar or even a [silver] dirhem and no garment to wear; I arrived naked in Tripoli." Only the luck of meeting someone who owed him money allowed him to continue on to Sicily. Joseph and his trade partners were part of the bustling regional "trade triangle" between Egypt, North Africa, and Sicily.

An even more dramatic account of a Mediterranean shipwreck is that of Ibn Jubayr, a Muslim pilgrim from southern Spain who traveled to and from Mecca across the Mediterranean between 1183 and 1185. His trip home went terribly wrong. Departing from crusader-held Acre on a Genoese ship, he and his fellow passengers had brought on board provisions for a two-week passage. But because they set sail in October (which was too late in the year for safe sailing), the storm-plagued voyage took 40 days and they nearly ran out of food and water. In the midst of a storm, the mast broke and a sailor had to climb the mast to repair it as the ship rocked wildly on the sea. The captain was able to keep the boat upright, but they lost sight of land and thus did not know where they were. The passengers began to give up hope – Ibn Jubayr wrote that both Muslim and Christian passengers wailed and prayed for safety. At last they spotted the shores of Sicily but, before they could dock in the harbor of Messina, another storm caused their ship to shatter into pieces and sink. The survivors clung to scraps of the ship to stay afloat. Sicily was by now a Christian territory, and the king, William II (r. 1166–1189), personally paid for the rescue of the Muslim survivors who could not afford the prices being charged for rescue by rowboat operators.

The Indian Ocean was no safer for seafarers. Shipwrecks and piracy were just as common in Cairo Geniza letters, written to and from merchants traveling in the Indian Ocean circuit like in the Mediterranean. Many traders from the Cairo Jewish community were active in the Indian Ocean, including the beloved brother of the most famous Jewish philosopher of the Middle Ages, Moses Maimonides. The final letter from David – who drowned on a mercantile journey in the Indian Ocean – to his brother Moses was found in the Geniza cache. In a later letter, Moses Maimonides admitted that his brother's death left him grieving for many years.

One of the most famous literary tales from the medieval Muslim world is about multiple shipwrecks endured there by a fictional merchant from Baghdad: Sindbad the Sailor. Stories about Sindbad circulated as early as the ninth century and were only later included in the compilation known as *One Thousand and One Nights*. These tales – seven in total, mirroring the number of voyages on which he sailed – tell of Sindbad's disastrous but enriching adventures in the Indian Ocean. Each tale follows the same pattern: at home in Baghdad, Sindbad squanders his money on a lavish lifestyle and goes to sea to regain his riches. He purchases local goods and loads them onto a boat headed downriver to a Persian Gulf port, whence he sails around the Indian Ocean from island to island buying and selling goods. At some point, his ship would wreck or he would be deserted by his shipmates and find himself alone and impoverished. After some kind of extraordinary adventure, he would become wealthy again and find a way home with his share of the goods. After vowing to give up the maritime life and settle down to enjoy his riches, he would again waste his money on luxuries and set out again.

The islands of the Indian Ocean – both in these fabulous tales and in reality – were places offering immense riches for merchants from the Middle East, with diamonds, coconuts, ivory, spices, aromatic woods, and other precious items that fetched high prices at the markets of Islamicate cities. The fantastical elements of Sindbad's adventures were crafted for entertainment, but if we read between the lines we can see a reality of both danger and wealth. Their high drama reflects both the risk and the reward to be obtained by maritime

Fig 6.8
This fragment of a letter written in Judeo-Arabic and found in the Cairo Geniza was sent from David Maimonides to his brother Moses Maimonides, the famous Jewish philosopher, in 1170. David writes that he had missed the departure of the caravan with which he intended to travel from Cairo to a port in Sudan. When he arrived separately at the port, he learned that the caravan had been robbed and many people killed. While he was grateful for his good luck, it did not continue. David chose to set sail for India – a risky proposition that his brother opposed – where his ship sank, and he drowned. The grief caused by his death plunged Maimonides into what he described in another letter as a years-long depression.
Cambridge University Library

mercantile trips within the Indian Ocean. Sindbad's stories are not just about mercantile profit, however. They also show him growing bored with a secure and predictable life and taking risks to satisfy his curiosity and ambition. The world of these tales was fantastical and wonderful – exploring it was scary and exciting at the same time.

Viking Longships

The Norse sagas portray colonization and exploration, and they also regularly mention trade expeditions between Iceland, Greenland, and Norway – suggesting that these voyages were quite common. Such extensive Scandinavian seafaring was made possible by innovations in shipbuilding technology. The Viking longships – so called because they were quite long compared to their width – were capable of covering long distances along inland river systems and across open waters. Viking vessels were built in a variety of sizes, from ships with a small cargo capacity of about 4 metric tons up to large ones that could transport around 60 metric tons. Warships were built to transport warriors and their horses, although some historians theorize that the close links between pillaging and commercial exchange meant that Viking boats would have been used for both purposes. Small fishing boats or dugout canoes were used regularly by Scandinavians of all classes. But, it was the sleek longships that were selected for burials of elite men and women.

    This tradition of burying important people in ship graves means that several complete examples of Viking longships have been discovered in burial mounds around the shores of the North Sea. One of the best preserved is a boat from Gokstad, in southeastern Norway. It was built between 885 and 890 and sailed for about a decade before being used in the burial of an important

Fig 6.9
The Gokstad ship, ca. 880–900, was preserved in the burial mound of a Viking chieftain. This boat was particularly suited to sailing quickly over open seas. It was rowed by 32 people and had room for passengers and moderate amounts of cargo. It is held today in the Viking Ship Museum in Oslo, Norway, along with two other Viking ships.
Scott Goodno / Alamy Stock Photo

man, perhaps a chieftain, who died as a result of battle wounds. As is typical for longships, the Gokstad boat could either be sailed or rowed. This ship had 16 pairs of oars, one per man, for a total crew of 32 – almost precisely the size of the one Leif Eiriksson hired for his first voyage to North America, as described in the sagas, suggesting that he would have used a boat this size. Sails, although rarely preserved as archeological remains, were depicted in medieval images as broad and square, which would have been necessary for powering these boats across hundreds of miles of open water.

Like the Arabic dhow (see Chapter 2), longships were double ended but, unlike the dhow, Viking ships used iron nails. Dhows were sewn together with ropes and made watertight with tree sap or other sticky gums. Longships were watertight by design: the body of the boat was constructed of slightly over-lapping planks secured with simple iron nails. Cargo could be stored below the removable plank deck, but the Gokstad boat was not crafted for carrying huge cargoes. Rather, it was built for speed across the ocean. Both dhows and longships were crafted for efficient sailing, but they were much smaller than contemporary Chinese junks, which could hold many tons more cargo. Later medieval galleys in the Mediterranean were built in sizes closer to the junks.

Sunken Treasure

Underwater archeology is one of the best ways we have of learning about the patterns and commodities of premodern maritime trade. Hundreds of ancient and medieval Mediterranean shipwrecks have been discovered, many on common sea lanes. One such ship is called the Serçe Limanı wreck, after its location near Turkey's Serçe Limanı harbor, or the Glass Wreck, after its cargo. It was a Greek Christian merchant ship that sank off the southwestern coast of Anatolia around 1025 while carrying three metric tons of broken glass (cullet) intended for recycling. It had been sailing toward Byzantine Constantinople from Fatimid Syria, where there was a significant glass industry. At Constantinople, the cargo would have been melted down and turned into new glassware – a process that required much lower temperatures and was therefore much cheaper than pro-ducing new glass from scratch. Other items onboard – such as intact glassware, ceramics, copper pots, gold jewelry, sumac (a spice), and raisins – were found in smaller quantities, suggesting that they had been purchased by individual sailors for resale or gifting back home.

With this shipwreck, we can both see a concrete example of Muslim-Christian trade in the eastern Mediterranean and a glimpse of the shipboard activities and lives of the sailors who carried out that trade. Many "daily life" objects were found that help us to imagine the lives of sailors onboard: grooming sets (with scissors, razors, mirrors, and beard combs), low-value coins (which help us date the wreck), well-worn ceramic dishes, weapons, tools, scales and weights for weighing goods for trade, games of backgammon and chess, fishing nets, and other items. Animal bones, dishes, and goblets help archeologists recreate the shipboard diet. Jugs of wine and olive oil were etched with names to indicate their owners; the most common name was "Michael," suggesting that he was the captain. This cache of undersea evidence helps us to imagine the lives of these Christians who sailed to Muslim ports: they played games, trimmed their beards, fished for food, mended their tools and nets, and hoped to profit from small bundles of Islamicate goods they had purchased to resell back home.

The ship sank in a shallow bay off the southeastern coast of Asia Minor, where it had probably sought safety from the harsh winds that battered this part of the coast. Several other ancient and medieval shipwrecks were found in this same area, suggesting that it was a difficult and dangerous section along a common sea lane. The search for safety failed, however, when more winds caused the anchor to snap and the ship to sink. Given the shallow waters, it seems that the sailors aboard were able to swim to safety – but they were not able to save their onboard possessions.

HOW IS NEW TECHNOLOGY CHANGING MARITIME ARCHEOLOGY?

Archeologists dig into the soil for the remains of past cultures, or dive under the oceans to bring up sunken ships and their treasures. But they also use a growing array of scientific tools and techniques to locate and study their evidence. Isotopic analysis of elements in human bones and teeth can tell scientists where an ancient person was born and where they migrated, what they ate and what diseases they suffered. Analysis of aDNA can reveal human family connections, migration patterns, hair and eye color, and sex. And, advances in sonar technology are revolutionizing the discovery and study of sunken or buried ships. Multibeam sonar rapidly creates a detailed three-dimensional image of the sea floor and objects resting on it. This allows scientists to quickly scan large areas, and thus find shipwrecks much faster than by previous methods. Similarly, ground-penetrating radar allows archeologists to use non-invasive techniques to study underground items. This technology has been used to locate several recent Viking ships buried in Norway, although they have not yet been excavated. Future technological advances will further help archeologists both study and preserve remains from the past.

Other recovered shipwrecks, like the Tang-era Belitung wreck discussed earlier, are transforming historians' understanding of globalized patterns of premodern trade. When this wooden sewn-plank dhow set out from a Chinese port around 826, it was carrying a huge cargo, with gold and silver pieces, spices, and thousands of mass-produced ceramics that had been made at the Changsha kilns in Hunan province. Many were bowls, but there were also pitchers, jars, and other shapes and sizes. Art historians note that these ceramics – as many as 60,000 pieces in all – were produced specifically for the export trade. Their polychromatic designs were popular throughout the wider world: shards of Changsha ware have been found in archeological sites from Southeast Asia and India to the Middle East and eastern Africa. Based on the ship's design and materials, it was likely bound for a port in the Persian Gulf, where the freight would be sold at markets in Baghdad, Cairo, and beyond. So, this one ship's cargo attests to large-scale mass production of ceramic ware, intended from the outset for export to foreign markets.

The bowls feature a variety of designs: animals, birds, human faces, sea monsters, inscriptions (in Chinese or Arabic, again suggesting that the intended destination was in the Islamic world), and poems. One of the bowls is clearly identified as a tea bowl, from both its shape and its Chinese inscription. While no actual evidence remains that there was also tea aboard, and no evidence that tea-drinking was popular in the central Islamic lands before the thirteenth century, at least one of the artisans crafted their product with a vessel for drinking tea in mind. Like the Serçe Limanı wreck, the Belitung wreck also contained items that show us glimpses of the people on board. Game pieces, sewing needles, small bottles that may have contained medicine, cooking utensils, and incense that may have been used in prayers all relate to shipboard life. Also found were a few individuals items that may have been purchased as gifts for loved ones back home: a ceramic dog, a bird whistle, and a low-quality gold bracelet.

Fig 6.10
Roughly 60,000 pieces of ceramicware like these were recovered from the Belitung wreck, ca. 830, packed into larger jars for shipment. This wreck was discovered in 1998 by Indonesians fishing for sea cucumbers, and some items were lost to looting before archeologists could begin their study. The first phase of its excavation was carried out by a commercial operation that did not follow western scholarly standards, and this has caused some controversy in Europe and the US. However, the project was approved by the Indonesian community's elders and the Indonesian government.
Metropolitan Museum of Art, Gift of Dianne and Oscar Schafer, 1986, 1986.97.3

Tea

By the Tang dynasty, tea, a hot drink brewed from the dried leaves of the *Camellia sinensis* plant, had replaced alcohol as the most important social, ritual, and alimentary beverage in China. Tea was initially popularized in China by Buddhists, who benefited from its ability to promote wakefulness and focus during meditation. It was a replacement for forbidden alcohol and used in preparation for enlightenment. Daoists promoted its medicinal qualities. Traveling Buddhist monks may have spread the popularity of tea throughout China, and on to Japan (where it did not really become popular until the late twelfth century), and also to Tibet (where it took off rather quickly and was traded in large quantities for Central Asian horses).

In China, tea was not simply a drink with religious or medicinal uses, but was widely enjoyed by people of all social ranks. It could be purchased by the cup from marketplace stalls, or prepared at home following elaborate rituals that included grinding the dried and roasted leaves into a powder, pouring it into a cauldron with water, and boiling it in three distinct stages at precise temperatures. It was then frothed with whisks, poured, and ladled so that the resulting drink was foamy and aromatic. Tang- and Song-era tea often included additives such as salt, herbs, leaves, fruits, and roots, but, by later periods, elite tea cultures were becoming more focused on green and black teas without such additions.

Tea was also a major agricultural product of China's economy, a marketplace commodity, a source of taxation, and an export good. Traded overland across Central Asia and by sea to Japan, it was also valued as a fitting tribute to the emperor. The tea trade was highly regulated by the Chinese government, as were several other items like silk, salt, and metals. In this period, Chinese porcelain reached new levels of refinement and beauty, and continued to be highly in demand and imitated in the Islamicate world. But, despite the long-distance trade connections that brought other Chinese and Southeast Asian goods, such as spices, paper, and porcelain, to the ports of the Persian Gulf and Red Sea and thence into the Mediterranean world, tea was not among the products imported into the Middle East or Europe until long after the medieval period had ended.

Spices

Even if they did not want tea, consumers in the Islamicate and Latinate worlds definitely wanted other natural products, most notably spices, medicinals, perfumes, incenses, and dyes harvested in China, India, Southeast Asia, and West Africa. Both culinary and medicinal in use, spices were in high demand and were hugely profitable for merchants. Pepper and cinnamon were the most popular spices, but so were ginger, nutmeg, mace (from the outside casing of the nutmeg), cloves, saffron, sumac, and many others that are less common today like spikenard (an aromatic oil from a plant that grows in the Himalayas), grains of paradise (also known as melegueta pepper, from West Africa), and mastic (a gummy plant resin from the eastern Mediterranean). Medieval European and Islamic cuisines were intensely flavorful from the use of all these spices, as well as vinegar and copious amounts of sugar (also considered a spice and regularly used in main course dishes as well as in medicines).

Contrary to popular belief, demand for spices did not arise because people were trying to cover up bad tastes from unrefrigerated food on the verge of spoiling. Rather, intense flavors were fashionable at the time; spices were considered good for health and digestion, and richly spiced banquets allowed the elite to demonstrate their wealth through conspicuous consumption of expensive imported products. Burgess families imitated these fashions – although using smaller quantities of spice – meaning that all but the very poor ate spiced foods. For example, later medieval European recipes for sweet-sour sauced meat called for pork or beef, sugar, vinegar, saffron, pepper, and cinnamon.

Bundles of saffron, pepper, and cinnamon would have been sold at Indian Ocean seaports and loaded onto ships sailing westward to ports in the Persian Gulf or the Red Sea. There, they might have been sold to overland traders who carried them to Alexandria, Egypt, where they could be purchased, for instance, by a visiting Italian merchant for shipment across the Mediterranean to Venice. Once there, an overland trader might have transported them northward, along with dyed fabrics, to the Champagne fairs, where they were bought by an English trader with the profit made from selling wool cloth. He might transport them to an urban shop in England, where an estate cook would purchase them to flavor a noble's meal or an urban housewife would make a recipe in imitation of noble banquets.

BANQUETS

As discussed in Chapter 2, diets in all parts of the medieval world differed by social status, as well as by region and culture. In general, we find that peasants ate simpler fare – based more heavily on grains and vegetables than the diets of the social elite. The nobility usually monopolized big game hunting, so their diets were often heavier in roasted meats, although peasantry would have eaten stews supplemented with small-game meat when it was available. As a form of urban "middle class" arose, their food preferences tended to mimic those of the elites, incorporating, for example, expensive imported spices.

Sumptuous banquets were a regular part of conspicuous consumption by wealthy elites in many parts of the premodern world. In the Islamicate world, banquets were intended to evoke all the senses – perfumes, oils, and scented waters and soaps were used to wash hands and scent the diner's hair, body, clothing, and air; entertainers performed music, poetry, and dances to delight the eyes and ears; elaborate dishes were designed to amaze the diner with their colors, arrangements, and delicious scents; and, of course, they were to taste wonderful, filled with spices and covered in sauces with several layers of flavor. Many of the most important dishes were highly spiced stews of meats and vegetables. Later, medieval European nobility likewise hosted feasts with elaborately prepared, highly colorful, and heavily spiced dishes for guests to enjoy.

Cookbooks in the medieval Islamicate and Latinate worlds were primarily aids to memory for cooks serving elite households. They did not list precise measurements like modern recipes do. For example, one recipe for "beef with rosebuds" from a fourteenth-century Egyptian cookbook directs: "Provide yourself with meat, rosebuds, lemons, onions, pepper, mastic, and cinnamon. Blanch the meat, then fry it with the onions. When it is ready, add crushed pepper, lemon juice, mastic, cinnamon, and rosebuds that have been crumbled by hand. Moisten with the necessary quantity of broth."

Viking Silver

In addition to the longship highlighted earlier in the chapter, the Gokstad burial mound featured a variety of grave goods meant to display the wealth and power of the dead man. Silk textiles with gold thread, shields, a gameboard with tokens, beds, a tent, and three smaller boats remained, but the expected weapons and jewels had been looted by grave robbers (perhaps already in the medieval period). Also buried with him were horses, dogs, hawks (for elite forms of hunting), and two peacocks. Peacocks are native to India, Sri Lanka, and Indonesia. They appear in ancient Roman art (and were one of many exotic animals imported into the Roman Empire), but this is the earliest archeological example of a peacock this far north. Likely an item of either trade or gift, the presence of peacocks in this early tenth-century grave demonstrates just how extensively the Vikings' international connections ranged.

The path taken by the Gokstad man's peacocks from Southeast Asia to Norway is not certain, but one likely route is the system of land and river paths between the Baltic Sea and the Black and Caspian seas. For at least a century before his burial in 900, Viking trade parties had been sailing the rivers across Russian territory – along the Dnieper River and across the Black Sea to Constantinople, or via the Volga River to the Caspian Sea and thence to Baghdad. Both Constantinople and Baghdad were, as we have seen, major metropolises with markets filled with products and people from around the hemisphere. There, the Vikings had access to wide arrays of commercial goods from China, the Mediterranean, Africa, India, Central Asia, and Southeast Asia, where the peacocks originated.

If the archeological record is a good indication, what the Norse seem to have wanted far more than exotic animals, though, is Islamic silver coins. Hundreds of thousands of silver dirhams, a mid-value coinage minted widely across the Islamic world, have been found in Viking hoards around the Baltic and North

Fig 6.11
The Vale of York hoard was buried near York, England (a Viking settlement) ca. 927 and discovered in 2007 by metal detectorists. A hoard is a collection of valued items stashed or buried for safekeeping. This hoard contained 617 silver coins and 65 other metal objects – mostly silver ingots and decorative items such as armbands but also a gilded cup containing coins. The items came from Iran, Central Asia, Russia, Ireland, North Africa, Scandinavia, and continental Europe, demonstrating interconnections among cultures in this period and the Vikings' roles as mediators of those connections. This silver dirham from the Vale of York hoard was minted under the Samanid dynasty (819–999), which ruled Iran and its broader region independent of the Abbasid caliphs at Baghdad. They had capitals at Samarkand (until 892) and then Bukhara, cities wealthy from trade eastward across Central Asia and westward with Baghdad and Constantinople. The coin had traveled to northern England by the time of its burial in 927. (right) Obverse and (left) reverse.

Sea regions. In exchange for silver coins, colorful glass beads from the Indo-Pacific region, and other eastern commodities, the Vikings offered enslaved people they had captured in raids, animal furs and skins, honey, wax, amber, swords, and walrus tusk ivory.

Although most of the direct contact between the Vikings and their trade partners from Byzantium and the Islamicate world took place in cities like Constantinople or Baghdad, we know that at least some Muslim travelers went north and encountered the Scandinavians and other peoples of the region. In 921, Ibn Fadlan, an envoy from the Abbasid caliph traveled north along the same route that brought the Viking traders south to Baghdad. He had been sent by the caliph to the ruler of a Bulgar territory along the Volga River. The Volga Bulgars, as they are known, had recently converted to Islam and wished to learn more about how to practice their faith. Ibn Fadlan and his party traveled overland from Baghdad to Bukhara, the capital of an independent Islamic state ruled by the Samanid dynasty (819–999). From there, they traveled north by a combination of river and land routes and encountered numerous seminomadic tribes in the steppes.

After arriving at their destination, they also encountered a group of traders whom Ibn Fadlan called the Rus, but who most historians agree were Scandinavians. As he described them, they shared many characteristics with the populations that had migrated out from Scandinavia and who were active in commerce along the Volga River. He described them as tall and attractive, with blond hair and pale skin, and carrying swords, axes, and knives at all times. They traded in animal furs, enslaved peoples, and other commodities. According to his account, they were interested in silver dirhams so that they could purchase jewelry including brooches, silver torques (neck rings), and green beads – all items that the Vikings are known to have traded for.

Despite their attractiveness and fancy apparel, however, Ibn Fadlan considered them to be incredibly unclean, with poor manners and disgusting personal hygiene. He found their habits and culture quite strange, including the custom of interring noblemen in boats, along with animals and enslaved girls who had been sacrificed, and then burning the boat. As we have seen, ship burials filled with animals and grave goods were common among the Vikings.

Games

Scandinavian communities also traded locally with the British Isles and northern Europe, where walrus ivory was particularly desired as a more accessible substitute for expensive elephant ivory. Some of the most spectacular pieces of European ivory sculpture from this period are ornately carved chess pieces. The three pieces below – a bishop, a queen, and a king – are among around 90 game

Fig 6.12
Isle of Lewis Chessmen: Bishop (left), Queen (center), and King (right), ca. 1150–1200.
PA Images / Alamy Stock Photo

tokens (parts of probably five chess sets and a game of tables, similar to back-gammon) that were dug up on the Isle of Lewis, Scotland. Crafted from walrus tusks at a Norse workshop, probably in Norway ca. 1150–1200, the pieces may have been buried for safekeeping by a merchant intending to transport them further.

The game of chess came to Europe from the Muslim world, where it was introduced from India via the silk roads and maritime routes. The spread of the game followed the same routes of transmission as many luxury trade goods. Originating in India during the Gupta Empire (280–550), by around 600 an early form of chess was played by the Sassanian Persians of Samarkand, a western outlet of the overland silk roads. When Persia and much of Central Asia were incorporated into the Islamic world ca. 700, so too was the game of chess. Europeans knew the game by around 1000 and, by the middle of the eleventh century, chess sets were items of art and commerce in the far north of Christian Europe. By the thirteenth century, chess was common among European elites as a characteristic pastime of the nobility, as were hawking and hunting. As it moved, the game altered slightly and took on new rules, with the modern form of the game – including a powerful queen – only forming by the end of the fifteenth century.

Chess may have been considered the most noble boardgame in the medieval period, but it was far from the only one played and shared between cultures. The Scandinavians who traded in game pieces like the Lewis chessmen also played a variety of games known as *hnefatafl*, strategy games played on a grid-like board, which spread around the North Sea area. The *Libro de los juegos* also contains illustrations of games of chance (such as dice); a variety of games called tables, related to modern backgammon; and nine men's morris, another strategy boardgame. In East Asia, a popular strategy boardgame was *go*, created in China and spread to Japan and other neighboring regions, where it is still popular today.

Looking Forward

The central Middle Ages was a time of increasing levels of commercial and cultural exchange, within local or regional networks and across huge expanses of land and sea. It was the linkage between various regional networks – the overlapping of individual travel circuits into larger connections – that allowed, for example, a spice harvested in China or Southeast Asia to end up on the plate of a banqueter in the north of England. The coming centuries will show the various economies of the medieval world deepening these interconnections, even as the disruptions of disease, conquest, and political disorder threatened, or made more difficult, some of the pathways by which trade occurred. In the later medieval centuries, we will also see the rise to prominence of European traders, who, for much of the earlier Middle Ages, had taken a back seat to merchants from the Indian Ocean and Islamicate world.

Fig 6.13
Chess was widely played at elite courts in the Mediterranean and European worlds.
The first known book of chess strategy was written in Arabic ca. 850; later, manuals
were also written in European vernaculars. This image is from a 1283 manuscript in
Castilian Spanish, called the *Libro de los juegos* (*Book of Games*), or *Libro de ajedrez,
dados e tablas* (*Book of Chess, Dice, and Tables*), commissioned by the Christian King
Alfonso X (r. 1252–1284). It contains specific chess problems and analysis of how to
solve them, with images of different people – Muslims, Jews, Christians, royals, enslaved
people, foreign visitors, men, women, and children – playing the game. For example, in
this image of game 88, a Black player wins a game against a white male cleric.
Album / Alamy Stock Photo

Research Questions

1. This chapter features the discovery of the Serçe Limanı wreck and its cargo. Explore this underwater archeological site further. What was its cargo, and what does the cargo tell us about trade in this period? Where did the ship sail from? Where was it going? How was the wreckage found?
2. Spices and herbs were valued as flavorings and for their medicinal properties. Modern science confirms the healthful properties of many spices; for example, cinnamon is an antioxidant and an anti-inflammatory. What are the valuable benefits of other spices and herbs as determined by modern medicine? How do these compare to medieval medical texts' discussions of their benefits?
3. Animals essential to survival were traded (oxen, camels, horses, and dogs). They were used for heavy labor such as carrying riders and supplies, turning mills, or hauling carts and plows. Other animals were purchased and gifted as signs of status. The macaw skeletons found at Chacoan sites and the peacocks from the Gokstad burial are two examples of animals bought and sold as luxury items or curiosities. What are other examples of medieval trade in live animals or animal parts?
4. Research historical ship trading routes and shipwrecks. Are there certain areas that are more prone to shipwrecks? Why?
5. Examine the place of women within economies. What labor did they perform? What goods did they produce? Did this give them any economic security? Political or social power? Why or why not?
6. Research the sea power of Srivijaya – a coastal state based in Sumatra that controlled transit through the Straits of Malacca from the seventh century to the tenth century. How did their geographical location aid their rise to power? What goods moved through their area?

Further Reading

Benn, James A. *Tea in China: A Religious and Cultural History*. Honolulu: University of Hawai'i Press, 2016.

Broadhurst, R. J. C., trans. *The Travels of Ibn Jubayr*. London: Jonathan Cape, 1952.

Constable, Olivia Remie. "Chess and Courtly Culture in Medieval Castile: The "Libro de ajedres" of Alfonso X, el Sabio." In *Speculum*, volume 82, no. 2. April 2007.

Crown, Patricia, and W. Jeffrey Hurst. "Evidence of Cacao Use in the Prehispanic American Southwest." *Proceedings of the National Academy of Sciences* 106, no. 7 (2009): 2110–2113.

Crown, Patricia, et al. "Ritual Drinks in the Pre-Hispanic US Southwest and Mexican Northwest." *Proceedings of the National Academy of Sciences* 112, no. 37 (2015): 11436–11442.

Frazier, Kendrick. *People of Chaco: A Canyon and its Culture*, rev. ed. New York and London: W.W. Norton, 2005.

Freedman, Paul, *Out of the East: Spices and the Medieval Imagination*. New Haven, CT: Yale University Press, 2008.

Goitein, S. D., trans. *Letters of Medieval Jewish Traders*. Princeton, NJ: Princeton University Press, 1973.

Haddawy, Husain, trans. *The Arabian Nights II: Sindbad and Other Popular Stories*. New York: Knopf, 1998.

Heng, Geraldine. "An Ordinary Ship and Its Stories of Early Globalism: World Travel, Mass Production, and Art in the Global Middle Ages." *Journal of Medieval Worlds* 1, no. 1 (2019): 11–54.

Jung-pang Lo. *China as a Sea Power 1127–1368: A Preliminary Survey of the Maritime Expansion and Naval Exploits of the Chinese People during the Southern Song and Yuan Periods*, edited by Bruce A. Elleman. Singapore: National University of Singapore Press, 2011.

Krahl, Regina, John Guy, J. Keith Wilson, and Julian Raby. *Shipwrecked: Tang Treasures and Monsoon Winds*. Washington, DC: Arthur M. Sackler Gallery, Smithsonian Institution; Singapore: National Heritage Board: Singapore Tourism Board, 2010.

Kunz, Keneva, and Gísli Sigurðsson, trans. *The Vinland Sagas: The Icelandic Sagas About the First Documented Voyages Across the North Atlantic: The Saga of the Greenlanders and Eirik the Red's Saga*. London and New York: Penguin, 2008.

Lunde, Paul, and Caroline Stone, trans. *Ibn Fadlān and the Land of Darkness: Arab Travellers in the Far North*. New York: Penguin, 2012.

Mair, Victor H., and Erling Hoh. *The True History of Tea*. London: Thames and Hudson, 2012.

Pollard, Edward, and Charles Kinyera Okeny, "The Swahili Coast and the Indian Ocean Trade Patterns in the 7th–10th Centuries CE." *Journal of Southern African Studies* 43, no. 5 (2017): 927–947.

Prange, Sebastian R. *Monsoon Islam: Trade and Faith on the Medieval Malabar Coast*. New York: Cambridge University Press, 2018.

Respess, A., and L. C. Niziolek. "Exchanges and Transformations in Gendered Medicine on the Maritime Silk Road: Evidence from the Thirteenth-Century Java Sea Wreck." In *Histories of Medicine and Healing in the Indian Ocean World*, edited by A. Winterbottom and F. Tesfaye, 63–97. Palgrave Series in Indian Ocean World Studies. New York: Palgrave Macmillan, 2016.

Zaouali, Lilia. *Medieval Cuisine of the Islamic World: A Concise History with 174 Recipes*. Translated by M. B. DeBevoise. Oakland: University of California Press, 2007.

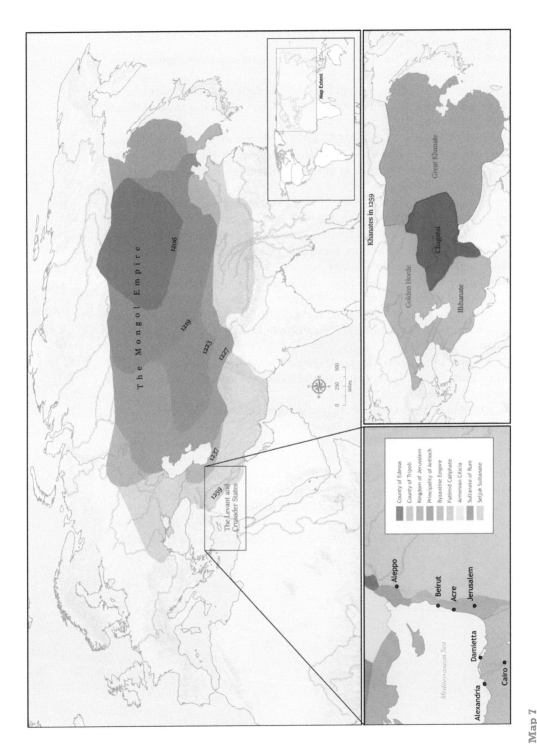

Map 7
Soldiers and Civil Servants

The Mongol Empire

1206
1219
1223
1227
1237
1259

The Levant and
Crusader States

Map Extent

Khanates in 1259

Golden Horde
Great Khanate
Chagatai
Ilkhanate

County of Edessa
County of Tripoli
Kingdom of Jerusalem
Principality of Antioch
Byzantine Empire
Fatimid Caliphate
Armenian Cilicia
Sultanate of Rum
Seljuk Sultanate

Aleppo
Beirut
Acre
Jerusalem
Damietta
Cairo
Alexandria

Mediterranean Sea

N
W   E
S

0   250   500
Miles

7 Soldiers and Civil Servants

Politics, 900–1300

With contributions by Paul L. Sidelko, 1967–2020

Introduction

In our first chapter on politics in the premodern world, we focused on how military men used their strength to create productive and defensible territories. The second section of our political discussion focuses on how those early territories solidified into states. Strength of arms alone was not enough to ensure continued political success. Even though continued warfare ensured steady streams of income, more was needed to move from petty territory to state. For those rulers who sought to control their borders, religion and philosophy aided in creating common identities among subjects, and administrative structures grew to manage revenue and governmental offices. The warrior ethos continued to permeate the political arena, as kings led armies and conquered new areas, but there was also an increase in the formalization of civil services.

Despite these actions, centralized power was threatened by rebellions and external invasions in states such as the Tang dynasty in China. In this chapter, we look at how some areas moved beyond the purely defensive and took steps toward administrative complexity, which is a hallmark of the modern nation-state. Using the same techniques of earlier rulers, leaders from 900 to 1300 focused energy on solidifying and expanding their dynasties (particularly by securing their lines of succession) and increasing their bureaucracies, while continuing to benefit from robust economic systems.

In the first section of this chapter, we discuss examples of centralization. Here, we see the effects of strong bureaucratic systems in Europe and Africa, including the expansion of the Mongols in the Central Asian steppes and beyond, and the western European incursions into the Middle East. The increase in power of one polity is necessarily at the expense of others. Under pressure from stronger states, some dominions in the Middle East and China collapsed and were claimed by the victors.

In the second section of this chapter, we focus on two genres of literature prized by the nobility of these increasingly centralized kingdoms and empires. As popular court and village entertainment, the romance explored the dramatic collisions of personal desire and public obligation – soldiers and their lovers must choose between their passionate relationships and duties to clan and king. Another genre, the military epic, also provided entertainment at banquets and army camps, inspiring loyalty to a particular leader, god, or cultural ideal of superiority over other peoples. Literature and art supported and glorified the projects and ambitions of centralized states, and, as more kingdoms moved to bureaucratic civil service, a tension between the older, familial clan model of leadership and the newer, formal civic-servant model played out in the epic narratives.

A: CONSOLIDATION AND FRAGMENTATION

Evidence: *The Tale of the Heike*

                 Anglo-Saxon Chronicle

                 Secret History of the Mongols

                 Al-Bakri's *Realms and Routes*

                 Gesta Normannorum Ducum

Introduction

In this section we examine the centralization and fragmentation of several political entities. The recognized definition of a state is "a sovereign organized political community under one government, that is concerned with both civil and military affairs." States have recognized territory, bureaucracies, and some control over their constituents. They levy taxes, operate a military and police force, and are comprised of bureaucratic institutions (like a court system) that administer and enforce laws. Although few of the political communities from 900 to 1300 can be classified formally as nation-states (nation-states are "imagined communities" where the people see themselves as one unit, tied to a political and geographic space), most of the political leaders were working to establish statehood. Bureaucratic stability became the key. With stability comes the ability to innovate (see Chapter 3) and to create lasting legacies. Leaders began creating political states by using their authority to create succession plans, administer justice and enforce laws, and levy consistent taxes.

While some areas grew toward statehood, others found themselves spread too thin, with challenges to their governmental institutions that caused retraction and fragmentation. Losing the bureaucratic center, these states often fell to internal and external fighting. The crusades of the Middle East and the growth of the Mongol Empire are two important events that show how external pressures, combined with internal disintegration, had far-reaching consequences.

Problems of Succession

China

In China, emperors followed the Mandate of Heaven, the idea that the gods gave the emperor the authority to rule over the people. This religious precept, however, was tempered by the belief that the emperor should always rule with the good of the people in mind. Conquering emperors justified their rule through the Mandate: if the gods had not wanted them to take over, they would not have succeeded. The Song dynasty (960–1279) began in this manner. The emperor Taizu had been a military commander of the Later Zhou dynasty, one of the many ruling houses in the Five Dynasty and Ten Kingdoms period (907–979), which followed in the wake of the fall of the Tang dynasty. Taizu staged a coup and forced the final Zhou emperor to abdicate.

In the beginning, Song emperors struggled to create a strong line of succession; for instance, Taizu's brother Taizong (r. 976–997) had Taizu's two living sons disinherited to become his brother's heir. The next several emperors were all succeeded by their sons but, due to high child mortality, many were succeeded by fourth and fifth sons. Taizong's sixth son, Zhenzong, inherited his father's estates after all five of his elder brothers died as youths. The mortality rate of children, even those at the highest echelons of society, dictated the need for many wives and many sons. Following the Confucian precepts of filial obedience and loyalty, Chinese political theory and traditional practice meant that a father's eldest son inherited his estate. Generally, emperors chose the eldest son to be the heir, designating him the "Supreme Son" (*taizi*) and conferring authority on him; however, sometimes a second or younger son would be chosen. This practice of choosing an heir while the emperor was alive allowed for peaceful transitions of power; however, this rarely worked easily. The practice of polygamy in the imperial palace complicated these relationships. Ostensibly, the empress's eldest son should inherit the throne, as she was the crowned consort of the emperor, but, in practice, sometimes a concubine bore a son prior to the empress. Chinese tradition got around this problem by stating that all the children of the emperor belonged to the empress as well. As we can imagine, infighting was common in most imperial households.

Emperor Ningzong (r. 1194–1224) was a second son who succeeded his father. Despite his multiple marriages, he had no living sons and adopted a young cousin to be his heir. The boy also died young and, at Ningzong's death, court intrigues saw two young men vying for the throne. One had Ningzong's approval but not that of the court bureaucrats; strangulation ended his bid for the throne, and Lizong (r. 1224–1264) moved into the palace. Ningzong's reign had been plagued by invasions by the Jurchen in the north and by rising domestic inflation, and Lizong's reign was as fraught as his predecessor's, especially because Mongol invasions began in earnest in the 1230s. Despite internal economic and external warfare issues, the process of crowning a prince with a living emperor did allow the Chinese Song dynasty some measure of stability and success during trying times.

Japan

Unlike China, Japan was highly decentralized. At the end of the Heian period (794–1185), the military system of local militias made up of mounted soldiers was widespread. The rise of a military class coincided with a decline of a central civil government. Law enforcement, taxation, and other civic duties fell to local lords, who spent much of their time in capital cities, vying for position within the government instead of ruling their territories. By the 1150s, the ruling clan, the Fujiwara, began to lose out to other large clan families. One of the major failings of the Fujiwara was its inability to prevent other families from gaining large amounts of private property with which these rivals could support large standing armies. Rival clans, like the Taira and the Minamoto, amassed considerable territory and had large numbers of soldiers on retainer. As the Fujiwara began to rely more heavily upon private armies, they often had to hire their rivals, which created political opportunities for outsiders to control the Fujiwara clan.

The Japanese clans established a military system based on local armies, composed mostly of professionally trained cavalry soldiers (*samurai*) who owed their loyalty to the clan leader. The three largest clans in Japan increasingly fought for control over the island. The Fujiwara influenced the emperor from Kyoto, located in the center of the island chain. Minamoto controlled most of eastern Japan, and the Taira held power primarily in western Japan. Improved military technology enabled these clans, their samurai and their leaders to be deadlier, and increased frustration at court caused civil conflict to spill out of the center and into the provinces. New, powerful bows caused a need for improvement in armor, and sophisticated sword-smithing called for new training methods – lighter, more flexible swords were not blunt-force, sharpened clubs, but instruments wielded with technique and skill. Horsemanship was crucial, and breeders raced to produce larger and stronger horses. Unfortunately, however, this focus on the aristocracy and their warriors led to a lack of a solid economic base in Japan. A bureaucracy tied to military life had less energy for the other civic functions of a stable, enduring state. The Fujiwara clan was not able to find a way out of the crisis of the late twelfth century, which saw a decline in food production (possibly caused by the Medieval Climate Anomaly) alongside a great growth in the population. Conflict and competition among the Fujiwara, Taira, and Minamoto clans escalated. Ruled as it was by the military elite in a loose confederacy of clans and families, Japan had no strong centralized government.

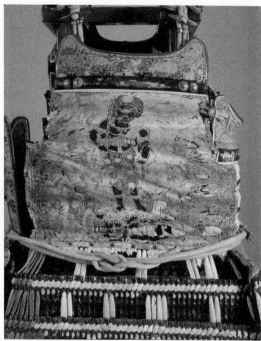

Fig 7.1 and 7.2
The medieval armor called a *yoro* wraps around the body and is secured by a separate panel. It has a flexible skirt for a warrior to ride horseback. The leather breastplate features the fierce-looking Buddhist spirit *Fudō Myō-ō*. Ashikaga Takauji (1303–1358), the founder of the Ashikaga shogunate, gave it to a shrine near Kyoto.
Metropolitan Museum of Art, Gift of Bashford Dean, 1914, 14.100.121b–e

In 1156, a clash between the retired emperor and his successor brought the Fujiwara, Taira, and Minamoto into military conflict. Known as the Hogen Disturbance, this struggle was the beginning of the end for Fujiwara control. Although the Minamoto sided with the Taira against the Fujiwara in this conflict, once they realized the weakness of the Fujiwara, they began fighting each other for domination of the imperial palace. From 1156 to 1185, the two clans battled for control; the Taira ruled from 1160 to 1185 and were overthrown in 1185 by the Minamoto, when Miyamoto Minamoto began ruling as *shogun* (military protector). The Genpei War of 1180–1185 between the Taira and the Minamoto clans was immortalized in the *Tale of the Heike*, which we will discuss in the second section of this chapter.

The Kamakura period (1185–1333) was known as the *bakafu* or "tent government" (because soldiers lived in tents), and either the Minamoto or the rejuvenated Fujiwara clan (from the Heian period) controlled the seat of government, and the emperor himself. Primarily concerned with military over civil affairs, the shoguns and their men let the civil servants control their personal areas; this decentralized Japan further, as local and national governments were not tightly connected. Emperors were displayed for religious purposes, but rarely had any formal political say. Although eldest clan sons were generally chosen to succeed their fathers, succession was often contested. In 1199, Hojo Masako took over when her husband died, and she ruled until her death in 1225. She and her samurai defeated several coups, even after she retired to become a nun, earning the title "nun shogun." The shoguns would rule the empire until 1868, when the Meiji Restoration brought power back to the emperor.

BATTLE OF MIKUSA AND BATTLE OF DAN-NO-URA

Through much of the Genpei War, the Taira were on the offensive against the Minamoto. They had superior numbers and better military positions. By 1184, unable to cope with the double impact of civil wars and devastating weather, the Taira fell to the defensive. In March 1184,

Fig 7.3
The legendary battles of the Genpei War between the Taira and Minamoto clans were popular subjects for high art. Here a fourteenth-century folding screen features the 1185 Battle of Dan-no-ura.
DEA / A. DAGLI ORTI / De Agostini via Getty Images

at the Battle of Mikusa, the Taira (also called the Heike) holed up in a fort at the edge of the sea. Three sides of the fort were tall and impenetrable; the fourth wall was a steep cliff. The Minamoto (also called the Genji) decided to scale the cliff walls at night to breach the fort. Men and horses began the treacherous climb that ended in a 70-foot drop to the ocean.

Through this dangerous action, the Minamoto entered the fort and defeated the Taira, forcing them to jump into the ocean and swim to boats moored offshore. The Taira regrouped, and, in April 1185, the two clans met at the naval battle of Dan-no-ura. The Taira knew the area and the tides well, and the battle seemed in their favor for much of the day. By the afternoon, the tides turned (literally and figuratively) and one of the Taira generals defected to the Minamoto side, using his ship to attack the Taira from behind, while the tides pushed their boats toward the Minamoto navy. Taira soldiers were surrounded, and many committed suicide; among the fallen were the six-year-old emperor and his grandmother. Thus ended the Taira's bid for control of the empire, and the Minamoto clan became the shoguns of Japan. Both these battles are enshrined in Japanese history: the subject of paintings, poems, kabuki, and other artistic forms. Today, both are also used as fodder for role-playing games (RPG), video games, manga, and movies.

England, France, Sicily: Intertwined States

England

A new era of peace settled over Europe's center during this time, and kings there began consolidating their bureaucracies and quelling internal dissension. The Vikings (another group well known to the RPG community) converted to Christianity and entered into political and economic commerce with the rest of Europe, and the Scandinavian kings and their descendants ruled in areas like Ireland, Iceland, England, Northern France, and Sicily. Once areas solidified, royal gazes looked to external military expansion. The mid-eleventh century, in particular, saw the start of multiple conquests by Latinate rulers at the borders of Europe: Christian Spanish kingdoms began pushing southward into Muslim al-Andalus, and armies of Latin Christians marched eastward toward Jerusalem in the crusades. The dukes of Normandy (northern France) conquered England, and another family of warriors from Normandy, the de Hautevilles, moved south into the Mediterranean region.

In Europe, the states of England, France, and Sicily are good comparators, as these neighbors and cousins had very different succession systems. The *Anglo-Saxon Chronicle* is one of our best sources of English history from this period, and the entries there give us information on many Scandinavian expansions throughout Europe. Actually a series of chronicles from different monasteries in England, this compilation was written by monks who often were eyewitnesses to the events they described. The monks show us the small kingdoms of Britain barely endured the Viking invasions and conquests of the ninth and tenth centuries, and, by 1066, King Edward the Confessor's death once again brought strife. Edward died without any children, and his brother-in-law, Harold Godwinson, was elected to the kingship in January 1066, leading to a series of fateful events. In September and October 1066, William, Duke of Normandy, brought war to the southern portion of the island, while Norwegians invaded the north. A powerful warlord, Harold Godwinson had the support of the royal council, but could not contend with war on two such distant and important fronts. Aided by his wife Matilda of Flanders, the Norman Duke William's fleet made the landing in southern England merely 20 days after Harold's major battles 275 miles north, meaning that his battle-weary army had to march for days to meet their next opponents.

The Battle of Hastings on October 14, 1066 saw the death of Harold Godwinson, and thus the Norman invasion became a conquest. The *Deeds of the Franks* (*Gesta Normannorum Ducum*), the history of the Dukes of Normandy, tells us that William was himself crowned king on December 25, 1066, at Westminster Abbey. The spectacle at the abbey, a church built by Edward the Confessor, created the veneer of a solid progression from Edward and the English kings to William, but it was a conquest and not a succession. It took him 20 years to subdue the island fully. Unfortunately for the people, William's succession plan was to part out his estates among his three living sons (the partible inheritance we saw as so problematic in earlier kingdoms). Because William prided himself on his strong Norman heritage, he bestowed this duchy on Robert, his eldest son. He rewarded his second son, William Rufus, with the kingdom of England, and gave riches but no land to his third, Henry, who eventually rose to power. In 1096, the eldest son, feeling slighted by his father's will and upset at his inheritance, mortgaged Normandy to his brother Henry and left for the First Crusade. When his brother, King William Rufus, died in a hunting accident without an heir, Robert was too far away to seize control, and Henry I (r. 1100–1135), the youngest, beat his brother Robert to the crown. For the next six years, the brothers battled in Normandy until the Battle of Tinchebray (1106), where Henry captured and imprisoned his brother Robert.

Henry died in 1135, just a year after his jailed brother Robert, also without a stable succession plan in place. He had 9 sons and possibly 15 daughters, but only 2 of his children were considered legitimate. In late November 1120, Henry's legitimate son William and a group of young nobles sailed from Normandy to England. Sources tell us that the young men and women had spent the voyage in revelry, with few sober people among the passengers or crew. The boats ran into foul weather, and over 300 people drowned, including William, several of his siblings, and many of the young nobles of northern Europe. Henry quickly recalled his legitimate daughter Matilda to England, the widowed empress of Germany. He anointed her his heir and made the men of his court swear to uphold her crown. They did not, and civil war wracked the island off and on until 1153, when Matilda's son Henry was crowned Henry II (r. 1154–1189). England's problems with inheritance and partible inheritance continued throughout the medieval period, culminating in civil war and reformation with Henry VIII (1491–1547).

France

Outside the problems of legitimate heirs, the kings of England were also, since 1066, vassals (landholders beholden to a lord) of the French crown (because they held their position as Duke of Normandy in vassalage to the French king). When Henry II married Eleanor of Aquitaine in 1152, he gained rights to her considerable French properties, now controlling more territory in France than the French king, Louis VII. However, as a vassal to the French crown, he owed fealty (loyalty) to Louis, who was also his cousin and his wife's ex-husband. The kings of France worked throughout the period of 900 to 1300 to unite their rule over all French territories, and the English kings were directly in the way of that consolidation. The French kings, however, were able to create peaceful transfers of power between themselves, which the English lacked. This gave them a decided advantage over their northern neighbors, but one that took several hundred years, including about 100 years of warfare, to resolve.

The French Capetian kings (987–1328) regulated their kingship by designating the eldest surviving son as the heir apparent during the lifetime of his father (similar to the Chinese system). This created a strong line of succession – everyone knew who would be the next king, because he sat right next to the current king. The elder king controlled access to his throne, but generally the eldest son was selected as co-king. In 987, Hugh Capet consecrated and crowned his son, Robert, king only a few short months after he himself was crowned king. Robert then ruled as co-king with his father until 996. Robert named his eldest son *rex designatus* (the designated king), and at his first son's death, he designated his second son. The Capetian kings secured hereditary succession through this manner until 1179, when Philip Augustus died prior to crowning his son. Until 1328, each Capetian king had just one surviving son, and kings themselves were often long-lived (most living between 50 and 70 years). This process of crowning their sons as co-kings enabled the Capetian family to control the French throne for over 300 years.

The combination of good fortune in producing adult male heirs and the foresight in managing royal succession helped the French monarchs in their process of consolidating and centralizing their kingdom. Hugh Capet was, in many ways, weaker than his vassals, but by crowning his son king during his own lifetime, Hugh created a stability for the French crown that it had previously lacked. When Hugh Capet became king, the French crown controlled only the Île de France, a small area surrounding the city of Paris. Centering his government in Paris, Hugh increased the French crown's connection with saints and churches, which created a cultural cohesion (as we have seen earlier) while also creating a stable administrative base for his small kingdom. Over the next 300 years, the French kings struggled with their nobles, not the least of whom was the king of England. In bids to increase their own territory and power, barons and dukes alternately backed the French or the English kings. However, despite the consistent struggles against their powerful nobles, the French kings extended royal authority from a small power base in northern France to ever-larger areas, mostly because of their decisions on kingly succession. And, by the end of this period, the French kings had control over nearly all the territory that is modern-day France, and their employment of administrative officials allowed them to govern it all closely.

Sicily

The descendants of the Scandinavian settlers in the north of France (Normandy) did more than conquer England in the eleventh century; a family of Norman lords, the de Hautevilles, also took over Sicily and southern Italy, creating a new Latinate kingdom in the Mediterranean. Known as the Norman conquest of Sicily (1061–1091), this effort gave Latin Christians power over an island that had been under Muslim rule for more than two centuries, with a mixed population of Arab and Amazigh (Berber) Muslims, Jews, and Greek Christians. Norman warlords also consolidated control of southern Italy, which had a long history of decentralized rule by independent city-states and a mixed population of Latins (western Europeans), Greeks (including Byzantines), Lombards, and Jews. By taking these lands, the Normans gained control over rich trade routes that reached across the Mediterranean, bringing in foodstuffs, spices, gold, and other valuable products from the Islamicate world.

In 1130, one of Sicily's Norman rulers, Roger II (d. 1154), declared his possession a kingdom (his father Roger I had conquered the island and ruled as Count Roger). By attracting officials from Byzantine strongholds and the Fatimid Caliphate in Egypt and adapting their administrative techniques, the Norman Kingdom of Sicily was a culturally complex and economically advanced state ruled from its capital at Palermo. The Normans sponsored art and architecture inspired by both Byzantine and Islamicate cultures – most famously at the private chapel in the Norman palace (Cappella Palatina) and the Cathedral of Monreale. They also capitalized on their island's centrality in the Mediterranean to attempt conquests in many directions: east into Byzantine territory and south to North Africa, portions of which they controlled for a few years in the mid-twelfth century as the Norman Kingdom of Africa.

Marriage and succession were matters of deep importance for Roger II. While sponsoring art and administrative forms borrowed from his Greek and Muslim peers, he sought wives from Latinate Europe. His first wife, Elvira of Castile, came from a region of Spain where, like Roger himself, a Latin Christian king ruled over a culturally and religiously mixed population. Elvira gave birth to six children, of whom four sons lived to adulthood. Roger II appointed his eldest son Roger III (1118–1148) as Duke of Apulia (in Italy) in 1134, only a few years after he proclaimed the Kingdom of Sicily. That ducal position over a region on the Italian mainland was a precursor to the royal throne. Unlike the Capetians in France, however, the Sicilian Normans did not co-crown the intended heir to the throne.

Roger's plans for a smooth succession of his realm were thwarted when his eldest three sons died in 1138, 1144, and 1148. Despite having one remaining son, these losses led Roger to fear for the future of his kingdom. Even though he had long remained unmarried after Elvira's death in 1135, the demise of his intended heir led him to seek another wife, this time from France in 1150. Sibylla of Burgundy (d. 1150) did not outlive the birth of her child, who also died, leading Roger II to try for more heirs with yet a third wife. He married Beatrice of Rethel (also French nobility) in 1151, and she gave birth to Constance in 1154; Roger died the same year. At his death, Roger II had two living children: his youngest son, William, who had not been raised with the expectation of becoming king and apparently did not learn it on the job (he was known as William the Bad); and his daughter Constance, who married Henry VI, King of Germany and Holy Roman Emperor. At William's death, his only surviving son took control, becoming William II, who died without any

Fig 7.4
Mantle of Roger II of Sicily, dated by inscription in Arabic to 1133–1134. This cloak was produced in a royal workshop in Palermo, Sicily, for King Roger II. Often called his "coronation robe," it was actually finished four years after that event. It is made of red silk, gold thread, gemstones, enamel medallions, and thousands of tiny pearls. The gold embroidery along the edges is written in Arabic in the style of Islamic *tiraz* (textiles with inscribed bands along the arms, cuffs, or edges that were produced exclusively by workshops under caliphal control). It is the highest-quality silk fabric produced in Byzantium and is dyed with kermes, an insect that produces the durable and vivid red color. It is likely the pearls were harvested from the Persian Gulf and may have been purchased in Constantinople along with the gold thread. Produced in Latin Christian Sicily, in the style of royal Islamic textile workshops, using materials from Greek Byzantium, Roger II's mantle demonstrates his extensive connections across the medieval Mediterranean world.
B. O'Kane / Alamy Stock Photo

heirs, and the title reverted to Constance's line and through her to the Holy Roman Empire. Thus, the Kingdom of Sicily was joined to German imperial lands, showing just how correct Roger II had been to worry about succession as a matter of prime importance for the future security and independence of his kingdom.

DYNASTIC MARRIAGES

The choice of a mate is a key decision in anyone's life, but particularly so for rulers wishing to cement their power and ensure the future of their realms. Marriage could be a way to forge connections with important families or even rival powers. Those links could also help introduce desired commodities and ideas to new places. The choice of a wife might also directly impact governance, as sometimes the mother of a minor might rule in the child's place as regent. And, of course, the choice of wife was directly related to the desire for offspring – infertility, pregnancy loss, and the death of young children were disappointments felt both personally and politically.

One example of a strategic dynastic marriage occurred in the Ottonian Empire (919–1024), a revival by the Dukes of Saxony of Charlemagne's claim to Roman imperial power. The title "emperor of the Romans" had long been held by the Byzantine emperors in Constantinople, who considered the western claimants to be illegitimate rivals. The Byzantine imperial family was also fiercely protective of their daughters, refusing to marry imperial women to anyone they considered a "barbarian." But, despite these odds, the first Ottonian emperor, Otto I (912–973) was able to secure a Byzantine wife for his son (Otto II, r. 973–983). Theophanu (955–991) was not a direct daughter of the emperor, but probably his niece (princes and princesses born to a reigning Byzantine emperor were referred to as "born in the purple," after the exclusive imperial color), and that was enough to satisfy Otto. She married Otto II in 972 and was crowned Holy Roman Empress at the same time.

When Theophanu came to Germany, she brought with her Greek clerics and intellectuals, as well as clothing, jewelry, books, and other objects from the splendid court at Constantinople. She also transferred considerable prestige to the Ottonian court, although she was criticized by some contemporaries for her luxurious, foreign clothing. Her only son, Otto III (980–1002), was thus raised with knowledge of Greek language and culture – quite rare in the Latin West at the time. When her husband died in 983, Theophanu took over as regent for Otto III, who was only three years old. She struggled against other members of the family who wanted to control the child king, but was able to successfully reign on his behalf until her own death in 991. Otto III attained his majority a few years later and he, too, was betrothed to a Byzantine princess (Zoe, who was "born in the purple"), but as she was traveling from Constantinople for the marriage, Otto III suddenly died (in 1002, aged 21). This kicked off a succession crisis that led to years of warfare before his cousin Henry assumed the imperial throne. When Henry (as Emperor Henry II, 1014–1024) also died without heir, the Ottonian Empire came to an end.

Abbasid Disintegration

The Islamicate world, while nominally centralized under caliphal rule, also experienced political fracturing during this period. Regional governors broke away from the caliph's direct control, and new powerful groups entered the scene. The Umayyad dynasty was accused by its critics of discrimination against non-Arab Muslim converts and of moral and administrative laxity. They faced succession crises, internal civil wars, and Shia-Sunni conflicts until the Abbasid revolt that overthrew them in 750. The Abbasid Caliphate (750–945/1258) ruled from the city of Baghdad, but they found that ruling an extensive empire from a base in Iraq was difficult, and many of the regional governors (emirs) across the wide Islamicate world governed independently.

In the early 900s, the Abbasids also lost control of North Africa and Egypt to a rival sect of Muslims who traced their roots to Muhammad's son-in-law Ali, who had married his daughter Fatima. The Shi'ites had supported Ali's right to succeed Muhammad's position at the head of the Islamic community because he and his sons, Hassan and Hussein, were Muhammad's closest direct descendants. When this group lost the conflict to the Umayyad (Sunni) dynasty, they became an underground religio-political sect in North Africa. But, in the early tenth century, one of the leaders of the Shi'ite community (using the title Imam) established a rival caliphate – one that was Shi'ite – and ruled from North Africa from 909 until 969, when they moved their capital to Cairo. This Shi'ite caliphate – known as the Fatimid Caliphate, after the Prophet's daughter – ruled Egypt, the holy cities of Mecca and Medina, and (for a while) Jerusalem, until the caliphate was dissolved by Saladin in 1171.

Also, at the time of the Abbasid revolution, a man claiming to be the sole surviving member of the overthrown Umayyad family fled to Muslim-controlled Spain. Named Abd al-Rahman I, he claimed power as emir and ruled (independent of the Abbasid caliphs) from the grand city of Cordoba. One of his descendants, Abd al-Rahman III, decided to proclaim his state a caliphate instead of simply an emirate. So, in 929, Cordoba became another rival capital to Baghdad – ruling the Sunni Umayyad Caliphate of Cordoba (until it broke up into smaller kingdoms in 1031). Although the Abbasid caliphs had had no hand in governance of al-Andalus for several centuries at that point, by the tenth century they were just one of three rival caliphates – two Sunni and one Shi'ite.

Even in places that remained under Abbasid command, their ability to rule directly was threatened by rival powers and break-away governors. In 945, for example, a Shi'ite tribe attacked the city of Baghdad and ruled as the Buyids; although the Abbasids continued to hold some power in and around the region, decentralization of their large territory became the norm. By the tenth century, the Turks moved eastward out of the Eurasian steppes and into the Middle East. The Seljuk Turks, seminomadic people from the steppes, converted to Islam in the tenth century and moved west and south, buoyed by the weakness of the Abbasid Caliphate and the Byzantine emperors.

The Seljuk Turks paid nominal allegiance to the Abbasid caliphs – but, in truth, they were independent powers over much of Syria, Asia Minor, Iraq, and Iran. Ruling as sultans, the Seljuk dynasty threatened Byzantine power in Asia Minor and united many of the previously independent emirates in the Abbasid Caliphate. The Abbasids continued to rule as religious figureheads of the Sunni world, but they were increasingly marginalized as political or administrative rulers – especially after the crusades saw the rise of newly powerful military leaders. The Abbasids were routed – the city of Baghdad destroyed, and the final caliph killed – by the Mongols in 1258, which ended the golden age of Baghdad and even nominal centralization of the Islamicate world under a caliph (no one would claim that title until the Ottoman sultan Selim I in 1517).

This decentralization and the emergence of new players in the region destabilized the long-held peace in the Levant, those territories on the eastern Mediterranean, including the city of Jerusalem, held sacred by the three major Abrahamic faiths. Since 636, Jerusalem was part of the Islamicate, ruled by Muslim caliphs but (mostly) open to members of all faiths for travel and religious pilgrimage. By 1055, this city was at a crossroads, passing back and forth between the control of two major Islamic dynasties (the Fatimid Caliphate and Seljuk Turks) and still connected to its Byzantine neighbor to the north. In 1071, the Byzantine army met with the Seljuks at the Battle of Manzikert, and the once-mighty Byzantine forces were dealt a significant blow: the emperor was killed and their forces routed. At this point, the Turks controlled all the access routes to Jerusalem; they did not prohibit pilgrims but charged heavy tolls and did not police the roadways of bandits.

The Crusades

A new dynasty in Byzantium changed the status quo in the twelfth century. Alexius Comnenus (r. 1081–1118) began a new campaign against his neighbors to the south. Eager to solidify his territory, and to perhaps regain some lands lost to the Muslim armies in the previous 50 years, Alexius needed to shore up his army. A lack of training and of men had depleted the Byzantine forces, and Alexius needed money to gain new warriors and arms. In 1093, he wrote to the pope in Rome, Urban II, and requested mercenaries for a new army.

Urban II responded and, seizing the opportunity, called on the warriors of Europe to travel to Constantinople, then on to Jerusalem, to liberate the holy lands from the infidel. In November 1095, Pope Urban II spoke to a crowd of bishops and laypeople in southern France, at the cathedral in Clermont. He called a council to discuss current reform movements in the Roman Church, but the letter from Alexius Comnenus prompted him to add a call for men-at-arms to aid Byzantine armies. Although many literate men attended that council and heard Urban's public speech, few could have predicted the importance of the moment, and few direct records of his words exist. After the conquest of Jerusalem in 1099, that importance became more obvious, and several accounts of Urban's text appeared. Five different records of Urban's speech exist and all five are different, some radically so. Only two writers, Fulcher of Chartres and Robert the Monk, are thought to have witnessed the speech, and all five versions were written down after the crusader victory at Jerusalem in 1099. The shortest account, from the anonymous *Deeds of the Franks* (the *Gesta* version), was the earliest recorded version and became the template for the four others. It expounds on Urban's use of biblical imagery and the ideas of heaven as a reward for the faithful warrior. Robert's account was written more than ten years after the event and, while it carefully copies earlier versions, it contains the most fiery and dramatic rhetoric; he records the pope as detailing supposed atrocities carried out by Muslims against the Christian inhabitants and visitors of Jerusalem. Fulcher's account, sometimes considered the most accurate, is also colored by the fact that he was part of the crusading armies, which shaped his later interpretation of the goals and messages of Urban's speech. Despite the differing descriptions of the speech, the result was that thousands made plans to equip themselves and conquer Jerusalem. The crusades had begun.

These wars were justified in Europe as "Holy Wars," based on theological ideas about warfare and Christianity. The early military victories of Christian emperors like Constantine and Charlemagne required a shift in the previously pacifist Christian attitude against the conduct of war to a more supportive, but qualified, acceptance of the legitimacy of war. War could be considered legitimate if it was defensive, obligatory, and, during the era of the crusades, not only *not* sinful but spiritually beneficial. Participation in these wars ensured salvation and entry to paradise. Just as the crusades drew their primary inspiration from a sense of religious duty or obligation known as "Holy War," the Muslim counter-crusade invoked the concept of "jihad," which in simple terms means "struggle." Muslim theologians and believers amplified the term *jihad*, which meant the struggle for an individual person to be more virtuous, into the larger struggle of a "just" war. Despite the shared divine commandment not to kill, Christian and Islamic theologians developed ethical and moral justifications for wars that were carried out with right intention toward a just goal.

For both faiths, under certain circumstances, warfare could be legitimate, obligatory, and spiritually beneficial. From its inception, Islam and its prophet Muhammad waged defensive wars to protect the new faith; leaders relied upon warfare for the defense and survival of their communities. As a result, during the crusades, Muslim leaders in the Middle East could look back to historic examples for defensive warfare. By the time of the launching of the crusades and the subsequent transformation of "Just War" to "Holy War," Christian and Muslim attitudes to war were very similar.

From 1094 to 1291, thousands of Europeans poured into the ports and cities in the Levant and Egypt, seeking lands, treasures, and indulgences (forgiveness for sins). Facing a divided enemy (the Turks, the Abbasids, and the Byzantines continued infighting; even Abbasid lands in the Levant were divided between independent petty governors), the Europeans were able to enter Jerusalem in 1099 as conquerors. They slaughtered the inhabitants of the city. Some of the European conquerors became rulers, creating western European-style kingdoms in the Levant: the County of Edessa, the Principality of Antioch, the County of Tripoli, and the Kingdom of Jerusalem. The remaining crusades were attempts to hold territory (this proved impossible) or take new lands in Egypt and beyond (also impossible). Other than the First Crusade (1094–1099), the western Europeans rarely won, as they became divided while fighting an increasingly centralized enemy.

As the Turkish rulers moved to consolidate their rule in the Middle East, there were fewer opportunities for European crusaders to take territory. During the Second Crusade, King Louis VII of France, and his wife, Eleanor of Aquitaine, stopped in Jerusalem before the French army headed out to Egypt, determined to retake the County of Edessa, which had fallen from European hands in 1144. The entire endeavor was a fiasco: the armies failed to win any major battles, in either Edessa or Egypt, and Louis and Eleanor fought incessantly. As the Seljuks eradicated internal rivalries, they focused more intently on capturing lost territory and this culminated in the Muslim capture of Jerusalem in 1187. This brought about the Third Crusade, well known for the rival leaders Richard the Lionhearted, King of England, and Saladin, the Kurdish commander of the Muslim forces that liberated Jerusalem. In the next hundred years, six more formal crusades would leave from Europe. King Louis IX of France fought in the Sixth and Seventh Crusades (in Egypt), dying in the Seventh but earning sainthood. The Children's Crusade of 1202 ended, as did the Peasants' Crusade, with the majority of the European "forces" sold into slavery. The final chapter in the crusades was the fall of the city of Acre in 1291, the last European stronghold. Ousted from the city to the islands off the coast, the crusaders never again held territory in the Levant.

WHY DO WE CALL THEM "CRUSADES?"

The word "crusade" was not used during the medieval period. It is a modern term applied to the wars for control of the Levant in the Middle East from the eleventh to the thirteenth centuries. First used in the sixteenth century in English, it comes from the Latin and French terms for "marked with a cross." The *Gesta Normannorum Ducum* tells us that men who heard Urban's speech "caused crosses to be sewed on their right shoulders, saying that they followed with one accord the footsteps of Christ, by which they had been redeemed from the hand of hell." In Latin *"cruces signatus"* denotes someone signed with the cross. In Europe, those we call crusaders may have been called by some vulgarization of the Latin word for pilgrim, *"peregrinus,"* or *"miles Christi,"* warrior for Christ. While a crusader would not be considered a cleric, he was placed under the peace (*pax*) of God and the authority of the Church. Using the word "crusade" today is an anachronism, and one that has a thousand years of problematic historical understandings by Christians, Jews, and Muslims.

The hundreds of thousands of Europeans who traveled to the Levant from 1095 to 1291 had differing goals. Medieval motivations and modern understandings of those incentives are often at odds. Some historians posit that the crusades were an expression of fanaticism and hatred; others argue the wars were "an act of love" inspired by piety and devotion. Despite the competing modern ideas, people involved in mass movements always have very individual, and occasionally contradictory, reasons for joining; they never completely lose their individual identity or autonomy. From existing crusader accounts, we know many went to reclaim the holy lands, with a sincere and pious belief in their righteous cause. Others believed the Day of Judgment was imminent, and pilgrimage to Jerusalem would atone for their sins. Some were ambitious for lands and lordships abroad, and still others had family-motivated choices (families with crusading ancestors tended to inspire later generations to go on crusade). Many had economic reasons – controlling trade routes could lead to immense wealth (the Fourth Crusade is a great example of this motivation). Some simply desired travel and adventure. We can say that the majority of men who went on crusade went as warriors, soldiers who killed and looted. They may have been inspired by faith, but love was rarely part of their action. Bernard of Clairvaux (d. 1153) gives us a good example when he tells us that the majority of those involved with the Second Crusade were "criminals and sinners, ravishers and the sacrilegious, murderers, perjurers, and adulterers."

The crusades are a bloody chapter in the history of the Middle East and of Muslim-Christian relations. Marked by ruthless mass murder of civilians and the destruction of armies of soldiers, they caused immense suffering for many, and death for others. They also, however, opened the knowledge and the education of the Islamicate areas to Europe in new ways. Arabic scholarship, new translations of ancient Greek texts, and Persian and Indian literature and scientific texts invigorated new universities in Europe. Trade intensified along the Mediterranean and northern African coasts, and further east into India and China. The Italian city-states grew in importance and wealth; money increased in circulation, and the European kings began to impose taxes more consistently.

Civil Administration: Taxation and Justice

West Africa

Taxes are levied by a government to fund public expenditures, like the common needs of infrastructure (roads and bridges) and security (legal administrations, law enforcement, and military). In fact, a "government" is defined as a body that raises revenue and uses it for the benefit of the larger polity. Tax collection and revenue distribution consistently aided in the consolidation of power and the stable rule of a kingdom or empire. Even when taxes were not levied in monetary form, they might be raised in labor – either military or agricultural.

In West Africa, the Kingdom of Ghana (ca. 300–1100) rose in importance, partially due to their sophisticated and detailed tax systems. The government taxed all items, both imported and exported. By 800, increased iron-ore production brought more wealth and trade to the village communities of West Africa. These older villages were transformed by a growth of urban infrastructure: entrenchment and walls surrounded larger villages, which had central squares, possibly for trade and civic duties. The surge of quarrying in the area led to a rise in gold mining. Most of our written documentation on Ghana in this period is from Muslim travelers, who wrote of a "land of gold." By the mid-tenth century, Ghana's kings controlled much of the neighboring territory, gaining tributes and taxes from the tribes and groups that settled near the large trade centers. With the use of the camel (introduced to the area in the 300s), the Ghanaians controlled the trans-Saharan trade in West and North Africa. Gold, salt, copper, iron weapons, and more moved between West Africa and trade centers further north and east.

The Islamic historian al-Bakri wrote on the kingdom of Ghana in his work *Routes and Realms*. Although he himself never traveled to Ghana, he based his work on interviews with people who had been to the kingdom. He wrote that Ghanaians excelled in education, and that jurists, religious leaders, and scholars held important positions within the government. Each major village had a center for justice, and taxes paid for the salaries of the civil servants. The kings of Ghana excelled at revenue and taxation: every import and every export required a payment to the central government offices. Imports were taxed more heavily than exports, and salt, in particular, garnered heavy taxation. Al-Bakri also noted the interesting succession pattern of the kings: they were succeeded by their sister's sons, as kings were always sure their nephews were directly related to them, and never sure if their own sons were. Ghana became an important and very wealthy kingdom, based in part on the steady leadership and administration of its government, and in part on its ability to control the mining and export of gold and other trade goods. As the Empire of Mali (1235–1670) began its meteoric rise in the thirteenth century, it overtook Ghana and subsumed this older kingdom into its empire.

Iceland

In all cultures, justice was and is very personal, often resulting in revenge killings and feuds. Medieval societies realized that social rifts could bring down an entire community: infighting jeopardized group survival. One interesting example of the link between justice, law, and societal order is the Icelandic Althing. In order to control for inevitable clashes between families, clans, and new settlers, Icelanders developed legal customs that discouraged retaliatory revenge and feuds, including an involved schedule of fines to be paid for the murder or maiming of an individual. In an effort to resolve such crimes, the family of the attacker paid "man-money" to the family of the victims. (In Old English, *wergild* is literally man-money. Gild is gold or money and wer is man.

We see the same connection in the modern word werewolf.) Negotiations happened every summer, when chieftains and their advisors gathered at Thingvellir, a large plain on the western side of Iceland. Each group set up its living and meeting shelters, ate fish from the Oxara river and Thingvallavatn, the largest lake on the island, and discussed and made decisions on all "things" (the English word "thing" comes from this source): murders, theft, sale or inheritance of land, exchange of livestock and crops, marriage contracts and dowry disputes, fishing and grazing rights, and new laws. Presiding over the Althing was a law speaker, who recited the laws by heart and reminded the assembled crowd of its duty to adhere to those laws. He spoke from the Logberg, the law rock, to the Logretta, the gathered group of lawmakers.

The Althing was most vital during the Commonwealth Period, which dates from the first Althing in 920 until 1292, when Norway claimed sovereignty over the island. Notable events of these summer sessions are recorded in Icelandic literature, most notably the Althing of 1000, when Icelanders voted to become Christians. By 1000, Iceland's North Sea trading partners – the Scottish, Irish, Swedish, Norwegians, Dutch, and English – had replaced their pre-Christian religious beliefs with Christianity. Although many Icelanders had converted as well, traditional practices were common, and there was no formal declaration

Fig 7.5
Thingvellir "Assembly Plain," Iceland. The outdoor law court at Thingvellir was surrounded by a thriving temporary marketplace for goods and services. Merchants set up booths, musicians and actors entertained from makeshift stages, and foreign traders and dignitaries came to make deals and alliances. Among the goods exchanged were enslaved people passed along the trade routes.
Kuntalee Rangnoi / iStock

against them. In danger of becoming economically and socially ostracized from these vital trading partners, Icelanders took up the matter of Christianity at the Althing of 1000. Those who favored converting to Christianity argued with those who did not want to convert. Each side had its own law speaker and attempted to take control from the other; however, as the story goes, it was decided that the trusted, non-Christian law speaker should rule on the question. After deliberation, Thorgeir Ljosvetningagodi Thorkelsson pronounced that all Icelanders would publicly convert to Christianity, but would not be prevented from practicing traditional religious rituals in private.

China

Tang and Song Chinese rulers followed the lines of long-established legal codes and taxation systems, dating from the Han dynasty (206 BCE–220 CE). During the Tang, the emperors took control of all land, parceling and leasing it to their nobles, then peasants worked the land for them. The Song continued and refined this practice. The nobles collected taxes from their peasants and then transferred these taxes to their rulers. This was a great way for the nobility to make money, as they could skim off the top prior to paying their dues to the government. Nobles charged their dependents in-kind taxes (goods), corvée (forced labor), and land rentals. The kings and emperors charged their nobles land rentals, a toll tax on dependents, and smaller compensatory fees (like fees to free a noble from military duty).

In China from 900 to 1300 there were constant tensions between the small, centralized Tang dynasty and the border states that surround it. Many central Asian peoples lived on the edges of the Tang dynasty; they traded goods and people (mostly soldiers) into the Chinese dynasty and in return received finished products and protection. With the Tang dynasty's dissolution in 907, China entered a period known as the Five Dynasties, where different groups vied for control of the centralized Chinese state. The Song dynasty, centered in the south, took control in 960, and they restored stability to some portions of China with a period of economic and social change and growth.

The Song dynasty (960–1276) continued Tang taxation systems. A strong fiscal capacity aided in repelling invasions; taxes paid the salaries of military men, and those men were often used to conquer new territory, thereby bringing new areas for taxation under control. The Song dynasty, however, did not maintain all the Tang taxation structures. In an effort to garner public approval, the Song bureaucracy lightened the tax burden on the individual farmer and decreased the land tax. They instituted a smaller poll tax on every subject, regardless of gender, income, or ability, but this did not equal the lost tax revenue. In response, the Song increased many state monopolies on trade goods and instituted heavy import taxes on goods brought into China (see Chapter 10). The government held monopolies on salt, tea, alcohol, paper money, and sulfur, and the taxes became so high that many Chinese stopped purchasing these items altogether. Inflation soared, and, despite their efforts, the government could not control it, and the overall decrease in income caused the Song empire to reduce its domestic military force and rely more heavily on mercenary armies. Civil servants within the empire began publicly denigrating their military brethren and the military lost its position within the civil bureaucracy.

The Song controlled a much smaller territory than the Tang dynasty did, and with a reduction in both number and status in their military forces, they did not expand either north or west into "barbarian" territory. They faced consistent pressures from the north and the west as different Central Asian steppe peoples encroached on the older Tang dynasty. The Song also had an intense commitment to being "Chinese" at the expense of any outside influence. The elite exhibited signs of xenophobia in their hostility to any foreign ideas or thought. They prevented innovations that came from other societies and emphasized their own distinctly "Chinese" character, which played out in the Neo-Confucian philosophical ideas that reinforced class and gender distinctions. These two ideas, the decrease in numbers and in the status of the military and the lack of innovation, caused a crisis within the system that facilitated the ease by which the Mongols overtook the empire in the 1270s.

Japan

Japan, too, struggled with taxation and the rising cost of governance during the Kamakura shogunate (1185–1333). Collecting taxes was left to local stewards (who could be male or female), who often took a hefty cut before passing along the remainder to the central government. This left a serious lack of money for the infrastructure in Japan; roads and waterways were controlled and maintained at the local level, as were policing and other important administrative duties. In 1232, the shogun published the Joei Code, which detailed the duties and responsibilities of the different levels of Japanese society. The code also established military structure and outlined inheritance practices for the upper levels of society. These 51 laws gave guidance on the issues of land and taxation, but the code was rarely explicitly followed. This continued the decentralization of the Japanese government and, without steady revenue, made it easier for internal fissures and external invasions.

In 1266, the Mongols invaded the island, after conquering China and portions of Korea. Kublai Khan had declared himself emperor of the east and was determined to take control of Japan. He sent representatives to the shogun's court, but, instead of capitulating, the Japanese stood their ground and sent the men back to China empty handed. Kublai gathered his forces and set sail for Japan in 1274, sending about 800 ships packed with soldiers to attack the island. Superior numbers and better weapons (including grenades – gunpowder packed inside thin pottery) allowed the Mongols to prevail in the first battles.

Local peasants prayed for relief, and it came in the guise of a storm, which swept many of the Mongol ships out to sea and caused the remainder to flee back to China. Kublai's second invasion, in 1281, had about 4,000 ships and 100,000 men. The Japanese had learned their lessons from the first invasion and set about defending their beaches. After several weeks of fighting, many Mongols had yet to land ashore and take territory. Stuck aboard, they were unprepared for another deadly storm, when typhoon-level winds sank the majority of the Mongol navy. Remaining warriors washed ashore were executed and the second Mongol invasion of Japan ended. These divine winds (*kamakazi*) defeated the Mongols, with some help from the poorly built Mongol boats and the Japanese defenders. Although the Mongols never attacked again, the Japanese government continued to pay for soldiers to defend the coasts, raising taxes and ignoring the peasantry. Despite their wins against the Mongols, these revenue and military problems defeated the Kamakura, who were to remain in power only another 50 years.

The Mongol Invasions

Earlier in the thirteenth century, the Mongols rose to prominence in the Eurasian steppes. The scattered tribes, plagued by competitive clashes, coalesced under new leaders in the early 1200s. Temujin (ca. 1162–1227), the orphaned son of a Mongol chieftain, rose to prominence in Mongolia. Through military might, decisive leadership, and political machinations, Temujin succeeded in uniting most of the Mongol tribes. He gained the title Chingghis (sometimes spelled *Genghis*), or "Great Khan" for his actions. As khan, Chingghis forbade looting of conquered areas, shared war spoils with his entire army, and welcomed the subjugated peoples into his empire (after the heat of war), often asking his mother to adopt children orphaned by his battles. From 1207 to his death in 1227, Chingghis traveled the Eurasian steppes and created the largest land empire in history.

Beginning his conquests in the eastern portion of Eurasia, Chingghis conquered the tribes living on the edges of the Chinese empire: the Western Xia, the Jin, and the Western Liao were his first major victories. His army moved westward along the trade routes, attacking the kingdoms along the Caspian and Aral seas. The attacks at Samarkand and Urgench were remarkably brutal, with Persian sources claiming that Mongolian soldiers slaughtered the populaces almost wholesale. He entered eastern Europe and the Middle East, but illness and politics forced him to withdraw before the defeat of Russian and other European territories. At his death in 1227, Chingghis controlled an empire that stretched from the western edges of China to the eastern edges of Europe.

RUSSIA AND THE RISE OF MUSCOVY

Formed in the 800s, the Russian Kievan state (primarily Scandinavian merchant traders governing Slavic populations) was tied to the Byzantine Empire in the south, connected to the emperors there through trade and familial relationships (see Chapter 1). The Rus did maintain relationships with other western European countries, mostly through trade. All this would change when Chingghis Khan and the Mongols moved through the Central Asian steppes. The conquest of the east Slavic states by the Mongols brought two centuries of Mongolian rule to the southern portion of Russia and effectively halted the state of Kievan Rus. At this point, the Grand Duchy of Moscow grew in importance and a Muscovite empire formed in the north. The northern areas of Russia had little Mongol interference, but they were also further from western Europe compared to the Kievan state. The Duchy of Moscow kept religious and political ties to the Byzantine empire and, when western European crusaders attacked the Christian city of Zara, Hungary, in 1204 and Constantinople thereafter, Moscow became a center of anti-Roman (as they called western Europeans) sentiment. The rulers in Moscow felt the Roman pope and western Europeans to have abdicated their duties both as Christians and as soldiers, which further separated Moscow from western European powers.

Chingghis valued literacy and education, bringing historians and artists into his sphere to glorify his reign and his family. Although a military man, Chingghis used Chinese ideas of civil service to help him control his widely flung empire. Controlling an empire that stretched from China to Turkey created a strong need for communication and for bureaucrats. He kept many Mongolian ideas, however, at the forefront of his rule. Race, ethnicity, and birth meant far less than action, and his civil servants gained their positions through merit alone. As polytheists, the Mongols did not require adherence to a particular religious ideal and they generally supported the religious practices of their subjects. (Mongols ruling in China would later adopt Buddhism, while those ruling in Persia adopted Islam. Others stayed polytheistic.)

Women held higher status in Mongolian society than in either Chinese, Persian, or European cultures, and Chingghis placed great stock in the advice of his mother, wives, and daughters. The *Secret History of the Mongols* gives us much of this information on the Mongols. It was written sometime after 1227 and was the first major work written in the Mongolian language. The original copy, however, has not survived, and our remaining work is a fourteenth-century Chinese copy. Containing the history and rise of Chingghis, the work is invaluable for understanding Mongolian culture and life in the thirteenth century. Combined with Persian and Chinese sources about the Mongols, this work allows us to glimpse how the nomadic steppe tribes united under their charismatic leader and expanded across a continent.

BATTLE OF AYN JALUT (OR AIN JALUT), 1260

Many battles can be said to have been pivotal in world history, one of which is the 1260 battle between Mongols and Egyptian forces under the Mamluk sultans. Mongol forces had rapidly conquered the steppe regions and central China over the preceding decades and pushed westward into both Persia and Russia. They appeared, from some vantage points, to be likely to sweep across the central Islamic lands and perhaps into central Europe. But in the mid-thirteenth century, their westward push was halted both north and south of the Black Sea. In central Europe, they withdrew their forces in 1242 despite having defeated Hungarian troops in 1241, possibly due to a succession crisis within the Mongol confederation and possibly for other, unknown, reasons.

The end of the Mongol advance in the Syria-Palestine area in 1260, however, was the direct result of their surprising defeat at the battle of Ayn Jalut by Egyptian forces. Just two years earlier, the Mongols had overrun the Abbasid capital of Baghdad, killed the caliph, and sacked the city, which had been a center of culture, luxury, and the arts. The Mongols destroyed libraries filled with books, elegant palaces, luxurious gardens, and grand mosques, and killed thousands of residents, ending a so-called golden age of culture, learning, economy, and political power in the city. The Mongol khan Hulegu then sent the Egyptian sultan a letter demanding that Egypt pre-emptively surrender to the Mongols.

The sultan of Egypt, named Qutuz, ruling a dynasty known as the Mamluk sultanate, refused to surrender and marched his troops from Cairo into Palestine to meet the Mongols. There, they met the Mongol Kitbugha and his large cavalry. Through several rounds of attack and counter-attack, Qutuz was able to lead his troops to victory. Kitbugha died in battle, causing Mongol warriors to flee and allowing the Mamluks to occupy most of Syria and surround the small coastal outposts of the crusader Kingdom of Jerusalem (centered on Acre since the loss of Jerusalem in 1187) and the crusader-held County of Tripoli to the north.

Despite his victory over the Mongols, Sultan Qutuz was assassinated by his rival, Baybars, who took over as sultan (1260–1277). Baybars turned his attention to the task of destroying the last remnants of crusader territory in the area, although it would be a successor who reclaimed the final city, Acre, in 1291.

Mongolian culture, like others in Eurasia, followed the principle of partible inheritance. As we have seen, the lack of a clear order of succession is a death-knell for any kingdom or empire, and the Mongolian empire was no different. Chingghis chose his third son, Ogedei, to succeed him as Great Khan, based on the tensions between his eldest son, Jochi, and his other children. Luckily, Ogedei proved a skillful leader, continuing his father's expansion and giving his elder brother, Chagatai, a strong stake in the invasions in Central Asia. As khan, Ogedei invaded as far eastward as Korea and into Song China. The eastern European areas of Georgia and Armenia fell to his armies in the 1230s, and, by the 1240s, most of southern Russia was part of the Mongol

Fig 7.6

The Mongols invaded Baghdad in 1258 and dumped the contents of the city's large libraries into the Tigris river. In this image from a Persian manuscript ca. 1430–1434, the river runs black with ink.

DeAgostini / Getty Images

Empire. In the 1240s, Mongolian armies pressed into the Indus river valley, meeting with the Delhi sultanate in battle several times. After Ogedei's death in 1241, the Mongol empire split among his family. Conflict over the matter of succession had begun in 1259 and accelerated over the next few years, until the huge expanse of territory conquered by the Mongols broke up into four distinct states (called khanates): The Golden Horde (ca. 1242–1502) ruled in eastern Europe and Russia; the Ilkhanate (ca. 1256–1335) in the region of modern Iraq, Iran, and Turkey; the Chagatai Khanate (ca. 1225–1680s) in central Asia; and the Yuan dynasty (ca. 1271–1368) established by Kublai Khan in China. By 1300, the Mongols had settled into ruling several large areas of Eurasia, and Eurasians, too, entered a more settled period.

B: TALES OF WARRIORS AND COURT LIFE

Evidence: *Mahabharata*, "Draupadi's Swayamvara"

Andreas Capellanus, *The Art of Courtly Love*

The Finn Cycle

The Romance of Gillion de Trazegnies

Tale of the Heike

The Bayeux Tapestry

Introduction

In this section, we examine the stories popular among the wealthy and elite in court settings. Tales of heroes in warfare-dominated stories were told in great halls and courtyards, but, alongside them, and often embedded in them, were tales of love and loss. In fact, despite the ravages of starvation, disease, and the degradations of war, all classes enjoyed these stories in which the fear of imminent death intensified the passion of love affairs, and high-stakes competition for lovers caused battles between friends, among relatives, and sometimes outright war against another clan. In these tales, love and war are of the same import. If the warrior's quest or the clan's war is one of earnest righteousness, the courtship answers that tone. If the quest is one of bewitched treachery, the love affair is enchanted and destructive. A valiant show of camaraderie on the battlefield may bring romance and joy into the heart of a castle, just as a fraught love triangle may result in many dead soldiers on a hillside. The discourse of courage, loyalty, reputation, and honor operates in both spaces.

As a genre, medieval romance was a story written in the vernacular, that is, the language commonly spoken by a people in a region. Vernacular French around the twelfth century was known as "romanz," and since these popular narratives usually included courtly love situations, the English word "romance" came to mean the feelings of excitement and mystery associated with love. In keeping with the older ideas inherent in the earlier European heroic epics, the romance genre also has the element of chivalry, a code requiring a hero to be true and loyal to his king and warrior brothers. A third element is the presence of the "greenworld," a landscape or seascape through which the hero travels and faces challenges. In the greenworld, he learns more about himself, improves his character, and resolves dilemmas for himself and his people. Although this definition of romance came from a European sphere, the generic concepts of love, marriage, betrayal, and warrior prowess are present in many cultures. In general, these tales also give us an insight into courtly and bureaucratic culture, even when they describe the tale as happening "a long time ago." Tales of love in India, Europe, and Japan all focus on the military and sexual exploits of their protagonist, while also relating in detail the political forces at play in their own times.

The *Mahabharata*

A reciprocal effect of war and love is represented in a sacred text of India, the *Mahabharata*. An elaborate epic of ancient India, this narrative has been a foundational text of the Indian subcontinent up to the present day. The story centers on a mighty clan war between two branches of one family, and it demonstrates the human tendency to define war by love, and vice versa. In the "Swayamvara Parva" or the Book of Choosing a Husband, a nobleman arranges a contest through which his daughter, Draupadi, is allowed to choose her own partner. She has "eyes like lotus-petals and of faultless features endowed with youth and intelligence," and her body "emits a fragrance like that of blue lotus for two full miles around." She also has a powerful father and brother, who seek to strengthen their alliance with the five famous Pandava brothers, the heroes of the greater epic. In this scenario, the brothers take on the robes of the Brahmana or religious leaders, thus hiding their warrior identity from the other competitors vying for the young girl's hand. The setting for this "battle" is a level field surrounded by grand houses. It is a domesticated, manicured arena for civilized combat, and the challenge is artfully constructed. Wielding an impossibly heavy and stiff bow, a suitor must shoot over his head and through a revolving wheel. His target is the eye of a wooden fish suspended above, but

Fig 7.7
Relief carving of Arjuna competing for the hand of Draupadi in the archery contest.
Hoysaleswara Temple, India, twelfth century.
AnandMorabad / iStock

in a challenging twist, the archer must aim by looking at the reflection of the fish in a pool of liquid at his feet.

Draupadi has organized the challenge so only a magnificent Pandava brother can win it. Arjuna, in his guise as a Hindu priest, surprises the rest of the suitors with his skill. They are jealous and humiliated, but also ineffective and impotent. Arjuna wins his bride (or she wins her husband), but that is not all. Emphasizing the sacred bond of brotherhood, Draupadi becomes wife to all five Pandavas. Delighted by his victory, Arjuna returns to his mother's hut and announces that he has brought a great gift. Thinking he has brought food, his mother, as parent to five boys, repeats a timeworn phrase: "Share it among yourselves." The ethics of the story require that a son obey the wishes of his mother; therefore, Arjuna shares his beautiful wife with his brothers, and, for a time, competition and desire are in balance. Five warriors devoted to each other over all else share equally and peacefully in love.

The Art of Courtly Love

In the twelfth century, Andreas the Capellanus, a member of the court of Marie de France, wrote *The Art of Courtly Love*, an instruction manual on the intricate social rules of seduction as developed in the love lyrics of French troubadours, traveling performers who came from Occitania, a region in southern France. Like Draupadi, Andreas presents love as a competition; however, it is an emotional battlefield where the lover is in the service of the King of Love, a soldier in pursuit of his chosen lady. Unlike the happy ending in the Indian tale, for Andreas love is an injury – an immediate, powerful blow to the heart. It is a stealth operation, conducted behind the backs of foes through strategic use of illicit temptation and covert tactics. It also provides for an inverse gender power structure. The knight is a slave to his lady, who is his mistress. She owns his heart and soul, and he labors to be worthy of her attention. Pale and melancholy, the true lover is jealous and tormented, besieged by emotion in the camp of Love. Lovers are victims, and the audience is meant to sympathize with them.

In *The Art of Courtly Love*, Andreas includes a story about King Arthur, a character of Welsh origin who became a popular centerpiece for European medieval romance; however, it is Andreas's contemporary, Chrétien de Troyes, who, in a story called "Lancelot of the Cart," introduced Lancelot into the Arthurian stories, and created tension around the code of chivalry. Since a true warrior only achieves glory and integrity through loyalty to his leader and his comrades, he never betrays his "brother," but sexual desire does not follow the same code. In the tales of King Arthur, Lancelot is Arthur's comrade and has a seat of honor at the Round Table. He is also infatuated with Queen Guinevere, and their affair is a model of courtly love in direct violation of the code of chivalry. The love triangle ends in the personal despair of all three characters. Arthur loses both his wife and his trusted ally; Lancelot forfeits his place in the honorable brotherhood and is forced to murder his friends on the way out; and Guinevere is confined to an abbey. Concentric rings of destruction extend out from the kingdom as the affair brings down the chivalric unity and mission of the Round Table.

The Finn Cycle

Many European romances focus on the danger of personal entanglements and politics. Chrétien de Troyes' works show the courtier the dangers inherent in placing the love of women and family above that of duty to lord and state. In the medieval Irish story, "The Pursuit of Diarmuid and Grainne," which exists within the Finn Cycle, we see how the struggle between private desire and political duty brings dire consequences. Finn MacCumhaill (MacCool), the elder chieftain of the Fianna, decides he wants to marry the maiden Grainne, the fairest maiden in the land. She is also the daughter of his rival, and marriage to her settles the disputes between their two clans. Finn's plan overlooks one detail: Grainne does not want him – he is too old, and she does not know him. At a prenuptial feast, she gives a sleeping potion to most of the guests and then sidles up to one of Finn's warriors, the "charmer" Diarmuid O'Duibhne. She puts a *geis* (magical obligation) upon him to take her away before Finn MacCumhaill and her father, the king, wake up. She threatens Diarmuid with destruction, disgrace, and unnatural punishment if he defies the *geis*. Her actions begin a political and military feud, where the entire region suffers intense disruption.

Grainne explains why she chose Diarmuid: one day while watching a sports match between two teams of Fianna, he was the best athlete and brought his team victory. Here the athletic match is a substitute for combat (much like that of Draupadi and her contest), and, in this story, the mock skirmish of intraclan athletic competition morphs into a real battle between Finn and his retainer Diarmuid. At one point in their feud, Finn even imports soldiers from other countries to fight against his own clan member. Finn's irrational behavior (inviting foreign warriors into one's homeland to fight against a kinsman) puts his clan in dire jeopardy. He places personal outrage over his communal responsibility, and, as he pursues Grainne and Diarmuid deeper into the mystical territory of the tale, their elusive behaviors cause more and more chaos. Stability and order cannot exist around passionate, competitive love.

This destructive rift in the clan structure is almost too horrible to consider, and so the narrative works itself into the realm of the supernatural. A guardian from the Tuatha De Danaan, the ancient Celtic gods, joins the fleeing lovers and protects them from venomous hounds and dangerous landscapes. In medieval romance, love does not rest in peace. In the end, Finn tricks Diarmuid by inviting him to a wild boar hunt and leaves him vulnerable to the beast, which kills him. Because of his treachery, Finn loses the faith of the Fianna, and Grainne perpetuates the feud, moving from the status of Diarmuid's beloved to that of his fierce and loyal avenger. She recruits women warriors to fight against

Fig 7.8
The Giant's Causeway, County Antrim, Ireland, is a geologic monument formed by a volcanic eruption. In Irish legend, Finn MacCumhaill (MacCool) built these steps to battle a rival Scottish giant. Finn's superhuman physical strength is matched by his furious jealousy of Diarmuid O'Duibhne and the maiden Grainne.
Deposit Photos

Finn and travels to the underworld to learn the secret arts of war. Grainne empowers a fierce martial force that comes from inside the family and the clan against the clan's ruler. This kind of conflict is the saddest of all, and Finn finally recognizes the destruction he has caused and learns a lesson in humility. He transforms into a good leader by setting out on a road to reconciliation, first and foremost courting Grainne in a proper and careful way "with sweet talk and tender cajolements until in the end he wore down her resistance." At last, she consents to be his wife, and their marriage resolves all conflict in the tribe.

The Romance of Gillion de Trazegnies

The French romance of Gillion de Trazegnies presents another fantasy of out-sized proportion where the conflicts are mighty, the love affairs incredible, and the geography vast. The chivalric exploits are wide-ranging, as the characters move from northern France to Egypt and beyond, by way of Venice, Dubrovnik, Corfu, Crete, Cyprus, Palestine, and Tripoli. The feats are superhuman, with the hero fighting for Christians and for Muslims. The courtly love seductions include Gillion's great loyalty to his aristocratic Christian wife, alongside his love affair with and eventual marriage to an Egyptian maiden, all set against the backdrop of high-adrenaline combat.

The lavishly ornamented manuscript of *The Romance of Gillion de Trazegnies* belonged to a courtier named Louis de Gruuthus, who was in the service of Philip the Good, Duke of Burgundy. Louis commissioned the manuscript on the event of Philip's call for a crusade to recover Constantinople from the Ottoman Turks, which fell in 1453. A year after the defeat, at an event called the Feast of the Pheasant, members of Philip's chivalric inner circle, the Order of the Golden Fleece, took an oath to join him in the crusade. It appears as if the legend of the fictional Gillion was referenced by many of this crowd, as Louis and his circle identified with the exploits of this heroic and romantic character. However, unlike Gillion, the patron of these lavish adventure stories had seen little real battle; his warrior reputation was made through participation in numerous organized tournaments. In fact, Louis de Gruuthus was more of a politician, acting as an advisor and diplomat for Philip in the Low Countries and England. He held positions of leadership requiring him to recruit or conscript men for Philip's army and to raise money for outfitting Philip's crusade.

Louis never went on crusade. It was planned for 1463 or 1464, but Philip the Good was under the control of a new French king, Louis XI, who did not grant leave to the duke to mount a campaign. Instead, Philip appointed Louis governor general of Holland, Zeeland, and Frisia, new territory important to Philip's realm. There is no record of Louis' travel outside Flanders and England. His job appears to have been raising money and armies for his lord as a sort of political campaign manager. The duke died in June 1467, and that was the end of this crusade program and of Louis' possible military career, but the high fantasy of Gillion that he commissioned was testament to his desire to be a romantic hero.

Gillion is an involved tale about courageous feats and forbidden love. With noble religious and political aims, Gillion journeys to the crusades to fight the Muslims, but his ship is attacked and he is taken prisoner. As a slave, he is forced to fight for the Egyptian sultan, and, as a dedicated warrior, he does his best. Because he fights so nobly for the Muslim army, he comes to the attention of the sultan, whom he eventually rescues. Meanwhile, his wife sends his sons to look for him. They experience parallel adventures in their quest to find their father. But, he does not need to be rescued; by his own incredible courage and skill, he has risen to a place of honor in the Muslim army. In fact, the sultan rewards Gillion by giving him his daughter in marriage.

One would think this plot would be undesirable as a way for a Christian noble to imagine his potential in a great and dangerous world, but Gillion provides a vehicle for a dreamer like Louis to have it all. The plot allows for Gillion and his sons to carry out harrowing rescues, both as soldiers of France and then as soldiers captured and conscripted by an Egyptian sultan. The plot allows Gillion to be a bigamist with one wife of high status from his native culture and another a high-status Muslim princess, whom he wins because he rescues her father, the sultan of Egypt. The amazing ending is that when Gillion returns to Burgundy as a war hero with an Egyptian wife, he discovers his French wife is alive, and the wives and the community accept the circumstance. Although

Fig 7.9
This image is a detailed and richly colored depiction of the moment in *The Romance of Gillion de Trazegnies* when Gillion's ship is attacked by the Egyptian sultan's army. The J. Paul Getty Museum, Los Angeles, Ms. 111, fol. 21

the women become best friends, retire to a convent, and resolve never to have sexual relations with Gillion again, they do revere him and pray for his soul. *Gillion* is a detailed, hyperbolic fantasy about the heroic and erotic possibilities of men who join the army.

The *Heike Monogatari*

By the Kamakura (1185–1333) period of Japanese history, the historical romance of the Heian moved more strictly into poetic forms, and the epic tales of martial prowess again became popular. The wars for control of the empire at the end of the Heian period were the fodder for several historical epics. The Japanese had many tales of romance and court life, like the *Genji Monogatari* (eleventh century), the first novel in history written by a woman, Lady Murasaki Shikibu. With the backdrop of the Genji clan and their rise to prominence, the epic focuses on the love affairs of Genji, a beautiful man of refined culture, an excellent lover, and a poet. His romantic relationships are deep, but short lived, as he moves through Japan and his clan wrests control from the Fujiwara.

Monogatari was a Japanese literary form with an extended prose narrative, generally an epic, that takes historical events and fictionalizes them for a courtly or noble audience. It was popular from the ninth to the fifteenth century, and, as we saw with the *Genji Monogatari*, both men and women wrote these tales. Most monogatari detail events and people well known to the elites, who expected poetry to be elegant and focus on themes of impermanence and personal ethical struggles. A noted new feature of monogatari in the Kamakura and Muromachi periods is the *emaki*, or picture scroll, which would combine artistic representations and the text of important scenes together. New forms of expression helped to spread the tales and leave for us impressive artistic pieces. The most prominent Kamakura military chronicles were the *Hogen Monogatari*, *Heiji Monogatari*, and *Heike Monogatari*.

The *Heike Monogatari*, completed prior to 1330, focuses much of its energy on the relationships and intrigues of courtiers, many of whom were also warriors. The tale details the battles and conspiracies between the Heike (Taira) and Genji (Minamoto) clans for control of the empire from the 1170s to 1190s (see above). When the Fujiwara clan lost control of the empire to the Heike, other major clans had to decide where they would situate themselves. Despite previous alliances, the Genji chose to position itself opposite the Heike, eventually supplanting the Heike to control Japan. The *Heike* is a tragic history of a failed clan. Most Japanese readers and viewers would have known that the Genji clan took control after Kiyomori's short rule (the last Heian emperor), and that the Japanese emperor would become no more than a figurehead. Rival clans continued to fight for power and control under the period of the Kamakura, where shoguns ruled Japan and its emperor, so much of the *Heike* would also have been relevant current history for Japanese nobles, as well. Presaging the actual historical outcome, the author shows the bravery of the Genji repeatedly. In one example, Yorimasa, an old general and courtier, mounts a failed rebellion against the Heike early on. We are told that this white-haired soldier "must have known that this day was his last, for he had left off his helmet." These scenes of war contrast to those that detail the court itself.

Court intrigue is one of the omnipresent themes of the text. Courtiers spend the majority of their time currying favor with whomever is in charge, gaining new posts and leaving old ones in an attempt to raise their own family's reputation and standing within the community. The theme of political impermanence is central to the text, which courtiers in the fourteenth century would also have found telling, within the early years of the Morumachi period (1333–1573). Unlike the Gillion tale, the *Heike* focuses less on the exploits, political and personal, of one man, and instead gives an almost historical account of the final days of the Heian period. One of the more tragic scenes in the text is the battle of Dan-no-ura, when the emperor's widow commits suicide by throwing herself and her young grandson into the sea. Near the end of the tale, the young emperor's mother, who escaped the massacre at Dan-no-ura, becomes a Buddhist nun and laments the suffering of her clan, bringing a tale of warfare and courtly intrigue to a close with a plea to understand the passing of time and the impermanence of this world. The political military epics like the *Heike* sought to teach the elites about the dangers of intrigue and hubris, couching the lessons in beautiful language and paintings.

The Bayeux Tapestry

Although we focus often on literature, historical presentation through artwork is another important facet of understanding medieval life. Much like the *Heike Monogatari*, the Bayeux Tapestry tells a pictorial story of historical events. The Norman conquest of England, begun in 1066, is displayed in detail within long linen. Commissioned by Odo, the bishop of Bayeux and King William I's half-brother, the embroidery (falsely labeled a tapestry) was completed by English nuns working in southern England. All the vegetal colors used for the eight dyes were sourced from areas near Kent, Odo's new territory. Probably completed prior to 1100, the work focuses on the events leading up to the conquest of England, including the famous Battle of Hastings.

More than twice as long as an American football field (231 feet long and 20 inches tall), the linen was "read" like a comic, from left to right, with scenes of the lives of Edward the Confessor, William, Duke of Normandy, and Harold Godwinson playing out through the frames. The upper and lower registers show Aesop's fables and other events that seem to offer a "counterpoint" to the official history of the embroidery. As Aesop's fables show the weaker defeating the stronger, perhaps the English nuns, now living in a conquered country, ruled by a king who did not know their language or even how large their country was, sought to subvert the sanctioned Norman narrative. There are only 57 phrases sewn into the cloth, in Latin, most of which label individuals or important events like "Here Harold is killed." All told, the tapestry features 626 individuals, 190 horses, and 35 dogs, among other animals and architectural scenes. Halley's comet appears in one scene, an omen observed by King Harold and his men as they look to the sky. The nuns include three women who appear in the main register: Queen Edith, a woman and her son fleeing a burning building, and an "Aelfgyva" fending off a lecherous cleric. Three anonymous women appear in the upper and lower registers.

The embroidery must be read in a different manner than all the other texts mentioned here. Nevertheless, its audience would have been familiar with the

Fig 7.10
The Bayeux Tapestry is a 231-foot-long visual epic depicting the Battle of Hastings (1066) where William of Normandy's armies defeated King Harold of England. The language of this heroic tale is the embroidery of nuns from southern England. FORGET Patrick / Alamy Stock Photo

history and followed the events as they walked the length of it, suspended around the interior of a church. With the separate registers and symbols within the text, the story probably changed depending on whether that viewer was English or Norman. We have many textual accounts of the conquest, from both the English and the Norman viewpoints; this embroidery is the epic of the conquest. Battles rage in the main register, as men and horses clash with each other, and, in the lower registers, we see the dead stripped of clothing and animals in mourning. This work allows for multiple interpretations and has done so since its creation, but the themes of deceit and hubris appear in this work, as in the others under discussion here.

Looking Forward

In this chapter, we have focused on the growth toward statehood by many political entities from 900 to 1300. A rise in the professionalization of the civil service and the creation of clear lines of succession created a new sense of continuity within many kingdoms in Europe. No territory in this period fully realized nationhood, especially as domestic unity was often disrupted by civil disturbances and outside invasion. As some states became more bureaucratic and centralized, others succumbed to internal and external pressures. As new rulers and new states formed and changed in the 300 years of the crusades, the wars between western Europeans, Byzantines, and Muslims changed the face of the Middle East, and the rise of the Mongols and the khanates they established created new states within Eurasia, as they also fragmented older polities like Song China and Kievan Rus.

All these changes, and others, were presented within the art and literature of the day. The romance genre was a popular way to experience the heroic deeds and fraught passions of a fantasy elite. Within these stories of ill-fated love lay the contest between loyalty to one's king or loyalty to one's heart and family. Epics centered on wars and battles reminded nobles of their own political histories and were cautionary tales against the perils of power: hubris, disloyalty, and destruction. Stories traveled across political and geographic boundaries and changed to match the interests of new audiences. On the whole, the political landscape of this period is one of centralization and connection, as we move forward to a new era of economic growth and political expansion.

Research Questions

1. Explain the relationships between the cultural ideas of marriage and parenthood and the political reality of a ruling family.
2. Research one of the crusades in Europe and the Middle East. How is this crusade related to the ones that came before it? What were the goals of the crusaders? Did they meet those goals? Why or why not?
3. How did the Mongols affect the existing regimes and power structures of Russia? China? Iran?
4. Examine medieval warfare. What technological advances occur during war? How do battles and wars change political, religious, and cultural boundaries?
5. Research several medieval European romances such as those by Chretien de Troyes (1130–1191) or Marie de France (1160–1215). Or research several *chansons de geste* (Tales of Great Feats) such as *Song of Roland* or *Song of El Cid*. What are the major themes within the tales? How do they relate to other fictional works we've discussed in this chapter?
6. Research visual representations of the *Heike Monogatari* or the Bayeaux Tapestry. How does the work represent the political intrigues and military strategies of its day? Can you find anything subversive in the presentation that seems to be commentary and not history?

Further Reading

Bowersock, G. W. *The Crucible of Islam.* Cambridge, MA and London: Harvard University Press, 2017.
Brook, Timothy. *The Great State: China and the World.* London: Profile Books, 2019.

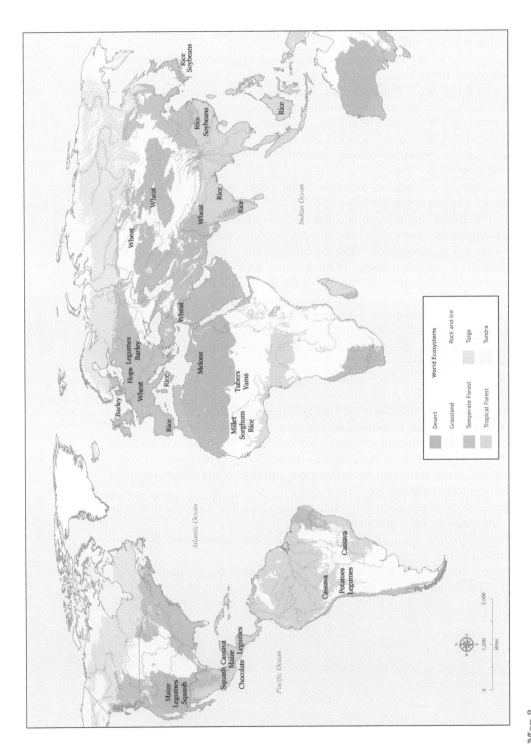

Map 8
Class Rites

8 Class Rites

Society, 900–1300

Introduction

Humans love to classify and sort; we will arrange things like our music, our photos, and even our pets. The Bible starts with Adam getting the right to name and classify the animals. We also categorize humans. For much of the Middle Ages, people were sorted into at least three major categories. The elite were defined by land ownership or control of armies and other resources. Warriors were a class unto themselves, sometimes part of the nobility, higher in status than agrarian peasants and laborers such as miners and sailors. As we discussed earlier in the book, the majority of populations were expendable peasants and laborers, doing work for the noble classes or fighting on the front lines of wars. Some cultures distinguished religious orders as a distinct fourth class, and, as the medieval period progressed, another class distinguished itself, that of the skilled laborers, artisans, and merchants who, through trade of goods and ideas, connected world cultures with commodities such as tools, armaments, books, textiles, medicinal knowledge, and house wares. This group, which will become the bourgeoisie (burghers/burgesses), were paid in money for their work, a departure from a barter economy or subsistence farming. In all societies and classes, women lived in subservience to patriarchal systems of power. While they did have avenues toward self-agency related to mothering and religion, and occasionally distinguished themselves in literary pursuits such as in Japanese court life, women and girls of all classes had fewer rights and privileges.

In the first part of this chapter, we look at how class systems changed from 900 to 1300. Stratification of people into a range of high-status and low-status roles continued to allow confederations and city-states to conquer large geographic areas, construct cathedrals, build roads, and dredge harbors. And, while some people benefited from these civilizing projects, others certainly suffered. By definition, a class system enforces disparities: those who owned land were separate from those who worked the land, those born of elite families were different from those born to peasants. The formally educated lived differently than the unschooled. The wealthy had access to materials and comforts that the poor did not. Sumptuary laws reinforced these differences.

The second half of the chapter explores what happened to people who existed outside the social class rankings – how did they become outsiders, and what were the terms of exclusion? Outlaws were banished because they had broken formal laws or committed social taboos; they were outside the law. Foreigners were born outside the system, and therefore often stigmatized. Some outsiders were insiders rejected by mainstream culture. These outcasts lived within a community but were scorned and mistreated because of disability, disfigurement, or differences deemed abnormal. A few examples from medieval culture give us a glimpse of how premodern societies distinguished insiders from outsiders and learned from their examples.

A: SOCIETY, CLASS, AND GENDER

Evidence: Cheng-Zhu school of Neo-Confucian scholars

Zhu Xi, *Family Rituals*

The Gossamer Years

The Pillow Book

Genji Monogatari

Letters of Abelard and Heloise

Hrostvita, plays and other works

Introduction

Class is an ordering of society, generally based on differences in wealth, inherited rank or position, profession, occupation, race, or gender. "Class" is a comparative tool used to define hierarchical social groups; although it is a modern term with ties to post-Industrial society, we use it because people in the Middle Ages were organized along economic, occupational, and institutional lines. Those within a particular class share similar economic or social status, which often aligns with political power. These separations make the people easier to control and organize, which, in turn, makes the creation of a stable state easier to manage. In the premodern period, class-based societies were closely linked to economic security. Those of the noble classes held legal, social, cultural, and political sway over the lower classes, and, although members of the military and religious organizations could occasionally come from lower classes, aristocratic nobles held the positions of leadership. This meant that almost all the positions of authority and power were held within one class, a small group of families that passed down resources and titles to their descendants and lived off the labor of the agricultural class. Medieval people believed these classifications were divinely determined, and religious organization reiterated these categories within their written commentaries, supporting social and political striations.

Since the advent of writing, codes have separated people by birthright, economic status, occupation, and gender. From ancient Mesopotamia, laws privileged free men of property over free men; after all, free men of property were the ones who wrote the laws. Enslaved people had no power at all. These ancient codes also defined religious leaders (priests) from the rest of society, and women almost always held a lesser position within their economic state – that is, free women of property were "worth more" than free women, and both classes were above enslaved women, but all women were less than men within their class. In all societies under discussion here, women held lower positions than men, socially, legally, and economically.

India

Populations on the Indian subcontinent derived their social order from sacred literature called the *Vedas* (ca. 1500–900 BCE). Known in the West as the caste system, this social structure has four major classes: priests (Brahmins), warriors/rulers (*kshatriyas*), merchants/craftsmen/farmers (*vaishyas*), and laborers (*shudras*); but hundreds of complex social groups developed within those categories based on occupation, ethnicity, language, religion, and/or gender. There is little mention of class or caste in the medieval Indian texts, and it seems that occupations were more fluid in the medieval period than in later history, allowing for some social mobility and assimilation of outsiders. The Indian subcontinent's size and diversity also meant that systems that held sway in one section of India rarely meant the same thing in another area. When Muslims began ruling in northern India around 1200, they found a social stratification they were able to use for taxation and political purposes, but nothing akin to the confines we see in the period post-1500, when the caste system was rigid, with stratifications set at birth and strict social barriers in crossing the castes enforced by both customary and written law.

Like most premodern societies, women in India lived under patriarchal family structures. Socially and legally, women were considered minors who needed the control of a firm male figure. Laws forbade women from inheriting men's wealth; in fact, most laws mentioned women and property in a single phrase, and there is evidence that women's labor was loaned out, much like property, throughout the premodern period. We do have evidence, however, that women did have wealth and property of their own, as there are numbers of religious inscriptions detailing the gifts made by women to temples and religious spaces.

Vedic texts dictated women's compulsory marriage and motherhood. Despite the burden and expense, these cultures prized large families. This social imperative kept men toiling in the fields and women in the homes to support their growing families. Women's primary occupation was to provide sons and to care for the family and its property. Few women received formal education, although noblewomen were often trained in statecraft and literacy – but their prime duty still remained birthing children. Despite what may seem to be a depressing existence, funerary inscriptions point to numerous wives and mothers who were deeply loved and respected by their families and to women acting to honor their own parents and grandparents. Northern India also made space for "third" genders (*hijra*), who lived a life dedicated to the goddess Bahuchara Mata. Androgynous deities like Ardhanari, whose iconography grew during the Gupta period (ca. 300–600 CE), represented a synthesis of masculine and feminine traits and showed there was room for nonbinary individuals within Indian society. Many nonbinary Indian people were seen as spiritually pure, and they were sought out to perform blessings for marriages and at births.

Religion allowed some women to live outside the traditional family sphere. In the Hindu faith, young girls could be sold to temples, either as offerings to the gods or simply out of desperation to pass off children who could not be cared for. Talented girls became temple dancers and singers, while the less talented became servants. Temple women enjoyed longer lives than their married sisters, as they did not have the liability of childbearing. Some temple entertainers earned salaries, created groups akin to unions within their temples, and aided in the administration of temple duties. The meaning and use of this religious space by women have changed significantly in the modern day, but, in the premodern period, these temple women enjoyed status and wealth that their secular sisters did not have. By 700, Buddhism also provided a way for women to live outside the household in nunneries. Most women who joined cloisters did so once widowed and, although they held subordinate status to male monastics, women did have the opportunity to study and teach.

China

Outside of the royal household, which was supreme, there were four traditionally ranked classes in Chinese society: scholar-officials, farmers, artisans, and merchants. Despite often being the wealthiest group in society, merchants, as people who did not "make" anything and lived on the labor of others, were always the lowest social class. As the Song Chinese economy expanded (960–1279), so too did the social status of merchants, but, nevertheless, traders were always a lower class than the bureaucrats, despite their wealth (see chapters 2, 6 and 10). Warriors existed throughout the ranks, but, by the Tang dynasty, warrior-aristocrats vied with the scholars for access to the emperor. Families could, and did, move among ranks, using marriage, wealth, and land ownership to gain social, political, and legal status. Like other cultures, there was no "middle class" – most people lived frugal lives of near-poverty, whereas a lucky few lived in luxury. These classes, while fluid, maintained themselves throughout all premodern Chinese history.

The ideal of the patriarchal family stood at the center of Chinese social systems. That family was based, like much of Chinese social life, on Confucian teachings. Confucius (551–479 BCE) lived during a politically unstable period, when warfare consumed the state and the place of the educated bureaucrat lessened. He wrote social philosophy that was fundamentally conservative: change brought disruption and warfare, so consistency in daily life was key. The social hierarchies were patriarchal in nature: the emperor was the father of the empire and all the subjects his children; a key precept for Confucius was "let the leader be the leader and the subject a subject." Customs and traditional laws based on Confucian values ruled society from the farmer class to the emperor. The Chinese family was patriarchal, patrilocal, and patrilineal: fathers were the head of the family, women married into and moved to a man's family, and goods were passed from father to son. The father stood supreme in the family unit; his will was law and all people within the household owed him obedience and respect. In turn, his goal was to assure the family's prosperity through work. Fundamentally, Confucianism held conservative ideals, centered on rule and obedience. Confucius felt relying on laws would eventually lead to disarray: "The Master said: Guide them with policies and align them with punishments and the people will evade them and have no shame. Guide them with virtue and align them with *li* [ritual] and the people will have a sense of shame and fulfill their roles" (*Analects* 2.3). Legalistic ideas, however, continued to hold sway in concert with Confucian ideals throughout premodern Chinese history.

Confucian ideas centered on the family: the ruler should be the ruler, the father should be the father, and the son should be the son – in essence, the ruler should rule, and the subject should be ruled (*Analects* 12.11). He insisted rulers be wise and lead ethically, but he also knew this was an ideal to strive toward and not a reality. Governing with virtue, which was practiced through proper rituals, showed the ruler's decorum and moral power to his subjects. As a ruler acted toward his subjects, a father was to act toward his family – an arbiter of law and the example of virtue. Confucian family roles were vertical, with one's place in the family dictated by gender and birth order. The younger deferred to the elder, the woman deferred to the man, and the eldest male held the prime position. The family was the microcosm of society, and Confucian ideals insisted on the vertical alignment within the farm, village, and state. He taught that the love of others was the center of all society, and that each person should practice self-restraint to be truly altruistic.

Women's roles followed Confucian thought – daughters were to obey their mothers and fathers, they were to marry at their father's direction, live under the tutelage (often brutal) of their mother-in-law, provide their husband with male heirs, and maintain the family rituals. They were in charge of spiritual practices of the home; ancestor worship was a major ritual attended to by the women of the family. Buddhism and Daoism gave more freedom than Confucianism to women to act outside the patriarchal family, by allowing women to exit the family and live as nuns (still under the direction of a male leader). Most women chose to enter the nunnery in old age, after the death of their spouse – perhaps to release their children from financially caring for them (a Confucian edict), perhaps to enter a quieter life of contemplation and education.

By the Tang dynasty, Neo-Confucian writers sought to counteract the growth of Buddhism within China. Assimilating ideas from Daoism, Buddhism, and native folk beliefs, Neo-Confucian thought sought to bring Confucian ideals into the contemporary world, while sticking to the Confucian ideals of ritual and obedience. Ancestor rituals became more common, and writers like Zhu Xi (1130–1200), a prominent Neo-Confucian author of the Southern Song dynasty (960–1279) wrote *Family Rituals*, detailing women's involvement and importance within familial customs, working to bring women back into the family and away from the nunneries. Neo-Confucian writers extolled the place of mothers within the family and they encouraged embracing marriage as a sacred space. Accepting marriage as sacred and the sole avenue to respectability for women was doubly difficult in China's polygamous society. While men in the Song dynasty could have as many concubines as they could afford, they only had one legitimate wife. Concubines were generally women of a lower social class, or women whose families did not have enough money for a dowry; often these women became servants within their new households, never able to enter that sacred space of marriage or attain its veneer of respectability. These women were not co-wives – they did not have the same rights as the wife, nor did they have the same opportunities. Their children were legitimate, but all children were officially considered "of the wife's womb," and the wife could raise any child within the household as her own. Some concubines could raise themselves up, especially if the wife had died and they had borne sons for the patriarch, but most lived lives near drudgery.

Despite the proscriptions against them, women engaged in business and legal affairs, aided in family farms, and almost single-handedly controlled the silk industry. In the noble classes, a prominent example of a powerful woman is Wu Zhao (625–706), whom we introduced earlier in the book. This remarkable woman rose from being a secondary concubine of one emperor to the wife of his son. She became "Wu Hou" (Empress Consort) in 655 and "Wu Zetian" in 690 when she ruled the empire alone. She named herself "Wu Huangdi" – a play on the first Chinese emperor's name (Shi Huangdi), as Huangdi means "first emperor." Her regnal name in Chinese combined the elements for sun (male) and moon (female) and, as such, she created a nonbinary space for her rule – she was more than male, more than female. (Many female rulers, from Hatshepsut to Queen Elizabeth I created identities that included both male and female attributes.) Wu re-founded the Zhou dynasty (originally 1046–256 BCE) to associate her rule with that long-lived and highly respected dynasty. Her Zhou dynasty, however, lasted only from 683 to 705, when she died at age 81.

Wu was a capable ruler; for example, she expanded the examination system to allow men of lower classes to take the exams, and her government prized talent over birth, giving rise to a system of meritocracy within the Chinese bureaucracy and allowing new men to rise in social classes. She promoted Buddhism within China, paying for temples to be built in several regions of China and patronizing large Buddha statues like the Lu She Na Buddha in the Fengxian Si Cave (Longmen Grottoes) that have, today, become tourist sites. Wu also promoted Daoism throughout her reign; scholars have seen her predilection for Buddhism and Daoism as a way for her to curtail the influence of Confucian practices that denied women political power.

The Tang and Song dynasties continued the Confucian traditions of family and the traditional ranked classes. The Neo-Confucian movement of the Song dynasty reinstated the proscriptions within the classes in Chinese society. A hostility to foreign thought and styles permeated Song social life; perhaps hewing strongly to the Chinese "golden age" would prevent further invasions. During the Song, living up to the ideals of Confucianism became the hallmark of being a good Chinese subject. There was a reinforcement of the class, gender, and age distinctions, and a new emphasis on rank and deference. Women's roles were severely curtailed, as women were seen as causing the downfall of the Tang empire (with Empress Wu and Yang Guifei the major instigators – see Chapter 3). Restricted to the house, women were excluded from public life (if the family could afford it; many women of the lower classes had to work in family farms and workshops). The adherence to Neo-Confucian thought, however, came at the expense of the military, which left the Chinese state open to attack. The Yuan dynasty (1279–1368), with its emphasis from the martial Mongolian society, reinstituted strong differences in both class and gender for northern Chinese society.

Japan

Japan's ruling class was the warrior-aristocracy; they ruled over a large class of lower nobles and peasants. There were few merchants in Japanese society during the period, and the nobles controlled access to governmental offices. Unlike China, where the scholar-gentry reigned supreme among the classes, in Japan the warriors presided over all people.

Japan's Heian era (794–1192) saw the rise of several powerful noble families who dominated the empire from their position as regents for the emperors. These clans controlled their own personal militias, and clan leaders trained and hired professional soldiers to go to war with other clans. This freed the clan nobles to focus on court intrigues. From 856 to 1086, the Fujiwara clan ruled behind the emperor's throne, manipulating and holding on to power through strategic marriage alliances and forcing other major families to spend much of their year in the court city. The government employed 6,000 people, with 4,000 employed in the imperial city alone. The Fujiwara court was a refined and graceful expression of an aggressively competitive militaristic dynasty. It also produced a class of bureaucrats who gradually lost touch with their warrior personas.

The professional soldiers hired by the increasingly courtly nobility became known as "samurai"; they became large private armies, owing their loyalty to the clan who paid them and not to the emperor himself. Largely illiterate and drawn from the lower classes, samurai were held in contempt by the bureaucrats who nonetheless needed their military acumen to survive. As time went on, the samurai moved up into the lower nobility, becoming educated and worldly. They were trained military men but were also expected to be culturally sophisticated. A warrior was to be highly trained in the arts: he was to appreciate and emulate the best of literature, poetry, visual media, and music.

Still constrained under a patriarchal system, noblewomen were often restricted to their home compounds and rarely allowed to leave or see non-family members. Women of the samurai class had more freedom of movement, and some received specialized military training and became "onna-bugeishi" or women-warriors. Peasant women tilled the fields alongside their families, much as peasant women did around the world. Elite women of the court were supposed to be beautiful and highly educated, and an elaborate sense of aesthetics was vital to all genders of the elite class. Hidden behind screens when in public, women wrote letters to lovers, and potential lovers, and worked within the familial bureaucratic system of feudal Japan. Wealthy women might wear up to 40 layers of kimono, and they would change the layers and colors to experience a change of the seasons. Elaborate hair and makeup created an artistic vision of women that reinforced the status of their upper-class husbands and lovers.

COLORS

Just as wealthy people desired highly spiced food (see Chapter 6), they also sought vibrantly colored clothing, hats, and shoes to ornament their bodies, and tapestries to adorn the walls of their homes. Similar desires for brightly colored textiles, and rapidly changing clothing fashions, are found among the wealthy classes in most regions of the premodern world and fueled a lot of medieval trade. Since clothing could be an important marker of social status and class in all regions, wealthy and high-ranking people around the premodern world chose to dress in quite colorful clothing as a sign of their expendable wealth and status. Materials for the dyeing industry and finished textiles were major trade items of the period. But, expensive dyestuffs could be used for more than just textiles – extravagant manuscripts also called for a variety of bright colors for decoration and embellishment. Some colors in various cultures carried symbolic meanings, of life, death, sacrality, the wisdom of heaven, or imperial power.

Blue and purple, in particular, have long been prized colors, in large part because they were difficult to source. In the Roman Empire, for instance, Tyrian purple (or imperial purple) was the essence of prestige, an exotic dye made from droplets of mucus squeezed out of a small sea snail called the murex, which was initially only harvested along the eastern shores of the Mediterranean (near the Phoenician city of Tyre, hence the name "Tyrian purple"). It took fluid from thousands of them to color one robe, and only members of the Roman senatorial class could afford this precious hue.

The connection between purple and exalted rank continued into the Greek Byzantine period, when use of purple for robes was restricted to members of the imperial family. A child of the emperor was said to be "born in the purple." Eager to connect themselves to Roman traditions, manuscript makers in early medieval Europe and Byzantium produced sumptuous codices of parchment saturated in purple. The purple pages were a statement of status and luxury, often accompanied by gold or silver ink. Purple had prestige in Asia as well. In China it was thought that the Heavenly Emperor lived in a purple palace illuminated by the Purple Star (Pole Star), and thus the imperial palace of emperors is the Purple Forbidden City. Purple orchids, silks, and shadows decorate the mysticism of Chinese poetry.

The murex dye (or that from a related species of sea creature) may also be the source of color in the ritual garments worn by the Jewish high priest in the temple. Known in Hebrew as *tekhelet* ("blue-violet" or "blue"), this bright or dark blue color was mentioned numerous times in the Hebrew Bible and carried great significance on ritual robes and the fringes and stripes on prayer shawls.

The deep blue-purple dye from the indigo plant was regularly traded in large bales across the medieval Indian Ocean and Mediterranean Sea. True indigo is harvested from the leaves of a flowering shrub that grows in tropical regions of Asia and Africa. Other plants could also produce similar shades of deep blue and purple, such as woad, which was much easier to access in northern Europe and therefore much less expensive there. Ultramarine came to

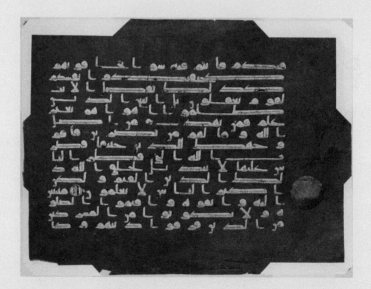

Fig 8.1
The Blue Qur'an was produced in ninth/tenth-century Tunisia in the tradition of dyeing parchment luxurious purple or blue (murex dye or indigo). For the main text, the calligrapher used ink made with gold. For the verse markers he used silver. This art of this luxury manuscript refers to purple-dyed parchment and gilded decorations popular in the Byzantine Empire. Metropolitan Museum of Art, Purchase, Lila Acheson Wallace Gift, 2004, 2004.88

be considered the luxury blue. Ultramarine was extracted from lapis lazuli, a stone mined in present-day Afghanistan or in parts of South America. In a painting or manuscript, the use of ultramarine was an expression of wealth and prestige, and the beautiful subtleties of this blue came to be iconic in European panel and manuscript painting as the color of the Virgin Mary's robes.

Another popular color was a vibrant red, which came in many different shades. One of the brightest and most resilient reds did not come from a sea creature but from a bug, the kermes, many pounds of which were required to make crimson. Similarly, in the Americas, Aztec and Inca royalty were distinguished by clothing dyed with a bright red color called carmine. Carmine also came from an insect – the cochineal beetle – which the Mesoamericans collected and grew on large farms of prickly pear cactus. Other natural sources of reds were the madder plant, the brazilwood tree, and rust. Red was the most widespread color in medieval European manuscripts, in large part because red ink was used to highlight chapter titles and important passages (called rubrication).

Fig 8.2
Discovered in 1994, the Tomb of the Red Queen is the grave of a woman of high status from seventh-century Mexico. Her remains and the objects buried with her were covered with vivid red cinnabar powder.
© Wikimedia Commons, public domain under the Creative Commons Attribution 3.0 Unported license.

Other popular shades of red are known collectively as vermillion, which is the term for a variety of hues created from ground cinnabar, a mineral that is the primary source of mercury. Vermillion carried a wide range of meanings in Chinese culture, from the color of life (because it looks like blood) to that of eternity. It was used for a number of items restricted to imperial use: seals, ink, and carriages. It was also used for a very popular type of vessel known as lacquerware, in which intricate designs were carved into wood, and gold, silver, or mother of pearl designs are inlaid, before it was coated with resin and left to harden. Produced extensively in China during the Tang and Song eras, Chinese lacquerware and the technology to produce it were also exported to Korea, Japan, and Southeast and South Asia. Vermillion was also used to decorate tombs of South American royalty such as the Maya Tomb of the Red Queen.

There were other rare and desired colors, like bright yellow and green. While also sold as a spice, saffron was used to make a rich yellow-orange favored by Buddhist monks for their robes. Only the Chinese emperor and the highest of officials were allowed to wear silks dyed imperial yellow, a tint made from careful handling of the root of the Chinese foxglove flower. Yellows, yellow-oranges, and yellow-browns could also be produced by a variety of natural clays (such as red and yellow ochre), plants (especially one called weld), and spices (such as turmeric). Green could be produced from plants, minerals (such as malachite), or verdigris (a solution made of copper patina). Access to particular colors and the right to wear and use specific colors were important markers of class status in most parts of the premodern world.

Upper-class Japanese women were highly literate, producing well-known and respected poems, epics, letters, and stories. Japanese writing used a combination of Chinese characters (kanji) and syllabic writing (kana). Educated men wrote almost exclusively in kanji, but it was difficult to directly correlate Chinese characters to the Japanese language, hence the syllabic systems. Hiragana was the syllabic version of kanji and, throughout Heian Japan, it was known as *onna-de*, or women's writing. Medieval Japanese women penned some great works of Japanese literature, many during the Heian era. The most popular genre, the *nikki* (autobiography), shows the inner workings of noblewomen's lives: their relationships with husbands and servants and with court dealings. *The Gossamer Years* (ca. 950) details the unhappy life and marriage of a young woman whose husband spent much of their marriage away at court, leaving her bound to a house without peers or close family. *The Pillow Book* by Sei Shonagon (ca. 990s) shows the intrigues of court life, written by a noblewoman who lived at court with her spouse. Perhaps the most famous work is the quasi-historical *Genji Monogatari*, or *Tale of Genji* (ca. 1020). Written by Lady Murasaki (a pen name, meaning "violet"), the tale is considered the world's first novel. The story centers first on Genji, a young aristocrat in the Heian court who seeks love and fame, and then on his son, whom fortune favors in love and at court. In no other premodern society do we find so many texts of

Fig 8.3
This scene from the Lady Murasaki's *Genji Monogatari Emaki*, or *Tale of Genji*, is
from the earliest existing illustrated version of this novel (early twelfth century). The
image highlights the use of painted screens as dividers and decorations. An emaki is
an illustrated scroll, in this case made of fine paper.
Matteo Omied / Alamy Stock Photo

poetry, biography, autobiography, literature, and history by women. Although
cloistered and separated, access to the written word allowed Japanese women
to become powerful societal players, both during their lives and for us today.

Mesoamerica

Mesoamerican societies also had social classes of nobles, commoners, and serfs/
slaves. Most Mesoamerican cultures had hereditary aristocracies that traced
their lineage to a divine or mythic hero. Military prowess was essential for men
within these societies, and a warrior-noble class formed as early as the Olmec
period (1500–400 BCE) and saw its peak at the Aztec civilization (1300–1521).
Noble status followed bloodlines and kin groups of both male and female lines.
Within the noble class, the subclasses included priests, judges, bureaucrats, and
highly decorated warriors. The commoners included lower-level bureaucrats,
farmers, artisans and merchants, and low-level priests. Peasant serfs and slaves
were generally prisoners of war or economically indebted to a member of the
upper classes.

    In most Mesoamerican societies, men could move up the ranks with mili-
tary prowess and elevate the family name. Mesoamerican cultures allowed for
members of all the lower classes to believe in their ability to attain a higher
status. Since every male in every class (except slaves) was trained in warfare,
there was always a possibility of gaining captives, which allowed advancing in
wealth and rank. The disparity between the classes gave incentive for men to

raise themselves and their families out of the lower classes into more prosperity, and the social structure allowed for movement. Heavily gendered expectations followed children in all castes, and primogeniture (eldest son inherits) gave family wealth to the eldest living son, leaving younger sons to seek their wealth in trade or religion. To symbolize their futures, parents gifted newborns with either a pottery shard or loom to girls and a knife to boys. Girls married at menses and, while marriage was considered essential to a woman's life, divorce could be contracted by either party. Women frequently inherited property from their mothers.

Food-processing was the central part of a woman's life. Female skeletons from the Maya period show women with enlarged, gnarled knees, calcified toe bones, and large arms, all the result of incessant grinding of corn. In Central America (as in China), women also held responsibility for weaving and textile production, which was often used as a method of tax payment. Wealthy women wove fine cottons with feathers and beads, whereas lower-class women wove rougher fabrics for daily use. Often, women worked together in public spaces, weaving large projects on looms in the central squares. We can imagine women weaving, dyeing, stretching, and creating these pieces, chatting among themselves, with young children nearby. Being in public spaces and working together for pieces that eventually became government property (either directly or through taxation) gave these women a feeling of belonging and a sense of value to the state, and showed the community the importance of women to its long-term survival. In essence, working publicly gave women a level of social power that societies who restricted their women to the home did not see.

WOMEN'S WEAVING

For much of history, women produced textiles for their families inside their homes. In fact, across the globe, textile production was almost always seen as a strictly female vocation, done in homes and monasteries around the world. In most cultures, women were also relegated to the home itself, out of sight of other men and often of other women as well. Being restricted to home compounds could be a lonely experience for women, especially of certain classes, as we learn from the Japanese writer of *The Gossamer Years.* Lower-class women often worked alongside their husbands in the markets and some produced goods to sell for the family, while also caring for children and running the household, participating in what one scholar called "the economy of makeshifts." While these efforts did impact the larger state economies, women's work was almost always seen as owned and controlled by men.

However, some Christian, Aztec, and Chinese women wove for more than their families; their weaving was part of their empire's taxation system, part of the state economy. Christian nuns wove intricate and costly vestments (garments for clergymen) and occasionally grand tapestries and embroideries. Some European women could even join professional guilds of textile workers. In China and Mesoamerica, silk and weavings were taken as taxation and used by those empires as trade goods, moving long distances within the Eurasian and American spheres, respectively. These women facilitated economic trade, and their goods became the currency of their empires. Chinese women, however, still worked alone within their households, whereas Aztec women worked publicly in the village centers. This public face gave women significance within the empire – their labor was seen and valued, which meant that, in some ways, Aztec *women* were seen and valued.

Motherhood was a sacred calling for Mesoamerican women, and giving birth was considered a blood sacrifice to the gods. Bloodletting was an important religious ritual, designed to prove to the gods, and the people, the worth and the sacrifice of the victim. The rulers, both male and female, shed their own blood to keep the world moving forward in time, to keep the weather stable, and the agricultural output secure. Noblewomen, particularly queens, took part in auto-sacrifices, the shedding of blood for ritualized purposes. Sculptures show elite women participating in blood sacrifices for the people; generally, women

Fig 8.4
Shield Jaguar II and his wife, Lady Kabal Xook. Lady Xook pulls a thorned rope through her tongue, while her husband holds a torch over her. The Yaxchilan Lintels, Classic Maya 723–726, Mexico.
Peter Horree / Alamy Stock Photo

are shown with a rope studded with thorns or a stingray barb that was dragged through the soft flesh of the tongue, cheeks, or labia. The bloodletting ritual aided in the completion of Mesoamerican time systems (see Orientation) and showed the commoners the belief and dedication of their rulers.

When the Spanish invaded Mexico, they found a social hierarchy quite like their own in Europe. It allowed for some small amounts of diplomacy between the noblemen, and meant that, for many farmers and slaves, the hierarchies remained similar between Aztec and Spanish rule. Some nobles worked with the Spanish to advance their own claims to rule and the Spanish used these relationships to cover more territory for their home country. Many in the peasant and slave classes saw little change in their lives after the arrival of the Spanish, until diseases from Europe spread throughout the Americas, devastating local communities. No amount of sacrifice by the rulers could prevent this destruction of the timeline, and Mesoamerican society was forever changed by the colonial conquerors.

Europe

Like Mesoamerica, European nobility was a warrior-aristocracy, in which military prowess, wealth, and land ownership went hand in hand. Not as proscriptive as Indian systems, nor as open as Mesoamerican ones, the European class structure was designed to ensure a steady warrior base with enough trade and farming to support the large nobility. Much European nobility was an outgrowth of the old Roman aristocracy and Germanic warrior classes, so from its inception the ideals of warfare and governance were entwined. Ideally, the warriors (those who fight) were to protect the church (those who pray) and the remainder of society (those who work). In truth, however, farmers and those at smaller church holdings had as much to fear from these aggressive and competitive elites as from outside attack. Unlike other regions of Eurasia, the warrior nobility in Europe shared power with religious leaders, much like the Mesoamericans did. In fact, the secular and the spiritual leaders were often members of the same family; for example, William I, king of England and Duke of Normandy (d. 1086) made his half-brother Odo the bishop of Bayeux, an important spiritual position in northern France. Conversely, the European priesthood held lands outside the bonds that tied lord and noble and therefore they could either act as a check on the aristocrats or reinforce aristocratic power by consolidating lands and supporting a secular lord's larger goals. In all areas, spiritual leaders aided in performing bureaucratic duties for the kings, as they were often the most educated and literate portions of society.

The farmers supported the upper classes through their labor. In many areas of Europe, peasant-farmers or "serfs" were bound to the land where they were born – they were not slaves, owned by a lord, but had little freedom of movement – they could not move to another village, or to the city, without the express permission of their land's lord. Serfs performed corvée labor (unpaid labor owed to lords) yearly, fixing roads, building dams, and constructing buildings, and owed rents to the landlords in the form of agricultural produce. Free peasants lived outside the protection of a lord but could pay for aid in the form of taxes. Since the nobles often lived and fought far from their villages,

Fig 8.5

John of Worcester, Those Who Work, Fight, Pray. For most of the European medieval period, Christian clerics and monks compiled and transcribed histories and recorded the events of their times. In this episode called *The Nightmares of Henry I*, the chronicler John of Worcester (1095–1140) recounts the story that the English King Henry I suffered from a recurring nightmare in which three layers of society – peasants, knights, and agents of the Church – harassed him for failing to uphold promises of justice.

© Wikimedia Commons, public domain

peasants administered their own justice, holding court and levying fines and punishments. By the central Middle Ages, almost every community had a core group of literate peasants to help with the legal and political needs of the group.

During the period 900–1300, merchants and artisans migrated from villages to European cities, creating, trading, and selling goods from Scandinavia to Africa. These groups developed from the peasant classes into a socially flexible force, often enjoying the rights and benefits of the upper classes. Over time, this "middling" group created their own laws, administered justice, and organized themselves to create advantageous alliances with the secular and Church elite. Several important towns in Europe created self-governing communes, whose elected officials negotiated with aristocracy and bishops. Other cities received "liberties" from their kings, who gave them certain freedoms from corvée labor in return for stable and reasonable taxation. Freed from the service of their lords, these cities also had to see to their own defense and created policing units, fire relief, and militias.

As economics improved the lot of the lower classes, several major changes happened in Europe. First, slave-owning fell from prominence in western Europe as an economic or social commonplace. Domestic slavery continued in the Mediterranean, Viking, and Russian areas, but, overall, slavery decreased for most Europeans (see chapters 2, 6 and 10). Second, increased trade brought more wealth for the burgher (merchant) classes, and they often became far richer than the landed aristocracy. War is an expensive business and agricultural activity could only bring in so much wealth. Trade, on the other hand, was highly lucrative, especially with the growth of luxury goods from India, the Middle East, and China (see chapters 2, 6 and 10). In this way, class functioned outside of just economic structures. This disconnect often created issues between elite landowners and wealthy burghers. Elites occasionally sought to "control" the lower class of merchants through sumptuary laws, or rules restricting the consumption or display of luxury items.

SUMPTUARY LAWS

Styles of dress and adornment – jewelry, hats, shoes – were important in medieval cultures around the world, not simply as matters of personal taste and changing fashions. They could also function as important signifiers of status, profession, gender, class, and even religious identity. Laws regulating dress and adornment fall under the category of sumptuary laws. In the medieval period, many societies around the world used sumptuary laws to enforce visible distinctions between people of different classes, professions, religions, or ethnic groups by means of regulating what could be worn, eaten, drunk, or displayed (on houses or personal graves) by each.

In Christian Europe, as centralizing powers of states and the church increasingly emphasized religious homogeneity as a unifying force, Jews and other religious minorities faced expulsions and violent pogroms as well as cultural and economic pressure. Both royal law codes across Europe and Roman Church councils, notably at the Fourth Lateran Council of 1215, stressed the need to be able to easily distinguish Jews (or Muslims, though fewer lived in European cities) from Christians and thus mandated that Jews and Muslims wear distinctive hats or clothing. The degree to which these laws were enforced, however, was uneven, varying from place to place and depending upon the will of local authorities.

Fig 8.6
This manuscript image of a banquet scene shows men and women dressed in the highest aristocratic fashions of the fifteenth century. The women wear many layers of sumptuous silk fabrics and elaborate headdresses. Men wear very short tunics that reveal their buttocks and legs covered in tight, colored hose. Sumptuary laws restricted the lower classes from wearing revealing clothing; this seductive luxury fashion was only for elites.
The J. Paul Getty Museum, Los Angeles, Ms. Ludwig XV 8, fol. 123

European municipal laws from the later thirteenth and fourteenth centuries often restricted the clothing, shoes, and headgear of city dwellers such as prostitutes, members of the clergy, and both male and female burgesses. While women's clothing was the primary target of these laws – legislating both the appearance of morality, luxury, and social status – some male clothing items were also targeted. Prostitutes, for example, might have to wear striped tunics or specific-colored collars to differentiate them from respectable women. Clergy were prohibited from wearing certain colors and had to sport identifying haircuts (tonsures) so they would not be mistaken for secular people. Non-nobles could not wear a variety of furs and fabrics identified with royal and aristocratic use only, and women might be restricted in the number of gold, silk, or fur items they could own. Many sumptuary laws were initially issued during periods of war, as cost-saving measures and attempts to curb conspicuous consumption. They also increased in European cities after 1348, suggesting that they were intended to enhance the sense of community structure and hierarchy that had been threatened during the plague years.

Both Aztec and Inca Empires also legislated clothing for different ranks in the social hierarchy. Building upon the textile traditions of preceding cultures and those they conquered, Inca women made finely woven and brightly dyed textiles that became a hallmark of both their artistic and political culture. The Inca maintained sumptuary laws that reserved the finest and softest cloth (especially that made from vicuña fiber) and precious metals for royal use, including both noble adornment and diplomatic gift-giving (see chapters 2, 6, and 10). Inca rulers would offer the finest royal textiles to conquered rulers as a sign of their submission. Non-royals could only wear rougher, plainer textiles. Inca sumptuary laws also mandated that conquered peoples wear distinctive headgear so that their ethnic origin could be easily identified. During the colonial period, Spanish sumptuary laws were enforced along not only class but racial lines.

Economic growth and political stability made European society more secure, which in turn allowed for change and movement. New classes, like the bourgeoisie (French for burghers), grew to become formidable opponents, and occasional allies, of the ruling elite classes. The elite sought to hold on to their status by legal and religious means, which worked, but the economic push to a monied economy meant that they needed the merchant class more frequently. Women within all classes found new avenues to education and economic security, even if they were often curtailed by the patriarchal standards of European society. Luxury, in fashion, jewelry, food, and goods, became a hallmark of elite and wealthy classes, much to the consternation of religious classes, who felt ostentation to be a sign of ego and pride. The growth of primogeniture (inheritance by the eldest son only) and monogamous marriages in the elite classes changed the patterns of land ownership in some of the larger countries, and many younger sons moved to work for their brothers, sought their own territories to rule, or moved into new professions. All these changes were made possible by the large class of peasant labor, who farmed and fed the elite and merchant classes.

The Place of Women in Europe

Women in medieval Europe lived within their social classes, as women did in all other cultures. Noblewomen began gaining more educational opportunities, and more merchant women gained literacy as long-distance trade opportunities for their husbands increased, leaving them in control of the shops. Some women owned their own businesses or workshops, which often employed other women of lower status. Despite these advancements, a woman's primary duty was to marry and bear sons for her husband's patrimony. Women of all classes could inherit and pass on property, but were legally minors and could not represent themselves in court. For most European women, property was handled by husbands and passed along to sons, but women could pass their property (including clothing, jewelry, books, and land) to their daughters. Burgher women (married to or acting as merchants in cities) often did control and give out their property, as did women of the elite classes. We know that some daughters of noble families also learned to fight, especially in the central medieval period, because most military training took place in the context of the noble household.

Christianity allowed some women to live outside the bonds of marriage and motherhood; however, only elite women were afforded this luxury, as monasteries required an entrance fee and women used their dowry (goods and money brought by women into a marriage) to enter monastic spaces. Nuns were often highly educated and wealthy women and, like their male peers, still connected to their natal families. Some nunneries, like Wilton in southern England, became "finishing schools" for elite girls, functioning as educational spaces for wealthy girls who would return to secular life and marry. Girls learned reading, writing, math, and how to comport themselves within their political and economic class.

An example of the connections between monastic and royal spaces is the monastery at Gandersheim in northern Germany. Their strong ties with the emperor of Germany and the connections aided both the empire and the abbey. One of the more famous abbesses, Gerberga, was granddaughter and daughter of kings and niece to the sitting emperor, Otto I (936–973). Her abbey became a center of learning and produced one of the finest writers of the medieval era: Hrotsvita of Gandersheim. Hrotsvita (pronounced "Roswitha") was the first German playwright and the first German historian. She was also the first northern European to write about Islam, which she references in her history of the Ottonian empire. She wrote hagiographies, theology, grammar and logic, poetry, and letters. She was specially chosen to write her history book, which she personally presented to Otto II. Her plays are rife with humor and show the female-only environments of the monasteries as places of joy and learning.

Other abbeys became centers of artistic excellence, creating beautiful handwritten books, tapestries, and vestments. Recently, a female skeleton from Dalheim, Germany, was found with flecks of ultramarine embedded in her front teeth. The color is created from the stone lapis lazuli, found only in Afghanistan and worth its weight in gold. She was an illuminator of manuscripts and she must have placed her paintbrush often in her front teeth, perhaps as she contemplated her next color or line. Ultramarine was often used to color expensive manuscripts, and this skeleton shows the importance of women to the luxury book trade in medieval Europe.

Wealthy women could also be educated outside monastic walls, although we find them only rarely. A prominent example is Heloise (ca. 1090–1164), a highly educated wealthy young woman in Paris. She was *nominatissima*, "the most renowned" woman of her day, literate in Latin, Greek, and Hebrew. Her education brought her to the attention of Peter Abelard (ca. 1079–1142), a famously exasperating philosopher who sought to tutor this most erudite young woman, whose learning was supreme and rare. Abelard's ego and his desire for Heloise overcame his professional obligations and it ended with him in desperate straits. He taught Heloise philosophy (his specialty) and soon their hands "strayed more to each other than their books." They began a tempestuous love affair that ended with a secret marriage, her pregnancy, and his forced castration. Heloise fought the marriage, preferring to remain Abelard's lover, saying: "Scholars and nursemaids, writing desks and cradles, a book and a distaff, a pen and a spindle – what harmony can there be in that?" At her pregnancy and with her guardian's insistence, Abelard married Heloise in secret and they sent their young son, Astrolabe, to be raised by Abelard's sister. (An astrolabe is an instrument used to make astronomical observations to determine latitude.)

The marriage was soon exposed; Abelard was castrated by hired assailants, his professional life destroyed, and his life ruined. Heloise's uncle insisted that she become a nun, and Abelard fled to monastic life in shame. At almost all points of their story, Abelard seems driven by his ego and his desires, and Heloise is the voice of reason and rationality. After years of wandering between monasteries, Abelard wrote a small book, today named the *Historia Calamitatum*, or the *Story of my Misfortunes*. Rightly furious at her treatment within the account, Heloise penned a scathing letter to Abelard, their first contact in ten years. Throughout the letter, she pointedly tells him, "Think of what you owe me," and she demands he answer her. Through the next several years, the two exchange letters on a variety of topics – all in Latin. Heloise's letters are written in poetic form while Abelard's are in prose. Although Heloise despised the idea of her enclosure, she became abbess of her small monastery. Despite being the Superior in the abbey, in a rare moment for medieval writing, Heloise shows her reluctance to be a nun and her inner turmoil that she thinks often of their carnal love and not of God's love. The letters between Heloise and Abelard show us a bright and driven woman, one who demanded to be treated as an equal, who stood toe-to-toe against one of the finest philosophers of the age, and who generally out-wrote and out-argued him. Today, one can visit a nineteenth-century monument to these lovers at Père Lachaise cemetery in Paris.

Religious structures in many places in the world dictated much of a woman's life from marriage, motherhood, widowhood, and death. Marriage in Europe changed during this period. To curb men leaving their wives and children, divorce was forbidden by religious edict, and setting aside a wife became more difficult than it had been in previous years. This brought religious bureaucracy into the realm of marriage, which previously had been strictly personal and civil unions. Consent of the bride became another important idea urged by religious leaders. To prevent child-marriages and coercion in early marriages, religious institutions insisted on consent to marriage: both parties needed to say "I do" in front of witnesses for a marriage to be valid. These movements on consent and divorce brought religious bureaucratic involvement in personal marriages; in fact, marriage became a sacrament in Christianity during the Middle Ages, as medieval theologians argued that marriage was an instrument of sanctification.

Conclusion

Separating people and boxing them within categories based on their birth and assigning social and political value to them based on class is incongruent with much progressive thought. Nevertheless, these premodern structures are vital to understanding how cultures viewed their relationships with each other and with the wider world. Although we see a large divide between the wealthy nobility and the lowly farmer, in reality, most cultures had a mix of people at each class who helped to check the privilege and power of that class. Legal and social rules followed class lines, with the law favoring those with power and wealth over poorer groups. Acting within one's class and following the traditions may have confined the individual, but it protected the group. In every case, women constituted a subset of any class, experiencing significant restrictions. As we see in the next section, those people who acted outside the bounds of their class, gender, or rank were seen as dangerous. They challenged authority and structure and, in doing so, showed the limits that class had within any society.

B: OUTSIDERS

Evidence: *Laxdaela Saga*

Ramayana

Journey to the West

One Thousand and One Nights

Maya *Dresden Codex*

Introduction

As the first section of this chapter showed us, premodern societies sought to create order through caste and gender. Social, political, legal, and religious needs followed class lines. Often, people work out their ideas of justice or outrage at injustice through stories about outsiders. Separating insiders from outsiders is a complex social practice. Sometimes an insider becomes an outsider through destructive behavior that threatens or disrupts communal norms, and incurs the punishment of imprisonment, execution, or exile. They have acted outside the law. Other times, people from outside the community are excluded because they are perceived to be a threat; they are "the other," with unfamiliar or stigmatized physical characteristics, food preferences, spiritual practices, or languages. For real and imagined reasons, insiders fear them and sustain narratives that support these fears. Whatever the root cause of social rejection, stories about outsiders in all their forms – outlaws, outcasts, out-groups, the "other" – are centrally important to defining social conditions and cultural norms. By thinking about and examining examples of what a culture deems to be criminal, dangerous, disturbing, and even evil, societies question and define what is respectable and just.

From a thousand years in the future, we can tell a lot about cultures by reading their stories; whether written or oral, tales compel us to ask important questions. What's at stake? When a tribe accepted new members, was it strengthened or jeopardized? If a ruling class tolerated people who were not of the mainstream religion, did the society flourish or fail? Below are four examples of treatment of outsiders. First, the story of a pagan ghost in the Icelandic *Laxdaela Saga* is a way of managing fear of social and supernatural disruption. It is superstitious and yet quite practical: ghosts exist and must be dealt with, so the living can do their work. Second, embedded in the Indian *Ramayana* is a story of exile in which Prince Rama faces challenges that teach him how to behave as a just king. Some of these lessons come from his loyal wife, Sita, and his noble brother, Lakshmana; however, the best model is Hanuman the monkey-man. By his very nature, Hanuman is outside humanity, but he is used as a model of an ideal heroic character. We can also examine conceptions of integrity and decency through another popular monkey character, the Chinese Monkey King, our third story. His hyperactive creativity and curiosity needed limits. And, finally the fourth story, the tale of Scheherazade – a sexual slave with no rights, who, through her crafty, unexpected stories, humanizes a despot with stories of outcasts.

Killer Hrapp

Composed in the mid-thirteenth century in Old Norse, *Laxdaela Saga* records the migration of a family from Sweden to Iceland and the experiences of generations that settled the lands and sorted out both real-life problems and ones that are more superstitious and fantastical. An unforgettable character of the story is Killer Hrapp, a ranting, offensive man whose behavior tests the laws and customs of this new society. Respecting his right to govern his own life and property as he sees fit, villagers steer clear of his house and his aggressive verbal and physical abuse. Finally, aged and debilitated, he demands that upon death he be buried feet down/head up under the threshold of his door. His burial demands are honored, a sign of the culture's respect for individual rights, and there his ghost exists at the threshold of life and death, terrorizing his home and neighbors from the grave.

But because his behavior had gone uncorrected in life, he is much worse when dead. He haunts the property, killing most of the servants and livestock and driving his widow and survivors to desert the farm. To secure this much-needed arable land, the farmers engage a leader of the community to dig up Hrapp's body and move it away; nonetheless, he continues to curse them all, even his own son, from the outlands. After having lived on the land a short time, Hrapp's son loses his mind, but Ghost Hrapp meets his match in Olaf Peacock, a responsible community leader who has the respect and trust of his kinsmen. He annexes Hrapp's property, and when he realizes that Hrapp haunts the barn and terrorizes Olaf's field hands, he goes to Hrapp's grave site, digs up the body (which is eerily preserved), cremates it, and has the ashes taken out to sea. This is the end of Hrapp's mischief.

What is at stake? Killer Hrapp did not steal fire from the gods and give it to humans. He did not lie to get someone killed. He did not imprison a noble and virtuous woman in an enchanted castle. In this case, the trickster terrorized the farmhands, disrupting the regular care and maintenance of the homestead, clearly an unforgivable and life-threatening act for this isolated group. Through Hrapp, we learn what these early Icelanders feared. Survival was difficult in this island touching the Arctic Circle, where the growing season is short and the nearest neighbor far across a frigid sea. To survive, these subsistence farmers and risk-taking fishermen relied heavily upon each other. No community could tolerate a disrespectful, selfish neighbor like Hrapp, whose nature was as unpredictable in life as in death. As the hero of the story, Olaf is not a demigod with superhuman strength or divine magic; instead, he is a good citizen with common sense and integrity toward his fellows. He stands for justice, defined as respect for one's neighbors, their property, and the power of nature to wipe them all out. The community cannot tolerate a meddling poltergeist. Killer Hrapp pushes the community to define a limit on personal freedom: it is against the law to kill people, other people's livestock, and drive them off their own property. And that is why Hrapp is an outlaw.

Rama and Hanuman

One primary issue of *Laxdaela Saga* is how rights and property are passed down to future generations, and this concern is a prevalent topic of medieval stories and mythologies. Who owns and rules the land? And who deserves to own and rule that land? This question is one of many taken up by the massive Indian epic *Ramayana* (*The Journey of Rama*), a 24,000-verse epic composed in Sanskrit possibly as early as the 6th century BCE. It is attributed to a poet named Valmiki, who supposedly lived in the Ganges Plain of northern India, but the epic was added to for over 1,000 years. The text became part of a powerful artistic tradition and across the Indian subcontinent to Persia, Arabia, China, and most parts of Southeast Asia artists copied, drew, and recited the *Ramayana*. The majority of texts of the *Ramayana* are from the medieval period, from the sixth to the sixteenth centuries, and one of the oldest written witnesses is on palm leaves dated to the eleventh century CE. It was and still is memorized and recited by oral storytellers called *bhopa*.

Rama is the son of a king and the embodiment of Vishnu, the god dedicated to fostering a moral balance. One of the most striking episodes begins when Rama's father, the king, lies dying. Rama is worthy, noble, and talented, but he is the son of a second wife and not the chosen heir. When the king dies, the first wife banishes Rama to the forest for 14 years. Rama dutifully obeys; he follows the divine law, dharma, which requires unquestioning honor and respect for fathers and wise elders. Rama's wife, Sita, and younger brother, Lakshmana, accompany him in his exile, also following the divine law and respecting their family unit. Adherence to dharma is to strive for ideal behavior in an imperfect world, and the epic rehearses the tension between earthly demands and desires and spiritual righteousness.

Rama has much to learn from the world beyond his kingdom. Outside the kingdom and outside the law, he has many experiences that test and define ideals of justice in dramatic terms. In a significant episode in Rama's exile, the demon king Ravana abducts Sita, his sister-in-law, sweeping her off in a flying golden chariot. She leaves a trail of veils and jewels, and these are found by a tribe of *vanara*, monkey-like humans. The epic takes this opportunity to show a race of outsiders, nearly human but not quite, who exhibit laudable self-governance and honor. They debate how to rescue the captive princess, and the *vanara* king sends the gallant and earnest Hanuman to investigate the situation. For a time, the focus of the narrative shifts from Rama to this wonderful hero with many powers: he can change size at will, morphing into a giant or shrinking to pocket size; he can travel by leaping from cloud to cloud; and perhaps his greatest skill is the ability to recognize truth and goodness and use his cleverness to protect both.

This episode of the *Ramayana* is called the *Sundarakanda*, the story of Sundara, one of Hanuman's nicknames. He taps into all his many extraordinary powers to rescue the virtuous heroine. Growing to behemoth size, he launches himself from a mountainside into the wind and flies to the demon's island. He evades the evil guardian of the island, the naga queen who turns into a giant serpent. He makes himself tiny, disappears into her cavernous mouth, tears out of her belly, and escapes. Eight hundred miles later, he arrives at Lanka and finds Sita; however, she forbids him from liberating her. Her loyalty dictates

Fig 8.7
Nearly human, Hanuman is marked as a monkey just by his face and tail. This eleventh-century figure is from the Chola Kingdom of southeastern India.
Metropolitan Museum of Art, Purchase, Bequests of Mary Clarke Thompson, Fanny Shapiro, Susan Dwight Bliss, Isaac D. Fletcher, William Gedney Beatty, John L. Cadwalader and Kate Read Blacque, Gifts of Mrs. Samuel T. Peters, Ida H. Ogilvie, Samuel T. Peters and H. R. Bishop, F. C. Bishop and O. M. Bishop, Rogers, Seymour and Fletcher Funds, and other gifts, funds and bequests from various donors, by exchange, 1982, 1982.220.9

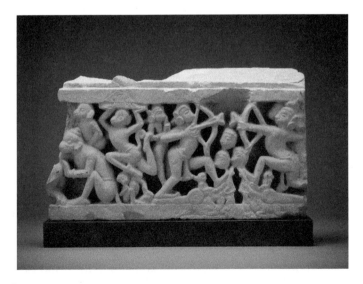

Fig 8.8
On the left of this tenth-century carving from India, Hanuman holds healing herbs, and on the right, he fights Ravana.
Los Angeles County Museum of Art, Anonymous gift (M.89.159.1)

Fig 8.9
Statues of monkey soldiers of Hanuman's army on guard at Banteay Srei temple at
Angkor Wat in Siem Reap, Cambodia.
kool99 / iStock

that she not be touched by another man. It is Rama's prerogative to make the
heroic rescue. Sita recognizes the human within Hanuman, the semi-human
forest dweller, modeling the best qualities of an honorable human being, but
he stays within his station as a not-quite human. As his character develops, his
courage expands to overcome obstacles, while his ego reduces to humble and
discreet proportion. He is flexible and accommodating, chooses discipline over
desire, and remains in his place in the social order. He is the intersection of our
animal tendencies and human intellectual potential – an example of how individual integrity contributes to communal justice.

Monkey King

The earliest Chinese Monkey stories are from the Tang dynasty (618–907) and
feature a monkey hero who resembles Hanuman in his capacity to conquer
demons. A written record of this version of the monkey-man exists in the Ming
dynasty (1368–1644) novel called *Journey to the West*. Considered in Chinese
culture to be one of four great works of literature, *Journey to the West* is based on
the life of Xuanzang (602–664), an early Tang-dynasty Buddhist monk who, in
629, traveled to recover original Buddhist thought from gurus in India. *Journey
to the West* presents Xuanzang as "Tripitaka," or three baskets, which alludes
to the Buddha's three baskets of scriptures. Early in Tripitaka's journey, he
encounters several traveling companions, most notably, Monkey.

Monkey has the superhuman powers of Hanuman but lacks humility and refinement. He is more of a light-hearted cautionary figure of how humans punish themselves by subverting and defying order. He is a happy and expansive character, delighted with himself and with others. He, however, cannot see beyond his own impulsive desires, moving from imaginative games to mischievous pranks, heedless of the egocentric destruction left in his wake. His very state of mind is ungoverned. His behavior is an admonitory tale, reminding us how lack of self-control has wide consequences for others. While it is fun to read stories about him, it would be no fun to be like him or ruled by him. Monkey is born out of a stone egg, half human/half animal, half real/half fantastic. Like Hanuman, he can call on many talents. He can change shape. He can cover great distances by bouncing from cloud to cloud. His "weapon" is a sliver of wood, and if he is threatened, or merely bored, he can make it into a giant club as big as a tree trunk. By blowing on one of his own hairs, he can create a phalanx of other little monkeys. Intoxicated with his own clever powers, Monkey calls himself "Great Sage Equaling Heaven." After his monkey cohort elevates him to be their king, he sets out to find wonders, encountering Tripitaka along the way.

Monkey dedicates himself, impetuously and thoughtlessly, to the monk's pilgrimage/mission, but cannot help seeking out glory or resist his own curiosity. He has only shallowly considered his own motives for joining the project. He is both the major force compelling them on and the major force resisting progress. He earnestly swears to help Tripitaka, but regularly puts the monk in danger. Nimbly moving between tiny acts and grand ones, Monkey exhibits how our everyday abilities can be amplified into incredible power. Humans have tremendous talent and capacity for invention, but those abilities can be used to create good or evil. In a combination of insecurity and hubris, we find ourselves in a paradox: creating destruction.

When Tripitaka is at his wits' end with Monkey's irresponsibility, he happens upon a spirit woman who offers him a solution – a magical cap and a spell for activating its power. Finding the hat irresistibly shiny, Monkey steals it and sneaks off to try it on. Tripitaka intones the charm, and the cap shrinks, constricting Monkey's mind and impulses until he is paralyzed in thought and action – stopped in his tracks and forced to focus on his behavior.

Much of Monkey's example comments on how quickly our human minds get bored and restless. When our lives are regular and comfortable, we itch for new challenges, new territory, or new company. We chafe against rules and laws that constrict our behavior. A fundamental challenge of human happiness is striking a balance between routine and novelty without causing ourselves and others anguish and despair. In addition, just like Monkey, we need company, an audience to show off for, and selfish, unpredictable behavior drives away that community. At any moment, just like Monkey, we can become our own worst enemies, destabilizing the social order that allows us to flourish and the delicate balance between social and spiritual law. Through a mythological creature, audiences are reminded of the benefits of maintaining the social hierarchies.

Monkey-humans

Across cultures, monkeys represent so many aspects and projections of human behavior that it is impossible to link monkey imagery to a specific culture or metaphor. Monkeys are physically similar to humans. To "ape" someone is to copy them. In fact, the English adjective simian is from Latin *simius*, which is also the root of "similar." Over the course of the European medieval period, monkeys and apes were used both as twisted images of human sin and comical parodies of human activities. They are less-than-human, and therefore representations of our less-sophisticated actions. They live in the jungles and forests outside human civilization but are also the monkey in our minds.

In Europe, people consulted books called bestiaries for information about animals. Not scientifically reliable, bestiaries mixed up facts about real animals with misinformation about animals from far-off places and mythological animals. Information about unicorns existed alongside information about foxes. In most bestiaries, monkeys took on the symbolic weight of good and evil. Initially used as symbols of the devil and of specific sins such as deviousness and greed, they were also represented as creative and joyful, at play in the world, both outsiders and insiders.

Within this period, monkeys roamed freely across Japanese islands. In Shinto, the indigenous faith of Japan, there was a spirit, or *kami*, named Sarutahiko, a

Fig 8.10

An illumination for a thirteenth-century bestiary depicts a monkey or ape carrying its two babies as it flees hunters. She clings to the baby she favors, ignoring the baby gripping her back. Eventually in exhaustion she drops the beloved baby, but the hated baby survives. One interpretation of the image was a lesson not to hold too tightly to earthly desire. The baby she grasps to her chest is riches and power and the baby on her back is the sin of greed.

Album / Alamy Stock Photo

Fig 8.11
Manuscript illuminators regularly placed humorous monkeys in the margins of otherwise serious texts. This illustration from a fourteenth-century Latin Christian prayer book features a monkey leisurely roasting a pig on a spit.
Stowe MS 17 f.176r Page from 'Book of Hours, Use of Maastricht' ('The Maastricht Hours') / Bridgeman images

monkey-man deity who served as a messenger between the human and the divine worlds, a god who stood between heaven and Earth. A god of strength and guidance, Sarutahiko is known as the patron of travelers, roads, aikido, and the father of female court and religious dancers. Today, students buy monkey masks from Sarutahiko's shrine to help them pass their arduous school exams, and houses display masks to ward off evil and bring proper guidance to the household. The monkey kamis were friends of horses, and, important to this chapter, a representative of those who do not fit into proscribed social roles.

The Maya culture of Mesoamerica worshiped a monkey god and respected the native howler monkey. The *Popol Vuh* is the central religious text of the pre-Columbian Maya. Prominent characters in this creation story are half-brothers or twins who have been turned into monkeys. Despite this punishment, the howler monkey gods are connected with writing and creativity, acknowledgment of the natural creativity and curiosity of monkeys in general.

Fig 8.12
In Mesoamerica, the howler monkey was the patron god of writing and creativity, and spider monkeys represented fertility and sensuality. This monkey-god statue is at the Archeological Site of Copan in Honduras, built in the fifth–ninth centuries.
Siempreverde22 / iStock

WERE IMAGES OF APES USED AS RACIST IMAGERY LIKE THEY ARE TODAY?

Many medieval cultures used images of monkeys to comment on human behavior because simians were close to, but not quite, humans. The Latin phrase "ars simia natura" means "art is the ape of nature," which describes one of the goals of the artist's craft: to imitate nature the way apes imitate human behavior. But, medieval artists did not make a clear link between monkeys and Africans. Christian beliefs about whiteness and light being associated with God, and blackness or darkness being connected with the devil, tropes which grew throughout the medieval period, however, led to dark pigment carrying anti-Black connotations. And in the early modern and modern periods, monkey images came to be associated with Blacks. From the mid-fifteenth century onward, white Europeans developed increasingly racist ideas about Black Africans as the trans-Atlantic slave trade escalated. Whites justified enslavement based on false ideas that Black individuals were subhuman, closer to apes than to "full" (meaning white) humans.

However, medieval European depictions of Africans and other marginalized people – including Jews, Muslims, and Mongols – in manuscripts, world maps, tapestries, stained glass, and more were filled with many derogatory symbols. By the twelfth century, Jews were regularly depicted in ways that suggested they were greedy, secretive, and dangerous to Christian society. Across the later medieval period, Jews were increasingly blamed for the death of Christ and were falsely accused of hoarding gold, killing Christian children, stealing and abusing the Christian sacramental wafer, and other nasty deeds. Images of Jews showed them wearing distinctive pointy hats, with exaggeratedly large, hooked noses (linked with evil and greed), dark skin, long beards, and threatening grins with bared teeth; they often carried bags of gold or daggers.

These images increasingly were related to images of demons and the devil himself, to whom they were also linked by evil behavior and a supposed formal alliance. Likewise, anti-Semitic imagery shared a number of symbols with negative depictions of Africans, Mongols, Muslims, and monsters – all of whom were shown in European art with disfigured or exaggerated physiognomy, often naked or wearing little clothing (a sign of "barbarity"), and with enlarged sexual organs to depict their supposed perversity. And, as the devil and demons came to be depicted regularly using black or brown paint, the link between darkness, evil, sin, and negative stereotypes of outsiders was cemented.

Slavery and Difference

Sometimes, the powerless are not on the physical outskirts of society but suffer in the very center of it. Even if communities have a strict rule of law, it favors a small elite class, and the rest suffer from ill treatment and disregard. Some of our favorite stories feature oppressed characters who become agents of much-needed change, disrupting an unjust system or using cunning deception to defend a community against exploitation. Although the stories known now as *One Thousand and One Nights* or *The Arabian Nights* were not collected into their current form until the late eighteenth century, many of the tales were known as early as the eighth century. They are an amalgam of Indian, Arabian, and Persian stories set in a frame tale about a harem concubine determined to change the behavior of a sultan who sleeps with a maiden every night only to murder her in the morning.

Eventually the sultan meets his match: Scheherazade, the daughter of his advisor. Although she has no choice but to join the sultan's harem, she determines not to lose her life. Night after night she narrates engrossing tales, and morning after morning the sultan cannot bear to kill his storyteller. Her survival depends on carefully constructing her dramatic episodes, so the sultan remains in perpetual suspense and cannot bear to destroy her. She promises her father that either she will die as a martyr to inspire other women, or live and deliver them from this fate. She is willing to use every trick she has and die trying.

One Thousand and One Nights is a frame tale, which means there is an outer story (Scheherazade's efforts to keep the sultan from executing her by enchanting him with her stories) and then stories within that story. Each story Scheherazade tells is about a narrator who tells his story, which is about other storytellers. Like nesting dolls, each folktale contains characters who invent other characters, all of them telling their own lies, excuses, and histories, until we are lost in a wonderful maze of narratives about commoners and outliers. And each nested tale has the same theme: characters who are falsely accused and mercilessly abused tell stories to save themselves from execution. They are focused on getting a powerful man to show generosity of spirit and pardon them, which is Scheherazade's message to the sultan.

Many are familiar with the stories attributed to Scheherazade of Sindbad the Sailor and Aladdin and his magic lamp. Both hapless men are marooned or trapped on islands or in deserts trying to find their way back into community through supernatural means. They are the definition of outlaws, stateless exiles, undesirables isolated outside a country. But other stories demonstrate the plight of those discriminated against for gender, sexuality, and disability. One of the story cycles begins as the "Tale of the Hunchback," and by the end sounds like a tasteless joke: a tailor, a Christian, a Jew, and a steward are brought before a king because of the violent death of a disabled beggar.

The story begins with the hunchback, a diverting street performer, whom a tailor and his wife invite to dinner. Thinking it a hilarious entertainment, the tailor's wife crams a large piece of fish into the hunchback's mouth and forces him to swallow it. The hunchback chokes and dies. From this brutal beginning, the story rampages through many episodes. To get rid of the evidence, the tailor puts the corpse out on a stairway, and a Jew trips over it, sure that he has killed the person lying under his feet. To escape blame, the Jewish man throws the corpse into his Muslim neighbor's yard. The steward of this household sees the corpse and thinks it is an intruder, pummels it with a mallet, and when he is sure he killed the trespasser, he throws the corpse in an alley. Here a Christian stumbles upon it. Unnerved by its grisly aspect, the Christian beats the body and calls the authorities. Ultimately it is all tracked back to the tailor, who, to stave off execution, tells an involved lie about how a barber killed the hunchback.

Scheherazade (or the folk tale attributed to her) then weaves together another series of stories, one from each of the six brothers of the barber, until we are looped back to the present state of the barber, on trial for his life and out of stories, who takes out iron forceps from his pocket, puts them down the hunchback's throat, and pulls out the fishbone. With a violent sneeze the hunchback springs to his feet and praises Allah. What does the officiating king do? He bestows robes of honor on the Jew, the Muslim, the Christian, the steward, the hunchback, and the barber, and then appoints the tailor to his court, where he becomes the king's drinking companion.

This is a lot of wishful fantasy about empowerment of the poor and the disabled, all persuasively narrated by a person less powerful even than they – a concubine. A harem is a culturally authorized form of sexual slavery, and *One Thousand and One Nights* is frank about that environment. Her job is to make her body available and alluring for sex. As a trickster figure, Scheherazade and her stories provide a voice for respecting and liberating the subservient. Should a disabled body be dragged and kicked around the neighborhood? No. Do a tailor, barber, and servant have any moral or ethical right to justice? They should. Can a woman be purchased, raped, and murdered? Not without consequences, because, in fact, she may be able to save them all; she has the power of creating life. During the course of 1,001 nights, Scheherazade conceives and delivers three boys for this sultan. A common ending for the story collection features the sultan as a reformed potentate, now merciful and fair, reigning over an enlightened kingdom, surrounded by his happy family.

Out-groups

Many people within societies performed work deemed "unsavory" by the upper classes and were also restricted and shunned by elites. Butchers, night-soil collectors, and dyers often lived on the margins of the towns, and of society. As we saw above, it took skill and extensive knowledge to source, create, and use color. Nonetheless, instead of being at the center of the artisanal neighborhoods, dye workshops were normally on the outskirts of town. The chemical processes used to extract or distill dye fluids often produced sulfur, which smells like rotten eggs, and actual rotten eggs were used as a binder for paints. In addition, great barrels of old urine lined the outside walls of a dye shop. The way to make a dye stick to fabrics is to first soak the fabric in a what is called a mordant (or fixative), and the best and most readily available mordant was the ammonia in stale urine. Urine was also used to soften and whiten cloth and leather. Another fixative was alum, which was harvested in Central Africa and commonly traded to the Islamic world and across the Mediterranean. Many common medieval commercial goods that were shipped under the broad category of "spices" were actually dyestuffs and mordants like alum.

Another reason that dye workshops were isolated at the margins of medieval cities is that many of the ingredients were poisonous. Orpimint, a vivid and popular yellow, is a highly toxic arsenic compound. Lead white caused madness. The prestigious royal red vermillion was made from the mineral cinnabar, which contains mercury, and mistakes in processing it caused mercury poisoning. The buildup of ammonia from urine could explode, if enclosed and exposed to high heat. Despite these risks, the reward of brightly colored clothing was too appealing for medieval people to pass up, and many urban craftsmen grew wealthy through participation in the dyeing trade.

Another measure of a culture is how it cares for the poor, sick, and disabled. Are there systems in place and moral imperatives to care for these individuals? Or are they outcasts, left to suffer and die? The Abrahamic faiths present a God who requires his worshippers to take care of those in need. In Judaic practice, taking care of the sick or providing food for the poor is a mitzvah, or a good deed that honors God's commandments. In Christian teachings, Christ and his miracles of healing provide models of decent behavior toward those who suffer. He enacts the Golden Rule: "do unto others as you would have done to you." Similarly, one of the five pillars of Islam is zakat, charity and giving of alms. This act does not require money; service to the community counts as much.

The disabled and poor often lived at the edges of society in medieval Japan and were seen as *ijin* or "different people." These people were liminal persons within Japanese society, at times considered favorably by villagers, other times outcast and seen as suspicious. For example, *Goze* were blind Japanese female musicians who entertained peasant communities in the winter. These independent women lived outside the regular social classes, and religious obligation dictated that they be sheltered, fed, and paid by their audiences (to deny this was to court bad luck for one's house). By the late Middle Ages, they had established their own guilds, which existed into the twentieth century. The medieval European play *The Cure of the Blind Man* encourages its audience to see the blind man as one's own neighbor and one's own kind, for disability is a universal human experience.

Many social supports allowed the disabled to participate in society, especially within the religious spaces of pilgrimage and the seeking of cures at shrines. In much of Africa, disabled individuals were seen as blessed by the gods and given special religious duties within a society, and, as the Middle Ages progressed, secular authorities in Europe began social welfare programs to aid the elderly, poor, and the disabled within their communities. Class concerns and resources often determined the fate of the sick or disabled. If a family had wealth already, disabled children might be viewed as bringing happiness and divine purpose to a family, but a poor family might regard a disabled child as a curse, as the money needed for their care could be difficult to obtain. Unfortunately, we often say one thing and do the opposite, but the models for compassionate and inclusive behavior are there to follow, even a thousand years ago.

Fig 8.13
Christ healing the blind man and raising Lazarus from the dead from a cycle of wall paintings in the church of San Baudelio in northern Castilla (Spain), possibly 1129–1134.
Metropolitan Museum of Art, Gift of The Clowes Fund Incorporated and E.B. Martindale, 1959, 59.196

Fig 8.14
A begging leper missing an arm and leg is painted in the margin of an early
fifteenth-century manuscript. Although the manuscript text is in Latin, the banner
above the figure is in Middle English and translates "some good my gentle master
for God's sake."
Album / Alamy Stock Photo

Looking Forward

Presumably you are reading this book for an academic course. That means you
are literate and seeking an education. These are indications that you live in a
culture that has social mobility, and that you expect to have some choice in
how you will put your talents, interests, and knowledge to work in your society.
You have the opportunity to develop your skills and choose how to use them
to attain economic and social security. It is difficult for those of us in this fortu-
nate position to understand how strict and even sacred class distinctions were
in the medieval period and in some cultures today. Some of this is protection
of resources. Those who have resources want to keep them and will support a
social structure that secures their privileges. These elites codify laws and rites
that ensure their power, and their ideas of justice prevail for a time. But communities also follow religious texts and customs, dedicated to a divine law that
proscribes their earthly occupation and status.

Members of every generation and class contemplate just, moral, and ethical
behavior for secular and religious practice. As an abstract principle, justice is
defined by its opposite. Until we take offense at an action or attitude, until we
find a behavior or an act repulsive and unacceptable, we do not know what

we consider to be fair and righteous. Whether fictional or historical, outsiders define the lines between acceptable and taboo, and the just and the criminal. The figures described here – Killer Hrapp, Rama and Hanuman, the Chinese Monkey King, and Scheherazade – challenge cultural norms about decent and constructive community conduct. They do so in story, but enduring stories, repeated and respected by figures with power over others. They demonstrate the dangers and the advantages of challenging authority. The big message is that, no matter how hard humans struggle to establish and sustain order, chaos is always lurking around the edges, and human beings make sense of this chaos through a constant process of evaluating who is in and who is out.

Research Questions

1. All societies have a class system, but the class categories differ depending on what a society values. In one community, strong, aggressive, young men may have elite status and elderly men are considered a burden. In another, elderly men who communicate with gods may have the highest status. How would you describe the class you belong to? Who might be your counterpart be in the medieval period?
2. How could motherhood confer authority upon a woman?
3. Read selections from Heian women's writing. What importance did the women place on class within their society?
4. There are many ways of identifying what class a person belongs to and stereotyping them by outward appearance. Sometimes outward appearance is a conscious act of self-expression. Sometimes outward appearance is controlled by societal norms. Choose a culture from this chapter and investigate how class was communicated through such things as the type and color of clothing, physical features, possession of goods and tools, and intellectual abilities such as literacy.
5. Investigate animal fables from one culture or follow the symbolism of a particular animal across a number of cultures. What do animal fables tell us about the personality of a culture? Which animals are seen as comic relief and which ones are part of teaching a lesson about human behavior?
6. Disability studies is a growing field. Investigate medieval peoples' ideas about disabilities. What were the social, medical, religious, and cultural aspects of disability?

Further Reading

Buckley Ebrey, Patricia, ed. *Chinese Civilization: A Sourcebook.* New York: Free Press, 1993.

Christenson, Allen J. *Popol Vuh: Sacred Book of the Maya: The Great Classic of Central American Spirituality, Translated from the Original Maya Text. Quiché Maya*

People. Norman: University of Oklahoma Press, 2003. Electronic version: Mesoweb: www.mesoweb.com/publications/

de Sahagún, Bernardino. *The War of Conquest: How it Was Waged Here in Mexico*. Salt Lake City: University of Utah Press, 1978.

Eaton, Richard M., and Phillip B. Wagoner. *Power, Memory, Architecture: Contested Sites on India's Deccan Plateau, 1300–1600*. Oxford: Oxford Scholarship Online, 2013.

Ebrey, Patricia Buckley. *Women and the Family in Chinese History*. Abingdon: Routledge, 2002.

Finlay, Victoria. *Color: A Natural History of the Palette*. New York: Random House, 2002.

Goldin, Paul Rakita. *The Culture of Sex in Ancient China*. Honolulu: University of Hawai'i Press, 2002.

Kellogg, Susan. *Weaving the Past: A History of Latin America's Indigenous Women from the Prehispanic Period to the Present*. New York: Oxford University Press, 2005.

Levitan, William. *Abelard and Heloise: The Letters and Other Writings*. Indianapolis, IN: Hackett Publishing, 2007.

Lutegendorf, Philip. *Hanuman's Tale: The Messages of a Divine Monkey*. Oxford: Oxford University Press, 2007.

McNab, Cameron Hunt. *Medieval Disability Sourcebook: Western Europe*. Goleta, CA: Punctum Books, 2020.

Metzler, Irina. *Disability in Medieval Europe: Thinking about Physical Impairment during the High Middle Ages*. Oxford: Routledge, 2006.

Mews, Constant. *The Lost Love Letters of Heloise and Abelard: Perceptions of Dialogue in Twelfth-Century France*. New York: Palgrave MacMillan, 1999; 2nd edition, 2008.

Morrison, Elizabeth, and Larisa Grollemond. *Book of Beasts: The Bestiary in the Medieval World*. Los Angeles: J. Paul Getty Museum, 2019.

Mvuyekure, Pierre-Damien. *West African Kingdoms, 500–1590*. Detroit, MI: Gale, 2004.

Rehman, S. A., and Balraj Verma, eds. *The Beautiful India – Andhra Pradesh*. New Delhi: Ess Ess Publications, 2005.

Scher, Sarahh, and Billie Follensbee, eds. *Dressing the Part: Power, Dress, Gender, and Representation in the Pre-Columbian Americas*. Gainesville: University Press of Florida, 2017.

Singh, Sabita. *The Politics of Marriage in Medieval India: Gender and Alliance in Rajasthan*. Oxford: Oxford Scholarship Online, 2019.

St. Clair, Kassia. *The Secret Lives of Color*. New York: Penguin, 2016.

Sundarakanda from the *Ramayana*. PDF download www.holybooks.com/sundara-kanda-hanumans-odysey/.

A Tale of Flowering Fortunes: Annals of Japanese Aristocratic Life in the Heian Period. Translated, with an introduction and notes, by William H. and Helen Craig McCullough. Stanford, CA: Stanford University Press, 1980.

Watson, Frank. *One Hundred Leaves: A New Annotated Translation of Hyakunin Isshu*. New York: Plum White Press, 2013.

Wu, Cheng-en. *Monkey*. Trans. by Arthur Waley. New York: Grove Press, 1970.

Section IV

1300–1500

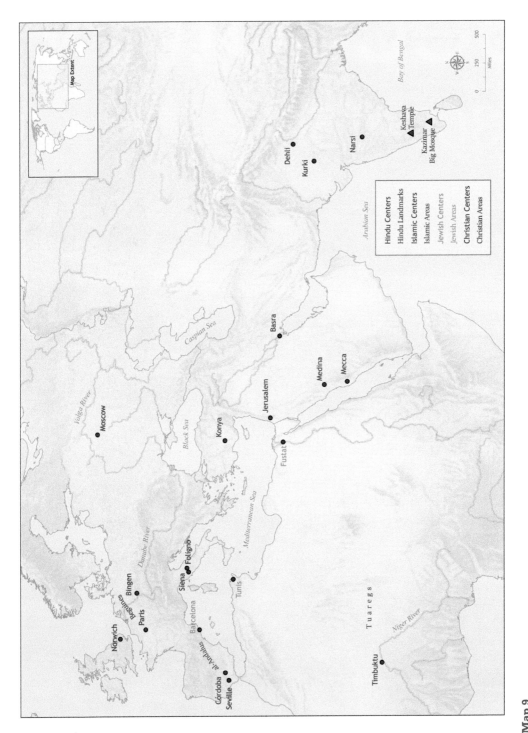

Map 9
Devotion

9 Devotion

Religion, 1300–1500

Introduction

In the first chapter on religion, we discussed the major monotheistic faiths that influenced Afro-Eurasia from 500 to 900. In the second chapter on religion, we discussed India, China, and the subcontinental region with the massive expansion of Buddhism during the central medieval era. In this last chapter, we discuss the rise of affective religious experiences that permeated several faith traditions. This key development of late medieval religiosity was endemic throughout many of the cultures we have been discussing. We focus, in this chapter, on women's experiences with the spirituality of the late medieval world. This chapter also expands its timeline to include women who lived prior to 1300 and who died after 1500. As Joan Kelly wrote, in her groundbreaking 1977 article "Did Women Have a Renaissance?", women's history must question all accepted historical periodization, as the development of men's history has differing effects on women, and, we might add today, all peoples outside a strict gender binary.

As we have seen in earlier chapters, it behooved sovereigns to have strong connections with religious leaders; religion created group cohesion while also motivating political, social, and cultural decisions and divisions. Throughout Europe, Africa, and the Middle East, the time from 1300 to 1500 was politically unstable, particularly after the traumas of the Black Death in the fourteenth century. Economically, politically, and socially, societies were changing, and we see this directly within the religious ideologies popularized during this time. So-called heretical movements and challenges to religious leadership increased, as people sought more personal and intimate relationships with their gods.

Although these changing religious ideologies affected people of all classes and genders, in this particular chapter we focus on how religion affected and was affected by women. In doing so, we highlight the particular roles of women within the larger movements of religious change, and learn about these larger trends through looking at women's spiritual lives. Despite constraints placed on them by male-controlled religious doctrine, women across the world created religious and spiritual opportunities and spaces for themselves and their concerns. It must be said, piety and spirituality themselves have no gender, except that which is socially constructed. People across time and space have lived within the gender constraints of their worlds, and certain types of customs, beliefs, and behaviors have become known as "female" since those who were coded female were the ones who practiced them. In the first section of this chapter, we discuss the spiritual practices of women within major religious groups around the world. The second section discusses how expanding spiritual consciousness affected literature and art just prior to the modern period.

A: DO NOT DENY ME YOUR ETERNAL BEAUTY

Evidence: Hildegard of Bingen, *Scivias*

Julian of Norwich, *Showings*

Catherine of Siena, *The Dialogue*

Marguerite Porete, *The Mirror of Simple Souls*

Mechtild of Magdeburg, *The Flowing Love of the Godhead*

Rabia al Adawiyya, poetry

Fatimah of Cordoba, poetry

Rumi, poetry

Mirabai, poetry

Akka Mahadevi, poetry

Janabai, poetry

Introduction

In this section, we look at women's major religious experiences around the world. We begin with the textual religions of Hinduism, Christianity, and Islam, and finish with a discussion of sub-Saharan African and Aztec traditions. Women in both traditional and textual religions found ways to express their faith in expansive ways. All religious structures were gendered, with particular ideas for men and women. Most faiths believed in spiritual egalitarianism – that is, all genders had the opportunity to better themselves and reach a promised afterlife. Nevertheless, men almost always occupied the positions of authority within religious structures, and women were denied access to much of the hierarchy. Furthermore, women were often considered as gateways to sin and error.

Women in Religious Traditions

On the whole, women across the world experienced their religions through rituals, oral traditions, and written texts. Men from textual religious faiths often derided female spirituality because women's spirituality seemed to exist outside texts and literate spaces. Women were said to be prone to "superstition" and "paganism," and many clerics thought their more "natural" minds could not understand the nuances of men's rational understanding of religion. And, since women practiced these syncretic beliefs, they could not be trusted with better religious instruction, since they would also pervert the texts and traditions found in formal educational contexts. An example is found in the trial of one of late medieval Europe's most famous women, Joan of Arc, who was arrested and tried for witchcraft and cross-dressing after leading French troops in battle. One question asked at trial was whether, as a child, she had decorated or danced around a tree that fairies were said to visit. She answered that many of the girls and women in her town did so – they sang, danced, and hung wreaths on the fairy tree. Whether this was just child's play or a particular form of local women's devotion is unclear. This practice was taken as evidence that Joan was not a proper Christian, did not fully understand her Christian faith and practice, and could not be trusted when she said saints spoke to her.

Why, we might ask, did women create different spiritual beliefs? Were they just more attuned to nature? Were they more emotional and therefore needed emotional connection to the divine? For some women, the answer may be yes; but, on the whole, the answer lies in the patriarchal notions of education, religion, and women's bodies. Women in many settled agricultural and urban Eurasian societies were viewed as sub-male, as less capable of intelligence, as earthy and animal (because of childbirth). Their presence eroded the rational and tarnished the divine; through their ungoverned thought and impulsive sexuality, they led men astray. Men denied women access to the religious texts and the education needed to understand them, then derided women for not knowing the texts and the commentaries (educated men's writings on the texts). Women, then, had to seek out other ways to engage with their gods, to interact with divinity, to understand their faiths. And, they did this in ways that also illuminate some of the larger trends in many religions during this time.

A woman's spirituality is as diverse as the individual; it is tied to her religious traditions, her background, and her status. Despite the diversity among women within the same religion, there are some connections we can make about women's faith and spirituality; for instance, women practiced a "householder spirituality" – one connected to her immediate family, extended family, and the larger female community, including ancestors whose spirits were acknowledged in practices of the living. In particular, this type of spirituality was found within rural or lower-class households, although wealthier and urban houses often had similar practices. Women, across cultures, imbued their daily lives with spirituality, using prayer and song to bring the divine into their daily activities. Food, in particular, was an important avenue for bringing faith into the house and into the family. In an era where companies bring fresh meals, ready to cook to our doorsteps, we may have forgotten the intensity of preparing food for families from dawn to dusk. Making flour from grain and creating breads from that grain (leavened or unleavened) took immense time and energy. Often, women worked together, singing, talking, and grinding flour, corn, or oats. Creating rituals around these activities alleviated the monotony; adding prayers, poems, and songs made the work easier, and it brought the divine directly into the activity of women.

Many communal activities centered around birth and death. Through childbearing, women were a portal between the supernatural world and the human world, and, through childbirth and tending to the dying and dead, they ushered spirits from the heavens, to Earth, and to the afterlife. Women washed, dressed, and prepared the dead just as they washed, dressed, and prepared infants. Women went to cemeteries together (in areas where people buried their dead), visiting family graves, providing food, companionship, and remembrance of the dead. These activities also became ritualized, with specific prayers and songs performed by women as they left their homes, arrived at graveyards, and grieved with their kin. Women, across time and cultures, have important (and often unrewarded) roles to play in the transmission of ritual practices. Women were often responsible for the home-related practices of faith; they passed on traditions and practices to the next generation: making food, caring for children and home altars, and teaching as they worked and cared for their homes and families. In times when the institutions of male textual scholarship are threatened, women's roles take on an even larger importance in the transmission of the religion itself. Without women, religions are nothing more than words.

And in many areas, these women's activities were considered doctrinally suspect; that is, not tied closely enough to the orthodox opinions of the elite hierarchy, particularly within textual religions. In Abrahamic faiths, women were viewed as responsible for humanity's fall from grace; Eve's transgression against God's injunction to avoid the Tree of Knowledge brought sin and death to the world. All women suffered for Eve's sin, through pain in childbirth, as men suffered through the pain of physical labor. For Christian writers, women were considered the "gateway to Hell" and men should do their best to remove themselves from the presence of women. Women in India and China also experienced negative patriarchal religious ideas surrounding their wicked nature. Hinduism believed only men of the highest caste could achieve escape from the cycles of death and rebirth, and women needed to be reborn as men prior to achieving full release. Confucian ideology stressed a woman's subservient nature, due to her less intelligent and feeble mind. Despite these harmful ideologies, women were not always passive victims; wealthy women had more ways to express their faith and to leave behind evidence of their devotion than did the poor.

WHAT IS THE DIFFERENCE BETWEEN A "TEXTUAL" RELIGION AND A "TRADITIONAL" ONE?

We are using the terms "textual" and "traditional" to differentiate those religions based on written texts and those based on more oral traditions. Traditional and folk religions are often called "cults," which denies the agency and authority these faiths held for their adherents. Some faiths, like those of the Mesoamericans, may have had more texts available for the elite than we have remaining today – the colonial practice of destroying religious artifacts of a conquered people erased much of the record of these beliefs and practices – but we use as much text, archeology, and oral story as possible to form historical ideas about the religion. In cases where there are few texts prior to conquest, as in many sub-Saharan African groups, archeology, oral stories, and historical writings by outsiders provide our evidence. Understanding and giving prominence to the historical memory of current practitioners of these traditional faiths is an important aspect of historians' study of past religions.

Mystics and Anchorites

One of most distinctive aspects of late medieval Christian spirituality was the rise and expansion of mysticism: the search for an emotional and sensual connection to the divine. Men and women of all classes sought new relationships to their God or gods, forged by personal and emotional bonds. Women's religiosity in late medieval Christianity, for example, was particularly focused on mystical practices. Mystics approached God, understood, heard, and felt the divine outside the text, outside the church walls, and outside the educational spaces preferred by the Church elite. The mystic or visionary might create a space that makes it easier for God to approach them – they retreat to a hermitage or their room, they eat and speak very little, they pray and beg for God's grace. They appeal to the divine individually and personally, without a priestly intermediary. God speaks through visions, emotions, colors, and scents to illuminate the individual's spirit with a direct experience of and with God.

This experiential learning was quite distinct from the educational and scholastic basis of Christianity in Europe. The religious movements of the tenth through fourteenth century often stressed an academic study of text; men spent their lives working to understand God and creation through a detailed study of biblical texts. Learned men parsed out and commented on the Bible, a process called biblical exegesis. Grammar and logical argument were the foundations of many great scholastic thinkers such as Thomas Aquinas who, through his *Summa theologiae*, sought to bring *all* Christian theology together in one text, arriving at divine faith through rational proofs.

Formal education in biblical languages, texts, and exegetical traditions was not a space open to many women. Nuns were not given the same opportunities

Fig 9.1
Hildegard von Bingen's twelfth-century *Scivias*, or *Know the Way to the Lord*, is a
record of her revelations. In this image she receives knowledge from God (the red
waves coming from above and connecting to her head) and uses a wax tablet on
which to record them. Her scribe, Volmar, leans in to hear her and read her notes.
Luckily, in 1933 this manuscript was carefully copied by nuns at the Abbey of
St. Hildegard in Ebingen, Germany. The original was lost during World War II and
has never come to light.
© Wikimedia Commons, public domain

as their monastic brothers, even though some became highly educated. Many
sought new ways to understand God's word outside the text, outside the school-
room, outside critique and analysis. They sought to *experience* God. Few women
were educated in Latin grammar, logic, and rhetoric. Several nuns did have the
education to engage in textual criticism, but most did not write biblical exegesis. An exception was Hildegard of Bingen (1098–1179), who did not have a
strong background in Latin, but still wrote large tomes explaining God's plan,
the creation of the universe, and the healing powers of music and plants. Her
authority to write with such purpose was God himself, who spoke to her through
a series of visions. She bypassed gender, educational, and social restrictions by
communing directly with divinity, and then recording her insights in detailed
and illustrated manuscripts. It is unclear how much actual writing and artwork
she did herself, but at the very least, she dictated her visions to a monk named
Volmar and oversaw the colorful depictions of her experiences.

Julian of Norwich (1343–1416) epitomizes another aspect of female Christian mysticism in the late medieval period: full withdrawal from the world. Born in 1343, just prior to the Black Death's arrival in England, Julian lived her entire life in the English city of Norwich. Famous for its strong religiosity, the city boasted over 90 churches and religious houses within its walls. At 30 years old, Julian fell very ill and, fearing death, chose to become an anchoress (one who withdraws from the world to focus on prayer and meditation), secluding herself in a small room attached to the side of a church. In her illness, she received a vision of Christ's passion. Educated well enough to read and write in Middle English, she recorded her visions in two redactions: a short text, written soon after the visions, and a long text, written years after her enclosure. Her vision, or *Showings* as she called it, described the Passion of Christ in intimate detail. The short text includes biographical information on Julian, along with the standard female apologies for her lack of formalized education, and it describes her vision in loving and sensual detail. She wrote she was a "simple creature" who begged God to give her three gifts: the story of the Passion, sickness in her youth (to move closer to death and God's grace), and the gift of three meta-phorical wounds (to emulate Jesus' physical wounds). From the twelfth cen-tury forward, a strong theme of mystical Christianity was a focus on Christ's suffering and an emulation of his pain and agony.

Julian's visions focused on the themes of motherhood, longing, love, and grace. She described her images vividly. She dared not look away from a bloodied Jesus with red garlands streaming down his face from the crown of thorns, or from his dead body. He gave her a token the size of a brown hazelnut that represented the steadfastness of God's love. In these descriptions, Julian framed her visions similarly to other medieval European mystics and vision-aries. The mystic denies her worthiness, only to have God announce he seeks the lowly, for the mighty do not listen. She revels in the absolute love and grace of her God, as he becomes her bridegroom and lover, and she suffers with him on the cross, or with his mother Mary at his feet. Julian also used her visions as allegorical tales to elaborate on God's love.

Anchorites chose to withdraw from a secular life to devote themselves to prayer and meditation in a way that was related to, but distinct from, community-based monasticism. They were walled into a small room, gen-erally attached to a church, and a priest said Last Rites as they entered (the idea being that the person would only leave the room upon their death). Most anchorites had servants who passed through their room, with food and waste, and a small window through which they could converse to people from the outside world. As such, this form of religious life was open mostly to people of means. More women than men chose this life in the thirteenth and fourteenth centuries; men had more opportunity to live apostolic lives of poverty within the world, wandering like St. Francis, while women were enjoined to enclosure by community and religious standards. But the high number of women who gained fame as anchoresses in the late medieval period shows women's wish to engage with God outside the monastery and shows people's longing for direct connection with God and with those spiritual individuals who spoke directly to him.

Several women sought to remove themselves from the secular world but did not, for various reasons, join monastic movements or enter into anchorholds. Catherine of Siena (1347–1380) was from a working Italian family who survived the first onslaught of the deadly plague that swept Italy in 1348. Siena's population dropped by four-fifths in less than two years and the plight of Italy must have affected Catherine's search for a personal relationship with God. Around 15, when she should have married, Catherine had a vision of a mystical marriage to Christ, where she vowed her virginity to him. She rejected an earthly marriage to a living man. Her family resisted, even locking her up and physically punishing her. She refused to relent, cutting her hair and refusing to leave her room except for attending Mass. She taught herself to read and write and began writing her visions, which she continued to have throughout her short life. At 23, a vision prompted her to care for Italy's poor and ill, and she became widely known for her patient skill and her gift of teaching theological ideas while nursing the sick. She strongly believed the Church hierarchy had failed to care for the people and she sought to bring those in power back to their rightful duties. She wrote over 400 letters, including letters chastising the bishops and the pope for their actions.

Despite her vociferous rebuke of what she considered corruption, her theology and her visions were clearly orthodox – she was herself invited to Rome to speak with the pope and impressed him with her knowledge and dignified behavior. Ill for much of her life, Catherine found it difficult to eat during her last months, and she died at 33. Angela of Foligno (1248–1309) was another Italian mystic whose visions and theology meshed with Church doctrine. Her visions began late, in her forties, when she was "wooed" by the Holy Spirit while on pilgrimage. She wrote how God moved toward her, wanting to know her, and she, in her doubts and shyness, turned away from him. Her mystic visions continued when she experienced the suffering of Christ (these gave her fits of screaming through the night, which embarrassed those who lived with her) and finally moved toward God in love. Like Catherine, Angela's writings never contradicted Church teachings or the hierarchy itself, and her works were widely copied and read.

Other women sought different ways to experience divinity. Beguines were groups of women (and a few men) who withdrew from their secular lives to live communally; they took vows of chastity and vowed to live apart from their families. While this sounds a lot like living monasteries, beguines never formally joined any religious order, instead living communally under a shared devotion to prayer and good works. Most were widows and women past childbearing age who left their natal and marital families to join with like-minded individuals. They often lived within cities and ministered to the poor and lowly. Some formed hospitals and schools, others worked in the silk and wool industry, and others lived solitary lives devoted to scholarship. They frequently skirted the bounds of heresy and were never fully recognized by the Church hierarchy.

Several famous beguines were also mystics. Hadewijch of Antwerp (1200–1248), Mechtild of Magdeburg (1207–1282/1294), and Marguerite Porete (1250–1310) from Hainaut all had mystical experiences of God and wrote them down for others to read. They wrote of their intense experiences with God's love in their native languages and not Latin. Hadewijch wrote of the soul as Lady Love, who sought to "become God with God." Mechtild's sensual descriptions of her encounter with the love of God, who kisses and embraces the mystic and calls her his queen, are detailed in her book *The Flowing Love of the Godhead*. Marguerite's visions were interspersed with condemnations of common Church practices, particularly against women preaching and talking publicly. Although she was burned at the stake in Paris in 1310 for being a heretic, her book *The Mirror of Simple Souls* was translated into four languages outside her native French, and it circulated widely both during and after her life. All these women, and many others, focused on God's love in sensual, emotional, and often erotic terms.

These women, and others, are indicative of the wider movements within late medieval Christianity. Men like Francis of Assisi, Bernard of Clairvaux, Ramon Lull, and many others also wrote about their mystical and physical unions with God. Whether considered heretical like Marguerite, slightly heretical like Mechtild, or completely orthodox like Catherine and Angela, all these women show the great longing for a personal connection to their God, a longing for a maternal/feminine side to this faith, within mainstream and less conventional positions within Christianity.

Islam

Like their Christian sisters, Muslim women also lived and worshipped within spaces created and controlled by men. Like the New Testament, the Qur'an lays out the ideal of spiritual egalitarianism – both women and men have equal access to God, have equal capacity to sin, and have equal ability to reach heaven. Both men and women are to act with modesty and morality. However, new ideas on women did enter the text and the religion. Muhammad and the Qur'an brought some changes to women's lives that many considered favorable. Women in Islam were guaranteed a portion of their father's inheritance, the ability to own and control their own property, the ability to divorce, and remuneration within the divorce (if the husband initiated the divorce). Pre-Islamic women in Arabia did have some economic rights – as we see Muhammad's first wife Khadijiah owning and running her own mercantile business – but the right of inheritance and divorce seems to be new within the religious system.

As Islam spread and new cultures embraced this religion, upper-class urban Islamic women took on practices like veiling (an ancient Syrian practice) and seclusion (an ancient Persian practice). Lower-class urban women and rural women were rarely secluded, as their work was a vital contribution to the family economy. Like in other religions, wealthy women had more opportunities to engage with education in ways their poor sisters did not; however, poor women had more opportunities to exist in public spaces. Veiling and seclusion became marks of wealth and status, and women in lower classes emulated their wealthier neighbors by veiling as soon as legally possible, although poverty often meant seclusion was a more difficult concept to implement. Most scholars agree the idea of seclusion and veiling are ideals much older than the religion of Islam and practiced in cultures in and around the Mediterranean. Polygamy, seclusion, and veiling were common gender restrictions in the Middle Eastern world from about 2000 BCE forward, but were not universal. Several Muslim sects did not require veiling for women, and in Tuareg society (North Africa) men were the ones who veiled more consistently than women did.

The most important advantage wealthy Islamic women held was as a patrons: as purveyors of art, education, and business expansion. Muslim inheritance laws were the basis for this patronage. Women were entitled to half the inheritance their brothers received, and this inheritance did not become part of their husbands' or sons' property. Therefore, wealthy Muslim women had access to monies that were unentailed by their familial relationships. Wealthy women in Africa and the Middle East opened schools, hospitals, and mosques. Although they could not engage educationally or in spiritual leadership roles in many of the same ways men did, Muslim women were prominent in the expansion of spirituality and Islamic arts in the medieval era.

Just like Christian women mystics discussed above, Muslim women created spiritual spaces within their homes, weaving prayers into their daily lives and adhering to mystical practices. In addition to less formalized female sanctity, during the late medieval period new forms of Muslim spirituality gained in importance. Sufism (Islamic mysticism) emerged early within the Islamic period, but, by the eleventh century, Sufi masters established schools of practice, and by the thirteenth century Sufism entered its golden age. A premise of Sufism is destruction of the ego in order to merge the soul more fully with God. Its practices varied by school but most centered on a master who taught disciples how to dismantle the Self and seek mystical experience of God directly. From the earliest days, women were involved in the Sufi schools. Some paid for buildings (using their own properties and inheritances), others supported the masters and disciples, and still others trained with Sufis and became masters themselves.

Many Sufi women were married or widows, and the language of domesticity and family permeated their poetry. The women acknowledged God as their protector and guardian, to whom they were willingly obedient. Most of the women were confident of his providence in return for their love and obedience. Rabia al Adawiyya was the most famous female Sufi. Born around 718 to a poor family in Basra, Rabia devoted herself early to an ascetic life, withdrawing to the desert to live alone and seek communion with God. She is the first Sufi to expound on Divine Love (a universalizing love between God and human) and love is the central theme in her poetry. One story tells of Rabia running through the streets, holding one bucket of fire and one of water. Upon questioning, she replied the fire was to burn down heaven and the water to quench hell, so humans could only look to God. "If I adore you out of fear of Hell, Burn me in Hell. If I adore you out of desire for Paradise, Lock me out of Paradise. But if I adore you for yourself alone, do not deny me your eternal beauty." Her aim, and the Sufi aim, was to deny her Self, to turn totally inward in order to reach out to her God. She died in 801.

Most female Sufis are known because of their disciples, who became masters themselves. Most of their work was orally transmitted, spoken and repeated for centuries. Fatimah of Cordoba (twelfth century) trained Ibn Arabi, introducing

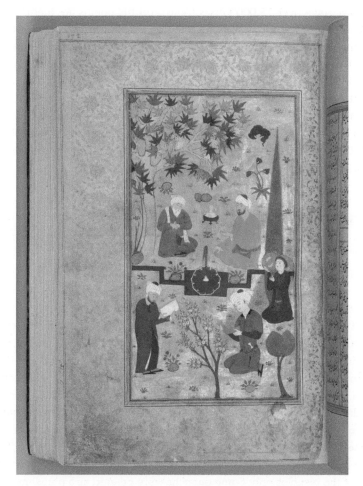

Fig 9.2
The *Masnavi* is a poem of epic length written in Persian by Jalal al-Din Rumi. Through it, he explores the mystical dimensions of achieving the complete love of God. This late fifteenth-century six-book manuscript features spiritual seekers in intense study and contemplation. Other painted pages include receptions, feasts, and gilded pages of calligraphy and intricate abstract design.
Metropolitan Museum of Art, Gift of Alexander Smith Cochran, 1913, 13.228.12

him to living with joy, as God created happiness. Shawana of Basra wept daily on God's love – joyful weeping for its existence and doubtful weeping at her worthlessness (this is similar to Angela of Foligno's nightly emotional outbursts or Margery Kempe's daily crying). Tahiya of Nubia is said to have ended every prayer with "O Who loves me, I love him." Although their male counterparts gained lasting fame, female Sufis used the same affective language of love and devotion within their verses, and much of it was similar to the mystical religion of their Christian counterparts.

Arguably the most famous Muslim Sufi poet was Rumi (1207–1273). A Persian poet and man of letters, his work is similar to writers like Rabia. Rumi was raised in a Sufi household and began work as a lawyer at 24. Well educated and highly prolific, we have over 75,000 verses today and his poems are memorized and recited around the world. Despite his education, Rumi felt learning could be won as much through inner experience as through study. Love and emotion are central themes to Rumi's poetry; he focused on the internal movement toward God and the love he experienced when his separation from God ended. He wrote, "Union with Thee is the root of all joys!" The inward spiritual journey figures prominently within his work, as does the need for selflessness and the removal of ego when approaching God. His passion and his emotion place him in a unique space within Persian literature, but also squarely with his Muslim sisters who also wrote ardent works to God.

GENDERING THE SPIRIT

Although we have used the terms "women" and "men" within this chapter and this text, we recognize these terms are socially and historically constructed. We also recognize many societies included genders other than male and female. Some cultures use the term "Third Gender" or "Two-Spirit" to refer to individuals we would see as nonbinary or trans. Gender designations could be announced by social behaviors or physically altered by clothing, presentation, or body modifications such as surgeries. India, Southeast Asia, Central and North America, and many regions in Africa recognize and celebrate people along the gender spectrum. Religiously, Third Gender, Two-Spirit, nonbinary, and trans people who took genders other than their birth designation often occupied important spaces as diviners and healers. These ideas and people have important histories that deserve full and nuanced discussion.

Many ancient and medieval societies granted special status to men called "eunuchs," who had been intentionally castrated, either through "total ablation" (full removal of both penis and testes) or removal of the testicles only. Some eunuchs were created as a punishment (in adulthood), but many more were castrated before puberty in order to cause the development of distinctive physical states (such as beardlessness and long, delicate limbs) associated with the special functions they served at royal or imperial courts or as guardians of sacred spaces (including a royal woman's bed chamber or the royal harem). Eunuchs were expected to be both sexually and spiritually pure.

Many eunuchs were castrated prior to sale on the slave market, where they could fetch high prices. Other ancient Greeks and early Christians castrated themselves in order to remove sexual temptation or to purify themselves for priestly roles. The expectation of purity led to their important responsibilities guarding temples, sacred precincts (such as in Islam at the Prophet's Mosque in Medina and the Sacred Mosque in Mecca), tombs, the entries to royal or imperial courts, and other significant or sacred passageways. Chinese and Persian emperors, Hellenistic kings, and many other ancient and medieval Near Eastern cultures also used eunuchs at court for ceremonial and administrative tasks and to serve and protect the women and children at court; these practices spread later to Byzantine (Greek Christian) and Islamic court cultures and appeared at some Latin Christian courts in the Mediterranean world, such as Norman Sicily (1061–1194). In medieval Chinese, Byzantine, and Islamic sources in particular, eunuchs are depicted as existing on a unique plane – neither female nor fully male, separated forever from their families, unable to reproduce, marry, or undergo puberty – and thus capable of transcending both physical and spiritual boundaries.

Hinduism

By the seventh century, Islam moved into northern India, bringing with it many of the ideals shown above. As Islam took hold in the north, a new wave of Hindu spirituality moved up from the south. Bhakti spirituality emerged in southern India and moved slowly north, beginning in the late seventh century and reaching its apogee in the sixteenth. Like their monotheistic neighbors to the west, this vibrant new spirituality within Hinduism focused on emotional and intellectual union with the divine. One of the more significant aspects of this new experience was how open it was to women and members of the lower castes. For centuries, Hinduism dictated and reinforced a social caste system in which only men of the upper classes were able to free themselves from the cycle of birth, death, and rebirth. Members of the lower classes and women needed to move themselves up the caste system in order to remove themselves from this cycle. In Bhakti, some of these structures were relaxed into a more democratic doctrine.

Hinduism is based on the Vedic texts, a series of religious texts written between 1700 BCE and 400 BCE. Written and studied by educated and wealthy men, the Vedas expounded views of Hinduism by and for the upper classes. Early educational centers have been found in Bronze Age cities, places where Brahmin-caste men met to study and write on their faith. Lower-caste men, and women of most classes, were excluded from studying and engaging with these religious texts, and, in many ways, excluded from formalized worship. That left many Hindus to find spaces outside formalized structures for their spiritual practice. The Bhakti movement focused on the god Vishnu, the second god in the triumvirate of Brahma (the creator), Vishnu (the preserver), and Shiva (the destroyer). Vishnu and his avatars (representations on Earth) were the impetus behind the *Mahabharata* and the *Bhagavad Gita* – two of the more famous religious texts in the Hindu world. In southern India, where Bhakti spirituality formed, followers focused on collective aspects of their spirituality. Public singing of Vishnu's praises, collective prayer, and a rejection of caste status marked Bhakti groups. Many, including women, found themselves drawn to this spirit of communal activism. Bhakti followers cooked and ate together, regardless of gender or caste – a very unusual activity in Hindu society. Bhakti poetry and song infused spirituality and piety into everyday activities, including cooking and cleaning. Current Bhakti followers say that Bhakti is the religion of song, of communal sharing, of common speech, and of common heart.

As Bhakti spirituality evolved, people discovered other individualistic ways of following a path of equality and spirituality. Later Bhakti ideals focused on a divine union between the individual and their god – an emotional connection that did not need texts, education, class, or gender to be validated. As Bhakti ideas moved further north, their followers encountered Muslims and Sufism. Some scholars suggest the newfound individualistic drive merged with the Muslim idea of complete surrender to God. Bhakti poets in northern India from the eleventh to fourteenth centuries stressed a single-minded devotion to Vishnu. The poet-saint Kabir (d. 1518) acknowledged a Sufi mystical element within his poetry, but he never strayed from his Hindu faith.

Bhakti women, poet-saints and singers alike, wrote poetry extolling their god while they engaged in their workaday lives of wives and mothers. Some women derided their mundane lives, eager to seek their divine spouse and leave their confining familial spheres. From the seventh to the twelfth centuries, female poets often rejected this world and sought the next; in effect, these women used Bhakti spirituality to critique the patriarchal world they found themselves within, even as they conformed to its roles as wife and mother. Akka Mahadevi (d. 1160) wrote over 430 extant poems. She declares she was female in name only – her body, mind, and soul belonged to Shiva. She sought the everlasting love from her god, a love no mortal man could give her, and, without her god's love, she lived a half-life, heartbroken as she wandered this world awaiting the next.

Janabai (d. 1350) was a servant who lived with the famous Bhakti poet, Namdev. She wrote over 300 poems herself, extolling the divine love of Vitthal (a Vishnu avatar). Her poetry denied the lowliness of her caste, showing that through her emotional union with Vishnu she lost all sense of ego and completely erased herself to become one with god. The poet-saint Mirabai (d. 1546) is the most famous of the female Bhakti saints of the medieval period. Born into a royal household, Mirabai also rejected the class of her birth. At her husband's death, Mirabai wandered the streets, caring for the poor. She declared Krishna (an avatar of Vishnu) as her spouse and that no mortal man had power over her. Her poems speak to the longing Mirabai had for her eternal husband, a desire to join fully with the universal self of the god and to lose her personal self in the process.

These female Bhakti poets wrote both of their earthly lives and their heavenly longings. Like women in other mystic spiritual traditions, Hindu women sought divine union with their god, outside the traditional male spaces of the university, the text, and the written commentary. Replete with images of wives, of sensual union, and of desperate longing, these poems influenced Hindu spirituality into the modern world. Female poets of the seventeenth to twentieth century and beyond continue the trajectory of their medieval ancestors, focusing on personal piety, rejection of societal norms, and communal ideals.

Sub-Saharan Africa

Talking about women's religious experiences in sub-Saharan Africa is much like talking about them in Mesoamerica: we use archeology and oral history where there is little written history. By combining oral, written, and material sources, there is much we can and do know about African religions. Oral traditions have been passed down for centuries to professional historians and storytellers, often called *griots* in West Africa. These stories are confirmed by Muslim accounts of Africa. Once we add archeological evidence, our view of African history becomes more expansive and more detailed than we would at first think.

Like most other areas in the premodern world, most African women lived under systems of patriarchy. We do know of some groups who followed matriarchal and matrilineal descent, and, in many of the smaller states, there existed a system of gender complementarity, where men and women had balancing roles, equally important, within their society. Women, especially grandmothers, were often the storytellers and moral teachers for all young people in a group, weaving tales of strong and beautiful women whose intelligence saved the day and won them praise and status. Post-menopausal women were often as valued as elder men, and gender became less important as a category of analysis for elders in many African groups. Women, especially elders, acted as intermediaries between this world and the next, giving advice to younger members of their families and communities. Their knowledge of plant life gave them the opportunities to be healers of both a person's physical and spiritual self. In many cultures, certain illness and spirits could, and can, only be cured by female healers.

As in Hindu and Aztec religions, there is a long history of female deities in Africa. Goddesses held important spaces within the spiritual realm for most Africans; songs and poetry, in addition to religious stories, show us the importance of the divine feminine in Africa. The role of women in reproduction is religiously significant in almost all faiths. In most African cultures, women were esteemed as life givers and often seen, dialectically, as life takers as well. Menstruation and childbirth were considered magical, sacred, hidden, and out of human control. Like women in other societies, African women tended to children, the ill, the dying, and the dead. Living and communing in the spaces between life and death, African women held important, and at times dangerous, religious and ritual wisdom. These dichotomies fit within patriarchal worldviews, as male leaders could both praise and fear goddesses and women.

By the seventh century, Islam had converts throughout North Africa and they began spreading the religion southward. Many in northern Africa converted to Islam, which linked them to the great trading networks of the Islamic world, stretching from the Straits of Gibraltar to India. Christianity still held sway in eastern Africa, despite Islamic incursions. Both Sunni and Shi'ite versions of Islam spread along the coast of eastern Africa over the next several centuries. In many ways, conversion to Islam was a slow process and women, such as the Hausa of western Africa, kept alive older pre-Islamic religious ideologies and brought them into their new faith. As Islam spread within Africa, women's roles changed – sometimes, with the advent of Islam, they came to play less prominent public roles. In other ways, the pre-existing religious ideals often merged with Islam, as they did with Christianity and other faiths, to become more syncretic and culturally specific. For example, some West Africans merged burial and death practices, which included songs and dances at various intervals after death, with Qur'anic scriptures and beliefs about the afterlife, or with griots, who added the history of Muhammad to their chronicles of local kings.

Mesoamerica

Because Spanish colonial priests and others destroyed so much of the religious archeology and texts of the Aztec world, we know very little about this advanced society. Nonetheless, we do know that religion in Aztec society was gender-segregated (men and women held different occupations and societal positions) with ideas of gender complementarity (both men and women were needed for a well-run society), as it was in earlier Mesoamerican states. At birth, girls were given a broken shard of pottery or a broom to indicate their life within the household, and boys were given a small bow and arrow to indicate their life as warriors or hunters. Most Aztec families used a system of primogeniture to pass along family wealth, with the eldest son inheriting the majority of the property.

As a continuation of earlier manifestations in Mesoamerica, Aztec male and female gods held complementary spaces within the religious realm. Texcatlipoca (husband, night, diffusion) and Texcatlanextia (wife, day, illumination) balanced each other and the world itself. This divine pair were also the patron gods of royalty. Kings and queens maintained the connections between this world and the next by "autosacrifice," where a royal would engage in ritual, and often public, bleeding, such as a woman pulling a knotted string through her tongue and cheeks, offering blood to solidify the connection between her people and to their deities. As in earlier Mesoamerican religions, blood sacrifice was also important for the Aztec.

Like in other faiths, both men and women had the opportunity to ascend to the afterlife, and both men and women had religious obligations. Household rituals and rites were essential and women were responsible for these daily manifestations of faith. These Aztec beliefs merged with Spanish Catholicism to create a new Central American Catholicism with aspects of the older Indigenous religion melded within the colonizers' faith. The importance of the Virgin Mary in Mesoamerican culture, for instance, can be directly linked to this syncretic movement. The Aztec goddess Tonantzin had an important altar near Mexico City and many Nahua (Aztec) people worshipped her as the Sacred Mother, goddess of fertility and the Earth. The Spanish destroyed her temple and built a small church there, dedicated to the Virgin Mary. Not long after, in 1531, Juan Diego (a Nahua peasant man) had four visions of a woman who approached him, saying to him, "I, who am your mother, is here." He told these visions to his local priest, who believed Diego had seen the Virgin Mary. She became the Virgin of Guadalupe, whose imagery and symbols point to her syncretic nature as a saint both of the Spanish and the native Nahua.

Conclusion

Although the majority of women in the medieval world lived under patriarchal cultural and social mores, they (and other marginalized peoples) were able to find ways to engage with their religions and find active ways to communicate and participate spiritually with their gods. Connecting with their deities outside spaces controlled by educated, wealthy men allowed disadvantaged peoples to have a stake in their religions. They also show us how the increasing "democratization" of spirituality was formed, particularly within traditionally female spheres. These movements track with larger trends in late medieval religion – movements toward the nurturing side of God, experiments with non-clerical leadership in places where clerics held power, and pushbacks against textual control over religious tenets. The next section looks at how these illuminations of the spiritual took shape within visual and textual fields.

B: ILLUMINATION

Introduction

The people discussed so far in this chapter sought enlightenment in many forms, and the metaphor of light and sight was as powerful for them as it is for us. They prayed and worshipped to access the light of the divine. They followed the light of gods. Sometimes, they described their faith in a contradiction of terms: because they were blind with earthly darkness, they could not see the light. They used light in terms of knowledge (to shed a light on an idea) and justice (to shine the light into corners of corruption). Light also indicated new ideas and innovations: fresh ideas occurred with the light of new day, and new discoveries illuminated human experience.

Illumination has a specific definition in book arts. It refers to the bright colors and gold and silver foil used in the paintings and decorations of a medieval manuscript. When a manuscript decorated with gold or silver foil was opened, light reflected from the page. The effect of candle flames or of the sun glinting off the metallic surface inspired medieval viewers to see it as divine light shining forth from holy images. Illumination is a term specific to manuscripts from the European tradition. Decorations and images in Islamic manuscripts are called illustrations or paintings. Comparable Eastern and Mesoamerican illustrations are described as paintings. Despite the difference in terminology, all of these works demonstrate an awareness of the spiritual experience of seeing glowing images. In this section, we explore many aspects of illumination, both intellectual and spiritual.

Evidence:	Christine de Pizan, *The Book of the City of Ladies*
	Guillame de Lorris and Jean de Meun, *Roman de la Rose*
	Hours of Catherine of Cleves
	Très Riches Heures
	Hours of Jeanne d'Evreux
	Icons of Andrei Rublev
	Chartres Cathedral
	Mosque-Cathedral of Cordoba
	Aztec Temple in Tenochtitlan
	Kazimar Big Mosque in Madurai, India
	Golden Haggadah
	Keshava temple at Somnathpur

The Light of Reason

Christine de Pizan is the first European woman who earned a living as a writer. The most powerful of her books highlighted ways in which men degraded women and their contributions to their communities. In 1364, when Christine was born, her father was a court physician and advisor in Venice, a powerful center of trade and intellectual exchange. Because of her father's reputation as a doctor and intellectual, he was hired as the astrologer and physician for King Charles V of France. As a young girl, Christine moved with her family from Venice to Paris. Christine acquired a significant education, in part because of her father's delight at her natural wit, and her access to libraries and the learned scholars of her father's circle. At 15, she married a man who, like her father, earned a living as a royal bureaucrat, but ten years later (1389) both her father and husband were dead from the plague. Christine now had three children to raise and support, in addition to caring for her mother and a niece. In order to make a living, she turned to writing and launched a successful career.

Initially Christine wrote courtly love ballads. These were a popular genre of elite poetry, connecting her to aristocrats throughout France, including women who sponsored her and her work. She often acted as her own scribe and illuminator, frequently dedicating books to patrons and illustrating them with

Fig 9.3
Christine de Pizan presents *The Book of the Queen* (ca. 1410–1414) to its namesake, Isabeau of Bavaria.
The Picture Art Collection / Alamy Stock Photo

beautiful portraits in lapis blue, vermillion, and gold leaf. When Charles V died in 1380, his son, Charles VI ascended the throne. Charles VI suffered from mental illness, and his wife, Queen Isabeau, was instrumental in providing stability to the realm throughout the chaos caused by the Hundred Years' War (1337–1453) and the tremendous disruption and fear caused by the plague. For this noblewoman, Christine created a book of stories from Ancient Greek and Roman sources called *The Book of the Queen*. In it, she included an illumination of herself presenting a book to Isabeau.

Well read and well connected, Christine engaged with the issues of her day, specifically objecting to and reframing the casual and vulgar way men presented women in literary and theological texts. It was through her public criticisms of a widely circulated book, *Le Roman de la Rose* (*The Romance of the Rose*), that she entered into public debate with the antifeminist forces of her culture. *Le Roman de la Rose* was a medieval European bestseller. Begun in the early fourteenth century by Guillame de Lorris and finished several decades later by Jean de Meun, the story is of an allegorical character named Lover who gains entrance to the Garden of Love in pursuit of a Rose. The characters are personifications of abstract ideas such as jealousy, old age, and beauty. The Rose is allegorical for virginity; she remains a mute, tightly furled flower that changes only by becoming ever more provocatively "open" to the Lover whose goal is to "deflower" her. Having gained one kiss, the Lover sets off alarms, and Jealousy builds a tower to protect or imprison the Rose, a fortified castle with moat, bailey, and guards at the four gates – Resistance, Shame, Fear, and Foul Mouth. Jealousy installs La Vieille (the old woman) and a character named Fair Welcoming (temptation) to guard the little flower.

There are very few allegorical males in the Garden of Love. Most of the characters are coded feminine, including Felony, Villainy, Covetousness, Avarice, Envy, Sorrow, Old Age, Pope-Holiness, Idleness, and Poverty, but also Joy, Beauty, Wealth, Generosity, Openness, Courtesy, and Nature. Jealousy is feminine, and so is Reason, but a feminized Reason will not prevail. Although the God of Love is masculine, he is under the control of Venus, and there are only a few other male figures: Time, Diversion, and also Resistance, a gnarly, snaggle-toothed, hairy monster. In other words, the Rose's entire entourage is an emotionally inconsistent and morally confused obstacle (the feminine) to the Lover (masculine) getting what he deserves. In the end, in a thinly disguised metaphor, he pierces the tower with his lance.

Christine found this representation of woman both ungodly and unproductive. She countered *Le Roman* and other viciously sexist texts with her own allegories, including *The Book of the City of Ladies*, published in 1405. Written in the first-person, the author/narrator begins in her own library. She thinks about all the books on her shelves that condemn women as agents of vice and corruption – in other words, all the books on her shelves – yet observes that her personal, daily experiences with women of all ages and statuses proves the opposite. Her friends are earnest and devout. The women in her community are capable and reliable. Royal women inspire her. As the fictionalized Christine

Fig 9.4
Illumination by Christine de Pizan for *The Book of the City of Ladies* (ca. 1410–1414).
On the left is Christine visited by Lady Reason, Lady Rectitude, and Lady Justice. On
the right, Christine and Lady Justice begin work on the city to be governed by women.
Photo 12 / Alamy Stock Photo

in *The Book of the City of Ladies* contemplates the contradiction between men's
assessments of women and the examples of women before her, she falls into a
dark space. Suddenly, she is illuminated, pierced by rays of light that shine from
three regal figures of intellect: Lady Reason, Lady Rectitude, and Lady Justice.
Through them, Christine builds a city organized by and ruled by women, and
presents the possibility that, if left alone, women could create a superior civilization based on reason, righteousness, and justice.

Books of Reflection

Christine populates her city with women from all walks of life, from peasants
and merchants to nobles and warriors. And, ruling over her city is the Queen of
Heaven, Mary, the mother of Jesus. One woman whom every medieval Christian
venerated, the Blessed Virgin Mary was a ubiquitous figure of personal worship
throughout Europe. Popular devotion to Mary increased throughout the
Middle Ages. She was ever-present in sermons, art, and cathedral decorations,
and as the subject of a popular and common book of religious devotion called

a Book of Hours. These small private devotional books dedicated to a study of the Psalms, prayers to Mary, and biblical extracts became popular for nobles to own and display. The title refers to the many times of day (hours) a Christian stopped to pray to Mary, with the expectation that those prayers would be relayed to Christ, her son, and from there to God the Father. The format included a calendar organized by "feast" days commemorating the martyrdom of a saint or significant events in the life of Christ and the Virgin. Historians can tell where a Book of Hours was made because of the local saints presented in it; for instance, Books of Hours made for use by Christians in Paris usually included January 3 as the feast day of the martyrdom of Geneviève, the patron saint of the city.

From 1250 to 1550, more Books of Hours were produced in Europe than any other text, including bibles. Copying a full-text Bible required immense resources – hundreds of sheep or calf skins prepared as parchment and cut into pages. It also required thousands of hours of trained scribes copying from exemplar texts to a new one. It also required access to an exemplar from which to copy; copying the Bible took scribes, illuminators, and others working for several months. Mistakes were easy to make and difficult to correct (the most

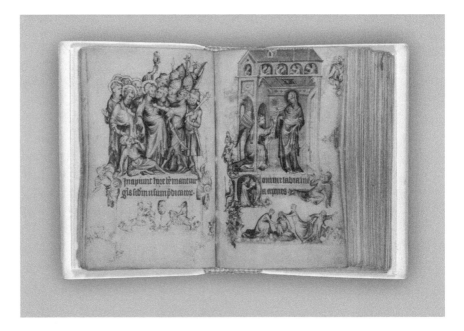

Fig 9.5
Two pages of *The Hours of Jeanne d'Evreux* (mid-1320s) depict the Annunciation, where the Angel Gabriel tells Mary she will be the mother of Jesus (right), and the arrest of Jesus in the Garden of Gethsemane (left). Below the image of the Blessed Virgin Mary is a tiny portrait of Jeanne contemplating a religious book, possibly this Book of Hours. Medieval artists are usually not identified, but in this case we know the illuminator was Jean Pucelle.
Metropolitan Museum of Art, The Cloisters Collection, 1954, 54.1.2

famous mistake is the scribe who misspelled "was" in the first line of the Gospel of John, in an 8th century Northumbrian manuscript). Thus, religious books for personal use were small ones, made up of only portions of the complete text, such as Gospels (the four books of the Evangelists, Matthew, Mark, Luke, and John), Psalters (collections of psalms), and breviaries (books of prayers recited by those in holy orders). Like these, Books of Hours were typically small and portable. Many of the owners were elite women, which shows us both the literacy and the devotion these noblewomen had. The books were discreet personal objects that made the owner feel directly connected to the Blessed Virgin and, through her, to Christ. Some were easy-to-carry accessories with embroidered silk covers and delicate silk pouches. They were a means to express gratitude and a comfort in despair. Many survive intact in the present day.

In its leather binding with tiny tabs, a pocket-sized Book of Hours was made in the mid-1320s for the French Queen Jeanne d'Evreux, wife of Charles IV. The pages are only 3⅝" by 2⁷⁄₁₆" by 1½", smaller than a mobile phone but three times as thick, about the size of a bar of soap and just the right size to nestle reassuringly in the hand. In it are elaborate illuminations by French artist Jean Pucelle that invite close study and concentration. Peering at the intricacies of the small images (too small for more than one person to look closely) draws the single reader into heightened spiritual attention. Through the eye, the mind concentrates on the examples of Christ's life and passion, and the spirit is absorbed in meditation.

On the right in Figure 9.5 is an image of the Annunciation when the Angel Gabriel arrives from heaven and announces to Mary that she will be the mother of Christ. Under this illumination is a historiated initial – an exaggerated capital letter with a story inside. This historiated letter D contains an image of Queen Jeanne herself meditating on a religious text; the metaphor is that through her intense focus, the devoted Jeanne has entered her own Book of Hours.

The Hours of Jeanne d'Evreux became part of Charles V's library of treasures and was then passed on to his brother, Jean, Duc de Berry, who in turn commissioned exquisite Books of Hours of his own. One of the most famous and beautiful of the books in his collection is the *Très Riches Heures*. Like Charles V (the patron of Christine de Pizan's father), Jean applied his great wealth and power to promotion of the arts.

Queen Jeanne was not the only woman commissioning Books of Hours and using them as a way to "see" themselves in divine context. Another good example of female literacy and religious self-agency is evident in *The Hours of Catherine of Cleves*. Catherine was Duchess of Guelders in the Netherlands. The primary artist of her Book of Hours produced nearly 100 miniatures for this luxury work. Completed in the 1440s, other artists contributed to the effort for a total of 168 illuminations.

In the depiction of the crucifixion of Christ, the grieving Mother Mary is on the left, and on the right side of the image, Catherine has joined the holy scene, kneeling at the foot of Christ. With her rosary beads draped over her arm and a representation of her Book of Hours open on the small stool in front of

Fig 9.6
The metaphor of hell as a great beast that devours wicked souls was inspired by the
biblical book of Revelation. The monster's great, gaping mouth of flame and torture
is prevalent in medieval European art. This example is from a Book of Hours made
around 1440 for the Dutch aristocrat Catherine of Cleves.
Album / Alamy Stock Photo

her, she communicates with the divine. She says, "Pray for me, Holy Mother
of God," and Mary responds by addressing her son, "Be gracious to her for my
sake and breasts that nursed you." Christ in turn appeals to God, "In the name
of my wounds, spare her," and God answers, "Your prayer has been heard with
my favor." Through this image of just one Book of Hours, we can understand
the hope that each hourly prayer to the Blessed Virgin Mary, repeated each day
of the year by countless women, would reach Christ who would in turn relay
it to God. Through intense consideration of an image, Catherine appears in
the image, collapsing the line of sight, sound, and spirit between her and God.

An arresting illumination from this Book of Hours is a mouth of hell.
Hellmouths appeared in medieval art as a caution that a lack of piety has
consequences. It is a *memento mori*, a reminder that all humans die, including
the creator, patron, and owner of this manuscript. *Momento mori* was an artistic
style well known around the world, and it increased in importance in Europe
during and after the Black Death as Europeans grappled with the enormity and
randomness of the disease's destruction.

Iconographies and the Faithful

We are accustomed to the word "icon" as a picture on a computer or smart-phone that represents an application or a program. We also use the term to identify a person who is famous for a certain talent or behavior. In religious traditions, "icon" was, and still is, used for an artistic representation of a holy character or event. The practice of the holy, of faith, and of religious duty and devotion are all part of understanding the various iconographies present in medieval religions. Two powerful iconographic traditions are held within Christianity and Hinduism.

As we saw through the discussion of the Iconoclastic Controversy within Christendom in the eighth and ninth centuries (see Chapter 1), the interpret-ation and use of religious images changed over time. By the later Middle Ages, icons had become a standard part of most Christian faiths and the growing wealth in the European and Middle Eastern world meant that more people had money to spend on purchasing and using holy images within their own homes. Often these smaller, portable icons themselves were regarded as being as holy as the person or divinity they represented, and icons of the Blessed Virgin Mary were increasingly popular from the thirteenth century forward. *Mariology*, or the theological study of Mary, as the mother of Jesus, grew from the third cen-tury forward. Known as *Theotokos*, the bearer of God, in the Orthodox trad-ition, poems, stories, and images of Mary populated churches and, increasingly, homes during the medieval period. Icons of Mary, as the Blessed Virgin or the Mother, were as available to Orthodox Christians as Books of Hours were to European Christians. One of the most famous Orthodox icons was painted by the Russian St. Andrei Rublev (ca. 1360–ca. 1427) who, at one point, was an abbot of a monastery near Moscow. Among his works is a panel painting of Mary holding the Christ child in her lap. The loving mother and her happy baby represent a time of innocence and grace before the trials of Jesus and his final suffering for humanity. The painting itself is regarded as having a miracu-lous power of healing.

In another of Rublev's great icons, he demonstrated a sensitivity to the Orthodox tradition of iconoclasm. One of the commandments God communicated to Moses was that man should not worship false idols. This rule was often interpreted to mean that people were not allowed to worship physical objects or images in place of the spiritual God; in other words, they may not pray to or privilege statues or pictures as if they were the real thing. All three Abrahamic faiths struggled with the question of how to represent the divine, or how humans could act as creators (a job only God could do) by trying to depict the physical world in artistic form. Humans cannot conceive of the divine, and therefore are hubristic if they try to draw it. If common people mistook the false images for the holy figures themselves, their worship was false and damaging. After the Iconoclastic Controversy of the eighth and ninth centuries, however, it was accepted and expected in Christian areas that artists could draw, paint,

Fig 9.7
The Theotokos of Vladimir, ca. 1405, by Andrei Rublev.
Album / Alamy Stock Photo

and sculpt direct representations of biblical characters, including the divine figures of saints, Christ, and God. Persian and other Muslims created art featuring humans, animals, and other representations of the natural world. All three monotheistic faith cultures produced representational art in many forms.

The ability to layer meanings within iconography aided in spreading Christian ideals to new areas around the world. Mary became important in the Mesoamerican world, in part because of the syncretism of Christian iconography. As a mother of a persecuted son, as a woman, and as a saint, Mary translated well into Mesoamerican cultures. She became conflated with goddesses of fertility, grain, and protection (similar to the movement of ancient pagan goddesses like Brigit to saints in northern Europe). Soon, Mary enshrined herself into Mesoamerican culture. Outside Mexico City in 1531, she appeared to a Nahua man, Juan Diego, who had converted to Catholicism a mere seven years prior. She appeared to him five times, each time encouraging him to approach his bishop, a Spaniard, with news of her visitations and a request for a new church. After her first appearance, Juan Diego did as she requested; however, the bishop did not believe the Native man and sent him away. Disheartened by his bishop and the illness of a favorite uncle, Diego attempted to dissuade the Virgin, and then to ignore her. In the most famous line of the visitations, Mary chides him, saying "Am I not here, I who am your

Fig 9.8
The Holy Trinity, ca. 1410, by Andrei Rublev.
PAINTING / Alamy Stock Photo

mother?" She directs Diego to gather roses with her, and she places them in his cloak. He returns with the perfectly red and blooming roses to his bishop, who recognizes the work of God, as it was December and roses should not be blooming. Mary's likeness was also emblazoned on Diego's cloak, which solidified the bishop's belief.

Mary appeared to Juan Diego in Tepeyac, outside Mexico City. The area had long venerated Tonantzin, the Mexica goddess of grain and fertility. Her name means "Our Lady" or "Great Mother." In another aspect, Tonantzin was known as "The Serpent Crusher," and, like the Virgin Mary, was known to have killed serpents who sought to inflict damage and mischief on humanity. She was often seen holding children or grains and flowers, all symbols of fertility and mothering. The new church built for Diego's Mary sat near the old shrine to Tonantzin. Mary, and Juan Diego's cloak, were soon worshipped by Indigenous people and newcomers alike. As she appeared to a Nahua man, she was also thought to protect the lives and rights of Indigenous Mesoamericans. She became known as the Virgin of Guadalupe, and her icon is found throughout Mexico, Central America, Spain, and the southwest and western United States.

Fig 9.9
Enshrined in the Basilica of Our Lady of Guadalupe, the cloak of Juan Diego features the image of the Virgin Mary surrounded by a mandorla, an oval halo around her body.
bpperry / iStock

The image of the feminine divine is also heavily present in Hindu iconography. Icons in the Hindu faith are different from Christian icons in that, for Hindus, icons embody the divine. The icon itself is holy as it becomes a housing for the god; it is part of the god, and not just a conduit to the divinity. Gods are worshipped through their images, but the image itself is not the true face of the god. Like faithful adherents in other religions, Hindus know their gods are more than the human image found in the material object – the divinity transcends human experience, but the image helps to ground the faithful. The three faces of divinity (Brahma, Shiva, and Vishnu) have specific symbols attached to them and to their different forms (avatars). In the same way a Christian recognizes Mary by her blue cloak, a Hindu recognizes Parvati by her lotus flowers and lions. As the wife of Shiva, Parvati represented the religion and faith of the householder and the family, and brought domesticity to her creator and destroyer husband. She is the Mother Goddess and is often portrayed as nursing Ganesha (the elephant-headed god), one of her sons, while her second son Kartikeya frolics nearby. When alone, she is often portrayed as dark-skinned, the epitome of divine beauty, one who encourages humanity toward reason, freedom, resistance, and action.

Fig 9.10
Keshava Temple in Karnataka, India is a model of Hoysala architecture. The main temple has a star-shaped platform and a series of steps for the faithful. Inner and outer walls are carved with gods and goddesses, historical scenes, and animals.

DreamStation / iStock

In Hinduism, like in Christianity, the creation of the icon is a holy act and everything carved or painted had numerous meanings behind it. Parvati herself has multiple forms, as mother (Parvati), as destroyer (Kali), as guard of harvest (Gauri), and others throughout India. Multiple arms symbolized the god's power, and gestures, objects, and skin tone all indicated different aspects of a god. Access to the icons themselves became an important aspect of Hindu faith, and those who could not afford to own personal icons had access to various forms of the gods depicted at temples, like Keshava Temple in southern India. A temple dedicated to Vishnu, today the complex holds over 1,500 Hindu and Jain temples. Consecrated in 1258, the temple quickly became a pilgrimage site, and visitors climbed the central temple complex and wandered through the inner and outer walls. Each part of the compound was intricately carved with icons of various gods, historical scenes of the Hoysala kingdom, and comic interplay between animals. The Hoysala controlled the area of south-central India from the tenth to fourteenth centuries. Mostly known today because of their temple architecture and literature, this kingdom traded with China and other areas of Southeast Asia, but kept tightly to their Indian cultural roots. Today, their temples, and others throughout Asia, provide us with important touchstones of Hindu iconography and the importance of the divine in daily life.

Fig 9.11
One of a multitude of images carved into Keshava Temple, Parvati is featured with a wasp waist and generous proportions, indicating alluring sexual beauty and good health. An elephant sits below her feet, and lotus flowers adorn the sculpture.
ERIC LAFFORGUE / Alamy Stock Photo

ELEPHANTS

Animals and animal parts could be potent symbols of power and status for medieval elites – sometimes indicating control over trade routes, wealth, favored status with spiritual forces, or positive relationships with foreign rulers. Some animals had to travel very long distances to get to their new homes. Medieval examples include the peacock feathers found in the Gokstad Viking ship burial (ninth century, see Chapter 6) or the gifts of exotic animals, including a giraffe, to the Yongle Emperor (r. 1402–1424; see Chapter 10) via the voyages of Zheng He's Treasure Fleet. Certain animals took on particular meanings in various medieval cultures and could be employed to symbolize human traits, spiritual status, or to critique human behavior. In Hinduism, gods often were part human and part animal (theriomorphic), where the god carried traits of both the animal and the human.

Elephants were especially favored as diplomatic gifts because of their impressive size and widespread use in warfare. Menageries in many parts of the ancient and medieval world, from China to Rome, often contained elephants and this brought prestige to their owners. They also appeared in many artistic cultures around the Eastern Hemisphere, often symbolizing power, wisdom, and loyalty. The Hindu deity Ganesha takes the form of a hybrid elephant-human and is associated with wealth and the removal of obstacles to success.

Because they only live in Africa and Asia, knowledge of elephants in other areas of the medieval world was restricted to that gleaned from books or legend. Such legends often contained fabulous and fantastical representations of animals from faraway places and imbued them with a variety of meanings. Personal interaction with an elephant could cause astonishment. Charlemagne's court was amazed in 802 at the arrival of an elephant named Abul-Abbas (d. 810), a diplomatic gift from the caliph Harun al-Rashid. The Europeans wrongly claimed the caliph had given Charlemagne his only elephant, making it seem as though the elephant was as rare in Baghdad as he was in Germany. Later European kings exchanged large animals – like the gift of an elephant from French King Louis IX to English King Henry III in 1255 – which they accessed by means of accelerated cross-Mediterranean trade.

Beyond the animals themselves, elephants were most valued for their ivory, which was an expensive trade item used for the most luxurious products. When elephant ivory was unavailable, or too expensive, ivory from walruses or imitations from whalebones might be used – but elephant ivory (especially from the large African savanna elephant, with long thick tusks) was highly prized for items carved from a single tusk. Arabic sources for the trans-Saharan trade often talk about yellow gold, red gold (copper), and white gold (ivory) – signaling the high status all three held within West African commerce. Between 700 and 1100, the Medieval Climate Anomaly caused the trans-Saharan routes to flourish; art historians find a correspondingly high number of carved ivory products from this period in Europe, al-Andalus, Byzantium, and the Fatimid Caliphate. This suggests that trade in elephants and elephant parts was increasing in pace and value.

Fig 9.12
An oliphant was a ceremonial horn to be blown at certain moments, especially in hunting. Even if it was not useful as a horn, a hollowed-out elephant's tusk was still a symbol of elite culture, connecting the owners to exotic African and Indian landscapes and the charismatic elephant. This one was made in the twelfth/thirteenth century in southern Italy.

Metropolitan Museum of Art, Gift of J. Pierpont Morgan, 1917, 17.190.215

Rainbows

Europe's most spectacular gothic cathedrals were dedicated to the Blessed Virgin Mary, among them Notre Dame (Our Mother) de Paris, Notre Dame de Chartres, Santa Maria del Fiore (St. Mary of the Flower) in Florence, Catedral de Santa María de la Sede (St. Mary of the See, or headquarters) in Seville, the largest gothic cathedral in Spain, and Sankt Mariendom Cathedral in Hamburg. The first example of Gothic architecture was the brainchild of Abbot Suger (1081–1151), who, as a boy, was given by his family (an oblate) to the abbey of St. Denis, just outside the center of Paris. Over the course of his career cultivating friendships and alliances with kings and bishops, Suger became a powerful and visionary leader. In 1137, he set out to rebuild the church at St. Denis, incorporating innovative engineering breakthroughs into a new style of architecture.

Since the eighth century, Romanesque architecture was the grand style of religious buildings in western Europe. It is characterized by large pillars, rounded arches, and few windows and was the extent of engineering and building capabilities left in the West after the loss of construction knowledge following the collapse of the Roman empire. Abbot Suger took advantage of new ideas about how to manage and support the tremendous weight of large structures made from stone. He oversaw teams of masons who innovated thinner pillars, pointed and ribbed vaulting, arcs of support, and other reinforcements, all of which allowed for larger openings for windows and the light of God to enter the building. In the centuries after, builders added flying buttresses, columns, and half-arches that distributed the weight of the roof from the inner walls to outer walls, supporting or buttressing the building. The arches "flew" outside the buildings and allowed for even more windows to be placed within the walls.

These new buildings were costly and took years to build, and many were perpetually renovated, enlarged, and further decorated. Most of these cathedrals were sponsored and paid for by wealthy patrons, from kings to city dwellers, and built by the large and wealthy guilds or artisans' companies of the cities. Masons, glaziers, sculptors, and painters cooperated to complete these large civic projects. In addition to being ultimate expressions of sacred devotion, they were a source of tremendous local pride. Cities competed to build the largest and most ostentatious cathedrals, showing off their wealth and craftsmanship to the world through the construction projects. The cathedrals were the epitome of a large and organized Church hierarchy, but also highlighted the growing wealth and influence of merchants, tradespeople, and craftspeople.

The structural innovations allowed for larger window openings such as the clerestory, a row of windows at the top of the walls, creating the illusion of heavy stone resting miraculously on delicate glass. Artisans filled them with elaborate designs in colored glass that filtered God's light into kaleidoscope patterns on the floors and walls of interior spaces. Medieval stained glass was like comic books or graphic novels. The images told the stories of the Bible, panel by panel, and provided visual cues to Bible stories and saints' lives that the people knew by heart.

Light changes throughout a day, changes by the season, and changes according to weather. The different qualities of light animated the stories in the glass panels through which it shone. Wealthy patrons and groups of artisans commissioned stained glass panels and story cycles, with silk-makers, haberdashers, and others donating money to see their windows completed and hung within the local cathedral. Congregations gazed upon the images while listening to choral music, human voices in mystical harmony. God brightened their souls with color and sound: heaven on Earth.

Notre Dame de Chartres is both a quintessential Gothic structure and emblematic of the worship of Mary. The massive structure is organized and supported by sturdy, but elegant, pillars extending from the foundation into ribs meeting at points in soaring domes. Flying buttresses fan out from the sides, holding the walls upright, and there is bountiful stained glass. A hallmark of Gothic ornamentation is a rose window or wheel window. Framed by tracery – openwork in the stone supporting each individual pane of glass – multicolored images radiate from a center in concentric rings of petals or spokes. In many churches dedicated to the Virgin Mary, the center of the rose window depicted the Mother and Child surrounded by the apostles, prophets, and saints inspired by the power of the child Jesus. Here, we also see the effect of a story cycle as the many characters and events of biblical stories pass information from one frame to another. A rose window is a metaphor of God's light, his holy community, and his earthly community. Unsurprisingly, the Blessed Virgin Mary sits at the center of Chartres' medieval rose windows with the Christ Child in her arms. Just as all Christian stories emanate from that point of light, the entire cathedral space and its congregation extend from the reliquary at its core. In the Roman Christian faith, no cathedral could be consecrated without a relic, a part of a holy person's body, or an object belonging to a holy person, or an object touched by a holy person. The relic of Notre Dame de Chartres is thought to be the tunic Mary wore when she gave birth to Jesus.

Al-Andalus

During the ninth and tenth centuries, Islamic Cordoba was a flourishing center of politics, scholarship, art, and trade. It had the largest library known in Europe and a bustling community of intellectuals. At night, the streets were lit with oil lamps, giving the city an ethereal glow. La Mezquita, or the Grand Mosque, was a worthy statement of a grand city. It was built on the site of a Roman Visigothic church. For 70 years, Muslims and Christians both worshipped there, but eventually the church was replaced with a splendid mosque. Named in honor of the Blessed Virgin Mary, the magnificent Cathedral of Our Lady of the Assumption

Fig 9.13
Notre Dame de Chartres Cathedral illuminated at night.
Deposit Photos

Fig 9.14
Interior arches and stained glass of Notre Dame de Chartres Cathedral.
Deposit Photos

in Cordoba, a Christian house of worship, was for nearly 500 years a mosque built by the Muslims who ruled most of the Iberian Peninsula from 711.

Like the Gothic cathedral builders, Muslim artisans designed structures with many windows. Rows and rows of double arches, arch upon arch, supported the weight of the walls and a higher ceiling. Light from the sunny Spanish climate streamed in through high windows, augmented by lamps suspended in uniform lines following the curves. In the heart of the great mosque was the mihrab – a niche built into a wall showing worshippers which direction pointed toward Mecca, so they could always pray facing that holy city. The arch surrounding the mihrab is decorated in mosaics made from thousands of pounds of tiny glass and enameled pieces, along with border paintings of blue lapis and gold paint. The dome above is entirely covered in gold leaf. All of these surfaces reflect the natural light of the Earth, the lamp light of human hands, and ultimately the brilliance of Islam.

The Kazimar Big Mosque in the Tamil Nadu region of India has similar styling, but it combines the elements of both traditional Muslim and Indian architecture. Built in 1284, the mosque has minarets and a domed center, along with scalloped edging reminiscent of other Indian worship centers. The mosque itself could hold up to 1,200 people for services, and a large complex soon surrounded the central worship area. Important Indian Muslims were buried near the mosque and it soon became a pilgrimage site for the faithful to visit.

In the 400 years of Muslim rule, al-Andalus was essential to the dynamic and robust trading, intellectual, and cultural networks of the expansive Islamicate world. In addition, there was significant cultural exchange between Muslims and the other inhabitants of the Iberian Peninsula – Christians and Jews who had been living in the region since the late Roman Empire. Greek and Roman manuscripts moved into Europe through the bustling intellectual centers in Spain. Writers like the Jewish philosopher Moses Maimonides (1138–1204) wrote prolifically while living in Spain, Egypt, and the Middle East. In 1236, King Ferdinand III of Castile and Leon captured Cordoba. He started an ongoing renovation of La Mezquita into a Christian church, which now includes a rose window over the arches.

Iberia (modern Spain and Portugal) was one of medieval Europe's most multi-cultural places, with Jews, Muslims, Christians, and converts between those three faiths living close together – sometimes peacefully and sometimes in con-flict. During the period of Muslim rule, Christians who kept their religion but adopted the language of Arabic and many of the cultural traditions of Islam are known as *Mozarabs*. They produced *Mozarabic* Christian art, architecture, and literature (during what is known as the Romanesque period) heavily influenced by Islamic traditions; they were allowed to keep their places of worship and their religious and local community leaders.

From the late eleventh through the thirteenth centuries, Christian kings took over Muslim territories in what is often called the "reconquest" (*reconquista*), but was really a series of military conquests of lands that had been under Islamic rule for hundreds of years. The new Christian lords were initially a

Fig 9.15
Christian and Islamic architecture combined in the Mezquita of Cordoba, Spain,
which has been adapted from a Muslim mosque to Catholic cathedral.
Deposit Photos

minority ruling class, with the great majority of the population being Muslim
or Jewish. The Muslim subjects of these Christian rulers are known as *Mudéjars*.
This is also a common term for the art produced during the Gothic period in
Spain, which imitates Islamic styles of art and architecture, although it was
often produced by Christian artisans for Christian patrons.

Jews lived and worked under both Christian and Muslim rulers. As the
Christian conquest of Iberia progressed, however, Jews came to be viewed
with increasing suspicion and many were encouraged or forced to convert
to Christianity. Known as *conversos* ("converts"), these Jewish converts to
Christianity were imperfectly integrated into the dominant Christian culture.
In contrast to "Old Christians" (those from families who had been Christians
for far longer), these "New Christians" were often accused of secretly practicing
Judaism – being "crypto-Jews" (secret Jews) and negatively influencing their
Christian neighbors. *Conversos* came to be the main targets of the Inquisition
from 1478 onward, as Church and State worked together to try to "root out"
nefarious secret Jewish practices and to homogenize Spanish Christian society.

Iberia's multiculturalism came to an end in the fifteenth and sixteenth centuries, as King Ferdinand and Queen Isabella (known even in their lifetimes
as the Catholic Monarchs) and their successors sought to impose a uniform
Christianity on their kingdom as they centralized royal control over the Spanish
state. In 1492, Ferdinand and Isabella expelled all the Jews from Spain and
its territories (including the Balearic Islands and Sicily) in what is sometimes

known as the Alhambra Decree. Over the first quarter of the sixteenth century, the practice of Islam was also outlawed in all parts of Spain; all Muslims were forced to convert to Christianity or leave their homes. These Muslim converts to Christianity are called *Moriscos* ("Moors" – although the term "Moors" is considered derogatory and is not the preferred term for Muslims). In 1609, the government ordered an edict of expulsion for the *Moriscos*, and by 1614 the majority of Spain's population was made up of old Christian families.

For many centuries, Jews lived productively but not always peacefully in the Iberian Peninsula under both Christian and Islamic rulers. The Sephardic Jewish community in Barcelona had been established since Roman times and was one of the most flourishing in Spain. Jews acted as advisors, physicians, and financiers to the various Christian kings and to the counts of Barcelona, who provided economic and social protection (Jews in Spain were even considered to be part of the king's royal treasury), and they offered the same services to Islamic caliphs. Caliphs sponsored scientists, artists, weavers, and builders, in addition to commissioning luxury manuscripts, leaving behind many examples of cross-cultural artistic and intellectual exchange. A good example of a luxury item reflecting this artistic synthesis is *The Golden Haggadah*, a book for the use of a wealthy Jewish family produced around 1320 in or near Barcelona.

A *haggadah* is a collection of Jewish prayers and readings that is read aloud and chanted during the Passover Seder, a ritual meal eaten on the eve of the Passover festival. *The Golden Haggadah* is named for the breathtaking effect of gleaming gold. Each image has a gold-tooled background, basically a layer of gold leaf carefully applied to the surface of the page, on which the figures are painted. It contains many illuminations, such as representations of the ten plagues God sent to torment and punish the Egyptians for their treatment of the Jews before the Jews gathered behind Moses to leave Egypt for the Promised Land. Intermixed with images from the Exodus (the leaving) is a highly stylized, nearly full-page depiction of *matzah* (matzoh, or matzo) the flat, unleavened bread central to the story. Along with bitter herbs, milk, and honey, *matzah* is a symbol of the deprivation the Hebrews experienced as Moses led them from slavery when there was no time to stop and let the bread rise. The fugitives subsisted on flat crackers and the sparse vegetation of the desert, but they believed in the Lord's promise of a land of milk and honey.

The Golden Haggadah is one of a very few surviving Jewish manuscripts from medieval Spain. They are rare for at least two reasons. Books such as this one were used regularly. Presiding over the ritual meal, rabbis and fathers read aloud from them to teach children the Passover prayers and stories, and eventually the text would wear out and be repurposed or discarded. In 1236 King Ferdinand III of Castile and Leon captured Cordoba. He started an ongoing renovation of La Mezquita into a Christian church, which now includes a rose window over the arches. This also began a diaspora of Spanish Jews, who moved, like Maimonides, into other spaces in the Islamicate world. Many books like the *Haggadah* were lost or left behind and destroyed after the Jews were expelled from Christian Spain in 1492.

Fig 9.16
This image of matzah from *The Golden Haggadah* was produced in Catalonia, Spain between 1320 and 1330. Jewish communities used haggadahs as part of the ritual of Passover, and this one shows the combination of Jewish, Islamic, and Christian iconography of medieval Spain. It is embellished in a gold, red, and blue pattern common to Islamic art of the period. It also resembles the tracery of a rose or wheel window, a primary architectural element of Catholic churches. The story of Moses and the Exodus is celebrated in all three faiths, and Passover commemorates an important chapter in the story. To punish the Egyptians, God sent ten plagues. The final punishment was that he would take the life of the first-born son of every Egyptian family. To distinguish Egyptian families from Hebrew ones, Moses instructed the Hebrews to paint the blood of a sacrificed lamb over the doors of their houses. In this way, the angel of death would know which houses to pass over. Passover is a time to honor and remember the sacrifices and hardships the early Hebrews endured, and Christian and Muslims consider it representative of their suffering as well.

Looking Forward

Throughout this chapter, we examined how people in the later premodern period understood and connected with their higher powers. Christian women found private spaces where their spiritual practices were safe and satisfying. Sufis and Muslim poets enjoined their peers to sing and dance, and Bhakti poets pictured themselves in loving communication with their gods. The ideals of light and illumination represented the divine in literary metaphor and artistic rainbows. New cathedrals soared over European villages, and illuminated manuscripts and stained glass physically embodied religious enlightenment.

In 1492, Isabella and Ferdinand achieved their goal of reclaiming Spain for the Christians. In 1521, the Spanish destroyed the Great Temple at Tenochtitlan. The Aztec temple complex was begun in 1325 and at least six major rebuilds happened prior to the arrival of the Spanish. It was the most important, and largest, Aztec temple. It rose over 300 feet high and housed the god Huitzilopochtli. The Spaniards were impressed with the grand temple complex, which held over 70 buildings, and with the dedication of the Aztec to their faith. Nonetheless, Spaniards razed the temple to build a church, a monument to the power of the Spanish crown and to Catholicism itself.

Just four years earlier, the German Catholic theologian Martin Luther had published his *Disputation on the Power and Efficacy of Indulgences*, commonly known as *The Ninety-Five Theses*. Through this tract, Luther called attention to at least three ways representatives of the Church abused their power over the people they served. He objected to the sale of indulgences, official pardons for sin that came in the form of a certificate or a token. He also criticized the sale of relics, which were pieces of saints' bodies or fragments of their possessions sold at high prices to ardent believers. Mostly, however, these were fakes passed on to devout worshippers who implicitly trusted agents of the Church. He also attacked the practice of simony, where Church leaders rented out parishes or offices to others who took advantage of the tithes and fees a clergyman could make. Many of the spiritual quests that had marked late medieval Christianity – the desire to find a personal connection to a nurturing side of God – caused Luther's message to find a ready audience. Luther's work catalyzed demands for Catholic Church reform all over Europe, and the protests erupted into a violent disruption of Christian religion and practice that informed the wars, immigrations, and nation building of the early modern period. In the following years, Christianity became a global religion, through conquests, colonization, and mission activities of both Catholic and Protestant groups.

Research Questions

1. Compare the writings of two authors listed here. What symbolism seems consistent among them? What is different? How might you account for those differences? You may choose authors within the same culture, across cultures, or across genders.
2. How did the political and social change affect the spirituality of this period?
3. Compare cathedrals from different areas of Christianity. What is the influence of local customs on the cathedrals?
4. What is the importance of the connection between the growing middle class and urban spirituality, especially as seen through the growth of the cathedral movement?

5. Imagine yourself as one of the marginalized peoples listed here (woman, peasant, colonized person, religious minority). How do you keep your own religious traditions and ideals alive within the majority culture? Can you connect this to the modern period?

6. How does the increase in movement in the later Middle Ages change religious traditions? Think of pilgrimage, commercial travel, and religions such as Christianity, Islam, and/or Hinduism.

Further Reading

Carrasco, David. *City of Sacrifice: The Aztec Empire and the Role of Violence in Civilization*. Boston, MA: Beacon Press, 1999.

Chandra, Satish. *Essays on Medieval Indian History*. New Delhi: Oxford University Press, 2003.

Clendinnen, Inga. *Ambivalent Conquests: Maya and Spaniard in Yucatan, 1517–1570*. Cambridge and New York: Cambridge University Press, 1987.

Cornell, Rkia Elaroui. *Rabi'a From Narrative to Myth: The Many Faces of Islam's Most Famous Woman Saint, Rabi'a al-Adawiyya*. New York: Bloomsbury Academic, 2019.

Cortés, Hernán. *Letters from Mexico*. New York: Grossman, 1971.

Joyce, Rosemary. *Gender and Power in Prehistoric Mesoamerica*. Austin: University of Texas Press, 2000.

Levtzion, Nehemia, and Jay Spaulding. *Medieval West Africa: Views from Arab Scholars and Merchants*. Princeton, NJ: Markus Wiener, 2003.

Miner, Earl R., Hiroko Odagiri, and Robert E. Morrell. *The Princeton Companion to Classical Japanese Literature*. Princeton, NJ: Princeton University Press, 1984.

Phillips, Charles. *The Lost History of Aztec & Maya: The History, Legend, Myth and Culture of the Ancient Native Peoples of Mexico and Central America*. London: Hermes House, 2004.

Rieff Anawalt, Patricia. *Indian Clothing before Cortés: Mesoamerican Costumes from the Codices*. Norman: University of Oklahoma Press, 1981.

Ruether, Rosemary Radford. *Goddesses and the Divine Feminine: A Western Religious History*. Oakland: University of California Press, 2005.

Sterckx, Roel. *Ways of Heaven: An Introduction to Chinese Thought*. New York: Basic Books, 2019.

Tiesler, Vera, and Maria Cecilia Loza. *Social Skins of the Head: Body Beliefs and Ritual in Ancient Mesoamerica and the Andes*. Albuquerque: University of New Mexico Press, 2018.

Wieck, Roger S. *Painted Prayers: The Book of Hours in Medieval and Renaissance Art*. New York: George Braziller, 1997.

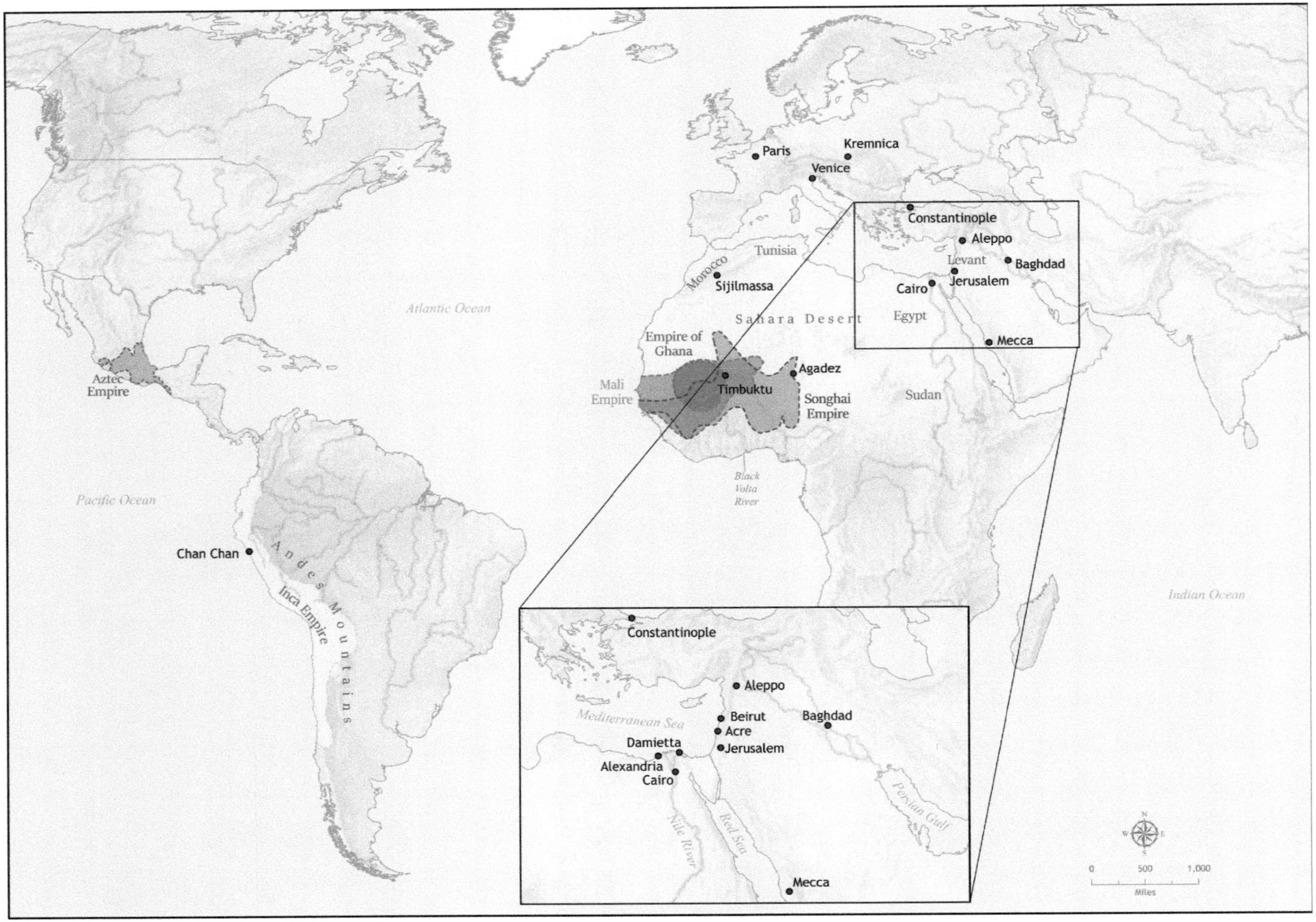

Map 10
Golden Opportunities

10 Golden Opportunities
Economies, 1300–1500

Introduction

Late medieval economic activity is generally characterized by three major themes: the growing volume and speed of long-distance connections along pre-existing routes, the expanded monetization (use of currency for economic exchanges) of several important regions, and the rise to dominance of Europe-based merchants within the Eastern Hemisphere. Many of the commercial goods along land and sea routes in the late Middle Ages were similar to those of earlier periods: silk and other textiles, Chinese and Islamic ceramics, spices, incenses, medicinal substances, ivory, precious stones and gems, metals, and more. But, in some ways, the story of the later Middle Ages can be told through gold. Gold's luminous shine, beautiful color, and malleability made it a highly desired luxury item in many cultures, and its rarity meant that those who controlled its supply held considerable political and social power.

The growing European hunger for gold and silver, along with spices and other luxuries from the East, helped fuel the race to discover faster routes from Europe to China, and from Europe to the Indian Ocean. These efforts were accelerated by development of advanced navigational technologies, which, by the end of the period, allowed the Portuguese to conquer ports along the coast of West Africa, and both the Portuguese and Spanish to sail into and across the Atlantic. Difficulties of access to gold – because of political problems or depletion of local mines – could cause inflation in prices and serious economic destabilization. Some people became very rich. Others were enslaved and annihilated. The devastating effects of European conquest on the populations of Africa and the Americas in the sixteenth century were the result of European desire for precious metals. Section A focuses on the main regions that exported gold and those where gold was imported for use in both coinage and decorative arts. Section B highlights objects and resources that were widely valued as signs of status, fashion, and glamour among the social elite.

A: TREASURE HUNTS

Introduction

The late Middle Ages was a transformative period for the world system, and economic exchange was at the heart of these developments. West African gold mines had long supplied the Islamicate and Byzantine economies, and gold from eastern Africa was one product among many traded in the Indian Ocean. But, over the thirteenth and fourteenth centuries, European traders established trade colonies along the southern shores of the Mediterranean, allowing them greater access to that precious metal. Mongol conquests across Central Asia and China facilitated trade connections across land and sea, but also changed the relationship between China and the rest of the hemisphere.

Although known as land-based warrior nomads, the Mongol Yuan dynasty (1271–1368) was in fact quite interested in maritime long-distance exchange. Under their rule, China's ships dominated commerce in the China Seas and eastern Indian Ocean. Their successors, the Ming dynasty (1368–1644), oversaw the further growth of maritime trade (to the disadvantage of over-land trade along the silk roads) and revived the tributary economy of earlier Chinese dynasties. In western Asia, merchants based in Europe and the Middle East took advantage of Mongol rule to trade for desired eastern products. After the breakup of the Mongol Empire, however, the flow of goods from eastern Asia became more difficult for merchants to access by land routes, so European merchants and explorers, already in control of Mediterranean Sea trade, launched out on new maritime routes to the Asia. In South America, the powerful Inca Empire facilitated the production and distribution of both basic foodstuffs and valued luxury goods. This system was demolished during the sixteenth-century Spanish conquest of the Inca.

Evidence:	Cowrie shells
	Mongol paiza
	European silk dresses
	Gold coins
	Women silkworkers guilds
	Inca textiles

West Africa

The thirteenth through sixteenth centuries was the peak of medieval long-distance trade both into and within West Africa, with gold at its heart. Africa was the primary source of gold in the Eastern Hemisphere: any place in the Mediterranean world that did not have trade connections directly to Africa (or with the Muslim states of North Africa that acted as the middlemen for the gold trade) did not have a significant source for the metal. For example, western Europe had no access to gold after the depletion of Roman-era mines in north-western Spain, but in the late Middle Ages European traders established outposts in the Islamic ports of the southern Mediterranean (and a few new European gold mines were discovered). Byzantium had long maintained a gold currency because of their trade relationships with Muslims, but European trade with the Islamicate world only intensified enough to import gold from the thirteenth century.

The trans-Saharan route was the primary one bringing West African gold into the Mediterranean region, and so it became an essential linkage in the late medieval economy. Gold was also exported from Ethiopia and eastern Africa, but at lower volumes and along different routes. Ethiopian gold traveled through Red Sea ports, and gold from Zimbabwe traveled via the Indian Ocean ports of Sofala (modern Mozambique) or Kilwa (modern Tanzania). Trade within Africa was also important for supplying local needs. Some regions participated in intra-African and long-distance trade as middlemen, or in products other than gold. In contrast to gold-rich West Africa, for example, the region further east, in the Sudan, was not a source of raw materials, but became an exchange center in the late medieval period, mediating between North Africa, the Sahara, and the savanna regions to the south.

Gold was of primary importance for the West African economy, but it was not the only commodity traded along the trans-Saharan routes: copper and salt were also vital for the north–south trade across the Sahara, and alongside them moved ivory, animal products, foodstuffs, finished cloth, enslaved humans, and items related to the textile industry. After the eighth-century consolidation of Muslim emirates in western North Africa, large quantities of gold – primarily in the form of bullion (processed bulk metal), but also in the form of dinars minted at Sijilmasa – were transported across the Sahara and into the Islamicate world. Gold was also sometimes exported as finished products, like fine jewelry made from long strands of gold filigree. In exchange, dyes and other raw materials for textiles, salt, and copper from Mediterranean regions moved southward. So, too, did the religion of Islam, which was adopted by most West African peoples (and often syncretized with indigenous religions) by the twelfth or thirteenth century.

SIJILMASA

The medieval city of Sijilmasa (or Sidjilmasa) is today a series of ruins in Morocco, but, for centuries, it served as one of the primary trading cities of the Maghrib (Arabic for "the west" and comprising modern Tunisia, Morocco, Libya, Mauritania, and Algeria). Standing at the northern edge of the Sahara Desert, it was perfectly located as an outpost for trade routes between West Africa and North Africa and, from there, eastward to Egypt and the central Islamic lands. Although Sijilmasa was not the only such entrepôt, it remained economically relevant through the end of the fourteenth century.

Sijilmasa was probably a temporary settlement until the mid-eighth century, when Arabic sources tell us that a revolt by the Berbers (an Indigenous North African people who call themselves Amazigh) against caliphal authority resulted in the establishment of an emirate, which built up the city from 757/8. By the tenth century, the city grew wealthy from its control of the gold trade from West Africa and was a site of competition between Muslim powers. In 1054 one of those powers – the Almoravids (who controlled the Maghrib and Spain, 1040–1147) – used the city as a provincial capital where gold coins were minted. Although conquered several more times in the later Middle Ages, the city continued to prosper from the great amount of wealth that circulated through its markets.

Gold – exported as dinars or as bulk gold – as well as enslaved humans, ivory, and other West African products, were traded for alum, ambergris, salt, and finished Mediterranean goods, especially textiles. These "regular" products, as much as the highly valued gold, were key to the wealth of Sijilmasa. The late fourteenth century saw a decline in trans-Saharan trade when the Portuguese ports on the Atlantic coast diverted the focus of trade, but Sijilmasa continued to trade in both directions until the sixteenth century. Destroyed sometime in the sixteenth century – likely due to its loss of economic centrality and political changes – Sijilmasa is today a protected historical and archeological site.

Muslim rulers in North Africa and Iberia sought to control access to the trade routes transporting gold across the Sahara in camel caravans. In many parts of West Africa, similarly, control over gold fields was the key to gaining and maintaining political power. In the case of the three major empires of West Africa – Ghana (ca. 700–1240), Mali (1230–1670), and Songhai (1464–1591) – the rise of centralized and expansive political states was the result of their control over gold fields and trade routes to the Mediterranean. When traffic shifted to new routes, political power might decline or transfer to new states. Trading cities such as Gao, Tadmakka, and Sijilmasa grew rich from the exchanges and markets that took place, then contracted and even disappeared when the caravans moved along different routes and used other trade hubs.

Three major gold fields were exploited in West Africa during the medieval period: Bambuk, Bure, and the Akan Forest. Smaller veins of gold were also mined, with some sources being exhausted and new ones discovered throughout the period. Gold was extracted using two primary techniques: in one, gold dust was separated from river water with baskets or calabashes; in modern West Africa this job is often done by women. In the other method, large chunks were extracted from underground veins using hand tools. Most small-scale extraction was done by local farming families during the agricultural off-season. Later, as political rulers used control over gold sources to cement their power, large-scale mining developed, and, in some places, enslaved people were imported as laborers. The human labor needed for gold mining increased when Europeans made direct contact with West Africa in the fifteenth century. The Portuguese arrived seeking gold, above all else, and between 1475 and 1535 they imported 18,000–20,000 slaves into Akan from other parts of Africa for intensive gold mining.

Long before the arrival of direct European trade, however, intra-African production and exchange were vibrant and active. Trade routes across the Sahara Desert and West Africa brought much more than gold north to the Mediterranean. Indeed, trade that supplied local needs was equally significant along these paths and in the trade hubs that controlled them. However, few of these everyday commodities appear in the archeological record because they were mostly perishable items (food, animals, ivory, cloth, and leather). Some archeological sites – such as the tombs at Durbi Takusheyi – show the many products that were traded within and into West Africa from elsewhere on the continent. Located near the Tuareg-controlled trading hub of Agadez (modern Nigeria), these burial sites contained products from around the region: ivory from the savanna to the south, gold from the west, and copper from the north.

One of the most important Mediterranean imports south into Africa was the biologically necessary natural product salt. Not available everywhere, yet necessary for all human life, salt was prized highly as an import from both the Mediterranean and from salt flats within the Sahara Desert. Medieval Arabic trade accounts dismissed the Africans as fools for exchanging gold for salt, but, without salt, humans cannot survive. Other desirable import goods were raw materials associated with the dyeing and textile industries – alum, indigo, and other dyestuffs imported from the Mediterranean region. And, cowrie shells from the Indian Ocean region were brought to West Africa via the Red Sea–Mediterranean route. Such items were key to trade and economy within Africa and across the Sahara: for example, even though West Africans mined gold, their currencies were imported products like cowries or copper.

Copper was a particularly valued import into West Africa, both as a raw material and as finished goods. Some copper came from eastern African sources, but some was imported from Europe. Not typically thought of as a valuable metal within Europe, copper in West Africa was treasured both because it was rare there and because of its color; thus, it became a component of ritu-ally important objects. For example, copper-alloy bowls were imported from Mamluk Egypt (1250–1517). Inscribed with Arabic, many such bowls have been preserved by the Akan people of Ghana as ritual objects even in the modern period. Local production of bronze (an alloy of copper and tin, copper and another metal, or copper and a non-metal such as arsenic) statues show advanced techniques and artistry. Other goods that were produced locally in West Africa included colorful glass beads, ivory items, tanned animal skins, brightly dyed textiles, and delicate jewelry.

Coins are used throughout this book to illustrate economic and cultural connections and important developments, but, as we have seen in previous

Fig 10.1
Important copper or bronze objects were produced locally in West Africa using
sophisticated casting techniques. Many of these items assumed important ritual
functions, even into the modern period. For example, this naturalistic and detailed
statue of a seated human figure (thirteenth/fourteenth century, Nigeria) was made
using an advanced lost-wax casting process. Thus, imported raw materials were
crafted into elaborate works of art and ceremony.
Photo © Dirk Bakker / Bridgeman Images

chapters, a variety of non-coinage items were also used in different parts of the
premodern world as currency: bolts of silk, colorful glass beads, sacks of grain,
and even small domed seashells called cowries. Because they are uniform in size,
small enough to carry in large quantities, and beautifully shiny, cowries have
long been used as units of exchange in places around the Eastern Hemisphere.
While there are many species of this marine mollusk, only two have historically
been used as currency and as ornament, both of which are found in the Indian
Ocean, near the Maldive islands particularly. Even in antiquity, cowries were
transported along various branches of the silk roads from the Indian Ocean into
northern India, Central Asia, northern China, and beyond, where they were
buried with high-status dead, given as gifts, used for religious or ritual purposes,
and may have been exchanged as a type of money.

In the medieval period, cowries were used as currency in northern India, West
Africa, and parts of Central and Southeast Asia. By the fourteenth century, they
were a common currency in the Mali Empire, followed by the Songhai Empire.
In most of these regions, they were imports from as far as 3,000 miles away –
and thus valued specifically because they were not something people could
easily find. Rather, they were gathered, prepared, and sold in large quantities

and shipped to foreign ports (often used as ballast, weight placed in the hull of a ship to improve its stability at sea). Because they are natural products rather than metal coins stamped with images, however, many people, both medieval and modern, have dismissed cowrie currencies as being valueless trinkets or mere "small money." But wherever they were used as currency, they played specific and well-defined roles in exchanges. In places that used both cowries and metal coins, there were agreed-upon equivalencies between cowries and coins of various denominations. And the role of low-value currency should not be underestimated: it shows that even small purchases of daily-life items were monetized.

Cowries were imported into West Africa across the Sahara from Mediterranean ports, where they were not used as currency. But they were important within the wide trans-Saharan networks exchanging gold, ivory, copper, salt, and more. In the early modern period, when European powers inserted themselves directly into the economies of West Africa, they took advantage of cowrie currency to exploit it for their larger aims. They used their direct access to the Indian Ocean sea lanes to import huge quantities of cowries into West Africa, flooding the market and causing them to lose value, thus destabilizing the local economy.

Mongol Asia and the Indian Ocean

The vibrant commercial networks of the silk roads and maritime silk roads were transformed by the triumph of Mongol warriors in the thirteenth century. Horse nomads from the steppe region north of China formed a confederation under Chinggis (or Genghis) Khan in 1206, and began rapidly conquering territories. Within 50 years, they had taken China, northern India, and Russia. In 1258, they destroyed Baghdad, capital of the Abbasid Caliphate, and killed the last caliph. Mongols were fearsome warriors, deft archers with composite bows, shooting while expertly balanced on their swift, nimble horses. Although known for their rapid and ruthless conquests, they also facilitated connections between China and its neighbors and were deeply interested in fostering craft production and long-distance exchange within their realms.

Mongol unification of extensive territory, even after its breakup into separate khanates, accelerated long-distance travel and trade. They maintained paths, like those along the earlier silk roads, and built miles of new roads. They created an extensive post-relay system (called the *yam*) for communication, travel, and government business. Mongol policies supported foreign merchants and encouraged trade: many foreigners, like Marco Polo, received the pass (*paiza*) that allowed them to use the roads and post-relay system tax-free. And, Mongol thirst for precious metals and pearls, in connection with demand for spices, porcelain, silk, and other eastern commodities among both Latin Christians and Muslims, stimulated strong connections between Mongol Asia and western merchants. Mongols valued trade and elevated the status

Fig 10.2
The *paiza* was an official pass that allowed the bearer to travel along the roads of the Mongol Empire freely and to obtain food, shelter, and fresh horses at government relay stations. Typically reserved for government envoys and officials, *paizas* were also granted to foreign merchants in order to attract their business. Marco Polo left a gold *paiza* to his heirs in his will. This example, in iron inlaid with silver, contains writing in the Mongol language warning that the khan's edict of protection for the bearer must be respected. Yuan dynasty (1271–1368).
Metropolitan Museum of Art, Purchase, Bequest of Dorothy Graham Bennett, 1993, 1993.256

of merchants both domestic and foreign. So, although relatively short-lived (Chinggis's empire broke into four khanates in 1294, and the Yuan dynasty in China was overthrown by the Ming dynasty in 1368), the Mongol impact on globalized connections in the Eastern Hemisphere was significant.

Mongol expansion came at a time when Europeans were concerned about losses of Christian crusader territories in the Syrian region: Jerusalem fell to Saladin in 1187, and, over the next century, all crusader lands went back to Muslim control. Mongol invaders from the east – considered as possible allies against the Muslims – aroused both Christian fear and curiosity and led to an increase in western travelers seeking entry into their domain. Part of European curiosity about the Mongols was connected to a long-held myth about a Christian priest and king called Prester John somewhere in "the East" (various accounts placed him in India, Central Asia, or Ethiopia). Theories that Prester John would in time rise up to conquer non-Christian enemies may have led to beliefs that he would help Latin Christians retake Jerusalem. Christian explorers and missionaries sought Prester John as they pushed into Central Asia and, later, into interior Africa and the Americas.

Merchants from Persia were especially active in overland trade along the silk roads, and Mongols valued and respected Persian medicine and science (particularly astronomy). They also revered artists and builders, sparing skilled artisans when conquering new regions and importing groups of them to their capitals. Among the most prized artisans were weavers, many of whom were women, and many of whom were moved from Persia to China by the Mongols. The most luxurious textile was called "cloth of gold" – woven almost entirely of fine gold thread and illustrated with embroidered images, many of which reproduce the earlier Iranian-Central Asian motifs of the mirrored animals within a roundel.

Another product greatly desired by the Mongols was pearls – ranked with gold and silver as the most preferred goods. Like the Song before them, Mongol rulers imported pearls in massive quantities from fisheries in the Persian Gulf and Indian Ocean. Used in elaborate headdresses, necklaces, earrings (worn by both men and women), and on clothing such as robes, belts, shoes, and head-gear, pearls were considered to have special qualities and to bestow good luck, virility, and fertility.

Other foreign travelers welcomed into Mongol territories were Latin Christians, who had previously depended on the mediation of merchants from the Islamicate world to access Central Asia and China. Diplomats like John of Plano Carpini (an envoy from the pope, 1245–1247), Christian missionaries like William of Rubruck (who visited the khan's court, 1253–1254), and merchants like the Venetian Marco Polo (who traveled with his father and uncle across Mongol lands, 1271–1295) were among the Latins who visited Mongol territory and returned to Europe with information about them. Similarly, Muslim travelers like Ibn Battuta (1304–1369) wrote about Mongol culture and the Muslim communities in their realm. Mongol rulers encouraged such visitors, not because they intended to accept conversion or submission to foreign rulers, but because they pursued their own enrichment and took advantage of opportunities to demonstrate their power.

However, the Mongol Empire's trade connections were not only conducted by foreign merchants seeking eastern goods. Even though the Mongols are traditionally known as an inland people, their focus on sea trade was significant. Building upon the maritime strengths of the Southern Song dynasty (1127–1279), when the Chinese gained control of the seaborne commercial routes in the Indian Ocean and China Seas, Mongol emperors encouraged maritime commerce among its coastal residents. In the China Seas, they relied upon the knowledge of Muslim merchants familiar with its ports and markets. Muslims brought to China more than trade goods and coins: they also participated in intellectual exchange, offering the Mongols valued knowledge of cartography, geography, medicine, and navigational technologies.

Under Mongol rule, merchants sailed both east to Korea and Japan, and south to places like Vietnam, Burma, and Java, to maintain both trade and tributary relationships. But, whereas the Song encouraged relatively unrestricted trade, the Yuan emperors mixed trade with demands for tribute from their neighbors. And, unlike the later Ming emperors (who initially outlawed private commerce in favor of the tributary system), they supported maritime merchants trading

Chinese commodities and paper money for foreign gems and precious metals. Mongol China was fully monetized – a process completed under the Song dynasty – but they restricted the export of coins, preferring that merchants use paper money so that precious metals could be kept at home.

As in earlier centuries, the ports of the Indo-Pacific in this period offered pearls, coral, gems, aromatic woods and incenses, ivory, ambergris, cowrie shells, and a wide variety of products in the category of spices (used in food, rituals, and medicine). Chinese porcelain, silks, and metals were traded at intermediary markets for products from the western Indian Ocean, as well as Southeast Asian spices and aromatics. Numerous shipwrecks filled with cargo attest to the thirteenth and fourteenth centuries as periods of expansion in maritime trade, especially active in Southeast Asia. As in the earlier periods, seaborne trade and overland routes worked together. In western Asia, camel caravans carried goods between Persian Gulf ports and Egypt, Constantinople, and the Black Sea. There, northern Italian merchants such as the Genoese and Venetians had access to the desired eastern products (until these routes began to break down after the Mongol collapse). Further east, overland routes across northern India and Persia continued to bring maritime products like pearls, coral, and spices to inland markets.

AMBERGRIS

One of the most valuable natural products traded throughout the premodern world is also one of the oddest: ambergris. It is a waxy substance formed in the digestive tract of sperm whales, which the whales expel if it is too large to be digested. Often referred to as "whale vomit," it is a rare substance dependent upon chance discovery. Found floating on the sea or tossed up on beaches, ambergris was highly prized as an ingredient in perfumes. It has a sweet and musky odor and is also a fixative, meaning that it helps scents stay fresh and last longer. In many cultures ambergris was also used as medicine, incense, or an aphrodisiac. Much of the premodern ambergris trade originated in the waters of the China Seas and eastern Indian Ocean. Still valuable today, lumps of ambergris found by beachcombers have been known to fetch prices in the thousands of dollars on the international market.

Following the Mongols, the Ming dynasty radically altered many aspects of China's economy, but eventually it grew to be the most powerful economy of its time. The Ming restricted Central Asian trade, erecting fortresses at their borders and discouraging the kind of long-distance journeys that had been possible through the Mongol *yam* and *paiza* systems. They also declared private maritime trade illegal, although this did not stop it, and did not mean that they were uninterested in business. But, the early Ming emperors did focus more on agriculture than on commercial markets, and conducted foreign exchange through the traditional tributary system. In the early fifteenth century, the Ming undertook a revitalization of the Grand Canal (see Chapter 6), which transported huge amounts of grain and other goods as both taxes and agricultural surplus intended for markets. The move of the capital to Beijing, at one end of the canal, in 1420 led to the growth of that city's population and markets. And, as foreigners in the markets of Japan and Southeast Asia continued to seek Chinese products, such as spices, silks, and porcelains, seaborne exchange continued. The Ming wanted foreign products less than they wanted silver, which they used as currency. The introduction of American silver into the globalized economy from the sixteenth century caused huge amounts of the metal to enter China. Thus, although the story of the late Middle Ages was, in some senses, one of gold, silver was the precious metal that took center stage in the early modern global economy.

Europe

The period beginning from the late twelfth century in Europe has been traditionally called the commercial revolution; this is not, as it might seem, because this period was the beginning of commercial exchange in Europe. As we have seen, the earlier periods also had thriving regional and long-distance commercial exchanges, both within Europe and beyond. Rather, the major changes during this period were both in terms of pace and volume of trade, and in the monetization of exchanges (rents, wages, taxes, salaries for government officers and military, and almsgiving) that had earlier been done "in kind" (that is, using goods or services rather than cash). By the time of the Black Death, money was the standard measure of everything in Europe – from the valuation of land or forest to that of a title or official position – and the basis for nearly all economic encounters.

Another characteristic of the late medieval period is the growth of urban populations and the concentration of political, social, and economic affairs within cities. Although aristocrats' hereditary wealth and status was based on ownership of rural estates, many of them began living in cities during this period. Because they now collected rents and taxes in money rather than produce, nobles had larger reserves of cash to spend. Their presence in cities fueled the growth of urban industries, not the smallest of which was food and craft production necessary for the maintenance of large households and opulent lifestyles. Urban merchants and artisans thus became wealthy from commerce, and could themselves afford luxurious food, drink, clothing, and entertainment in imitation of aristocratic fashions. These burgesses (non-noble urban dwellers) challenged the cultural primacy of aristocrats, because their wealth often far outstripped that of the old landed nobility. They became targets of laws restricting social behavior (burgesses were restricted from wearing clothing more opulent than the aristocracy), and they were excluded from social trends such as "chivalry," which was meant to emphasize the cultural superiority of the aristocracy over the newly rich, but untitled, burgesses.

Transregional trade, banking, and coin production in late medieval Europe were led by the Italians, but eventually the English, German, and other northern European merchants became involved in these networks, especially at regional circuits like the Champagne fairs (discussed in Chapter 6). The primary exports of England were wool and tin, the demand for which was high, but never high enough in this period for them to become leaders in trade or banking. Cities in the Baltic Sea region formed a new circuit called the Hanseatic League (thirteenth to seventeenth centuries). It was intended to provide trade privileges and protections to the merchants from League cities, thus allowing them to dominate the northern trade routes from Novgorod to London. Mostly German towns, they exported wool, wheat, beer, timber, furs, and amber to the Mediterranean region in exchange for silver, cloth, and, eventually, gold.

These economic systems were transformed by the disruptions of the fourteenth century – famine, plague, extended wars, monetary debasement, and declining productivity of gold and silver mines. Successive crop failures (1315–1317) caused disastrous famines that killed millions of people, reversed the population growth of the preceding centuries, and weakened the surviving population so that it was hit especially hard by the arrival of the plague of 1348. Dense cities fostered rapid spread of the plague, which moved along the trade routes that had intensified since the late twelfth century. At the same time, centralizing monarchies vied with each other in increasingly disastrous and expensive wars, such as the Hundred Years' War between France and England (1337–1453). Rulers across Europe faced economic burdens that were created by these wars, as they contested territories and titles using armies of soldiers who expected to be paid with monetary wages rather than with land. These wars sent kings and princes deep into debt. They responded by taking loans from bankers, debasing their coinages, and exacting heavier taxes from their populations. These forces, combined with a restricted labor market due to population declines after the Black Death, led to peasant and worker revolts that destabilized both the economy and the political power of European rulers.

Many of the developments in this period are exemplified by Europe's silk industry. Textiles had long been a major driver of medieval long-distance trade (in both finished goods and raw materials such as fibers and dyestuffs), and silk had long been the most desired type of cloth. The later medieval period also saw the growth of Europe-based silk industries and guilds, associated with many stages of textile production, from spinning yarn to weaving, dyeing, sewing, and embellishing with embroidery, beading, or gold thread. One reason for this growth was the rise of a newly wealthy urban middle class, whose fortunes were made from trade and industry. With greater expendable wealth, they could afford displays of luxury in their clothing, adornment, and consumption of food and drink, all of which further fueled the growth of industries that enriched the artisanal groups within European cities. Clothing fashions for wealthy men and women were both lavish and rapidly changing. In some places, this resulted in a backlash of attempts to regulate public displays of luxurious clothing through sumptuary laws, as discussed in Chapter 8.

Fig 10.3
This late fifteenth-century illumination depicts four of the seven liberal arts – Music, Geometry, Arithmetic, and Astronomy – as elite women dressed in exquisite finery. We can see here a variety of styles in their dresses' shapes, colors, and designs – many with elaborate gold-thread embroidery and gold trim – and their elaborate headdresses. (The three liberal arts not pictured are Grammar, Rhetoric, and Logic.) J. Paul Getty Museum, Los Angeles, Ms. 42, leaf 2v

By 1300, Paris was the largest city in western Europe, with a population of about 200,000 people, and the site of an active silk industry. Tax records give a range of the city's businesses, including production of high-value items such as armor, leather, chests, saddles and other items for horses, swords, glass, and metalwork. But, silk was the most widespread industry in Paris, and a source of great wealth and status for many of its workers. Silk fiber was imported from China, or near the Caspian Sea, the Levant, or southern Italy – its prices varied depending on the quality of the product and also on the reputation of its point of origin. Italian merchants imported the fiber on reels, either as raw silk or dyed silk yarn, and, in Paris, professional women turned this fiber into yarn, preparing and spinning it before weaving it into cloth.

In fact, women dominated the Parisian silk industry, forming around 80 percent of the city's silk workers. Paris also developed women-only guilds for silk workers. Only three towns in Europe had guilds exclusively for women (Paris,

Cologne, and Rouen), and all were related to cloth production, although many other guilds allowed women to participate if their husbands or fathers were guild members. Women worked in the textile industries of other cities as well, but often did jobs with lower skill levels, lower mechanization, and lower status and wages. In Paris, however, some women even rose to become mistresses of their own workshops, who profited from the labor of apprentices and other lower-skilled women. Some women-led workshops were the sole providers of certain types of silks to the royal household, suggesting that these women were producing high-quality work and being paid well for it. But, other working women remained relatively poor and relied on charity, petty theft, or pawn-broking to meet their family's needs. So, even though they worked – often as single women or as widows – not all professional women were wealthy. By the mid-fifteenth century, Paris's silk industry had essentially disappeared, due to economic changes in the wake of the Black Death, and political turmoil that led the French royal court (and many wealthy elite) to leave Paris.

Women's participation in the labor force – making and/or selling goods for profit, earning wages, and often joining organized labor guilds – peaked in Europe during the thirteenth and early fourteenth centuries, but began to decline in the later fourteenth century. This decline was due, in part, to economic destabilization after the Black Death, and in part to male efforts to control increasingly lucrative trades. For instance, the English beer industry was, prior to the Black Death, dominated by brewsters (female brewers); by the sixteenth century, women were excluded from positions of ownership or control in the industry. Brewsters worked from their homes brewing ale (unhopped beer) as an extension of food production for domestic use. Some sold excess ale for profit, and many women transformed these home-based efforts into commercial operations. It was not until the fifteenth century, however, that English brewers were organized into a labor guild. By that time, changes in technology and the increased profitability of the industry had essentially driven women out of brewing, or consigned them to working with and behind their husbands, who took on the public-facing roles. At the same time that men took over profit-making industries, they also developed restrictive notions about women's work. By the sixteenth century, beer and ale production in England was dominated by men, and women's opportunities for paid work in this and many other fields had sharply declined.

The Mediterranean Sea

Even though vibrant local industries arose in European cities, their markets continued to demand imports of goods and materials from faraway places. And, while the North Sea route was the most active one in the early Middle Ages, by the late period the Mediterranean Sea saw the bulk of cross-cultural exchange. As Europeans sought increasing amounts of gold and silver for minting the coins they needed to buy valuable imported goods like spices and silks, European merchants also sought to push deeper into the places where those commodities were available. In the Mediterranean region, this meant establishing trade colonies in ports of the Islamicate southern Mediterranean, and on Byzantine islands of the eastern Mediterranean. These sites became even more important for European traders after the return of all crusader territories to Muslim control. After 1291, Latin Christians no longer had a foothold in the area of greater Syria.

The main agents of the movement of goods within the Mediterranean were northern Italian merchants, taking over from southern Italians, Muslims, and Jews from the Muslim world of the earlier periods. While in the early medieval period the Mediterranean Sea was primarily under the economic and political control of the Islamicate world, during the central Middle Ages that began to shift toward Christian (especially Italian) powers. By the late Middle Ages, the Mediterranean was sailed almost exclusively by Christian ships, especially Italian and Aragonese ones. By 1500, Europe-based merchant fleets were solidly in control of Mediterranean sea lanes, and Europeans seeking direct access to West African gold also set up ports along the Atlantic coast.

As transporters and suppliers for the crusades, Italian city-states had gained concessions and control over eastern Mediterranean ports. This near-monopoly allowed them to dominate regional trade and begin to establish economic empires. Pisan, Venetian, and Genoese merchants established outposts in Muslim Mediterranean coastal cities such as Alexandria, Damietta, Aleppo, Beirut, and others, from which to purchase both imported goods and locally produced items like cotton, linen, glass, and sugar from Syria and Egypt, and hides, beeswax, olive oil, ivory, and gold from North Africa. Italian merchants also mediated trade between Muslim North Africa and the Middle East, since, by the thirteenth century, they (especially the Genoese) controlled the sea lanes and piloted most of the ships on Mediterranean waters. Florentine merchants were in control of many land routes, as they moved goods northward into Europe from the Mediterranean world. Florentines were major players in the Champagne fairs of France (see Chapter 6) and in the textile trade that involved Mediterranean silk and wool from England and the Netherlands. Florentine merchant houses developed into some of Europe's earliest banking firms, such as the Peruzzi of the fourteenth century and the Medici of the fifteenth century.

While Genoese came to dominate trade in the western Mediterranean Sea, and Florentines the northern land routes, the Venetians held increasing control over the eastern Mediterranean. When crusaders conquered Byzantine Constantinople in 1204 during the Fourth Crusade, the Venetians were the main beneficiaries. Their political control of Constantinople, which had long been a nexus of trade between the Mediterranean Sea and the Black Sea ports and overland routes to Central Asia, allowed Venice to fortify an economic empire in the eastern Mediterranean that consisted of port-cities and islands that the Venetians dominated with their impressive naval forces. Even after the return of Constantinople to Byzantine control in 1261, the Venetian fleet tried to monopolize the sea trade of the eastern Mediterranean, with competition

Fig 10.4
The Republic of Venice, an independent city-state ruled by a doge who was elected
by a council, used its massive naval fleet to control both commerce and territory
in the Adriatic and eastern Mediterranean Sea regions. Warfare with the Genoese,
Byzantines, and later the Ottoman Turks was waged by its armada of oared galleys
built at the public shipyard called the Venetian Arsenal. Galleys – used for both naval
warfare and carrying commercial cargo and passengers – were the primary ships
of the Mediterranean until the seventeenth century. The final all-galley battle in the
Mediterranean was the 1571 Battle of Lepanto, in which an alliance of Catholic states
(called the Holy League) defeated the Ottoman Turks. This is a model of the flagship
galley of the Holy League.
Photo by Sarah Davis-Secord

from Genoa; naval battles between the two were waged intermittently between
1256 and 1381. The commercial economy and warfare were thus closely linked,
as competition for control of profitable routes led to armed conflict, which, in
turn, increased the need for money in order to fund wars.

The increased pace and volume of international trade also meant increased
high-value coinages, both because of economic need and because of greater
access to sources of precious metals. New discoveries of silver mines in Europe
during the twelfth century increased minting of silver coins, which fueled the
export trade. The Venetians began minting large silver coins in 1201, which
were then imitated in other European regions. Stronger direct links with
Muslim traders also gave European merchants access to gold from Africa. In the
earlier medieval periods, gold coinages had been restricted to Mediterranean
territories with direct trade links to Byzantium and the Muslim world. In 1252,
Genoa and Florence both began minting their own gold coins, but it was not
until 1284 that Venice followed with a gold coin of its own. These new Italian

coins were in regular use at the Champagne fairs, alongside silver coins from around Europe. However, it was not until the mid-fourteenth century that northern European kings in France and England produced gold coins that met local needs well enough to succeed economically.

Part of the triumph of gold in Europe came from the opening of a gold mine at the Hungarian town of Kremnica (modern Slovakia) in 1320. Coins minted in Kremnica were modeled on Florentine coins because the Florentines dominated the economic distribution of this gold. Hungarian gold traveled northward to Germany, England, and the Netherlands, carried by Italian merchants. By the fifteenth century, however, both Hungarian gold reserves and European silver mines were essentially depleted, resulting in a drought of precious metals. Combined with heightened demand because of the full monetization of the economy, this sudden downturn resulted in a monetary crisis that caused mints across Europe in the mid-fifteenth century to cease coin production either temporarily or permanently. This, in turn, brought the economy of many European cities to a halt, since even small daily exchanges now required coins.

Greater quantities of regional and long-distance trade, all with higher monetary values, went hand in hand with the development of sophisticated business and banking practices, including double-entry bookkeeping, letters of credit, and bills of exchange (used to transmit large sums of money without needing to carry heavy loads of coins). Money changing – exchanging coins from one denomination or mint for those of another – was originally the job of mint-masters, but became a specialized role among merchants. Merchant money changers were increasingly important, especially at transregional markets, since long-distance and regional exchanges came to be conducted in a wide variety of coin values from mints across Europe and the Mediterranean. Money changing involved assessing the purity of a coin's metal content, validity, and denomination, and then weighing it to determine its exchange value. Sometimes money exchange could be used to hide an interest charge (to avoid accusations of usury), but often it simply facilitated international exchanges. By the late Middle Ages, merchant-banking houses had evolved into account banks, which could accept deposits and issue letters of credit, transfer money, invest in commercial enterprises, and offer personal and commercial loans.

Jews had long worked as merchants in the multicultural Mediterranean world, and in urban industries throughout Latin Europe. Jews were initially integrated into the urban economies of Europe, and served important roles as merchants and moneylenders. But, by the late period, many European monarchs owed them massive debts – money that the kings needed to fund their many wars and lavish lifestyles. Royal legislation in many parts of Europe came to restrict or repress Jewish economic activity and community life, in part because this allowed them to seize Jewish property and cancel Christian debts. Combined with the growth of anti-Semitic ideas and imagery, such economic pressures caused serious harm to Jewish communities. Late medieval Jews faced

Fig 10.5
Because of their involvement with long-distance trade, many European Jews
became moneylenders, supposedly aided by freedom from the restrictions on
usury (charging interest on loans) by Christians. However, these restrictions were
circumvented as often as they were observed by Christians, even in the earlier
periods; by the thirteenth century, Italian bankers openly offered loans at interest.
Jewish bankers are here shown accepting and sorting gold coins in the *Cantigas
de Santa Maria*. Caricatures of Jews in medieval images often looked like the man
in the red hat: wearing pointy hats and having large, crooked noses. Pictures like
these contributed to negative and stereotyped images of Jews as greedy, ugly, and
secretive. This was connected with the rise of anti-Semitism in the late Middle Ages.
Codice Rico produced during the reign of Alfonso X (1221–1284), Biblioteca de San
Lorenze el Real at El Escorial, Madrid.
Prisma / UIG / Getty Images

periodic violence and cycles of expulsion and return from Christian lands that
diminished the size and economic agency of the Jewish community. Between
the twelfth and fifteenth centuries, a cycle of expulsion and return seriously
diminished the size and economic agency of Jewish communities. During
the 1306 expulsion of Jews from French domains, for example, an estimated
100,000–150,000 Jews were forced to leave behind their property and money
as they fled. They were invited back later, but the Jewish community that faced
the final expulsion from France in 1394 was much smaller, poorer, and less
involved in the economy, because recovery of their earlier property and status
was impossible. Similar patterns of expulsion and property seizure happened
in England, and elsewhere in Latin Christendom, until 1492 (see Chapter 12).

Inca South America

In the Western Hemisphere, late medieval commercial exchanges worked quite differently than those in the Eastern Hemisphere, which were highly monetized and interconnected over both land and sea. Unlike the Aztec Empire of Mesoamerica (1300–1521), the Inca Empire in South America (1438–1533) had nothing that functioned as commercial markets or money, in coinage or otherwise. This does not mean, however, that there was no long-distance movement of goods and people among the Inca. In fact, the lands of the Inca Empire were closely interlinked through a network of about 25,000 miles (40,000 km) of roads that were used, in part, to move agricultural produce and other goods throughout the Andean region and beyond.

Known as Qhapaq Ñan, or "road of power," in Quechua, this network of paved paths is often called the "Inca royal road." It covered forests, rocky mountains, foothills, and deserts, and connected all parts of the extensive empire to the capital at Cuzco. First developed prior to the Inca, possibly by the Wari Empire (Peru, 540–1000), the Inca extended and connected the roads into an expansive network in the fifteenth century. While not its only purpose, one major use of the road system was redistribution throughout the empire's population centers of agricultural produce and other commodities. Another was exchange of highly desired products from beyond the empire's borders.

The Andes mountains, with steeply vertical terrain and a wide variety of altitudes and life zones, had been home to many culture groups who practiced agriculture there for thousands of years, long before the Inca. When the Inca Empire – which they called Tawantinsuyu, or Land of the Four Quarters – conquered and united 3,400 miles (5,470 km) of Andean territory, its leaders adopted and built upon pre-existing traditions of agriculture and artistic production from a variety of conquered cultures. They terraced mountainous hillsides to maximize productive land and minimize loss of water and soil through erosion. The development of terraces and irrigation allowed Incan farmers to produce enough food – corn, potatoes, tomatoes, peppers, avocados, and a variety of tubers and grains – to feed the estimated 12 million people of the empire's peak population. That food was distributed over a huge swath of Andean territory.

Agriculture, like the rest of the Incan economy, was managed through a labor tax imposed upon the entire population of the empire for some portion of each year. Production of food, metalwork, ceramics, featherwork, textiles, luxury items, and other goods could be assigned as the annual labor tax for a family or community, as were services, such as the construction and maintenance of roads, bridges, and buildings, military service, mining, communications, and carrying items for redistribution. The road network facilitated that redistribution by making it easier to bring foods from where they were best grown, to population centers outside those life zones. Thus, the Incan authorities could manage a huge population and its food needs far beyond what local subsistence farming could do.

The roads were not simply paths for travel, but also featured regularly placed storage facilities, llama corrals, and hostels, where runner-messengers could rest and replace each other in a post-relay system similar to the Mongol *yam* or the *barid* of the Islamic caliphates (see Chapter 3). The primary users of the road system were government officials, military troops, llama caravans, and official messengers, and commoners were not permitted to use the roads without permission. This network of storage and relay stations made it possible for the Incan authorities to send and receive communications quickly, manage the empire's populations, and redistribute its surpluses. Roads also carried military and government officials who kept records, conducted the census, gathered tribute and tax payments, and managed other government business using knotted strings called quipu.

Quipu cords are evidence of sophisticated Incan recordkeeping. One struggle historians face when seeking to understand pre-Hispanic American cultures and economies is the lack of written records, in part due to intentional destruction of texts by Spanish conquerors, and in part due to the rarity of writing systems. Mesoamerican peoples did have formal writing systems, such as the Maya glyphs and Aztec (Nahuatl) pictograms. However, South American peoples, such as the Inca of the Andean region and their many neighbors, did not develop graphic writing systems in a style recognizable to European conquerors. Yet, both the Inca Empire and its predecessor, the Wari Empire (ruling from modern Peru, ca. 600–1000 CE), used a system of woven cords, pendants, and knots called *quipu* (or *khipu*, from the Quechua word for "knot"), that served as a way of preserving records and stories.

Made from animal hair or cotton and dyed a variety of colors (which held clear meanings for users but have not been deciphered by modern scholars), strings were wound, wrapped, and knotted in complex formulations that likely combined numerical and narrative values. Easily portable, a quipu could be used for accounting, census-taking, recording tribute payments, and more. Spanish conquerors learned of quipus from the Incan quipu-makers and -keepers, who explained that the colors and knots were a memory aid, allowing them to recall historical and cultural information as well as administrative records. In 1583 the Spanish declared that all quipus had to be destroyed, on the theory that they were idolatrous objects. But the Spanish also incorporated quipus into their colonial regimes of governance and religion. This contradiction ensured some continuation (or reformulation) of the practice in Peru until the nineteenth century.

CAMELIDS

Throughout history, humans have developed interdependent relationships with animals, which they used for food, labor, entertainment, transportation, status, and companionship. Animals from the camelid family have played particularly important roles in the regions where they live. This group includes camels (dromedary and Bactrian), llamas (and their wild cousins guanacos), and alpacas (and their wild cousins vicuñas). The two types of camels live in Asia and Arabia, while llamas, alpacas, and their wild kin live in South America. Camelids are all able to walk long distances over rough terrain, carrying passengers and cargo. Camels can carry up to about 500 pounds of goods and humans. Llamas can carry up to 100-pound loads, but not human passengers. They are herbivorous and well adapted to harsh environments like hot, sandy deserts and high-altitude, rocky mountains. They were, and are, also sources of milk, meat, and fiber for textiles.

In the Sahara Desert and across Central Asia, camel caravans were better adapted to the environment than wheeled carts, and, thus, were preferred for long-distance transportation. Likewise, in the high-altitude regions of the Andes, a combination of llama caravans

Fig 10.6
Since no culture in the pre-Hispanic Americas developed the use of wheeled transportation, distribution of military supplies and various goods along the Inca royal roads was facilitated by llama caravans. Camelids were both economically and also spiritually important to the Inca, who used them in important ceremonies and rituals, as well as for transportation, food, and textile fibers. Many small gold camelid figurines have been excavated from burial sites in South America, where they were placed as sacred objects. Figurines like this one from the fifteenth century were crafted of an alloy of gold, silver, and copper using the lost-wax technique. Metropolitan Museum of Art, Gift and Bequest of Alice K. Bache, 1974, 1977, 1974.271.36

and runner-messengers constituted a more advanced technology for the irregular terrain than wheeled vehicles would have been. Large herds of llamas were staples of the Incan economy: llama caravans traveled the Inca royal roads, carrying military supplies and goods for distribution. Their ears were decorated with colorful bits of yarn, and the leader of the train wore around its neck a bell and a bag filled with coca leaves, to mark its status as leader. Corrals for llama herds were evenly spaced along the road network, alongside the huts and storage facilities. Similarly, camel caravans were the key to trade and long-distance commerce across the Sahara Dessert, North Africa, Central Asia, and the Arabian Peninsula.

Items transported by llama trains included staple foods such as corn, tubers, and salt, as well as obsidian (for tools) and high-value luxury items like gold and jade, brightly colored feathers and featherwork textiles, coca leaves (used ritually, socially, and medicinally), and the highly desired *spondylus* shell. These sea creatures – referred to as "daughters of the sea, the mother of all waters" – were revered by many South American cultures, both as offerings at water shrines and as decorative items. The Inca transported them from the Mesoamerican tropical coastlines (modern Ecuador and further north) where they were found, southward to the workshops where they were made into beads, pendants, figurines, and more. Likewise, the Mexica (Aztec) capital of Tenochtitlan maintained both trade and tributary relationships with *spondylus*-harvesting regions. In similar fashion, jade, turquoise, and other highly prized green stones were traded for use as ornaments and offerings. Both the stones and ornaments themselves, as well as the techniques and artisans who crafted them, were transmitted among various cultures throughout both South America and Mesoamerica, although the specific meanings of particular items could differ significantly in each culture.

Perhaps even more important to Incan culture than gold, jade, or shells, however, were textiles. They were considered the highest art and the most important indicators of status and ethnicity within the empire. Textiles were used in daily life, imperial rituals, diplomatic exchanges, and were sacrificed during religious rituals and buried with the dead. Spun from cotton and camelid fibers, brightly dyed yarn was woven into elaborate designs and then crafted into rectangular tunics. Coarser fabrics were made into rugs or blankets, and slightly finer cloth was used for clothing for lower-status people. The softest yarns – those made from alpaca or vicuña fiber – were reserved for the nobility or for royal diplomatic gifts. The production of high-grade cloth was undertaken by skilled artisans, typically women who worked in royal workshops controlled by the state. Textiles were so important to the Incan economy that they imposed a cloth production tax on all households – all families were required to spin, dye, and weave a certain amount of fabric each year.

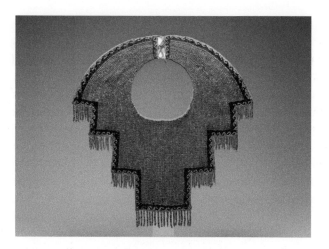

Fig 10.7
Spondylus shells were regarded as religiously significant by most Andean and
Mesoamerican civilizations. This is a collar made sometime in the twelfth to
fourteenth centuries from hundreds of shells and black stone beads by the Chimú of
northern Peru. One of the last states conquered by the Inca Empire (in about 1470),
the Chimú ruled from their capital at Chan Chan for many centuries. They grew
wealthy in part because of their control over the *spondylus* trade, which was highly
desired throughout the Americas.
Metropolitan Museum, Purchase, Nathan Cummings Gift and Rogers Fund, 2003,
2003.169

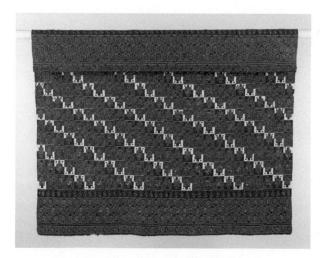

Fig 10.8
Men in the Andes region typically wore sleeveless tunics over loincloths, while
women wore wrap-around dresses belted and pinned at the shoulder. The highest
textile grades were colorful ones woven of camelid fibers, like this woman's dress
from Chuquibamba, Peru (fourteenth to early sixteenth centuries). Textiles for both
men and women were woven into repeated symmetrical patterns out of brightly
colored wool, with the softest fibers reserved for the social elite.
© The Metropolitan Museum of Art, public domain

Conclusion

From 1300 to 1500, merchants, traders, and adventurers transported an array of staple products and luxury items along regional routes such as the silk roads, the Indian Ocean, the Mediterranean and China Seas, and the Inca roads. The gold trade was a driving force in political changes, consolidation, and competition. Europeans' growing demand for gold and silver drove their expansion along the Atlantic coast of West Africa – seeking direct access to its gold – and across the Atlantic at the end of the fifteenth century. The massive influx of American gold and, especially, silver from South American mines, however, caused sixteenth-century European coinage to tank in value, sparking rampant inflation. This was especially true in Spain, the main importer of American precious metals, which provided space for the English and Dutch to gain economic predominance on the global stage by the seventeenth century.

While it had been Italian merchants who monopolized trade routes in the Mediterranean, by the end of the fifteenth and into the sixteenth centuries, the Portuguese and Spanish displaced the importance of Mediterranean trade by sailing around Africa into the Indian Ocean and across the Atlantic to the Americas. By doing so, they fundamentally altered the world system: European commercial markets came to dominate and subjugate regional networks like those of the Americas and the Indo-Pacific, which had previously operated as economic centers. In the early modern period, these formerly essential emporia became peripheral supply points or sources of riches rather than autonomous economic agents. The European economic enterprise was increasingly the dominant global power.

B: STATUS SYMBOLS

Introduction

In the late Middle Ages, patterns of long-distance trade that were established in the earlier centuries continued, but at a significantly increased pace and volume. Conspicuous consumption – the public display of one's purchasing power – by wealthy and powerful elites drove much of the commerce in the later medieval period. Members of the Mongol ruling families, both noble and non-noble wealthy Europeans, Muslim elites, and Inca royalty all sought to surround themselves with signs of their wealth and status. They threw sumptuous banquets with imported foods, spices, and drinks. They wore gorgeous silk or alpaca clothing and jewelry, adorned with gold, gems, pearls, coral, and precious stones. And, they purchased, patronized, and gifted a wide variety of artistic items that also helped fuel long-distance commercial connections.

Evidence: Mansa Musa's gold

Gold dinars and their imitations

The Colmar Treasure

Islamicate bronze incense burner in the shape of a lion

The travel accounts of Marco Polo and Ibn Battuta

Treasure fleet of Zheng He

Inca tunic with gold panels

Mansa Musa's Gold

Because gold was so highly desired by Mediterranean markets, control over gold fields and trans-Saharan trade routes was a focus for empire-building within West Africa. The power of gold is observable above all in the pilgrimage of Mansa Musa (r. ca. 1312–1337), the tenth ruler of the empire of Mali (1230–1670). Often referred to as the richest man who ever lived, Musa's fame comes from his travel to Cairo and Mecca carrying displays of his vast wealth. The Mali Empire had grown rich and powerful within West Africa by conquering cities and regions, many of which were connected to the gold trade.

The religion of Islam arrived in West Africa along with North African traders who traveled across the Sahara. But, it was not until the reign of Mansa Musa that Mali had a ruler as dedicated to the religion as he was: he built mosques, patronized Islamic learning, and departed on the *hajj* (pilgrimage to the holy city of Mecca). Between 1324 and 1326, he traveled along some of the same trans-Saharan paths long followed by commodities. Arriving in Cairo with hundreds of elephants, camels, and enslaved men and women, Mansa Musa had with him what is estimated to have been a literal ton of gold in the form of dust and bullion. The impact of his arrival in Cairo was immense: not only did his entourage impress observers with its opulence, but also the gold that he brought into the city's economy depressed the price of gold and caused inflation that was said to have lasted a decade. Arabic written records of King Musa's visit to Cairo also focus on his generosity and the many distributions of gold he made to various officials.

Mansa Musa's pilgrimage represents one of the earliest moments of European awareness, not of African gold, but of the places where it came from and the people who controlled it. African empires like Mali and kings like Musa were now located on Europe's physical and mental maps of the world. For instance, the 1375 *mappa mundi* (world map) known as the *Catalan Atlas* displays Mansa Musa as a king with a golden crown and scepter, sitting on a throne overseeing all the known (to Europeans) cities of Africa – for example, the trading hubs of the western Sahara Desert, such as Sijilmasa, Gao, and Timbuktu. He holds a large nugget (or disk) of gold, signifying what Europeans thought was most important about him and his kingdom.

Gold Dinars and their Imitations

The primary reason Europeans were so interested in gold was for producing high-value coins with which to buy other luxury goods and fund warfare. Europeans purchased gold from Muslim traders and modeled their gold coinages on Muslim ones. One of the most widespread denominations in the western Mediterranean region was the Almoravid dinar, minted by a Muslim dynasty ruling North Africa and al-Andalus 1040–1147. When they conquered Sijilmasa in 1054, they gained control over the gold trade and began striking massive quantities of dinars in the city.

The dinar was the standard gold coin of the Islamic world, introduced in the late seventh century with a weight standard of 4.25 grams of gold. Initially based on the Byzantine Empire's solidus, the dinar underwent a reform by the Umayyad caliph Abd al-Malik (685–705). Because of the dominance of Muslim merchants in the economy of the Mediterranean, and because Muslim rulers controlled trans-Saharan gold trade routes, the dinar became the standard gold denomination across the Mediterranean and Islamicate worlds. Between Spain and Central Asia, dinars were minted by local authorities, each of which contained the name of the caliph to whom that region was loyal. Rulers across the Muslim world had been minting gold dinars for hundreds of years before the Almoravids came to power, but their dinars were of the best quality because they had direct access to high-purity West African gold. In order to produce a lot of them, the Almoravids opened new mints across their united territory of western North Africa and Iberia.

WHAT CAN WE LEARN FROM MEDIEVAL COINS?

Medieval objects – whether prized artistic pieces that made their way into museums, or daily-life items found in archeological sites, shipwrecks, or buried hoards – can supplement our use of textual sources for studying the past, and often they answer questions that surviving texts do not. Coins are some of the most commonly found medieval objects, and they are rich with meanings: some economic, but others related to political authority, religious ideas, long-distance connections between cultures, technology, and political propaganda.

Premodern coins were issued by a wide variety of rulers – not only kings or caliphs, but local governors, emirs, dukes, counts, and princes. So, one thing a coin or set of coins might tell us is who the authorities were, who could issue money, and how much control they had over its value. Local rulers might issue a few low-quality coins, which indicates a different level of political and economic power than a king or emperor minting numerous high-value coins, and an historian would be curious about a leader who issued no coins at all. If a state sought centralized political power, they might consolidate their control over minting and outlaw the coinages of their predecessors or of rival authorities in their realm. And, in some places, coins might be issued by regional governors, but in the name of a higher power. For example, coins in the Islamicate world were issued by local emirs, but listed the name of the caliph to whom the emir was loyal – so a coin might tell us which of the competing caliphates a particular region was allied with.

Coins were minted by placing a thin metal blank disc between two halves of a die – one with the image to appear on the front (obverse) and the other with the image for the back (reverse). Studying these images helps us understand the values, propaganda goals, and influences of the ruler who minted them. Which symbols or ideas did they want circulating? Did they choose to depict the ruler, a religious image, or one with historical meaning? Which other cultures' coins did they imitate? In the case of medieval Islamicate world coins, however, it is the lack of images that is noteworthy: the earliest Islamic coins minted looked like Byzantine coins, showing the ruler on one side; but after a coinage reform by the ninth caliph, images were replaced by words alone – typically quotes from the Qur'an. This came to be standard across the Islamicate world, which produced numerous high-value coins throughout the Middle Ages. They were also imitated in parts of the Christian world where trade with Muslims was common (for example the Crusader Kingdom and also Sicily and southern Italy), sometimes with fake Arabic inscriptions and sometimes in real Arabic carrying Christian messages.

Coins were not only political and symbolic items, they were also units of economic exchange. Thus, they can teach us about a society's volume of trade, access to precious metals, partners in trade, and how far away their trade goods traveled. Coins of high metallic purity are considered signs of a high volume of trade and access to precious metals; debased (alloyed) ones indicate the opposite. Likewise, the metals used in a ruler's coins tell us important things about what types of trade were happening: bronze or copper coins were typically used for small purchases, silver for medium-value ones, gold for large and expensive items. If a society had coins of all three metals, it could indicate that exchanges at many economic levels were taking place with money, not just barter. If a society used only high-value, or only low-value, coins, we might presume that barter was used for small exchanges instead of coinage, or that valuable luxury items were not available for purchase. Some premodern societies used non-coin commodities as money, such as cowrie shells, bolts of silk, metal ingots, glass beads, or other items with intrinsic value. The use of such a "commodity money," either in place of or alongside metal coins, can teach us much about a society's system of value and exchange.

The location in which coins are found can also tell us about the extent of a society's communication and exchange networks. If, for example, a society only minted low-value coins found in archeological sites close to home, we might surmise that they were not engaged in long-distance trade for valued goods from far away. If, on the other hand, we find gold or silver coins in graves, sites, or hoards, in distant regions, or copied by faraway cultures – as with Roman coins both found and imitated in China or the coins from Iran discovered in a treasure hoard in the north of England, both discussed in Chapter 6 – we can tell that their economies and societies were linked across long distances.

Fig 10.9
This *maravedí* of Alfonso IX el Baboso (the Slobberer), King of León (1188–1230)
retains the style of its model, the Almoravid dinar, which had Arabic inscriptions: one
in a circular band around another in the center. On the Spanish Christian coin,
the circular inscription is in Latin and the center is replaced with a portrait of the
crowned king on the obverse and the heraldic image of a lion on the reverse
Numismática Pliego, Spain

Almoravid dinars were so highly valued that even Christian merchants in
the Mediterranean world used them as valid currency. They have been found
in treasure hoards in Europe and were used as currency by Italians trading with
the East. They also formed the basis for some of Christian Europe's first gold
coins. As Spanish Christian kings pushed southward into Muslim territory
during the so-called *reconquista*, they gained control over areas that regularly
used gold currency. Christian kings in Spain and Portugal took over minting
Arabic-style gold coins from the late twelfth century, modeled quite closely on
the Almoravid dinars.

Other Latin Christian gold coins minted before the thirteenth century were
restricted to lands that had been conquered from Muslim rulers. For example,
Sicily was taken from Muslim control by Latin Christians called Normans in
the mid-eleventh century. They continued to produce the gold quarter-dinar
that had been the island's primary denomination for centuries. Reconfigured
to include Christian symbols, it was a popular currency in Mediterranean
transregional trade because it could be used for smaller exchanges (at only
one-fourth the value of a dinar). Similarly, crusader territories in Syria minted
gold coins in order to do business with Muslim merchants from neighboring
regions who were accustomed to using dinars for high-value exchanges. The
crusader states minted coins that looked like Fatimid (Egyptian) dinars but
mostly used "pseudo-Arabic" – squiggles that look like Arabic script but are
illegible as Arabic language. Called the *bezant* (from "Byzantium," which also
used coin currency), this coin style was altered in 1250 to include a Christian
cross, after the pope objected to the use of Islamic images and inscription styles
on Christian coinages.

In 1252 both Genoa and Florence had enough supply of gold bullion to mint
their own gold coinages. Unlike all earlier Christian gold coins, these were not
based (in either value or style) directly on Islamic-style coins. Venice followed

in 1284, modeling its coin on the Byzantine coins of the eastern Mediterranean. Most future European gold coins were modeled on these Italian golds, since Italian merchants controlled many of the trade routes linking Europe with the rest of the hemisphere. However, in 1266 when the French King Louis IX (r. 1226–1270) tried to issue a gold coin of his own, it was not a success. Neither was the "gold penny" introduced by English King Henry III (r. 1216–1272) in 1257, which rapidly failed. Northern Europeans were not yet ready to consider gold as coinage material, although they were accustomed to it as a valuable metal for prestige items and as decoration in valuable manuscripts.

It was not until the mid-fourteenth century that English and French kings found success in introducing gold coinages to their realms. King Edward III (r. 1327–1377) first issued a gold coin soon after starting the Hundred Years' War (by declaring himself heir to the French throne in 1337). The French King John II ("the Good," r. 1350–1364) responded by issuing a gold coin in 1360, after being released from English captivity. As these and other wars were conducted across Europe in the late Middle Ages, money became increasingly important for kings who needed to pay soldiers, ransom captives, and supply troops. By this period, all of these exchanges used money, unlike in the early Middle Ages when lands and titles could be used to reward loyal soldiers.

By the late fifteenth century, however, European gold supplies had dropped sharply. The collapse of a unified state in western North Africa meant that less West African gold was transported across the Sahara to Mediterranean ports. And, the Hungarian gold mine at Kremnica was essentially depleted, causing European mints to slow or even cease production of coins. And yet, European markets still needed money to function. All regular economic transactions took place in cash, and wealthy European consumers, in particular, continued to seek desirable products from the Islamicate world and Southeast Asia. Kings continued to wage expensive wars using professional soldiers who expected to be paid in cash. The drought in precious metals meant that, when Europeans began to exploit the natural resources of the Americas in the late fifteenth and sixteenth centuries, they sought gold and silver above all else.

Gold and Silk in European Fashions

European demand for gold was tied to two main developments in the later medieval period: the first was the growing trade imbalance with China, the source of highly desired spices and silks. So, most gold and silver was used for making coins with which to purchase these luxury goods, and European coins (in both silver and gold) flowed eastward in ever-increasing amounts. The second development was the rise of local European industries in growing cities, whose economies came to be completely dependent upon coins by this period.

But, gold was also desired as a decorative element itself – gold leaf was used in luxury book production, gold thread was sewn into fashionable clothing, and gold was cast into fine jewelry. In the early Middle Ages, silk was an imported luxury in Europe, either purchased or received as diplomatic gifts from silk-producing regions of China or Byzantium. It was preserved for the most sacred uses (like wrapping holy relics), or ceremonial robes for the highest elites (like emperors and popes). Silk production facilities were introduced to the Islamicate Mediterranean (and formerly Muslim places like Sicily and Spain) by the central Middle Ages. But, by the later thirteenth century, local European silk industries had also developed in northern Italy and Paris, which imported not only silk fiber but also technologies and skilled silk workers from the East and the Mediterranean world.

The European silk industry, as well as those for other textiles, shoes, jewelry, hats, purses, leather goods, and woven belts, all speak to the styles preferred by the wealthy for fashionable clothing and adornment. Both men's and women's fashions changed regularly, and urban burgesses and aristocrats alike wanted to keep up with new styles. European clothing and textiles were made from a wide variety of materials, including wool, cotton, linen, silk, and velvet, all in a range of quality and fineness. Wealthy people wore several layers of clothing, often designed so that the top layer opened to frame layers of rich color and design. Color was a particularly important part of fashion, and vibrant colors were in high demand. So, too, were stripes and patterns, made either by weaving or by

Fig 10.10
A silk purse, made in early fourteenth century Paris, was embroidered with brightly colored silk yarn and gold thread. It depicts a scene associated with the cultural concept of "courtly love," a literary and artistic construct that was closely connected to the idea of chivalry. Chivalry was a social code of honor that supposedly differentiated the knightly class from the wealthy but non-noble burgesses. The themes of courtly love and chivalry were popular images for tapestries and embroidered items.
Metropolitan Museum of Art, Gift of Irwin Untermyer, 1964, 64.101.1364

Fig 10.11
Like the silk purse above, shoes were another item of clothing subject to changing fashions. All levels of society wore leather or fabric shoes, although the elite turned shoes into sensational objects. This example of a leather shoe from fourteenth-century England has an extremely long and pointy toe. This was a man's shoe, cut quite low to display the wearer's ankle. Medieval aristocratic men wore tunics with colored tights (called hose) underneath, and a shoe like this would accentuate the length and shapeliness of the leg. In the mid-fifteenth century, shoes like this were the target of sumptuary laws on the grounds that they were both impractical and sexually explicit. Short tunics were also restricted by such laws, often intended to keep lower classes from imitating high-class fashions, especially ones that revealed so much of the body.
© Museum of London

embellishment with beads and embroidery. Some of the most spectacular silk fabrics were embroidered with gold thread.

The shapes, colors, and decorations of shoes and clothing went in and out of fashion relatively rapidly. Tunics changed length, hats and headdresses changed height and style, and popular colors and patterns shifted. Embroidery, striping, and decoration were important aspects of fashion, and late medieval clothes were thought to "speak" through words, images, and designs. By the fourteenth century, buttons (of metal, ivory, or bone) and decorative clasps were found on the fronts and backs of tunics, and on both sleeves. Poorer people wore fewer layers of clothing, typically made of coarse wool and other animal hair fabrics. Burgesses tried to imitate elite fashions, although usually with less sumptuous materials.

Gold, Silks, and Spices in the Islamicate World

Just as European consumers desired spices, silks, and precious metals from afar, so, too, did people throughout the extensive Islamicate world. Merchants from Muslim-ruled lands controlled many of the markets and transit ports that brought spices, porcelains, incenses, silks, and precious stones into both land

Fig 10.12
Noble Christians were not the only ones who adorned themselves with gold and silk
in later medieval Europe: so too did Jews, many of whom were wealthy burgesses.
The gold wedding ring at the center of these jewels is just one of many items of high
value found buried in what is known as the Colmar Treasure. Enameled in red and
green and inscribed with Hebrew letters spelling "mazel tov" ("congratulations')
and with a gold dome in the shape of the Temple of Jerusalem (destroyed in 70 CE),
it held both monetary and cultural value. It was buried in the wall of a house along
with many other items of gold and silver jewelry and coins around 1348, when
the Jewish community of Europe was suffering doubly – both from the disease of
the plague and from attacks against Jews carried out by Christians who thought
that Jews might be the cause of the epidemic. The treasure was collected and
hidden, probably in an attempt to safeguard it from attackers. It was not discovered
until 1863.
Photographer: Jean-Gilles Berizzi. Paris, Musee National du Moyen Age et Thermes
de Cluny. © 2020. RMN-Grand Palais / Dist. Photo SCALA, Florence

markets and Mediterranean Sea ports. But, it would be a mistake to see the
merchants of the Muslim world as only middlemen rather than purveyors of
precious commodities to their home markets.

Islamicate world consumers had been using coinage for exchanges for many
more centuries than those in Europe or China. They purchased a wide variety
of products from Southeast Asia and around the Indian Ocean: spices like cinnamon, pepper, star anise, sumac, cumin, and nutmeg for elaborate banquets
and home recipes – all of which were grown in China or Southeast Asia. The
category of "spices" could also include a number of other things like dyes,
medicines, and perfumes. Among the latter category, incenses and aromatic
woods were among the most highly desired items, and were traded in large
quantities. Incense and coals would be placed inside a burner, and perfumed
smoke would exit through its many small holes. Such items both exemplify the
luxurious products bought and sold at marketplaces in the Islamicate world
and demonstrate the fact that medieval Muslim art was often comfortable with

Fig 10.13
This bronze incense burner is shaped like a lion and elaborately decorated
with scrolling designs and Arabic inscriptions, which provide details that are
rare for medieval works of art: the names of the artist and owner, and the date of
manufacture. Made by Jafar ibn Muhammad ibn Ali in 1181/82 for an elite patron
in Iran (then under the control of Seljuq sultans, Muslim Turks who paid allegiance
to the Abbasid caliphs of Baghdad but operated independently), this item also
displays words – like the Jewish ceremonial ring above – that wished happiness and
prosperity on its owner. Animal and bird forms were popular shapes for incense
burners, and lions were particularly used to represent bravery, ferocity, and nobility
of bearing.
Metropolitan Museum of Art, Rogers Fund, 1951, 51.56

representations of humans and animals. This was particularly true of art used
in secular contexts.

Consumers in the Islamicate world also greatly desired porcelain ceramics
from China, which were among the earliest drivers of Indian Ocean trade. By
the later medieval period, the technology for producing fine porcelain dishes
had transferred to the central Islamic lands, and Muslim artisans were producing delicate ceramics in a variety of styles. Bright blue, green, and gold were
favorite colors, and many featured geometric or calligraphic designs. Later,
medieval Europeans also wanted fine ceramics, both porcelains from China
and brightly painted stoneware from the Islamicate world.

The use of gold as a decorative element, like in the gilding on ceramics, was
quite commonly used to emphasize the magnificence and splendor of an object
and its owner. One of the most spectacular gilded items from the premodern
Muslim world is known as the Blue Qur'an (see Figure 8.1). Written entirely
in gold and silver leaf on parchment dyed with indigo, the style of this manuscript evokes the gilded purple-dyed manuscripts produced in early medieval

Fig 10.14
A bowl from late twelfth- or thirteenth-century Iran is enameled in turquoise glaze with gold and brightly colored decorations. Showing a scene of elite courtly life, it depicts a lute player at the center with ten seated people either singing or watching the performance. All wear gorgeous robes and jewelry, speaking to the importance of elaborate textiles and adornments among wealthy Muslim elite. Bowls of fruit suggest a banquet scene, where people would enjoy music performances, poetry recitations, aromatic perfumes, and lots of highly spiced foods and drinks.
Metropolitan Museum of Art, Henry G. Leberthon Collection, Gift of Mr. and Mrs. A. Wallace Chauncey, 1957, 57.61.16

Byzantium. Indigo was one of the medieval world's most popular dyes and was regularly traded in large bales. Indigo was typically used to dye fabrics in shades of blue and purple, but many other natural products were used to color textiles in a range of other bright colors. Wealthy and high-ranking people around the premodern world chose to dress in quite colorful clothing as signs of their expendable wealth and status.

Clothing, along with the raw materials for producing and dyeing fabrics, represented a huge part of the commerce of the Islamicate world. In addition to fashionable clothing for regular consumers, many textiles were created by and for the rulers and elite. For example, *tiraz* silks are finely woven silk robes with bands of embroidered Arabic inscriptions. These bands would appear at the cuffs, along the bottom of the robes, or, as in the robe worn by the lute player on the bowl in Figure 10.14, as a band along the upper arm. Often, the inscriptions were created in gold leaf or gold thread and contained messages about the name of the textile's patron and the date of production. The inscriptions might also include blessings and good wishes for the wearer – just as the turquoise bowl in Figure 10.14 is ringed along the edge with Arabic conferring blessings and happiness on the owner. *Tiraz* workshops were closely controlled by rulers and, unlike other fine textiles of the Islamicate world, could not be purchased in the marketplace. Instead, a ruler would bestow a *tiraz* as a gift, honoring the recipient, or use them as ceremonial robes.

The Travel Accounts of Marco Polo and Ibn Battuta

Much of the splendor of later medieval culture is known from travel accounts, such as that of Marco Polo (1254–1324), a member of a Venetian merchant family accustomed to trading in western Asia. In 1271, he joined his father and uncle on their second journey, which resulted in a 17-year stay in Mongol China, diplomatic work on behalf of the Great Khan, Kublai (1215–1294), and a return to Venice via the Indian Ocean route. Although some of the claims in his *Travels* are demonstrably false or exaggerated, most historians accept that he really did make the trip, and his account contains important details about the economy and society of Mongol China as well as the cultural and economic riches to be found there. Most importantly, perhaps, is the fact that later medieval travelers and authors – such as Christopher Columbus and the creator of the Fra Mauro world map (see below) – relied upon Polo's text as a source of information about the East.

Similarly, the Muslim scholar and explorer Ibn Battuta (1304–1369) wrote a travel account that contains a mix of fact, error, and fantasy. He traveled for most of his adult life, starting from his native Morocco and covering around 75,000 miles across Africa, Central Asia, and the Indian Ocean. In addition to descriptions of locations and cultures across both the Islamicate world and non-Muslim lands, Ibn Battuta's text shows the depths of the interconnection between Muslims and others in maritime Asia. He visited mosques, Qur'anic schools, scholars, and Muslim merchant communities around the Indian Ocean and eastern Africa. In China, he visited port cities like Quanzhou and Guangzhou, which had been home to Muslims since the eighth century and testified to the importance of the exchange of ideas, science, technology (especially in navigation), and commodities between the Islamicate world and China.

Tributes and Technologies

Marco Polo and Ibn Battuta were primarily (although not exclusively) travelers over land. But the late medieval period also saw an increase in maritime voyages for exploration, not just for profit. The successors to the Mongol Yuan dynasty in China, the Ming dynasty (1368–1644), reversed many of the Mongol economic and commercial policies of openness to foreigners. For example, Ming policy outlawed private maritime trading; all foreign exchange was to be under official control. But, the third Ming emperor, known as the Yongle Emperor (1402–1424), sponsored a fleet of treasure ships under the admiralty of a court eunuch named Zheng He (1371–1433). Between 1405 and 1433 Zheng He captained seven voyages to Vietnam, Java, Sumatra, Sri Lanka, southern

India, the Persian Gulf, Red Sea, and along the eastern coast of Africa. His fleets comprised hundreds of massive ships, which carried thousands of sailors and thousands of tons of Chinese products.

These were not simply trade voyages, however. They engaged in tribute trade, or the official exchange of valuable items. The primary goal of these voyages was to impress foreign leaders with the power and might of the Chinese imperial navy and to reinforce China's tributary relationships. They offered and sought gifts of high value – all of the expected trade goods plus exotic animals, such as ostriches, lions, leopards, and even a giraffe. For a time, these "treasure voyages" established the Ming as the dominant naval power of the period.

On the other side of the hemisphere, late medieval Mediterranean sea-faring was solidly under the control of northern Italian sailors, especially the Genoese and the Venetians. After the withdrawal of the Ming from maritime concerns in 1433, Muslim merchants directed the seaborne trade of the Indian Ocean. But, by the end of the fifteenth and beginning of the sixteenth century, it was the Spanish and Portuguese who dominated the newly established sea routes around Africa, and across the Atlantic, and were thus able to control the new global trade routes. Portuguese sailors were the first to establish trading ports along the Atlantic coast of Africa, and were first to round the Cape of Good Hope into the Indian Ocean (under captain Bartolomeu Dias in 1488). Spanish ships were the first to reach the Americas across the Atlantic a few years later.

This shift in power was partly due to geographical accident: states with access to the western Iberian Atlantic coast were shut out of Mediterranean sailing, but in the long run that proved to be advantageous because they could focus on Atlantic sailing. Another major reason was the efforts of a Portuguese prince named Henry (1394–1460), who lives on in history as Prince Henry the Navigator. He sponsored naval expeditions along the African coast and invested in the technology and cartography that allowed Portuguese sailors to successfully navigate the difficult Atlantic waters. For these new types of ships, sailors adapted technologies from other cultures, such as the Chinese magnetic compass (discussed in Chapter 6) and the Islamic mariner's astro-labe and quadrant, used to determine latitude. Using improved instruments alongside new styles of maps called portolan charts, Iberian vessels could sail across open water, into the wind, and at night without getting disas-trously lost.

Inca Gold

Gold was also an important and valuable item transported along the Inca roads, although not as a commercial product or coinage as in the Eastern Hemisphere. Mined throughout the empire, it was especially plentiful in the area of modern

Bolivia. Most of the gold workshops were located in the Inca capital of Cuzco, so the mined ore would be transported along Incan roads and processed there. Gold was worked in the Andes and across Mesoamerica from around 2000 BCE, so Inca goldwork incorporated thousands of years of tradition. Because gold, silver, and copper objects were so valued by the Inca, metalworkers were highly specialized artisans working in royally controlled workshops. In 1470, Inca rulers imported expert artisans from the Chimú Empire.

Not used as currency, gold was primarily made into ritual objects that indicated political power and status. It was fashioned into bracelets, earrings, nose ornaments, crowns, ritual cups, and other items of adornment often reserved for the use of the Inca royalty and those to whom they gave diplomatic gifts. Most Incan metalwork is now lost to us because the Spanish conquerors melted down the vast majority of it for production of coins sent back to Europe.

The visual and aural properties of gold were among the most significant of its features and part of its value within Andean cultures. Many Inca goldwork items were breastplates that were meant to shimmer and create noise when worn into battle or during imperial rituals. Tunics covered in gold plates also took advantage of the metal's sensory properties. The finest alpaca fiber was brightly dyed and woven into a tunic, which was then festooned with small squares of gold that would have glimmered in the sun and clacked as its wearer moved. Figure 10.15 is an extremely high-value tunic that belonged to a person of very high rank and honor within the Incan hierarchy.

Fig 10.15
A sign of luxury and status, this tunic with gold panels sewn onto an alpaca textile belonged to a powerful nobleman from the south coastal Inca Empire, 1430–1532.
Werner Forman / Universal Images Group / Getty Images

Looking Forward

In 1532, the Spanish conqueror Francisco Pizarro defeated the troops of the last Sapa Inca (ruler of the Inca Empire) Atahualpa, ending both the political and economic autonomy of the Inca. Atahualpa promised Pizarro an enormous ransom in gold and silver for his release, but despite delivery he was kept in captivity and executed the next year. Pizarro's actions inaugurated mass appropriation of Incan wealth by the Spanish. Seeking to exploit the natural riches of the Americas, with gold and silver at their heart, the European invaders decimated the political, cultural, and economic infrastructure that had been established by Indigenous peoples. Thus, the Native resources of the Americas came to be integrated into the networks of connections that were increasingly dominated by European merchants and their market demands – the beginnings of an entirely new phase of globalized economic systems called the early modern period.

Some historians have thought that the rise of European trade along the Atlantic coast of Africa in the fifteenth century caused a significant decline in trans-Saharan trade, but others find evidence for continued trade into the sixteenth century. The true end to the dominance of West Africa's gold trade came from the mid-1600s rise of South American silver exploitation. Mines like that of Potosí (in modern Bolivia), which was discovered in 1545, flooded the European market for precious metals. This initially helped Europeans pay for the commodities they desired from China and Southeast Asia, but eventually caused monetary deflation and economic instability across Europe and the Mediterranean. From the early sixteenth century, the main export from West Africa shifted to enslaved humans, who were exploited to work the mines and agricultural fields of the Americas. The massive transatlantic slave trade that arose from this process both dominated and defined the early modern global economy, while bringing to an end the power of the African gold trade and the autonomous economies of West Africa.

Research Questions

1. Compare and contrast monetary systems in two different regions/countries/locales. Remember to include non-coinage systems!
2. How did the Mongols both disrupt and encourage trade in their empires?
3. Compare some of the entries in Marco Polo's travels to those of Ibn Battuta. What seems to interest both of these men in their travels? What differences do you see in the narrative styles? What do these narratives tell us about the economic, political, and/or cultural worlds of each of these men?
4. How is clothing and adornment a signal of wealth and power? What types of clothing/adornment were important signs in South America? Europe? Africa? The Middle East?

5. Numismatics is the study of coins. Investigate a local numismatic society and inquire if anyone there has studied or traded in medieval coins. What types of coins are most favored by modern numismatists? What coins are abundant?

6. The mariner's astrolabe and the quadrant allowed sailors to navigate open waters and unchartered seas. How did sailors use these tools? How did they operate?

Further Reading

Allsen, Thomas T. *The Steppe and the Sea: Pearls in the Mongol Empire*. Philadelphia: University of Pennsylvania Press, 2019.

Bennett, Judith M. *Ale, Beer and Brewsters in England: Women's Work in a Changing World, 1300–1600*. Oxford: Oxford University Press, 1996.

Berzock, Kathleen Bickford, ed. *Caravans of Gold, Fragments in Time: Art, Culture, and Exchange Across Medieval Saharan Africa*. Princeton, NJ: Princeton University Press, 2019.

Boehm, Barbara Drake. *The Colmar Treasure: A Medieval Jewish Legacy*. London: Scala Arts Publishers, 2019.

Farmer, Sharon. *The Silk Industries of Medieval Paris: Artisanal Migration, Technological Innovation, and Gendered Experience*. Philadelphia: University of Pennsylvania Press, 2016.

Gomez, Michael A. *African Dominion: A New History of Empire in Early and Medieval West Africa*. Princeton, NJ: Princeton University Press, 2018.

Hansen, Valerie. *The Open Empire: A History of China to 1800*, 2nd ed. New York: W.W. Norton, 2015.

Lane, Kris. *Potosí: The Silver City that Changed the World*. Oakland: University of California Press, 2019.

Lo, Jung-pang. *China as a Sea Power, 1127–1368*. Singapore: National University of Singapore Press, 2012.

Mendieta, Ramiro Matos, and Jose Barreiro, eds. *The Great Inka Road: Engineering an Empire*. Washington, DC: Smithsonian Books, 2015.

Pillsbury, Joanne, Timothy Potts, and Kim N. Richter, eds. *Golden Kingdoms: Luxury Arts in the Ancient Americas*. Los Angeles: Getty Publications, 2017.

Russell, Peter. *Prince Henry 'the Navigator': A Life*. New Haven, CT: Yale University Press, 2000.

Spufford, Peter. *Money and its Use in Medieval Europe*. Cambridge: Cambridge University Press, 1988.

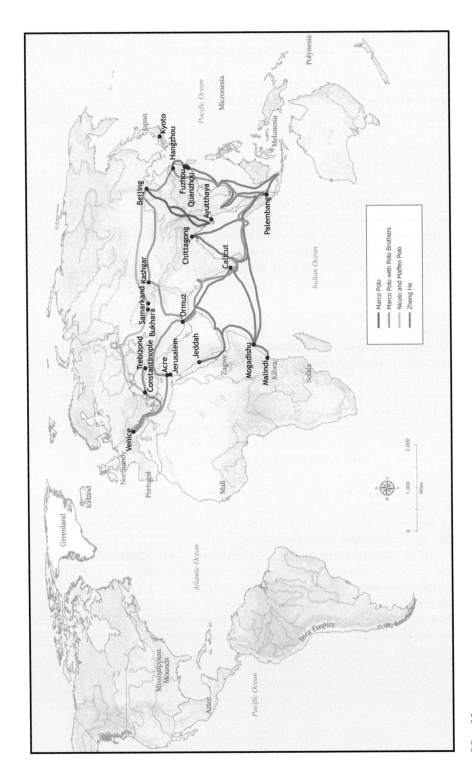

Map 11
World Connected

11 World Connected

Politics, 1300–1500

Introduction

The Earth's surface is composed of about 30 percent land and just over 70 percent water. Attempts to explain and explore this vast world have been voiced and recorded in myriad languages, often tied to political endeavors of rulers and regimes. The boundaries of continents and oceans on maps have shifted considerably over time. Historical linguistics – the study of language or speech patterns in the past – provides a tremendous amount of evidence for the long-distance movement of people and products. For example, across the Pacific Ocean – from the islands of Southeast Asia to the coast of South America – the spread of the sweet potato can be traced from community to community across oceans and over mountains through local words. The sweet potato is native to western South America and began its global travels with the Polynesian voyages to the Americas around 1000–1100 CE. A similar phenomenon can be glimpsed through the history of the tea trade: in general, those communities with overland contact with China, where the leaves have been traditionally harvested, adopted variants of the word "cha/chai" for the beverage, whereas those cultures with maritime links to East Asia refer to the drink as a form of "tea." Sweet potatoes and tea are just two of the commodities that helped fuel the trade economy, which in turn supported policies of regulation, taxation, and border management as many of the centralized governments that would define the modern world began to consolidate and expand their territories. Sweet potatoes and tea do not know political boundaries; those are made by humans.

This chapter discusses the politics of boundaries by focusing on islands and nautical networks in Section A and on the harsh terrains of deserts, mountains, plains, and other overland routes in Section B. Land and water often create natural boundaries between places, or at least the demarcations on maps make it seem that way. We intend to disrupt the idea of fixed borders, including those of continents and oceans, empires and territories, and also of concepts of marking, recording, remembering, or dividing history and time into periods or eras. As you have read in Chapter 1, mapmaking strategies and oral traditions have varied and been expressed in a multitude of forms across the Earth. The relationships of rulership to resources, and of kingdoms to commodities, guide our travels in this chapter. We will venture to many courts and encounter several forms of governance, each of which can serve as an inspiration for greater research on the entanglements of local and global in the medieval world.

A: ISLANDS AND NAUTICAL NETWORKS

Introduction

From 1300 to 1500 CE, ambitious rulers followed in the footsteps of traders and explorers, laying claim over territories and resources, natural and commercial. The familiar borders of present-day nations or states began to take shape for some parts of Eurasia, and these centuries also witnessed the rise of European colonial exploitation that we must continually keep in mind while looking at the politics of naming, erasing, acknowledging, and reclaiming the histories of land, water, and, most importantly, of people, in large parts of Africa, Southeast Asia, Austronesia, and the Americas. Consider as you read that despite their small size and disconnection from land masses, several island-nations – from Great Britain to Indonesia and Japan – ruled considerable territory and contributed to the trade examples discussed at the beginning of this chapter.

Maps assist in the creation of national history and in the process of state formation. As an example, consider a letter written on 21 August 1501 by Angelo Trevisan, secretary of the Venetian chancellor to Spain, to the Venetian naval captain Domenico Malipiero (1428–1515): "The map of the voyage to Calicut (India) is impossible to acquire, as the king has decreed the penalty of death to anyone who gives it away." Trevisan is referring to the prohibition by King Manuel I (r. 1495–1521) of spreading information about the voyages of Vasco da Gama (1460s–1524) and Pedro Álvares Cabral (ca. 1467/68–ca. 1520) to India. This mandate exemplifies the maxim that knowledge is power. More specifically, that knowledge of geography is power: geography is political.

Evidence:	Cantino Planisphere
	Kitab al-Sulwa (*Kilwa Chronicles*)
	Maqamat al-Hariri (The Assemblies of al-Hariri)
	Imagawa Sadayo's *Michiyukiburi* (*Travelings*)
	Codex Borbonicus
	Pacific Island stick chart

The Mysterious Island of Socotra

Speleologists are cave explorers, and, in 2000, Belgian geologist and speleologist Peter De Geest made an exciting subterranean discovery on the island of Socotra. Located about 150 miles off the coast of Africa, Socotra is today governed by Yemen and is an official UNESCO World Heritage site. Inside Cave Hoq – one of about 50 underground formations on the 1,466-square-mile landmass – De Geest encountered a trove of writing in various scripts and on a range of surfaces. From the second century BCE to about the thirteenth century CE, people stopped on the island – stranded or en route to other ports – and chiseled in stone or painted on bark short inscriptions in Indian (Brahmi) and South Arabian languages, as well as in Aksumite (from Ethiopia), Greek, and Palmyrene Aramaic (from present-day Syria). The names of people or deities and short phrases of exultation or pleas provide tantalizing evidence of Indian Ocean trade throughout antiquity and the long Middle Ages. There is even a petroglyph (or rock carving) of a ship.

Socotra is often described today as one of the most inaccessible places on the planet, due in part to visa restrictions (politics) and in part to the challenges in accessing the island (geography). It is also seen as a pristine paradise due to its natural wonders. What were all these medieval sailors searching for, and how did the island fare with the changing political landscapes (and seascapes) of the fourteenth and fifteenth centuries? A look at maps and manuscripts from the time provides some answers.

Remarkably, in late 1502, a man named Alberto Cantino, a representative (or spy) of Duke Ercole I d'Este (r. 1471–1505) of Ferrara, smuggled a 7' 2"-long world map on parchment from Portugal to Italy. Known as the Cantino Planisphere – which is a projection of the Earth on a flat or planar surface – this map records impressive details about the recently encountered (for Europeans, that is) coastline of Brazil (reached by Cabral in 1500), the Caribbean islands (known to Christopher Columbus from 1492 onward), the Florida Peninsula (Ponce de Leon waded ashore in 1513), and Newfoundland (ventured to by Gaspar Corte-Real by 1501). The Cantino Planisphere also depicts the land of India and the "spice" and "jewel" islands in Southeast Asia. Africa is at the center of the six sheets of parchment, and by following the flow of the Red Sea one reaches the island of Socotra (labelled Çacotora). Socotra is one of the few islands on the map to receive additional place designations: we also read Calissia ("Qalansiyah"), which is still a major town on the island and was said by Marco Polo (1254–1324) to be home to a Christian enclave.

The mapmaker indicated cities and provided descriptions of local commodities on other, larger islands such as Madagascar, Sri Lanka, and western Indonesia, specifically Sumatra and Java. The presence of Portuguese flags along coastal West and East Africa, and again on the shorelines of western India, suggests that Socotra held a strategic position in the Arabian Sea and greater Indian Ocean as a crossing for Christian merchants. Flags indicating Islamicate

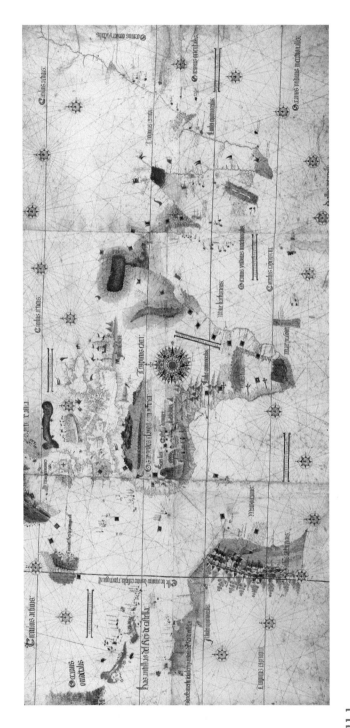

Fig 11.1
The Cantino Planisphere, 1502.
World History Archive / Alamy Stock Photo

polities mark the Arabian Peninsula and Southern Persia, limiting access to the waters of the Red Sea, except along a southern, Portuguese-controlled route, and to the Persian Gulf. The Portuguese eventually established a military presence on Socotra from 1507 to about 1511, continuing a long history of Christian presence on the island. Following Portuguese occupation, Socotra was ruled by the Mahra sultans, who governed from southern Arabia (present-day Yemen).

On the map, Socotra's natural riches are catalogued. The cartographer included this phrase in Portuguese next to the site: "On this island there are many date palms and herds of cattle." The global commodities prized by the Portuguese feature in several other inscriptions near islands across the map: porcelain can be found on an island called "Ganaor"; cinnamon, spices, and pearls can be found on Sri Lanka; brazilwood trees grow on Tioman Island (off the east coast of peninsular Malaysia), where silk is also traded; gold and silver can be sourced on Madagascar; and so forth. But while numerous texts throughout the Middle Ages signaled the abundance of dates and livestock on Socotra, above all they identify the island as the prime source of dragon's blood. This mysterious red resin can be obtained from certain trees, including the *Dracaena cinnabari* or dragon tree that is native to the Socotra archipelago and which secretes red sap. Elsewhere along global waterways, dragon's blood could be obtained from the Spanish Canary Islands in the Atlantic Ocean off the coast of Northwest Africa. The point to remember is that even seemingly remote and inaccessible islands, like Socotra, could be hubs of transoceanic trade and desirable territory for rulers.

DRAGON'S BLOOD AND MEDICINAL WONDERS IN THE CONNECTING SEA

For more than a thousand years, people all over the globe have used dragon's blood for such purposes as healing wounds (it calms inflammation and kills harmful bacteria), for increasing blood circulation, for reducing skin rash, and for stopping diarrhea and vomiting. Modern-day scientific analysis has confirmed the efficacy of dragon's blood for these and other ailments. Because of its all-purpose effectiveness, medieval doctors and faith healers attached some spiritual properties to dragon's blood. It was used in folk rituals and magic. Because of its beautiful red color, it was also prized as an ingredient in dyes and paints.

Plant-based medicinal remedies have been developed throughout human history. During the Middle Ages, recipes and descriptions of all known herbs, spices, vegetables, and fruits used in healing (including religious rituals and physician-directed care) were compiled from Baghdad and Mosul in Iraq to Salerno in southern Italy and Canterbury in England in manuscripts commonly known as *De materia medica* (On Medicinal Material). These collections of texts were often richly decorated and referenced ancient Greek and Roman writers, as well as scholars from the Islamicate world, including Dioscorides (40–90), Galen

(129–220), Ibn Sina (also called Avicenna; tenth–eleventh century), and Ibn Butlan (eleventh century). Similar manuscript traditions existed in India. The *Sushruta Samhita* is a compendium of the ancient Indian physician called Sushruta (sixth century BCE), whose practices form the foundation of Indian traditional medicine (known as Ayurveda).

Traditional Chinese Medicine (TCM) still prescribes treatments developed by the Ming dynasty physician Li Shizhen (1518–1593), whose writings covered acupuncture, pharmacology, and medicinal tinctures. In the Americas, Maya codices or codex-style ceramics reveal the many uses of natural cures, and oral traditions across North America provide glimpses into the sacred connections made through natural medicinals.

The Indian Ocean World

If we continue looking at the Cantino Planisphere and proceed down the eastern coast of Africa, we encounter additional Portuguese flags at Mogadishu, Malindi, Kilwa, Mozambique, and Sofala. Regarding Kilwa, the mapmaker writes, "The king of this city is a very noble king and rules this coast, from here to Sofala. In this kingdom there is an abundance of gold and other things." An interest in gold is revealed through other inscriptions along the Swahili Coast (as this region is also called) as is the declaration that these rulers are loyal to the Portuguese crown.

Kilwa – or Kilwa Kisiwani as it is more formally called – is a fortified island that ruled over the vast coastal area from the eighth century CE until 1513, when competing powers in Oman and from Portuguese colonizers arose in the region and struggled for control of the island kingdom's territories. Islam was known to this part of Africa as early as the mid-ninth century, but by the tenth and eleventh centuries, more eastern Africans had converted to Islam, and the Kilwa sultanate began sometime in the tenth century. The archeological remains of a congregational mosque and a palace (the Husuni Kubwa, or "Great Fort") still dominate the landscape and testify to the might of this sultanate in the Indian Ocean world. The tides have also revealed intriguing facts about cosmopolitanism and trade at Kilwa. Sherds, or fragments, from a range of pottery routinely wash ashore. In 1974, the British Museum in London received a donation of 150 fragments of ceramic vessels found at Kilwa that can now be identified as originating from China, Persia, and East Africa (tenth to fourteenth century). No doubt the original objects were intended to be traded but likely sank with a merchant ship.

The thirteenth-century Iraqi painter Yahya ibn Mahmud al-Wasiti depicted one such barge to illustrate the *Maqamat al-Hariri* (The Assemblies of al-Hariri), a series of 50 anecdotes that take the form of fables, satires, romances, and proverbs. Al-Wasiti is often praised for his attention to the racial diversity of the Islamicate and Indian Ocean worlds, as well as for his interest in textiles, architecture, and engineering. Most of all, al-Wasiti's text and the archeological finds at Kilwa and across the Indian Ocean region bear witness to the role that trade played in establishing a robust economy.

Beyond the Swahili coast, similar ceramic objects have been found at the Great Zimbabwe – a royal palace in present-day Zimbabwe in southern Africa – dating from the tenth through the fourteenth century. A coin from the reign of the Yongle emperor (1403–1424) of Ming China was discovered on the island of Manda (part of Kenya), and coins from Northern Song China – from the reigns of emperors Renzong (1022–1063) and Shenzong (1067–1085) – have been excavated in Harla, Ethiopia. Copper coins from the Kilwa sultanate have also been found at the Great Zimbabwe, and further afield in Oman (on the Arabian Peninsula) and, remarkably, in Arnhem Land in the Northern Territory of Australia. This circulation of precious objects and currency suggests a complex network of commerce with significant island hubs, and a sophisticated knowledge of how to navigate the monsoon winds and tidal currents across the Indian Ocean. The material evidence that the sultans and their subjects participated in long-distance overland and maritime trade can be further corroborated by textual records that describe such encounters. The legacy, global reach, and

Fig 11.2
A Ship Sailing to Oman in *Maqamat al-Hariri* (The Assemblies of al-Hariri) by Yahya ibn Mahmud al-Wasiti, Baghdad, Iraq, 1237 CE/AH 634.
World History Archive / Alamy Stock Photo

maritime dominance of each of the rulers just mentioned continues to spark scholarly research and ignite our imagination about the possibility of seeing a connected and intricately entangled premodern world whose politics revolved around commerce and control of borders and resources.

The history of the Kilwa sultanate was recorded in two sixteenth-century texts (possibly derived from earlier sources, including oral traditions): the *Kitab al-Sulwa* (*Kilwa Chronicles*), a genealogy of rulers in Arabic, and the text *Decades of Asia* by João de Barros (1496–1570), who presents an account of King Manuel I and of Portuguese travels in India, Asia, and East Africa. Both authors tell us that the Swahili sultans originated from Shiraz in Persia (Iran), that fishermen discovered gold along the coast, and that the Yemeni Mahdali dynasty established rule in Shiraz and had conflict with the Kilwa rulers over succession throughout the fourteenth and fifteenth centuries. As we have seen, the Indian Ocean hosted a busy network of shipping ways that characterized the medieval period and would continue to define the political horizons of subsequent times. Our focus now shifts to other global oceans: first to the Pacific and then to the Atlantic.

"If You Have Little Leisure, Read Books": The Samurai Code in Japan

The island of Japan was besieged in 1274 and in 1281 by armies and navies under the command of Kublai Khan (1215–1294). Grandson of Chingghis Khan (ca. 1162–1227), who founded the Mongol dynasty, Kublai went on to establish his own court in mainland China as the Yuan dynasty (1271–1368). The dramatic events of this invasion include catastrophic naval battles and the destructive use of explosive devices engineered by the Mongols (gunpowder had been used in China since about the ninth century). Less than a century prior to this invasion, at the start of the Kamakura period (1185–1333) in Japanese history, a new system of government emerged: the shogun, a military dictator with power over the country (a position that lasted until 1868), replaced the emperor in sovereign matters of state, and the warrior caste known as the *bushi* or *buke* (more commonly known as samurai) protected the security of the realm and of provincial lords called *daimyo*.

During the Mongol-Japanese conflict, Takezaki Suenaga (1246–1314) proved a valiant fighter and skilled battle strategist. To commemorate his victories, and in accordance with the religious practices of Shintoism to offer gratitude to one's ancestors and to nature spirits, Takezaki Suenaga commissioned two painted handscrolls. Both are kept in the Museum of the Imperial Collection in the Imperial Palace in Tokyo, Japan. Together, the scrolls provide compelling visual detail about armor, ship construction, weaponry, and infantry movements. Above all, the scrolls highlight Takezaki Suenaga's bravery and virtue.

Fig 11.3
A scroll of the *Illustrated Account of the Mongol Invasion*, Japan, 1293. Called the *Moko shurai ekotoba*, the first measures over 75 feet long (23 meters), and the second stretches over 65 feet long (20 meters).
© Wikimedia Commons, public domain

The middle of the fourteenth century ushered in a new phase in the history of Japan, as Ashikaga Takauji (1305–1358) became the first shogun of the Muromachi period (named for the district in Kyoto where Ashikaga and his descendants ruled). One of the most remarkable and rare objects associated with Ashikaga is a *yoroi*, or suit of armor, now in the Metropolitan Museum of Art in New York City (see Figs. 7.1 and 7.2). This particular suit was typical of those worn by warriors on horseback. It consists of iron and leather scales, connected by leather and laces, and featuring lacquer decoration (produced from the sap of a tree, which hardens and can be imbued with sprinkled flakes of gold or painted during the drying process). The breastplate is stenciled with an image of a Buddhist protective deity called *Fudo Myo-o*, venerated by kneeling figures. Engulfed in flame, the deity holds a sword, symbolizing a severing of delusions or ignorance, and a rope, representing the binding of those ruled by violent passions and emotions.

In addition to the patronage of works of art that displayed military might and social status, the samurai class also gained honor through poetry. General Imagawa Sadayo (1326–1420) was learned in the writings of Buddhism and Confucianism and was trained in strategy and horse-back combat. He also wrote lyrical verse, a travel diary (the *Michiyukiburi* or *Travelings*), and committed his life to meditation as a Buddhist monk, taking the name Ryoshun. Of politically corrupt leaders he wrote, "In your actions you disregard the moral law by evading your public duties and considering your private benefit first." And another maxim is, "It should be regarded as dangerous if the ruler of the people in a province is deficient even in a single of the cardinal virtues of human-heartedness, righteousness, propriety, wisdom, and good faith."

Like earlier periods of Japanese history, Buddhism and diplomacy were also entwined in the Muromachi period. The monk Tensho Shubun (1414–1463) embarked on a mission to Korea in order to acquire manuscripts of important Buddhist texts, a journey that demonstrates the versatility of trade between polities and the way communication networks operated over land and sea.

Recalling the theme of paradise that we discussed in Chapter 5, in fifteenth-century Japan, lush and verdant gardens in domestic and elite spaces were gradually replaced by arid landscapes as aids for meditation and release from earthly desires or attachments. Thus politics are as much about competing factions and consolidation of power as they are about changing societal and religious ideals of how to govern.

Perspectives on Contact and Conquest

In the late fourteenth century, a successful and learned farmer on an island in the North Atlantic Ocean called Iceland, commissioned two scribes to write the so-called *Flateyjarbók* (*The Flat Island Book*). The stories in the manuscript transported readers and listeners to the time of Eirik Thorvaldsson (ca. 950–ca. 1003), known as Eirik the Red, and of his son Leif Eiriksson (ca. 970–ca. 1020). Among the 225 pages are sections that scholars refer to as the *Vinland Sagas*, Icelandic texts that include *The Saga of the Greenlanders* (about European settlements there) and *The Saga of Eirik the Red* (see Chapter 6). We learn that Eirik's father was banished from Norway, and thus Eirik's early life was spent in Iceland. Eirik, too, was later exiled and sailed with a crew to Greenland. His son, Leif, would eventually venture west to an area of coastal North America known as Vinland, which includes the archeological site of L'Anse aux Meadows on an island in Newfoundland and other establishments in the Gulf of Saint Lawrence and New Brunswick. Today, anyone around the world with a computer can page through the manuscript.

Books preserve memories of the past, but these accounts often reveal the biases of their authors. Comparing the *Vinland Sagas* and letters from the local bishops to popes in Rome – specifically the characterization of encounters with the Greenlandic and Canadian Inuit (the Kalaallit, Tunumiit, Dorset, and Thule) – with evidence from archeology and Indigenous oral histories provides counterpoints to understanding how each group adapted to the environment and interacted with each other. Conflict may have been a factor in the decline of the Greenland settlements, as manuscript evidence often indicates. But the cool climate may have more directly contributed to the eventual disappearance of a sustained European presence there. Indeed, another way to think about the chronology of the Middle Ages is to look at climate science, which creates timelines for the Medieval Climate Anomaly (ca. 900–1300) and the Little Ice Age (1300–1600). The latter centuries can be characterized by a slight cooling in the Northern Hemisphere. The last written records of Norse presence on Greenland were from 1408, and Hvalsey Church (in present-day Qaqortoq, Greenland) is the best-preserved ruin of this lost civilization.

The legacy of Scandinavian warrior-travelers, more commonly called Vikings, in other regions is also attested in manuscript and architectural traditions. For example, the *Chronicle of Normandy* by Benoît de Sainte-Maure (active

Fig 11.4
Flateyjarbók (The Flat Island Book), 1387–1394.
The Arni Magnusson Institute for Icelandic Studies, Reykjavik

1150–1180) or the *The Great Chronicle of Normandy* by an anonymous French author (ca. 1350) provide ancestral accounts of the Normans, descended from Viking settlers in present-day Normandy in northern France. An early fifteenth-century copy of Benoît's *Chronicle* from Paris depicts the Vikings as destructive and bloodthirsty, with scenes of churches in ruins and vicious attacks. But the text also notes the importance of the conversion to Christianity by Rollo (ca. 860–ca. 930) and champions the military victories and building activities of William I (ca. 1028–1087), "the Conqueror," in England. The manuscript was later owned by Claude de Lorraine (1526–1573), Duc d'Aumale, who had his coat of arms added as a frontispiece to the book, thereby asserting his dynastic link to his Norman predecessors.

Norman architecture – characterized by grand, rounded arches and massive drum columns with intricate patterns – can be seen from Canterbury and Durham cathedrals in England to Monreale in Sicily. One of the great centers of Norman power was the island of Sicily, especially during the reign of Roger II (1095–1154) (see Chapters 6 and 7). Claim to rule over Sicily was hotly contested throughout the Middle Ages, with claimants from England, France, Italy, Germany, Tunisia, and Egypt, among others. Remarkably, the Norse managed to colonize and establish a long-lasting dynastic presence in England, Italy, Russia, and North America – feats that continue to capture the imagination of filmmakers and video-game developers today.

The Aztec Island at the Heart of Mexico

Another empire as legendary as it was formidable is that of the Aztec, the Nahua-speaking Mexica who ruled across Mexico. Their civilization reportedly arose from Aztlán, generally believed to have been an island (today associated with Mexcaltitán de Uribe in the state of Nayarit, dating to the eleventh century). Their capital later moved to Tenochtitlan (present-day Mexico City), which was built on an island in the former Lake Texcoco. The first page of the Aztec codex (book) known as the *Codex Mendoza* – made around 1542 and named after Don Antonio de Mendoza (1495–1552), the first viceroy of New Spain (Mexico) – visualizes the legendary discovery in 1325 of the site that would grow to become one of the largest city-states in Mexico. According to an ancient prophecy, the peripatetic ancestral tribes would one day settle in a place where an eagle wrestled a serpent in its beak atop a cactus. This image is now one of the national symbols of Mexico. The 3 to 5 square mile (8 to 12 sq km) city included public administrative and agricultural buildings, palaces, and several temples, including the *Hueyi Teocalli* (Great Temple) dedicated to the gods of war (Huitzilopochtli) and rain and harvest (Tlaloc). Elsewhere in the *Codex Mendoza*, the Indigenous artists depicted the prized luxury objects of trade and tribute. These goods include turquoise, feathers, and textiles, and each are brightly colored and wonderfully arranged across the pages in an inventory of the status symbols of regional governance. Thus, as we have seen throughout our study on politics, economic access to desired goods (through both trade and taxation) is an important part of the consolidation of political power.

Precious few preconquest manuscripts from the Americas survive, and most are named for the collector, historic owner, or institution that owns that object (in the past or today). Some have been referred to by multiple names in the past. Efforts have been and continue to be made to digitize and present these treasures online. A short list of these codices shows us that most of them are very far from their point of origin. The *Codex Borgia* and *Codex Vaticanus B*, both from Puebla Mexico, are now in the Vatican. The *Codex Cospi*, also from Puebla, spent time in Rome but is now at the University of Bologna, Italy. The *Codex Fejérváry-Mayer* and *Codex Laud*, also Nahua texts, are in the UK, at the World Museum in Liverpool and the Bodleian Library in Oxford. Knowing where a text is from, and the paths it has been on, is known as provenance, and knowing the provenance of texts helps us to understand how colonialism has damaged and changed works all over the world.

Several of these codices record the rituals and religious practices of the Aztec, as well as their systems of marking time and tribute. *Codex Cospi* contains painted decoration from before and after the conquest, effectively revealing the change in political regimes. For the Mixtec people, the three surviving manuscripts are *Codex Colombino-Becker* (National Museum of Anthropology, Mexico City), *Codex (Zouche-)Nuttall* or *Tonindeye* (British Museum, London), and *Codex Vienna* (in the Austrian National Library). *Codex (Zouche-)Nuttall/ Tonindeye* is remarkable for its genealogies of Mixtec rulers and their alliances and conquests. And for the Maya, whose empire centered on the Yucatan (including parts of Mexico, Guatemala, Belize, Honduras, and El Salvador), there are four known manuscripts from among the hundreds that were burned by the Spanish in the sixteenth century: the *Maya Codex of Mexico* (formerly *Grolier Codex*; housed in the National Library of Mexico in Mexico City), the *Dresden Codex* (in the Saxon State Library), the *Madrid* or *Tro-Cortesianus Codex* (in the Museo de América), and the *Paris Codex* (in the Bibliothèque nationale

Fig 11.5
These pages from the *Dresden Codex* provide a glimpse into the Maya hieroglyphic system of recording calendrical and divine cosmic content, including eclipses, multiplication tables, and an account of a flood.
© SLUB Poster, Wikimedia Commons, public domain

de France). The content of these codices ranges from administrative and clerical to astronomical and sacred writings.

CHRONOLOGIES FOR THE AMERICAS IN A GLOBAL MIDDLE AGES

The centuries between 500 and 1500 often constitute the general chronological boundaries of the Middle Ages in Europe and parts of the Mediterranean world. But for Mesoamerica, the history of pre-Hispanic civilizations is often organized as Classic (250–900 CE), Postclassic (900 to 1521), and Colonial (1521–1821). As we will see in Section B, timelines of the civilizations in South America located across the Andes Mountains are often organized as Middle Horizon (600–1000), Late Intermediate Period (1000–1470), and Late Horizon (1470–1532). Remember, from the first chapter "Orientation," that both the Aztec and the Maya conceived complex, round calendrical systems, with a 365-day solar year and 260-day system (consisting of periods of 20 and 13 days). The Inca method of calculating time, census information, and economic transactions consisted of a system of color-coded knots called *quipu* (see Chapter 10).

A Sea of Islands: The Case of Rapa Nui (Easter Island)

The Pacific Ocean is a vast sea of islands that includes the geographic region known as Oceania. This area of the Southern Hemisphere includes Australia, Melanesia (New Guinea, Fiji, Vanuatu, New Caledonia, and others), Micronesia (Caroline Islands, Marshall Islands, Palau, and more), and Polynesia (with an excess of 1,000 islands, including New Zealand, Samoa, Hawai'i, Marquesas, and Rapa Nui, known in English as Easter Island). In Aotearoa (the Maori name for their land, which is currently also known as New Zealand), Indigenous chronologies refer to the period from 900 to 1200 as *Nga Kakano* (The Seeds), 1200–1500 as *Te Tipunga* (The Growth), and 1500–1800 as *Te Puawaitanga* (The Flowering). This form of periodization reflects a view of increased movement into the Pacific by the many island inhabitants, a common theme for expanding the political reach of peoples in the region during the period we are studying. The phenomenon that often Aotearoa (New Zealand) does not appear on world maps, which filled social media platforms throughout 2018, provides a real-time example about the politics of mapping.

The ancestral voyagers of *Aolepan Aorokin Majel*, or the Marshall Islands, devised a system for tracking ocean swells and determining the distance between islands, effectively allowing them to move across great distances to acquire resources or to expand their territory. This technology is called a stick map and has been passed down generationally. It involves limited raw materials: coconut

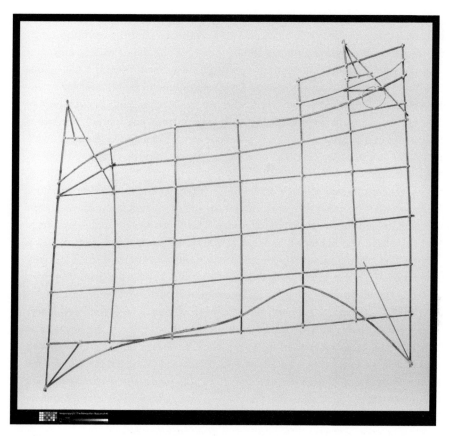

Fig 11.6
Navigational Chart (Rebbilib), Marshall Islands, nineteenth or early twentieth century.
The Michael C. Rockefeller Memorial Collection, Gift of the Estate of Kay Sage Tanguy, 1963. Acc.n. 1978.412.826 © 2020. Image copyright The Metropolitan Museum of Art / Art Resource / Scala, Florence

midrib fibers and fronds, sticks, and shells. The sticks are held together by fibers and fronds in an open framework. They represent the direction of waves and currents as they approach an island. An island is indicated by a shell. Might a similar device have allowed sailors to voyage from island to island until ultimately reaching Hawai'i or Rapa Nui?

ASIDE FROM WRITING AND PRINTING, WHAT ARE OTHER WAYS OF RECORDING THE PAST?

Throughout this book, we turn to written documents from the period 500–1500 as evidence for global events. Except for a few in the final chapter, all were written by hand, and even if they were copied, each copy had features unique to the scribe. Manuscripts were the property of aristocrats or secured in religious spaces; they were not circulated widely, and only a small percentage of people could read them anyway. The way most people knew about the past was through their oral storytellers, who trained and practiced techniques for memorizing great quantities of information. They were, and are, walking, talking encyclopedias of triumphant leaders, heroic ancestors, challenging losses, former homelands, remedies, customs, and geography. In a general sense, they are often considered to be shaman, a word that comes from the Tungen people of Siberia and describes a person as having a mystical connection to the spirit world.

One way oral storytellers transformed or transform a group of active individuals into a listening audience was and is by using musical instruments and other props. For Anglo-Saxon storytellers of *Beowulf*, the singer, or *scop*, used a harp. The Yugoslavian songtellers were called *guslars* because they accompanied their tales with a stringed instrument called a *gusle*. Chinese storytellers still embellish the dramatic, acrobatic cloud surfing of the Monkey King with swooshes made on a *xianci*. The West African storyteller is called a griot. The griot often uses a kora (slide) to accompany his tales and sometimes flourishes a "talking stick."

In India, oral storytellers, called *bhopas*, still travel to small villages and set up their storytelling space in the town square or on a wealthy person's estate. In addition to the *Ravanhatta*, the storyteller's instrument, the *bhopas* have a *phad*, a large backdrop with images painted on it. As the *bhopa* recites, he can point at a scene on the *phad*, reminding the listeners of the characters or events of the story. The *phad* is sacred. After it is made, the divine spirits are invited to inhabit and inspire it, and when the *phad* is old and tattered, it is ceremoniously desanctified. The heat of the storytelling gods must be cooled and extinguished by a ritual washing, and then it is just fabric. Persian storytellers, *naqqal*, also used canvas backdrops.

All of these traditions are called Indigenous Ways of Knowing, a phrase that reminds us how much we should value the vast amount of knowledge held by Native communities, their practices, and their worldviews. For generations, the Ancestors, Elders, and storytellers of Native and Indigenous groups have passed down essential information, from land management to locating natural resources to using astronomy for determining seasons. Only gradually has what we call "settler science" begun to catch up with Indigenous knowledge, and, as scholars of history, we have to be mindful to continually educate ourselves and others about the importance of Indigenous Ways of Knowing.

Across the Blue Continent of the Pacific Ocean, carved stone figures reveal evidence of early medieval human settlements. In the northwest Hawaiian Islands, on Mokumanamana (Necker) Island, mysterious stone carvings of a figure (head and torso with broken arms and legs) suggest habitation from about the ninth to eleventh century. In the case of Rapa Nui, local tradition holds that the island was populated by Polynesian sailors, possibly from the Mangareva Islands (Gambier Islands) or the Marquesas Islands, during the eighth or ninth century (or possibly as early as the fourth century). Another view sees potential early settlement by South American sailors. Whatever the date of the first settlers, somewhere between 1250 and 1500, a group of people constructed at least 1,000 monolithic human figures (nearly 1,000 survive intact, or as fragments) – a colossal undertaking of quarrying, transporting, and refining stone into larger-than-life forms. At the sanctuary-site of Ahu Tongariki, *moai* were positioned to face toward villages and away from the ocean, perhaps symbolically protecting the people, whereas those at Ahu Akivi face the sea as if guiding those seeking the island.

With the arrival of Europeans from the eighteenth century onward, word spread quickly of the iconic *moai* statues. In 1868–1869, when the British excavated and later removed one figure from the island, they were told by the Indigenous people that this particular *moai* is called Hoa Hakananai'a. Traces of paint and refined carvings on the back of Hoa Hakananai'a suggest that these sculptures were once highly decorated. As with other objects from the medieval past, including the Benin plaques from southern Nigeria discussed in Section B, this and some of the other *moai* in museums have been formally requested by the government of Rapa Nui for repatriation. These issues will continue to be at the forefront of the politics of museum and medieval studies in the future as the objects themselves retain special significance for present-day Indigenous communities.

Conclusion

The intertwined histories of islands and island nations that we have just explored bring us to the dawn of the early modern world. Historians sometimes use the dates 1453 (for the Fall of Constantinople), 1492 (for Columbus's voyages to the Caribbean and the ensuing genocide there), or, more generally, ca. 1500 as end points for the Middle Ages. The centuries that followed were marked by sustained and large-scale transhemispheric contact among peoples across all continents, as European travel to the Americas constitutes the beginning of colonization on a fully global scale. National or imperial boundaries drawn on parchment and paper maps on one side of the Atlantic would extend to the forests, mountains, waterways, and people on the other side of that ocean, and ultimately to the Pacific realm as well. Claimed areas would be traded back and forth between political rivals and united through the arranged marriages of royal figures. These paper boundaries were contested through large-scale wars and resulted in the enslavement and often decimation of entire races of people.

As we discussed in "Orientation," maps are not the only tool of political control over peoples. Although timelines are a neat and orderly way to arrange dates and events into periods and other contexts, they leave out quite a bit of information, by necessity of brevity or space constraints. There are countless ways to conceptualize the sequence of events from the past, and even when we work within one method of defining human time and history, we must remain aware and respectful of others. Many of the historical periods we are accustomed to (for example, the medieval period or the Middle Ages) were defined by Europeans after 1500 and imposed on the histories of people whom they conquered. These cultures have other interpretations of their pasts that may not sync up with events in Europe. "Periodization" is a significant topic of debate for current historians.

B: OVERLEAPING THE MOUNTAINS

Introduction

In addition to seas and islands, the political horizons from 1300 to 1500 were transformed in deserts, highlands, plains, and overland routes. On the one hand, we see an excitement for "discovery" – a word that you should read with a critical eye because it often denies or ignores Indigenous histories – and the search for real and legendary people or rumored treasures, but on the other hand we witness painful histories of theft, extortion, enslavement, appropriation, and more. Although Europeans and Africans had traded captive humans since ancient times, the circumstances surrounding this subjugation always depended on the local or regional context. The kinds of expansions that we will see in this section required greater labor forces, and the increased distances that came with governing vast empires often correlated with an increase in dehumanization of foreign subjects. As we have seen, maps and manuscripts from the period provide insight into this paradoxical past. Likewise, luxury objects made for the elite ruling class continue to provide evidence of long-distance trade, prejudices toward outsiders, and imagery related to one's right to rule.

Evidence:	*Epic of Sundiata*
	Letter from the King of Kongo to the King of Portugal
	Kebra Nagast (*The Glory of Kings*)
	Great Mongol *Shahnama* (*Book of Kings*)
	Jean Froissart's *Chronicles of the Hundred Years' War*
	Felipe Guaman Poma de Ayala's *Nueva crónica y buen gobierno* (*New Chronicle and Good Government*)

African Kingship

Griots (storyteller-sages) of West Africa have passed down a centuries-old tale of a king who united many chiefdoms and performed wondrous feats. His name was Sundiata Keita, and the events of his life can be traced to the 1200s. The griots speak that, "In all these villages, Sundiata recruited soldiers. In the same way as light precedes the sun, so the glory of Sundiata, overleaping the mountains, shed itself on all the Niger plain." The *Epic of Sundiata* derives from a combination of oral traditions from medieval Mali, and the story has inspired such films as *The Lion King* (1994/2019) and *Black Panther* (2018).

African rulers gained international fame during the Middle Ages, including the kings of Aksum (from the first through tenth century) and the Zagwe (ca. 900 to 1270) and Solomonic (1270–1636) emperors in Ethiopia and Eritrea; Mansa Musa of Mali (d. 1337); and Qaitbay, the Mamluk sultan of Egypt (1416–1496). As we have read in Chapter 10, Mansa Musa's wealth in gold was heralded across the Sahara Desert and over the waters of the Mediterranean Sea. Mansa Musa was a pious Muslim ruler, and when he embarked on *hajj* (pilgrimage) to Mecca in 1323/24, the vast sums of gold that he brought with him altered the economy of Europe and Africa. The Arab scholar ibn Fadl Allah al-Umari (1300–1349) lived in Cairo at the time and later reported on the ruler's expenditures and benevolence in one of the 20 volumes of his encyclopedia:

> This man flooded Cairo with his gifts. He left no court emir nor holder of a royal office without the gift of a load of gold. The people here profited greatly from him and from his entourage in buying, selling, giving, and taking. They traded gold until these lessened its value in Egypt, making its price fall.

A Spanish Jewish cartographer called Abraham Cresques memorialized Mansa Musa in the famous 1375 map known as the *Catalan Atlas*. On the second of eight sheets of parchment, Cresques included a depiction of Mansa Musa, shown enthroned and holding a golden orb and scepter. An inscription declares: "This king is the richest and most distinguished ruler of this whole region, on account of the great quality of gold that is found in his lands." This characterization of Mansa Musa contrasts with that of the "King of Organa" (constituting Senegal and inland West Africa), who is referred to as, "a Saracen who waged constant war against the Saracens of the coast and with the other Arabs." The word "Saracen" was generally used in reference to North African Muslims (see "Orientation" for why this is no longer considered an appropriate term for Muslims). Near Mansa Musa on the map are several key cities, including the trading hub of Sijilmasa (Morocco), a major source of gold, and the scholarly city of Timbuktu (Mali), known for its libraries that hold thousands of rare or unique manuscripts (see Chapter 3).

Cresques' view of Africa stops at the Sahara Desert – from Mali and Niger to Egypt and Nubia – and does not include the rest of the continent. From his perspective, Africa is a site of Christian-Muslim conflict – demonstrated by the cross and crescent flags (identifying each religion, respectively) and from the inscriptions – and is a racially diverse continent in which Arabs, Amazighs (Berbers), Black Africans, and others live. Another important ruler identified in Africa is Prester John, the mythical Christian priest-king who was said, according to medieval Christian legends, to live either in Ethiopia or in India.

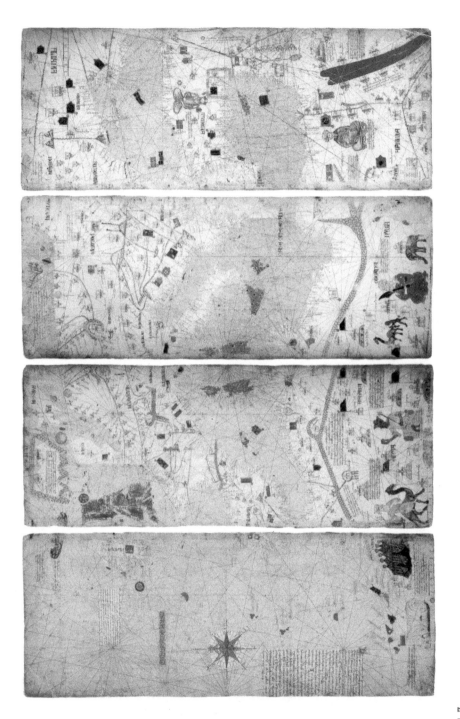

Fig 11.7
Mansa Musa is one of numerous rulers depicted on this map of Afro-Eurasia. He is shown on the second panel from the left, and he holds a golden orb.
Science History Images / Alamy Stock Photo

Reports of his existence became popular in the twelfth century and were quite varied, with some authors citing origins of a powerful Christian ruler in India following the preaching of Christ's apostle called Thomas, while others located him in a generic "Eastern" land somewhere in Central Asia. Geographic uncertainty among European scholarly networks often conflated India and Ethiopia, a fact that might seem incredible to readers today. By 1487, the Portuguese sailors Pêro da Covilhã (ca. 1460 to after 1526) and Afonso de Paiva (ca. 1443–ca. 1490) were sent to find an overland route to India and to gather information about Prester John's kingdom in Ethiopia.

Looking again at the Cantino Planisphere of 1502 (see Figure 11.1), discussed in Section A, we see that Saharan Africa is hardly of interest to the mapmaker: a landscape labeled as "The Clear Mountains of Africa" occupies the desert region. We read a caption that the "King of Organa [Senegal]" is very noble and rich, and that the King of Nubia is constantly at war with Prester John. The land of Prester John is indicated on the map beneath the large wind rose at the heart of Africa and above the equatorial line. Similar to the power dynamics presented by Cresques' map, the Cantino Planisphere also visualizes Christian-Muslim conflict, seen here by the prevalence of golden crosses that line the coastal areas of the continent and by the crescent-moon flags of Muslim rulers. This map also includes a grim reminder of Portugal's long history of enslaving Native peoples: Elmina Castle (*Castello damina*) with its flying Portuguese flags is occupied by nude or partially clothed and turbaned Black Africans. Close by, in an unmarked land between a series of rivers (labeled in red), the bodies of three Black Africans hang from gallows. Elmina Castle was established by the Portuguese in 1482 and was the first trading post for enslaved Africans. The fortress appears with regularity on European maps from that time onward to the present day. Estimates of upwards of 20 million women, men, and children were violently taken from their homes in West Africa and forcibly transported in horrific conditions to Europe and the Americas. Many died during the voyage.

A firsthand West African perspective from this period survives in the form of a letter written by King Nzinga Mbemba (called Afonso I; ca. 1456–1542/43) of the kingdom of Kongo, a convert to Christianity, to King João III of Portugal (1502–1557). On July 6, 1526, King Nzinga wrote,

> My Lord, Your Highness must know how our kingdom is being lost in so many ways that it is convenient to provide for the necessary remedy, since this is caused by the excessive freedom given by your agents and officials to the men and merchants who are allowed to come to the kingdom to set up shops with goods and many things which have been prohibited by us … And we cannot reckon how great the damage is, since the mentioned merchants are taking every day our natives, sons of the land and the sons of our noblemen and vassals and our relatives, because the thieves and men of bad conscience grab them wishing to have the things and wares of this kingdom which they are ambitious of, they grab them and get them to be sold; and so great, Sir, is the corruption and licentiousness that our

country is being completely depopulated, and Your Highness should not agree with this nor accept it as in your service ... That is why we beg of Your Highness to help and assist us in this matter, commanding your factors that they should not send here either merchants or wares, because it is our will that in these Kingdoms there should not be any trade of slaves nor outlet for them.

The King of Kongo wrote again on October 18, 1526, this time indicating that diseases were weakening their resources and made another plea against the enslavement of Black Africans living freely there.

Fig 11.8
This grid of brass plaques (1550–1680) came from the palace of the Oba in the Kingdom of Benin, Nigeria – they were brutally taken by the British in 1897 when British forces launched a punitive expedition on Benin City. From February 9 to 18, the British sacked the palace, burned the city to the ground, and looted more than 2,000 plaques, hundreds of which can now be found in museums in Europe and the United States.

The Portuguese also brought raw materials of copper and zinc, used to make brass, to West Africa in exchange for human lives, as well as for gold, ivory, pepper, and rubber. In the Kingdom of Benin (southern Nigeria), adjacent to the empires of Mali and Ghana, the Oba (or king) and Iyoba (queen mother) memorialized their ancestors on brass plaques that adorned the walls of their palace and through carved elephant tusks that chronicled the lineage and history of their civilization. Craftspeople still create brass works to commemorate the reigning Oba, and their skills working molten metal earn them high rank in the community.

On the other coast of the continent, toward the Horn of Africa, the Ethiopian Empire experienced a less violent history than that of Ghana, Benin, and Kongo. Ethiopia claims one of the longest unbroken histories of Christian kingship, dating to the time of King Ezana (r. 320s to 360) of Aksum who converted to Christianity and minted coins with his image on one side and a cross on the other as a testimony to his beliefs. Like his counterpart in Kongo, Emperor Gelawdewos (r. 1540–1559) of Ethiopia also wrote to King João III of Portugal. Gelawdewos expressed a unity of Christian faith in the recommendation of a knight who would serve at the European court. The letter begins:

> In the name of God, indivisible Trinity, who sees the exterior and scrutinizes the interior, who weakens the strong and strengthens the

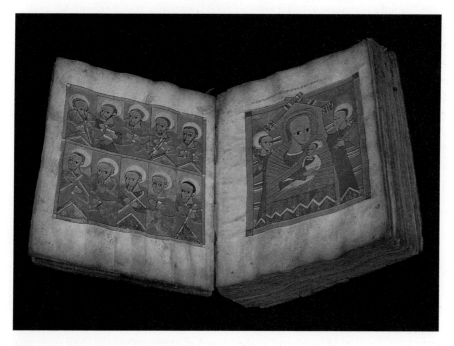

Fig 11.9
The Seventy-Two Disciples and *The Virgin and Child with Archangels Michael and Gabriel* in a gospel book (1480–1520) from Gunda Gunde Monastery in Ethiopia. The J. Paul Getty Museum, Los Angeles, Ms. 105, fol. 9v

weary. This letter is sent on behalf of the King Galawdewos, descendant of King Zar'a Ya'qob, son of King David's son, King Solomon, Kings of Israel, on whom be peace, to be delivered to João, King of Portugal, lover of God, lover of the faith.

Note the importance of lineage in the letter. Emperor Gelawdewos evokes the names of powerful rulers. Emperor Zar'a Ya'qob (r. 1434–1468), together with Empress Eleni (d. 1522), established strong ties to the papal court in Rome and ushered in a period of significant artistic patronage. David and Solomon are biblical kings; Gelawdewos alludes to these rulers to show another Christian king that they share sacred beliefs.

EMPEROR ZAR'A YA'QOB AND EMPRESS ELENI OF ETHIOPIA

Since the birth of Christianity in the first century, church leaders across Afro-Eurasia have called together large gatherings of dignitaries and theologians to discuss matters of doctrine (belief) and practice. Ethiopian presence was especially important in 1441 at the Council of Florence, which lasted from 1431 to 1449. On behalf of Emperor Zar'a Ya'qob and Empress Eleni, the delegates brought to the papal court letters and manuscripts, which are still housed in the Vatican Library, together with similar objects from the representatives of the Coptic (Egyptian), Syriac, Armenian, and Greek churches. Zar'a Ya'qob and Eleni championed an important visual tradition in Ethiopia, that of the Virgin Mary and Christ child shown enthroned and flanked by archangels. The *Chronicle of Emperor Zar'a Ya'qob* details the emperor's use of honor guards for official ceremonies, and thus the image of Mary and Christ in manuscripts and in church wall paintings from this time may refer directly to this imperial practice. In other manuscripts, the presence of King Solomon – dressed in Ethiopian regalia with a diadem, textile headcloth, earplugs, holding a spear, and shaded by a parasol – creates a visual link between the biblical ruler and the Ethiopian court. This connection was developed in the Ethiopian history the *Kebra Nagast* (*The Glory of Kings*).

The link to Jewish (Hebrew) rulers had powerful resonance in Ethiopia, and we can explore this importance through a text known as the *Kebra Nagast* (*The Glory of Kings*). The earliest manuscript of this chronicle survives from the fourteenth century, but earlier versions likely existed, especially as oral tradition. Ethiopian rulers of the Solomonic dynasty (1270–1636), in particular, traced their royal line to Solomon and to the Queen of Sheba by way of their only son, Menelik, reportedly the first emperor of Ethiopia. The *Kebra Nagast* begins by praising the Abrahamic God, then traces the generations of Jewish patriarchs (including Adam, Abraham, Noah, and Moses), and next focuses on Solomon's story and the origins of Christian Ethiopia. Upon Solomon's death, Menelik leaves Jerusalem for Aksum, bringing with him the Ark of the Covenant, which is still believed by Ethiopians to reside in the country. The final section of the text connects the relationships among the pope in Rome, the patriarch of the Orthodox or Eastern Christian churches, and the Ethiopian emperor. The chronicler concludes the text with a series of exhortations to the Ethiopian people to remain faithful and proclaims, "Thus God made for the King of Ethiopia more glory, and grace, and majesty than for all the other kings of the earth because of the greatness of Zion, the Tabernacle of the Law of God, the heavenly Zion." The reference to Zion names both the hill on which Jerusalem is built but also the concept of a heavenly Jerusalem or eternal paradise.

Manuscript copies of the text survive in Berlin, Oxford, and Paris, and in 1872, another copy was sent from London to Ethiopia when Prince Kasa (later King Yohannes IV; 1837–1889) wrote to Queen Victoria (1819–1901) requesting the volume as part of his country's patrimony. Each of these volumes includes information at the very end of the text about the circumstances of copying the account in a section known as a colophon. We are told that the scribe Isaac found the text in a Coptic manuscript (likely from Egypt) that was translated into Arabic in the thirteenth century and later, in the fourteenth century, to Ge'ez, also called Classical Ethiopic, the liturgical language of the Ethiopian Orthodox Tewahedo Church today. The histories of African kingship and of the lost kingdoms across the continent – fragmented due to centuries of enslavement and colonialism – are still being written. This field of study is central to advancing our understanding of a global Middle Ages.

A Game of Thrones across Medieval Eurasia

The Venetian merchant-author Marco Polo (1254–1324) is one of the best-known travelers of all time. His fame is due in part to the various writings he authored – especially the *Devisement du monde* (*Description of the World*) – about his trip from Italy to the court of the Mongol ruler of China, Kublai Khan (1215–1294), and back to his homeland by way of Southeast Asia, India, the Middle East, and through lands governed by the Byzantine Empire. But he was not the only individual during the Middle Ages to traverse great distances and to record his journeys. A century earlier, Benjamin of Tudela (1130–1173), a Jewish-Spanish traveler, wrote the *Sefer ha-Masa'ot* (*Book of Travels*) about his journeys from Zaragoza in northern Spain to major cities in present-day France, Italy, Greece, Turkey, Syria, Lebanon, Israel, and Iraq.

Other travel writers inspired European travelers, including Giovanni da Pian del Carpine (called John of Plano Carpini in English; ca. 1185–1252) and Odoric of Pordenone (1286–1331). Marco Polo's contemporary, Ibn Battuta (1304–1368/69), an Amazigh (Berber) scholar from Morocco, undertook several global itineraries, which he dictated as *A Gift for Those Who Contemplate the*

Wonders of Cities and the Marvels of Traveling. His first trip covered a pilgrimage to Mecca (Saudi Arabia) and travels in Iraq, Persia, and East Africa along the Swahili coast. His second voyage took him to Anatolia and across Asia by way of the Black and Caspian Seas, the Indian subcontinent, South and East Asia to Beijing and Egypt. On his final excursion, he ventured to al-Andalus (southern Spain), and then throughout Morocco, the empire of Mali (including Timbuktu), and back home.

The Chinese mariner Zheng He (1371–1435/44) embarked on expeditions south to the Majapahit Empire in Java and east to Sri Lanka, India, the lands along the Persian Gulf and Red Sea, and along the Horn of Africa down the Swahili coast to Malindi (Kenya). Guru Nanak (1469–1539), founder of Sikhism, spread his teachings on foot across South Asia, China, the Middle East, and on to Rome. Sikhism emerged in India in the fifteenth century CE. Sikhs follow the teachings of faith and meditation described in their sacred text known as the Guru Granth Sahib, and they are devoted to equality of humankind and selflessness. And, there is also the fictional travel memoir known as *The Travels of Sir John Mandeville*, which circulated between 1357 and 1371 and was possibly written by a French or Flemish author under a pseudonym. These many accounts can all be read in various translations today, in print and online.

Marco Polo's journeys would have taken him through Mongol-ruled lands long before he reached the capital of Beijing in China and the court of the Great Khan (a title for the supreme Mongol ruler). From 1256 to the mid-1300s, the territories of Persia (Iran) to Anatolia (Turkey) and parts of what is now western Afghanistan and Northwest India were ruled by a khan as an appanage (or land-grant) that became known as the Ilkhanate. This form of regional governance expanded Mongol influence and necessitated the loyalty of familial or appointed leaders to the Great Khan. As we have already seen in this and the previous chapters, Marco Polo wrote about several of the major islands and harsh terrains, whose political seascapes and landscapes fluctuated greatly at the time. Notwithstanding the popularity of Marco Polo's writings – which survive in 141 manuscripts and portions of text in many European languages – a more insightful view of the Mongol world, its ceremonies, and customs comes from a luxurious fourteenth-century copy of Ferdowsi's eleventh-century text of the *Shahnemeh* (*The Book of Kings*). The *Great Mongol Shahnemeh*, as this manuscript is known, was planned as a two-volume royal commission for the Ilkhanid rulers of Tabriz, the capital of the western Mongol empire. Only 58 pages survive today in collections around the world. The illuminations present the blending of Chinese and Persian painting styles, an appropriate hybridity for a vast continental empire.

In the early fourteenth century, as the Ilkhanate was dissolving, a major military conflict ignited between France and England (and it is important to keep in mind that, from around 1348 onward, the Black Death or Great Pestilence spread quickly across Asia, Europe, and Africa, as addressed in Chapter 12). The French historian Jean Froissart (ca. 1337–ca. 1405) recorded the events of the first half of the Hundred Years' War (1337–1453), as it came to be known, in a multiple-volume compendium known as the *Chronicles*. The primary players in this lengthy political skirmish were the House of Plantagenet in England and the House of Valois in France. Both vied for titular and terrestrial claims to the crown for rule over land on the French mainland and beyond. The Plantagenets forged alliances with the pope in Rome, the Spanish kingdom of Navarre, and the kingdom of Portugal, while the Valois formed pacts with the kingdoms of Scotland, Bohemia (in central Europe), Castile and Aragon in Spain, and the Republic of Genoa (in Italy). In large part these loyalties centered on political succession.

Froissart's *Chronicles* takes readers on a journey across the Mediterranean to throne rooms, battlefields, and distant lands alongside kings, soldiers, dignitaries, and popes and anti-popes. As a result of the Great Western Schism (1378 onward), cardinals of the Roman Church elected three different popes – one ruling from Rome, another from Avignon in southern France, and a third in Pisa in Italy. Even in the context of the fragmentation of the church and numerous battles in Froissart's account, the military conflict at Agincourt (northern France) in 1415 stands out as it was memorialized in Shakespeare's history play about King Henry V, who took the victory over the French. This medieval saga of conflict, intrigue, and shifting alliances enjoyed lasting esteem, as copies of the text were commissioned well into the late fifteenth century. The Hundred Years' War was followed by the Wars of the Roses, a civil war in England between the House of Plantagenet and the House of Lancaster. These many events inspired the author George R. R. Martin in the writing of *A Song of Ice and Fire*, which became the worldwide sensation known as HBO's *Game of Thrones*.

While feuding raged between the kings and popes of western Europe, formidable rulers emerged across the African continent, and Japan's Ashikaga shogunate renewed relations with imperial China, two additional powers emerged in the Middle East and in the Mediterranean: the Timurids and the Ottomans, respectively. Founded by Timur (Tamerlane) in 1370, the Timurid dynasty ruled over Iran, Iraq, and parts of Syria, Russia, and India. Two of the political strategies used to unify this vast area included gathering craftspeople from all conquered regions to Samarkand (Uzbekistan) and Herat (Afghanistan), important capital cities, and sending sumptuous gifts to neighboring courts. Timurid manuscripts reveal numerous moments of exchange with rulers in Mamluk Egypt, Ming China, and more. A famous gift of a giraffe sent by Sultan al-Nasir Faraj ibn Barquq is recorded in a text celebrating Timur and made for his grandson, Prince Ibrahim, in 1436. This diplomatic exchange was also recorded by a Spanish ambassador to the region, Ruy González de Clavijo, thereby further demonstrating the long-distance movements of people, their ideas, and their activities in the late Middle Ages. In 2020, a Qur'an produced during this same period made headlines when it sold for about $8.8 million. What makes the manuscript remarkable is that the words of God as revealed to Muhammad were written on multicolored sheets of Ming paper with gold painted landscapes, architecture, and flora and fauna. The vibrancy of art in Timurid lands testifies to the ideal of internationalism held by the rulers.

Fig 11.10
In this large, luxurious copy of John Froissart's *Chronicles* (1480–1483), the English prince John of Gaunt (1340–1399) sails for Brest, France as the battle between the English and the Bretons ensues.
The J. Paul Getty Museum, Los Angeles, Ms. Ludwig XIII 7, fol. 116v

The other power that grew in the Mediterranean in the 1400s was the Ottoman Empire, which would rule until 1922. The imperial foundations for this group can be traced to Osman, who died 1323/24. For over a century after his death, the dynasty expanded throughout Anatolia (present-day Turkey) and in 1453 the Ottoman sultan Mehmed II (1432–1481), known as "the Conqueror," took the city of Constantinople, forever ending the Christian Byzantine Empire. The fear of Ottoman advancement into the Mediterranean percolated for over a decade prior to the fall of the great city and required Christians to unify against the Muslim invasion. One of the major political figures present at the Church councils convened in Italy from 1431 to 1449 was Basilios Bessarion (1403–1472), a priest and scholar who soon became a cardinal and was named papal legate and governor of the university city of Bologna. Bessarion commissioned expensive decorated books, including a copy of Ptolemy's second-century CE *Geography*, which opens to a lavishly painted frontispiece showing the ancient geographer in a library surrounded by astro-nomical devices. It features a stunning world map showing Africa, Europe, and Asia from the Canary Islands to Thailand. The volume contains an additional 26 regional maps.

Mehmed II also gathered a vast library and commissioned Greek, Turkish, Persian, and Italian scribes and artists to his court with the goal of self-fashioning as a powerful Muslim sultan and European prince. He sent ordinances in Arabic, Greek, and Demotic, declaring his protection and patronage of the sacred sites across the eastern Mediterranean and eastern Europe, including to numerous Christian monasteries. At his court, luminous copies of the Qur'an were acquired as gifts or as goods from Persia, the heart of the Safavid dynasty (r. 1501–1736). Therefore, as we have seen in previous chapters, illuminated manuscripts continued to play an important role in forging alliances, crafting identity, unifying communities, and advancing political aims, especially in times of territorial expansion and war.

Indigenous Byways

The relatively flat landscape of what is now the central, southern, and south-western United States was once dominated by large civic complexes organized around ceremonial earthen mound-and-plaza centers. From the Great Plains, located between the Rocky Mountains and the Mississippi River, to the Coastal Plains along the Gulf of Mexico, and to the Eastern Woodlands beside the Atlantic seaboard, Indigenous communities undertook the incredible engin-eering feat of transporting earth to form burial mounds that resemble pyramids or tall hills. One of the most famous of these sites is the once-great Mississippian culture city of Cahokia, located in St. Clair County, Illinois, which is about 12 miles (19 km) east of St. Louis, Missouri. Although relatively abandoned by the 1300s, archeological evidence from the region – in the form of carved and painted objects – demonstrates possible long-distance travel or trade to sites in Mesoamerica. Moundville Archaeological Site in Alabama is another Mississippian earth-structure that was occupied from around 1000 to 1450 CE. An online project of scholars is attempting to recreate these small-world networks using three-dimensional augmented reality.

Evidence from ceramic vessels – both their decoration and the organic residue found within, as well as local raw materials (stone, shell, bird and animal skeletons, and plants) – reinforces the view that Native Americans moved across vast expanses of territory. The Ancestral Pueblo peoples, such as those at Chaco Canyon, appear to have used cylindrical vessels to drink cacao, a plant that grows in the Yucatan and which was sacred to the Maya. Scarlet macaw skeletons in Pueblo lands further testify to these connections. Steatite (soap-stone), a type of metamorphic rock quarried from the Channel Islands off the coast of present-day California, was made into a range of portable objects (from bowls to jewelry), which have been found well beyond the seaside homeland of the Chumash people in the deserts of northern Los Angeles County where the Kawaiisu, Tataviam, Yuhaviatam, and Maarenga'yam have resided for centuries.

Beyond these overland links, peoples around the globe looked up to the stars and planets and recorded their position in, and movement across, the sky, respectively, in works of art. For Indigenous artists in the Americas, petroglyphs offer rare glimpses into this rich past. There is a theory that the Ancestral Pueblo peoples at Chaco Canyon may have recorded a similar astronomical event to one(s) depicted by the Shoshone-Bannock peoples in Idaho, phenomena marked by sun, moon, and star forms. In consultation with Indigenous communities, some archeoastronomers – those who study potential astronomical content at archeological sites – propose that the 1054 supernova that formed the Crab Nebula inspired petroglyphs in the same way that this cosmic event was recorded in Eurasian manuscripts. There are several examples of rock art that visualize the cosmos at a specific moment in time, such as at an equinox or solstice. Much research continues to be undertaken by Indigenous and non-Native scholars to add to our understanding of the power and sacrality behind these artworks produced within and beyond the chronological scope of this chapter.

The fortified citadel of Machu Picchu in the Cuzco Region of Peru draws nearly 5,000 visitors a day during high season. The wonder of this site, however, was not known to the Spanish conquistadors. In fact, after the conquest of the Inca civilization by Francisco Pizarro (ca. 1471–1541) in 1532, Machu Picchu remained hidden at an elevation of nearly 8,000 feet in the Andes Mountains until about 1874, when it appeared on maps, and until its global rediscovery in 1911 by American historian Hiram Bingham (1875–1956). Built as a royal estate during the reigns of Pachacutec Inca Yupanqui (1438–1471) and Tupac Inca Yupanqui (1472–1493), Machu Picchu was organized with temples, dwellings, and agricultural sectors in an upper and lower region based on the topography of the range. Despite its seemingly isolated and difficult-to-access location, Machu Picchu was well connected to other centers of power by the *Qhapaq Ñan*, the famed Inca "royal road" system. These roadways traversed the highlands and lowlands of six present-day countries, from Colombia to Argentina, and included Ecuador, Peru, Bolivia, and Chile. Evidence for these contacts can be seen in the archeological record: obsidian objects (made from naturally occurring volcanic glass) at Machu Picchu can be sourced to the Lake Titicaca Basin on the border of Peru and Bolivia.

Written histories of the Inca empire survive in three post-conquest manuscripts: two copies of the *Historia general del Piru* (*General History of Peru*) of about 1580–1600 and of 1616 by Spanish (Basque) friar Martín de Murúa (ca. 1525–ca. 1618); and the *Nueva crónica y buen gobierno* (*New Chronicle and Good Government*) of 1615/1616 by the Quechua scribe Felipe Guaman Poma de Ayala. Although these texts were written beyond the chronological limits of the Middle Ages, their contents provide important insights into the history of Inca rulership. Beginning with Manco Cápac (d. ca. 1230), the authors chronicle key events from the lives of each emperor up to the time of Atahualpa (ca. 1502/

Fig 11.11
Tupac Inca Yupanqui and a Quipucamayoc in *Historia general del Piru* (*General History of Peru*) by Martín de Murúa, Southern Andes, South America, 1616. The J. Paul Getty Museum, Los Angeles, Ms. Ludwig XIII 16, fol. 49v

26–1533), the last Inca king. Tupac Inca Yupanqui, for example, reportedly discovered many silver mines in the mountain region of Potosí and in what is now Sucre, Bolivia (which the Spanish called La Plata, meaning "silver"). The account of Tupac Inca Yupanqui spans three chapters in Murúa's history, demonstrating the importance of silver to the Spanish crown, on whose behalf Murúa wrote his text. In one of these chapters, Tupac Inca Yupanqui consults a *quipucamayoc*, a recordkeeper or accountant in the Inca Empire responsible for reading the *quipu* (see Chapter 10), whose color, width, and placement communicated census or tribute data. This Indigenous form of recording the past is still being deciphered and promises to, one day, shed greater light into the technological advances of the Inca.

Looking Forward: A Long Middle Ages

Looking at global political entanglements on islands and harsh overland environments from 1300 to 1500 has revealed the many ways all places and cultures are inherently hybrid. The study of a global Middle Ages is also something of a hybrid field, one that requires the perspectives of all kinds of people (rulers, artisans, and enslaved populations among them) and that necessitates inclusion of a range of disciplines and specializations. Part of this approach has been to stretch the chronological context to allow for various understandings of time periods and modes of remembering the past. In fact, the medieval world is always present, as each generation thinks anew about those distant centuries through the texts and objects that still survive.

In 2015, scholar Robert Rouse shared one approach for bridging past and present, and for including parts of the globe that have not traditionally fit under the rubric of "medieval." Rouse described what he termed "indigenizing the medieval" as seen in two manuscripts now located in Australia. The first is a sixteenth-century Book of Hours produced in France that was gifted between British settlers of the Wellington colony in Aotearoa (New Zealand) in 1842. Dedications in Latin, Greek, and Maori were added to the manuscript by a settler-scribe, indicating that the recipient of the book was "Doctor to the Maori people." The second manuscript was penned by minister Lancelot Edward Threlkeld (1788–1859) in 1858 and includes a complete translation of the Gospel of Luke in Awabakal, an Indigenous language of Australia. Illumination reminiscent of French manuscripts was added to this one. These two hybrid objects serve as reminders of a long colonial history that privileges a European past and painting style while also suppressing the perspectives and pasts of Indigenous peoples around the world.

The Spanish missions of the eighteenth century in California offer another link to the past, through the pages of manuscripts and printed books. Mission San Gabriel, for instance, preserves a 1399 Latin deed for land in Spain, a 1488 printed copy of St. Thomas Aquinas's *Summa theologiae*, and dozens of additional codices produced in Europe prior to the Spanish foundations at the site, which were brought there by the mission founders for study and to aid in the conversion of Indigenous populations. One hope for a global Middle Ages is to reveal the views and the lives of those individuals whose stories are otherwise lost in time, and to show that our world is one of constant connections.

Research Questions

1. Select one of the following islands or island geographic regions and research the history, art, literature, and religion there from 1300 to 1500: Sri Lanka, Madagascar, New Guinea, the Caribbean, Polynesia. What has survived? How do scholars reclaim these histories?

2. We have studied the politics of several natural resources in this chapter, including herbs and spices, gold and silver, and birds and animals. Undertake a comparative study of the value placed on one of these or other materials or living things in different locations around the globe. You might wish to explore precious stones (including diamonds and rubies), beautifully plumed birds (parrots, peacocks/peafowl, and macaws), or lustrous pearls and coral.

3. Gather material (from the list of additional readings or online) that introduces Indigenous Ways of Knowing or Native perspectives on the past and write about these views. Consider the relationship between human experience and the landscape and resources of a place.

4. Research the Inca "royal road" system. Where did these roads lead? What goods were traded on these roads? How far did the networks extend into Central and North America? How did the transportation system indicate the politics of the region?

5. Research what happened to the Easter island *moai* called Hoa Hakananai'a that was removed from the island. Where is it now and where did its journey take it? Should it be returned to its home on the island?

6. Some of the cultures that rose to power or individuals who lived from 1300 to 1500 have received popular acclaim through film, video games, comic books, or social media memes. These include the Mongols, Marco Polo, Ming Dynasty China, Mansa Musa of Mali, and the competing factions of the European Hundred Years' War. Research how popular presentations compare with the historical sources.

Further Reading

Alt, Susan, and Timothy Pauketat. *Medieval Mississippians: The Cahokian World*. Santa Fe, NM: School for Advanced Research Press, 2015.

Budge, Sir E. A. Wallis. *The Queen of Sheba and Her Only Son Menyelek (Kebra Nagast)*. Cambridge and Ontario: In Parentheses Publications, Ethiopian Series, 2000.

Crown, Patricia L., ed. *The House of the Cylinder Jars: Room 28 at Pueblo Bonito, Chaco Canyon*. Albuquerque: University of New Mexico Press, 2020.

Delmas, Adrien. "Writing in Africa: *The Kilwa Chronicle* and Other Sixteenth Century Portuguese Testimonies." In *The Arts and Crafts of Literacy: Islamic Manuscript Cultures in Sub-Saharan Africa*, edited by A. Brigalia and M. Nobili, 181–206. Berlin: De Gruyter, 2017.

Fauvelle, François-Xavier. *The Golden Rhinoceros: Histories of the African Middle Ages*. Princeton, NJ: Princeton University Press, 2018.

Heng, Geraldine. *The Invention of Race in the European Middle Ages*. Cambridge: Cambridge University Press, 2018.

Jennings, Jesse, ed. *The Prehistory of Polynesia*. Cambridge, MA: Harvard University Press, 1979.

Kelly, Samantha. "Ewostateans at the Council of Florence (1441): Diplomatic Implications between Ethiopia, Europe, Jerusalem and Cairo." In *Afrique* [online], placed online June 29, 2016, consulted July 1, 2019. http://journals. openedition.org/afriques/1858.

Krebs, Verena. *Medieval Ethiopian Kingship, Craft, and Diplomacy with Latin Europe.* London: Palgrave Macmillian, 2021.

Malotki, Ekkehart, and Ellen Dissanayake. *Early Rock Art of the American West: The Geometric Enigma.* Seattle: University of Washington Press, 2018.

Nash, George, and Aron Mazel. *Narratives and Journeys in Rock Art: A Reader.* Oxford: Archaeopress Publishing, 2018.

Patterson-Rudolph, Carol. *Petroglyphs and Pueblo Myths of the Rio Grande.* Albuquerque, NM: Avanyu Publications, 1993.

Roullier, Caroline, Laurie Benoit, Doyle B. McKey, and Vincent Lebot. "Historical Collections Reveal Patterns of Diffusion of Sweet Potato in Oceania Obscured by Modern Plant Movements and Recombination." *Proceedings of the National Academy of Sciences of the United States of America* 110, no. 6 (2013): 2205–2210.

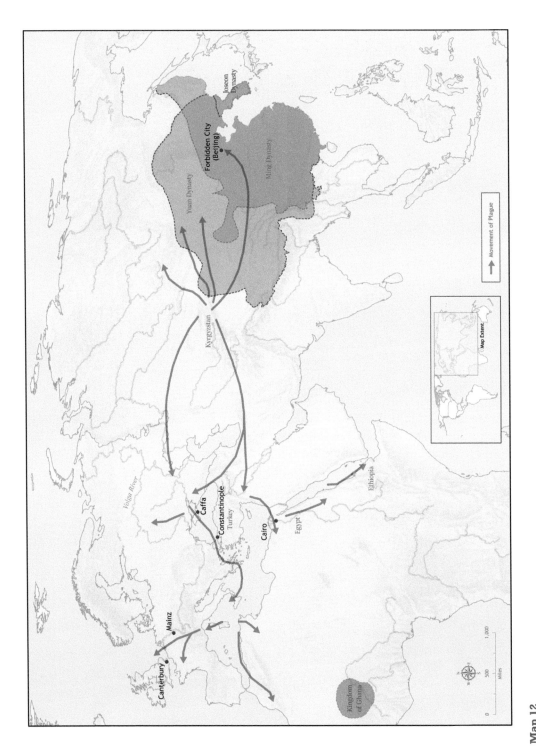

Map 12

Everyone Believes it is the End of the World

12

Everyone Believes it is the End of the World

Society, 1300–1500

Introduction

A primary topic of this chapter is the massive devastation created by the fourteenth-century plague, which traveled with merchants and warriors over long-distance routes. The intensifying globalization from 1300 to 1500 allowed people, ideas, products, and diseases to cross geopolitical boundaries, and although many historians have focused their study on the European sphere, new scholarship shows how the spread of this pathogen was a semiglobal catastrophe. This chapter explains the Second Plague Pandemic as an event that affected multiple regions and peoples, causing labor shortages, famine, and tremendous social anxiety. In Section A we cover the plague itself, looking at possible origins of the disease, its spread around Eurasia, and human reactions to it, including advances in medical knowledge.

In Section B we look at how people responded to the stresses caused by death and suffering on such a large scale. It was the end of some cultures and empires, but it was not the end of the world. People survived, reorganized, rearranged, and innovated. Artists, writers, philosophers, and religious folk created works expressing human despair and extolling human strength. In Section B, we also introduce trends that mark the end of the Middle Ages and the beginning of the modern period. Newly empowered leaders emerged, overseeing construction of architectural monuments and sponsoring explorers and traders to find new routes to riches.

A: DEADLY ROUTES

Evidence:	Giovanni Villani, *Chronicle*
	Michele de Piazza, *Chronicle*
	Rochester Chronicle

Ibn Sina, *Canon of Medicine*

Ibn al-Wardi, *History*

Introduction

The common understanding of the Black Death is that it was European in scope and generally limited to the period from 1347 to 1353. While partially true, this limits our understanding of the extent of this pandemic that lasted from the early 1220s to the late 1370s. Widening our lens to 150 years and including an Afro-Eurasian context reveals how much more virulent, dangerous, and devastating the disease was, as well as showing us the resiliency, adaptiveness, and determination of humanity. We begin with a medical understanding of the bacteria, move to the thirteenth-century plague in China, and then shift westward to the Middle East, Africa, and European spaces. The growth of technology (a direct by-product of globalization) intensified long-distance travel and the spread of knowledge, which both helped and hindered responses to the plague. It is estimated that over 150 million people died across Eurasia and Africa, with significant consequences for the societies, cultures, and economies of the impacted communities. Labor shortages led to major changes in wages and labor practices in Europe, and long-distance trade was slowed for a time as quarantines were imposed.

Yersinia pestis

The Second Plague Pandemic is commonly called the Bubonic Plague or the Black Death, but medieval people called it the Pestilence or Universal Plague. The disease itself is caused by the bacterium *Yersinia pestis*, which had been present and active across Afro-Eurasia for many centuries. The full genome of the pathogen was tested in 2011 by using the teeth of victims from a plague burial site in England, and new analysis from 2018 suggests that the oldest plague strain is from the Bronze Age, but the pathogen itself is much older. Modern scholarship suggests that there were eight or more major pandemics from the Late Bronze Age forward, but historians often concentrate on three major plagues in Afro-Eurasia: Justinian's Plague (the First Plague Pandemic) of 400–750, the Second Plague Pandemic of 1220–1400, and the Third Plague Pandemic of 1855–1960. Testing has revealed that all three pandemics came from *Yersinia pestis*.

Between 3,000 and 4,000 years ago, the disease moved slowly from a soil bacterium to a host-borne bacterium, and the late Bronze Age variant survived within fleas, which were easily transmitted from rodent hosts to human hosts. The oldest-known victims, from the Samara region of Russia in the Central Asian steppes, died and were buried together over 3,800 years ago. Their teeth allowed researchers to connect their deaths to the later, virulent strains of *Y. pestis*. By Justinian's Plague, over 200 species of rodents and 80 species of fleas could carry the plague, as could humans. Around the thirteenth century, *Y. pestis* diverged into novel strains that exist to the present day. This "Big Bang" brought a new and especially devastating disease out of the Central Asian steppes, bringing death and destruction to China, the Middle East, Europe, and Africa.

Today, the *Y. pestis* organism is endemic to rodent populations (marmots in Mongolia, rats in Europe, prairie dogs in the western United States) and it is believed that fleas and lice from the rodents spread the disease from animals to humans. Scientists continue to research and study the modes of transmission but do not have precise knowledge on the mechanism of transfer. They do know that rodents were not totally responsible for the disease spreading so quickly throughout medieval Eurasia. Human travel and contact played a major role. Once humans became ill, they easily infected others through coughing and fluid transfer.

There are several different clinical forms of plague: the three most common are *bubonic, pneumonic,* and *septicemic*; a fourth type, *gastrointestinal*, is the subject of various studies today. The vectors and method of transmission are different in each case. The most commonly known and widespread type was the bubonic plague. The primary vector, or transmitter, of this strain was the Oriental rat flea (*Xenopsylla cheopis*), which fed on rodents but could move to humans. Once a human was bitten, the bacterium infected the lymph nodes. The lymphatic system attempted to destroy the bacteria by creating antibodies, which caused the lymph nodes to swell. Victims developed high fevers, headaches, chills, and body weakness. The lymph nodes closest to the bite swelled the largest, and these distended nodes were called "buboes," giving the disease one of its many names. Oftentimes, as the disease progressed, blood pooled and coalesced in the lymph nodes, forming a ring around the bubo, darkening into black and purple bruises – the black death. The incubation period was usually two to six days, and, during the medieval era, 60 percent of people who contracted the disease died, but the 40 percent who lived developed some level of immunity.

The second type was the pneumonic plague, where the human is the vector and the plague settles in the lungs. Pneumonic plague becomes airborne via infected droplets and is transmitted from person to person. This variant caused extremely high fevers, weakness, mucous and coughing, and then pneumonia. It was highly contagious and probably the most common type in the medieval period. Pneumonic plague was usually fatal within 18 to 24 hours of exposure. Even if victims lasted a bit longer, they always died.

The third major type was the septicemic plague, where blood itself is the vector. If a person had any cuts or abrasions and handled an animal or came into contact with another human with plague, the bacteria could enter directly into the bloodstream. It could also be transmitted by flea bite, or through a burst bubo. A victim with a strong immune system might survive that erupting node, but, more likely, the bacteria entered the bloodstream and became lethal. In the European sphere, plague was also commonly transmitted by doctors who

Fig 12.1
In a fifteenth-century fresco from the Chapel of St. Sebastian in Villard-de-Lans,
Rhone-Alpes, France a doctor treats a plague victim with buboes.
DeAgostini / Getty Images

bled patients, a therapy thought to rid the body of unhealthy fluids. The doctor
would pierce a patient's vein and wait for an amount of blood to drain out,
inadvertently transferring and inviting infection. Once the bacteria entered the
bloodstream, it caused systemic, multi-organ failure. The bacteria overwhelmed
the patient's vital systems, and organ failure set in within a day or two. Victims
experienced high fevers, abdominal pain, shock, and exhaustion prior to
succumbing to massive bleeding and death. Occasionally, if a victim lived past
the day, they might also get necrosis in their soft tissues and their fingers and
toes could turn black. Septicemic plague had a 100 percent death rate.

There are other, more minor categories of plague: variants that infect the
spinal cord and brain (always fatal) and throat (less fatal). The last type is the
gastrointestinal plague, where food is the vector. As seen in earlier chapters,
grain from Central Asia was a prime commodity for European markets, where
townspeople specialized in trades other than farming. Recent scholarship
suggests that contaminated grain supplies from around the Black Sea entered
Europe, and this contaminated grain could have infected large swaths of the
southern European populace. The gastrointestinal plague strain, like the others,
is studied in labs today, and forensic researchers are reinterpreting the historic
record through this forensic study.

Determining how many people died of plague is difficult and can only be estimated. Few governments kept specific enough statistical data on their populations. The Chinese kept records of tax-paying "households" – but only the households that owed taxes and not the number of inhabitants in that household. European episcopal records of the fourteenth century recorded births and deaths (as these events required a sacramental ceremony that was often paid for) and these documents give us some idea of population, but only in certain regions of Europe. From these sorts of records, scholars suggest that the plague had an average mortality rate across the globe of 40–60 percent, and some areas were totally depopulated.

PLAGUE TODAY

Many areas of the world still experience plague, including India, Africa, and western areas of the United States. As in the fourteenth century, rodents and fleas are generally the vectors in modern cases. The bacteria can lie dormant within rodent populations, allowing it to survive without causing serious rodent die-off. Once the disease moves past the rodents (the enzootic cycle) and infects other animals (the epizootic cycle), humans are at risk of catching the disease. Cats can catch and transmit the disease to humans and are a common source in many areas. Cooler summers and wet winters seem to precede modern outbreaks. Eighty-five percent of people who contract the bubonic plague today survive with antibiotic treatment, yet people succumb to the disease each year. The pneumonic plague is still commonly fatal, with only 50 percent of people surviving, even with treatment.

As mentioned above, all three of the major "modern" pandemics are variants of the *Y. pestis* plague bacteria. The first major outbreak, Justinian's Plague (541/2 through to the 700s) killed between 25 and 40 million people from the Persian Sassanian and the Greek Byzantine empires to the British Isles. Genome research on the bacteria suggests this plague began in the Kazakhstan region of the Central Asian steppes. The historian Procopius (500–565) blamed the Egyptians for bringing the disease to Constantinople, but genetic testing has proven this false. Other traditional scholarship placed the plague's origins in China. Recent scientific and scholarly research traces the spread back to the Central Asian steppes. In 2013, scholars proved the "Big Bang" theory, which identified the new strain of *Y. pestis* as originating in the Qinghai-Tibetan plateau in Central Asia. More research, both medical and textual, points to the steppes as the birthplace of the modern plagues, with movements east and west, moving along with the Mongolian armies.

In Kyrgyzstan, scientists found a way to study the plague through local cemeteries. At one location, 106 headstones have a death date of 1338, and 10 percent are labeled as dying from "pestilence." In 2019, scientists showed the fourteenth-century plague variant that infected Europe spread out from the Volga region of Russia, an area bordering the steppes. This research is the work of several paleomicrobiologists who discovered a plague bacteria variant in two skeletons that matches the plague bacteria found in the major plague burial sites in Europe. Although two skeletons are not a large sampling, they do offer some evidence of how the fourteenth-century plague moved from the Central Asian steppes westward.

The pestilence mirrored the movement of armies, goods, and peoples throughout Eurasia. The Eastern Pandemic, in China, began in the 1220s. The Western Pandemic, in the Middle East, Europe, and North Africa, began in the 1340s. The plague hit the Kingdom of Ghana and the Niger River valley in the mid-fourteenth century, and new research indicates the likelihood that there were pandemics in both West and East Africa later in that century. It reached the southern portions of India in 1619. Plague reached more far-flung regions of the world during the Third Plague Pandemic of 1894, when places like the Americas (South, 1899, and North, 1900) and Australia (1900) were introduced to a new strain of *Y. pestis*, which had now become a worldwide disease. The map of the plague's movement matches the overland and overseas routes throughout Eurasia and across the globe. The bacteria spread in fits and starts, in what scientists call "metastatic leaps," as humans moved across both land and sea and took their diseases with them.

Mongols and Movement

Central Asia and China

Following recent research on the plague in the Central Asian steppes, we see that China had its first encounter with the pandemic in the 1220s. Current evidence indicates that Chinese cities were decimated by the plague after the arrival of the Mongols. Creating the largest land empire in history, these Central Asian steppe peoples extended their reach from Europe to China and also from Russia to India. As we have seen earlier, environmental and political changes often caused the nomadic herders of the steppes to invade their neighbors, with periodic incursions throughout the medieval period. This changed, in the thirteenth century, with the rise of Chinggis Khan (ca. 1162–1227). He united the nomadic groups into one unit and used their superior weaponry, horsemanship, and military skill to carve out an empire that crossed Eurasia. The Mongolian army was a fast and agile light cavalry (horseback warriors with little armor and light weapons) reinforced by a small infantry. Since all Mongolian children learned to ride and shoot from a young age, Mongolian tribes had plenty of warriors at the ready.

As the Mongolian armies moved into northern China, they passed through the Qinghai-Tibetan plateau, where the new strains of *Y. pestis* were emerging. The plague bacteria was endemic in the native rodent population of marmots, an animal highly prized by the Mongolians for its meat (fat and protein) and hides (carpets, coats, and leathers). It is possible that plague moved from marmots to humans at this stage, or that fleas brought the plague to their human hosts. Whatever the mode of transmission, Mongolians seemed to have spread a pandemic in their military wake. The invasions of Jin China (northern China) in the 1220s, and the incursions further south in the 1230s, brought this new disease into China. By the 1230s, Chinese doctors and historians began to detail the disease and its death rate. Dr. Li Gao wrote in 1232 of one million dead of a new disease in Kaifeng after the Mongolian invasion. He, and others, wrote of a disease that caused fevers and large lumps on the body. While we do not yet have scientific data to prove these epidemics were bubonic plague, textual evidence leads scholars to believe the disease to be the same bacteria that later affected western Asia. Quantitative analysis shows us that about 30 percent of northern China's population was lost in the latter part of the thirteenth century.

Some scholars believe that plague also hit the Yuan dynasty from 1330 to 1380. The Chinese governments kept very detailed annual historical records, but there is little mention of large-scale deaths. Some scholars have argued that this is because the government sought to keep massive deaths out of the accounts. The instability in the Yuan Empire from 1320 to 1333 saw seven emperors and factional political warfare. Keeping a pandemic out of the historical record may have been an attempt to stabilize a rocky empire. Our best sources on plague in this period are archeological medicine, which traces the disease through its variant strains on the bodies of the dead (as seen above), and the meticulous Chinese census. Although not a perfect method of determining population statistics, the Chinese did keep fairly detailed records of the number of households within their territories. In 1291, the Yuan dynasty counted approximately 13.6 million households. Regions outside Mongol control also kept records, and their records show another 13.4 million households. Despite the problematic recordkeeping of the Yuan, scholars believe the total number of households in China was approximately 26 million (or about 130 million people). The next major census was completed by the Ming in 1381. They controlled the majority of China and counted 10.6 million households. This is a loss of about 16 million households in 100 years. Other, more localized sources show that 20 percent of southern China's population died between 1350 and 1380. As in Europe, Chinese history was filled with famines, wars, and, we suspect, a plague pandemic.

Asia Minor and Africa

As the Mongols and other Central Asian steppe peoples moved around the large swaths of land in Eurasia (possibly because of a climate shift, as we saw earlier), the plague moved with them. The site in Kyrgyzstan shows evidence of plague in 1338, and new sites in southern Russia may also reveal plague victims, as research continues to track the plague across the steppes. Several historical sources wrote that "pestilence" affected portions of Muslim North India in 1335, but we do not yet have proof that the disease was plague.

The first major historical mention of the Black Plague is in the Middle East and Byzantine Empire in 1346/1347. It spread quickly throughout the Middle East, North Africa, and Europe. It moved along military and trade routes set up and, in many cases maintained by, Mongolian authority. Perhaps infected grain, perhaps infected camels, or furs (an important trade good), or fleas moved along the routes across the great grasslands to find another unsuspecting populace. Once it arrived in ports, ships carried the disease further and faster than it had traveled before. Areas along the Black Sea and the coasts of the Mediterranean all saw infection in 1346 and 1347. The disease hit Alexandria, Egypt, in 1347 and spread south and eastward quickly throughout the Muslim world. As we saw in earlier chapters, the robust trade between North Africa, the Islamicate, and the European countries created a tightly connected web of goods and humans who traveled throughout the region.

Ahmad ibn Ali al-Maqrizi, an Egyptian scholar and historian, wrote of the plague's entry into North Africa, which he witnessed firsthand. He wrote that Cairo had become "an abandoned desert" and the world itself could think of nothing outside of death. Upper Egypt was "deserted" and fields were left unplowed and unplanted. We know plague hit Egypt especially hard and it moved further south into Ethiopia and the Kingdom of Aksum, where trade sent the disease across the Red Sea and into southern Arabia. The pestilence moved quickly across North Africa, decimating the caliphates along the coast. Until recently, scholars believed plague did not reach sub-Saharan Africa until the fifteenth century; recent archeological evidence has proven this narrative false. Particularly in West Africa, the major states and kingdoms seem to have been ravaged by the plague in the mid-fourteenth century, the same as North Africa. Several African kingdoms experienced serious depopulation around this time. Archeologists have found evidence of entire villages and large towns being deserted. Scientific research is in its early stages, but scholars believe plague to be responsible for people moving away from some coastal cities and small groups of survivors moving inland. Trade along the coast was fairly robust during this period, and the Saharan desert, despite its reputation as uncrossable, had many routes and merchants plying the sand to north and west. The plague could easily have entered West Africa by these routes and there is no reason to believe that it would not have devastated these communities the same as it did in North Africa.

Europe

The disease hit Europe after the famine of 1313–1317, infecting people already weakened from decades of malnutrition. The plague, which entered Mediterranean Europe and the Middle East in 1347, arrived there on ships sailing from the Black Sea. It may have entered on trade ships from Kaffa, or with

Fig 12.2
An image of Death strangling a victim of the plague from a fourteenth-century
manuscript called the Stiny Codex.
Fine Art Images / Heritage Images / Getty Images

infected grain from further east; nevertheless the results were the same: unprecedented death. Italian cities were unprepared for the death and devastation
brought to them by sea. From southern Italy, it spread rapidly northward along
commercial routes and took advantage of the increased population in Europe's
cities to inflict a massive death toll. The dead lay unburied, children wandered
without parents, civic society faltered, and kings and lords struggled to keep
governments running. From 1346 to 1353, approximately 40 percent of the
European population, or about 30 million people, perished. That equates to
almost 10 million people every year, for three years in a row.

One of the more interesting facets of studying the plague in western Europe
is the responses of those left to suffer from the virulent disease. One group,
called the flagellants, believed that the plague was a punishment from God
for the sins of humanity, and if human sin could bring disease, maybe human
repentance could end it. If they could repent before God for the sins of *all*
humanity, perhaps God would spare the world of the devastating disease. From
1347 into mid-1349, roving groups of men traveled from village to village in

Europe calling on locals to prostrate themselves in village squares and beg God for forgiveness. Many flagellants whipped themselves to show their repentance before God. Their whips, called flagella, gave the group their name. Surviving liturgies demonstrate flagellants calling on all humanity to flee from evil and to repent, to suffer as Christ suffered. "Because of God we spill our blood, so that it will precede the sin" reads part of a flagellant liturgy; it continues, begging for God's forgiveness, "Now God may avert the Great Death!" Like bloodletting, the flagellants' actions merely spread plague to new areas within Europe. Bishops and priests decried the movement as full of lies, and city officials called the adherents "nuisances." The pope, Clement VI (1342–1352) soon called for their disbanding, labeling them heretical for their actions.

Much more devastating were pogroms against Jews. Following the medical idea that poison must be causing the plague, many sought out *who* was poisoning towns and villages. This "poison conspiracy" targeted vagrants, the poor, and Jews. Anti-Semitic tropes of well poisonings were endemic in many areas of Europe, and as murders of Jews during the crusades show us, Christians in Europe were quick to blame and kill Jews for a multitude of false claims. Thousands of Jews were murdered in 1348 and 1349, and the conspiracy only died out when people realized that the plague kept killing residents long after the local Jews had been executed. Clement VI's papal bull of September 1348 (*Quamvis Perfidiam*) sternly warned any Christian against violence against the Jews, stating that God alone was responsible for the plague.

Remedies and Responses

Doctors from China to Sweden did their best with the scientific knowledge at hand to ameliorate the effects of this terrible disease and to improve survival rates among their patients. In some areas, physicians suggested avoiding baths for fear that a clean body would allow disease entry into the body, and, in other areas, particularly in the Muslim world, victims were told to take baths more frequently than they normally would. The most common advice was to flee infected areas, which unfortunately just led to the spread of plague. Fumigation and quarantine were two other popular medical treatments and, as we might expect, the second one worked better than the first. It might seem unusual, but doctors also suggested to plague-stricken cities that they bury their dead and clear their refuse. Many of the early deaths were among gravediggers, and soon the dead and city refuse began piling up on the edge of town, becoming almost unbearable as those who cleared trash and buried bodies died. Cemeteries and graveyards turned into large pit burials, where villages sought the most expedient way to cover the dead. The most unfortunate medical treatment, without a doubt, was bloodletting. According to Galenic medical thought of the Classical west, which both Christian and Muslim doctors used, removing blood from the body could help to balance the humors that provided health and indicated disease within a body.

DID MEDIEVAL PEOPLE BATHE?

Stereotypes about people in the Middle Ages claim that they neglected personal hygiene, did not clean their teeth, and were afraid to take baths. But, to the contrary, evidence from nearly all premodern cultures indicates that bodily cleanliness was important, especially as related to preparing and eating food, as an aid to health, after hard physical labor, and for ritual purification before or during worship. Elite members of each society had more access to bathtubs than did peasantry, as well as to the fuel needed for heating water and servants to manage the tubs. Many elite cultures were deeply concerned with personal beauty, pleasing bodily scents, and fashions, which intersected with personal hygiene. Washing hands and face was particularly important before eating, and decorative water jugs for handwashing were quite popular in Europe from the twelfth to fifteenth centuries. Descriptions of banquets in the Islamicate world detail several steps in the cleansing of face, hands, beard, and hair with soap, water, oils, and perfumes. People of lower status and wealth washed their faces and hands daily – typically with soap and jugs of water – and cleaned their whole bodies perhaps weekly. Teeth would be cleaned with picks or by rubbing them with cloth or herb leaves.

The origin of this false stereotype is the truth that Europe did not have public bathhouses like the Roman Empire. In ancient Rome, many bathhouses were built and sponsored by wealthy politicians, and bathing was an important part of social life, even for members of the lowest social ranks. Christians in early medieval Europe thought that a better use of personal wealth was to donate land to monasteries or churches. At the same time, urban structures in general were in decline, so the use of public bathhouses declined in northern Europe. However, Roman-style bathhouses continued to be in regular use in the Islamicate and Byzantine regions. By the later Middle Ages, communal bathhouses had revived in Europe, and numerous public bathing facilities were found in many European cities (for example, thirteenth-century Paris had more than 30 bathhouses). They contained steam rooms, public pools, and dining rooms; some were places where sex workers could be hired, but others were restricted to cleansing only. It was only in the early modern period that public bathhouses fell out of favor in Europe.

In many societies, bodily and spiritual cleanliness played important roles in preparation for prayer, worship, or religious feasts. Ritual purification was particularly important, for example, in Judaism, Islam, Japanese Shintoism and Buddhism, Hinduism, and many Indigenous American religions; Christianity required priests to cleanse their hands before administering the sacrament. Full bodily immersion in water was required by some religions, either after the loss of ritual purity (through menstruation, ejaculation, or contact with something unclean, like a dead body) or in preparation for or during worship. For example, in Judaism, use of the mikveh (ritual bath) is attested in Jewish communities throughout the medieval world. Other religions mandated cleansing of hands, face, arms, and feet – such as Islam, in which ablutions are to be performed before prayers. Water fountains are thus an essential part of a mosque complex.

Medieval Japanese society placed a particularly high importance on bathing, in its many religious, health, and social functions. In the early medieval period, access to bathing was typically restricted to a privileged few, largely as a form of spiritual practice. Ritual ablutions (often in cold water) took place within temple and court complexes. Extended series of bathing treatments using steam baths, hot water tubs, and herbs were considered therapeutic but were only available to the elite. However, charity baths were sponsored by those elites and gave the poor the chance to have a warm bath at a temple or bathhouses at springs. By the fifteenth century, public baths, private bathing tubs, and hot spring baths were all common. In the late medieval period, bathing was not only considered hygienic and healthful, it was also a prominent social activity open to all members of society – a place for people of diverse status to gather and enjoy themselves. In large urban centers like Kyoto, public bathing facilities were important aspects of the commercial and social world. Socializing, eating, tea ceremonies, and other entertainments took place at public bathhouses and, for the wealthy who could afford them, at private bathing facilities where they gathered with friends.

The Greek physician and writer Galen (ca. 200) popularized the idea of the four humors that doctors promulgated and believed from around 200 BCE until the Scientific Revolution. Possibly as old as Mesopotamian medicine, the classical philosophers and doctors believed that the four humors, four seasons, and four elements, along with a list of other concepts, had to be in balance for the body to be working properly. Illness in a patient could be traced back to either an excess or deficiency of one of the four humors. These four, black bile, yellow bile, blood, and phlegm, also had the qualities of cold, hot, moist, and dry, and were related to mental and emotional temperaments. It was thought that the balance of the humors with their qualities (seasons, elements, planets, etc.) was what kept any individual healthy. An excess of black bile created melancholy: reserved and detailed individuals who were prone to anxiety and depression. Too much yellow bile caused a choleric personality: independent, domineering, and short-tempered. An increase in blood caused a sanguine personality: extroverted and social, hot-blooded, and prone to anger. Too much phlegm created a phlegmatic person: easy-going but with a tendency toward apathy. To remedy these imbalances, doctors encouraged bloodletting, emetics, and purges. They also prescribed herbs and foods that would rebalance the body.

Medieval Islamic doctors from Ibn Sina (980–1037; known in Europe as Avicenna) forward leaned heavily on the four humors method in diagnosing and treating ailments of their patients. As Islam moved east, west, and south, these ideas traveled with their adherents and their doctors so that people from Pakistan to Africa were practicing medicine with the Galenic method. Medieval Islamic medicine was among the most advanced in the world; Islamicate medical scholars combined elements of ancient Greek, Roman, and Egyptian medical texts, Persian ideas, Aryuvedic (medical) texts from India, and modern elements of analysis and experimentation. And the four humors theory was still top of their minds in all cases. Doctors in all regions did their best to help their ailing and dying patients. Many contemporary texts hold physicians accountable for failing to discover the root cause of disease and for fleeing from infected areas, but recent scholarly research indicates that doctors died early in the plague months, probably as they treated the patients and were then infected themselves. We know doctors followed early ideas of medical experimentation along the lines of the scientific method. For example, they understood that occasionally a bubo opened on its own and the person was restored to health. Therefore, some doctors lanced buboes to repeat what they had seen as positive medical treatment. Unfortunately, what this often did was spread the infection directly into the bloodstream, creating septicemic plague, and a dead patient within 48 hours. Many quickly stopped lancing buboes. Nevertheless, we see this as an early attempt at scientific experimentation as doctors saw a problem, experimented with a solution, and then revised their ideas based on the results of those solutions.

Outside of the four humors theories, doctors in Europe and the Middle East worked desperately in search of causes and cures for this pestilence. One major advancement in medical science was the "poison thesis." Doctors believed that poison must have infected people – they could see no other reason for so many people to be ill all at once, unless they all got the disease from the same place at the same time. Most doctors believed the poison traveled by air, and that it stuck to inanimate objects, such as beds and clothing. They determined this by observation (the first step in the scientific method) and tried to find reasons why families in the same house died together, or why clothing resellers and their customers died after handling clothing from sick people. In their experiences, only poison could affect so many so quickly.

Doctors treated their patients through the same methods they treated poisonings – with herbal drug remedies. Modern study has shown that some of the sweet-smelling flowers and herbs they used were antibacterial, but not enough to defeat the plague bacteria. Oregano, garlic, and ginger, all used in the medieval medical tisanes and tinctures, have small antibacterial and anti-viral properties. Echinacea, yarrow, and calendula were used, in addition to rosemary and lavender, which also all have small amounts of antibacterial qualities. The flowers and herbs also helped to cover the stench of sickness that permeated plague victims. Some medieval doctors in the Islamicate and Christian worlds believed that small "bodies of poison" infected their patients causing sickness and death.

Given the limited number of effective remedies, the disease took its toll, and paranoia and fear overtook survivors who looked for someone or some-thing to blame. Literature of the period derides doctors for abandoning towns and villages to the plague, but they were not the only group of people who were seen negatively by those who lived through the plague. Particularly in western Europe, we see frequent condemnations of village priests and others within the Roman Church hierarchy. Doubtless, some priests did flee their posts, but records show that many of these local priests also died soon after the first victims in their towns. In many cases, post-plague criticism of the clergy arose from the fact that new priests were hastily trained newcomers, which indicates that high numbers of plague-era clergy died because of their attention to the sick and dying – thus the need for them to be replaced quickly.

Social Mobility and Movement

The bubonic plague was an equal-opportunity killer. No class, gender, or ethnicity had more resistance than another. As a result, the drastic reduction of the population shook up social structures. Despite the horror and destruction of the plague years, as the disease slowed its course, people in the lower classes saw their economic and social situations improve. The labor shortage that the plague created meant surviving workers could demand wages – some for the first time – and they could leave their lords' estates for greater opportunities in the cities. This became especially true for women, who had greater economic opportunities in cities than they did in rural environments. If there had been three brewers in the town, for example, two men and one woman, and only the woman survived, she had a corner on the remaining market, despite her gender. If a land-holding noble were short on labor to work and manage his estates, surviving tenants could demand better terms. Nominal wages (actual pay) increased and, for a short time, real wages (the purchasing power of those wages) did as well.

As the lower class began earning more, they spent their money on housing, land ownership, and higher-quality goods. This angered the upper classes, who began to demand that members of the lower classes return to their reduced station. These anxieties were aided by inflation, which rose drastically in the 1360s. By the 1370s, the wealthy looked to their monarchs and governments to curb rising wages and costs. England, in particular, passed laws designed to deflate wages and stem the increasing social tensions within the country (as seen in Chapter 10). These laws, called sumptuary laws, were passed to restrict luxurious spending by the lower classes (see Chapters 8 and 10) and applied to clothing, jewelry, and modes of transportation. For example, fur was confined to the upper classes, gold and purple clothing could only be worn by the royal family, and lower-class people had to ride in carts pulled by donkeys, not horses. These laws and subsequent ones that fixed wages at pre-plague prices did negatively affect the lower classes, but economic advances for the lower classes in mid-century allowed them to acquire more wealth throughout the next several decades.

In the countryside of England, peasants who survived the plague had some leverage to protest such taxation policies. They objected to serfdom, the system by which they were enslaved to a landowner to work his estates in return for shelter and often meager supplies. They objected to being conscripted for the Crown's wars, and they protested the unfair and random practices of the justice system, which did not represent them. By 1381, a radical religious leader named John Ball and a farmer named Wat Tyler led a march on London to present their demands for reform to 14-year-old King Richard II. When he refused to face them, protestors became rioters. Fortified by their London counterparts, the angry peasants liberated prisoners, destroyed the city palace of Richard's uncle, set fire to the law courts, and murdered many officials, including high-ranking court advisors. Forced to meet with the peasants, Richard made concessions, but, during negotiations, Richard's army killed Wat Tyler and dispersed the crowd. Over the next few months, the Crown's forces rooted out the agitators and killed them, but the Peasants' Revolt of 1381 left a lasting impression.

In addition to rebelling against an oppressive and unjust nobility, English commoners who survived the plague resented the abuses of power committed by clerics and monks. Judging from literature of the period, corrupt priests and self-serving monks took copious advantage of the congregations they were meant to support. *Piers Plowman*, a popular English text, offered a scathing criticism of Church practices. At the beginning of this story, the narrator falls asleep next to a stream and dreams of a "field of folk" – people of all kinds – going about their work. The poem celebrates these common people and their industry and satirizes representatives of the Church, allegorical figures of greed and wealth, who seek only more riches and earthly delights. Piers Plowman rejected the rituals and customs of the Roman Church for a simple life dedicated to Christ's example of charity. There is dignity and purpose in plowing one's own half-acre. The many extant versions of the poem exposed and criticized the exact abuses of Church power and privilege that triggered the Protestant Reformation a century later.

There were other activists for Roman Church reform. As an Oxford University theologian, John Wycliffe (ca. 1330–1384) spent his life studying the Bible and Church doctrine. He believed priests should more closely represent the simple lessons of Jesus: humility, mercy, and care for the poor. Scripture did not, he wrote, authorize or call for the worship of saints, the existence of monastic institutions, or even the office of the papacy. In his view, there was no reason to submit to the authority of the Church of his day, and, in fact, many reasons to rebel against it. He advocated for a Bible written in English, arguing that each worshipper could and should interpret holy scripture for themself, and even though the Roman Church forbade such work, he began his own translation. His calls for reform attracted a network of followers across England, who called themselves Lollards. They inhabited every section of society; some participated in the English Peasants' Revolt and others were members of the royal courts.

Though Wycliffe did not live to see the changes he argued for, his ideas gained momentum in the fertile ground of late fourteenth-century England. The ascension of Henry IV in 1399 saw a return to strong monarchical and ecclesiastical authority, and, in 1415, the Council of Constance declared Wycliffe's movement heretical. Wycliffe's texts were discredited and destroyed, he was posthumously excommunicated, and his body was removed from consecrated ground and burned. The Lollards were persecuted, and Church leaders in England went as far as to make it a heresy for a someone not in clerical orders to translate the Bible. Even as late as 1536, another religious reformer, William Tyndale, was burned at the stake for translating parts of the Bible into English.

Pressing On

Tynedale's Bible was the first English Bible to be printed, and the invention of the printing press is a marker of the end of the medieval period in Europe. In the 1440s in Mainz, Germany, Johannes Gutenberg synthesized a variety of mechanical innovations into a successful, movable-type press. Until that time, reading material of any kind was copied by hand, making it unlikely that there would be many copies of any one text, and it was impossible for copies to be identical. Because of the labor involved and the expense

Fig 12.3
This woodcut is the earliest known illustration of a printer's shop (ca. 1500) and is an image from the *danse macabre* artistic genre of late medieval Europe. In *danse macabre* images, people from all classes and activities are visited by the skeletal figure of Death, usually at their most productive moments. It is a *memento mori* emblem, which is Latin for "remember we all die." Reminders of death were a common apotropaic gesture of post-plague Europe. In this picture, Death actively participates in the daily bustle of a printer's shop. The compositor arranges type in a tray with Death's hand on his shoulder, the worker with the inking ball fights Death's grip, and Death greets a customer.
Album / Alamy Stock Photo

of prepared parchment writing surfaces, manuscripts were rare and belonged to the upper classes. The printing press, or letter press, allowed for a printer to "set" a tray with type (individual blocks of lead stamps with letters set in relief), place the tray in a depression on the table top of the press, spread ink on it, place a sheet of parchment or paper on top, and clamp down a block that pressed the image of the letters onto the page. Impressions of the page could be made again and again. Gutenberg experimented with his invention by printing copies of the Bible in Latin. His invention revolutionized communication and made it possible for popular movements to gain power, most notably the demands for Church reforms like those that began in late fourteenth-century England.

During the last decade of Gutenberg's life, a feud between two archbishops – one appointed by the citizenry and the other by the pope – caused considerable violence and disruption in Mainz. For a time, Gutenberg himself was exiled from the city, and printers trained in the new technology went in search of work in cities where there was a need for recording international trade transactions (Venice), universities (Paris), or religious administration (Rome). The technology spread, and the printing press revolution caused many social changes. For one, the Church no longer had control of printing and therefore could not enforce the requirement that religious writing be in Latin and produced by clerics. Printers began publishing texts in vernacular languages, that is, the language the common people spoke, such as dialects of English, French, and German. This accelerated religious reforms that mark the end of the medieval period and the beginning of the early modern period in Europe. In the sixteenth century, uniform vernacular bibles could be produced for everyday, individual use, and it became a religious duty for people to read scripture for themselves. The printing press also made it possible for dissenters to announce their views in broadsheets and pamphlets, thus significantly changing religious and political communication.

Conclusion

The plague was a cross-cultural connection with dramatic results across Eurasia. Adding in the famines and wars, about two-thirds of the European population was lost in the 100 years between 1345 and 1455. Societies managed the catastrophe in different ways, both positively and negatively. The trauma of the random onset of disease and death forced some into superstitious mindsets that often drove them to scapegoat marginalized peoples and accuse their neighbors of bringing on the wrath of God, or the gods. Others carried on with the collective work of a village or smaller community, and, in many places, depopulation created room for adjustments to the social hierarchy, allowing some groups access to resources and rights they had not had before.

B: SURVIVORS

Evidence: Dante Alighieri, *Divine Comedy*

Giovanni Boccaccio, *The Decameron*

Geoffrey Chaucer, *The Canterbury Tales*

Thomas Malory, *Le Morte d'Arthur*

The Forbidden City

Machu Picchu

Sancta Sophia

Introduction

Despite the psycho-social disruption of plague and the justified fears that it was the end of the world, it was not. Communities and greater societies survived, with renewed direction and purpose, sometimes achieving astonishing new feats of ingenuity and scientific advancement. The literature, art, and culture of the late medieval period are ones of innovation and change; the printing press, vernacular bestsellers, and early Renaissance art brought more people into the sphere of art and writing. However, these enlightening artistic trends existed side by side with early Reformation strife, pogroms against the Jews, the Inquisition, and the beginnings of conquest and colonialism. Post-plague social momentum inspired Europeans to sail out of their territorial bounds, and rulers in China, Turkey, and the Andes solidified their authority over large empires, demonstrating their power through monumental and expensive architectural buildings.

Surviving Hell

From 1308 until 1314, Dante Alighieri (1265–1321) composed the poetic masterpiece the *Divine Comedy*, a trilogy of the *Inferno* (hell), the *Purgatorio* (purgatory, the in-between space from which imperfect souls hope to improve and pass on to heaven), and *Paradiso* (heaven). In the *Inferno*, Dante, in a desperate mid-life crisis, learns important lessons from a tour through hell guided by the great Roman poet Virgil. Each of the nine circles of the underworld is reserved for the souls of those who have committed specific sins, and as the two descend, the severity of the sins increases.

At the bottom of the funnel of hell is Lucifer or Satan, in a freezing, colorless, suffocating lair. Inferno is a word we associate with fire, like a furnace, but the

Italian word Dante used connects with inferior – hell is massively inferior to heaven, an imperfect, joyless place deep underground. And the *Divine Comedy* is not a story of hilarious jokes and funny incidents. Here *comedy* is used in the way the ancient Greek philosopher Aristotle defined it – a story that ends with all conflicts resolved, maybe happily. In the case of Dante's *Divine Comedy*, the character Dante and all of those who atone for sin and are humble before God's majesty have the potential of an afterlife of eternal peace.

Dante must have desperately wanted an afterlife of peace. In the fourteenth century, Florence was a turbulent and dangerous place of feuding

Fig 12.4
At the end of the fifteenth century, which in art history is the early Renaissance, Sandro Botticelli illustrated the *Inferno*. In this drawing he depicts the tricky moment in the text when Virgil guides Dante down, down, down, suddenly twisting so they are facing down and yet moving up and out of hell. On the right side of the image, follow the figures of Virgil and Dante as they descend along the hairy, frost-covered body of Lucifer. As the poem tells us, at about the top of the monster's thigh, Virgil turns them upside down, but impossibly, they are now climbing up to Lucifer's feet. When they reach the surface, Dante looks down to see the devil's body inverted. They have flipped over and emerged in Purgatory on the other side of the world.
The Picture Art Collection / Alamy Stock Photo

Fig 12.5
Botticelli's *The Birth of Venus* (ca. 1485).
World History Archive / Alamy Stock Photo

noble families, political treachery, and warring factions, most notably the feud between two groups called the Guelphs and the Ghibellines. Dante himself fought in several battles and participated in the fractious politics of his city. Once the Guelphs defeated the Ghibellines, they split into two parties, and Dante backed the White Guelph faction, which lost out to the Black Guelph faction in 1301. Dante, along with other White Guelph members, was tried and convicted of financial corruption. Exiled from Florence on punishment of death if he were to return, he moved among cities until his death, all the while working on his masterpiece. His hell stands for the real world as Dante saw it, with hypocrites, liars, and double-crossers in the lowest levels, below those who committed crimes of passion such as adultery and murder. In 1321 he died from malaria.

Instead of writing his verses in Latin, Dante chose to write in his Tuscan dialect of Italian, and, with the success of the *Divine Comedy*, Dante's Italian became the standard dialect of the language. Circulated in hand-written copies, the *Divine Comedy* was quickly recognized as an intellectual classic, and it inspired the great Italian writers Boccaccio and Petrarch, who, along with Dante, had a tremendous impact on subsequent European writers, including the English writer Geoffrey Chaucer, whose *The Canterbury Tales* alludes to their work. In addition, Dante's work was a portal into the Renaissance; for instance, the painter Sandro Botticelli (1445–1510), who painted early Renaissance classics such as *The Birth of Venus*, produced illustrations of the *Inferno*.

Medieval European Bestsellers

Just two decades after Dante's death and only eight short years prior to plague arriving in Europe, the English writer Geoffrey Chaucer was born. From an early age, Chaucer worked as a bureaucrat for Edward III and his powerful sons, with both plague and war ravaging the island. Like Dante, Chaucer fought in battles (at one point being ransomed back to the king of England) and during a long career of working for the English royal family, he also wrote literature, including a frame tale called *The Canterbury Tales*. The outer story of this tale begins with a group of people gathered at a tavern on the south bank of the Thames River preparing to depart on a pilgrimage to Canterbury Cathedral. There they will ask God's forgiveness at the shrine of Thomas Becket, an archbishop who was murdered on the altar steps in 1170. The tavern owner proposes a contest. Each of the pilgrims will tell a story on the way to the cathedral and one on the way back. The pilgrim who tells the best story gets a meal on the house.

Chaucer borrowed the idea of tales within tales most directly from the Italian writer Giovanni Boccaccio (1313–1375), whose frame tale *The Decameron* is about ten noble men and women who retreat to one of their country estates to escape the plague. To entertain each other and calm their fears, each one tells a story for ten nights in a row – ten times ten, the "deca" in *Decameron*. Both Chaucer and Boccaccio mimic frame tale story traditions popular in Arabia, Persia, and India, similar to Scheherazade's *One Thousand and One Nights* discussed in Chapters 6 and 8.

For *The Canterbury Tales*, Chaucer borrowed specific stories from *The Decameron* and adapted them to his purposes; however, in sharp contrast to Boccaccio's storytellers, not one of Chaucer's band of travelers is an aristocrat. The highest-status character is a knight who has recently returned from the crusades, but not as an attractive, adventurous hero; he is bedraggled and confused, perhaps suffering from PTSD. The rest of the company includes a bawdy miller (he operates a mill used to grind wheat into flour), a reeve (a handyman caretaker for a young noble's estate), a shipman (probably a pirate), and a pompous man of law. It also includes guildsmen: a haberdasher, a carpenter, a weaver, a dyer, and a tapestry maker. Medieval guilds were unions of tradespeople or artisans who banded together so each individual member had more power to control trade and collect accounts payable. These pilgrims are not princes and princesses, emperors, or caliphs. Instead, each character is identified by jobs or social roles – merchants, property managers, and agents of the Church – evidence that the decimations of the plague created room for social advancement and change.

One of Chaucer's most intriguing characters is Alison, more famously called the Wife of Bath. Alison's prosperity comes from two sources, and she is proud of both. One of her careers is as a fine weaver. We are told that the cloth she produces is as beautiful as the fine fabrics woven in Flanders, an area now part of Belgium that was known for its luxury textile production. Maybe to show off her skills or maybe for a bit of vacation flare, Alison has chosen red stockings for the journey. Her second career is as a serial wife, which we learn about in great detail.

When it is her turn to entertain the group with a tale, Alison spends most of the time recounting the business of her marriages, from her first one at age 12 through her most recent one to a man 20 years younger than herself. The major error of her career? Being so in love with her fifth husband that she gave him control of her land and money. The major triumph of her career? Manipulating him into giving it back. Chaucer leaves it a bit vague whether she is on pilgrimage to find another husband (has her fifth husband died?) or is able to travel freely without a man. Either way, she is a sensational example of social mobility in the wake of the plague. She is a female artisan and landowner, an independent person of means who challenges the patriarchy and conventions of marriage.

Chaucer's characters are imperfect and quirky, and he makes fun of some of them with light humor, but, like Dante and Boccaccio, he is scathingly critical of others, especially agents of the Church and the religious orders. The summoner is named for his job as the person who finds accused sinners and brings them to ecclesiastical court for questioning and trial. A person with such power could and often did abuse it by falsely accusing innocent people and extorting them for bribes. The summoner's outward appearance reflects his corrupt soul. His face is red and diseased, covered with oozing pimples and infected sores that no salve can heal. His breath reeks, and children are afraid of him. Another character is a monk, someone who should spend his days on Earth confined in a cloister, denying his own needs in fervent praying for the

Fig 12.6
Chaucer's Wife of Bath as depicted in the Ellesmere Chaucer (1400–1410).
© Huntington Library, Pasadena, California

souls of the community; instead, he is fat, well clothed, and loves to spend the days hunting with his wealthy patrons. There is also a prioress, whose thoughts should be focused on the starving poor, but is preoccupied with feeding fine meats to her little dogs.

Chaucer's most degenerate character is the pardoner, who is utterly honest about what he does: he peddles fake relics and indulgences, items and documents supposedly authorized by the pope (and therefore God) that forgive the purchaser of all sins. He feels no guilt for how he cheats poor people with his phony wares. He says out loud that he does not care if he takes money from the poorest widow with children to feed; he likes fine food and comfort, and he supports his tastes by preying on naive people burdened with a sense of guilt. In 1517, a little over a hundred years after Chaucer invented his pilgrims, Martin Luther set in motion the Protestant Reformation by publishing his *Disputation on the Power and Efficacy of Indulgences* (also known as *The 95 Theses*). His outrage over the sale of relics and indulgences, the pardoner's merchandise, is the primary topic of that document. Chaucer tapped into the distrust of representatives of the Church that was a precursor to philosophical shifts that led into the Protestant Reformation of the early sixteenth century.

William Caxton and Printed Texts

The Canterbury Tales was one of the first works of literature in English to be printed in a movable-type edition. From one press in Germany in 1450, printing expanded rapidly to the major cities in Europe; by 1480 there were printers in over 100 cities. Dante's *Divine Comedy* was first published in 1472 in Foligno, Italy. In 1471, an English merchant named William Caxton (1422–1491) studied printing in Cologne, Germany and brought it to England. Having fulfilled a term of service as the Governor of English Wool Merchants in Bruges, Belgium, Caxton's career took him to Cologne, Germany, where he observed the potential of the printing press. He decided to purchase one, and, in 1476, he had it delivered to his newly established printing shop in London. Having made a considerable financial investment in the new contraption, Caxton had to make it profitable. In addition to the purchase and maintenance of mechanical parts and pieces and trays of lead type, printing required skilled and literate typesetters, who had to learn a sort of braille proofreading system in order to check their work by running their fingers over the compositor's block before it was inked up and imprinted on paper.

Fonts also cost money. Early fonts were a simplification of human script. Since the public expected a book worth purchasing to look like a manuscript, successful type design had to imitate handwriting, which is not uniform. Handwriting, in order to be fluid and efficient, uses all kinds of ligatures, connections from one letter to the next that are unique – for instance, an e written before an s is formed by a different ending stroke to that of an e flowing to an h. This made for very complicated fonts. For Caxton's press,

15 different forms of lower-case e were necessary to make a page of script that resembled handwriting. And yet another impediment to recovering the costs of printing a book was that, in comparison to manuscripts, they looked and felt cheap. Patrons thought of a book as pages of laboriously prepared animal skins (parchment), with elaborate calligraphy, fine painting, and gold leaf. Black symbols marching across a rag surface (paper) did not seem worth paying for.

KOREAN HANGUL

During the period from 500 to 1500 CE, China, Japan, and Vietnam all used *hanzi* (or *kanji* in Japanese), the writing system of the Chinese. These shared characters created a mutual literacy among these cultures even when they could not understand each other's oral language. Instead of being bilingual, they were biliterate; for instance, while the Chinese and Japanese might use a similar symbol for "house," the spoken Chinese word for house and the Japanese word for house were not the same. As a result, Chinese and Japanese diplomats negotiated through "brush talk," writing their different languages in mutually intelligible symbols.

Initially, the Koreans used *hanzi*, but, in the fifteenth century, King Sejong of the Joseon dynasty (1392–1897) commissioned the development of a writing system with symbols that corresponded to the shape the mouth makes when pronouncing the sound. In 1446, Koreans adopted *Hunmin chong-um*, which means "the correct sounds for the instruction of the people." Hangul, as it is now called, is used by North and South Koreans and Koreans all over the world.

Literary texts were not the profit center of the first printing businesses. In fact, the bread and butter of the operations was handbills, indulgences, and other blank forms, usually to order for a particular customer. An entrepreneurial printer such as Caxton had to create new outlets, and if he turned to literature, it was best to stick with the familiar. Knowing that the works of Geoffrey Chaucer were popular, Caxton had his workshop print a version of *The Canterbury Tales* with carved woodblock illustrations. In 1485 William Caxton used his printing press, the first one on English soil, to publish a hefty collection of stories about King Arthur, his knights, and their adventures. Caxton entitled this collection *Le Morte d'Arthur* (the death of Arthur) and organized the text by subtitles and chapters to make it reader friendly, but he was not the author. The author was Thomas Malory, a thief, kidnapper, rapist, sheep rustler, and political operative who spent his ample prison time writing down all the adventures of Arthur he knew. These stories had roots as far back as a thousand years – Celtic oral-storytelling traditions, early English culture, Roman Christian motifs, and medieval French romance. The names Arthur, Guinevere, and Merlin are Celtic Welsh; Lancelot is French.

Because continental European printing shops and monastic scriptoria had the corner on Latin books for university and theological use, Caxton decided that his market would be books in English. But in order to appeal to the most customers, he had to decide on how words were spelled. In late fifteenth-century England, there were many regional dialects and no standardized way of writing them down, no dictionaries to check, no authorities to ask. Caxton chose pronunciations and spellings that he thought would be understandable to the largest group of readers. Because he was based in London and sold materials to more Londoners than any other group, he favored English as it was spoken in London. His spellings of basic words as they were pronounced at the time are the "correct" spellings of modern-day English. In addition, because he printed *The Canterbury Tales* and *Le Morte d'Arthur*, those works became canonical literary texts in English.

The year 1485, when Caxton printed the *Le Morte d'Arthur*, is also notable for the end of the destructive civil war called the Wars of the Roses, a feud between two branches of the Plantagenet dynasty, which had ruled England and parts of France since 1154. (In *Le Morte*, we see evidence of Thomas Malory's political cynicism as his life was informed by the ruthless tactics of both sides.) At the Battle of Bosworth Field, the armies of King Richard III (symbolized by a white rose) and Henry Tudor (symbolized by a red rose) clashed a final time. Richard III was hacked to death and his rival was crowned Henry VII, the first monarch of the powerful new Tudor dynasty (symbolized by a red rose with a white center). The Tudors are major figures of the transition from the premodern to the early modern period in Europe. In 1522, Henry VII's son, Henry VIII, separated his country from the Roman Church by declaring himself the supreme head of the Church of England. In 1558, Henry VII's granddaughter ascended the throne as Elizabeth I, and during the course of her 45-year reign united her people into a nation, funding and directing merchant explorers to claim property in the New World.

The printed texts of Malory, Chaucer, Dante, and Boccaccio were immediate bestsellers, if not money-makers. Dante's *Divine Comedy* had over 500 copies in 1472 alone (fewer than ten of those remain today), and Malory's *Le Morte d'Arthur* inspired new works on the Arthurian legends. Reading entered a new phase in Europe, done for pleasure and not just for edification, and the advent of the printing press meant more people could access the written word. With the constant warfare and recurring plagues, escapist literature with moral lessons found ready audiences.

Prejudice, Pogroms, and the Inquisition

Fear and privation were relentless during the fourteenth and fifteenth centuries. This often manifested as terror of anyone different or unfamiliar. Throughout the years of pestilence and war, no person of any faith, class, or homeland had any better chance of surviving than another, but to calm their anxiety, people needed to find someone or something to blame for their suffering. In Europe, deep distrust and resentment, specifically toward Jews, resurfaced in pogroms and the Inquisition. Prejudice survived plague.

The mid-fourteenth-century plague pandemic caused a rise in violence against Jews, who, as we saw, were accused of poisoning wells and causing the disease. The Black Death was not the only cause of difficulties for Europe's Jewish populations in the later Middle Ages: they also suffered periodic violent attacks (often called pogroms), pressures (both subtle and overt) to convert to Christianity, and a variety of restrictions on their freedom of movement, living, and worship. In the earlier medieval period, the predominant theological position was that Jews should not be forced to convert to Christianity – although there were episodes of persecution and violence, such as those carried out by troops in the First Crusade and the massacre at York, England, in 1190. But, across the later Middle Ages, Christian attitudes against Jews hardened, often connected with the theory that even conversion could not overcome their nature. Jewish sacred texts, too, came to be viewed as blasphemous. For example, in mid-thirteenth-century Paris, the Talmud was put "on trial," found guilty, and ordered destroyed – many thousands of copies of Jewish religious books were burned.

One idea that became a dominant part of anti-Jewish discourse in the later Middle Ages was the notion that Jews were forever guilty for the death of Christ. By extension, in some places they were falsely accused of killing Christian children, ritually murdering the eucharistic wafer (ceremonially, the body of Christ), and other evil deeds. While the papacy never endorsed these accusations, they did find support among some local secular and clerical authorities. And because Jews were active in commerce and as moneylenders, they came under increasing pressure from rulers who owed them large sums of money. All of these ideas were accompanied by a growth in defamatory stereotypes of Jews as greedy and diabolical.

The combination of anti-Semitic ideas and imagery with the efforts of later medieval rulers to centralize political power over their territories led to a series of edicts expelling Jews from different European regions – each time requiring they forfeit their property to the royal treasury, thus enriching the kings who owed large sums of money to Jewish and other bankers. For example, in 1182 they were expelled from the French royal domain (although they were invited back in at the end of that century); in 1288 from Naples; in 1290 from England; and in 1360 from Hungary. Similar edicts of expulsion were issued in cities and regions across Europe. Across the fourteenth century they were expelled from and re-admitted to the kingdom of France more than once – first in 1306 and finally in 1394.

Jewish communities remained the longest in Spain, where they were the most populous and deeply rooted. In Christian Spain, Jews were formally protected, considered part of the royal treasury. But there, too, from the fourteenth century, they were often mistreated and subjected to intense pressure to convert – in some regions being forced by law to listen to Christian sermons, having their sacred texts outlawed, their synagogues destroyed, or their neighborhoods burned. In 1391, a series of massacres in the Kingdom of Castile and Crown of Aragon led to the deaths of thousands of Jews and the conversion to Christianity of many thousands more. The massacres began in Seville, where a local preacher had been advocating violence against Jews for many years. Because Jews were royal property, these attacks were also considered challenges to royal authority – in large part because the kings were seen as favoring Jews. As the riots spread from Seville to dozens of other cities, thousands of Jews were killed, and their homes and synagogues burned. The end result for Spain's Jews was disastrous, and their once-vibrant community was much diminished.

Despite the death or conversion of much of Spain's Jewish population, hatred and fear of Jews and Jewishness continued. Many of the *conversos* (converts) were suspected of secretly practicing Judaism and were treated as enemies of Christianity. These developments came to a head in the later fifteenth century, after the rulers of Spain's two largest Christian kingdoms – Queen Isabella of Castile and King Ferdinand of Aragon – married in 1469 and thus dynastically (although not administratively) united Spain into one Christian kingdom. Intensely devout themselves, they also saw Christianity as a useful tool for uniting their territories and solidifying a common culture despite linguistic and historical differences.

One of Isabella and Ferdinand's most effective and vicious weapons in this effort was the Spanish Inquisition (founded in 1478 and operational from 1481). While the Roman Church had used inquisitorial trials – in which a suspected heretic would be questioned, sometimes using torture – since the late twelfth century, the Spanish Inquisition was a new development in that it operated under royal control. The purpose of the Inquisition was to discover and punish *conversos* and, later, *moriscos* (converted Muslims) who were not "real" Christians but heretics. The Inquisition had no power over those who remained openly Jews or Muslims.

The first appointed head of the Inquisition – called the Inquisitor General – was Tomas de Torquemada (d. 1498), a member of the Dominican order of preaching monks and Queen Isabella's personal spiritual advisor. Under his leadership, the Inquisition became a highly organized institution that operated throughout Spain to try to discover and either reform or punish Christians who had strayed from belief or practice that was considered correct (or orthodox). Torquemada was accused, even by his contemporaries, of excessive use of force and harshness in carrying out this project. Torture became a customary practice during the trials of suspected heretics. Those who repented – expressed their guilt, asked for forgiveness, and sought re-admittance to the Christian community – were publicly recognized as penitents in a large public spectacle called an *auto-da-fé* ("act of faith"). Those who did not repent but were found guilty were handed over to the secular authorities for punishment or execution, many by burning at the stake.

EDICT OF GRACE

The methods used by the Spanish Inquisition are notorious for their harshness, but inquisitors claimed that they were motivated by a sincere desire to benefit the eternal souls of heretics and to purify the Spanish Christian community. To that end, the first action when inquisitors came to a town was to issue what they called an "edict of grace" – the invitation for the guilty to present themselves and thus receive a more lenient punishment. People were also invited to inform on their neighbors and their so-called accomplices in heretical behavior. Thus the inquisition trial records often include what sounds like neighborhood gossip – accusations that a neighboring woman prepared food in the "Jewish manner," refused to eat pork, swept her floors and lit candles on Friday nights (in preparation for the Sabbath), bathed and went to bed early on Fridays, refused to cook or do other domestic work on Saturdays, or carried out other home-based practices associated with Jewish customs. In fact, women were some of the main targets of the Inquisition because of the importance of domestic rituals in the preservation of faith traditions. Those who refused to confess were subjected to an inquisitorial trial, in which witnesses and evidence would be presented, and torture might be applied.

Most of the Inquisition's targets were converts to Christianity who were accused of secretly practicing their old religion, but others were old Christians who were accused of adopting practices from their Jewish neighbors. This accusation – of "Judaizing," or spreading Jewish religious practices to otherwise faithful Christians – came to be the basis for continued pressure on Iberian Jews. In many cases, the charge was that converts who secretly practiced their Jewish faith ("crypto-Jews") were a negative influence on other converts who were trying to live a Christian life but were being enticed back to Judaism through continued communication with Judaism.

In fact, Judaizing was the main charge levied against the Jews in the decree issued in 1492 by Isabella and Ferdinand, kicking Jews out of all their territories in Spain, southern Italy, Sicily, and other Mediterranean islands. The edict of expulsion (often called the Alhambra Decree, after the Islamic hilltop-fortress in Granada, southern Spain, where the monarchs issued the proclamation) declared that all Jews in Spain had to leave within four months and were not to take with them Spanish coins or most other forms of property. Granada had been the last remaining Muslim-ruled territory in Spain from 1250; Ferdinand and Isabella decided to finish the "reconquest" of all Muslim territories and so, in early 1492, their forces marched in and ended Granada's independence. Now in control of all the formerly Muslim lands in Spain, these deeply religious monarchs took the opportunity to further homogenize their kingdom by expelling all remaining Jews based on the idea that they were threatening (intentionally) the spiritual wellbeing of their Christian neighbors.

The expulsion led to a massive dislocation of communities that had lived in Spain for more than a thousand years; the resulting migrations fundamentally changed the patterns of Jewish settlement across the globe. Jews were forced to flee Spanish territory with few possessions and no money, seeking a new home abroad in a welcoming place. Since most of the other Christian kingdoms of Europe had already expelled Jews, their choices were limited. Some Spanish Jews fled first to Morocco, but few were allowed to stay. Many others went to nearby Portugal, but the Inquisition followed only a few years later. Others migrated to the Ottoman Empire, which had taken over Byzantine Constantinople in 1453 and welcomed the Jews. Jews fleeing violence in fourteenth-century Germany migrated in large numbers to the Kingdom of Poland. So Christian Poland and the Muslim Ottoman Empire became the centers of Jewish community and culture in the following centuries. Some Iberian Jews eventually made their way to the Americas.

Other exports from Europe to the Spanish colonies in the Americas include the institution of the Inquisition and the imagery associated with the *reconquista*, both of which were useful in Spanish administration over the Indigenous populations they had conquered. Inquisitorial trials were held in both North and South America, monitoring the Christianity of both the converted Indigenous populations and the local European colonizers. Likewise, images and ideas associated with the Spanish "reconquest" of Muslim territories in Iberia were imported into New Spain. One of the most striking images of Christian triumph over Muslims was known as Santiago Matamoros ("Saint James the Moor-Slayer"), a heroic avatar of Saint James associated with the Spanish Christian pilgrimage site of Compostela, who was often said to appear in battles between the Christians and Muslims in Spain. He is depicted as wielding a sword while on the back of a horse that tramples a slain enemy underfoot. In the Americas, that image came to be identified as Santiago Mataindios, "Saint James, the Indian-Slayer," and played a significant role in solidifying, at least in the minds of the Spanish conquistadors, the connection between their domination of Muslim regions in Iberia and that of Indigenous territories in the Americas.

Monuments of Time

Monumental architecture has, since Mesopotamian times, been used as a way to indicate power. Leaders with enough money, means, and clout constructed public and private buildings in order to exhibit affluence and authority. In Chapter 9, we detailed the Grand Mosque in Cordoba and the Kazimar Big Mosque in the Tamil Nadu, but not all monumental building was religious in nature. In this section, we detail several large noble complexes around the world: the Chateau de Lusignan in France, the Forbidden City in China, and the palace complex at Machu Picchu. During periods of intense change and anxiety, the wealthy chose to demonstrate their prosperity through massive and beautiful complexes.

In western France, the ancestral home of the counts of Poitou grew to rival the greatest estates in Europe. Making their names in the First Crusade, the

Poitevin lords ruled the Kingdoms of Jerusalem, Cyprus, and Cilicia, bringing money and prestige back to their homelands in France. The original castle, known as the Chateau de Lusignan (from the first count's name), was first built in the tenth century, and it was small, but made of stone, sufficient for a borderlands count. Post-crusades, the castle was rebuilt to match the distinction of being the home of kings. At its grandest, in the fifteenth century, the castle was a marvel of white stone and bright blue roofs. Grand walls surrounded the estate and towers stood at each corner – much the way an imagined medieval castle would look. Aspects of the castle mirror those European strongholds of the Levant region, like the barbican (fortified) tower that loomed over the main gate.

Today, only foundations remain of this once-great estate. Combining several written accounts with artistic representations of the castle shows us the scale and beauty of the construction. The best visual evidence is in *Très Riches Heures du Duc de Berry*, a luxury manuscript commissioned by Jean, Duc du Berry (1340–1416), who was also the Count of Poitou. Of his many castles, Lusignan was his favorite. Earlier, in Chapter 9, we described Books of Hours, collections of prayers usually to the Blessed Virgin Mary, recited and meditated upon at certain times (hours) throughout the day. The format for these books included a calendar organized by "feast" days commemorating the martyrdom of a saint or of significant events in the life of Christ and the Virgin. The *Très Riches Heures* (*The Magnificent Hours*) is a masterpiece of this genre. Jean hired a trio of artists from Belgium, possibly the greatest painters of their age, the Limbourg brothers, to produce his lavish masterpiece. The Chateau de Lusignan is prominently painted on many of the pages.

In Figure 12.7, hard manual labor in extreme circumstances is glorified and romanticized by the grand castle that serves as a backdrop to the peasants' toiling. Looming over these peasants is the forbidding and inescapable seat of power, the fantastic Chateau de Lusignan. The gleaming stone, capped in blue, is overseen by a large golden dragon, who hovers over one tower. This recalls a famous folktale of the castle, which said that it was too large, too beautiful, and too impassive to be human-built; the counts of Poitou must have had help from the fae Melusina, a water faery who was often seen in dragon form.

Jean and his fellow aristocrats were extraordinarily rich and the Limbourg brothers were extraordinarily talented, but, like the peasants they lived off, all were mortal. In 1416, the duke and the artist brothers died suddenly and unexpectedly, most likely from the bubonic plague, but Chateau de Lusignan survived for centuries as a reminder of Jean's wealth and impact. Because of its strategic position in the center of France, later rulers fortified the buildings for military purposes. In fact, Louis XIV's (r. 1643–1715) government used it as a prison, but over time it decayed and disintegrated, and in the eighteenth century it was destroyed to make way for a public park. We would expect that such a grand stone structure would have survived in total, but today only parts of the foundation and underground passageways exist. It is memorialized only in the illuminations of a delicate and vulnerable manuscript.

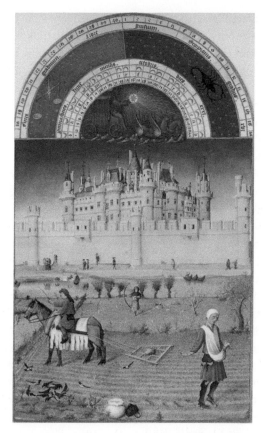

Fig 12.7
In an image from *Les Très Riches Heures du Duc de Berry* (1413–1416) peasants sow a field in front of the Chateau de Lusignan, the favorite estate of Jean de France, Duc de Berry (1340–1416).
The Print Collector / Heritage Images via Getty Images

Forbidden City

Once an imposing statement of royal power and human ingenuity, Chateau de Lusignan did not survive, but other architectural monuments of the fifteenth century did, even if their significance changed. In 1417, the year after Jean, Duc du Berry and the Limbourg brothers died, the Yongle emperor of China, Zhu Di, began building the gigantic complex of buildings known as the Forbidden City. When completed in 1445, it was the world's largest walled city, constructed primarily from the trunks of the *nanmu* tree, some as tall as a six-story building.

Everything about this project was extreme. It was the home of the god on Earth and therefore must imitate the imagined palace of the celestial emperor who was thought to inhabit a lavish 100,000-room palace on Polaris, the

North Star. (In deference to the great ruler of heaven, Zhu Di's grand facility had slightly fewer rooms.) Historians estimate that it took a million laborers, some of them prisoners of various dynastic wars, to build the infrastructure and buildings, and another 100,000 skilled craftsmen, masons, and artists to provide the exquisite ornamentation of both the exteriors and interiors. Chinese engineers invented solutions to the most impossible of tasks; for instance, there is a grand staircase carved from one gigantic 300-ton slab of marble. It was dragged about 40 miles from the quarry to the construction site, mostly over a manmade ice-way. In the frigid cold of January, crews stopped about every third of a mile and dug a well. They directed the flowing water to extend a path of slick ice over which hundreds of men and horses dragged the monolith slowly and torturously toward Beijing.

Zhu Di (1360–1424) was third emperor of the Ming dynasty (1368–1644). When he came to power, it had not been very long since the Yuan dynasty, the dynasty founded by the Mongol Kublai Khan, had been overthrown. Zhu Di rebelled against a rival emperor in the south, seized the throne, and conquered the capital, Nanjing, but he was not secure in that city, facing hostilities that escalated to assassination attempts. In addition, the expelled Mongols continually threatened to reclaim territory, and all efforts to shore up and extend the Great Wall did not prevent invasion. In order to protect himself from danger in Nanjing and to position his armies strategically against the Mongols, Zhu Di uprooted his court and relocated from Nanjing north to Beijing.

There, he claimed space and authority with his grand building project. As a statement of the growing power of the Ming dynasty, he had Kublai Khan's palace razed and built his compound on the ruins. The centerpiece and tallest building was the Hall of Supreme Harmony. Sitting atop three white marble terraces, it contained the throne room of the emperor, the moral leader of the Chinese people, the supreme judge, the military commander, and the curator of artistic taste. Officials of the empire bureaucracy – mandarins – gathered in the courtyard to hear imperial proclamations and to be granted audience to the emperor and his closest advisors. Entry into China's mandarin class was through a set of difficult exams that included knowledge of classical Chinese literature and good handwriting, but, once in, a bureaucrat could rise through the ranks. Levels of influence and accomplishment were indicated in mandarin attire by the color of buttons on their hats or emblems on their robes.

Everywhere a visitor looked there was shock-and-awe ornamentation. Carved mythological figures populated the roofs and walkways, especially statues of dragons, but never of the fire-breathing variety. Since the Forbidden City was built almost entirely of wood in an environment with frequent lightning storms, the greatest threat to it was fire; therefore, the protective stone dragons are water creatures, featured prominently on roofs, gutters, and downspouts. The dragon motif continued in the interior spaces, where precious metal and gem figurines and paintings were everywhere. If a visitor had the status and good fortune to enter palace rooms, they would be overwhelmed by gilded woodwork, rich red walls, fine porcelain objects for decoration and use, and

Fig 12.8
Forbidden City, Beijing, China.
zhaojiankang / iStock

ornate carpets and textiles crafted from richly dyed silk and wool fibers – the most precious and advanced luxuries of the silk roads. And it was all maintained by eunuchs. Other than the emperor, his male family members, and maybe a few religious or other advisors, no men who could procreate were allowed in the Forbidden City (it is called Forbidden for a reason). Instead, a multitude of eunuchs managed the property, tended to the imperial family, oversaw food service, preparation for ceremonies, household tasks, and gardening. They were the heart of the enterprise.

For 24 emperors, the Forbidden City was the political and religious center of China, until 1911 when the six-year-old Pu Ye abdicated the throne. Eventually, the complex became a museum with some, but not all, parts open to the public.

Machu Picchu

In the heart of the Inca Empire, nestled in the jungles of the Peruvian Andes, lies an architectural and engineering marvel that has stood the test of time. Historians believe this city palace complex was built by the Inca emperor Pachacuti during the height of the Inca rule in western South America, around the mid-fifteenth century. The five-mile complex of carved stone steps and citadels is thought to have been a royal estate and spiritual center. The city holds multiple temples and towers throughout that led historians to believe it had significant importance to Inca rulers and spiritual leaders. It was possibly a

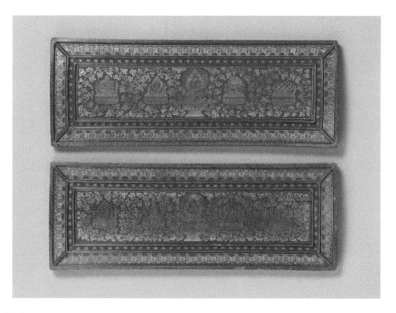

Fig 12.9
The court of the Yongle emperor Zhu Di of early Ming China had close ties to Tibetan Buddhist monasteries, which provided manuscripts for the Chinese emperors who desired accurate and complete translations of the major texts of Buddhism. A pair of sutra covers once preserved part of an edition of the 108 volumes of a Tibetan Buddhist text – likely including the *Prajnaparamita Sutra* – produced in Beijing, China. Surviving manuscripts from the reign of the Yongle and subsequent Xuande emperor (Zhu Zhanji; r. 1426–1435), some of which were enclosed by such lacquered boards, may have featured block-print illustrations, while others were lavishly decorated with costly materials and golden calligraphy. At the center of both covers are the three flaming jewels that represent the Buddha, his teaching, and the monastic community. This particular symbol, called the *triratna*, corresponds with the concept of an auspicious and wish-granting gem, or *çintamani*, which appears frequently in Buddhist, Hindu, and Jain art.
Metropolitan Museum of Art, Gift of Florence and Herbert Irving, 2015, 2015.5001.52a, b

trade hub linking the Inca Empire's 25,000 miles of roadways to other communities, such as the Aztec and Olmec people of Mexico, and the Chavín of Peru.

The Inca were brilliant architects, manipulating massive gray granite slabs, cut from the foundation of Machu Picchu and dragged up steep paths, to construct the nearly 200 buildings there. The Inca did not have use of heavy metal tools, wheels, or draft animals, so it is believed that hundreds of men dragged the stone blocks to the construction. The temples were built using polygonal blocks that fitted together perfectly, like a puzzle. Expert Inca masons did not use mortar, but made the polygonal blocks using stone axes to cut the blocks, with obsidian pebbles and sand to smooth the edges. This mortarless masonry method of fitting the stones together perfectly with a little ease, accommodated frequent earthquakes. Often thought of as dragon-like creatures, both the deity

Fig 12.10
Machu Picchu.
DoraDalton / iStock

of earthquakes and the deity of the oceans feature in many temples of the Inca empire. The most revered structure in Machu Picchu was the rounded Temple of the Sun, but the gods of earthquakes, the ocean, and the moon also hold prominent places. Priests observed and interpreted the shadows and light that entered the windows of the divine temple of the sun god, Inti.

In the early twentieth century, Machu Picchu was "discovered" by an American archeologist who unveiled the ruins to the world. Multiple expeditions were sent to Peru to learn about who lived there and what daily life was like at the city's peak. Hundreds of skeletal remains were unearthed. Initially, they were believed to be mostly women, but upon further examination, it was discovered the remains belong to people of all ages, sizes, and genders. Archeologists also identified various sectors of the city that were used for different purposes, such as farming, residential neighborhoods, a royal palace, and a spiritual center. Although Machu Picchu was considered a "lost city" by white explorers, the local Indigenous people were still farming the terraced region, and had been for centuries. These stepped agriculture terraces were nurtured by a complex aqueduct system still used in the twentieth century.

Machu Picchu was never considered lost to the locals, who likely kept a strong record passed down through oral tradition, but the modern historic record is primarily that of foreign archeologists. As we work to reclaim these cultures that were oppressed and nearly obliterated by colonization, there is much we do not know. Future discoveries in collaboration with local authorities will help to decolonize our views of conquered cultures. What we do know is that the Inca were a superpower in South America, with sophisticated agricultural, military, economic, and architectural techniques. In the sixteenth century, Spanish conquistadors invaded South America. They brought with them plagues and superior weaponry that ended Incan rule. Machu Picchu was abandoned about a hundred years after its completion, possibly due to the invasion of the Spanish.

TRAVELING ARTIFACTS

Although Machu Picchu was known to the local people of Peru at the time of its "discovery" in 1911 by American archeologist Hiram Bingham, the ruins were unknown to the world. The awestruck Bingham immediately wrote a book called *The Lost City of the Incas*, which sent swarms of tourists to Peru to find the magical city. In order to learn about the function of this intriguing site, Bingham began to excavate artifacts and send them to Yale University to be studied. The exportation of these historic treasures sparked a feud between the United States and Peru that would last a hundred years.

Fig 12.11

Chicha, a kind of beer made from fermented or non-fermented corn, is a traditional beverage of the Inca and other peoples of the Andes and the Amazon region and was part of Inca religious ceremonies and rituals. This vessel from Machu Picchu was probably used for *chicha*. It is part of the vast collection of artifacts "jointly" owned by Yale University and the Museo Machupicchu. Frank Scherschel / The LIFE Picture Collection via Getty Images

When Bingham returned to Peru to retrieve more artifacts, he found the Peruvian government had passed a law forbidding artifacts to be removed from the country. Peru was anxious to preserve its cultural heritage from looting and offered a resolution that would allow the artifacts to go to Yale to be studied under one condition: the items taken would be returned to Peru whenever the government requested them back.

For a hundred years after receiving these artifacts, Yale denied the validity of this agreement, claiming that the laws at the time of the original excavation of the artifacts did not apply in this scenario. It was not until 2008, when Peru's President Alan Garcia lobbied President Barack Obama and then sued the United States for failure to comply with the agreement that Peru gained ground. In the end, Yale University President Richard Levin agreed to a settlement. He argued that Yale was meeting the original agreement by studying the artifacts at Yale's Peabody Museum in Hartford, Connecticut; however, he agreed that since millions of people are now flocking to Peru to learn about Machu Picchu, all parties would be better served if the artifacts were returned to the Museo Machupicchu at the San Antonio Abad University in Cuzco.

The Church of Holy Wisdom

Throughout this book, we have provided information about events and ideas that define global cross-cultural, transregional connections and comparisons from 500 to 1500 and continue to inform our present-day reality. In conclusion, we offer one example that embodies the layering of cultural exchange over time, the massive and ingenious building now known as the Hagia Sophia Mosque.

Early in the fourth century, the Roman emperor Constantine converted to Christianity. He was the first emperor to do so, and his recognition of the Christian religion informed the eventual conversion of all regions and peoples that were part of the empire. He ruled from the city named for him, Constantinople, and had a church built near his grand palace. Later Christian emperors improved on that church, but none more grandly than Justinian (482–565), who oversaw the construction of this complex and stunning structure. Justinian hired scholars in mathematics and physics to advise the architects on how to erect dense stone walls to support a high, central dome, and how to incorporate heavy marble design elements and profuse windows to let in the light of the divine.

As emperor, Justinian appointed patriarchs and bishops, presided over the Council of Chalcedon (see Chapter 1), and felt that the unity of his empire needed also unity of Christian faith, thus Hagia Sophia (Holy Wisdom) was a symbol of the theocratic power of the Byzantium. At the center of trade routes and political clashes, the empire became more and more cosmopolitan, and its decoration reflected diverse cultural interactions. Initially, interior decoration included plentiful gold-leaf mosaics of abstract designs with symbols such as

Fig 12.12
Hagia Sophia Mosque in Istanbul, Turkey.
iStock

Fig 12.13
The famous *Theotokos* (image of the Mother of God with the infant Christ) hovers
in the apse dome of Hagia Sophia, and rondels around the interior feature ornate
Arabic calligraphy that celebrates Islam.
kotomiti / iStock

the cross. Earlier in this book, we discussed the Iconoclastic Controversy and the strict rules against depicting holy figures, such as Jesus and Mary, in art. But, by the mid-ninth century, the rules were relaxed. Patrons, supported by the emperor and patriarchs, funded large, beautiful mosaics of Christ and his holy companions that were installed in Hagia Sophia. A primary subject of the new art was a *Theotokos* (mother of God), an image that includes Mary and the baby Jesus. Replacing a similar image destroyed a century earlier by the Iconoclasts, an artist installed in one of the domes a 16-foot tall *Theotokos* – a seated Mary and the Christ child in her lap.

Hagia Sophia remained a grand emblem of Orthodox Christianity until 1204, when a disgraced and excommunicated western European army sacked Constantinople during the Fourth Crusade and occupied the basilica. The crusaders looted the city's monuments, including Hagia Sophia, which was repurposed as a Latin Christian cathedral until 1261, when the Byzantines recovered their capital. Because of the subsequent decline of the Byzantine Empire, the basilica was not entirely restored to its former glory, but it was impossible to ignore it as a symbol of world-class status and authority. In 1453, the powerful armies of the Ottoman Turks conquered Constantinople, changing the name to Istanbul. Long a symbol of the Byzantine Orthodox Church and very briefly a symbol of the Roman Christian Church, Hagia Sophia was redesigned as a mosque surrounded by minarets. Changes to the interior included installation of a *mihrab*, a special spot in a mosque indicating the direction of Mecca, and a platform from which a *muzzein* called the community to prayer. Like the Iconoclasts and Jews, Islam considered most representations of holy figures to be taboo; nevertheless, Jesus, Mary, and other biblical figures are also holy in Islam, and the Christian mosaics of them remained in place until 1739, when they were plastered over and the sculptures removed. In their place, master calligraphers painted Qur'anic phrases and verses.

Hagia Sophia Mosque remained a place of Islamic worship until 1934, when the newly established Turkish Republic changed it to a public museum, a living representation of the rich layers of ebb and flow of intercultural exchange throughout a thousand-year period. Sculptures and mosaics returned, sharing space with the Qur'anic phrases and Arabic calligraphy. In 2020, the Turkish government reversed this decision and Hagia Sophia is once again a mosque. Many of the images are being covered in fabric (itself a medieval Byzantine Christian practice within the basilica) as this building reverts to a functioning mosque instead of a museum.

Looking Forward

Throughout this chapter and all of Section IV, we offer many dates and events that mark the end of the period 500–1500. Certainly, European global exploration is a significant marker of the modern period. Its effect on the rest of the world is both a powerful accelerator of human ingenuity and also the destruction of many cultures. Ambitious leaders, such as Prince Henry the Navigator (1394–1460) of Portugal, funded and commanded a new generation of merchants and seamen to find new resources. Later, King João of Portugal sponsored Diogo Cão, who, from 1482 to 1486, explored the Atlantic coast of Africa and located the mouth of the Congo River. In 1487, his countryman Vasco da Gama rounded the Cape of Good Hope, creating the possibility of a sea route to India as an alternative to overland travel. His escapades were written in epic form in the Portuguese *Lusiads*. In 1501 Gaspar Corte-Real made it to Newfoundland, a feat the Vikings achieved centuries earlier; while from 1519 to 1522, Ferdinand Magellan's ships rounded Cape Horn, the southern tip of South America, and crossed the Pacific. Although Magellan was killed in the Philippines, one of his ships and a handful of original crew members made it back, the first to circumnavigate the globe.

In the 1490s, Italian Christopher Columbus (sponsored by the Spanish monarchs Ferdinand and Isabella) traveled several times to the Caribbean, while another Italian, Amerigo Vespucci, traveled south along the contours of eastern South America. In 1507, a German mapmaker named Martin Waldseemuller applied the Latin form of Amerigo to a map showing Vespucci's travels along the coast of Brazil, and it stuck. Other emerging nations in Europe followed the trend, often claiming "discovery" of Eurasian and African routes and geographies that were common and ancient reality to other peoples. The early explorers made it possible for further invasions we have discussed, such as Hernan Cortes's conquest of the mighty Aztec in 1521, and Francisco Pizarro's decimating of the Inca in 1533.

Exploration made a path for conversion of other cultures to Christianity, and the near eradication of written and artistic evidence for earlier religious and cultural practices. One culture successfully defended its heritage. In the sixteenth century, Spanish, Portuguese, and Italian missionaries arrived in Japan and were able to convert many Japanese, especially in the larger cities. These priests and monks required converts to reject their traditional Shinto and Buddhist practices. In 1597, angered about these religious restrictions and other political issues, the *daimyo*, or regional ruler, Toyotomi Hideyoshi, had a number of Christian missionaries executed. All trade with the barbarians was restricted to Nagasaki, and only Portuguese and Chinese ships were allowed entry, until 1605, when the Dutch ("red-headed barbarians") arrived in Japan. Fearing encroaching Catholicism in the country, the government forbade Portuguese ships soon after, and only the Dutch traded in Japan from 1638 to 1853, when Commander Matthew Perry of the United States coerced his way into the country.

What other dates, people, and events spark your interest for further study? What people were living in the places when Magellan's crews traveled around the world? For instance, what did the Chamorro people of the Mariana Islands in Micronesia call their island? And what strategies did the

Indigenous peoples of southern Chile have for navigating the area called in English the Straits of Magellan? Maybe you will study the life of Bartolome de las Casas (1484–1566), a Spanish priest living in Hispañola who took up the cause of the Indigenous peoples and advocated against their enslavement. Maybe it is 1470, when the Inca conquered the Chimú, who were wealthy because of the *spondylus* trade. Maybe it will be 1500, when the Safavid rulers conquered present-day Iran and Azerbaijan and forced conversion of Sunni Muslims to Shia, setting the Persian Muslim state at odds with neighboring Sunni societies. What happens to control over the West African gold trade at the end of the great empires of the Ghana (ca. 700–1240), Mali (1230–1670), and Songhai (1464–1591) peoples? In 1542 or 1543, the long reign of the King of Kongo, King Nzinga Mbemba (Afono I) came to an end, and 1517 is the end of the Mamluk dynasty in Egypt (1250–1517). How does African trade and culture continue on in the next era?

Old Discoveries, New Approaches

Another way of taking the knowledge you have learned from this text to the next step is to consider how new technologies and cultural sensitivities change the questions and hypotheses of scholars who study history and culture. In our first chapter on religion, we discussed how radiocarbon dating science changed historians' views of the Ethiopian Garima Gospels, elevating them to pride of place as possibly the earliest surviving illustrated gospel texts known. In the economies chapters, we saw how advances in underwater archeology reveal new dimensions of trade and travel across the seas. Maybe your intellectual curiosity will take you into the work of ongoing attempts to understand and translate Mesoamerican hieroglyphs, such as those in the *Dresden Codex*, or the mysterious languages recorded in documents preserved in the Dunhuang Caves of China.

As we have stressed, sensitivity to cultural identity, languages, and spiritual customs calls into question assumptions made about evidence from this period and all human history. This book challenges the idea that "globality" is a new phenomenon. Other new frameworks emphasize the experiences of those discriminated against and oppressed, re-reading documents and artifacts from the point of view of those without status or representation: religious or ethnic minorities, the disabled, enslaved, and gender or sexually nonconforming. As the perspective of global histories develops, you will be able to tell where a scholar begins an inquiry, how a museum frames an exhibition, and why an artifact or archeological site is suddenly "rediscovered" as a topic of great discussion. Maybe your curiosity will lead you to ongoing legal battles over which governments and museums should possess historical treasures. Whichever dates or cultures linger in your imagination, use these as a reckoning point, by which to orient, as you delve into further study of global connections and comparisons.

Research Questions

1. How did the Second Plague Pandemic affect systems of government? Research social and economic changes to society from a region that was affected by the plague.
2. Read some of the English sumptuary laws. What do we learn from these laws about growing tensions among the classes?
3. Imagine yourself as a doctor living in Salerno, Italy. What knowledge do you use to understand and treat the plague? What if you are from Baghdad, Iraq? Cairo, Egypt? London, England?
4. Read up on the Genome Project on the Black Death. How does modern science help us to understand the past better? How do we use that information to aid our modern struggles against disease and pandemics?
5. The second half of this chapter discusses large buildings of the empires in China, Peru, and Europe. How are architectural projects related to political power, religious worship, and/or class status? What modern projects can you compare to these medieval ones?
6. We go to museums to see objects from all over the world, but is it right for them to be in museums far from their original contexts? Is it justified to take artifacts from an archeological site and place them in another country, even if those items are secure and available for study? Research a contemporary example of cultural artifacts that have been sent from one area to another. Or research an example of artifacts repatriated to their original home.

Further Reading

Aberth, John. *Doctoring the Black Death: Medieval Europe's Medical Response to Epidemic Disease*. Lanham, MD: Rowman & Littlefield, 2021.

Boccaccio, Giovanni. *The Decameron*. Translated by Wayne A. Rebhorn. New York: W.W. Norton, 2021.

Boeckl, Christine M. *Images of Plague and Pestilence: Iconography and Iconology*. Kirksville, MO: Truman State University Press, 2000.

Caferro, William. *Petrarch's War: Florence and the Black Death in Context*. Cambridge: Cambridge University Press, 2018.

Chaganti, Seeta. *Strange Footing: Poetic Form and Dance in the Late Middle Ages*. Chicago: University of Chicago Press, 2018.

Chouin, Gérard. "Reflections on Plague in African History (14th–19th c.)." *Afriques* 9 (2018).

Cohn, Samuel. *Epidemics: Hate and Compassion*. Oxford: Oxford University Press, 2018.

Cohn, Samuel K., Jr. *The Black Death Transformed: Disease and Culture in Early Renaissance Europe*. London and New York: Arnold and Oxford University Press, 2002.

Dante Alighieri. *Inferno*. Translated by Michael Palma. New York: W.W. Norton, 2021.

Dodd, Robin. *From Gutenberg to Open Type: An Illustrated History of Type from the Earliest Letterforms to the Latest Digital Fonts*. Vancouver: Hartley & Marks, 2006.

Dols, Michael. *The Black Death in the Middle East*. Princeton, NJ: Princeton University Press, 1977.

Fancy, Nahyan. "Knowing the Signs of Disease: Plague in Arabic Medical Commentaries Between the First and Second Pandemics." In *Death and Disease in the Long Middle Ages*, edited by Lori Jones and Nükhet Varlik. York: York University Press, forthcoming.

García-Ballester, Luis, Roger French, Jon Arrizabalaga, and Andrew Cunningham, eds. *Practical Medicine from Salerno to the Black Death*. Cambridge: Cambridge University Press, 1994.

Gertsman, Elina. *The Dance of Death in the Middle Ages: Image, Text, Performance*. Turnhout, Belgium: Brepols, 2010.

Green, Monica, ed. *Pandemic Disease in the Medieval World: Rethinking the Black Death*. Amsterdam and Kalamazoo, MI: Arc-Medieval Press, 2015.

Hatcher, John. *The Black Death: A Personal History*. Cambridge, MA: Da Capo, 2008.

Herlihy, David. *The Black Death and the Transformation of the West*. Cambridge, MA: Harvard University Press, 1997.

Hsy, Jonathan. *Trading Tongues: Merchants, Multilingualism, and Medieval Literature*. Columbus: Ohio State University Press, 2013.

Little, Lester, ed. *Plague and the End of Antiquity: The Pandemic of 541–750*. Cambridge: Cambridge University Press, 2007.

Malory, Thomas. *Le Morte d'Arthur: Selections*. Edited by Maureen Okun. Peterborough, Ontario: Broadview Press, 2015.

Palma, Michael, and Lee Butler. "'Washing off the Dust': Baths and Bathing in Late Medieval Japan." *Monumenta Nipponica* 60, no. 1 (Spring, 2005): 1–41.

Soifer Irish, Maya. "Genocidal Massacres of Jews in Medieval Western Europe (1096–1391)." In *The Cambridge World History of Genocide*, Volume I: *Genocide in the Ancient, Medieval and Premodern Worlds*, edited by Ben Kiernen, Tracy Maria Lemos, and Tristan Taylor. Cambridge: Cambridge University Press, forthcoming.

Index

Note: Headings in *italics* indicate a publication title. The prefix al- is ignored in the filing order. Page numbers in italics refer to information in figures or their captions.